BY LOVE POSSESSED

JAMES GOULD COZZENS

By Love Possessed

+ + +

Thereby to see the minutes how they run—
How many make the hour full complete,
How many hours bring about the day,
How many days will finish up the year,
How many years a mortal man may live.
             —*Henry VI*

HARCOURT, BRACE AND COMPANY · NEW YORK

first edition

LIBRARY OF CONGRESS CATALOG CARD NUMBER: 57-10062

PRINTED IN THE UNITED STATES OF AMERICA

CONTENTS

PART ONE

DRUMS AFAR OFF

ONE

Love conquers all—*omnia vincit amor,* said the gold scroll in a curve beneath the dial of the old French gilt clock. To the dial's right, a nymph, her head on her arm, drowsed, largely undraped, at the mouth of a gold grotto where perhaps she lived. To the dial's left, a youth, by his crook and the pair of lambs with him, a shepherd, had taken cover. Parting fronds of gold vegetation, he peeped at the sleeping beauty. On top of the dial, and all unnoticed by the youth, a smiling cupid perched, bow bent, about to loose an arrow at the peeper's heart. While Arthur Winner viewed with faint familiar amusement this romantic grouping, so graceful and so absurd, the clock struck three.

The struck notes succeeded themselves in the quiet room with a pleasant silver tone. When his mother got up, Arthur Winner, too, got up. Left alone, he remained standing, thoughtful in a pose of habit. He held his tall, big-limbed body, whose suit of tan linen was rather wrinkled by the hot day's wearing, erect. He carried his head, in its good proportion made more distinguished by being now for the most part bald, at a reflective angle—composed face lifted a little; strong-boned chin raised, as though he scanned, scrutinous and unhurried, the middle distance; big beaked nose up, as though to scent the air. On the air hung, in fact, a faint spiciness, a barely apparent fragrance of potpourri given off by a Canton jar on a coffee table in front of the couch. The room was mostly shadowed. Big maples on the lawn grew close, shading the house; yet the September afternoon's lowered sun had now begun to slant an occasional

3

beam through their branches. The tall screened windows, open on the warm day, admitted these declining rays. Bright, they came and went as the leaves stirred, casting themselves across the polished dark floor.

Sight of the old gilt clock had made Arthur Winner think of his father—indeed, the room was full of such mementos. A little-disturbed museum, its collection, informal and unassuming, preserved evidences of that many-sided mind, of the grasp and scope of interests, of perceptions so unobtrusive as to be nearly private, of quiet amusements and quiet enjoyments. Seeking Arthur Winner Senior's monument, you could look around you. You could ask yourself, for example, how many lawyers—or, to give the point proper force, how many small-town lawyers, born and brought up in a fairly-to-be-called rural county seat like Brocton—would, fifty or more years ago, have had the interest —let alone, the taste, the eye—to pick over, unaffected by then current ideas of what was fine or beautiful, of what was rare or valuable, the then next thing to junk—the secondhand, the old-fashioned, the discarded—and select, exchanging a few dollars for them, exactly the items that the antique trade (at that time hardly born) was going to look on as prizes half a century later. Would you guess one in a thousand, or one in ten thousand?

From the room beyond, Arthur Winner heard his mother's movements. She was in search of a list she had made of the things she meant to speak to him about, things she did not want to forget. That she should then forget where she put the list of things not to forget had, she was quite aware, touches of both humor and pathos. Liking the one in connection with herself as little as the other, his mother indignantly summoned her forces. She was compelling herself to an organized effort of recall, a determined methodical review of what she had been doing, on the not-bad chance that she would be shown suddenly where the list must be. As, in her seventies, had become her practice, she spoke aloud, relating what she could remember, interpolating comment as comment seemed to her called for.

She said loud enough for Arthur Winner to hear: "I know I had it just before Maud went out. Where was I? Upstairs? I don't think so. And she wanted me to speak to Arthur about

4

her bonds. And I put that down—" Her voice was carefully, cultivatedly clear; yet from time to time some slightest involuntary tremble of the old muscles of the larynx put into the distinct words a hint of quaver. She said: "It's Luella's afternoon off. So she came in to ask me if she could bring me tea before she left—who would want tea at half past two? Still, we're fortunate to have her; though she's not very clean." Speaking still louder, meaning him not to fail to hear—perhaps a realization that the clock had struck a moment ago prompted her—she said: "If I don't find it, he'll start saying he has to leave; and I might not see him again for days—"

With compunction, Arthur Winner must realize that his mother stated there, advertently or not, one truth about these lists she usually had ready for him, about the innocent, even perhaps unconscious, stratagem. The more things she noted down, made sure she would speak of, the longer she could legitimately keep him. That she might forget something important was not the danger; if she did, when she remembered, she had only to pick up the telephone. The danger was that, his duty too quickly done, the too-few things coming to her mind at the moment all mentioned, taken care of, he would have no reason to stay. He would be going; when, if she'd planned better, he could have been caused to remain longer. She called: "Do you hear me, Arthur?"

"Perfectly," Arthur Winner said.

"You didn't say anything. I suppose it means you're in a hurry."

"Not particularly," Arthur Winner said. "I told Clarissa I'd try to be out by five—"

"Well, you must, then! Give her my love. And Ann. Ann came to see me—did I tell you?—one day last week. We had a nice time. Suddenly, she seems quite grown up—more than fifteen, I mean. But I would be glad if you could persuade her not to call me Granny. That's quite new. I imagine she got it from a friend, or read it in a book. She's at an imitative age. Now, what was I—"

Arthur Winner said: "You're looking for your list, Mother."

"Don't be impertinent, Arthur," she said, almost sharply.

5

"I've not entirely lost my wits, whatever you may think. Now, I believe I *did* leave it upstairs—"

Arthur Winner said: "Would you like me to look?"

"No. How would you know where to look?" He could hear her steps pattering rapidly into the hall; and he said: "Don't rush around. It's not good for you. Take your time."

She answered: "All very well to say that, but how can I take my time when you're in such a hurry, when I know you'll say you have to go in a minute?" However, reaching the stairs, she began to mount them with careful slowness. She called out: "Your father was *never* in a hurry. He said that when you saw a lawyer in a hurry you saw a man who didn't know his business. You should be more like him."

"I believe that," Arthur Winner said.

The remark was, indeed, his father's; yet this use might seem to show that some quality of serious directness in his mother's thought, her natural way of viewing things in terms of yea and nay, white or black, so or not so, made her miss his father's whole meaning—the dry overtone; the sidelong ironic look at the law's infinite utilizable resources of obstruction and postponement, and the wily, knowing lawyer's habit of profiting from them. Arthur Winner said: "The truth is, I'm only now starting to see how well father knew his business. He and Noah Tuttle made quite a firm in the old days. Getting old myself, I can realize how good they were."

As though shocked, his mother said: "Arthur!" Clearly she had stopped on the stairs. "You're absurd to think of yourself as old! Fifty-four's no age!"

Laughing, Arthur Winner said: "It's kind of you to reassure me; but I don't see how I could be called young. Moreover, I'm glad to be where I am. It occurs to me that youth's a kind of infirmity. You don't have the use of your logical faculties—or, at least, most of us don't."

His mother said: "Well, you *are* like your father—in many, many ways, Arthur. I often notice. He was—" She interrupted herself. Taking this turn, her thought, it could be guessed, revived a neglected, most of the time dead, grief. The force of grief, the active shock of losing, was gone. Grief recurred as a

6

forlornness grown of the loss. Now that she thought of it, what, in fact, was this life of hers but a staying, a waiting solitary, without real use, while death hesitated over the multiple choice of ways to kill her? She called, beginning to go upstairs again: "You didn't say who else was at the lake, Arthur. Tell me when I get back."

With a wish to change his thoughts, too, Arthur Winner moved. He crossed the room to an ample *étagère* between the side windows. On the middle shelf reposed a music box of burled walnut veneer intricately inlaid with mother-of-pearl patterns. Arthur Winner lifted the lid. Not sure anything would happen, he depressed several times the handle that wound the spring. The little control lever's nickel plate was pitted. Pushing hard, he managed to push it to *play*. A jar of cogs, forced, creaking and dubious, together, sounded. Beneath the inner lid's oblong of plate glass, the tarnished cylinder bristling with pins stirred, stopped, quivered, started again. In the room a ghost of music materialized. Spaced apart, elegiac and slow, note on faint plunking note formed a pensive tune: *'Tis the last rose of summer left blooming alone. All her lovely companions . . .*

Arthur Winner's father, poking (how many years ago?) through the jumble of some secondhand store (who would give houseroom to an old music box? Up-to-date parlors had phonographs with a horn), spied one day the elegant veneer, smudged and dull with dust. Removing whatever was piled on top, he noted the much dirtied, fancy and delicate inlay. Smiling to himself, he lifted the lid and peered at the mechanism. On his way out, he dropped a casual, take-it-or-leave-it offer. The shopkeeper was sure to take it. An expert perception, an aptitude for estimating people, their situations, their intentions, seemed always to let Arthur Winner Senior know what *would* be just enough. In the case of the music box, the offer need not be much. Obviously the old piece of junk had been there some time. It didn't even work; and where, after all these years, could you find anyone able to fix it?

7

Arthur Winner Senior, unconcerned, laid down his dollar or two. Someone to fix a music box would not be far to seek. He himself could fix anything; just—you might say—as he could play the violin, and not badly; or, getting out a box of colors and a palette, paint in oils an excellent likeness of whatever he set himself to paint. He could root slips or cuttings, and graft fruit trees. He tied dry flies with unexampled dexterity. Given a setter puppy to his liking, he could train a gun dog certain to take field trial ribbons. He could bowl (sometimes) a three hundred game; and he could beat (anytime) almost anyone at croquet.

Getting the music box home, Arthur Winner Senior would remove the works. Patiently, with the loving care of a man who understood wood, he did what mending the veneer needed and restored the original fine finish. Some rainy Sunday afternoon, he would then attend to the mechanism. His neat-featured, narrow, but strongly shaped face thoughtful, Arthur Winner Senior, with the loving care of a man who understood machinery, proceeded to take the works apart. The trouble soon became plain. If adjustments were faulty, he saw how to correct them; if this or that were broken, he devised a repair; if a part were missing, he found (or, even, made) something that would serve the missing part's purpose. Reassembled, the music box did not fail to play.

Remembering such accomplishments of his father's, so impressive in their variety, Arthur Winner could, of course, now see that they were not the separate or unrelated wonder-workings at which the child or boy once looked open-mouthed. The youth, the young man, might dimly feel their interrelation —that they were the fruits, the natural yield, of a temperament, a mental temper, a special make of mind—yet of course the youth, the young man, could not be equipped to know the thing he felt. Arthur Winner Junior, brought fresh from law school into the office of his father and Noah Tuttle, would need years of being himself a practicing lawyer to appreciate his father as a lawyer. To appreciate his father as a person, he would clearly have to wait until time made him wholly adult, gave him the

8

full status—was it given to anyone under forty?—of a grownup. The slow, seldom painless accreting of self-knowledge must take place before there could be reliable knowledge of other people, before Arthur Winner Junior would recognize, in sharp illuminations of retrospect, his father for what his father was—the nearly unique individual; the Man, if not perfectly, at least predominantly, of Reason.

By his fruits, you knew that man. They, the many accomplishments, were for his father a simple matter. Uncluttered by the irrelevant, uncolored by the emotional thinker's futile wishing and excesses of false feeling, the mere motion of his father's thought must usually prove synonymous with, the same thing as, perfect rightness. Any end being proposed, the Man of Reason considered means. At a glance, he separated what was to the purpose from what wasn't. Thus simply, he determined the one right way to do the thing. You did it that way; and there you were.

The music box's stiff old spring, no more than part wound, faltered. Hesitating, dying on a last reluctant note or two, the melodious tinkle stopped. The tune had not been finished; yet a silence of served purpose fell. How long since anybody had played it? How long before anybody would play it again? The questions seemed to put themselves, to be put inevitably by the sudden silence, yet these were questions, Arthur Winner, with a certainty of intuition, could realize, of his father's proposing.

Played, the faltering thin music spoke to you, with meanings unqualified by use of words. In a way that words, too specific, too obvious, could not tell you, you were told of time, of what was gone, of what was going, of what was to go. With the tinkle of the far-off notes, with the dying of the half-heard melody, mortality touched the mind. Intimated in the following stillness were the tears of things—those only tears the Man of Reason stayed to drop. The Man of Reason, from his inward, nearly unbroken solitude, looked out. He regarded the world of men, mostly, in respect to reason, unlike him. Rarely mistaken, he saw them as they were. With hope no higher than became the lonely student of mankind, Arthur Winner Senior, in earth

9

now rotten, speaking to whom it might concern, addressed those surviving him through these things, once his. Somehow, sometime, his messages might or might not reach someone.

Through the silence, the gilt clock ticked on. The clock, too, could be thought of as waiting. It, too, without words, stood ready to say a particular piece. In place of the tears, here was the joke of things. Arthur Winner Senior, dryly smiling, wryly nodding, had appraised the tableau presented by the silly, charming figures. He noted the motto's incontrovertible asseveration. Monkey business proposed the grand truth. The boy, surprising a naked girl, hiding to titillate his thoughts with peeks at her, was himself surprised. The little god was about to take a hand. Indeed, *he* did conquer all. *L'esprit est toujours* —yes, always!—*la dupe du cœur!* So cuddlesome in form, he was the heart, the baby lord and master of the head. His victory was love—love's bliss of thoughtlessness. Love pushed aside the bitter findings of experience. Love knew for a fact what was not a fact; with ease, love believed the unbelievable; love wished and made it so. Moreover, here where love's weakness seemed to be, love's strength resided. Itself all unreality, love was assailed by reality in vain. You might as well wound the loud winds, kill the still-closing waters. Would someone, sometime, read the motto; ponder this figured triumph of unreason, see the joke?

Upstairs, distantly, Arthur Winner's mother was calling. She said: "Arthur! Can you hear me?"

Going to the hall door, Arthur Winner said: "I can. Are you all right?"

She said: "Arthur, look in the book on the table by my big chair, please. I marked a place. What did I mark it with?"

Crossing back, Arthur Winner saw the book closed near the middle on a gold fountain pen and a folded sheet of paper. Drawing both out, he looked at the paper. His mother had written in her still-pretty but no longer quite firm script: *1. keeping up big house 2. my medicine—why I don't like calling Reggie Shaw 3. Oil burner—not O'Brien 4. Ann being a*

10

lawyer 5. Rector and his m.—sunset years 6. L. and sherry. 7. Lawrence? 8. explain to Marjorie P. 9. Maud and bonds.

Arthur Winner called: "You marked the place with your list, Mother."

"Well, what a relief! Please don't read it. You couldn't understand it. I meant to speak about the rector and his mother calling on me with his fiancée. That reminded me of a line he'd quoted—misquoted, I was sure. I put a check by it."

"It's too late. I've read the list," Arthur Winner said. "Only about two things aren't clear to me. Most of them I think we've covered."

"I'm coming down. Don't go on looking at it. I know you're thinking how funny it sounds. Read what I put a check by on that page."

Arthur Winner took the book up. It was covered in faded green watered silk, a type of binding surely not used for years. Stamped on the cover in worn gold was what he took to be the facsimile of a signature—*Robert Browning*: a poet, he would think, for years little read. The book, opening, showed him the flyleaf. Written there with time-dimmed ink in a hand he recognized as his father's were the words: *For Miss Harriet Carstairs from her sincere friend Arthur Stanton Winner.* A little lower, the same hand had written: *"O Lyric Love, half-angel and half-bird—" Midsummer Eve, 1893.*

Arthur Winner said: "I've lost your place, I'm afraid. So I don't see what I was to read."

Downstairs now, his mother said: " 'And I shall weigh the same, give life its praise or blame.' " She moved briskly into the room. " 'Young, all lay in dispute; I shall know, being old.' Well, sometimes I think so. Sometimes I wonder. This Doctor Trowbridge said something to me about sunset years, and then quoted that. He seems very young."

Exertion had pinkened slightly the clear soft skin of her face, now almost everywhere finely lined, traced with innumerable delicate wrinkles. Not conscious of doing it, she lifted a practiced hand, whose once-slender fingers showed arthritic enlargement at the joints, to make sure that she had not disordered her

11

carefully blue-rinsed white hair, carefully dressed under the hairnet—nowadays she had trouble finding white hairnets. Her eyes, a soft brown, rested on Arthur Winner a moment, and she said: "How stupid of me! I could have been talking to you all that time. I know you have to go, but—give me the list." Taking her glasses from the table, she put them on and held the list up. She said: "Well, it *is* a great expense. Your Aunt Maud and I could live more cheaply—we have to have Luella, and a cleaning woman one day a week to help her, and a laundress Mondays because Luella doesn't do laundry. Oh! What that other note means is that we're missing a great deal of sherry. I'm very much afraid Luella's taking it. Maud and I couldn't be using as much as that. I don't quite know how to deal with it. I don't like to keep the cabinet locked—that seems so pointed."

Arthur Winner said: "About the house, that's settled. The only reason to move would be if you and Aunt Maud weren't able to be comfortable here. About the sherry, if I were you I'd simply say to Aunt Maud, when Luella can hear you, that it seems to go fast. If she's making off with some, very likely it's because she's sure you never notice. I think she'd stop. She wouldn't want it to get to Alfred that one of his family was taking things where she worked."

"I could do that," his mother said. "But I like it when you can trust people. You used to know you could trust any of the Reveres—I suppose, as you say, Alfred, or old Paul, saw to it. Well, I only wanted to tell you that I know you have many expenses; and your father left me as well off as any old woman is entitled to be. If your Aunt Maud and I didn't try to keep up a whole big house—all right, I won't go on about it. I just hope you're making a lot of money—what about that case you mentioned, those out-of-town people who wanted to bring that suit here. Did you get it?"

Arthur Winner said: "I'm afraid that fell through."

"Oh, Arthur! I hoped you were going to get it. From what you said, it sounded like a very big fee—"

His mother, Arthur Winner reflected, had not been a lawyer's wife for nothing. Her practical grasp of such matters was good. Smiling, he said: "We're doing all right. With Julius still

12

tied up with the Ingoldsby thing—which may be quite big—we really have all we can handle. So, don't feel badly."

"I don't like them not giving it to you after they thought of giving it to you. As though somebody else could do it better."

Arthur Winner smiled again. "Then you'll be glad to hear it was the other way around," he said. "Mr. Sutphin and the board were quite anxious to retain us. I'll have to treat what they told me as a confidential communication, so I can't go into it; but there were points about their legal position Noah didn't like—not in matters of law; in law, they have a strong case. I'd expect to win it for them. But there were aspects, if you regarded them as Noah chose to regard them, the least bit—well, dubious. That side only developed this week. When I mentioned it to you, I thought I'd heard the whole story. When the rest came out, Noah balked. Julius had left for Washington on the Ingoldsby thing—"

"Remind me to tell you about Marjorie coming to see me," his mother said.

"I will. So I called Julius, and we agreed, Noah's attitude being what it was, that we'd pass it up—tell Sutphin that, when we'd estimated the work involved, we found we simply couldn't handle it because of other commitments. An untruth, I'm afraid. Sutphin was rather set down; but I think he accepted it—that is, his interest would make him see his position as absolutely just and right; so it wouldn't be likely to cross his mind that our trouble was a scruple. In fact, I don't know that Julius and I would have felt any need to be quite so scrupulous."

"Oh, Arthur," his mother said, "nobody could be more scrupulous than you are! I've seen that time and again. Character's a thing you can always sense in people. It's absurd to suggest that you, or Julius Penrose either, would ever touch anything dishonorable. I know you wouldn't—any more than your father would have. Or Noah Tuttle would."

Arthur Winner laughed. He said: "Of course, you mustn't say anything about this to anyone; and certainly you mustn't say *that* about it. That amounts to defamation. In law, Sutphin's people have a case. So they have every right to litigate it. All they want is what the law, as I read the law, would award them

—the defeat of certain claims against them. There's no impropriety in counsel trying to show those claims, however fair or just in point of principle, are for various technical reasons without legal merit—it's what counsel's for. The fact that some pretty sharp practice may be involved is immaterial."

His mother said: "When Noah had that trouble, there were suggestions made to him, your father told me—things quite legal which would have saved him a great deal of money. Noah wouldn't hear of them. He assumed, because he thought them honorable and right, obligations he needn't have assumed. Your father respected him for it as he respected very few men—"

"I respect Noah, too," Arthur Winner said. "I even respect his scruple about Sutphin's business. I didn't like it either; and while we could always use a good fat fee, we're quite comfortable. So, why not be high-minded?"

"Now, you're teasing me," his mother said. She gazed at him with mild reproof. "There's right, and there's wrong; and needing, or not needing, fees hasn't anything to do with it. As you'd be the first to say. If what this man meant to do wasn't right or honest, I know you and Julius Penrose didn't want to appear for him any more than Noah did."

"Perhaps not," Arthur Winner said. "In so far as a practice of law admits of honesty, Julius and I are, I trust, honest—"

His mother said: "You're still teasing me. I know those jokes about lawyers. People are always trying to say that if you're clever you won't be good; and if you're good you won't be clever. That's silly and untrue."

She spoke with tranquil positiveness. Matters of principle, she wished to point out, were all settled, all immutable, all clear and simple—and hardly material for joking. Here was at least one moment when she did not wonder. Being old, she knew! The positiveness, as well as touching, was a little disconcerting when you realized that the things thus known came to neither more nor less than what the girl she used to be had known. Years and years of living had affected no change in the beliefs that were hers when she attained young lady's estate. The convictions of Harriet Carstairs, a properly brought-up miss of eighteen, were hers still. Some singleheartedness, magnificently

14

strong and unswerving, some resolute will-not-to-know, by treating as nonexistent, made nonexistent anything she did not care to know. She was protected from the usual process of experience, from experience's progressive resolving of all things, at first taken to be clear and simple, into their essential baffling complexity. There was, as she said, right. There was wrong. Good was good, and bad was bad. Good people did not do wrong, bad things.

Wrong or bad things were, of course, done; everybody knew that; but, to this grown simplicity of understanding that was also clear and simple. The doers were unfortunate people, people of few advantages or little education, hapless in being too unintelligent to know better. Luella, poor young colored girl, had perhaps abstracted, from a supply she could get at, a bottle or so of sherry not hers. Distressing to think that she would steal—but explicable enough. To Luella's limited mind, the temptation of any opportunity was irresistible. Slips in such quarters could not call in question the honesty and uprightness of the naturally honest and upright.

Patting her hand, Arthur Winner said: "Agreed. Now, what else?"

She said: "Still, I wish you didn't say things like that. Why should you want to be facetious?" Raising the list, she studied it distractedly. "Oh—Lawrence. I didn't ask about him, did I?"

Arthur Winner said: "I believe I showed you his last letter —in July, I think. Julius was going to look him up, so I'll hear when Julius gets back—that ought to be Monday or Tuesday."

"Then, of course you don't know how the children are. Washington's so hot during the summer. Sometimes that makes me feel queer—I mean, to realize I have great-grandchildren. I remember when just having grandchildren—" She paused. "Then, to have *them* grown, and having children of their own—do you suppose I'll ever see them?"

"I feel sure you will. Perhaps they can all come up for Christmas."

She said: "I never have been able to understand why Lawrence wasn't willing to stay in Brocton, go into the firm with you. So much simpler for him—"

Arthur Winner said: "No doubt he had many reasons. I think

15

the reason he took the government job is that he knew he wouldn't be satisfied to be a small-town lawyer all his life. He saw, I think quite shrewdly, where a main chance lay. In a few years, he probably plans to quit the department. With what he's learned, he'd expect to have valuable services to offer clients who needed more expert than average advice. Not impossibly, as an important and well-known legal luminary in Philadelphia or New York, he could find himself coming back as secretary of state, or something. In Brocton, what could he, in that sense, ever amount to? At law school, I thought myself very fortunate because I knew my father had a good practice he wanted to take me into as soon as I finished. I wouldn't, like a lot of the others, have to start on my own. Lawrence didn't see it that way at all. The sort of thing that was good enough for me wasn't good enough for him. He was more ambitious. I think, of course, he may find he's mistaken in supposing that what he's ambitious to get will be worth all that those things usually cost; but I'm I, and he's he. Lawrence clearly does want it; and I believe he has abilities that can get it for him; so I wouldn't for a moment wish to stand in his way."

"Oh, no; one wouldn't," his mother said. "Everyone seems agreed that Lawrence is brilliant. Still—" She hesitated, gazing at Arthur Winner thoughtfully. "Still, I know you were disappointed. And though Lawrence was a boy I always liked, I didn't like his not saying anything, beforehand. You'd done everything for him—and, well, a child should not be a thankless child."

Arthur Winner smiled. He said: "I think Lawrence appreciated as much as necessary my giving him the support I would have been compelled by law to give him, and whatever else I may have felt like adding to that. Yes; I was disappointed when he didn't choose to do what I'd planned for him to do; I suppose anyone is disappointed when he's worked out a plan that suits him, that he likes the idea of, and it falls through; but the fact that it *did* fall through—"

His mother said: "You'd even had a plate made to go by the door."

"True," Arthur Winner said. "I did. I've still got that some-

16

where—in the crate it came in. I think it's a good thing to keep. A useful reminder that you should be careful about what you assume. Because Lawrence didn't say anything to the contrary, I gladly went on assuming he still wanted to do what he said he wanted to do—actually, perhaps, let me tell him he wanted to do—when he went to law school. Long before his first year was over, he'd have realized there was a lot to the law besides small-time county court practice; and if you meant to amount to something, going into *that* was no way to do it—"

"Yes, Arthur; but how could he not tell you? He must have known that if he'd explained to you, nobody would have been more reasonable, or readier to help him—" She hesitated again. "No," she said. "That was a little bit of Warren in him. Hard! It's in the family, I'm sorry to say. A total disregard of the feelings of others. There was my father's brother, my Uncle Gregory—well, I won't drag that up. Much of it you've never heard —but, because of him, I *knew* what was going to happen to Warren—"

Arthur Winner said: "I don't agree, Mother. I think the point was that Lawrence *did* have a regard for the feelings of others —my feelings. He knew what I was assuming, and that I would be disappointed; and, very humanly, he didn't like to tell me. Very humanly, too, I think he may have felt that I'd made too many of his decisions for him while he was growing up. That was all right as long as he didn't know what he wanted to do. Now, he did know; and he was going to make his own decisions, take charge of his own life. There was a change in him soon after Warren was killed—he started to assert himself a little. As boys together, as the older brother, I think Warren had Lawrence at some psychological disadvantage—I mean, Warren both alarmed and impressed him. To be like Warren wasn't in Lawrence's temperament, so I suppose for a long time he accepted it as in the nature of things that Warren was the one who did what he pleased; that he was the one who did what he was told. With Warren gone, definitely never coming back, I think Lawrence was released in a curious way—he could be himself, not merely Warren's subdued, reasonable, levelheaded little brother. It was really high time he paid less attention to what

17

I wanted. I'm glad to have him acting for himself. I'm glad to help him."

"Still, I wish we saw him sometimes," his mother said. She looked at her list. "Oh—that about Ann. One thing she told me when she was here was that *she* had decided to be a lawyer. I suppose you know. She talked quite intelligently about it."

Smiling again, Arthur Winner said: "Yes; that's the latest. I don't doubt her generous idea is to gratify me; but I think, too, she may have seen something of the sort on television or in the movies—I mean: Lawrence went to Washington; so she enters the firm instead; and, though a girl, amazes everyone with her legal acumen. If she wants to study law when the time comes, she certainly may; but I don't think there's much danger. Any minute now, she'll be realizing there are other males in the world besides Father. When she starts setting her cap at one or more of them, her plans may be expected to change."

"There's a certain truth in that," his mother said. "Though I don't know how much I care for today's ways of putting it." She consulted her list quickly. "Yes; you said you would see about a different oil burner man to look at the furnace. I do hope nothing very expensive will be necessary—that's what I mean about this huge house. And if you get my medicine from Reggie Shaw, you'll ask him to stop and see me when he can. I don't want to call him, as if there were some emergency, when I know how busy he is. There's nothing in particular wrong—simply, one or two things I'd like to speak to him about." She appeared to be reviewing them for a moment; but what she said was: "I suppose I might as well mention this. I don't know whether Reggie's not well himself; but, lately, each time he's been here I've had the impression he'd been drinking. Once, at least, quite noticeably; he really didn't make sense. Of course, he came late; and I suppose he was tired, so he might have been unusually affected."

"Probably that explains it," Arthur Winner said. "Reg always liked a drink now and then. I never saw him seriously affected. I wouldn't worry."

His mother said: "I didn't say I was worried; but I think most people, when they consult a physician, would like to feel that

18

he was in full possession of his faculties. You were going to tell me who is at the lake."

Arthur Winner said: "Oh, there was to be a party for the children—because of school, Monday. Then everybody seemed to decide to have supper there. Miss Cummins, Doctor Trowbridge's fiancée, had remarked to Clarissa that she liked swimming; so she was asked. And it followed that he and his mother were asked. They all went out this morning. Willard Lowe and Fred Dealey are going with me—and I'm taking a Mr. Woolf, a New York attorney who was down with the McCarthy boys for the auditor's meeting. The McCarthys had to go back, or did go; but we weren't finished, so Mr. Woolf stayed over. He seemed rather at loose ends—"

His mother said: "I don't believe Mrs. Trowbridge much likes her son's marrying. I felt that when they were here. Did I say the girl came with them? She's thoroughly nice; but certainly she's a plain little thing. Well, that's suitable, I suppose. One couldn't altogether care for the idea of a clergyman marrying a raving beauty. It might seem to suggest interests not particularly appropriate to his calling. I thought their coming to see me was polite—even if I didn't take kindly his 'sunset years' observation. That young man has a lot to learn about handling old women. Did you tell him I almost never went out?"

"I believe I did," Arthur Winner said. "I thought he'd better be prepared not to see you in church often."

"Well, he didn't inquire as to my devotional habits. He spoke enthusiastically of you—what a help he'd found you. He told me that since Judge Lowe wished to resign, he hoped you'd be willing to let him name you senior warden. I told him your father had been Doctor Ives's senior warden for many years."

"We'll see," Arthur Winner said. "As a new man, he might be wise to put off things like that until he knows his parishioners better. Christ Church has a very old charter. A warden, once appointed, is there for good, unless he resigns. Just as a vestryman, once elected, is there for good. The charter makes no provision for removing incumbents the rector doesn't like. I believe I'd be more use to Doctor Trowbridge if I just went on as clerk of the vestry. The truth is, I don't very much want to be senior

19

warden—for various reasons. The rector's an earnest young man; and I feel that I may not be in every way qualified—"

Absently, his mother said: "Well, I hope you have a nice party. I don't suppose you remember when we used to drive up to the lake from Brocton in buckboards. You were a very little boy. I don't know whether I'd like to see it now or not. You're still using the lodge?"

"And the boat house," Arthur Winner said. "There's nowhere else you could stay now."

"No; I don't think I care to see it again—ever," his mother said. "It could only be sad. I remember, before your father died, driving up once. That was when Clarissa had the children's camp in summer. I remember they used her parents' place, and the lodge, and the boathouse. The other places were lost in the woods—everything overgrown. It gave me the most forlorn feeling—" Indeed, the feeling must have come again; for Arthur Winner could see a momentary quiver of her lips. She said decidedly: "I've pleasant memories of those early summers. I'd like to remember it that way. We used to sing around the fire. I think of things like that—you don't remember, I suppose."

Arthur Winner remembered. Surprised to be able to, he could recover perfectly the child's impression; see the people of those days in the clothes of those days joining each other from their bungalows in the woods along the lake shore, gathering after dark. Perhaps more strongly than they knew, the bonfire, the big blaze of wood, spoke time-out-of-mind meanings to them —warmth for the half-apes in the cave; food for hairy men whose artifacts were stone; safety's bright zone for protohistoric hunters in the wilderness. They sat or lay relaxed in a circle while flame lit their faces. They were singing. Against the summer night's polyphonic murmur, the ceaseless chirr of insects, their voices lifted out of the firelight, mounted together in darkness a little way toward the overseeing stars. That was long, long ago; the singers had dispersed; most of them were gone now; but at the time they sang: *How can I leave thee? How can I from thee part* . . .

Arthur Winner said: "You had something down about Marjorie Penrose. And what about Aunt Maud's bonds?"

20

His mother said: "Yes. Marjorie stopped to see me one day—I think, Monday. I wasn't very well; so I didn't see her. Your Aunt Maud said she appeared to be rather hurt. I hoped you'd find out if she was; and say whatever seemed necessary. She's quite tiresome, poor woman; but I wouldn't willingly hurt her. Is she going to be at the lake?"

"I think not," Arthur Winner said. "I know that Stewart and Priscilla went up with the others this morning."

His mother said: "One feels always that Marjorie's rather pathetic. Possibly for that reason—things hurt her that aren't meant to hurt her. She's too intense about everything—sometimes, I've thought, to the point of being actually unbalanced. People like that are never to be relied on—you can't tell what they'll do next. Creatures of impulse! I remember when Julius married her I didn't see how it could work out well—they were so unlike. I know your father was very doubtful about it; though I don't think he said so to anyone but me. I know he felt it didn't start on the right footing—Julius being the attorney in the divorce from whatever that man's name was; and then, if you please, marrying her himself. Your father used to say: Business is business and you should never let it be anything else. Of course, I suppose things are far from easy for Marjorie—Julius is such an impatient man; and, then, his misfortune—"

Arthur Winner said: "In his way, Julius is attached to her. She may be often unhappy; but I'm not sure she wouldn't be unhappier still with anyone else. What about Aunt Maud and the bonds?"

His mother said: "She wasn't to be out long. It's much too hot. I thought maybe she'd get back and she could tell you. I think she's quite set on the idea. What she wanted to know was whether you thought Noah would be willing to sell some bonds for her."

"Why does Aunt Maud want some bonds sold?"

His mother said: "There's an old friend of Maud's whose husband died—I used to know her, too; I don't believe you would. Sally King. Sometimes I think the world will end by being entirely populated by old women. At any rate, a friend of her husband's has been advising her on investments. He's a broker. He tells her stocks to buy. They only cost a few dollars; and they're called 'over the counter'—would you understand what that meant?"

"I would understand what that meant," Arthur Winner said.

"So, as a result, every year for a number of years, Sally's been making several thousand dollars' profit—as much as five or six, last year. She offered to tell Maud what the man advised her to buy; and Maud could buy it, too. Having extra money would be such a convenience to her—"

Arthur Winner said: "And what Aunt Maud wants to know is whether Noah would think this a good idea? He would not. He'd say old ladies have no business using their principal to speculate in any stocks—let alone, those not even listed on the exchange boards."

"Well, of course, I wouldn't approve of speculation, either," his mother said. "But I read Sally's letter; and the way she does it, it seems perfectly safe—" Arthur Winner smiled; and his mother went on at once: "Yes, I see you smiling! Perhaps it's not *perfectly* safe. But at my age and your Aunt Maud's, how much longer can you reasonably expect to need an income? Aunt Maud understands that she may lose all she thinks of putting in. If she did, what she'd lose would be about eight dollars a month in income. She thinks a chance of making what would be quite a good deal from her standpoint is worth taking—after all, Sally does it all the time. And, after all, it's your Aunt Maud's money, not Noah's."

Arthur Winner said: "While Noah's handling the money as trustee, just as long as the trust isn't revoked, for all practical purposes, the money is his, you know. The trustee's duty is to preserve and protect the corpus of the trust. What he does must be what his best judgment directs. And also, what's legally permissible. He couldn't, as trustee, legally invest in stocks of that sort; because the law doesn't regard them as safe enough—"

"I'm sure I don't understand the technical side," his mother said. "D'you mean Maud can't sell her own bonds if Noah doesn't want her to?"

Arthur Winner said patiently: "I mean, I feel sure that Noah, as trustee, would say he couldn't in conscience allow her to do

22

what he thought unwise. If Aunt Maud wants to use any of her money that way, she'd have to begin by revoking the trust—which she can do. Noah would then hand everything the trust holds over to her; and she could, of course, do what she liked with it. In my opinion, she'd be making a mistake. Noah's handling her money a great deal better than she could. Perhaps she'd like more than she has; but what she has, she can be fairly sure she'll always have while Noah's there to take care of it—"

"Well, here she is, I think," his mother said. "Wasn't that the door?"

Arthur Winner said: "Mother, I don't want to argue with her. You just tell her I'm sure Noah won't agree; and I don't think she ought to do it either. I must get on. Willard and Fred were hearing a case in chambers; and they expected to be through by half past four—"

His Aunt Maud, walking with heavy steps, said loudly from the hall: "You here still, Arthur?" She breathed with an audible wheezing sound. Coming to the door, she rested her hand in a black net glove against the jamb. Wearing, as she always did, black, her heavy-set frame had a dumpy look. Her solemn, somewhat puffed, face made Arthur Winner think of pictures of Queen Victoria in her old age. "Very oppressive afternoon," she said. "We'll have thunderstorms tonight." She moved slowly across the room to the other big chair, by usage, "hers." Subsiding, she said: "Hattie, did you tell him what I want to do? Arthur won't approve, of course." She paused with composure to wheeze a moment. "As it happens, I've just seen Noah. I met him by the courthouse a few minutes ago." From the table beside her chair, she took a black fan, opened it, and began with measured waves to fan herself. "He seemed to be in a hurry; so I simply asked him if he could see me sometime tomorrow. He said he couldn't. Maybe he didn't intend to be rude; but the fact remains that he was. That was all he said. He didn't suggest a time when he could see me; nor even ask me what I wanted to see him about. He just gave that head of his a wag; and, I think, was going to walk on—"

Arthur Winner said: "He's had rather an upsetting day—"

"One guessed that," his Aunt Maud said. "But, through no

fault of mine, surely! I think everyone spoils him. So I said: 'I want to see you within the next few days about a change in my trust.' He said: 'What change? Doesn't need changing. When it does, I'll tell you.' I've never liked that attitude of his. Noah Tuttle acts as though what he does about your affairs is none of your business—he'll never tell you how they stand—"

"Oh, now; his accounting's always regular, Aunt Maud," Arthur Winner said.

"That may be," she said. "I get accounts, yes; but I'm not an accountant. I think he might sometimes explain them to me. When I once made that suggestion, he said he hadn't time; if I couldn't understand, bring whatever it was in to Helen Detweiler, and she'd explain—"

"It's Helen who does them," Arthur Winner said. "So I'm sure she could answer any—"

"And suppose I haven't time to take myself to your office and consult Miss Detweiler? Well, just for once, I thought I wouldn't let him browbeat me. I said: 'If you'd prefer formal notice in writing, Noah, you may have it. I'm going to want you to sell one or two bonds.' Arthur, do you know what that offensive old man said to me? He said: 'You're getting senile, Maud. Try not to be more of a fool than you can help.' Now, why should I put up with being talked to that way? I won't put up with it!"

"It doesn't mean anything, Aunt Maud," Arthur Winner said. "You know it doesn't—"

"Senile!" she said. "The impudence of him! What's he, I'd like to know! More of a fool than I can help!" She uttered a sudden harsh laugh. "And it's not as if he'd heard what I wanted to do with the money either! It was most uncalled-for." She fanned herself vigorously.

Arthur Winner's mother said: "Maud, you mustn't get excited. Do you feel some asthma?"

"I'm not excited; I'm merely mad," his Aunt Maud said. "And yes I do, since you ask; and what of it? When don't I feel something? When don't you? I've no doubt we're both losing our wits, into the bargain. But who's Noah Tuttle to say so? What's Arthur say?"

Arthur Winner said: "I'm afraid I don't—"

"That is as I expected," his Aunt Maud said. "Goodness, what a gawk you are, Arthur! Don't stand towering over me! If you're going to argue, sit down."

Arthur Winner's mother said: "Arthur told me what those things Sally buys are, Maud; and I couldn't help thinking perhaps it was imprudent. I wonder if you ought not to—"

"How much does Arthur really know about it?" his Aunt Maud said. "When Sally buys what this man tells her to buy she makes hundreds of dollars. She has, for years. Inconceivable as you may find it, Hattie, there could be things Sally's friend understands better than Arthur does. It's his business. I'm not asking Arthur to advise me on what to buy. You've let him talk you around, as usual. *You* thought I should do it. Remember? People do make money in the stock market, you know, Arthur."

Smiling, Arthur Winner said: "I know. And some of them also make money on the daily double at a race track. I'm not going to argue. All I was going to give you was my opinion. You asked for it. I was telling Mother; I know Noah won't agree; and I think you'd be wise to let yourself be guided by him."

"That doddering old man! Talking to me that way! I'm going to write him a note right now; and tell him I'll thank him to keep a civil tongue—"

"Why not wait until tomorrow?" Arthur Winner said.

"What will be different tomorrow? Will I like abuse better then?"

Arthur Winner said: "Noah will be different. This, as I said, was a bad day. We had a long auditor's meeting with a lot of legal and other squabbling that tired him—it even tired me. And, then, he was upset this morning, earlier. When he's upset, Helen Detweiler usually handles him—she knows how to quiet him down. Unfortunately, today Helen herself was upset— that's what started Noah off. When I got in, she was in Noah's room in tears."

His mother said: "Why, what had happened? That certainly doesn't sound like Helen!"

"From most people's standpoint, nothing very earth-shaking, perhaps," Arthur Winner said. "It was brother Ralph. He was supposed to be off for college next week. This morning, he seems to have told Helen he didn't want to go, or wouldn't go. It would be a blow to her, I suppose. She's worked for years, you might say, to make certain he'd be able to go to college. At any rate, she *was* very much upset—"

Distressed, his mother said: "Poor Helen! How can children be so inconsiderate—?"

Arthur Winner said: "In the first place, Ralph, after all, isn't her child; she only acts as if he were. And if he's inconsiderate—well, after all, that's, I'm afraid, what she's brought him up to be—Ralph was the only one to be considered. Now, he takes her at her word. What's in Ralph's mind, I don't know. From something Noah said, I gathered that there might be a girl—someone Ralph's decided he's in love with; so his idea may be to stay in Brocton and marry her."

His mother said: "Well, what would he live on?"

"The thought seems to have occurred to Ralph, too," Arthur Winner said. "He devised a scheme of sorts. He turned up at the Union League while Noah was having breakfast, and tried to borrow money. Over the summer, Ralph was working—though I'd judge, not too hard—as a brush salesman. He earned a small commission on orders he took—"

His mother said: "I'd forgotten that. He came here once or twice. I must say he's a good-looking boy—except, I think he has a weak face. We ordered something from him; though I'm not sure we ever got it. I must ask Luella."

Arthur Winner said: "Well, the brush company has more advantageous—advantageous for whom would remain to be seen, I expect—arrangements when a little capital can be put up. I daresay Ralph thought he'd dispose of some of Helen's objections if he could show he had, or was arranging to have, an established 'business.' I don't think he stood much chance, anyway; but I gather he had the poor judgment to make his proposition the next thing to a demand—insinuating that Helen's work for Noah, the way Noah undoubtedly does depend on her, entitled him, Ralph, to a loan. People, let alone boys of eighteen, don't 'demand' things of Noah. Noah sent for Alfred Revere and told him to get Ralph out of the club. So Noah was still fuming when he reached the office; and there was

26

Helen, who didn't know about Ralph's trip to the club—Noah didn't tell her—but *did* know about Ralph's not wanting to go to college—"

"It's an explanation," his Aunt Maud said, fanning herself. "How far it's an excuse, I'll sleep on. Let Arthur go now, Hattie. Can't you see he's fidgeting?"

"I'm doing nothing of the sort," Arthur Winner said. "However, I do have to go. Aunt Maud, if it's the only way you can be happy, I'll personally advance your account a thousand dollars—that's quite enough to start—and you can let your friend's friend make you a fortune."

His Aunt Maud said: "Are you a bank, or a provident loan society? I don't need money; I have money. Not that I don't feel the offer does credit to your good heart, Arthur. I won't say what it seems to show about your head. Do I remember that jarring expression I heard my grandniece, your daughter, use when she was in last week? Yes! Bye, now!"

"Good-by," Arthur Winner said. He bent and kissed his mother.

His mother said: "And you'll remember all those things?"

"I will."

"And you'll all be here for tea Sunday?"

"They will," his Aunt Maud said.

"Well, have a nice time at the lake, darling. And give Hope my dearest love."

His Aunt Maud looked, her eye rolled in silent askance, from Arthur Winner's mother to him. An ordinary inadvertence, surely; the tongue's lapse, of course! But Aunt Maud, contemplating the state of age, understood well enough that the lapse was possibly of the mind. The immediate present, for the space of a thought or two, sank in mental oblivion. The mind's momentary time of life was yesterday; and Arthur Winner's mother might, for the duration of that moment, be wholly unaware that Hope, to whom she sent the dearest love, lay some seven years now in her grave.

27

TWO

Driving under the big maples behind the Brocton County Court House, Arthur Winner brought his car to the empty parking space nearest the rear entrance. Painted on the pavement in yellow letters were the words: PRESIDENT JUDGE. The courthouse's big double back doors stood open. Framed there, loosely ambling out, blinking into the hot sunshine, appeared Ephraim Todd, one of the tipstaves. His folded coat hung on his arm and he carried a straw hat. His lugubrious long face assumed an expression of mock disapproval. He called: "Judge Lowe catch you, you'll be in contempt, Mr. Winner."

Arthur Winner said: "I think not this time, Eph. I'm here to pick him up. I see Judge Dealey's car. I thought I was picking him up, too."

"Don't know," Ephraim Todd said. "Fellow from the garage brought that over. Judge Dealey must have telephoned for it. Oh; a minute ago, I saw Helen Detweiler. She was up in the hall, coming from the recorder of deeds' office. She asked were you over here. Want me to find her?"

"I'll go in," Arthur Winner said. "Court adjourn?"

"We did, outside," Ephraim said. "Judge Dealey told Mike, go ahead adjourn; wouldn't be anything else. Judge Lowe's still in chambers with the district attorney. Earlier, know what he was hearing? Witnesses on that Caroline Dummer girl. You seen her? Eighteen years old. Not so bad-looking either. First count: murder. Second count: concealing death of bastard child. Third count, you ask me: getting herself knocked up."

28

Arthur Winner said: "This is Mr. Woolf, of the New York bar, Eph. I don't think you're maintaining our legal dignity very well."

Mr. Woolf's face, full in cheek and chin, of a complexion whose cast was at once pale and swart, showed amusement. The large liquid eyes brightened; the melancholy mouth, small for the face, smiled. He said: "Even in our jurisdiction, I believe the court's view is a girl can't be too careful, Mr. Winner."

"See?" Ephraim said. "Same all over! Had the baby by herself in an outhouse. Could have been born dead; but the coroner says not, I hear. Baby's father's supposed to be Caroline's boss at the laundry where she worked. Used to call her into the sorting room and do it on the dirty clothes. But, then, I heard, too, anybody who asked her nice, she would; so I guess they can't hook *him*. What they say: Good time, had by all! Name of Dummer. Ha! What Judge Lowe wants is to take a plea of manslaughter—"

From behind Ephraim, Fred Dealey, coming out the door with a quick stride, said: "You aren't supposed to know what he wants, Eph. And if you do know, you aren't supposed to tell the world." His sharp jaw up, his sharp somewhat hollow eyes fixing Ephraim Todd with a critical, not wholly humorous stare, he came over to the car. He said: "Try knowing a little less from time to time. And talking a little less."

Arthur Winner said: "Mr. Eliot Woolf, I believe you know, Fred."

Fred Dealey said: "I do. Had the pleasure of admitting him *pro hac vice* this morning. Get through with the meeting?"

"Not quite," Arthur Winner said.

Mr. Woolf said: "I'm afraid I held the auditor up, Judge. There were a few figures the old gentleman, Mr. Tuttle, didn't have ready. I wasn't sure I understood the account without them. So I had to ask Mr. Winner for a continuance while they were worked out. I was sorry to do it—ask all these good gentlemen to be there on a Saturday; but I don't expect to keep them long—"

"Every day's a working day here," Fred Dealey said.

Ephraim Todd said: "Well, got to get along. Good night."

"Yes; good night," Fred Dealey said. He turned his head, looking after Ephraim. To Arthur Winner, he said: "I think perhaps we might review the appointments of some of our court attendants before very long, Arthur. Del called me. There seem to be things she wants picked up downtown and dropped off at Roylan. So I thought I'd better drive myself out to the lake. I'll see you there. Good night, Mr. Woolf."

Mr. Woolf said: "Mr. Winner has very kindly asked me to come out to supper, Judge. So I'll see you there, too."

"Oh?" said Fred Dealey. "Good; good! Arthur, you'd better let Willard know you're here. They finished in chambers. He's just talking to Jerry Brophy." Moving with decision, he snapped open the door of the car next to Arthur Winner's. Sliding his thin but muscular form along the seat, he shoved in the ignition key. Turned over, the engine caught. The car backed out, was swung impatiently around, and went off with a rush.

Mr. Woolf said: "Young, for a judge, isn't he?"

"Fred's forty-one," Arthur Winner said. "I'm inclined to think that's to the good—with a younger man, you get a fresh viewpoint, more flexible thinking. He's been writing admirable opinions."

"I know the type," Mr. Woolf said. "Hard to fool. Likely to be a little abrupt on the bench, isn't he?"

"Sometimes," Arthur Winner said. He resisted the instinctive movement of the mind, the mind's mild bristle to hear the outsider hint a fault. "Though I'm not in favor of easygoing judges. Fred's rulings are arbitrary now and then; but they're perfectly impartial, and nobody's found a reversible error yet. He's been on the bench almost two years; and I know that, in general, the bar's very well satisfied with him."

"That's one thing about this kind of practice," Mr. Woolf said. "You can really get to know your judges. When I prepare a case, I always wish I knew who's going to be sitting; and half the time, with us, we'll have somebody we might never even have seen before. Of course, some arranging can be done if you get the calendar. By continuing at the right time, you can do something about where you'll come up. But the other side may be doing the same thing—probably is; so there you are!"

Arthur Winner said: "Well, I think most of us here have an idea when we study a case which of our three judges we'd like to have sitting. But when our list's called, you have to explain why you're obliged to ask a continuance; and if your reason's something you ought to have done that you didn't do, you may not get it—" He felt, Arthur Winner must acknowledge, an awkwardness—a scrupulosity, he supposed (no doubt, the thing his mother had in mind), that did not quite like the matter-of-fact calculation by which Mr. Woolf sought, outside due process, to favor any cause of his; the experienced astute smelling-out of every little advantage; the assiduity in wangling advantage whenever possible. He said: "If you'll excuse me, I'll see where Judge Lowe is."

✦

In the back hall, whose unfinished masonry walls were painted white, the damp coolness of a stone building's basement hung. Halfway to the steps that led to the upper hall on the courtroom level, a little group waited at the heavy grill of polished steel bars, the entrance to the adjoining jail—Mrs. Morton, the matron, a stout placid woman who was the warden's wife; Walter Joy, a deputy sheriff; Henry Titus, the deputy clerk of quarter sessions; and what Arthur Winner realized must be the unfortunate Dummer girl Ephraim Todd had spoken of. Mrs. Morton was saying: "Now Caroline, there's nothing in the world to cry about—"

On Mrs. Morton, the girl had turned a broad face, blank and childish, with wide dark eyes whose tearful expression seemed that of great disappointment. The gray-green prison dress she wore fitted her quite trimly. Above the gently mooning face the straw-colored hair was waved and set with surprising care. Mrs. Morton said: "It'll only be a minute, dear. Then, we'll have supper pretty soon. You can have ice cream—"

The girl, flushed suddenly radiant, turned, clasping Mrs. Morton in her arms. "Now, Caroline!" Mrs. Morton said, remaining passive. "Now, Caroline!"

Walter Joy said: "You want me to—"

31

The girl docilely relaxed her hug. Instead, she grasped Mrs. Morton's arm in both hands and laid her confiding head against Mrs. Morton's shoulder. Seeing Arthur Winner, Mrs. Morton said, not without embarrassment: "The trouble is, I haven't my key, Mr. Winner. Gus must be in the cell block. He doesn't hear the buzzer. There! Joe's coming now—"

Henry Titus said: "Mr. Winner, Miss Detweiler was looking for you. I think she's in Mrs. Keating's office—" He nodded along the passage to the top of the stone steps and the doors open on the marble-lined upper-level hall. Beyond the gleaming frame of bars, a uniformed jail guard approached at a trot. Releasing locks, he drew back the grill enough for Caroline Dummer, tugging Mrs. Morton with her, to press in. Walter Joy said: "How you, Joe? Okay, ma'am?" With a clang, the grill returned, closing.

They moved up the passage. Henry Titus said: "Ever see anything to beat that, Mr. Winner? Hotel Morton's got one satisfied customer."

Walter Joy said: "Notice that hairdo, Mr. Winner? Mrs. Morton fixed her up to see the judge. She never had one before."

Hearing them mount the steps, Edna Keating looked out of the door of her office, next before the hall door to the judge's chambers. She lifted her glasses off, peering toward them. Over her shoulder, she said: "He's here now, Helen." To Arthur Winner, she said: "Mr. Winner, Judge Lowe rang for me to bring my book in. He won't be long. I was just telling Helen to tell you if you came. She wanted to see you a moment, if she could. Oh, dear! There! He's ringing again." She darted back to her desk, caught up a stenographic notebook, and opened the heavy mahogany door to the judge's chambers beyond.

Helen Detweiler had been sitting beside Edna Keating's desk. When Arthur Winner came in, she arose with what he could recognize as one of her spasms of resolution, a taking-in-hand of herself and her strung-up nerves. Strain stiffened Helen's straight and slender figure. A reflection of the same strain mysteriously, disturbingly, worked in Helen's face, the face of a young woman, and even of a pretty one, to drain out youth and

32

prettiness both. Helen's worn expression was almost old. Her features had a thinned, sharpened look, as though the nerves, preying so actively on flesh, consumed flesh. Helen's delicate-shaped thin mouth, where no lipstick had ever been used, looked paler than usual. The tired sensitive blue eyes, undercircled markedly, had a look of incommutable anxiety. Her blonde hair, drawn tight and neat, seemed to lack its usual brushed luster.

She said: "Mr. Winner, I didn't have a chance to tell you how sorry I am about this morning. It was awful of me to upset Mr. Tuttle right then. I can't think what happened to me—"

Arthur Winner said: "My dear, don't think about it. You couldn't help it. It's all right."

Answering his tone, Helen said: "Oh, you needn't worry, Mr. Winner." She managed a smile. "I don't feel that way now. It's over. It won't happen again. Ralph told me so suddenly, I suppose I got a kind of shock. I suppose I looked so funny when I came in, Mr. Tuttle had to say: What's wrong? And, well, I couldn't seem to help crying. I'm so ashamed of myself."

"Don't be," Arthur Winner said. "It was natural enough. What you do often depends a lot on how you feel at the moment; and there are times, I think most people understand, when how you feel at the moment is something you can't help—"

Whatever Helen might think or say, the strained appearance, the tense tone, suggested that she remained not too far from a possible second breaking point. By the frequently useful device of a soothing flow of mere words, Arthur Winner had intended to get Helen past an emotional juncture that could be critical. Astonished, he saw that she had colored vividly. She then cast her eyes down, declaring what unmeant meaning she took from his suggestion, announcing a distress of new embarrassment; different, indeed; but, in Helen's case, perhaps even more acute. Unless she had very present reason to take it, the meaning was one she would surely not be apt to take. In private recital of her troubles to Edna Keating, Arthur Winner could imagine her saying: "And on top of everything, I have to have the curse." Admitted in feminine confidence to Edna, the circumstance might be not altogether unwelcome—an explanation, in part at

33

least, for that unheard-of, never-before-seen flood of tears in the office. Detected, adverted to, by Mr. Winner, the circumstance was now—poor Helen!—reason to sink through the floor.

To get by this absurd little contretemps, to cure Helen of her confusion, Helen must be categorically but indirectly assured that he never thought of such a thing, that the supposed near mention of what Helen shrank from admitting—how silly could a grown woman be?—was, after all, no mention. Affecting not to have noticed the color of absurd shame, the downglance of modesty's disgrace, Arthur Winner, talking on, said: "There was nothing at all to be ashamed of, Helen. Noah quite understands; and I can understand. Of course you were upset. Naturally, you were disappointed. Naturally, you're worried about Ralph. But remember this: None of us can ever be really sure he knows what's best for another person. No one can live Ralph's life for him. If he feels he doesn't want to go to college, I think he's sensible to say so—he'd be wasting his time there."

Helen said: "Oh, I realize that, Mr. Winner. I don't imagine for a minute there'd be any use in trying to make him go, if college isn't what he wants." Helen had taken eagerly the lead he offered. Quick with relief, she concluded that her indelicate secret had been safe all along. By a fast reach of the will, by a practiced retightening of her nerves, she steadied into composure, she even reduced her telltale color. What was beyond the will's reach—the base functions, fastidiously abhorred with all her heart, of the vile body—she now excluded from her mind. Almost animated, she said: "But that's what worries me so, Mr. Winner. Can Ralph tell what he really wants? Would I be right to let him decide a thing like this all by himself?" She hesitated. "Mr. Winner, what I wanted to ask you—I know I'm asking a great deal—well, could you, would you talk to him? Ralph—" She hesitated again, as though she foresaw what the admission might convey. She said: "You see, I think he's just too used to me talking to him. Maybe he thinks I don't know. But he'd know you knew, Mr. Winner. If you told him why he ought to go to college—"

"Yes, I'll talk to him," Arthur Winner said. The answer was the necessary one; but he could not help adding: "Only, I'm afraid there's very little to say; and Ralph must know most of it already. He ought to remember, of course, that as things are today, not going to college closes most professional careers to him. But, then, he'd be bound to know he needed a college degree if a professional career interested him—" Would anything be gained by putting bluntly his own guess that Ralph, as well as not having the interest, probably hadn't the capacity for such careers? Arthur Winner thought not. He said: "I can make sure he fully realizes that part—in case he doesn't; and supposing he cares to listen to me."

Helen said: "Oh, if you only would, Mr. Winner! I know he'll listen to you. He has the greatest respect for you—" She looked at him with an excitement of hope so remarkable that Arthur Winner was moderately taken aback. Where, you might ask, could Helen have got the idea that Ralph viewed him with respect? Was Ralph in the habit of saying to her: "I have the greatest respect for Mr. Winner"? What reason could there be to imagine that Ralph, a not-unamiable (and, why shouldn't he be amiable? He mostly had his own way. He got everything he wanted that Helen could give him. He could easily talk her into agreeing that he needn't do anything he didn't want to do), a rather spiritless and spineless, and by all accounts indolent, and not-too-bright, brat of eighteen, gave any thought to old men in their fifties—unless it was to envy idly what money or power they might have; or to wonder what they could possibly be getting out of life? As for the old man in his fifties, *he* might not be insensitive to the brat's impertinence in venturing to have the greatest respect for him.

Arthur Winner said: "Did I understand from Noah that there might be a girl involved?"

Helen once more colored a little; but she smiled. "Ralph did say so; but that's just silly, Mr. Winner. I know what that is. Ralph was trying to find some reason to give me. He thought he'd try saying he was engaged. He's been having dates, going out with girls; but I know he wouldn't be serious about any of them. He wouldn't want that kind of—well, responsibility."

Arthur Winner heard her with an inner start of surprise. The new faint show of color, signal that Helen had been brought, by way of thinking why boys went out with girls, and how marrying and giving in marriage followed, to think again of nature's sexual contrivances, was expected enough. What was unexpected, what, in a small way, took Arthur Winner aback, was the downright estimate, direct and clear-eyed, of Ralph's habit of shirking. Observing, over the years, this intense Helen-and-little-brother relationship, you tended to think of Helen as completely fooled by a selfish, idle boy. Hoodwinked, bewitched, infatuated, victimized, Helen, you too readily assumed, was kept blind to all disparities between the actual Ralph and the ideal, imaginary Ralph of her head and her heart. More disturbing than that assumption, might be this truth. Seeing Ralph's weaknesses quite as well as you did, Helen said: No matter!

Arthur Winner said: "Then you don't think there's anyone in particular?"

Helen said: "Oh, of course, to say he was engaged, he had to choose a girl. He told me it was Joan Moore."

"Moore?" Arthur Winner said. "I don't place her. The only Moores I know—"

"You wouldn't know them, Mr. Winner," Helen said. "They're people who haven't been in Brocton more than a year or so. Nobody knows much about them. I was asking Edna; because Edna's brother rented them the house they live in. Mr. Moore's a butcher—or, at any rate, has charge of the meat department in that new supermarket on Hamilton Street. This Joan was in the high-school play last spring—that's the only time I ever saw her. That's how she got to know Ralph—being in the cast with him. The truth is, she's not even pretty, Mr. Winner. But I think that's all part of it."

Arthur Winner gave her a puzzled look. Helen said: "Well, Mr. Winner; if Ralph suddenly wanted to be engaged to someone, to be able to say he was engaged, I can see he might think of her. He might have noticed, while they were in the play, that she was—well, interested in him; and of course he'd know most boys didn't pay any attention to her. So he'd probably know that if he took her out a few times and then asked her to be engaged to him, she would, all right."

Granted that Helen (able, when she chose, to be undeceived

about Ralph's weaknesses; and able in passionate devotion to be unperturbed by them) might track better than Arthur Winner Ralph's moves of deviousness, Ralph's practice to deceive, Arthur Winner must ask himself if this reconstruction was in all respects plausible. He said: "Then you think he really did ask a girl to marry him?"

Helen said: "Oh, he wouldn't actually be planning to marry her, Mr. Winner. It would never be anything but an engagement. I think he's thinking this way. He'd know I wouldn't want him to marry her; I'd say he was too young; and I don't believe Joan can be more than seventeen, so he could probably count on her parents saying they'd have to wait. So, after a while, he'd find a way to get out of it, call it off. I mean, Ralph knows by now that girls like him. Why would he want to marry someone who wasn't pretty, and—well, whose father was a butcher, and hadn't any money? I mean, I'm not worrying about his really going ahead and marrying Joan. I know he wouldn't. He wants her as an excuse for staying in Brocton."

As well as devious, as well as deceiving, this pretty project might seem a little on the dastardly side—but, Helen calmly made plain, not to her! Of course, in Ralph's defense, you could reasonably say that Ralph's fault was youth. Not Ralph alone, but most young men, needed more experience than could be got in eighteen years to modify or overcome all their natural propensities for acting the fool and cad; or, failing that, to learn how to hide better these unhandsome parts of their nature. Ralph would probably claim, and truthfully, that he meant no harm. He was not old enough to see that his conduct was contemptible.

And in Helen's defense? With calm entire, Helen could be perceived to have let go by the board that any number of scrupulosities—more, certainly, than Arthur Winner ever entertained—which governed in flawless niceness of feeling the rest of her life. This was not the same; this concerned her dearest dear —his comfort and well-being; his all-important happiness; the future she meant him to have. Those ends so far justified these means that Helen, the fanatic, could not find a thing amiss in them.

Helen said: "So that's all that is, Mr. Winner. That's not

really why he doesn't want to go. Ralph doesn't admit it; but, for one thing, I know he's afraid college might be a lot of work. And because he doesn't look ahead, doesn't realize how sorry he may be—that's what really upsets me, Mr. Winner. Because, you see, I have to ask myself if everything I've done about Ralph was wrong, if the whole plan was a mistake, if I've failed him. I mean, I just know, if Father had lived, if things had gone on the way they were, Ralph wouldn't be saying now he didn't want to go to college."

She had a point; and the point raised other points. Upset, Helen asked herself whether this present Ralph, with his dislike of work, with his unambitious indifference to what he might become, was a result, the end product of Helen's mistaken decisions, Helen's errors in judgment, Helen's doting failure to impose on Ralph an instruction and discipline out of which character is said to be built. With George Detweiler alive, would Ralph today have his established habit of doing only what he felt like doing? George Detweiler, kindly, but also just and firm, would have taken care that any son of his learned to do the right and the reasonable whether he wanted to or not. Ralph would have been made to know that the results of work and obedience are rewards and pleasures; while the results of loafing or trying to get out of doing what ought to be done are all highly unpleasant. And today there would be a Ralph fundamentally different?

You were tempted (what could be more logical?) to say: Of course! But might you not do better to say: Who knows? Who can tell? From the past, Arthur Winner heard voices. His son Lawrence, a child, spoke in amazed alarm: "Yes, we *do* have to! Father says we have to." Cheerfully jeering, his voice bold, his son Warren, an older child, rejoined: "*You* might have to. *I* don't have to. . . ."

Helen said: "Then, another thing, Mr. Winner. I mean, that would have been different, if Father hadn't died. I mean, money. Of course, Ralph knows what he's going to have. It's enough to pay his expenses—he won't need to get a job, or anything. But other boys are bound to have more—and, well, Ralph's sensitive about things like that—not being able to do what the others can do—"

Arthur Winner put down an impulse to answer, with surely appropriate dryness, that all of us are under the necessity of cutting our coats to fit our cloth; that not a few boys would be only too happy to take jobs if they needed jobs to help pay their way; that Ralph, all his life, was going to find that some people had more money than he had, and, so, the sooner he adjusted himself, the better. He said: "Well, Helen, as far as that goes, I can say—I knew your father well enough to say—that he'd have been particularly careful to keep Ralph from developing extravagant tastes. If Ralph had let him see that his idea of college was a chance to throw money around with rich boys—"

Helen said: "Mr. Winner, it wouldn't be fair to say Ralph had that idea. I didn't mean, throwing money around. But he could feel at a disadvantage—I know sometimes he has. It's not his fault that things are different for him—well, he knows I have to work. And I don't suppose he likes us taking boarders—he might wish he had a home more like other boys' homes. That's what I meant about the plan being a mistake. I thought, by keeping the house, things could go on, be the same for him. I wanted what was best for him; and that's where I failed. I suppose you're right, Mr. Winner; we don't ever know what's best."

Arthur Winner said: "My dear, a person who has done all you've done, who has tried as hard as you've tried, has nothing to blame herself for. Every plan is a gamble. Wise is what a plan turns out to have been if everything happens to go right. You've done your best; you've been very brave and very faithful; and that's all anyone can do—or be."

"Yes; I have tried hard," Helen said. She could be seen to tremble in exquisite balance on the edge of tears. She held her lips together and the muscles of her throat moved in stiff successive little swallows. Opening her mouth, she said: "The others, I'm not, Mr. Winner. I'm not brave; everything frightens me. Ralph—doing things for him made me happier than anything else. I couldn't have not done them—"

By making herself speak, by obliging those throat muscles to obey her will, Helen resumed her measure of composure; yet this, Arthur Winner must realize, trembled in a balance, too. Close to Helen's consciousness, nearly impinging on it, was (everything frightened her) the forbidden horror, the dreadful eyeless face of our existence. In a desperation how different from the placid firmness with which Arthur Winner's mother successfully rejected knowledges she did not care to have, Helen pushed back the horror; refused to look. On the world she never made, she imposed with all her strength a pattern of the world she wanted—a place of peace, of order, of security; a good and honest world; the abode of gentle people, who, kind-minded, fair-minded, clean-minded, remarked the perfect man and beheld the upright; and who, once believed into existence, could alleviate—their unspotted life was serene; their end was peace —Helen's recurrent anguish of trying not to know, yet always knowing, that in the midst of life we are in death.

On a Saturday evening toward the end of the May of thirteen years ago, George Detweiler; his wife, Alice; his daughter, Helen, who was sixteen; and his son, Ralph, who was five, were at their lakeside bungalow. May was early in the Ponemah Association season; and the only other people up that weekend were the Hendersons—Tom Henderson; his wife, Edith; and their daughters, Clarissa, who was twenty-one, and Adelaide, who was eighteen. Like the Detweilers, the Hendersons had come to open their bungalow, which was on the point, a quarter-mile along the lake from the Detweilers'. Tom Henderson, helped by the girls, had been pleasantly busy all day with small jobs of carpentry and painting. For the jobs he had noted to do tomorrow, he needed a number of small items that the general store at Hancock, a village five or six miles away on the Eatontown pike, would probably have. After supper, a list prepared, Clarissa and Adelaide took the station wagon to get them. They stopped to see if the Detweilers wanted anything; and Helen Detweiler thought she would go with them for the ride.

The station wagon left. Darkness fell, with a fine full moon rising. At the Detweiler bungalow, little Ralph was put to bed. The night was balmy, the moonlight brilliant on the lake. George Detweiler carried a canoe down to the water. He helped Alice, who was recovering from a surgical operation, and was still not very strong, to settle herself in the canoe; and they went for a paddle.

About fifteen minutes later, while the canoe idled along well out from shore, something happened—what, was hard to guess. George Detweiler had been handling canoes since he was a boy, and the lake was perfectly calm; yet the canoe, in one way or another, overturned. The mishap, though awkward and inconvenient enough, was hardly to be regarded as serious. George, a strong man and a fine swimmer, aided by the floating canoe, could not have anticipated the least difficulty in getting himself and his wife to land, only a few hundred yards away, even if no other help was to be had.

As it happened, there was help. The full moonlight had brought Tom and Edith Henderson out to sit on their veranda overlooking the lake. They saw the Detweilers' canoe glide by; and though they did not see whatever the accident was, George's prompt shouts reached them easily. Tom Henderson ran down to his float. Moored there was a rowboat with an outboard motor. The motor, by bad luck, refused to start; and Tom Henderson lost time with that; but he had called to George, and George had called back cheerfully to take it easy; they were all right; they could hold on.

Tom Henderson hurried to his boathouse for a pair of oars. Returning with them, he unclamped the outboard motor and tipped it up onto the float. Plain to be seen in the bright night was the upside-down canoe, perhaps two hundred yards away. George and Alice, with no apparent trouble, were holding on. George, swimming, had even begun to steer the canoe and his wife toward shore. Casting off, Tom Henderson swung his bow at them, and rowed. A practiced rower, he had no need to look over his shoulder to keep his course, so he didn't look until he judged himself near at hand. Turning then, he saw the drifting canoe, right enough, some twenty feet from him, but no one was holding to it.

Even after the bodies were recovered, what happened to George and Alice Detweiler was as hard to say as what overturned the canoe. Though Tom Henderson had his back toward them, his oars made little noise, and he couldn't have failed to hear a cry, or any considerable disturbance in the quiet water. He had heard nothing. The likeliest-seeming explanation would be that Alice Detweiler, with no warning, lost consciousness. George, when she let go the canoe, moved hastily to keep her from sinking. The lake was chilly still; possibly, his muscles were chilled. A too-sudden movement might have set on general, totally incapacitating, cramps.

Aghast to find the canoe floating alone, Tom Henderson shot his rowboat up. In the water, he saw a movement; or perhaps only imagined that he did. He pulled off his sweater and trousers, kicked his shoes away, and dived in. The dive found him nothing; and neither did succeeding dives, which he made from the surface, until he was obliged to stop, exhausted, and hang onto the gunwale of his boat. Edith Henderson had left the bungalow veranda and come down to the float. Now she was calling, frightened; so he called back to reassure her. He managed to climb into the boat; and since he could do nothing more, he rowed for shore.

Arriving at the float, he found waiting for him not only Edith, but Clarissa and Adelaide, and Helen Detweiler. They were late, because, not able to get all the things at Hancock, they had been to Brocton. As the station wagon passed the Henderson place to take Helen home, they heard those last calls across the water. Knowing something must be wrong, they stopped, and came running down. Tom Henderson tied his boat to the float. He was obliged to tell them, including Helen, what had happened. Sitting in his wet clothes in the boat, he told them with difficulty, greatly winded. Stepping onto the moonlit float, still unable to get his breath, Tom Henderson suddenly suffered a heart attack. Telephoned for, young Doctor Shaw drove right out; but when he reached the Hendersons', the only service he could perform was to pronounce Tom Henderson dead.

If shocks of emotion could in fact put permanent marks on the mind, that moment's shock, Arthur Winner must admit, might well do so. The hideous, the incredible, impossible—a few hours ago the Detweilers were at supper, and what danger threatened anyone?—news was spoken up to Helen by a hard-breathing, moonlit man—how little like the Mr. Henderson Helen had always known!—in a boat. The wet man, gaining the float, shaking in the silver light as he tried to straighten himself, was suddenly struck dumb, collapsing on his bony bare knees, falling forward, his face on the planking under which lapped the lake water. Hours of night, of horror, of terror had to follow before Helen, in spite of everything, was no longer able to stay awake.

The exact effect of such a shock could never be predictable—people have supped full of horrors with no result other than that direness cannot start them; people, after the most dreadful griefs and losses, will in more cases than not, be observed a year, or even a few months later, in ordinary self-occupation quite themselves again. In Helen's case, the indubitable effect —Helen would never be the same again—the observable marking of the mind, might be a matter as much of this blow's timing as of this blow's force. For some years now not a child, yet with final adjustments to being a woman far from complete, Helen, by her unsureness, was left in the open, in every direction defenseless. The Helen thus caught might be thought of as destroyed root and branch—not only the hesitant but mostly unalarmed girl of the past (the happy-enough Helen, having fun helping her mother earlier with the evening meal; the carefree Helen, pleased to be treated as a grownup, allowed to drive off, for the ride, with girls as old as Tom Henderson's daughters), but also a future woman, very different from Helen today, that Helen was, until then, going to be. Feeling the brute blow of death, made to realize death's physicalness, how bad, then, the physical body must be, seeing that death was its appointed portion! How bad, then, must Helen be—how bad, perhaps, had Helen been? Were there wicked thoughts or secret experimental acts, known to her, which made her deserve her punishment? Had her parents done that which, half known to her, made them deserve theirs?

43

From the now-loathed body of this death, what, what would deliver Helen?

Next day, the world went on. Doctor Shaw had taken Helen, and little Ralph, roused in the middle of the night, back with him to his Roylan home. They remained there, while the whole of Brocton, staggered, really stunned, talked over and over the grotesque compounding of tragedy; while the lake was dragged; and while Noah Tuttle, George Detweiler's attorney, and Arthur Winner Junior, coexecutor with the First National Bank of George's will, went into George's affairs. These involved mostly the First National Bank, with which the Detweilers had a long association. George's great-grandfather had been one of the bank's founders; his grandfather had been president, and so had his father, and so had his Uncle Ned—though developments were to suggest that Uncle Ned did not bring much to the management but his name. When Uncle Ned, a certain pressure put on him, retired, George, though then a mere assistant cashier and no more than thirty-five, was hastily elected to succeed him.

High time! If not exactly known to be, the First National under Uncle Ned was strongly suspected of being overextended —in difficulties. Later, George Detweiler was to tell Arthur Winner that the suspicions were well founded, that "in difficulties" was a gross understatement. For several months they didn't know from day to day whether they could keep their doors open; and there had been one desperate session with the bank examiners, who only at the very last minute let themselves be persuaded that part of the bank's actually worthless paper might not be actually worthless. Clearly, Uncle Ned had to go; though, in his extenuation, it might be fair to note that the nearly fatal bad management or judgment could have proved of little real consequence if a then country-wide depression had not conjoined with a local financial catastrophe—the final going-out-of-business of the Brocton Rapid Transit Company, an electric interurban railway in whose expensive construction and

44

always unprofitable operation many Brocton people had unwisely invested.

George Detweiler (not unhelped by better times; and by a succession of payments, at first thought out of the question, on the transit company's bonded indebtedness) put the bank back on its feet. Five years after George became president, the First National was in good shape; once again Brocton County's leading bank; and obviously thriving. As befitted a banker, George was closemouthed about matters of policy and management. What arrangement he and the directors had, only they and he knew; but with the bank prosperous (thanks to him) it seemed safe to guess that the board would have no reason to be, and certainly would not want to risk being, niggardly.

So guessing, both Noah Tuttle and Arthur Winner Junior (who had taken legal custody of George's papers) were astonished to discover that George as the bank's president received in salary exactly what he had received as assistant cashier. Of course, this went a long way to explain the next discovery—that George's estate was, for a man of his position, modest, or, even, meager. Helen and little Ralph would take a good-sized Greenwood Avenue house (with a good-sized mortgage); an unimproved property out at Roylan whose tumble-down relic of an old fieldstone farmhouse George was planning someday to restore as a country home; and the bungalow at the lake. In addition to real property, George had qualifying shares of bank stock and a certain amount of savings and insurance—much less of both than a man like George Detweiler, clear-sighted and careful, would be expected to have.

Further investigation did something to resolve these perplexities. George, the size of it was, had not intended to die that night; nor this year; nor for many a year. It had not, naturally, been any niggardliness of a directors' board that determined George's salary. George meant to hold down the bank's expenses. To make his compensation commensurate with his services, he was accepting options to buy stock. At no present cost to the bank, options would enable him to take, in due course, an ever-larger share of profits he had good reason to believe the bank, managed by him, was bound to earn. A shrewd and forward-looking man, George had planned well. By his prudence and economy he was making as good as certain that before he was old he would be rich.

As it was, this exiguous and insufficient estate—by no means the provision, ample, secure, and ordered that George, far in advance of possible need, would certainly have meant to prepare—presented problems. As it was—well, Noah hawed and hummed, those options, for instance! The bank, in order to express regret, would probably be willing to do something fairly handsome about recovering them; still, nothing like what George might one day have realized. Then, the Roylan acreage —other Roylan property owners had first refusal; and they might— Then, at the lake; that couldn't go on the open market! Shaking his old head sadly, Noah would see what would be best. Arthur Winner Junior, the actual executor, was sent, with a nod, about his business.

All that could be done, Noah Tuttle duly and quickly did. In two weeks he came up with a worked-out settlement that must excite everyone's admiration. The estate, liquidated as he proposed, and the resulting funds handled as he proposed, could be made to give the Detweiler children an assured income to more than pay their expenses if they lived, as he supposed they would, with some cousins of theirs at Eatontown until such time as Helen might normally expect to marry, and Ralph would be old enough to earn a living. Noah went over his figures very carefully with Arthur Winner's father. He even (more perfunctorily) told Arthur Winner Junior what had been decided. To Helen, still pale in a silence of seeming extended shock, Noah then undertook to explain his plan, fully but simply, so a child could understand. Helen heard him with understanding. When he was done, Helen thanked Mr. Tuttle for his trouble. She then answered with a plan of her own, putting things fully but simply, so Mr. Tuttle could understand.

Most of the selling that Noah proposed she approved of; but, no, she did not wish to sell the Greenwood Avenue house. She did not wish to live with the Eatontown cousins; nor did she wish them to be appointed guardians. She hoped that Mr. Tut-

46

tle would consent to act as guardian for her and Ralph until she came of age, when she would ask to be appointed Ralph's guardian. A little money spent on the Greenwood Avenue house would make it possible to take boarders. Long employed by the Detweilers was a colored cook, one of the estimable Reveres, named Marigold. Helen had talked with Marigold; Marigold would stay; so they could manage. Helen herself meant to get a job as soon as possible. In this way, Ralph's home would not have to be broken up; current expenses would be met; and when the time came, there would be money for Ralph to go through college on.

The really extraordinary thing was that Helen, sixteen, with no practical or financial experience, in the end overbore Noah Tuttle, sixty-nine, ripe with such experience. At the time, Arthur Winner Junior was filled with astonishment. He was even dismayed. This was not business! Helen purposed to put money, a good deal, into an enterprise—taking boarders— which she knew nothing about. What made her think she could meet her expenses? Helen's plan was open to a dozen obvious objections. Moreover, Arthur Winner Junior, disapproving, was fairly sure that he understood Noah's unbusinesslike reason for not raising objections, or not raising them conclusively. The reason was no more than Helen herself; Helen, putting forward without confusion, her thought-out complete scheme of self-abnegation.

Helen was a good girl and a brave girl, and Noah was touched. He revered goodness and bravery. Helen's candid innocent face and slight girl's figure touched him. Toward women as women, Noah held an attitude shaped by the conventions, the presumptions, the social uses of the nineteenth century's notion of chivalry. This chivalry required not only a genteel, a courteous looking-away from anything that the notion must exclude, but also an actively constructive idealization that could, for instance, associate rosebuds or lilies with young females, girls still maiden. Resulting feelings, softening an old man's brusque manner and even moistening his matter-of-fact eye, appeared gravely to have impaired his judgment. Could Arthur Winner Junior in seriousness recommend a scheme devised by

47

a child to his coexecutor, the bank? He had been disturbed enough to speak to his father.

Arthur Winner Junior's astonishment at this going-into-reverse of Noah's was not, he found, shared by his father. Why should Arthur Winner Senior be astonished? Would Noah's partner of forty years—and such a partner!—be ignorant of Noah's occasional propensity to act emotionally, of Noah's sometimes sentimental sensibilities? Required to pass on Noah's almost certainly emotional capitulation, Arthur Winner Senior's cool, inquiring mind would not waste time on causes; he weighed consequences. To judge those, he had only to bend on George Detweiler's young daughter his detached acuteness. Though far from disparaging them, though acknowledging their personal and social utility, his father, Arthur Winner felt sure, never would submit to being moved by mere goodness and mere bravery as Noah was moved by them. The idle question with which Noah so involved himself—ought goodness and bravery, ought Helen's valiancy and selflessness, to be revered?—Noah's partner dismissed at once. His question was: Could this thing work?

Detached acuteness's survey seemed to have satisfied Arthur Winner's father that work this could. When he had listened, patient and reflective, to his son's statements of concern, he offered one of his characteristic explicative observations; a little dry, but spoken as usual to help rather than to reprove: "No; you're not able to be sure the plan's safe or wise. But it's what Helen wants to do. Son, when you can, always advise people to do what you see they really want to do. So long as what they want to do isn't dangerously unlawful, stupidly unsocial, or obviously impossible, you can, and you should. Doing what they want to do, they may succeed; doing what they don't want to do, they won't succeed."

In an understanding of his father, even then almost full-grown, Arthur Winner could take his father's meaning. The penetrative eye, quietly considering Helen, had come on and identified that type of true resolve whose force is as nearly inflexible as any human force can be. What Helen proposed was no momentary notion which she would be free to tire of or to think better of. To this plan of hers, Helen's whole nature was

48

unappealably committing her; the will-to-do was fixed in her fiber; the compulsion was applied at levels of unconscious desire that reason with reason's counterarguments of unhappiness, of disappointment, of exhaustion, could never hope to reach. Don't worry, in short! Helen's surface proposal, that part of her plan she had outlined to Noah Tuttle, was not beyond her physical and mental capacities. The plan—to make a home for little Ralph; to support him, and bring him up—in so far as doing it depended on Helen, was, then, practicable. No faltering need be feared, no possible conflict arising later between Helen's own interests and those interests of little Ralph to which she meant to give her life. To that anguished inquiry: What, what would deliver her from the body of this death? an answer had miraculously come. Little Ralph would!

Arthur Winner did not doubt that his father divined this truth, that he saw this inflexible resolve's real object. In the way of that too, too natural assumption of Noah's—Helen's marriage within a few years—Helen was putting the most formidable impediment she could devise. Through years when Helen would be looked on as most nubile, when all the other girls were marrying and having children, when men were most likely to press her to marry, no one could be really surprised if Helen refused. For everybody to see, she had a child already; and the duty of taking care of him wholly occupied her. Afterward, because she had never married, people would hardly expect her to. Having undoubtedly divined so much, did Arthur Winner Senior go on, divine more by applying himself to why this should be? Arthur Winner could not say. Though blinking no truths, his father, like Noah Tuttle, like the well-bred of that whole generation, preferred, unless he had a practical—say, legal—reason, not to spell some truths out.

And, indeed, no certain spelling-out would ever be possible here. From a marriage bed, from that loathed warmth, Ralph was plainly Helen's deliverer, her boy savior. Had a little girl, outside a big bedroom's blank closed door in the perfect quiet of a hall's late night or early morning, heard a big bed, during the day always neatly made, silent, and motionless, now sounding with dim persistence, with the quicker and quicker rhythmic

49

creak of a horror that was in the end to prove punishable by drowning? Who knew? Helen herself might not be allowed to remember! No; on the whole; Arthur Winner Senior had probably sought no further. What he did not need to know, he did not care to know. What he needed to know, he did know. Helen had a practicable plan; very well, Helen would be helped.

Of good omen might be the fact that he and Noah had at hand the very means to help Helen. Noah Tuttle's secretary was a Mrs. Hunt, a woman of sixty—actually, an inheritance from the days when old Judge Lauderdale was the firm's senior partner. To Mrs. Hunt, Judge Lauderdale had left an annuity when he died, so she could stop working: but for a few years, Mrs. Hunt worked on—as a matter of habit, perhaps; or because she did not know what else to do with herself. Now she had begun to express a wish to retire—though only, of course, when Mr. Tuttle had been able to find someone to suit him. Noah, therefore, proposed to Arthur Winner's father—to consult Arthur Winner Junior, or Julius Penrose, who had just joined the firm, was not deemed necessary—that Helen be taken into the office. Helen would start a secretarial course at the Brocton Business Institute; and in the afternoons she could do filing, things like that; and let Mrs. Hunt show her the work. Eventually, when Helen's typing and shorthand became good enough, she would take Mrs. Hunt's place. In six months, Helen's plan was fully operative. She had her proposed job; she had her house; she and Marigold had their selected paying guests. The future Helen wanted for little Ralph was assured; and with his, hers—the future she wanted, at heart, for herself. Arthur Winner Senior was not wrong; this plan, so far as the plan depended on Helen, had proved feasible. Helen made it work. She would go right on making it work.

And in so far as this plan, that assured future, didn't depend on Helen? Looking at her with a strengthened stir of compassion, eying with compassion Helen's tired face and tense body, Arthur Winner said: "We—everyone who knows you—know what you are perhaps better than you do, Helen. All of us will help you any way we can—"

The door of Judge Lowe's chambers opened. Edna Keating, refolding her dictation book, crossed to her desk. She said: "The judge will only be a minute now, Mr. Winner. He had to go on the bench again. He's through. He'll be right out."

To Helen, Arthur Winner said: "We're coming down from the lake tonight; so I'll be in early tomorrow. We won't be going on with the hearing until ten; so if you want me to see what I can do with Ralph, tell him I'd like to have a talk with him— around nine. Possibly I can change his mind about college; but if I can't, we ought at least to be able to work out something definite for him to do instead." (No doubt that "business loan" Ralph didn't get from Noah!)

Helen said: "Oh, if you would, please, Mr. Winner! I'll tell him. You're so kind—"

Arthur Winner said: "Good night, my dear. I've a feeling this will turn out all right."

From beyond the open door, Judge Lowe called: "That, Arthur, did my heart good! Work's not often such a pleasure." Coming into the room, Judge Lowe unhooked his robe, twitched it off, and threw it on a chair. His massive domed forehead gleamed lightly with sweat; his solid cheeks showed a color of heat; but his strong-lipped mouth had a humorous twist and his eyes shone with grim amusement. "This Ballard fellow has been in a couple of times—nonsupport; wouldn't live with his wife. Been before a justice of the peace once or twice; assault and battery on her—that sort of thing. Last time they were in, Lew Studdiford, who's appearing for him for some reason, asked me to continue—thought they could be got together; and meanwhile Lew said Ballard agreed to give her some money each week. I didn't put much stock in the getting-together; but I didn't mind continuing, because I wanted Morris's office to have a chance to find out what Ballard really earned—I knew he was lying about that. Well, I had a letter from the wife early this week; he hadn't paid her anything. I told Morris to send him a card to appear today. This morning, no Ballard. That was a

51

little too much. So I said: 'Let a bench warrant issue. I want him picked up right now and brought right in.' "

Judge Lowe nodded his head several times. Producing an enormous yellow silk handkerchief, he thoroughly wiped his forehead. "Well, Lew, who *was* here—he's also appearing for the Dummer girl—said he was sure it was some mistake; fellow had the day wrong. He'd find him, bring him in. So I had the warrant held. Fifteen minutes ago, Lew turned up with him. Ballard admitted right away he hadn't paid any money. When I asked him why not, hadn't he agreed he would; he said that was *then*. Mr. Studdiford had been saying they'd get back together so he supposed she'd be giving him a little. She said no; so he'd just tell me now she wouldn't see any of his money while she acted that way. The idea was one I thought I could help him get over—in jail you have lots of time to think. 'Your personal relations,' I said, 'don't concern me; that's between you and your wife. You haven't paid; and you've just told me you have no intention of paying. Take this man, Sheriff; I'm holding him in contempt.' Up pipes Lew: 'No order yet, your Honor.' "

The grim shine of amusement in Judge Lowe's eyes increased. He said: "One on me! True, I'd continued without making an order. I couldn't very well cite him for noncompliance. That really hurt; I could see this lout getting off; and what to do? Then, I had it. I said: 'There's an order as of now. Forty dollars a week for the support of wife Carol, and minor children, Doris, three, and Donald, two. The court further orders that a bond be entered, *with surety,* in the sum of one thousand dollars for faithful compliance. Is he in a position to post that bond, Mr. Studdiford?' Lew whispered with him for a while; and then said he wasn't. Just what I'd been hoping! I said: 'Then he'll have to stand committed until he can. The sheriff will take him to jail.' " Judge Lowe chuckled. "Pretty quick thinking for an old man, if I do say so! Are you driving me to the lake? What are we waiting here for? I'll have to stop by Roylan for a report Reggie Shaw has on the Dummer girl."

Edna Keating said: "Oh; Judge; will you want me to start

typing the Fabian opinion again? I thought maybe Mr. Winner would know about Mr. Penrose—"

"So he might, so he might," Judge Lowe said. "When's Julius coming back from this Washington jaunt?"

"Monday, perhaps," Arthur Winner said.

"Well, I'm preparing to gladden his heart about Fabian; but I've one or two questions I want him to answer. He's right. I'm going to hold; no analogy between a personal action against a minor and a tax sale of a minor's property for nonpayment. Of course, the legal effect of a judgment against a minor not represented by a guardian *ad litem*—yes; a very nice point! In principle, I think it really goes back to the right of *cestui qui use* as an equitable title—distinct from legal title vested in a trustee. Noah see the brief?"

"He made a few suggestions. The brief was Julius's, though."

"And, as Blackstone would have said, a bloody good one! Yes; when he gets back, tell him I'd like to talk to him. Good night, Edna."

Edna Keating said: "Good night, Judge. Good night, Mr. Winner."

THREE

The MASSED FOLIAGE of those big trees more than half hid the marble-cased courthouse building, classic in conception, but in execution falsely elaborated. Above the treetops, the structure raised, clear against the sky's hot haze, a small dome. The dome was surmounted by a pillared cupola in whose round base four faces of the courthouse clock were set. Crowning the cupola, stiffly poised on the summit, stood a bronze effigy—Justice. The copper carbonates of time had turned this effigy greenish-blue. The epicene figure's verdigrised hands held the verdigrised sword and balance. The verdigrised head stared south with blindfolded eyes. From the cupola's base now issued a mighty bong, whose power of sound could carry everywhere in the not-very-large borough of Brocton. Given grave deliberation by the full second's pause, another bong followed; and another; and another.

Over the way, diagonally across the intersection of High Street and Greenwood Avenue, Christ Church's heavy-shaped tower of brown sandstone 1880 Gothic seemed to hear and answer. Out high louvers, a sudden airy burst of musical sounds volumed, the chiming, quite equal in power, of simulated bells. A four-octave clavier attached to Christ Church's organ as an additional manual was activating little leather-tipped hammers to hit and rebound on a range of metal bars chromatically tuned. An electric pickup fed the struck tones into stages of amplification. Instantly, they were delivered to speakers in the tower, from which could issue a range of harmonic effects that true

54

campaniform chimes could never compass. In the ingeniously added, artificial sweetness, down floated the tumble of reverbrating notes on the three-sided close formed by church, parish house, and rectory. Words learned long ago, wedded to the simple hymn tune, produced themselves in Arthur Winner's head: *There's a friend for little children above the bright blue sky.* . . .

At the carillon's sudden outbreak, Judge Lowe and Arthur Winner had exchanged glances. Starting his car engine, Arthur Winner said: "Yes; I suppose something should be done. I still don't know quite what—nor, I think, does the rector."

To Mr. Woolf, in the back seat with him, Judge Lowe courteously said: "That's our church organist, Mr. Woolf—a Mr. Abbott. He's recently taken to coming in and playing the carillon—it's an electronic one—for fifteen minutes every afternoon, maybe at four, maybe at five, maybe at six. We've just inducted a new rector, who feels that the hour should be fixed. Mr. Abbott, one deduces, does not feel that way. His services have been many and devoted; and he's never been willing to be paid for them—so, as Arthur says, we hardly know what to do."

With cordial pleasure, Mr. Woolf said: "Are you an Episcopalian, Judge? So am I. I attend St. Bartholomew's in New York."

By the blink of eye, Arthur Winner could see that Judge Lowe had involuntarily composed, then voluntarily put away, a question that Arthur Winner, too, had asked himself when, earlier, Mr. Woolf had felt called on to declare this religious affiliation. What line of thought brought Mr. Woolf to perceive error in the faith of his fathers? What considerations produced the formal abjuring? Had light blasted him, like Saint Paul, a little this side of Damascus? Had he, like Saint Peter, seen a multitude of fishes and fallen on his knees?

The blink, the second's silence, must be not unfamiliar to Mr. Woolf, for his handling of it showed practice. On his own last words, without waiting for an answer, he craned over, as the car turned the corner, to look into Christ Church's cloistered close, where the reproduction of an English market cross was centered at a meeting of flagged walks. With casual alacrity, he went on: "You have a very attractive church here, Judge."

55

Judge Lowe said: "About that, sir, I understand opinions now differ. What was supposed to be the best ecclesiastical architect in the country at the time designed it; and everybody, at the time, admired it. Now, I hear it called fake Gothic. Like our courthouse, it doesn't recommend itself to what I'm told is the best taste of today." The judge's tone, a little tart, made plain enough his human irritation at having to acknowledge that what seemed all right to him did not seem all right to those who claimed to know. "Well, I'm afraid Brocton will have to put up with both for a while longer! Whatever they look like, they were built to last; and we'll be some time finding any good excuse for tearing them down." Meditating on what he had just said, he gave an incensed grunt. "Arthur, did Harry Minieri tell you about the interior partitioning he found in the rectory when they started work upstairs on the second bathroom? Our new rector's to be a married man, Mr. Woolf. The arrangements of our former rector for forty years, Doctor Ives, wouldn't have been convenient; so we've just now finished, or nearly finished, a remodeling of the rectory."

Over his shoulder, Arthur Winner said: "I don't think he did."

To Mr. Woolf, Judge Lowe said: "Three courses of pressed brick, sir; fourteen inches thick! Where could you find work like that nowadays? Our Union League clubhouse was built the same way. There, they supported the floors with three-by-ten joists, spaced on sixteen-inch centers, double cross-braced, and with every eighth joist also doubled. Elephants could walk around on them! Yes, sir, taste they may have lacked; but when they wanted to do a job, they knew how to do one."

"I guess labor was cheaper in those days, Judge," Mr. Woolf said. "And materials. Even so, that kind of work must have come to a lot of money."

"It did," Judge Lowe said. "No doubt there's far more money in Brocton now than there was then, even if you reckon one of their dollars as worth three or four of ours; but then money was concentrated in the hands of the relatively few. You had no taxes to speak of; so a rich man, when he chose to be charitable, could lay out sums for purposes such as church-building no individual could lay out today."

"You can say that again, Judge!" Mr. Woolf spoke with eagerness. "*We* see it all the time. Fortunes once pretty considerable, practically expropriated! The power to tax is the power to destroy, all right; and even the law's no protection—quite the opposite; they destroy you by statute! Winning an action against the commissioner of internal revenue in the tax courts we find, under present ruling cases, practically impossible. If we carry up, all we can really expect to get is more costs on petitioner. You're simply reduced to working out ways to escape tax liability. And as soon as you do, the act's amended to stop you; you have to start over."

Judge Lowe said: "Well, sir, I don't think it's all to the bad. In principle, I approve." Silently amused, Arthur Winner felt sure that, behind him, Mr. Woolf was doing the next thing to dropping his jaw. Judge Lowe said: "A society's not stable where the rich are very rich and the poor are very poor. When the disproportion of wealth becomes glaring, I regard the state as having, in the public interest, not only a right but a duty to rectify by due process a socially dangerous condition. A man is, of course, entitled to any reliefs or advantages that he, or counsel for him, can find in the statute as written. But I wouldn't, in a court where I was sitting, feel much sympathy for maneuvers whose object was nullification—a defeat by chicanery of the legislative intent to make large incomes pay large taxes."

"Oh, there I entirely agree with you, Judge!" Mr. Woolf said. Fast on his mental feet, Mr. Woolf, however astounded, repaired his mistake with zeal. "The law's the law. We make sure our clients understand that. If they have anything irregular in mind, they know they needn't come to us. All we ever say is what you just said. If they retain us, we'll undertake to see they aren't deprived of benefits they're legally entitled to—something our experience, they all realize, makes us better informed about than they are." Mr. Woolf paused, for what, Arthur Winner could see, must be a quick, a lightning, check on how he was doing. He went on: "I agree, too, Judge, about the danger of too much money in a few hands—conspicuous waste, and so on. But I think it must disturb us all a little when we see good people, like those you mention, no longer in the position to do the charitable works they once did. I don't know what size fortune these benefactors of your church had—"

Judge Lowe said: "They owned the Brocton Potteries—once, enormously profitable. They were among the first to make modern porcelain-covered plumbing fixtures, and held some vital patents—since expired, of course. Samuel Orcutt must have been several times a millionaire. His gifts made a new church, or at least a church on the scale you saw, possible. So much so, that the irreverent for many years used to refer to it as St. Sam's Cathedral."

Mr. Woolf uttered an obliging laugh. "Not bad!" he said.

"Yes," said Judge Lowe, "the Orcutts did very well by Christ Church. And the good wasn't all interred with their bones either. Even with shrunken values, we're one of the best-endowed churches in the diocese—most of it, Orcutt money. They're gone now. None of the name left in Brocton; though I believe a grandnephew of Sam's—he must be an old man—is still living, I think, in Philadelphia; or, perhaps, Baltimore. They had quite a history, locally—well, local history only interests local people. Even to them, old Brocton names now mean nothing."

In Judge Lowe's voice appeared a grumpiness from the acknowledgment forced on him by his own words. The days of the Orcutts were gone; and those days were really his days, too; so where did that leave him? Judge Lowe said: "A good example's Mike McCarthy, whose estate you're working on, Mr. Woolf. Twenty years ago, everyone in Brocton knew that name. A little after that, Mike moved away. If the widow's election to take against the will has come up yet, I daresay you learned some of the circumstances. You know how such things are in small towns, Mr. Woolf—or perhaps you don't. His second marriage amounted to a sensation—many people said, a scandal. Everybody knew about it, and everybody talked about it. Today, it's all forgotten. Mike's name's unknown."

Mr. Woolf said: "Yes, I heard enough to get the idea, Judge."
Arthur Winner did not, for a moment, identify the faintest pos-

sible alteration in Mr. Woolf's tone. He saw then that it was the entry, covered with care, yet not altogether covered, of an aroused interest. Mr. Woolf was entertaining an idea. Gathering his sharp wits about him, he hovered in alert speculation. Was it practicable? Was it feasible? He said: "Mr. Winner, and I thought him very right, ruled that the matter of the election would be heard first, going as it did to a first claim on the corpus. So Mr. Davis presented his argument for Mrs. McCarthy; and then we heard her; and Mr. Winner permitted me to cross-examine her. From the fact of the postnuptial settlement—agreement, I mean—I could see the marriage couldn't have been very—well, happy; and that was confirmed in testimony. Being so much older than she was—"

"Yes, there was that," Judge Lowe said. "Her age, the age of this then June Day—so-called—was unproved or uncertain. I believe she put down twenty-nine on the application for the license. No doubt thirty-nine would have been nearer the truth. I'm afraid that what really weighed in the matter of scandal was the sort of person she was. Her previous life hadn't been exactly secluded. Let's leave it at that, since I presume she's representing herself as having lived respectably from the marriage until Mike's death."

Arthur Winner admired Judge Lowe's reticence—a charitableness that sought to bury old scandal. If Mr. Woolf hadn't found out, why need Mr. Woolf know what everyone knew at the time—that the second Mrs. McCarthy was an entertainer at a roadhouse the police often raided; that she had a record of arrests for prostitution; that Mike first laid eyes on her at a stag party. Put upon a banquet table, "June Day" there stripped herself and danced naked for fifty men.

Judge Lowe said: "No; there were no elements likely to make for success. On Mike's part, we can suppose an aberration of a kind not uncommon in men of a certain age. From time to time, we have it in court in the form, very sad and painful, of indictable offenses. Those, we have to punish; though often they seem to be less willful acts than irresistible compulsions, not perhaps essentially different from any normal falling-in-love. On the new Mrs. McCarthy's part, I think mistake could be pleaded. I don't think she realized that Mike had lost almost all his money. In exchange for making her person available to the old man, she expected, I suppose, to be well-off for life."

"That's interesting, Judge," Mr. Woolf said. He spoke again with studied casualness; but his project was now plain. You could imagine Mr. Woolf, behind the desponding eye and melancholy mouth, secretly exultant, whispering to himself that here might be a gold mine, a means to mend one disadvantage he had been at throughout the hearing. This old boy, this Judge Lowe, had shown that he knew all about Michael McCarthy, deceased—the whole background, the ancient situations; everything, probably, that that other and still older boy, Mr. Tuttle, knew. A smart man, Mr. Woolf doubtless kicked himself for the error he'd fallen into *there*. A smart man, his mistake made, didn't proceed to the mistake, still more serious, of pretending to himself that he hadn't made one. That first mistake was irreparable; there it stood; but, as the alert and heedful so often do, had Mr. Woolf stumbled on a possible chance to make up, to recoup?

If Mr. Woolf kept, as Arthur Winner wouldn't doubt he did, a careful mental register of mistakes to the end that two of the same kind could never occur, he might have been obliged to enter that mistake as a bad one; yet, if it was any comfort to Mr. Woolf, the mistake was not fairly to be called a fool's. A fool, because his observation was slipshod and his powers of conclusion slow and inefficient, would very likely not have made it. Meeting Mr. Tuttle, Mr. Woolf inspected him attentively. He marked the doddering movements, the wagging head of snowy, silky hair. He took note of the doubtful poutings and workings of the shaky-looking blubber lips, the seeming aphasia of statements delayed. He considered the presbyopic fussing, so full of what seemed uncertainty, with papers. There'd be no trouble here! A stern manner ought to be enough to alarm this ineffectual old gaffer into obedience. A firm line would then keep him doing what he was told. Of course, Mr. Woolf couldn't have been more wrong. In the way of law, of legal acumen, he was to find that he might as profitably try teaching his grandmother to suck eggs. In the rencounter of minds, of sparring practice, he was offering to course a rabbit. He met an old lion, whose still doughty paw swung him a swipe or two that tumbled him. Far from defeated, indeed, dumbfounded more than hurt, Mr. Woolf picked himself up. He promptly continued the engagement; but from a prudent or respectful distance, warily.

Reconnoitering Judge Lowe, Mr. Woolf was (a lesson learned?) again wary. To help him, he would have the well-known craving of the elderly to talk, to be listened to; but the matter was, after all, in the judge's court. One misstep, and the judge might decide that something to be regarded as *sub judice* was touched on. Mr. Woolf perhaps heard his own too-interested undertone. That would not do! Things must not be rushed. The risks of openly going after what he wanted were too great; what he wanted must be caused to come to him.

His tone now simply obliging, Mr. Woolf repeated: "Very interesting! That's all very interesting. Of course, I never had any personal acquaintanceship with old Mr. McCarthy, Judge. We'd done a good deal of legal business for the McCarthy sons, so I knew them well; but this was only brought to us after their father was dead." He interrupted himself adeptly. "I see you have some fine early houses. Before the Revolutionary War, I suppose. I'm interested in history. History's a hobby of mine."

The claim, by being so general, naturally denied itself. Judge Lowe, somewhat dubious in tone, said: "Yes; Brocton still has a few eighteenth-century houses left. Perhaps the oldest structure around here is a gristmill at Roylan, where we'll be stopping on the way to the lake. The mill is known to have been in operation in seventeen twenty. You'll see the walls. Those along there—" his gesture, seen by Arthur Winner in the rearview mirror, was toward the east side of Court Street, warm in a refulgency of afternoon sunlight beyond the tree-ranged wide sidewalk of old brick—"aren't as early as that. The large building, incidentally, is the Union League's house I mentioned." He himself gazed a moment at the red brick mass peppered with the trim of white stone pediments over doors and windows and the consoles that supported them. "People don't think much of it, now, either," he said. "Of course, that's very much later—eighteen sixty-nine. Several houses on the other side do date back a long way. Well,

I think you've seen Arthur's office. Perhaps you found that interesting?"

"Yes, I did, Judge," Mr. Woolf said. "Yes, I had an opportunity to see that. I hadn't known I'd have to stay over, so I needed to make some long-distance calls. Mr. Winner was kind enough to take me there, and put a room at my disposal."

Judge Lowe said: "That was built about eighteen hundred— a little more elaborate than the earlier ones. The old Tuttle house. Noah's great-grandfather built it. Noah was born in it, as a matter of fact. When the Tuttles moved to a new house out Greenwood Avenue in the late nineties, Noah and Arthur's father, and former Judge Lauderdale, whose partners they were then, turned it into law offices—"

Swinging the car to go down Market Street to the river, Arthur Winner glanced in the rearview mirror again. Swayed a little by the turn, Mr. Woolf's face appeared. A shift of change, a darkening or shadowing went over the full pale cheeks at the naming of Noah Tuttle. Judge Lowe must have seen the change; for he said suddenly: "A stubborn man, Mr. Woolf. Sometimes he can be difficult. At his age—and I'm near enough there myself to speak—one isn't always in the best of moods. He can be fractious, I know. But in law, in his field, eighty-odd or not, you won't find many abler. The truth is, we're very proud of him. He's truly learned in the law, Mr. Woolf. This is a small town, and our bar's not large, so you'd hardly expect it; but he was chosen, out of the whole state, to be chairman of the advisory committee a few years ago when a general revision of the Decedents Estates Law was undertaken. He himself drafted entire the new, the present, Fiduciaries Act and Fiduciaries Investment Act. The committee, composed of many distinguished and prominent lawyers, didn't, as I recall, find a thing they wanted to change in the drafts. As Noah wrote them, they were enacted into law. A number of other jurisdictions, perhaps you know, have since used them as models."

Mr. Woolf said: "Oh, I can quite believe you, Judge. From what I saw today, I have every respect for his abilities."

Judge Lowe said: "We who know him can go further than that. We have every respect for his character. A man of complete

62

probity, of absolute integrity, Mr. Woolf. He may differ with you; and he may even be unpleasant about it; but you can trust him—you need never fear anything even faintly smacking of trickery, of underhandedness. We must both, I think, admit the painful truth that that's not invariably the case in our profession."

By a not-quite-easy laugh, Mr. Woolf appeared to acknowledge the reading of his thoughts. He said then: "Well, Judge, I'm really very glad to have you tell me that. I'll have to confess, he and I did have one or two little arguments. I mean, I'm glad if I can think he has them with other people, too—not just me. I couldn't see quite what I'd done to make the old gentleman so angry. He said some things I'm sure he didn't mean; but I suppose I must have provoked him. I'd be glad—I'll say this to you, too, Mr. Winner—to express my regrets, if you think that would help matters tomorrow. And if I knew what to express them for! I mean, I'd be happy to show Mr. Tuttle there're no hard feelings on my part."

"That's handsomely spoken, sir," Judge Lowe said. "All of us who are getting older must sometimes pray the indulgence of you younger men, I'm afraid. However, I don't know that I'd speak to Mr. Tuttle. He's as likely as not to be in better humor tomorrow. If he didn't behave very well, he'll express *his* regrets. If you have no hard feelings, you could tell him then."

"Oh, absolutely, Judge," Mr. Woolf said. "I realize he's all you say. I'd like to be his friend. I'll certainly do all I can to be." Glimpsing Mr. Woolf's face in the mirror again, Arthur Winner could see his lips form a smile, deprecatory, intentionally ingratiating. Was something there of the patient shrug, something of the bated breath and whispering humbleness? Were you right or wrong, were you fair or unfair, to guess the kept account? Had you been warned? Did you forget at your peril the ancient grudge that might be fed if Mr. Woolf could catch you once upon the hip?

Arthur Winner touched his brakes, slowing the car; and the air, eddying slower off the broad sun-heated paving of the

63

Eatontown pike, blew warmer across his face. Planted at the roadside to the right, a small metal shield on a metal standard bore the words: HISTORICAL MARKER AHEAD.

In the rear seat, Judge Lowe was saying: "Yes, I think I know what you have in mind, Mr. Woolf. I was getting to that. Community standing, we might say. Well, of course, Mike was Irish, a Roman Catholic. Those things were more attended to then than they would be now. A certain prejudice existed."

Judge Lowe paused; clearly considering how best to phrase a point that Mr. Woolf might find a sore one. He said: "At the time, I mean, when Mike was a boy or young man, I don't know that the prejudice was altogether arbitrary or unreasoned. Seventy years ago—and even thirty years ago, the number of people still around whose attitude had been formed seventy years ago was great enough to make them a majority—the term 'Irish Catholic,' at least to this community, meant the base and obscure vulgar. Few had anything that could be called education. Their mostly low standards of living—all they could afford— resulted in objectionable habits and manners. Politically, they were a troublesome mass vote at the disposal of their own highly purchasable politicians. Religiously, they seemed to be the willing dupes of their priests, of a superstition to the Protestant mind corrupt and alien— There, incidentally, is the Roylan sign, Mr. Woolf, if you're interested."

The car, slowing still more for the turn, approached a double-faced yard-square tablet of cast bronze supported by a bronze post. It was headed: ROYLAN. Below, the embossed letters proceeded: ONE MILE EAST OF HERE ALONG THE FORMER KINGS HIGHWAY STOOD THE ROYAL ANNA TAVERN ERECTED IN 1710. . . .

"Gone, of course, now," Judge Lowe said. "Much of the original structure was burned in seventeen seventy-eight, in connection with what's described as the massacre of a party of local militia, surprised there by a larger party of raiding loyalists. Rebuilt as the Thirteen Stars Tavern in seventeen eighty-five. Burned again, by accident, in eighteen fifty—"

Not without amusement, Arthur Winner reflected that Mr. Woolf had himself to thank. His hobby was history, wasn't it? Judge Lowe said: "Some years ago the Brocton Historical Society, to whom Arthur's father and Mr. Tuttle—they had acquired all the properties here around nineteen ten; and for a song, sir! Nobody then wanted the old fieldstone houses, or what was left of them—had deeded the tavern site, made excavations. A number of interesting implements and kitchen furnishings were turned up—now in the society's Brocton museum. You can still trace the original foundations where the old crossroads used to be—just beyond Doctor Shaw's house, where we'll be stopping."

If Mr. Woolf was disgruntled by what he'd let himself in for, by such a waste of precious time away from the subject of the late Michael McCarthy, he gave no sign. He said: "This is certainly an old part of the country, Judge. I'm glad to have a chance to see something of it. I'll be interested to read up about it when I get home."

Judge Lowe said: "Well, you won't find much on the particular business here. Incidents of the kind weren't infrequent; and the details are really not known. Across the road from the tavern foundations, you'll see that the Historical Society has enclosed with an iron railing a plot supposed to contain the common grave of twenty-three militiamen bayoneted without quarter in the tavern; and put up a stone with their names, or such of them as could be ascertained—"

The road, through rolling fields and fringes of trees, came now to the dip down, by which, curving, it dropped a couple of hundred feet into the miniature valley, the pleasant hollow where the houses stood. From the little eminence, you had a moment's view of the slated roofs below enwreathed by the great boughs of a venerable stand of sycamores—Arthur Winner's own house, the walled garden, the wink of sun off the mantling gilt eagle on the weather vane above the garage; the front, cool in shade, the right-angle wing hot in sunlight, of Julius Penrose's house across the road; the old gristmill's thick roofless walls, hung with masses of honeysuckle and buried in trees, by the tenderly preserved short covered bridge over the brook; and across the brook, past the Dealeys' place, past a meadow in which the doctor pastured three Guernseys, Doctor

Shaw's place. Down into the stillness of sun and shadow the car swept swiftly while nearer treetops closed the prospect.

Judge Lowe said: "It was, therefore, a matter of some awkwardness when old documents, coming to light soon after, seemed to prove that what was actually buried in a pit there was about that number of pigs. They had died of, or were killed to prevent the spread of, a sort of swine fever."

With a hearty laugh, Mr. Woolf said: "Not so good! I see what you mean, Judge."

"The question's been left unresolved," Judge Lowe said. "Perhaps, wisely! Proposals to dig and examine the bones were rejected on the grounds that disturbing them would be a desecration if they were in fact those of the honored dead. Not that there isn't also a question about how much they ought to be honored. Most of the so-called militia seem to have been no less bad a lot than the so-called loyalists. In forays of their own, they'd undoubtedly done enough in the way of horse-stealing, house-burning, murder, and rape for the others to have a score to settle."

Mr. Woolf said: "Isn't that the truth, Judge! If only we knew! That's a thing that interests me about history. Most of what you read's ex parte—we're used to studying evidence, so we see *that* right away. What *aren't* they telling you? A lot of men they put up statues to might not look so good if we knew what they really did; or why they did it. Or some of the other things they did that they managed to keep dark or have hushed up."

"Yes; men, perhaps unfortunately, are men," Judge Lowe said. Mr. Woolf's knowing triumph over the dead might have disturbed his sense of justice; for he went on: "If all hearts were open, all desires known; and if no secrets were hid—each of us, I think, might do well to consider just where that would leave him personally, whether he'd still be quite so well regarded as he may be now."

Judge Lowe paused, as though he invited Mr. Woolf to ponder for a minute that situation—the regrettable good guess to be made. Behind what man's honorable-appearing face, his airs of sound principle, his manner of rectitude, lay no self-knowledge

66

of at least a few mean secrets? More or less successfully not thought on, more or less safely out of public sight, some old matters of shame, some shoddy episodes—follies of appetite; lapses of honor—always (the virtual certainty was) lay hid in each man's heart. Judge Lowe said: "Who's that, Arthur—Rodney?"

"It is," Arthur Winner said. "He seems to want to speak to us."

By a rural delivery box at the road's edge was parked a convertible coupé, not new, but with a new paint job of brilliant scarlet enamel. Beside the car stood Rodney Revere, rapidly waving a large envelope at them. Slowing down, Arthur Winner swung over to the close-mowed grass of the wide roadside.

Mr. Woolf had looked sharply at the A. S. WINNER on the neat big mailbox. Then he looked past the gate, set back with formal curved wings and white posts with urn-topped finials, to the drive and up the long lawn under the sycamores to the ample house whose solid walls in harmonious shades of aged, uncoursed fieldstone rose luminous and warm in the dappling of sun across them. He said: "You certainly have a nice place here, Mr. Winner!"

The exclamation's surprise of respect was unmistakable. While Mr. Woolf would hardly, in what he saw, be finding evidence of actual wealth, of great amassings of money of the kind he must have come to know something about (even if he was only the little man hired to protect them), Mr. Woolf, in the space of a glance, had plainly made a rapid computation and revised upward certain estimates. The admiring comment with which he relinquished it, declared the opinion that Mr. Woolf, with efficient tact, had been concealing all day—that these semi-hicks weren't of any account. Small-town and smalltime, how much were they likely to make a year? When, as the moment always did, the moment came for money to talk, what would their insignificant affairs enable them to say?

Mr. Woolf nodded, confirming his new findings. In his sad eye a light of satisfaction briefly gleamed. This Brocton might remain an inconsequential town; but he could guess, gratified, that this company he kept was the most superior the town had to offer—people with nice properties; and, so, it followed, people who were successful, people of weight, people looked up to; and, so, it followed further, in a flash of conviction that lifted his heart, the real society of the town, the best—not, as he might have feared his getting an invitation meant, the second best.

With an ease of familiarity, black face brightly shining, Rodney Revere, who wore a sport shirt of many colors and a pair of tan sharply creased slacks, approached the halted car. "Glad I got you, Mr. Winner!" he said. "First thing: I have this for Judge Lowe. Doctor Shaw got a call; so there's nobody home at his house. So he drove by here; and said this was something Judge Lowe wanted, would I give this to him." Rodney came to a thoughtful halt. He said: "The truth is, I couldn't quite understand him—whether you *were* going to stop by; or whether it was in case you happened to. So I didn't know just what to do—if you had to have it, or not. So when I happened to see Judge Dealey's car come down the hill, I knew he was going out to the lake, too; so I thought I'd give it to him to give to you." Rodney smiled again. "Man, he was driving so fast, he was by before he could see me! Here you are, sir."

Judge Lowe said: "Much obliged to you, Rodney."

"You're quite welcome, Judge," Rodney said.

Half turned in the front seat, Arthur Winner could observe on Mr. Woolf's face the shadow of new amazement or incomprehension. The shadow would seem to show that, though holding with religion the concept of all men as equal, Mr. Woolf, humanly enough, meant to say that *he* should be any man's equal, not that every man should be *his* equal. Kindly given liberty, this young colored fellow with his fancy shirt and natty pants would seem to be helping himself to license. Ought not somebody to speak up: *Remember who you are, and whom addressing?*

Rodney being there, Arthur Winner could not very well help Mr. Woolf with more local history, explain to him that the extra service the judge acknowledged—Rodney's waiting for them with Doctor Shaw's envelope—like Rodney's very presence at Arthur Winner's gate, was, in fact, a piece of obligingness on Rodney's part. For a couple of years now, Rodney had been away from Brocton most of the time, attending a college of dentistry; but, during vacations, there were Brocton people he would "help"—you might say, less for money than for old times' sake. Not that Mr. Woolf made any mistake about who Rodney was. Rodney's great-grandfather had been a runaway slave. As a youth in the 1850's, he got north, where, associating the name with freedom, he called himself Paul Revere. Abolitionists in Brocton found him work. By his diligence and intelligence, Paul Revere prospered. A highly respectable man, he rose to become, when he was older, sexton of Christ Church, and steward of the Union League—positions, it might interest Mr. Woolf to know, descendants of his had ever since held.

Paul Revere was also a prolific man. In him originated a complicated connection of aunts and uncles, of nephews, nieces, and cousins of various degrees, on whom parishioners of the church and members of the club could rely for high-type doers of domestic work. Supervised first by old Paul, and then by his grandson Alfred—Paul outlived all his sons—no Revere, over a good many years, was permitted to take such situations with any other people—a family discipline that Arthur Winner didn't doubt still operated; his mother's Luella, though surnamed White, was a daughter of a daughter of Alfred; and the day she was found filching bottles of sherry, Alfred could make a bad day for her! Rodney was to be, was now within months, another year, of being, a professional man, a duly licensed dentist; but if Rodney was home and available, Rodney's Aunt Em, who worked for the Winners, had only to speak to Alfred. Rodney would be directed to go and give her any help she thought she needed. Rodney had been all week doing, with energy and no apparent feeling that he was demeaned, those parts of a house cleaning that Em (she was strong as a horse) held to be too hard for her now that she was getting on. After a conscientious eight hours of intelligent toil, Rodney hung his work clothes in the garage lavatory, washed up, donned garments suited to a social evening, and drove off cheerfully in his secondhand but newly painted and brightly shined car. Mr. Woolf's not-unnatural mistake would lie in his supposing that Rodney, because he gave service, was somebody's servant.

Rodney said: "Second thing, Mr. Winner: Mr. Tuttle's trying

to get hold of you. He was ringing here; but I didn't get to the telephone in time. When she left this morning, Aunt Em said Mrs. Winner wanted all the brass polished; so I was just finishing up, working on the front door knocker, when I heard the telephone inside. Only, I'd been coming around, so the door wasn't open; and I had to go to the back to get in. They'd stopped ringing then; and they didn't know who was calling. The way I found out; it wasn't more than a few minutes before Mrs. Penrose came over. When Mr. Tuttle didn't get any answer here, he called there. Said for you to call him right away."

Frowning, Arthur Winner said: "Mrs. Penrose didn't say why —what he wanted?"

"I don't believe he told her, Mr. Winner. She only said he told her he knew you were going to be driving through here, and he had to talk to you. He was calling from the office, he said. That was about fifteen minutes ago. I didn't know would you want to call him from here; so the front door's not locked—"

"No, on the whole," Arthur Winner said. "I'll wait till we get to the lake. I can call him from there. I don't want to hold the judge and Mr. Woolf up—"

Judge Lowe said: "Oh, call him, Arthur, call him! Only, don't let him talk all night."

Rodney said: "The other doors are all right; I locked them. So I guess I'll go along. Good night, Mr. Winner. Good night, Judge." With the obvious benevolent idea of not leaving the stranger out, Rodney gave Mr. Woolf a separate nod, and said affably: "Good-by!"

In the telephone he held, Arthur Winner could hear the throb of ringing, mechanically reiterated, and vain. He felt the coolness of the house contrasted with the heat of the afternoon beyond the open front door. From the car, drawn close to the steps, came Judge Lowe's voice, not loud but distinct, accustomed to making itself reach every corner of a courtroom. ". . . could fairly be called a wealthy man. He'd built up one of the largest and most successful contracting businesses in this part of the state; and that, ironically, was how he came to lose almost all his money."

Five miles away, the Brocton operator said: "One-one-two does not answer, sir."

"Please try one-one-one again," Arthur Winner said.

He controlled as well as he could his irritation—in part, to be laid, he supposed, to the heat of the long hard day; in part, to his certainty, a virtual foreknowledge, that Noah didn't "have to" speak to him at all. There was hardly the remotest chance that anything important in a business way could have come up; and even if something had, it wouldn't be of such a nature that it couldn't wait until tomorrow. What, then, did Noah want? With weariness of spirit, Arthur Winner knew. Returned from the hearing (and his encounter with Arthur Winner's Aunt Maud!), shut up in his room, Noah had doggedly been going over a mass of figures, locating at last what he was looking for. About some disputed, inconsequential item in the account, he now had the proof that he was right, quite right. He just wanted Arthur Winner to know. On the contrary, on the other hand, shut up in his room, Noah might have been doing nothing, slumped there in a stupor of brooding, afflicted to think how he had behaved. Like a child, Noah, at the end of the day forlornly conscious of his naughtiness, sought to make amend. He wanted to tell Arthur Winner that he knew, he knew; he hadn't meant to! It was all his fault. All he did was make everybody trouble—

Judge Lowe said: "As we go on up the valley, you'll be able to see still remains of the right of way—gradings; bridge piers; even an old tunnel. I suppose, since many electric interurban lines were showing big profits in the early nineteen hundreds, the project seemed sound. But, I suppose, too, the handwriting was on the wall, if they'd only looked. I suppose they ought to have counted the number of automobiles owned in Brocton even then."

Too true! The right of way, now abandoned, was planned to compete with those buckboards his mother recalled to Arthur Winner, with horse-drawn drays proceeding at a couple of miles an hour to Eatontown. Once the new line was operating, how greatly shortened were trips from Brocton to the lake; and how much more interesting! Any boy must be impressed by the transit company's great maroon cars. They were three times as long as the little streetcars in Brocton, and they had formidable iron cowcatchers, like steam locomotives. Coming back from Eatontown, on the favorable grades down to Brocton, they could, and often did, attain speeds of sixty miles an hour. People going to the lake would be carried up the line as far as Shelby's, a farm near the foot of the hill. There, you left your things for Mr. Shelby to bring along later in his wagon, and walked the trail as before. After a few years, the trail was improved enough to let early model T Fords be driven—a jolting, adventurous ride—to the lake. Arthur Winner's father bought one and kept it in Mr. Shelby's wagon shed. That, too, was not long in changing. The old Eatontown turnpike was straightened, widened, and paved; and there (yes, the handwriting had been on the wall!) was the real end of the Brocton Rapid Transit Company. Arthur Winner's father's Pierce-Arrow, before, driven only around town, or on the "improved" road to Riverside or Mechanicsville, could henceforth get to Shelby's as quickly as the trolley and much more conveniently. Soon, it could even go on to the lake.

The throb of ringing in Arthur Winner's ear ceased suddenly. Out of breath, a voice cried: "Tuttle, Winner and Penrose! Miss Mills."

Arthur Winner said: "Gladys, I'm at Roylan, on the way up to the lake. There was a message here that Mr. Tuttle had been trying to get me."

Gladys Mills said: "Oh, I'm so sorry, Mr. Winner! Yes; he did want you. Hasn't he answered? I was out a minute. Perhaps he didn't hear the bell. He's in his room. I'll go and tell him."

"Looking back," Judge Lowe said, "the astonishing thing is how everybody could be so slow to realize the hopeless situation. The Brocton Rapid Transit Company could not be said ever to have made any money; for a while, the operating expenses were earned, with enough over to pay the interest on the bonds. Almost to the end, people who should have known better believed dividends on the stock would be paid soon. Moreover, most of them never seemed to realize that if the line couldn't be made to do a paying business, the bonds were secured by nothing at all. True, what secured them had cost a lot. Everything—roadbed;

power plant; substations; carbarn; rolling stock—had been to the highest specifications of the day. But, as they stood, all they were good for was a trolley line. In the late nineteen twenties, that was to say; they were good for nothing—"

"Mr. Winner!"

Arthur Winner said: "Yes, Gladys."

With perplexity, Gladys Mills said: "Mr. Tuttle isn't here, sir. I don't know where he could have gone. He was waiting for you to call him."

"You don't know what he wanted to talk to me about? Mr. Penrose hadn't called from Washington again, had he?"

Gladys Mills said: "No; Mr. Tuttle didn't tell me what it was, Mr. Winner. And as far as I know, there wasn't any other call from Mr. Penrose—not after the one when you were here this morning." She was silent a moment. She said: "There's only one thing, Mr. Winner. He sounded sort of funny when he was asking me for an outside line. I hope he wasn't not feeling well—"

"But you've been into his room?" Arthur Winner said.

"Oh, yes; I went in, sir. And he's not in the little room, either. I thought he might be taking a nap. And he's not in the wash-room—I made sure."

"Of course, Helen's not there?"

"No, sir. She left fairly early. I think she said she was going over to the courthouse to see Mrs. Keating about something. Before that, I know she was reading some of her transcript of the hearing to Mr. Tuttle; and I think she said she might be coming back this evening to help him with some of the McCarthy figures."

"Nobody came in to see him, I suppose?"

Gladys said: "Why, no, sir. Well, Mr. Breck came in; but—"

"Bernie?" Arthur Winner said. Bernie Breck was chief of the five Brocton Borough policemen.

"Yes," Gladys said. "I was filing; and he just went through the office and I heard him knock on Mr. Tuttle's door. I think Mr. Tuttle may have forgotten and left his car in a no-parking place again. Oh, I hadn't thought of that! Of course, Mr. Tuttle usually gives Mr. Breck the key; and *he* moves it. I didn't see

73

Mr. Breck leave; but I know he didn't come back with the key. So perhaps Mr. Tuttle went out to move it himself. He might have met somebody; and—"

And, Gladys knew as well as Arthur Winner did, Noah's urgent need to reach Arthur, his supposedly important communication, would then slip the old man's mind altogether. Incidentally, Arthur Winner must reflect, Noah really ought to stop driving a car; but who would venture to say so? Who would call his attention to his malady without a cure—the yellow leaves, or none, or few; the twilight of the day; in the ashes, the doubtful glow of the expiring fire? This was the time of year on which Noah was congratulated; these were the mental powers whose persistence was often and admiringly mentioned. Remarkable? Yes; so remarkable that admiration posed the query of astonishment: Can such things be?

To that question, a question must be returned. The answer depended on what you meant. In his own field, on those probate and fiduciary matters to which Noah had given a lifetime, half a century, Noah could sound as acute and sagacious as ever. There, nothing unknown or new could now confront him; the right answers, formulated over and over so often that he had them by heart, came of themselves. If unimpaired mental powers was construed to mean competence to do today that job of ten years ago on the Decedents Estates Law that Willard Lowe had praised, Arthur Winner would be inclined to agree that Noah, unequaled in technical knowledge, unexcelled in practical estate and trust management, with so much of the special sort of legal experience needed in this special sort of work, probably still kept that competence. If, by unimpaired mental powers, you meant an unaffected judgment, a continuing sound sense of proportion, a reliable balance, a firmness of command in coming to decisions and a promptitude in acting on them— what was to be said about that?

As though to counterpoint the subduing thought, an offer in evidence, a proof of loss, Judge Lowe could be heard. ". . . this, you see, was soon after the failure of the transit company. Mr. Tuttle represented the bondholders, he was the trustee in bankruptcy confirmed by the Federal district court, in the windup of affairs; and he did a masterly job, Mr. Woolf. The business, of course, remained bad enough; but Noah so handled it that liquidation wasn't utterly disastrous. Due entirely to him, the total loss most of us thought impossible to avert was averted. Thanks to Noah, and no one else, Mike and a lot of other Brocton people didn't find themselves penniless. Mike knew that. It was their relationship in that business that led to Noah's consenting to be Mike's executor."

Breaking the silence in which Gladys, perhaps a little subdued herself to see the wrecks of time (though such things were so unimaginably distant from her), waited on him, Arthur Winner said: "Yes; I think we may assume he's all right. That's probably what happened."

Gladys said: "Would you like me to stay here until he comes back, or I hear from him, Mr. Winner? I could ring the Union League. He might have moved the car to over there; and then he might have just gone in."

"I think not, thanks," Arthur Winner said. "Put a note on his desk, in case he and Helen come back this evening. Say I called; that I'll be at the lake from about twenty minutes from now until ten or so, and he can get me there if he needs to. Close up then, and go home. You ought to have been off before this."

"Oh, I don't mind, Mr. Winner! With Mr. Penrose away, and you and Mr. Tuttle over at the courthouse all day, Mary and I hardly had a thing to do. You'll be in tomorrow, won't you?"

"In the morning," Arthur Winner said. "Tell Mary we'll shut at noon."

His hand still on the telephone, Arthur Winner stood motionless a moment while he thought of calling the Union League himself—not to ask what Noah wanted; for Noah had presumably forgotten that he wanted anything; but simply to speak to him. Since the closing of the house on Greenwood Avenue, Noah had lived at the club; and he was comfortable enough— more comfortable, and certainly better taken care of, than he could have been anywhere else. That undoubted fact did not much affect the picture of Noah, by himself, laboriously mounting the wide main flight of stairs; fumbling with his key; tottering a little as he entered a deserted room—though commodious, though containing everything an austere old man could possibly want, surely without cheer. Good, and, so, still sound, shabby only, not shoddy, everywhere in the Union League the furnishings were those of the 1870's—they, too, were very old; they, too, were left from another day.

But, of course, Noah, if he had entered the club absently (instead of going back to the office across the courthouse square, as he intended), would pad at once to the antiquated barroom; to the mahogany glow, perfumed by the slopped spirits of decades; to the massive last-century magnificences that probably comforted him. One of the boys, or Alfred Revere himself, would receive the old man with salutes of deference, set him in his corner, pamper him respectfully with their service. As Noah, aches of age warming away, glooms of age dissolving, took heart from his couple of ounces of whisky, he would be heard, all attention, if he chose to assure himself by denouncing in detail to-day's news, by complaining in general against the time and the customs. Unless Arthur Winner could show good reason for calling, Noah would resent the interruption.

FOUR

RUTH SHAW said: "They're all, or almost all, down at the boathouse, swimming, Arthur. Out there, do they have everything they want, now? I suppose if they haven't, the judge can bellow."

Arthur Winner said: "They have Scotch, they have rye, they have bourbon; they have charged water; they have ice. What would they be expecting? Dancing girls?"

"Willard Lowe wouldn't mind a few," she said. "Don't you believe he would!" In her wide, tanned, and competently composed face, Ruth Shaw's eyes turned, ironic and cheerful. "Men!" she said. "What a cave this place is! A real chamber of horrors. Heaven be praised, we aren't cooking much." She looked around the lodge's vast old kitchen with the long-disused wood-burning range that stretched several yards across the chimney wall. "You know, what people would put up with when we were children is simply extraordinary! Don't talk to me about the good old days. Em! Are we going to have enough plates?"

From the oversized pantry beyond, a voice called back: "How many is there now, Mrs. Shaw?"

"Let's see," Ruth Shaw said. Her solid and matronly figure posed itself as though for thought. She began to count on her fingers. She said: "The little ones. Mine; and Ann; and Priscilla Penrose and Stewart; and the Dealey boys—that's eight of *them.* Doctor Trowbridge, and his mother, and Miss Cummins. Fred and Del. You and Clarissa. Judge Lowe and your Mr. What's-his-name. Was Reg at Roylan? Did you see him? He said he was coming; but you never know."

"He'd got a call," Arthur Winner said. "He'd left before we got there—"

"Sure, sure!" Ruth Shaw said. "If he goes back to Brocton to the office—a stop's got to be put to this. He has too damned many patients. Three men couldn't do what he tries to do." Her brown eyes glinted again, coming around to Arthur Winner. Dropping her voice slightly, she said: "That's what's driving him to drink, in case you wondered."

"Well, I'd need a drink, too," Arthur Winner said.

"When you need one at nine o'clock every morning, you'd better start doing something about it," she said. "That man was at the hospital all last night. There's this hydrocephalic baby— and if you don't happen to know what *that* is, all the better for you!—Reg and Bruce Lamont are trying to keep alive. So he comes home for breakfast—they'd done a third operation. So he goes back to the office. After that, I don't know; but he swore he'd get some sleep this afternoon, and come out here to supper. Em! I make it eighteen. Can we manage?"

"Yes, ma'am. We got twenty. I just counted."

To Arthur Winner, Ruth Shaw said: "I don't know how you men are going to like it, but all you're having's a sort of buffet. We'll put things on the big terrace table and people can help themselves. There's plenty, Lord knows; but nothing's hot but Em's beans, which I hope are all right. Em's worried because that beat-up electric stove seems to come on and off—"

"They all right, Mrs. Shaw. I just tried them."

"Then, everything's all right. Just tell Clarissa, Em and I have the feast under control. There's nothing for her to do; so she needn't come up—she's not to come up. That Mrs. Trowbridge has been harrying her all day—" Putting a hand on Arthur Winner's arm, pushing him, Ruth Shaw moved with him and went out on the back porch with him. "Forget that about Reg," she said. "He's had a hard summer. I'll get him fixed. Reg thinks because he's only a little tight most of the time nobody notices. I felt like having you know that I know that everybody notices. When this damned horrible infant dies, Ruth's going to lower the boom. Was he tight this afternoon?"

Arthur Winner said: "I didn't see him, Ruth. He'd left."

"That's right," she said. "I forgot." The brown eyes, ironic and amiable almost ogled him. "Arthur cannot tell a lie! It's nice when you're able to count on something about somebody." She clasped her hands over her full arms and breathed the warm air deeply. "I love that smell," she said.

Sunlight had left most of the lake. The lengthening shadow of the tree slopes across the water to the west reached far out; but a late blaze of sun still rested on this shore. The heat was that of summer, heavy with brooding thunderous quality; yet the light, though so full and splendid, by a different angle, by the creeping trend of withdrawal to the south, was no longer summer light. The near-evening sunshine held a gauzelike haze in which every outline softened. If there had been a breeze, the breeze had fallen. The lake was motionless; yet from the woods around, slow currents of air moved. Wafted with them was viridity, a smell of coolness, of shadowed tree trunks, of shady leaves, of ferns, and not-quite-dry moss, which Arthur Winner, too, breathed gratefully.

Ruth Shaw said: "Somewhere, there are thunderstorms. I suppose we'll get them just when we start to eat. Do you ever wish this were forty years ago, Arthur? We used to have such wonderful summers. Or don't you remember? Or don't you think so? Or didn't you?" She had turned her head with an almost sensuous smile, as though of dreaming. The broadened, hearty face, rapt in reminiscence, seemed to be replaced, an instant's tricking of the eye, by another face—all the while hidden there; long overlaid; yet abruptly, perfectly, recalled by Arthur Winner. The face was the face, not seen for years, of a girl named Ruth Fentriss—pert; cool; pretty only in being young, but what older prettiness could compare with youth's prettiness? The light lighting up that earlier face passed; and the face passed, too. Ruth Shaw looked as though she could have wept. She said: "Be off, you oaf! You don't know what I mean."

Particulars of what Ruth Shaw, gazing back down her life until she came on Ruth Fentriss, then selected to remember could not be known; yet, being such stuff as dreams are made on, the gen-

eral nature of their baseless fabric was not hard to know. That
drifting bosky smell, a fragrance too subtle to be called sweet,
signaled the mind; and, from an immense repertory, the mind
pulled out associated thoughts. Here at the lake, hours were
sunny, and every day a happy day. Every night was deep and
starry, a peace into which one sank; and, led beside still waters,
slept.

As seen by a child, coming to the lake had been to go on a
journey; and, in fact, a journey it then was. Being fifteen miles
from Brocton, the best part of half a day, not the present's best
part of half an hour, was originally required. Longer than miles
from Brocton was a distance that lay, in those days, between
the one life there and the other life here. Brocton was winter—
a world of sidewalks, dead lawns, storm windows, and temporary
wooden vestibules; a schedule of school without end; a passage
of slow time with everything done indoors. The lake was summer. Clothes were fewer and more agreeable to wear. Meals
were different—more like constant parties. Families at the lake
lived in their separate bungalows; but they walked up to the
so-called lodge and ate together. Rooms for living and sleeping
were different. In the taste of the nineties, the bungalows were
very rustic. Exteriors of half-round bark slab, of rough juniper
veranda posts and rails, of roofs whose shingles were hand-hewn,
enclosed consciously simple and bare interiors, puncheon-
beamed—the rooms had no ceilings; floored with broad knobby
planks, walled with unfinished knotty pine. Cobblestones had
been used to build the big fireplaces. Originally—a difference
of great interest to a child—there was no inside plumbing.
Modest, retired among plantings of hemlock, stood trim, commodious outhouses.

In those days, the days of Arthur Winner's earliest memories,
the trip to the lake, as his mother had reminded him, was made
in horse-drawn buckboards. Along the valley road from Brocton
the buckboards carried everybody; but for the last mile and a
half, all uphill, following what was more a trail than a road,
everybody, to spare the horses, got out and walked. Short cuts
could be taken on foot; and, going ahead, the children were al-

ways up first. With them, leading them, was generally Mr. Detweiler—George Detweiler's Uncle Ned. A conscientious outdoorsman, Ned Detweiler was versed in woodcraft. He toted packs and portaged canoes for the fun of it. He cooked skillfully at open fires. Taking several of the boys, he would hike into the woods; and though they could easily have got back to the lake, they pitched camp and spent the night bedded on the ground under shelters that Mr. Detweiler showed them how to put together with no other tool than a sheath ax.

Up ahead of the rest, gaining the top of the hill, the children found themselves deep in a preserved strip of first-growth forest. Spanning the road or trail, a rustic gate arch confronted them. Close by was an immense glacial boulder to which bronze letters had been attached. They spelled: PONEMAH. With no effort, Arthur Winner could hear Ned Detweiler's voice, years ago silenced. Mr. Detweiler liked to recite for them: *Thus departed Hiawatha* (emphatically "poetic," insistently solemn, the mechanical trochaic tetrameters trotted along) *to the islands of the blessed, to the kingdom of Ponemah, to the land of the hereafter. . . .*

To go to the boathouse, Arthur Winner was coming down the path that passed below the lodge terrace. Sunlight, getting through a grove of pines planted half a century ago along the gentle lower slope, struck dazzling into Arthur Winner's face. From above, Judge Lowe's voice carried to him. Like Noah Tuttle in the Union League bar, Willard Lowe was ingesting some old man's milk, and now, gratefully, was beginning to get the good of it. An earlier edge of tired concern, of active or vigorous disapproval, had gone. What residue of regret his voice held was passive, pensive. Sad, but not dissatisfied, he was saying: ". . . dead, today, every man Jack of them! Well, Mr. Woolf, it is not growing like a tree, in bulk doth make . . ."

Smiling, Arthur Winner could be sure that the judge, his mind comforted, a physical pleasure in being alive recovered, enjoyed a mild access of the senses of sentiment and of eloquence. Arthur

Winner suspected him of gesturing at the great oak on the terrace, calling it, magniloquent, to Mr. Woolf's surely startled attention. This tree was, indeed, worth attention.

Out over the edge of the terrace parapet, out over Arthur Winner on the path below, and far beyond, the big lower boughs extended. The oak stood well removed from the old lodge's rustic front; yet Judge Lowe and Mr. Woolf, not far from the door, could be said to sit under it. The trunk, a ponderous short pillar of whitish gray bark, furrowed with massive perpendicular ridges as though to show its strength, was seven feet through. The highest twigs of the broad rounded crown were ninety feet in the air. Those low first boughs, nearly horizontal, reached sideways almost as far. Some of them were thicker than a man. Mounting in intricate symmetry, lesser boughs spread out branches too many to count, lifted in hills of leaves, leaves innumerable. Even now in September, they were kept green and lustrous by what must be a gigantic root system, boring down to the water table, searching half an acre for food. When they came to fall, those leaves would, not a few, measure eight or more inches.

Arthur Winner's idea as a boy had been that the Ponemah oak was the biggest tree in the world; and though he presently learned differently, learned that this tree was nothing compared to trees of the Pacific coast, here was at least a king of its kind—you would go a long way before you found as big an oak. On a visit—and this was years ago—a friend of Arthur Winner's father, a college professor who was an eminent—the new word still stayed in Arthur Winner's head—dendrologist, had painstakingly measured the oak. He gave his expert's opinion that no *Quercus alba* of such dimensions could be less than three hundred years old; and in all probability was very much older. Past the Ponemah oak when the country had seemed permanently theirs, Indians a good deal more real than Hiawatha might have filed.

What you knew at fifty—that a hundred years, far from being forever and ever, was not long; that all wonders, in time, will prove supposititious—left untouched the amazing thoughts you were at liberty to have at ten. The oak was the certificate that those days had not been merely imagined. Unchanging itself, the oak was living proof of afternoons when children (among them, a child, Arthur Winner Junior), by means of a ladder of cords that Arthur Winner's father dexterously tied together and hung for them, had played in the tree. With monkey agility (somewhat limited, since their feet were not hands, too) they made their excited way upward from point to point, exploring as far as they dared the dizzy aerial world.

Those children had been real; as, in their time, the Indians, possibly passing by, had been. The innocence of that stage of life was real; for innocence's essence was a rapturous unknowing, a bliss of doubt-free ignorance. The folly of being wise, those children had never yet committed. They knew nothing of life's unkept promises and impossible tasks. Soon to disappear, soon to be no more—the men and women they were fathers to, the grownups now found to bear their names, were total strangers to them—their sole existence was had as of there and as of then. In random flashes of memory, they peopled, all spirits, though clearly seen, that pageant. High in the green afternoon shade of the great tree, they hung and swung. Running to gain the Ponemah rock, the long-lost children could be heard shouting to each other through the woods above the bright lake. In clear echo, Arthur Winner, now close to the boathouse, where it lay with the last shafts of sunlight still on it, could hear today's children, the young voices, the sportive shouts from the water.

✦

"Darling," she said, "did you have a dreadful day?"

With quick ease, stepping neatly, light on her feet, Clarissa mounted the stairs from the landing to the veranda, running the width of the boathouse, that overlooked the lake. Strapped under her chin, a white rubber bathing cap framed in tight smooth lines her reposed clear features. Her firmly formed body moved, tall and athletic, under a plain bathing suit of black fabric. She said: "It was so hot! I hoped you'd be able to get out earlier."

Arthur Winner looked at her with pleasure. "So did I," he said. "So did we. I adjourned our meeting before three; but Wil-

83

lard was tied up in chambers. So we waited. And how were things here?"

"All right—I trust!" she said. "The children seem to be having a lovely time. The water's wonderful. I just got out myself—I'm wet."

Coming close to him, she set her fingers against his shoulders, holding him off, while she put her head forward and kissed him. Speaking low, she said: "Our other guests made motions of enjoyment, anyway—and I'll venture that Mrs. T. really *did* enjoy herself. I'll tell you about that. But not right now." She nodded past him, down the veranda. "Miss Cummins!" she murmured. "She and I had our clothes in the end room. She went up to dress a few minutes ago. She's in there. So if you want to go swimming, you'll have to wait—I'm afraid your bathing trunks are in there, too. She won't be long."

"No, I don't think I'll go swimming," Arthur Winner said. "I have another guest for you; which, I gather, is all right. Ruth, who says to say everything's under control, seemed confident there'd be enough to eat. He's a lawyer from New York. I left him on the terrace having a drink with Willard, so I can sit a moment; but for various reasons I don't want him to feel he's neglected."

"Arthur, at least take your coat off," Clarissa said. "Yes; there's tons to eat. What time is it?"

Removing his linen jacket and laying it on the settee by the veranda rail, Arthur Winner said: "A little after five." He sat down on the settee. Taking her hand, he said: "Sit here."

"No, darling; I'm soaking wet," she said. "And really I suppose I ought to get dressed. Was Adelaide helping Ruth?"

"I didn't see her," Arthur Winner said. "Though I thought I heard Fred talking to her. He drove out by himself and got here before we did."

Clarissa said: "Adelaide wasn't feeling very well. She went in after lunch to lie down. You mustn't say anything; but she believes she's going to have a baby—or hopes she is. She hasn't told Fred; and she doesn't want to see Reggie Shaw; because she's afraid he'll make her take some tests and she'll find she isn't.

Either that, or he'll say, after last time, she mustn't try it again—"

"I think she would be foolish to," Arthur Winner said. "I think you ought to talk to her about it."

"I'm merely her sister, darling," Clarissa said. "Anyway, this must be considered mostly hope—to date. I know about that." Half turning, she half sat on the veranda rail, her back against the center post.

Reaching to take her hand again, Arthur Winner said: "Do you find that entirely comfortable?"

She said: "Yes; I'm afraid I do. I'm only too well padded." She moved her free hand, feeling her long bare rounded thighs and her hips through the tight cloth of the bathing suit. "I try to tell myself I've always been a big girl; but I know better. I'm putting weight on. I don't take it off the way I used to when I played tennis."

"Nonsense!" Arthur Winner said. "There's no fat on you anywhere. Let's not have dieting. Russ Polhemus was telling me this morning that Betty's started it; and they now subsist on nothing but lettuce."

"Whatever happens, you'll be fed, my darling," she said. "If it's after five, I suppose those children ought to come out. They've been in the water almost all day." Turning her head, she called: "Ann, dearest! Priscilla! Winifred! Esther! All of you! The boys, too! I think that's enough, now."

From below, arose a wail in chorus: "Oh, Hendy! Oh, not yet!"

Arthur Winner could see their faces turned up in protest— Stewart Penrose, the Dealey boys, and George Shaw, who had been busy, not far from the plank walk to the float, climbing into and pushing each other out of an old rowboat, now nearly swamped. The girls were together at the float, their hands resting on it. There they lolled in the water, four heads just showing over the float edge in a row. Noticing Arthur Winner on the veranda, Ann shouted at once: "Hello, Father! Aren't you coming in?".

"Not just now," Arthur Winner said. "Aren't you coming out?"

"Oh, ten more minutes! Only ten more minutes!"

"All right," Clarissa said. "Exactly ten more minutes. Then everyone must go and get dressed." Withdrawing abruptly the hand that Arthur Winner held, she stood up, smiling.

Miss Cummins had come out of the door of the room at the end of the veranda. Her short boyish face was flat-cheeked, with small lips curved in what seemed a firm, permanent agreeableness. Her dark hair was braided, and she had coiled the braids tightly round and round her head—an arrangement, Arthur Winner suspected, that her fellow women would take at sight as conclusive evidence that Miss Cummins had no idea of how to make the best of herself. Miss Cummins, thin-hipped in a dark green frock with sprigs of small white flowers all over it, approached in a manner of decision and directness. Answering Clarissa's smile, her lips parted on her even, small upper teeth.

To Arthur Winner, who had arisen, Miss Cummins said, gazing earnestly up at him: "Mr. Winner, I can't tell you how we've felt for you, in town all day! It's been just delightful here. Such fun!" Making plain her awareness that she might have interrupted a conversation, she said: "I saw Mrs. Trowbridge and Whit coming back along the point a minute ago. I believe I'll walk over that way and meet them. Unless there's something I could help with about supper, Mrs. Winner. I'd love to—"

"There's not a thing, thanks," Clarissa said. "All we do now is eat it. We'll be up soon and have something to drink. My dear, let me have that bathing suit and towel. I'll hang them with mine. It's so warm, I think they'll be dry by the time we go home."

Miss Cummins said: "Oh, Mrs. Winner, no! Tell me where to hang it, and I'll—" With smile encountering smile, Clarissa gently took the damp bundle away from her. To Arthur Winner, Miss Cummins said: "I do feel people ought to get more work out of me." To Clarissa, she said: "Well, thanks so much! I did so enjoy getting a swim." She began to move again. "I just go out through here, don't I? I see I do." She offered them a last smile and went into the open passage that led through the boathouse to the back.

While Clarissa carried Miss Cummins's bathing suit and towel to the end of the veranda and attached them with clips to the line there, Arthur Winner sat down again. Coming back, Clarissa said: "Yes, Doctor Trowbridge went for a walk with his mother—or, she with him. She has lots and lots to tell him." Perched on the rail again, her shoulder against the post, she let Arthur Winner have her hand. "He adapted himself wonderfully, I must say. Good with the children. Oh; before I forget, there's something I must ask you. We've a little problem, he and I. I take it he's come to call you 'Arthur.' What's the etiquette? I mean, because of his—er—cloth, or something, do I keep calling him 'Doctor Trowbridge' until he calls me 'Clarissa'? Or, is he waiting for me, a matron a trifle his senior, to call him 'Whit' before he stops calling me 'Mrs. Winner'? Incidentally, every time Miss Cummins calls him 'Whit,' his mother's at pains to make an occasion to call him 'Whitmore.' "

"I expect he'd be pleased if you called him 'Whit'—or 'Whitmore,' " Arthur Winner said. "We got to it gradually. I imagine he feels he's known me, in a relative sense, quite a while. His correspondence was with me, as clerk of the vestry. When he was here to preach last June, we were, of course, quite formal. It only began to be Arthur after the induction. The spirit of the age, I suppose." He laughed. "*His* age. It's not particularly relevant; but I can't help remembering that having had him as vestryman and warden for nearly twenty-five years, old Doctor Ives always said 'Mr. Winner' to my father; and I'm sure he'd have been struck speechless if Father had ever addressed him as 'Jonathan.' Yes; I thought you'd find him easy to get on with. I do—" Arthur Winner smiled. "Which may be because he takes great care to ask my advice. Then, if I make any suggestions, he at once follows them. In matters of parish business, that is. In matters of faith and morals, I daresay I'd find him less malleable. I can assure him I won't intrude there. What has his mother to tell him?"

"Everything," Clarissa said. "Really, that woman! There's nothing about me—and not much about you—she doesn't know now. I don't think her son—well, fills her in very fully. At any rate, nobody happened to have informed her that I wasn't your first wife. So she had a horrified moment—I could see it—of

87

wondering if one of her son's vestry had been *divorced*. I couldn't do less than assure her you were a widower when I married you. Not that she hadn't decided by then that I wasn't much of a—what she calls—Churchwoman. Well, at least I didn't tell her my people were Presbyterians. Let go, darling; I must take this cap off. Some water got in."

Unsnapping the chin strap, Clarissa pushed her fingers under the cap's edges, stretching them until she could lift it off. Dropping the cap on the floor, she began to feel over her pinned-up dark hair. "Mrs. T. got at it by asking me how old Ann was. I said: 'Fifteen.' She said—I could see she thought it might be useful to butter me up—'My dear, you must have been married very young!' So I had to say I wasn't Ann's mother. 'Oh,' she said, quite obviously put out, 'I suppose that's why she calls you —"Hendy," is it?' So—you see how it goes—I said my maiden name was Henderson; and that Ann had known me before you married me—in fact, that I'd run a little summer camp up here at the lake for Brocton girls; that the girls all called me Hendy; and that Ann, for a couple of seasons, had been one of the girls. Yes; my hair's good and wet—"

Deftly, she began to unpin it, shaking her head to loosen it. "So, Mrs. T. said: 'Oh; that's how you happened to meet Mr. Winner. Has he other children?'" Clarissa laughed. "Do you see what an expert she is? I told her obediently that yes, there was Lawrence, who was married and a lawyer in Washington; and that another son, Warren, a year or so older, had been killed in the war. But of course she'd fixed it so I had to go on by myself then. Explain just who I was—that I hadn't come cruising in from God knew where and picked you up; that our families had always known each other; that my father had been a great friend of your father's; and so on, and so on. I admit I couldn't help saying—I suppose it was quite nasty of me—that far from marrying very young, I'd been almost Doctor Trowbridge's age. Well, if it's any compensation, I found out a few things about *her*."

"She doesn't plan to stay in Brocton, does she?"

"I expect she could be persuaded," Clarissa said. "But I don't believe she's going to be. I really feel for Doctor Trowbridge, poor fellow. He must know better than anyone else what a trial she is! Of course, she's far from happy about the marriage. I don't know that she has anything against Miss Cummins personally—she said she was a dear girl, and came of very good people. But having Whitmore live with her must have suited her down to the ground. And, no matter how he put it, the net effect—accepting a new job; getting married—was to shake her off. Just how old is he?"

"In the statement he sent me to read to the vestry, he said he was thirty-three that month—last May."

Dropping her handful of hairpins on the settee, Clarissa took her hair, hanging to her shoulders, with both hands and began to fluff it out vigorously. She said: "Miss Cummins is twenty-six. I had some semiconfidences from her, too. They've been engaged several years. She said she wasn't getting any younger; and she'd begun to wonder if she were going to go on being engaged for the rest of her life. Women have a way of understanding women, so I expect she pretty well knew *that* was Mrs. T.'s whole idea. Mrs. T. meant it to last out her time. She was all for the engagement—a kind of insurance, I suppose. I suppose she saw that Miss Cummins was the sort of girl a man can be sensible about; and as long as she was officially Whitmore's intended, he couldn't very well start taking an interest in girls a man couldn't be sensible about. I admit I wonder just what Miss Cummins did to beat the game."

Smiling, Arthur Winner said: "I'm not sure Miss Cummins did anything. I think we did it at the vestry meeting that voted to offer him the incumbency here. That changed the picture. Christ Church is well enough endowed for his stipend to be considerably more than the average parish could pay. He was an assistant, really a curate, while he did postgraduate work for his doctor's degree. Naturally, he wasn't making a great deal. I believe his mother has money; and, living with him, she must have helped with the expenses. While that was his situation, he might not have seen his way to marrying. Miss Cummins simply had to wait until he did see his way. I'm glad if we've been of service to her."

"Yes; good!" Clarissa said. "And that also clears up something

Mrs. T. said. It seemed to be about money—rather veiled. I suppose she never realized I hadn't the faintest idea what a minister—a term she much dislikes—gets; what would be more, or what would be less. But I *could* understand that, for some reason, she wanted me to know that Whitmore had made important sacrifices to come here. I'm afraid she doesn't find us very fashionable—or stylish. In short, Whitmore, as a matter of religious duty, because Brocton needed him, had stepped down from the more distinguished social circles he was used to; and, by his own Christian choice, had come to live among the lowest of the low —I'm glad I didn't really know what she was talking about. I'd have had trouble keeping my big mouth shut. Now, those children must come out." Turning, she called: "All right, everybody—"

Yells at once arose. From the float, Ann cried: "Oh, Hendy! Judge Dealey's just come! He's showing us—"

On the float, Arthur Winner could see Fred Dealey in swimming trunks. He had moved out on the springboard, which bent a good deal with his added weight, to where Priscilla Penrose stood at the end. He was rearranging her pose. Fred's dark muscular hairy arms brought Priscilla's narrow, pale tan, child's arms to a different angle. Putting his hand to Priscilla's blonde hair, plastered dank with water behind her ears, he set her head straight. He tapped her back to make her straighten that.

"Now, Fred!" Clarissa called. "Honestly, they've been in all day—"

"One dive apiece!" he called back. He steadied Priscilla a moment in her new position. He stepped away from her then, leaving the springboard.

Clarissa said: "Poor child! She was just born clumsy. Priscilla's pretty in many ways. That lovely hair—at least when it isn't wet. I suppose you could say, feature by feature, she's prettier than Ann; but—you notice every time you see them together—the really attractive one's Ann, not Priscilla."

Shading her eyes against the sun, now fairly on the rim of the rise across the lake's half-mile of unmoved water, she continued to watch the children clustered about Judge Dealey on the float. Thoughtful, she said: "The truth is, Priscilla looks more and more like Marjorie every year. Have you noticed? They move the same way—all over themselves. You even begin to see that expression of Marjorie's—you know; that really odd slant-eyed look, with her mouth open just a little when she listens to you, so you see the edges of her teeth. It's a pity the children didn't take after Julius more. When he was young, I think he was the handsomest man I ever saw. I remember starting to play tennis at the club—Julius used to spend a lot of time coaching the kids. When he'd stand over me, making me change my grip on a racquet, I'd nearly swoon—"

At the float's end, the springboard dipped slightly to the thrust of Priscilla Penrose's slim knees. It snapped up with her; and she left it, jackknifing uncertainly. She hit the water with a shattering splash.

"You see?" Clarissa said. "Her timing's all off. Marjorie does everything that way. Speaking of that, she's definitely getting queerer and queerer."

"Priscilla?"

"No, my love—Marjorie. You should have seen her this morning! The rector and his mother and Miss Cummins got out to Roylan quite early—you probably passed them on your way in. As a matter of fact, I didn't expect them so soon. I was still having coffee; so I had to ask them to have some. Stewart and Priscilla turned up presently; and then, for no special reason, Marjorie herself appeared. She was wearing a red pullover sweater, very tight, with nothing on under it; and a pair of quite dirty white linen slacks with, all too evidently, nothing on under them; and no shoes. Of course, you might say it's only a step across the road from the Penroses'; but the effect was certainly strange. The rector and Miss Cummins had gone down to see your rose garden. So I introduced Marjorie to Mrs. Trowbridge, simply saying Mrs. Penrose was the wife of one of my husband's law partners; and our near neighbor—passing it off as well as I could. I suppose not looking at Marjorie's feet was hard for Mrs. T.; so Marjorie suddenly said to her: 'Don't you love walking barefoot in wet grass? It's the most wonderful feeling.' If only for a moment, Mrs. T. was really stopped— Oh, that was Ann! That was a good one! You'll have to say you saw it."

From the float, Fred Dealey's voice came up heartily: " 'Ata girl, Ann! You show 'em! All right, Stewart. No, no; wait!"

Clarissa said: "Of course, Mrs. T. had to get this straight at once. I suppose the woman has real strength of personality, or something. I mean, as I was to find out later, you never think of not answering. You only realize afterward that half the things she wants you to tell her are absolutely none of her business. So she went right into Marjorie—where she was born; how long she'd lived around Brocton; how many children she had. Then she asked where Mr. Penrose was. Marjorie, rather dazed, said he was away for a week in Washington on business; he'd be home tomorrow—"

"That reminds me," Arthur Winner said. "He won't. He called me this morning. Somebody offered to drive him up; and it's so much easier for him, he said he'd stay over. He won't be here until early next week. I meant to call Marjorie; but things were much upset in the office this morning; and I never thought of it again. I suppose I ought to call her."

"We can tell Priscilla to tell her," Clarissa said. "She doesn't have to know right now. Well, the point was: Mrs. T. just nodded several times. Meaning: *That* went without saying! What man, if he were there to see her, would let his wife go around with no shoes?"

Up the stairs from the landing came a multiple sound of light running steps. Esther and Winifred Shaw; Ann; and then Priscilla appeared, their brief soaked bathing suits and flashing active limbs spattering water. Esther and Winifred said together: "Hello, Mr. Winner!" Priscilla turned a shy smile at him. To Priscilla's still little-developed rump, Ann swung a smart slap; and, giggling, jostling each other, they slipped in the door of the first room. After them, running too, came George Shaw and the Dealey boys, their cropped light hair almost white above their deeply browned faces. Tom Dealey said: " 'Lo, Uncle Arthur." To Clarissa, Jack Dealey said: "Where's mother?"

"She had a headache, dear," Clarissa said. "She's lying down for a while."

After them, without haste, as though separating himself from little boys—he was approximately eighteen months the eldest—

92

came Stewart Penrose. He carried his skinny twelve-year-old frame with an air of gravity and haughtiness. He said: "See me dive, Mr. Winner?"

"Very good, too," Arthur Winner said.

Stewart Penrose stared at him closely for a moment. Injured and contemptuous, he said: "I took a belly-flopper." He moved off, following the others to the room down the passage where their clothes had been left.

Smiling, Arthur Winner said: "At any rate, there's a lot of Julius in him, you must admit. No nonsense wanted!"

Clarissa said: "That child's too thin. I wish they'd do something—find out why. Darling, I've got to finish my story. At that point, the rector and Miss Cummins came back from the garden; and they looked rather startled. So I did the introducing; and, to occupy the moment, asked Marjorie if I couldn't give her some coffee. She said: 'Oh, no, Clarissa. Fridays, I fast.' Mrs. T. more or less gulped; and said: 'You mean, for religious reasons, Mrs. Penrose?' Marjorie said: 'Yes. You see, I've a great deal to atone for. I led, many years, a life of entire materialism. I did many wicked things. Now, I'm trying to do better.' I could see the rector looking at her with a certain, I suppose, professional, concern. Maybe Marjorie noticed, and didn't want him to think she was appealing to him. She said: 'I hope to become a Catholic, when I'm able.' That was the first I'd heard about that. D'you imagine she really means it? Does Julius know?"

Somewhat uncomfortably, Arthur Winner said: "It has been discussed. That friend of hers who visits her—that Mrs. Pratt, I believe—is a Catholic. She and Marjorie were at college together; and then I don't think they saw each other for a number of years—"

"I've met her," Clarissa said. "She's quite mad."

"Yes; I met her myself, I remember," Arthur Winner said. "I had a curious exchange with Marjorie about her last week. She —Mrs. Pratt—planned to drive down for a day. Marjorie called me at the office. Would I let her and Mrs. Pratt—Polly—talk to me; it was vitally important to her. Put that way, I couldn't very well say no—"

Clarissa said: "And you did talk to them?"

93

"No, I didn't," Arthur Winner said. "As far as I know, Mrs. Pratt never came. At any rate, they didn't come to see me. Perhaps Marjorie changed her mind. I've no idea what there could be to talk about."

"That's easy," Clarissa said. "You're to speak to Julius. Marjorie probably has trouble getting him to listen to her. They'll tell you what to tell Julius. Arthur, you're always doing things for people; and it's wonderful of you; but—" She hesitated in embarrassment. "But this once, here, I think you'd be very unwise to let her involve you. As I say, I don't know what Marjorie's up to—until this morning, I really hadn't seen her for at least two weeks. I took it for granted that she was in one of her moods. When she is, she more or less shuts herself up." She hesitated again. "I don't think I ever told you; when we were first married, when I was first living out at Roylan, Marjorie used to come over all the time for 'talks' with me. That was when she was doing a lot of drinking; but it wasn't just that. She works herself up. Then she tries to get everyone around her worked up, too. If you don't go along, take your hair down with her, she's hurt. Whatever the present thing is, it has to be between her and Julius. Arthur, I really beg you not to mix into it."

Arthur Winner said: "Well, the plan was probably to have the talk with me while Julius was away. I know he doesn't like this Polly; and I imagine Marjorie sees they meet as little as possible. Since it didn't come off this week, and Julius will probably be back Monday, I expect I'll hear no more."

"I do hope you don't," Clarissa said. "And if you do, you really ought to tell her that you don't feel able to advise her, that there's nothing you could say to Julius. She has no judgment—"

"Yes, I know that," Arthur Winner said. "You need to think of her as a child. Mother was speaking about her this afternoon. Marjorie'd come there; and Mother hadn't been able to see her. She didn't want Marjorie to feel, as you say, hurt. For all I know, Marjorie was going to talk to *her* about this. I suppose Marjorie had one of her impulses. Still, I think it's fair to her to say that her impulses are generally kindhearted—a sort of child's hoping-to-please. She doesn't refuse anyone anything; she can't under-

94

stand how anyone can refuse her anything. You're right; it's a fault in judgment; but—"

Taking his hand, Clarissa said: "Well, it isn't always quite as pretty as that. You've been so close to Julius for so long, he's able to make you see her as I suppose he sees her. When her feelings are hurt, and you never know what's going to hurt them, Marjorie's anything but kindhearted. There's no telling what she'll do, let alone what she'll say. It takes a woman to understand another woman—like Miss Cummins and her prospective mother-in-law. Women don't fool themselves about each other."

"I'll bear that in mind," Arthur Winner said.

Clarissa said: "You mean you just won't bother to argue. All right, darling; don't bother. But do steer as clear as you can." She tossed her hanging hair, with her free hand catching a handful. "I'm starting to get gray," she said. "Have you noticed? Would you like me to touch it up?"

"Nonsense!"

"There's a gray hair—right there. Well, if you don't mind, I don't—much!"

Arthur Winner said: "If you don't mind my having close to no hair at all, and the fact that I look, and am, nearly old enough to be your father—"

Tightening her strong fingers on his, Clarissa said: "Not too nearly old enough, I think." She smothered a laugh. "Not unless you were awfully precocious—" She broke off.

From the room where the girls were dressing murmurs of conversation could be heard; little by little, as their chatter absorbed them, getting louder. Now Ann's voice said clearly: "For somebody that old, I think she's kind of cute. D'you know what her name really is?"

Priscilla Penrose said: "Miss Cummins's name?"

Winifred Shaw said: "He calls her 'Midge.' I heard him."

"Yes," Ann said. "I think that's kind of cute, too. It's probably what she asks her friends to call her."

Esther Shaw said: "D'you suppose when they're alone he— well, you know; kisses her, and everything?"

"Of course, silly!" Ann said. "They're just like anyone else. But I saw her real name in the paper. Mrs. Gifford Trowbridge,

95

and Miss Hermione Cummins, at the Federal House. *Hermione!* But, actually!"

Enunciating those words, Ann, Arthur Winner knew, would be giving her head a jaunty little jerk. Moved from side to side in a mannerism she had come to practice during the last year, Ann's delicate-featured, sun-browned face would be expressing a fatigued resignation. With a dramatic drop of her long-lashed eyelids, Ann would be veiling her light blue eyes as though she prayed for the strength to bear it.

Priscilla murmured something; and Ann said: "Oh, it's from Shakespeare. Queen to Leontes. *The Winter's Tale.* It's there in that collected works we had to buy. Of course, Mrs. Pollard didn't assign *that!* It's the craziest play! Everyone's nuts. But, definitely! This Leontes suddenly gets the idea, because, when he asks her to, his wife—that's Hermione—asks this best friend of his to stay longer, that his best friend—" She lowered her voice.

"Oh, Ann!" Esther Shaw giggled. "You're awful."

Ann, plainly complimented, said: "I'm only saying what it says. 'And his pond fish't by his next neighbor, by Sir Smile—' "

Raising her voice, Clarissa called: "Ann!"

"Yes, Hendy?"

"You girls finish dressing, dear. And, Ann; unless you talk very quietly, anything you say in there people may be able to hear on the porch, you know."

There was an explosive faint sound of general dismay, and some choked giggles. Ann then said, composed enough: "We're dressed. Winnie's just putting her sandals on. Hendy, we're terribly thirsty. May we have some tomato juice, or something?"

"Yes. Take the boys, too. Em will give you all something. And tell her I'll be along pretty soon." To Arthur Winner, she said: "I suppose I should dress. Yes, I should. There's Doctor Trowbridge and his women—just past the pines, there. They'll go on up, I hope; but I'm sure Mrs. T. will think it very odd if there's no sign of me." Rising from the porch rail, she bent, caught up her bathing cap and collected the little pile of hairpins on the settee. "Come in while I get my clothes on. You didn't tell me about your hearing, or whatever it was."

Following her into the room at the end, Arthur Winner said: "I was sitting as auditor. All of it was long; much of it, complicated, and of merely legal interest, if that. None of it was of any consequence—unless you're able to feel it of consequence for the McCarthy sons, an unattractive pair, to succeed in their fairly ugly attempt to keep a cousin of the old man, who took care of him during his last years, from charging the estate what she says he cost her. The boys say, adducing no proof, that she was paid in cash from a horde he kept in his mattress. Or, for the widow, a distressing creature, to succeed in Lloyd Davis's I fear disingenuous attempt on her behalf to take against the will. By her own agreement, and for due consideration, she was years ago excluded. Her election will certainly be vacated. You couldn't possibly want to hear the details."

Clarissa closed the door. Turning in the warm shadow, she said: "I am not, and will never be, one of those wives who's bored by her husband's business. Oh! Another point of etiquette. I'm right in thinking it's proper to offer the rector a drink?"

Smiling, Arthur Winner said: "He's not a Presbyterian. It is proper." Looking out the screened window over the cot set against the unfinished pine plank wall, he said: "Yes; they're going on up—not coming here; if that's what worried you. I don't think you finished telling me about your talk with Mrs. Trowbridge."

Clarissa said: "Arthur, how patient you are!" Coming back to him, she lifted a hand to his cheek. "Do I chatter all the time? I believe it's because I haven't any intellect. Good at games—that's all I ever was. Why did you marry me? Aren't you sorry you did?"

"As most people would see it," Arthur Winner said, "I think the pertinent question might be: Are you sorry I did?"

"You don't know how lucky I am, Arthur," she said. "You'd have to be me to understand that." Coloring, she looked steadily at him a moment. She looked away then; and said: "Do I need a shower? I always feel as if the lake might be full of dead fish. No; I don't. Mrs. T. would probably take it less amiss if I appeared sooner, without soap and water, than if I appeared

97

later, with soap and water. I'll just throw some clothes on."

Sliding a thumb under the narrow worsted strap of the bathing suit, she freed her left shoulder. She said: "All the time I was young, I never, never, wanted to be married. When I saw boys looking at me as if—well, I suppose, as if I were a girl—I just hated it. I tried every way I could to make them stop. I remember when Adelaide got engaged—as late as that—she seemed to me completely insane. Fred might be all right; but why on earth did Del want to have to put up with a man for the rest of her life? I couldn't see it."

Pausing, she got the strap off her right shoulder, and said: "I'll tell you something I never told you before. I really kept right on not being able to see it until one evening when you'd come up, when Ann was at camp here. You had supper with us; and you stayed until taps. And I walked out to your car with you; and suddenly I realized that what you'd been thinking about was asking me to marry you; but for some reason you'd just decided not to. I can't tell you what a shock I got then. I mean, a minute before, I'd have been perfectly positive I'd never consider marrying anyone. The next minute, it was all settled—settled as far as I went! I was going to marry you if it was the last thing I ever did—you just *had* to ask me! So then I began to be in a kind of panic. There I was, thirty-one years old; and I'd never learned what any girl of sixteen knows—how to get a man to ask you."

Arthur Winner sat down on the chair at the foot of the cot. He said: "And how does she? I've often wondered."

"Not in any of the ways I thought of trying," Clarissa said. "I thought of trying to make you see there wouldn't be anything too funny about it—it wasn't as if I were in my teens; and, for you, I wouldn't be too tall either. Then, I thought of using Ann—I mean, of making you see that the child was quite attached to me, that you didn't have to worry about whether she and I would get on, that it would be so much better for her if she had someone like me to take care of her, make a home for her, while she was growing up. And, of course, that *you* needed a home, that living with Ann at your mother's, the way you were, with your own house shut up, was no way to live. I

98

knew you went out and took care of the gardens at Roylan, so it was pretty plain you wished you lived there. If you'll think back, you'll realize I took several months to work it; and it was pure Providence that I didn't bitch it for fair."

"This is not uninstructive," Arthur Winner said. "By your account, what concerned you was how to get me to ask you. I'll now tell *you* something I never told you before. What concerned me was a feeling that I had no business to ask you, that it would be an extraordinary piece of presumption and imperceptiveness, that you would be annoyed and offended. If men your own age hadn't seemed attractive enough for you to want to marry any of them, why on earth would you want to marry a middle-aged friend of your father's? That's the only reason it took you several months. Yes; let's ascribe it to Providence. I'm much obliged to Providence."

"Are you?" Clarissa said. "Arthur, I love you."

She worked the bathing suit down to her waist, turning away a little, with a swing of her freed breasts and a swing of the loosened dark hair that hid her face as she bent her head. She said: "It really never was that I didn't like men. I thought they were marvelous; and anyone could see that girls were just terrible—so silly; and always a nuisance. That's what I meant about Julius Penrose—the way he looked to me when I was a child. I never did the kind of mooning about him normal little girls might do—about how when they grew up he'd marry them. That would spoil everything; because what married him would have to be a detestable girl. All I meant was that I wanted to be a man like that so much I could hardly stand it—the shape of his hands was so beautiful; hands you could do something with, not ridiculous girls' hands. I knew it was no good; I'd have to go on being a girl. And I just loathed it. I don't know what was wrong with me; but that went on all the time I was growing up—very neurotic, I can see now. Quite horrid, really. It's nice to think you couldn't possibly have noticed me then."

In simple penetration of the heart by a tenderness of regard for her, Arthur Winner reflected that Clarissa was wrong. He had noticed her; he remembered her as a child. The notice he took might not have been consciously taken—conscious notice would do no more than mark her, identify the child as the elder Henderson girl—yet something in her expression, her carriage, her manner, could have left an impression. His mind had probably been prepared for the definite notice of her that he could remember taking later.

Hardly more than a child, Clarissa Henderson, by her remarkable tennis playing, had begun to make herself a name. To the Brocton club, she brought all the state cups available to girls of her age; and she was soon winning matches in invitation tournaments even farther afield. There had been hopeful local talk—too hopeful, as it proved—that Brocton was producing here a girl who might get the National Junior title away from the young California champions who kept succeeding each other. That was asking the impossible. A real amateur, who played tennis only in season, whose coaching was amateur, too, could never by any mere natural aptitude make herself a threat to what amounted to professional amateurs—girls who played tennis all year round, whose aptitude might equal hers, and whose training and coaching were highly professional. Coming up against some of these players, Clarissa, if not beaten easily, was beaten soundly. They outclassed her. A girl of good sense and good temper, she acknowledged it. She would have to be content to win from those with no greater advantages than she had.

This was the point at which Arthur Winner's recollections could become specific. He had observed Clarissa Henderson as an individual. He could clearly picture her, dressed for the evening, among young people at the club dances—say, twenty years ago. On many of the girls, dressing up of that kind worked an arresting, sometimes amusing, often touching, transformation into likenesses of grown women. The party dresses heightened femininity; they showed off insinuatingly the pliable lines of their new-found, fully female bodies. For the Clarissa of the middle teens, these garments of innocent allure did nothing good. They looked all wrong on her.

The right costume for Clarissa Henderson was the white

broadcloth shirt and shorts, the laced canvas shoes and green eyeshade that she wore on the courts. A highly developed muscular co-ordination would not let her be physically clumsy about anything; yet a timing of her motions to music, an according of them to those of a dancing partner who led her, broke the fine rhythms into which that co-ordination, left to itself, would fall. If you wished to see what those rhythms were like, you had to follow Clarissa Henderson, side-stepping sure and swift, as she passaged with zeal along a clay court's back line. You had to study her as she pressed with mastery, springy on her fast feet, every muscle in harmonious play. She walloped the ball back nearly as hard as a man; she carried, irresistible, the rally toward the net, toward the final deft lob placed with precision out of her opponent's reach. While she paused, motionless at last, her sweat wetting her shirt, resting her racquet in her hanging hand, the warmth of the short spatter of applause sure to sound from the stands acknowledged, not the incidental won point, but the pleasure that watching her had been.

Beside these pictures, that picture of Clarissa (who even if she had failed in the grand essay remained little the less a youthful local heroine) brought out to dance, of Clarissa obliged to put on the clothes that made other girls pretty, but did not become her, must cause a twinge of sympathy. Arthur Winner's sympathy had been, of course, altogether detached, impersonal. In what conceivable way could Tom Henderson's half-grown daughter come to be of the least intimate interest to him —let alone, to be his wife? Arthur Winner already had a wife; and, indeed, it was Hope who really brought him to notice Clarissa, to see what (being no concern of his) he might otherwise have failed to see, or failed to take in. It was the kind of thing that did concern Hope. It went to a generous general concern of Hope's, the prompt representations that a heart made, indignant and mutinous, when shown again how little common sense and common kindness went into the ordering of the world. Hope Winner, sitting with her husband (they were able to think of themselves as an old married couple, ages removed from the kids across the room) to watch the young people indulgently, was moved to the sudden complaint that it was a shame, it was too unfair, it was really cruel. She indicated Clarissa Henderson to him. The fact was, though none of the child-women over there could be said to have a figure better joined or more justly proportioned, Clarissa Henderson stood an inch taller than the tallest boy present.

That this should be so often a fact; and that to the fact was joined those other facts—no boy of her age in Brocton could face her successfully on a tennis court; every one of them, diving off a landing beside her, would be several yards behind when she lifted her face from the water and put a hand on the raft —might have, Arthur Winner thought, more to do than Clarissa now remembered with her hating it when a boy (in passing; how many such boys had there been? Hope Winner's compunctious concern, her woman's pitying appraisal, was not to be shrugged off. Would hurts to his manly pride incline a youth to love?) looked at her as if she were a girl. The hate, no doubt, was real; but what were the reasons for it?

Did Clarissa Henderson, her blood warmed with adolescence, really manage to think never of boys except in terms of athletic games and races to the raft? Aroused, she was physically ardent; and, with her vigor of health, as good as certainly she early became so. Forgotten in the years of wishing to forget, there must have been times when Clarissa, well past the stage (now preferred in memory) of the child who yearned to be a man, looked at some particular boy with funny feelings. What was she to do? She would have the flustering consciousness of her splendid tall athlete's body. She would have the disconcerting foreknowledge that she must be careful, or she would very likely humiliate him in fields supposed to be his. Those good but timid suggestions that instinct would not fail to offer her, she could not follow—they were all for small girls, cuddlesome little creatures. Suppose she ventured inviting an advance; and then (anguishing thought!) none was made? Suppose, thinking of her as a big lummox, he saw what she was trying to do, and laughed her to scorn?

Practicing themselves on Clarissa, these fears might perfect their wretched power. The game, the thing toward which the funny feeling tried to push her, was not worth the candle. For no gratification that such a feeling could possibly portend, not for anything, was she going to hazard the agony of finding, speechless in her shame, that she had been a public fool. She did not have to hazard it. She needed only to be first—rebuffing advances before they were made; arranging to have the laughing-to-scorn immediate, and hers; conveying at once, to any boy who in the least perturbed her, that there was nothing doing, don't be silly! So conducted, life was reasonably safe. Clarissa was fairly secure, un-get-at-able in her bright parthenic status of just Hendy, a grand girl, a good sport, a real pal—and, no, thank you, nobody's sweetheart now—or ever!

Since practice must here, too, make perfect, there was reason enough to think that Clarissa did not deceive herself about what her attitude of mind as a girl had usually been. Since the secret fearfulness was genuine, she genuinely wanted this state of her affairs; and, so, having established it, could be genuinely at peace in it. Most days, with all her free time going into games, she would be both too busy, and, because of the exercise, feeling too good physically, for any effective brooding. Most nights, putting herself to bed in a happy, drowsy tiredness, she went right to sleep. Her nature's real temper would have trouble finding its hours. How often would she be idle and by herself during the day; or, at night, gone to bed but wakeful? How often was the incubus able to creep upon her, to reach and to toy with that cribbed, that pent-up, ardency until, in her distraction, he compelled her to let him have his way, compelled her to go on and help him stay her and comfort her, compelled her to confess, by consent to her unavowable present engagement, what she secretly lay sick of?

Standing in the warm shadow, Clarissa pressed the tight bathing suit down over her hips to her knees, where, deftly balancing, she stepped with neatness out of it. Coming erect, her gainly white back poised with candid grace between her brown arms and her well-shaped long brown legs, she crossed to a chair by the dressing table where she had laid an undergarment and a slip.

The barefoot movement in the indoor twilight, the simple

103

unself-conscious display of the breasts in clean curved motion, of the narrowed waist and well-held hips, the straightness of limb, set up in Arthur Winner a stir of the senses—to be, of course, ignored; yet an ache of force persisted in the imagination's moment of fantasy. If they were alone, if he and she had been up at the lake by themselves this afternoon, if no people waited at the lodge, if no children were running around everywhere, if Fred Dealey weren't still down swimming—

Alone here, he could have touched her arm, turned her about. Coming late to the act of love, Clarissa came frank and fervent, unhindered by the juvenile bride's shy maneuvers of anxiety, or the untried recent schoolgirl's fits of embarrassment. The start of her surprise would instantly be gone. Getting, by one tender look at him, the answer to her grave smile of query, her color would come up—the warmth of a flattered quickening of heart, relish in his unexpected importunity, a warmth of fore-tasted pleasure, of the body's concentration, intent and inward, on the joy proposed, the bliss now soon to be in proof. She would, half in his arms, move toward the cot with him, helping him lead her, bring her, where he liked—flowers were the couch!

Clarissa said: "Who's this man who came out with you? Anybody?"

"He has a certain air of consequence," Arthur Winner said. "His name's Woolf. I don't believe he thinks much of us, or the kind of law we practice. He began the proceedings by challenging me as auditor. I had to explain to him that he couldn't do that—that I couldn't hear him. I wasn't competent, as an instrument of the court, to entertain objections to the legality or propriety of the court's appointment. His remedy would be to except to my report. He then wanted his protest against the whole of the proceedings noted as a part of the record. I didn't think we could do that either. The issue was in every sense de-hors the record."

With quick efficient movements, Clarissa had drawn on a pair of panties. She said: "He sounds quite unpleasant."

"Purely professional unpleasantness, I think," Arthur Winner said. "He's accustomed to seeing a surrogate, or something of that kind, handle all probate matters—at any rate, an ordinary member of the bar named by the court was new to him. I'd say he was right; he has a duty to his clients to scrutinize the proceeding for irregularities. He seemed to think he saw at least one. He understood, he said, that the executor, Mr. Tuttle, was what he called the principal trust and estate officer—you can see the scale of things he's used to—of a firm in which I was a partner. Supposing this to be true, how was it that I hadn't disqualified myself? Of course, he was still misunderstanding my function, and, perhaps, Noah's position. Neither of us was there in any capacity that made our business relationship relevant."

Dropping a slip over her head, Clarissa said: "Did he mean—"

"I suppose he did," Arthur Winner said. "I suppose he wondered if he was up against some cabal of small-town lawyers who had fixed things to play into each other's hands. Then, he wasn't long in displeasing Noah; so Noah proceeded to behave as only Noah, on occasion, can. Mr. Woolf's really owed an apology; and I expect even Noah thinks so now. He was trying to reach me by telephone about an hour ago; and I think that was what was on his mind. But one wishes he could remember that—that he's going to be sorry—before he says it."

Clarissa, sitting down to the mirror of the small and inconvenient dressing table, took up a comb. Tossing back her hair, she went to work on it. She said: "Arthur, Noah's just *too* old! He hardly remembers anything. A week or so ago I met him on the street in Brocton; and he stopped to talk to me; and I happened to tell him I'd driven Ann in to the dentist. He said to me: 'Ann? Ann? Who's Ann?' "

Rubbing his head wearily, Arthur Winner said: "Things like that depend a good deal on how he's feeling. Some days; he's quite all right. Some days; he gets upset, and then he gets confused. Helen Detweiler can handle him; but today Helen needed some handling herself. She'd had a shock of sorts. Brother Ralph is refusing to go to college. He says he wants to get married."

Clarissa said: "Heavens, is he old enough?"

"That's how time passes," Arthur Winner said. "Ralph's eighteen. Anyway, Helen seemed to see it as the end of the world."

Gathering together her combed-out hair in both hands, Clarissa drew it tight at the back of her head. "Well, I do feel sorry for Helen," she said. "That boy always was thoroughly selfish." Holding her hair, she picked up a narrow black ribbon, caught the held hair in a loop, and tied the ribbon firmly. She said: "Who does he want to marry?"

"Well, I think there's also that," Arthur Winner said. "Or, would be, if Helen took the marrying part seriously. The girl's father's a chain-store butcher. I don't doubt she's perfectly all right; but since Helen's idea is that nothing's too good for Ralph, this wouldn't be the match of her choice. But, as I say, she thinks Ralph's only using that to get out of having to go to college. She was a good deal more realistic about him than I expected. It doesn't seem to make her dote on him any less; but she said quite simply she knows Ralph; and Ralph isn't going to saddle himself with somebody to support—"

"I should hope not!" Clarissa said. "Eighteen years old! And I know who'd do the supporting, too." She stood up. She went to the wall where a frock of white linen on a cleaner's hanger was suspended from a hook. Slipping the hanger off the hook, she turned the frock around, looking critically at it. "I won't give those Acme people any more of our cleaning," she said. "Their work's getting worse and worse. Helen has a peculiar mind, you know." The frock on, she came over to Arthur Winner and faced about. "Zip me up, darling," she said. "Back when that happened about her father and mother, for a long time— several years—Helen was very strange with me and Adelaide. It was so marked, you couldn't miss it. Later, I found out why. She couldn't bear, she told someone, being with us; because she felt we must think Father's dying was her parents' fault. I mean, things that would never cross the average person's mind, I'm sure cross Helen's mind all the time. Could Ralph get married if she didn't want him to?"

"In theory, no," Arthur Winner said. "Helen's now Ralph's legal guardian. In this state, he can't marry without her consent until he's twenty-one."

Opening the door to the veranda, Clarissa said: "Then, she doesn't have to worry about that. I suppose that's why she doesn't take it seriously. She knows he couldn't do it."

"Not in this state," Arthur Winner said. "But if he took the girl into another jurisdiction; and if, there, neither of them was under statutory age, nobody could interfere with his marrying her. If he's legally married there, the full faith and credit clause makes him legally married here. Twenty-one or not, that's all he'd have to do if, tomorrow, he felt like contracting a marriage—"

Coming up the stairs from the landing below, Fred Dealey said loudly: "Who feels like contracting a marriage? Bring 'em before me! I'll marry 'em! Now, who's sticking his head in a noose?"

"I don't know that anyone is," Arthur Winner said. "Ralph Detweiler just told Helen he might be thinking of it."

"Best thing that could happen to him," Fred Dealey said. "I've wondered if that boy was ever going to do anything for himself. After all, he's George Detweiler's son. There ought to be something in him—if he's ever given a chance to show it."

Clarissa said: "Oh, Fred! That's utterly absurd, and you know it is! When Helen's done everything for him, made it possible for him to go to college—"

"Your thought's mine," Fred Dealey said. Balancing his hairy and limber, almost youthful, body tautly on the balls of his feet, Fred Dealey also balanced his sharp-chinned, severely narrow face, pulling back a little to stare at her with a penetrating shine of eye, cool and critical. He said: "I was afraid he *was* going to college. Four more years of living on his sister, and he won't be good for anything. What he needs is to have to work, not have Helen helping him find ways not to. Wasn't he supposed to be working this summer?"

"He was working," Arthur Winner said. "I don't know how hard—"

"Of course! Does he have to work hard? No! What was he doing?"

"Selling brushes," Arthur Winner said.

107

"Did he make any money?"

"Perhaps not," Arthur Winner said. "Helen had to buy him a car—"

"Why?" Fred Dealey said. "What's wrong with walking? Is Brocton so big you have to have a car to get around it? Helen had to buy him a car! There it is! No, sir! If Ralph can find the guts to get out from under and marry someone, more power to him!"

Clarissa said: "Now, Fred; really! A boy of eighteen. Wouldn't you want Jack and Tom to go to college?"

"Not if they don't do any better in school than I hear Ralph did," Fred Dealey said. "If they'd like to go to college, they'll have to show me they could get something out of it. What's Ralph going to get out of it? Nothing!"

Clarissa said: "You don't know that, Fred."

Pulling his chin down farther, Fred Dealey rose springily on his toes, making himself nearly as tall as she was. He gave her a look, friendly but derisive. He said: "Well, nobody would be making Ralph work; so he wouldn't be working; and when he isn't working, I happen to know something about what he does. Selling brushes didn't take all Ralph's time this summer. We've just had a report from the juvenile office on that Old Timbers Tavern place, down the Mechanicsville road, and who hangs out there. We want to see if we can't catch up with that Ropel fellow and his wife; and I only hope I'll be the one who has the pleasure of throwing the book at them. They encourage these kids to come in. Ropel knows none of them's twenty-one; but he sells them all they want to drink. We have Ralph's name. He's not one of the regulars—yet! But he's practicing for it. They're a no-good lot—two or three reformatory graduates who don't seem to remember they're on probation. Several girls who appear to be well-established teen-age tarts. The sooner Ralph has to support a wife and stay home evenings, the better."

Setting her arms akimbo, her strong hands on her linen-covered hips, Clarissa said: "Now, you're just talking, Fred! A boy Ralph's age hasn't any business to marry anyone. He's not old enough to buy a drink; but you're trying to tell me he's old enough to have a wife and family. Arthur says there isn't any law to keep him from getting married. I say, if you don't have one, you ought to make one. Heavens, I must get up there! Are you coming?"

"Well, get up there, Toots!" Fred Dealey said. "I've something to speak to Arthur about."

"That's a good sign," Clarissa said. "Maybe he can talk some sense into you. Darling, did you say your man's name was Woolf?"

"I did. No doubt Judge Lowe will see that he's introduced to you. They're on the terrace."

FIVE

Staring after Clarissa, Fred
Dealey said: "Big or small, these Henderson girls are great ones
for knowing their minds. When they say it, it's so! Why'd you
bring Woolf out, anyway?"

"Well, we had to continue—"

"Why did you have to? I didn't think you'd need more than
one day."

"I didn't either," Arthur Winner said. "In a sense, Mr.
Woolf can thank himself, if he doesn't like staying. He insisted
on going into detail on the inventory. Noah was prepared for
exceptions to the account, and for the widow's election; but
that he wasn't prepared for; so sums of money—an item of
bonds, in particular—were unaccounted. Any other morning,
Helen would have seen he had all the figures, just on the off-
chance he might need them; but today there was this Ralph
business. Helen got hold of herself. She was able to report the
meeting, all right. But she'd pretty thoroughly upset Noah; so
he got out of hand. Woolf, of course, bore the brunt."

"Well, he doesn't look exactly helpless."

"Far from it," Arthur Winner said. "And if trouble's what
you want, he'll oblige you. He's got a good head; and he hangs
onto his points. So, of course, he infuriated Noah. Noah's not
used to having statements of his questioned. Moreover, Mr.
Woolf must have had our probate law looked up for him. He'd
noticed that the amended statute lets us cite an executor to account after six months; and since nobody had told him we just
don't do things like that here, he was hinting pretty strongly

that that might be his next step. That really tied it; because Noah didn't like Mr. Woolf anyway. As you saw, Mr. Woolf's obviously Jewish. Noah made several references to 'you people' —very pointed; and getting madder all the time. Finally he said: 'I'm not ready to answer. I know why you ask. Never imagine, Mr. What's-your-name, that I can't tell typical Jew lawyer tricks when I see them.' "

"A highly improper observation," Fred Dealey said. "And is that what they were?"

"Woolf was perfectly in order," Arthur Winner said. "He had a job to do; and he was doing it. He's a very capable examiner; and the effect may have been a little rude once or twice. But it wasn't on him to know local customs of our courts; or that Noah's to be treated with tact and deference—the dean of the bar, and so on."

"How did you handle it?"

"Mr. Woolf didn't give it to me to handle; and I was very grateful to him," Arthur Winner said. "He certainly had a right to appeal to me. He simply said: 'If my religious faith interests you, Mr. Tuttle; I'm an Episcopalian. If you say you're not ready to answer, that's answer enough.' I had only to say to Helen: 'Strike Mr. Tuttle's concluding remark.' And we could proceed. That's the real reason I asked Woolf out. I didn't want him thinking we all shared Noah's prejudice."

"Well, Noah's outlived his times," Fred Dealey said. "This matter of so-called prejudice always interests me. Take a man like your father. Anyone who knew him would agree that if there ever was a fair and just man, a man absolutely unbigoted and unprejudiced, he was it. Back when the Ponemah Association was formed, and they were building the bungalows here, do you think your father would even have considered admitting a Jew, letting him come and build a bungalow with the others? He would, like hell! Why not? A perfectly reasonable reason. What—probably, little—he'd seen of Jews, persuaded him he didn't want them for neighbors. Today, for me to feel that way wouldn't make much sense. My personal observation is that Jews behave as well as other people; and you can trust them just as far—which isn't saying much! Take our brother of the bar

Dave Weintraub. Like our good district attorney, J. Jerome Brophy, he has, I know, some low-life customers in Mechanicsville; but, personally, I find him better company than half the alleged Christians. If he wants to live next door to me, he's welcome to. The same goes for J. Jerome—or would go, if he could manage to be a little less of a slick article; and I'm the first to say he could be that without having come from Water Street or being a Catholic. Speaking of Catholics, what's this about Marjorie Penrose? Is she serious?"

"I know very little," Arthur Winner said. "I think she may be."

"How's Julius going to like it?"

"I haven't asked him," Arthur Winner said.

"No; I suppose there's no need to," Fred Dealey said. "If he's been able to put up with her all these years, he must be able to put up with anything. Sometimes I think the crazier she is, the more he somehow feels responsible for her—have to be something of the kind." He looked closely at Arthur Winner. "Don't imagine I mean that to reflect on Julius," he said. "I mean just the opposite. How long would I be able to do unto a sort of idiot girl as I would that people should do unto me? And he's never been any professional saint, acting noble about it, either." He paused moodily. He said: "Well, what the hell! Let everybody do what he wants. Or she wants. They don't have to ask me."

Arthur Winner said: "Has someone been asking you?" He picked up the jacket he had laid on the settee.

"No," Fred Dealey said morosely, "no one! I suppose you want to get up there, Arthur. Come on. This isn't going to take long." They moved together through the open passage. "I don't know what to do, really," Fred Dealey said. "What would you do? Del, the damn fool, thinks she can have another baby. I say she can't—not after what happened three years ago. She says she can and will; she's going to. So there we rest."

The sunlight, moving up the slope, no longer lay on the path behind the boathouse. Shadow had mounted past the glimpsed terrace and the rambling front, partly seen, of the old lodge;

but the whole upper range of the great oak was sunny still. The bright enormous tree stood against a sky that looked heavier and darker—perhaps, only the shades of night to the east; perhaps, thunderstorms developing out of the close air. Arthur Winner said: "Clarissa mentioned it—that she thought she might be pregnant. I gathered that Adelaide was pleased."

"So the story goes," Fred Dealey said. "I don't know what got into her— Strike that!" He gave a rough, bitter laugh. "I wouldn't have to look too far to find what got into her, I guess. The bees and flowers weren't involved. It's not as if we hadn't two children already, for God's sake! Her idea seems to be that she wants a girl. Why? What's good about them? And, anyway, does she think she can order what she wants?"

Arthur Winner said: "If having a baby's really dangerous—"

"Well, you ought to know!" Fred Dealey said. He shut his mouth sharply, turning his strained severe face on Arthur Winner. "That was the goddamnedest thing to say! I'm sorry I said it, Arthur. I suppose I meant, because you'd seen how it could come out with Hope, you'd understand better than most people. When something like that goes wrong, I guess you do some thinking—if it weren't for you, it wouldn't have happened; you did it to her. Not much fun! That was still a hell of a thing to say."

Arthur Winner said: "You've a point. There's that to think of. I ought to know; and I do. I don't mind your saying it, Fred."

In a way that Fred Dealey, intent on his immediate anxiety of looking forward, imagining what could come, not able to see things as a looking-back would see them, might be unable to understand, Arthur Winner spoke the truth. The truth was one that took getting used to. Discovering it, the heart relucted, had recourse to customary defenses, tried to add one more to the index of prohibited thoughts. This truth, the fact that the heart's dear feelings, conceived as spiritual, could also die; that the poor flesh, supposed to be ephemeral, outlasted them with ease, at first sight simply would not do. For a second sight; for an adjustment to the knowledge that this, being so, would simply have to do, a little more time was needed. Contrite, Fred Dealey swore when he thought of the pain he must have caused any man of decent feeling. Forgiven, he was crediting Arthur Winner with magnanimity, not with a plain statement of the case. What, in actual fact, was left today of that live nausea of guilt and grief—Fred Dealey's "not much fun"?

The retentive mind could reproduce at once, sharp and exact, what was needed—evidences of the senses; things then seen and heard—to show Arthur Winner the corridors of the Brocton hospital's Grace Giddings Orcutt Memorial Pavilion on a January morning nearly eight years ago. He was walking through them. On the third floor, at the corridor's end, was a small sunroom, today without sun. Beyond the glass, snow was falling. The sunroom was furnished with a quantity of plants in sickly condition—pots of things sent to patients and left by them when, in one way or another, they departed.

Along the corridor, stepping with a swing that seemed to say he was at home there, now came Reggie Shaw. He wore a white operating-room gown. He was carrying his cap, and the square of fabric that had masked his mouth and nose. When he reached the sunroom, the sweat finely beading his broad bony forehead could be seen. He tossed the cap and mask on the table. "Buck up, Arthur!" he said. With hands that showed a tremor of strain or tiredness, he produced and lit a cigarette. Poised in his lips, the cigarette had a tremor, too. He spoke around it. "I think we've licked the thing. We're all right. I don't mind telling you we've had a time. We couldn't get it tied off—" Near his elbow, unobservable by him, the sleeve of his gown showed a good-sized bright stain of fresh blood.

In memorable shakiness of relaxing nerves, Arthur Winner looked at him. Reggie Shaw said: "She'll be all right. Now it's just a matter of starting transfusions and keeping them up a while. They're bringing the stuff down now." He flexed his hands, his breathing audible, as, relaxing, too, he drew deeply on his cigarette and slowly breathed smoke out.

The next moment, from behind them, from a suddenly

opened door down the corridor, a nurse was calling, her voice alive with urgence: "Doctor Shaw! Doctor Shaw . . ."

Arthur Winner said: "What I started to say, Fred, was that if it's really dangerous, too dangerous, you can depend on Reggie Shaw. He'll stop her."

"Him, and how many policemen?" Fred Dealey said angrily. "If Del's made her mind up to have a try—I don't even know that I believe her about *that!* The human mind's a cockeyed contraption! She had this gadget and some stuff Reggie gave her she was supposed to use. Then, says she, she got this idea. So she began, without telling me, not to use it. I don't know whether she did or not! I can generally tell what she's doing or not doing. I think this was a slip-up; but, God knows why, she doesn't want to admit that. So she's trying to say she planned it this way. I don't know what's going on."

By Fred Dealey's impatient scowl, Arthur Winner could guess that Fred was reviewing some of the many devices known to him of that cockeyed contraption, the human—or, here, specifically feminine—mind. He might see, though he was not going to say, that Adelaide, caught this way, could need him to share her trouble, not to get off free. She could feel impelled, a need not incompatible with human loving, to make him bear his ratable share. She revenged herself a little on him for what, even if only by accident, was (as he said) his doing. At the same time (a need frankly loving) she might want those proofs of his attachment to be found in his anger and alarm at the risk she was proposing to take. The two needs once sufficiently satisfied, she could have every intention of giving in, of, in good time, agreeing to run no risks.

Fred Dealey said: "So, at the moment, I'm supposed, says she laughing merrily, to leave it to her. The other, says she, could have happened to anyone. This will be different—wait and see! I suppose, if you're a woman, you may have a natural instinct to go on with it—unless, maybe, you forgot to get married. And even then! Look at our Caroline Dummer case—she seems to have wanted to have the baby; she only lost what little head she has after she'd delivered it." He paused. As though involuntarily, he said: "I suppose Hope wanted to have it, too."

"No," Arthur Winner said. "It wasn't that. She didn't know. It was one of those cases—Reggie said they weren't uncommon, particularly when they were going to terminate that way—in which there wasn't any reason to think she was pregnant until she had what turned out to be a miscarriage. If we'd known, there couldn't have been two opinions. She'd never been very strong; and she'd had a bad time when Ann was born; and she was in her forties."

Moodily, Fred Dealey said: "Well, that's a lot different—just bad luck. You can't blame yourself for not doing anything about what you don't know about. What creates liability?" His tone, sardonic, took on energy. Mimicking an attorney in argument, he said: "I offer Restatement of the Law: Torts. Volume what. Paragraph something or other. It is negligence to use an instrumentality, whether a human being or a thing, which the actor knows or should know to be so incompetent, inappropriate, or defective that its use involves an unreasonable risk of harm to others. Right on the nail! At my time of life, I'm not having any of this let's-take-a-chance stuff. That's no way to run a railroad!"

In the positive, irritable assertion appeared, for Arthur Winner to see, what Fred Dealey might not see himself. Angry and anxious, Fred was retorting to a faint disturbance of doubt, to a first enigmatic intimation that all might not be well with the unconscious assumption that underlay his settled view of things. At forty, Fred saw himself with living enough back of him to know what was to be known of life. He was able, sometimes sadder, always wiser, to survey the successive stages of himself. With the knowledgeableness of today, he could consider his own transitions—the onetime college "man" (he would have to smile); the zealous and optimistic law student (he had been number two in his class); the new attorney, not insensible of his own merit, and, so, hardly surprised (though pleased) to have the Winners, father and son; Noah Tuttle; and Julius Penrose soon agree together to offer him a job with what most people conceded to be the "best" law firm in Brocton. He had duly taken a wife; and, so, taken instruction in women. He had begot children;

and, so, made himself acquainted with the not-otherwise-to-be-understood pains and pleasures that the existence of offspring must afford a father. He had even come finally to know some law, actually to be little if any less learned in law than he had fondly (if privately) seen himself as being when he left law school. Then, with everyone's approval, and much earlier than might be expected, he became a judge on the bench.

Fred, of course, knew that someday he must grow old and die; but for the moment, probably for a number of years now, the course of his life lulled him with a reassuring steadiness—everything under control; nothing coming up that his gained experience couldn't unhesitatingly deal with. Having learned to understand both, he could handle himself, and he could handle other people. He might reasonably ask where any major formative changes, like those of the past, could now come from. At Fred's age, fourteen years ago, Arthur Winner, no more aware then than Fred was aware now of what he rested on, rested, too, on some such assumption. Intimations (like whatever this one was that he could see Fred now half feeling) had surely offered themselves—hints that the lute could rift; premonitory catchings and hitchings in the smooth run of the scheme of things; silences in which there seemed to be sounds. Were they from behind? Were they of hunting, of pursuers? Were they from ambushes ahead? He could not tell. He had done then what Fred would presently do. He dismissed them as fancies.

Arthur Winner said: "I don't know that much blame attaches to not doing anything about what you can't do anything about either. All I'd be able to suggest, Fred, is that you make Adelaide see Reggie. You can do that. And you could try to get her to promise that she'd have Reggie, not you, or her, decide."

"Well, yes," Fred Dealey said. "Smart move! The thing to do is really have an argument about that. I'll start right after supper." He gave a grimace as though of self-contempt. "What else? I didn't really want advice; I just wanted to shoot my face off. Thanks for listening." He paused where the path to the side door went off. "Maybe I can even get some licks in right now. Del was feeling lousy; so she'd gone to lie down in the old gun room. That's how I heard; she had my swimming trunks in there, and called me in. If she's still there, and feeling really bad, this might be a good time to beat her up."

"If you decide to, keep it quiet if you can," Arthur Winner said. "The Trowbridges, and Woolf, don't know us very well. If they heard anything, they might not understand."

Fred Dealey said: "Whatever happened, Del wouldn't yell. You've got to give her that." He took two steps away and stopped. Scratching his hairy leg thoughtfully, he said: "Well, I know what you mean about how much blame attaches, Arthur. I've a little thing I'm working on. I haven't got it done yet; and, anyway, I couldn't use it in my business. There, you just note how things came out, and say: The sentence of the court is—. You're dealing with what has happened; and that's always all over now. But, how about what's going to happen? By any chance, could *that* be all over now, too?"

Frowning almost diffidently, he looked at Arthur Winner. He said: "This may sound like a lot of words. I just notice how often, afterward, you think: If only I'd done this, if only I'd known that! But, observe: You *didn't* do this, and you *didn't* know that. Make you think of anything? *Quaere:* Could you ever have changed what's going to happen? You know this much: Whatever happens, happens because a lot of other things have happened already. When it gets to where you come in—well, it's bound to be pretty late in the day. Things have been fixing for whatever this is for a long time; and that includes you— whether you know it or not, what you're going to do or not do has been fixing for a long time, too. Freedom, I read at college, is the knowledge of necessity."

Standing still on the path, hearing mingled cheerful voices from the terrace above them, Arthur Winner looked at Fred Dealey. The nature of the intimation could be seen—a query directed at human struggle and human failure, and at the kinds of victory attainable in life. Might all of them be forms of defeat: givings-up; compromises; assents to the second best; abandonments of hope in the face of the ascertained fact that what was to be, was to be?

"And, maybe, just as well!" Fred Dealey said. This intimation was dismissible, too; and Fred was now dismissing it. He gave a scornful laugh. "Can *you* tell what's good? This looks wonderful; this is for you! Yeah? Wait a year; and check that. This worries you to death; this is terrible! And what does this turn out to be? Only—the best break you ever got! Sure! Listen to me! I'm the boy to call them!"

Down from the terrace came a burst of laughter. With everyone gathered around, Willard Lowe had perhaps condescended to tell a story; and often he told good ones. After the laughter, Clarissa's voice said: "Del, this is Mr. Woolf, a friend of Arthur's—my sister, Mrs. Dealey."

At the same time, Ruth Shaw said: "I actually believe that was Reg's car coming in. Poor lamb, I didn't really think he'd make it—"

A voice, not familiar to Arthur Winner, but surely Mrs. Trowbridge's, said: "I wouldn't, I'm afraid, care to be a physician's wife. It must be so hard to plan things—"

Still standing where Fred Dealey left him, Arthur Winner could feel—he was taken unprepared; he had been feeling cheerful enough—a deep sudden depression of mind, a reluctance to walk on, to face the weary, flat, stale, and unprofitable uses of taking up his part of the not-negligible burden of Mr. Woolf; of Doctor Trowbridge; of Doctor Trowbridge's mother. Sun had gone from the summit of the great oak, and from the wooded slopes beyond the lodge. Now the day was over. Though not anywhere near a dusk, though broad and lucid, the light was now the light of evening, the close warm air was evening air. Below Arthur Winner, the lake, with everyone gone from it, spread silent, flat as glass. Standing still, Arthur Winner seemed to see himself, the motionless big-limbed, taller-than-average figure, with his balding head tilted up, paused (past the middle of his journey) at loss. Laughter and idle voices above him made sounds how vain, how futile, before the coming night and the possibly coming storm.

119

An activity of mind, marginal, not pressed on Arthur Winner's immediate attention, would seem to have proceeded from that reference to Hope that he had not minded Fred's making. The marginal activity might first have been no more than vague formal feelings of a regret to realize how seldom today Hope was remembered, of discomfort at the heartlessness (Sleep on, my love, in thy cold bed!) of that necessary, and, so, inevitable, adjustment; of sadness to see how quickly and willingly the dead were not only allowed, but helped, to bury the dead. The change from the vague and formal to the definite, from remote regret to the pressing and depressing present grief of heart, came, of course, when Fred, after his half-embarrassed essay in minute philosophy—whether a man is a necessary or a free agent; and the possible teleologies of what happens to you—dropped his sardonic phrase: *the best break you ever got!* You might reserve judgment on whether or not an unalterable, already finished design determined your future; but could you deny the iron chain of effect following essential cause by which the past had so plainly determined your present?

From the tranquillity of today's slowly ending afternoon; from Clarissa, her hand in his, on the veranda rail above the placid lake; from Clarissa moving with grace about the shadowed room in a candor of nakedness; the chain, link after link, stretched back, a nexus unbroken to the winter morning with a cold and gloom of snowfall outside when, even as Doctor Shaw declared his triumph, his words were mocked. *That* was essential! This present, quite simply, went back to, originated in, was made possible by, the giving-way of a little tied ligature. A pack of gauze sopped at once with blood. Over linen covering the impervious undersheet, appeared a widening moist spread of blood—too copious to be controlled by anything at hand; too rapid for anything to be fetched. Presently, Hope's half-emptied heart fell silent.

There, too, of course, a chain was ending. Step by step, the present of that woeful morning in the hospital could be retraced from caused effect after caused effect to effective cause after effective cause. Each of them firm, the links of circumstance stretched back to another morning, a day in June in Christ

Church, Brocton. The day was the wedding day of a lanky tall young man of twenty-five, a figure long lost in the past, called Arthur Winner Junior. Apparent aspects of that occasion—one of local social consequence—were all fair. To the parents of Arthur Winner Junior and the parents of Hope Tuttle no more agreeable arrangement could be imagined. Every material prospect was fortunate. For the happy couple, a home of their own was ready and waiting. Arthur Winner Senior's splendid wedding present had been a deeding-over to them of the first of those old Roylan houses that he had caused to be restored with taste and fitted with every modern convenience. The charming house to live in was not all. The lucky pair was easy about their livelihood. The well-starred bridegroom had, in the law offices of his father and his father-in-law, not merely a job, but a position. He started where any other young lawyer, the newest member of the county bar, might expect to spend years getting.

Not material, not connected with money, yet perhaps to be counted on the practical side, was another, again surely favorable, aspect of this marrying. Bride and bridegroom had known each other a long time. Though the easily determined date must make him not quite three years old, Arthur Winner could recall (with a distinctness and insistency that suggested an actual remembering; an early first lifting of the oblivion that lies on infancy) himself being held up so that he could see into a crib which contained a small bundle of lace with a face. To sounds of an enthusiasm he did not share, he was informed that what he saw was the darling new little baby that God had given Mrs. Tuttle. But even if this episode was quite imaginary, a mistake in fact and a mistake in date, the bridegroom had, from a few years later, and thereafter continuing clearly, indubitable recollections of his bride-to-be. There was an often-seen slight girl child in rompers. Above her dainty pale face, still babyishly round, her hair formed a dense soft cap of curls of a remarkable dark red. A girl of ten or eleven, skinny in black stockings, bloomers, and a middy blouse wore that hair, unaltered in its arresting shade, braided to pigtails.

At such stages, Arthur Winner Junior—in age so far ahead of her; and she just a girl—would view little Hope Tuttle with a mild disdain of indifference; yet the more or less sissy world in which she lived overlapped his. During summers at the lake, during the winter in houses whose lawns merged together on Greenwood Avenue, she was there, insignificant, but well known to him. When (about the time she was seventeen) Hope astonishingly began to overtake him; when, a year or so later, he found Hope at home in his circle, his full contemporary, both of them were able to see themselves as having grown up together. It was true, at any rate, that they had a common background. They recalled together the same people, places, and incidents. Consciously or unconsciously, for years he had been observing her and she had been observing him. If he liked her, if she liked him, that liking was informed and tested. Neither need anticipate those appalling surprises that people who marry on short acquaintance, who had not perhaps even met a year before, may spring on each other.

Remaining, of course, were considerations that came, in young love's estimate, not last, but first—the powerful part of love; the pretty part of romance. What had this bridal to show of rapturous feelings, of elevated thoughts, of fine sentiments? To be true, to be real, love (everyone knows) must be innocent of calculation. Did this match, as far removed from imprudence as any match could be, fail that test? Surely not! He and Hope, in view of their feelings, would unhesitatingly have declared themselves to be in love. Why not state that they were?

With eagerness, such a young couple might seek to love; with longing, such a young couple might wish to love; but, could they? In effect, born yesterday, they were unversed in adult living. They were hardly aware of that main principle of life that all things pass and all things change. The knowledge they would need in their relationship could not be got in advance, so they were ignorant. They were imperceptive, because perception is an acquirement of experience. When they spoke of love, were they really given to know what they were talking about? That person of so long ago, the Arthur Winner Junior who protested

his passion to Hope Tuttle, now dead, could not be here to answer; but, to help with an answer, the lost and gone young man
had laid by some recoverable recollections—acts done; sensations experienced; thoughts entertained. They might bear on
the question, shed light.

In recollection's light, first to be noted was the plain fact that,
by standards of what was later learned, the feelings affording a
young man his state of love, of being in love, were largely facti-
tious. This was not by any means to say that they were false or
pretended; but, still, they had not, as the young man himself
was likely to imagine, arisen spontaneously. In theory, the feelings resulted when love magically and mysteriously seized on
him; in theory, that was what love did. In practice, love did
nothing of the kind. He, the truth usually was, seized on love. A
young man heard and read of a thing called love. Love was
praised everywhere as pure, noble, and beautiful. Love *did* have
to do with the commerce between the sexes; but love as described clearly could not have to do with sex—the physical urges
of nature that he knew about. Those had been denounced to
him as evil and impure, the associates of what he joined in calling (even if he fairly frequently indulged in them) dirty jokes,
dirty thoughts, dirty practices. What those were, must be everything true love wasn't. Love knew them not. Love, manifestly,
was out of this world. Love's high feelings, at once so exciting
and so presentable, could, moreover, be had, apparently, by anyone. A young man would not be long in resolving to have some.

By the time Arthur Winner Junior's eye came to cast itself on
Hope Tuttle, the resolve to love had made strides. An ordinary
number of awkward preliminary ventures lay behind. At first
timid and incpt, the resolve had tried forcing romances into being, practicing for the right feelings. The labored quality of
such ventures would soon dissatisfy the resolve; this was no
good. The venture had to be written off. He let the always-ten-
tative affair fade. He then tried again elsewhere. Thus, the eye
that cast itself on Hope had learned to look more critically. The
resolve to love had a better idea of what was needed. To pros-
per, the resolve now knew that the loved one would have to be

this, and she would have to be that. Until such requirements were, by trial and error, established, Arthur Winner Junior naturally had no way of knowing Hope Tuttle would do, would fill the bill, could be the girl of his dreams. That love was something one fell into, might, this far, be true. The frustrate resolve to love was searching, a formed idea now well in mind, for a one and only. The day came when, startled, Arthur Winner Junior looked at Hope; and Hope, a friend, laughed or smiled; and there she was!

The bill filled by Hope, never having been consciously formulated, could not be exactly stated. For one thing, Hope as an object of sight greatly pleased; and this was, of course, important since her proposed lover had gained at least an inkling of the great truth that people, if you have the eyes to see, are what they look like. Anyone would say that Hope was pretty; which was good; and a growing discernment could say the prettiness was not that of too-formal beauties—always warning you to watch out: their possessor's main business in life may be to admire herself in her glass. Was never face so pleased his mind! He liked Hope's looks; so, immediately the resolve to love improved them. They were interfused with light and radiance— the enchanting mysteries of the female; her delicatenesses of difference; her charms of strangeness. Arthur Winner Junior with a new eye, a re-created mind, took, marveling, these wonders in, entranced by them.

For another thing, Hope, as well as so wonderful to look at, was observed, with some of the same suddenness, to be fun to be with, to be nice to be with. Things she said and did were constantly delighting her now-acknowledged swain. Hope had, for example, a habit of silent laughter. Breaking in on what she was saying, or making her leave for a moment what she was doing, ebullitions of happiness appeared to take her by surprise. They buoyed up abruptly, too strong for a smile to contain them. Quietly exultant, Hope laughed to herself. Toward the end of the period of their engagement, feelings, clearly intense, of tenderness appeared to affect her in the same way. Not impossibly, pacing his resolve to love, parallel to it, equal in its success, a resolve of Hope's, a young woman's love of love determinedly applied, had been proceeding. With a look of amazement, she would say suddenly: "Think how I love you!"

Coming at last to stand in the flower-bowered chancel of Christ Church, with a dressed-up crowd behind him, and outdoors, a beautiful day—the sun was to shine on this bride—the bridegroom had undoubtedly (these sensations were recoverable) brought there a budget of excited emotions. At some moments, he had not failed to feel the joked-about male trepidation, the awful wish to run, the panic of goneness to realize that this, as they used to say, was "for keeps." At others, he might fairly be said to have felt all the exaltations that he practiced to feel; the high-minded, even holy, joy that he knew he ought to feel. Stumbling on a word or two, pronouncing after Doctor Ives the sonorous phrases put to him, he said, genuinely dizzy, that he, Arthur, took her, Hope, to his wedded wife, to have and to hold. Still dizzy, he heard her, Hope, their loosened hands again formally joined, take him, Arthur, to her wedded husband. Proffered Hope's other hand, whose immaculate glove had been slit for the purpose, he pushed, after an instant's unforgettable fumbling, the ring over her narrow finger tip and down Hope's bare finger. Taught by Doctor Ives, he dizzily endowed her, since she was agreeable to being had and held, with all those worldly goods, so luckily his, or in prospect to be his.

That was the place; that was the day; that was the moment. Revisiting the pretty solemnization's scene, one saw now (and might not one have seen then?) the presages. Did a prophetic whisper sound at Hope's appearance on her father's arm? Beneath the cascading veil, Hope's notable head of hair made the admired contrast with that face, from which all extra flesh was beautifully chiseled away, and with that skin's delicate sheerness, the pallor near-transparent. A liquefaction of lace and satin folds of a wedding dress that had been her mother's (taking in the dress enough to fit Hope had been a problem) suggested Hope's slender shape, the slim conformation of the body to the light bones. That slenderness could charm the male eye; that slimness could cost older women, who wiped a tear, pangs of envy; yet, though Hope did not look in ill-health, any physician, putting together the fined-down face, the sheer skin, the too-slight figure, was likely to be of the decided opinion that she needed to put some weight on. Professionally, he might ponder the prognosis. What about the practical side of this business? Pretty; yes; but was that a body to breed and bear? For the flesh's earthy function, was this mold all too ethereal?

An answer of yes could be made. The practical side, the earthy function, was, indeed, to bring about Hope's untimely cutting-off. On the other hand, to show you that doctors didn't know everything, that frame that looked so fragile must have been not unsturdy: her spouse, by that frail venter, was to have three children. Here, the ethereal mold, the outward and physical Hope, might mislead. Where appearances, as usual, did not mislead was in what they said of the inward Hope, of the body's tenant; and of that tenant's tastes and temperament. Not the one, nor the other, you might rightly guess, would be likely by itself to have prepared Hope to regard that practical side, the earthy function, with physical enthusiasm. Neither could the uses of courtship, which often effect a preparation, effect one in Hope. They could heighten her feelings of fondness or affection; they could not alter her temperament.

The fact of apparent paradox was that, in those uses, Hope had been by no means backward. To her fiancé, she offered herself to be hugged and kissed as much as he pleased. Hugs and kisses were an accepted, understood expression of pure affection. Hope liked them, in the sense that she enjoyed, innocently relished as compliments, their proof that she was attractive. Her nature unaroused, and in her experience, unarousable, Hope, with calm desireless happiness, was ready to (as it was then called) pet at every opportunity. Not really affected, she had no reason to proceed with caution. How far was far enough need never trouble her. The result, not without irony, was that Hope could and would consent to "pet" longer and oftener than girls whose temperaments were warm, than girls, conscious of natures not, they knew, to trust, who must call a halt fairly early in the game, must stop then, if they were going to stop at all.

To this ingenuous practice of Hope's, her fiancé adapted himself as well as he could. One important element in his resolve to love had, of course, been all along that attempted exorcising of everything base and gross. The resolve decreed that Hope's purity (of which there could be no possible doubt) and, indeed, the beauty and nobility of this relationship in general, should never be affronted by the taking of any liberties that were also indecencies. Embracing Hope, her lover comported himself with conscious high-minded restraint. As far as possible, he meant to take care that the object of his affections occasioned in him no thoughts that were low, no feelings that were dirty.

Given Hope's innocences of consent, this was not always easy. To the rules of high-mindedness, the flesh is imperfectly amenable. Kisses however chaste, caresses however decent, if the exchange of them is kept up, must have the flesh soon shaping to its natural end, projecting its actual objective. A discipline of mind was required. The witching hour was to be saved intact by a division of consciousness; one part excluding rigidly all that engaged the other part. Held separate, thoughts on the plane of moonlight and roses could proceed regardless of the lower animal. Or, at least, they could so proceed to a point. Due to that blameless neglect of Hope's to call the halt she (the fair, the chaste, the inexpressive she!) had no need to call; and to her partner in petting's reluctance to leave, since he was free to remain, there had been awkward occasions when the animal (disregarded by the hour and teased too far) reacted of a sudden, put to the shilly-shally so long imposed its own unpreventable end. Arthur Winner Junior—confusion in the moonlight; dismay among the roses! —was obliged to conceal as well as he could a crisis about which his single shamed consolation was that Hope, anything but knowing, would never know what had happened.

Recollected with detachment, these self-contrived quandaries, these piffling dilemmas that young love could invent for itself were comic—too much ado about nothing much! Arthur Winner Junior was entangled laughably in his still-juvenile illogicalities and inconsistencies. Absurdly set on working contradictories and incompatibles, he showed how the world was indeed a comedy for those who think. By his unripe, all-or-nothing-at-all views, he was bound to be self-confounded. By the ridiculous impracticalness of his aspirations, he was inescapably that figure of fun whose lofty professions go with quite other performances. The high endeavor's very moments of true predominance guaranteed the little joke-on-them to follow.

In unedited, unglossed fact, an endeavor of high-mindedness really had kept that dizzy morning in Christ Church free of all gross thoughts. Purity prevailed. To Arthur Winner Junior's unsteadiness, not the smallest part was contributed by thoughts that soon he could enjoy Hope physically. Entrance of smutty ideas—say, imaginings of Hope as she would look undressing, as she would look undressed—would be an outrage, unthinkable; even a glance at them would amount to piacular pollution. But, come night; what then?

Well, not that night. For that night, untied Hope still her virgin knot will keep! After all, Hope was worn out by the happy day's festivities; and, moreover, when they retired, they were under the inconveniences of retiring on a train. Hope's new husband's consideration for her, not unjoined by the subduing effects of a nervousness great enough to threaten incapacity, with a kiss put off what-then. But, come tomorrow night? At the resort where they had arrived safely, in the very expensive hotel suite reserved for them, high-mindedness could continue to set some comic difficulties in passion's way; but, never fear, they would not prove insuperable! A somewhat uneasy dinner over, Hope soon went upstairs; and while Hope was being allowed, to spare her modesty, to do her undressing by herself, those rejected imaginings of yesterday morning now entered unopposed. That concept of piacular pollution, much diminished as the idea of the undressing Hope was entertained, received, with the autoptic fact of the undressed Hope, its *coup de grâce*. Not ungently, not heedlessly nor unfeelingly, yet quite determinedly (that nervousness, though considerable, did not prove incapacitating), Hope, before the night was much older, was deflowered. With some unskillfulness, yet with technical success (and, perhaps, with a certain pause-giving sense of letdown; a certain is-that-all?), Hope was duly enjoyed.

128

And the enjoyed Hope? What, in this coming-together, had been the role of Hope Tuttle, the new Mrs. Winner? What comedy of cross-purpose did youthful errors of hers produce? What had the reluctant maiden been professing on the one hand, and actually doing on the other? In professing herself agreeable to being had and held, Hope's consent could be judged full and fair—her hand, with her heart in it. This was of Hope's considered choice; this was her deliberate decision—the more certain, the more definite, and, yes, the more loving, because no passion colored her judgment. Nor was Hope consenting in any serious ignorance of what she consented to. By a convention then dying, yet not then dead, a mother, otherwise devoted and affectionate, had seen no reason for Hope to know of such matters before marriage discovered them to her; but Hope had been to college. Naturally, she had not been there long before girls more knowledgeable saw to her instruction. Since Hope's temperament made the subject of greater embarrassment than interest to her, much detail remained obscure—her fiancé had been right in supposing Hope unlearned in male physiology— but she was quite clear about the capital point. She knew exactly what a girl must let a man start doing to her as soon as they are married.

Far from feeling any warmth, any faintest stir of personal desire, when Hope reviewed this knowledge of hers, she undoubtedly felt a chill. If stirrings of curiosity sometimes troubled her; anxious wonderings about what *it* was *really* like; attempts of the mind, revulsively fascinated, to imagine how two people would look, what they could find to do and say, as they prepared to accomplish, and then (how could they!) went ahead and accomplished their joint obscenity, these speculations would be against her conscious wish and will. The more or less hateful compulsion that occupied her with them left her distaste still stronger. She did not like any of it.

Nevertheless, what Hope did not like, Hope was going to do. Undeterred by chill or revulsion, Hope was going to agree, consent, submit. To help her, would be a girl's settled impression that marrying was what you did when you grew up. If you didn't marry, what would people think but that no man had ever liked you enough to ask you? To help her, too, was the fact that she was a woman; and, so, though unknown to her, her alarms, while real, were in the mind, were, at most, only skindeep. The ethereal mold, and the temperament so bespoken, were hers, all right; but they didn't mean that the female's saving, tough-spirited, matter-of-factness had been left out of her. Gestures of taught modesty, of conventional timidity, might cover it most of the time; but it was there; and it was always ready. Unaware of what it was, Hope could still be conscious of its presence. When really needed, it would appear, enabling her, like any woman, to face unblenching and unsqueamish every anguish and every nastiness that life could inflict on her.

With this undefined but perfect assurance, Hope might know that, though she was frightened and repelled, what she had promised to do she would be able to do. Hope's character, that other aspect of temperament, put duty as a matter of course before any conflicting personal wishes. Duty would keep her from entertaining so much as a thought of not doing what she ought to do. Meaning to love, obligated to love, she loved. If being the devoted helpmate of a man she cherished involved permitting him in his inexplicable pleasure, her pleasure would be to permit him, her pleasure would be to pleasure him. If being the mother of children she would cherish required of her (as she knew it did) acts of darkness, acts of darkness would be done. Wanting what came of them, she could even fairly say she wanted them.

So many years later, surveying the young states of Arthur Winner Junior and Hope Tuttle Winner, did the mind hesitate, form a query, feel a doubt about what to call their feelings? The doubt was really not particular. It did not reflect on him; certainly it did not reflect on Hope. The gist of the doubt was general; the query only this: All sayings aside, is youth in fact love's season?

✦

"Father!" Ann said. "Father!"
She was standing at the top of the stone steps to the terrace.

Following a fashion or fad (incomprehensible to Arthur Winner; since it was not attractive, and did not even look comfortable; yet it had persisted several years now with the girls of Ann's generation), Ann wore a white boy's shirt and coarse dark blue workman's dungarees whose trouser legs were rolled halfway up her shins. The garments gave her the air of a small male impersonator—a Rosalind or a Viola, at the requirement of a complicated and ridiculous dramatic plot, got up to act an unconvincing boy. Careless of her part, Ann had bunched her not-quite-dry hair together and tied it with a big blue little-girl's bow. She said: "Hendy says: Telephone."

"Thank you, my dear," Arthur Winner said. "Do you know who's calling?"

"Unh-unh!" Ann shook her head. She remained, her sandaled feet planted apart, looking down at him. "I think it *may* be Grandfather Tuttle—or some message from him." As he approached, mounting toward her, she moved, jumping. From two steps above, she threw her arms around him and kissed him. "Hello," she said.

Smelling the damp hair, the agreeable fresh odor of young skin, Arthur Winner said: "Goodness! What am I going to be asked for now?"

Ann giggled. "Oh, nothing much!" she said. Turning to move with him, she ran her arm through his arm and clasped it securely with both her hands. She said: "Father, if Mr. and Mrs. Penrose don't mind, could Pris and I have a car together?"

Arthur Winner said: "Would that be useful? Neither of you can get a driving license until she's sixteen."

"I know," Ann said. She rubbed her head hard against his arm. "But—Pris *will* be sixteen, right after Christmas. So she could drive then. We'd be awfully careful. We know a jeep we could get for two hundred and fifty dollars. If I didn't have any other presents for Christmas, could I go halves?"

Arthur Winner said: "That seems a very reasonable price for an automobile. I think I'd like to look it over, before you settle anything."

"But *after* you've looked it over, I can, can't I? We know it's all right. Rodney Revere's seen it. It belongs to a dealer he knows who sold him his car. We were asking him how much he paid for *that;* so then—"

"Has Priscilla spoken to her parents about this?"

"No," Ann said. "She hasn't had a chance. You see, we only just decided. And I said I'd speak to you first."

"And then Priscilla is to tell her father that you've spoken to me; and that I feel you and she ought to have a car right away?"

"Oh, Father!" Doubling her fist, Ann punched his arm several times. "I never said, right away! It wouldn't be till next year. But we have to know now; because we have to save our money to run it." She looked at him with an expression of virtue.

"At the moment, I think I must answer the telephone," Arthur Winner said. "I'll take the matter under advisement."

"Please, please, please!" Ann said. She turned her innocent gaze up at him. "And you'll tell Mr. Penrose you're thinking about it? Then, Pris wouldn't have to. Sometimes, when she tries to tell him something, she says he may just laugh at her. Or tell her he doesn't want to hear anything more about it before he even knows what she's going to say; when if he'd just *listen* a minute—"

Obliged to laugh, Arthur Winner said: "Now you think about it, since his daughter's involved, I'd really have to speak to him, wouldn't I?"

"So, you will!" Ann said. "That'll be simply super!"

"Have we a meeting of minds?" Arthur Winner said. "I've engaged to look into the question further; and to find out how Priscilla's father feels. Nothing more is implied; nothing else is to be inferred."

"Natch!" Ann said. Reaching the terrace with him, she let go of him. Poising a moment, cocking up an eye to a great limb of the great oak, she gave a giggle. *"That,"* she said, "is what *he* thinks!" She scampered away.

Along the terrace, the evening light, with so much of the sky shut off by the spread of the tree and the front of the lodge, was vitreous, holding uncolored, transparent preliminary hints of dusk. On the extensive trestle table burned two lighted candles in big hurricane glasses, their motionless flames a little brighter than the air. Along the table, which was spread with a red-and-white checked cloth, platters had been distributed, each carefully covered by a sheet of waxed paper. At the near end was an array of glasses and bottles and a cocktail pitcher. Fred Dealey, who must just have come out, stood there with Doctor Trowbridge. Their backs were to Arthur Winner.

Taking a swallow of the cocktail he had poured himself, Fred Dealey said: "Why in God's name do women like to eat outdoors? Do they like bugs?" To one who knew Fred well, it was apparent that, even as he spoke, the quick if belated thought that his companion might find the phrasing objectionable came to him. To pass it over, he said with annoyance: "They want to; we have to!"

Doctor Trowbridge's head turned, showing Arthur Winner his not-unhandsome profile, his straight nose, his pleasant-looking somewhat small-lipped mouth. He surveyed Fred Dealey with an expression that was dry but urbane. Casual and clear, with a little of a liturgical overtone's elegance, he said: "Yes; I believe it has been written that what Woman wants, God wants, Judge. With no irreverent intent, we should perhaps accept that in principle." The grave and friendly correction having been offered (and Arthur Winner must agree, with some deftness), Doctor Trowbridge smiled and raised his glass.

Down the expanse of flagstones, beyond the other end of the table, Willard Lowe could be seen. He remained sitting in state in his chosen chair; but talking to him now were Ruth Shaw and Miss Cummins. Mr. Woolf, Arthur Winner observed, had been somehow taken over by Mrs. Trowbridge. Mr. Woolf stood silent, his sallow face civil and serious. He held a two-thirds empty highball glass in the unmistakable manner of the man who, drinking only for politeness's sake, avoids, in order not to have to make a point of refusing more, finishing what he has. Since Mrs. Trowbridge held no glass, Arthur Winner judged that she did not drink even for politeness's sake. A dark purple straw hat was pinned to her masses of nearly white hair. Her features, large and formidable, seemed drawn to a focus, commandingly, searchingly, intent on Mr. Woolf's bland melancholy eyes. She was saying: "Your usual legal work, then, is mainly in New York City—"

Not pausing, Arthur Winner crossed over behind the oak to go to the other door. Here, out under the open sky, the light was brighter; yet you could see, in a violescent haze, the east's increasingly somber tone. Around the several cars, scattered in the morning beneath trees that would keep the day's hot sun off them, the boys, tireless, were playing tag. Their yells and cries were sharp on the heavy air. By the side door, another car, with Reggie Shaw's physician's number plate, stood. Arthur Winner went in.

The telephone, an old instrument, really an antique, with a handle by which you rang, was affixed to the wall near the pantry. Clarissa, who had in her hands a big bowl of potato salad, stood there with Adelaide Dealey, who was carrying a pitcher of iced tea. Confronting them was Reggie Shaw. He was saying with a roughness that sounded more jeering than bantering: "What's your trouble, baby? Or can I guess? Just let me have a good look at you." He put out a hand to touch Adelaide's chin up.

With her free hand, Adelaide struck away Doctor Shaw's hand. Her small face, trim-looking, with something of the shape, something of the delicacy and neatness of a cat's, hardened, growing pale in the weak electric light of the hall. Though she kept her voice low, she said with fury: "Just you mind your damn business!"

Clarissa said: "Oh, Reg; let her alone!"

Reggie Shaw said: "Be my damn business before you know it! Tell Pappy how many periods you've missed."

Adelaide said: "If you don't stop, if you don't shut up—" Her hand was shaking enough for iced tea to slop from the lip of the pitcher.

"Now, baby!" Reggie Shaw said. In his voice was that faintly maudlin benevolence of a man who might have had a few drinks; yet he would pass well enough for sober. In Reggie's broad bony face, his eyes, hollow-appearing, regarded Adelaide reproachfully. He rubbed his cropped patches of wiry matlike hair whose onetime rust red had now grown almost gray. He said: "Why don't you do what you're told? You can't get away with it. You know as well as I do you're one of those girls who only has to look at him to get herself knocked up." He gave his head a distressed shake. "Now, what are we going to do?"

Moving with violence, Adelaide stepped back, brushed past Clarissa, and carried her pitcher indignantly up the hall. Glancing after her, still shaking his head, Reggie Shaw said to Clarissa: "I knew it as soon as I looked at her. Sure. One night she thinks: Too much trouble to get up; the hell with it! You two ought to trade apparatus. Then, everybody'd be happy."

Clarissa said: "Reg, you're not being very funny—"

"That's right. I don't feel very funny," Reggie Shaw said. "Sometimes you get your bellyful of women—their goddamn notions; their goddamn talk-talk-talk; their goddamn sacks of tripes! Hello, Arthur. Are you here? Where did you come from?"

Arthur Winner said: "I came from the side door."

"Well, don't apologize!" Reggie Shaw said. "You aren't interrupting a consultation. The patient wasn't co-operative. But she will be; when the be-jesus is scared out of her, she will be!" He made an irritable waving gesture of dismissal and went down the hall toward the terrace door.

Clarissa said: "Did you hear any of that, Arthur? I don't like it. I think somebody ought to speak to him—tell him people will only take so much of this kind of thing."

"And if he were to answer that those who didn't like it knew what they could do?"

"Well, he wouldn't," Clarissa said. "Not to you." She nodded at the telephone. "Darling, I don't know what's going on. There was a call that seemed to be from your office—only it was a man, a voice I didn't recognize—just asking for you. Then, I don't know how, he was cut off; and Marjorie Penrose was on the line. Noah had called her at Roylan, she said, again—"

"Yes, I know," Arthur Winner said. "That is, I knew he called her before."

"Well, she was disturbed; because he was more and more excited or something. So I said I'd tell you. Oh; I also took the occasion to tell her what you said about Julius not coming home tomorrow. She said: 'Oh!' in a rather funny way. 'He won't be

135

here? Well, I've someone I must call then. I'll hang up.' So she did. Lord, I thought—I remembered what you said—now, she's going to get her Mrs. Pratt down! I wish I hadn't told her. So then, I asked the operator to try to find out who was calling first. So she's trying, I suppose—"

"Undoubtedly, Noah," Arthur Winner said. "Someone from the Union League might be putting in the call for him. I think it can be only what I spoke about—nothing of any importance. Why don't you take that bowl out and get rid of it? And if you'd care to bring me back a drink, I'd be most grateful. If it's Noah, he may want to talk some time—"

"Well, don't let him, darling. We're going to eat very soon. What do you want, Scotch?"

"Yes," Arthur Winner said. The telephone rang and he took down the receiver from the wall.

A man's voice, known to him, though he could not, for a moment, place the speaker, said: "Hello! Mr. Winner there?"

"This is Arthur Winner."

"Well, look: Bernie Breck, Mr. Winner. I'm here at your office—"

Astonished an instant, then instantly feeling a heart-fall of apprehension—the police were calling; and calling on Tuttle, Winner & Penrose's line—Arthur Winner said: "Has anything happened to Mr. Tuttle?"

Bernie Breck said: "Oh, no, Mr. Winner! Sorry if I frightened you—nothing like that; no accident or anything. I just came back here with Mr. Tuttle. But we have something—a little trouble—he was trying to get you about since four o'clock or so. He was trying all over, before we went out. He's kind of worried; so when we got back, he thought he'd rest in his office a while. So I said I'd keep trying to get you for him—"

"Yes," Arthur Winner said. "Thanks. But what is the trouble?"

Bernie Breck coughed. He said: "I guess maybe he should tell you. I don't know any details. What I have is this warrant issuing on an information before Joe Harbison. Joe called us around half past three; so I picked it up. It's for Ralph Detweiler, charging him with this offense, see? So before I served it, looked for Ralph, I thought I'd go around to Mr. Tuttle, show it to

136

him. On account of Miss Detweiler working for him, I mean—"

"Ralph?" Arthur Winner said. "What's he charged with?"

Bernie Breck said delicately: "I don't know if you want me to say a whole lot over the phone, Mr. Winner. There's an alleged offense against this girl, see? Well, that he attacked her. I didn't actually look at the complaint, Mr. Winner—"

"But I presume the name of whoever signed the complaint's on the warrant. It isn't Moore—M-o-o-r-e, is it?"

"Name's Veronica Kovacs," Bernie Breck said. "I happen to know who she is. She's from Mechanicsville; but she works at the Elite diner on Water Street."

"You haven't served it yet?"

"Yes, I have, Mr. Winner. We got him here." He lowered his voice. "That other name you mentioned; she's here, too. What we did was: Mr. Tuttle said right away, could we pick up Ralph and bring him here first, so you could talk to him. So he was trying to get you; and he couldn't. So then he went along with me in the police car, while we looked some places; but Ralph had gone home, see? Mr. Tuttle wanted to keep Miss Detweiler from knowing, was the thing. So I found this fellow I knew knew Ralph; and he said he'd go and get Ralph to come out, come down the street. So we went and parked out Greenwood Avenue; only I don't know what this boy did; he must have let something out; because Miss Detweiler came with him, Ralph. So I had to show them the warrant. And she's in the other room, with this Miss Moore. I better let you talk to Mr. Tuttle; he's here now—"

Some muffled noises followed; and Noah Tuttle said: "Arthur, Arthur—"

"Bernie's been telling me," Arthur Winner said. "I'll take care of it. What's Ralph say?"

"He didn't do it, Arthur. He swears he didn't do it. She's just making it up, he says. Now, she's not a good girl, Arthur. Bernie says that, too; he's heard that—"

Arthur Winner said: "Do you mean Ralph doesn't know her?"

"Yes, he knows her, Arthur. Only, he says he never knew her well; he was only out with her once."

137

"When was that?"

"Well, last night, he says." Noah Tuttle's voice quavered a little. "He says he offered to give her a lift in his car—she was waiting for the Mechanicsville bus. Then they went and had a drink; and, well, he admits he did what he shouldn't have done. But not against her will, Arthur; she wanted him to; she led him on, he says. He knows he did wrong; this girl he's engaged to, he even told her this morning."

"I see," Arthur Winner said. "Make sure Ralph understands that he mustn't, for any reason, say anything more to anyone else, will you? And will you ask Bernie if Harbison knows the warrant was served?"

Noah Tuttle said: "Yes, he does, Arthur. I told Bernie to tell him; tell him I had to wait for you. He said all right— What did he say? Here, you tell Arthur about that—what Harbison said."

Bernie Breck's voice cut in: "Mr. Winner; Joe said all right, I needn't bring Ralph over until you came. Only, he has the Kovacs girl and her mother on his hands—the mother didn't want to go home. So he said if you can make it he'd like to set a hearing at eight—"

Arthur Winner said: "Yes. Would you let him know that you've reached me; and I'll appear with Ralph. And may I speak to Mr. Tuttle again?"

Noah Tuttle said: "Arthur? Arthur?"

"I haven't had anything to eat," Arthur Winner said. "And I don't suppose you have. You'd better all get something; and I'll get something. I ought to be down by quarter to eight—"

Clarissa, approaching with a glass in her hand, said: "Oh, darling—no!"

Arthur Winner said: "I think we'd better meet at Harbison's. I won't need to see Ralph first; because what I'll be planning to do is ask Harbison to continue. I'll want the hearing reported; and we couldn't arrange that tonight. But don't say anything until I get there. Bernie tells me the prosecutrix and her mother are waiting; and I don't want her by any chance to go home. I want to have a look at her. We'll get a continuance; and bail set for Ralph; and then I'll hear what he has to say."

"All right, Arthur," Noah Tuttle said. "All right. I know you'll do everything."

"How is Helen taking it?"

"Fine, Arthur," Noah Tuttle said. "Just fine. She knows he didn't do it. And we'll go over to the justice of the peace; and you'll be there."

"I'll be there," Arthur Winner said.

Clarissa said: "Ralph? Helen?" She put the glass in his hand. Raising it, Arthur Winner took a swallow. "The brat is in a jam," he said. "Appropriately enough, about a girl. They've arrested him. Noah, quite rightly, thinks he can't handle it. So I'll have to get down. I can't tell you any more; because I don't know any more."

"Darling," Clarissa said, "should I ask—I wasn't forgetting! —Doctor Trowbridge to say grace right away, then?"

SIX

BRIGHT LIGHT filled the room
that Mr. Harbison used for his office. It was down toward the
back of his house, with an outside entrance by means of a small
porch several steps up. From the gate where a sign hung out on
North Federal Street—JOSEPHUS D. HARBISON. JUSTICE OF THE
PEACE. DOG LICENSES ISSUED. MARRIAGES PERFORMED. NOTARY PUB-
LIC—a brick walk led to the steps. Coming along the walk,
Arthur Winner was tall enough to see, through the uncurtained
two windows, the people who waited in the office. Walking
quietly toward the steps, Arthur Winner took a careful look at
them.

He had half expected that Noah Tuttle, worn by the
agitations and excitements of the day, would not feel able to,
or would not, come over with the others; but Noah was there.
Against the wall across the room, Noah sat with a weight of
presence. Under the unsparing light, Noah's loose mop of hair
was white as snow. The speaking old face, a venerable work of
time, was set in rugged folds and massive saggings. Noah
brooded formidable and forbidding on the bare room. Whatever his earlier states of upset, Noah now showed no agitation.
For Noah, Arthur Winner could guess, things had resolved
themselves. Noah knew where he was. Though not the part of
the law that occupied Noah, this was still law. The law, all of
a piece in its imposed waitings, its slow evolutions of due process, its calm impersonality of attitude, soothed and supported
him. Human or emotional factors with their power to perturb

could not get in here. Waiting on the law, Noah might be, in fact as well as in an appearance of habit, quite collected, quite unmoved.

Next to Noah sat Helen Detweiler; and with concern Arthur Winner gave an instant to studying Helen's face. Relieved, he saw that Noah, claiming Helen was "fine," was partly right. Now he thought about it, this was something reasonably to be foreseen. The practices of Helen's life, her stretched nerves, her disciplines of sacrifice and self-denial, her feats of sheer willing and wishing, provided her with effective equipment to meet genuine emergencies. By saying he did not want to go to college, Ralph might cause her to cry; but now she had no time for tears; now she was stirred up to fight. What the control of her emotions cost her was not hidden—the delicate narrow lips were stiff; the blue eyes had a tense shine—but the control was absolute. Helen held her blonde head up with an angered pride.

Next to Helen sat what must be the Moore girl—this Joan, that Ralph either did or did not seriously propose to marry. Short and slight, she had attractive hair of a light brown. Her face, though not pretty, might be called interesting—a small oval; sensitive; not unintelligent. Whether because of her youth, whether because of the softness and pliability suggested somehow in her little features and in her young girl's figure, Joan Moore plainly lacked Helen's equipment to meet emergencies. Miss Moore was slowly crying. In the space of Arthur Winner's glance of inspection, new tears forced themselves from her swimming sad eyes and slipped over the curves of her immature cheeks. With a soaked handkerchief, Miss Moore wiped them miserably away. At her movement, Ralph Detweiler, who sat beside her, undertook halfheartedly to give her arm a pat.

Ralph Detweiler's face, in the full light, was very pale—a wanness, Arthur Winner judged, of consuming alarm, of plain fright over this predicament of his. The cast of Ralph's face was the classic cast of Helen's face—a good nose; a good-looking line of forehead and cheek. Anyone would guess them to be brother and sister. At the mouth, however, the resemblance ended. Ralph's naturally larger, fuller lips were nicely shaped. Ralph had been a pretty little boy; and in a little boy, a child, prettiness might even be attractive; but, retained, continued, in the face of a young man the quality was faintly disturbing. The pretty mouth looked irresolute; the shapeliness was wistful. Not quite feminine, it was not manly either. The weak face was, of course, the weaker for being unnerved by fear; and the fear could, of course, be guilt's, yet Arthur Winner, concluding his quick look, thought with conviction: He didn't do it; he wouldn't have it in him!

The steps to the door reached, what would be the prosecutrix and her mother were to be seen, across the room from the others. They, too, were unsparingly lighted; and Arthur Winner instantly observed—would it be a satisfaction to Miss Moore, or to Helen?—that Veronica Kovacs, if he had the name right, must at some time have done some crying of her own. She kept her face averted with a sullen air; but the dry stain of tears could be seen. Miss Kovacs looked older than Miss Moore—a point that Arthur Winner, in automatic professional calculation, was glad to note. For doing "what he shouldn't have done," Ralph wouldn't, then, be faced (even if Miss Kovacs had consented) with a statutory rape charge. At the same time, to be noted was that Miss Kovacs, high-cheeked, sloe-eyed, with an ample soft mouth, would be likely to strike the average male as pretty, in the sense of attractively sluttish or desirable—much more so than little Joan Moore. From this appearance, one could probably infer the history of pursuit by boys that seemed likely to bear out the "not a good girl" business.

Dismissing that for later consideration, Arthur Winner looked comprehensively at Miss Kovacs's mother. A massive woman, Mrs. Kovacs was gross in feature, dark, big, and menacing. She was thick in body and hefty in limb. She sat with a glowering air of keeping her daughter in custody. She looked as though hers would be a hard and heavy hand—which might have something to do with those tearstains on Miss Kovacs's face; which, in turn, might have something to do (another point for later consideration) with Miss Kovacs's sworn complaint, with her sulky presence here.

142

Arthur Winner drew the screen door open. Stepping into the hot bright room, he said: "Good evening."

They had not heard him coming. There was something between a general stir and a general start. Noah Tuttle jerked his head up commandingly; and then gave a curt nod or two; as to say: Good; get on with it! Visible relief crossed Helen's face; the passionate compliment of her confidence. At last Mr. Winner was here! Now, everything would be all right! Mr. Winner—as she so well knew, a tower of legal strength—would, with his quick wisdom and unparalleled abilities, confound the enemy, demolish this false and malicious charge. When Mr. Winner got through with her, that horrid girl would be sorry she ever made it! Ralph Detweiler, with a grimace of nervousness, cleared his throat, though he did not attempt to say anything. Miss Moore gave Arthur Winner a stupefied look—as though she had no hope; as though no one could help.

Joe Harbison, seated at his roll-top desk in the corner, said: "Hello, Mr. Winner! Right on time." He had been turned away from the desk, facing Bernie Breck, a stout man who filled his uniform tightly, in a chair beside him. Bernie Breck said, nodding: "Mr. Winner."

Swiveling about, Joe Harbison moved the quarto blank book he used for a docket. He picked up a sheet of paper. Assuming a consequential manner, he raised the paper, peering through spectacles that sat on his small ruddy cheeks, tilting his hairless head and gnarled or knobby chin in a formal, surely needless verification of the form. He nodded then and said: "Now, this is the information, Mr. Winner." He coughed with dignity; and half rising, extended the paper. "You'd like to look at it, I guess."

Arthur Winner said: "Thanks. I would like to, if I may."

Taking the filled-in form without haste, Arthur Winner, without haste, drew from a case in his pocket the glasses he had recently come to need for reading and put them on. Ostensibly considering the rows of printed words: *Before me the Sub-*

scriber, a Justice of the Peace in and for the County of Brocton
. . . Arthur Winner set himself to a double effort. He meant to
receive, without appearing to seek them, all he could of those
usually important first impressions that Miss Kovacs, five feet
away, might contribute. While she and her mother supposed
him otherwise engaged, he hoped to take the sense of the situation—the small disclosures made by face or manner, the motive
or interest they might hint.

Holding himself open for anything of the sort, Arthur Winner
moved his eye with care to word after word: . . . *personally appears Veronica Kovacs of 147 Ferry Street, Mechanicsville* . . .

The position of the lifted paper let him have another look
at Veronica, hanging her head of coarse and rather oily black
hair. He looked then at Mrs. Kovacs. Darkly scowling, Mrs. Kovacs
seemed also to be holding herself open to impressions. With a
simple nature's blunt discernment, she perhaps (how rightly!)
felt this lawyer fellow, after making them wait all this time, was
now taking longer than he needed to. Her lips opened in a mutinous movement. Her remark was not intelligible; but, at the
sound, Joe Harbison, in a way to show he had been obliged to
speak to her before, said: "Now, just kindly be quiet please,
ma'am!"

Mrs. Kovacs uttered another mutter. A tremor of sorts had
passed through Miss Kovacs—that guess had been good! The
girl was scared to death of her mother. She was here because
she was afraid not to be. With deliberation, Arthur Winner
read: . . . *who upon her solemn oath taken according to law
deposeth and says that on or about the 14th day of September*
. . . However, the complaint, though made promptly, had been
made, Arthur Winner reflected, not this morning, but late this
afternoon. Did it take that long because they had to find out how
to lodge a complaint? Or did it take that long because Veronica
had to be beaten into lodging one? Aware that Miss Kovacs was
allowing herself a furtive stare at him, Arthur Winner suddenly
looked back. Her eye shifted so quickly that he did not catch it.
He read: . . . *in the Township of Lower Brocton, one Ralph
Detweiler did ravish, and unlawful carnal knowledge have of
her, forcibly and against her will; and further saith not* . . .

Inclining his head to Joe Harbison, Arthur Winner returned the form to Joe's desk. "I see," he said. "Now, if the court please—"

Joe Harbison said: "Yes; that's the charge, Mr. Winner. And, yes; I know that before proceeding further, you'll want to consult with accused. Glad to have you use the parlor, if that would be satisfactory. Just across the hall, here—"

"Good; thank you," Arthur Winner said.

Though perhaps not strictly necessary, changing his plan would, Arthur Winner saw, be advisable. Having occasion so seldom nowadays to come before a magistrate, he had forgotten, the truth was, the touchiness and self-importance of these usually pompous little men. Joe, clearly, would see a slight to his office if he were asked as peremptorily as Arthur Winner had been about to ask him, to postpone his hearing and set bail. Cost what it might in waiting around, Joe wished to stand on the ceremony of having counsel make such a motion with due deliberateness—not out of hand, having not even heard his client's story. Trusting Joe had not realized the original intention, Arthur Winner said: "We'll be as brief as possible."

Ralph Detweiler got up with uncertainty; and, seeing him rise, Mrs. Kovacs uttered a new growling sound. She said: "Where's he think he's going?"

Turning, staring at her through his spectacles, Joe Harbison said: "If you don't mind, ma'am; I'm running this. Accused has a right to counsel; and counsel's got a right to consult with him in order to advise him how to answer; and we're going to do things according to law. We'll hear prosecutrix and you when the time comes."

Getting to his feet, he said: "I'll just put a light on for you, Mr. Winner. And don't hurry yourself none."

✦

Arthur Winner could have wished for a better light than the one Joe Harbison put on. Sitting down himself, he had motioned Ralph to a seat at the round table on which stood an ornate lamp with a shade of stained-glass panels in a metal frame. There was more light here than anywhere else in the furniture-cumbered room; but Ralph's shifts of agitation kept moving his face back into the dusk of shadow.

The agitation was indeed considerable—enough to remind Arthur Winner that, as well as merely unmanly, this agitation *could* be guilty. Told to tell what happened, Ralph started out, eager and rapid, but also jerkily, interrupting himself every minute or two. He had been driving. He'd seen Miss Kovacs and offered her a lift. They'd gone to the Old Timbers Tavern and had a couple of drinks. Then they drove to Still Pond at Miss Kovacs's suggestion and parked, and—Ralph said: "I swear to God, Mr. Winner; she's absolutely lying, is all." Pausing, swallowing, his pale face's expression not clear in the shadow, he then said shakily: "Only, what if they don't believe me, Mr. Winner?"

Wishing to see whether Ralph, by himself, would do, would get by, Arthur Winner had been sitting silent, designingly, deliberately giving Ralph nothing in the way of help. Ralph, by himself, would not do! Arthur Winner said: "Now, just slow down, and calm down. The only people who've heard your story are Mr. Tuttle and Helen and, I gather, Miss Moore. They seem to believe you." He looked directly at Ralph. "Do you know some reason why others won't?"

As Arthur Winner intended, the sharp question caught Ralph unprepared. Ralph gaped, confused; yet, viewing this expected confusion attentively, Arthur Winner felt able to conclude, somewhat relieved, that it was confusion not so great as a guilty person with Ralph's weak nerves would show when touched where he was vulnerable. Ralph made a feeble explanatory gesture. He said: "Well, that's what I mean, Mr. Winner. They know me—that I never would have done it. Only, somebody that doesn't know me—I mean, like this Mr. Harbison out there; if he believed *her,* I guess, he could just find me guilty—"

Arthur Winner said: "I think you'd better understand this process. Mr. Harbison is a committing magistrate. A complaint against you was made to him and sworn to. On this information, a warrant issued, directing a peace officer to find you and bring you before Mr. Harbison. Because the charge is a felony, Mr.

146

Harbison has the power to do no more than hold a hearing. A hearing is not a trial. Mr. Harbison simply determines whether the charge *might* be true. He could dismiss it, if he found no real evidence against you. However, you're right in this sense. If Miss Kovacs can repeat her story without being shaken, Mr. Harbison couldn't properly hold there was no evidence. He'd have to send the case up for the grand jury. His jurisdiction ends there. Is that clear?"

Still paler, Ralph said: "Mr. Winner, you mean if she just says I'm guilty—"

Arthur Winner said: "I mean that Mr. Harbison can, and probably will, direct that you be held. Meanwhile, on the basis of Mr. Harbison's transcript and return—his record of what was put in evidence at the hearing—the district attorney will draw a bill of indictment, formally charging you with the offense. That bill will be submitted to the next grand jury. Miss Kovacs will have to go before the grand jury and give her evidence again. If they, or a majority of them—"

Ralph said: "But can't I say anything, sir?"

"No, you may not," Arthur Winner said. "Only evidence against you is considered. The grand jury isn't trying the case; they're just deciding whether you can reasonably be required to stand trial. If they think not, they'll throw the bill out. But, here again, if Miss Kovacs sticks to her story, we must expect them to find a true bill. The case will then be put on the criminal trial list. None of this has shown you to be guilty of anything. Miss Kovacs has still to convince, and convince beyond a reasonable doubt, a traverse jury that her story is true. If her story is not true, if she's lying, I've no doubt she'll fail. You can leave that to me. If she's lying! You're quite certain she is?"

"Oh, she's lying all right," Ralph said. "We don't have to worry about that, Mr. Winner." He attempted a laugh, as of ease or assurance; but his unsteadiness produced a sort of snigger. "It's just—I keep thinking—well, I certainly see this terrible position Veronica's got me in. I know what really happened; but—"

Arthur Winner said: "I'll take care of your position." He glanced at the windows open on the night. A stir of warm air

147

came from them. "At any hearing before Mr. Harbison, there'll be nothing you need to do. You won't be testifying. I'll simply cross-examine Miss Kovacs on her story; and we'll reserve your defense. But at a trial, if there is one, it will be necessary for me to place you on the stand; and when I've finished questioning you, you'll be cross-examined."

Regarding Ralph's obscured face a moment, he said: "As long as what you're telling is the truth, that needn't worry you. But the district attorney and his assistants are men of experience. Don't imagine you can fool them. If, on any point at all, you let yourself say what you know isn't the exact truth, you'll be in great danger. When jurors are shown that defendant lied, even on a small point, they may, and often do, elect to reject everything he says."

Ralph said: "Oh, I know that, Mr. Winner." He moistened his lips. "I understand how they always try to mix you up—"

"That's not quite it," Arthur Winner said. "That's done only in stories, or motion pictures. What the district attorney will be doing is testing your statements where they're in conflict with those of his witness or witnesses. If your statements are nothing but the truth, what really happened, you're quite safe. Unless you're trying to say you did one thing, while all the time you know you did another, nobody can mix you up in any way that will damage you. I must impress that on you. Don't deny what you know is true, no matter how you think you're being made to look. And don't put in things you think might make you look better. If, in what you've told me so far, you've done either; go back and correct it."

Ralph said: "Everything I've told you's true, Mr. Winner. I swear to God."

Stern being what Arthur Winner had meant to be, for him to read from his success in frightening Ralph again evidence of a greater than usual cowardice was hardly fair. Arthur Winner said: "Don't be alarmed. If you didn't do it, I'll be able to show that you didn't. All right; just go on. Give me the facts. When I have those, I'll take care of presenting them."

Ralph's shadowed face grew firmer. Regarded kindly, the frightened look, Arthur Winner supposed, might be only a sensitive look. Ralph had a quickness of nervous perception. For a bad moment, he felt that he was alone, that Mr. Winner was against him, too. Now assured that this was not true, that he was not alone, his relief might be going to carry him too far in the other direction.

Ralph said: "Oh, I'm not alarmed, Mr. Winner. It's only I wish I could figure out why Veronica would pick on me—try to do this to me—" He broke off. Not quite looking at Arthur Winner, but with earnestness, he said: "It isn't I care so much about me, Mr. Winner. I admit I did wrong. Lies about me could serve me right. It's Joanie and Helen I care about—that they have to go through this."

Arthur Winner looked toward the darkened window screens. Federal Street formed the north side of the courthouse square. A street light showed him the empty pavement. Across the street, through the thick foliage of the big ill-lit maples, a lighted window or two shone from the looming dim marble of the courthouse building. Behind, in the adjoining jail, a good many more lights appeared.

In fairness, Arthur Winner could allow that Ralph's protestation was probably sincere, his regret real. That Helen and Miss Moore—must he call her "Joanie"?—had to go through this was something Ralph might very well care about. He had no more meant to hurt them than he had meant to hurt himself. Arthur Winner said: "I think you do well to consider Helen and Miss Moore. We'll have to face the fact that it's a pity you couldn't have considered Miss Moore, at least, last night. I'm afraid that most people, most jurors, are going to feel that a man who's engaged to one girl should leave other girls alone. I say that, because it doubles the importance of the impression you make testifying. That means it's essential that they see you're being perfectly truthful."

Ralph said with alacrity: "I certainly know that, Mr. Winner. Oh, I agree it was a terrible thing for anyone engaged to do. Not it's any excuse—only, then, at that time, when I stopped to give Veronica a lift—well, doing anything with her was the last thing I ever thought of. Then, I just let myself get in this situation where I wasn't strong enough—"

149

Looking at Ralph thoughtfully, Arthur Winner put down as well as he could an increase in impatience. Given the "situation"—the young woman willing, the offered opportunity, was Ralph the only young man who wouldn't be "strong"? He was not!

Ralph said: "I certainly didn't use good judgment, Mr. Winner. I see that. I admit I ought to have known—I mean, that Veronica might get me into the situation if I ever gave her the least chance. I'd had the eye from her lots of times."

Arthur Winner said: "By that, you mean you'd got the impression, other times when you'd seen Miss Kovacs, that she'd like to go out with you?"

"Oh, absolutely, sir!" Ralph said. "I never knew her too well. But several times I remember she was practically hinting around. I remember once she even said to Joanie, at this place where we were dancing: 'You got a good-looking fellow there; you better watch him.' "

Arthur Winner was, indeed, going to need patience. He could feel at once his distaste of prejudice for "this place"—naturally, one of those tawdry roadside establishments; by day, sinister in their desertion; by night, with their signs lighted, filled to blares of idiot music with brainless young louts and the girls they brought—little near imbeciles often not much past puberty, dizened with fake jewelry and dime-store make-up, who would later pay for the public entertainment by going in the boys' dangerously driven, broken-down cars to dark byroads or lanes in the woods. Approaching now the point at which he would have to have the details, Arthur Winner could feel himself holding back—wishing not to hear much, to touch on the repellent business as little as possible, to take it as told.

Ralph said: "Of course, there's that, Mr. Winner. It's not a thing a fellow wants to do unless he has to; but plenty of people can tell you the kind of girl Veronica is. If she's going to make out she's pure and innocent, that's just a laugh."

Arthur Winner said: "Miss Kovacs's reputation for chastity would be admissible as bearing on the probability of consent. But unless you have, know you can adduce, ample evidence to destroy character, character should never be attacked—those attacks can boomerang. Plenty of people may know a girl's reputation is bad; but, as you say, people don't like to give that kind of evidence, and probably you'd have trouble finding even one witness who was willing to. In any event, it's collateral. The sort of girl Miss Kovacs may be doesn't go to the charge. You understand that?"

Ralph said: "Well, Mr. Winner, if we can show how many other fellows she was willing to do it with—"

"You can't show that," Arthur Winner said. "Only her reputation's admissible—witnesses may testify that they know people who know her, and that her reputation with those people is bad. That's all. They may not testify to specific acts of unchastity. How many men she may have had relations with has no bearing on the issue. If the prosecution can establish that on this occasion intercourse was had with her forcibly and against her will, rape is made out. Occasions, however many, when she consented are irrelevant. You are, of course, sure there wasn't any use of force? You didn't keep her from getting out of the car; or hold her down; or put your weight on her so she couldn't move—anything like that?"

Ralph attempted a laugh. He said: "Why should I, Mr. Winner? I mean, be using force? Putting up any struggle was the last thing she was doing."

Arthur Winner said: "You have a habit of answering a question with a question. You mustn't do that on the witness stand. Now, I think we'd better make sure you know what the law means by rape—what Miss Kovacs has to prove. The elements of rape are held to be; carnal knowledge; force; absence of consent—" He paused, searching his mind. Though the specific points of law came easily, he hadn't attended to points of this kind for years; he'd better check the annotated statutes tomorrow—find out what, if anything, had happened while he was away. He said: "The prosecution can show the first. You're not denying it. I may say that carnal knowledge is defined to mean penetration. You don't deny that you introduced your penis into Miss Kovacs's vagina?"

Ralph said: "Yes, sir. I mean, yes, I did; but—"

"There's no 'but,' " Arthur Winner said. "Either you did, or you didn't. You did. That constitutes fornication, of course; but to make you guilty of any higher offense, force and absence of consent must be proved. You say you used no force?"

"Not the least bit, sir," Ralph said. "I—"

"Yes," Arthur Winner said. "Understand that. The least bit's enough. Even if the force is only the force needed to perform the act when, for instance, the woman's been rendered unconscious by a blow. If you've put her in fear—fear for her life if she resists; that is force. Or if she has been drinking, and is too drunk to resist or know what she's doing, connection with her is held to have been by force. If there were none of these circumstances; if Miss Kovacs did fully and freely consent, knowing what she was doing, and not resisting or objecting in any way, rape can't be made out. You understand?"

"Yes, sir."

"Very well," Arthur Winner said. "Now, tell me exactly what happened after you parked the car in this lane—I believe you said, about half past ten—near Still Pond. Get the facts clear in your mind. After you stopped the car, you said you were embracing each other in the front seat. Miss Kovacs not only offered no objection; but, you say, encouraged you. What next?"

Ralph said: "Next—I wouldn't know exactly how long; not long; and Veronica said: 'Why don't we go in back, honey?' So we got in back—"

Arthur Winner said: "That's all the conversation you had?"

Ralph hesitated. "Well, no, sir. She did say: 'Do you have a thing—you know.' Something like that. Or, 'You have a thing, haven't you?' I told her no, I didn't—"

Arthur Winner said: "By 'thing,' I take it you both understood a contraceptive device?"

"Yes, sir. So I said no; I hadn't. Not with me." Ralph moistened his lips. He said anxiously: "Mr. Winner, isn't there that, too? If this was something I had any idea of, was planning, wouldn't I have had? Doesn't that go to show—"

"What that goes to show is, I'm afraid, nothing you want shown," Arthur Winner said. "In the first place, the point's not what you planned or didn't plan, but what you did. An inference might be drawn; yes. The one a jury would be likeliest to draw is habitual conduct—you do a lot of this. Fornication is not a felony, like rape; but it's an indictable offense, punishable by law. For most jurors, a serious moral offense is involved, too. If they got the idea that you made a regular thing of having unlawful relations with girls, or had them often, that would set a jury against you at once."

"Yes, sir," Ralph said. "I just thought—"

Arthur Winner said: "That's one point; the jury won't like it if they think you show no regard for morality. This would perhaps be a good time to mention another point—in effect, the converse, which you must remember, too. If you seem to be trying to tell the jury that *you* never had a wrong impulse, that everything was the girl's fault, they won't like that either. If you make a good impression, if they feel your testimony's frank and honest, they'll conclude for themselves that the girl was at least as much to blame as you were. You admit you did wrong; you're sorry. Leave the rest to them. Was there further conversation?"

"No, sir. Except I think I said a couple of times I didn't want to get her into trouble. And Veronica laughed, and said not to worry, she knew how to take care of herself."

"Go on," Arthur Winner said.

"So, we got in back; and Veronica pulled up her dress; and laid down on the seat—"

"This was, of course, your car," Arthur Winner said. "The one Helen got for you. What kind of car is it?"

"It's an old Chevy, sir."

"Not a big car," Arthur Winner said. "In the other room, I noticed that Miss Kovacs is fairly tall. You're certain the seat's long enough for her to lie down?"

Ralph said: "Yes, sir. I don't mean she was down flat, all the way. She lay back, kind of—her legs out. They were partly bent over the edge of the seat. So, then I went ahead and had relations with her—"

"Wait," Arthur Winner said. "You're not there yet. These are details that can be very important. Miss Kovacs lay back on the seat with her legs partly over the edge, and with her dress pulled up. What was done about her underclothing? Was it taken off? If so, by whom?"

Ralph hesitated. He said: "Of course, I couldn't see so well, Mr. Winner. I can't be absolutely sure; but what I guess is, she didn't have such a lot. She wasn't wearing pants, I know. I think she had a kind of, like a girdle; but not a regular stiff one. What she did about that, I think, after she had her dress up, she pushed that up, got it up around her as far as she could. I could feel something, the edge of something—"

"Well, go on!"

Ralph wiped the back of his hand across his forehead. He said: "Well, then I know she was saying: 'Come on, honey, what's the matter?' " Ralph moistened his lips. "So she began to fool with my trousers—"

Arthur Winner looked out at the dim night, the lights of the courthouse beyond the screens. With a rising, groaning racket, a heavy truck and trailer climbed the slope of Federal Street and went by. On the close air's movement, fumes of the exhaust came in. Arthur Winner said: "Yes; now, your trousers. Did you take them off; or merely open them?"

Ralph said: "Veronica started opening them. So then I undid my belt. So then I had them about half off; and Veronica was unbuttoning my shorts, getting those open. Then she was saying: 'Now, can't you, honey? Can't you now—' Then she was trying to get her own clothes up higher, more above her waist. I guess she thought maybe the girdle thing was still in the way—"

Arthur Winner waited in a distaste of mind so acute that a formal act of will was needed while he held the picture before him, visualizing the encounter, checking coldly detail against repellent detail, watchful for discrepancies or contradictions. He said: "Miss Kovacs was, in fact, drunk?"

Anxiously, Ralph said: "Oh, no, sir! I admit she had these couple of drinks at the Old Timbers. I don't say that couldn't have made her—well, sort of more passionate. So she could do these things—not care what way she talked. But not like—say, I was taking any advantage of her. I admit it was wrong—"

"Yes," Arthur Winner said. "You've admitted that. Were *you* drunk?"

154

With new agitation, with a deprecatory look of worry, Ralph said: "Well, without the drinks I had, maybe I wouldn't have done it, Mr. Winner." He gave Arthur Winner another look, plainly doubtful about what he ought to say. He said: "That is, except for the drinks I had, I might have been able to stop myself—see that it was wrong; tell Veronica we oughtn't to do this. But I could drive a car perfectly all right—everything like that."

Arthur Winner said: "The only point at this time is: Were you sober enough to be sure of what really happened? Miss Kovacs couldn't have protested or resisted without your now remembering?"

Ralph attempted a smile. He said: "Oh, no, sir. I wouldn't have the least trouble remembering everything. Resisting was the one thing she certainly wasn't. Just the opposite. What she was saying was: 'Lover, why don't you do it—' "

More sharply, Arthur Winner said: "That isn't what you told me Miss Kovacs was saying a minute ago. If you're not certain what was said at any point, don't try to give it."

With alarm, Ralph said: "Those were some of her exact words, Mr. Winner. I'm certain. Other times, she might be saying different things—only, all like that; couldn't I do it now? Like, at different times she was doing different things."

"When was that specific remark made? What was she doing? What were you doing?"

Ralph said painfully: "Well, right then, when she said that about why didn't I do it, I think she was kind of squeezing me with her knees, in between them; kind of working up and down. I had hold of, I guess, her hips. Trying to get them under me more, get her over more to the edge of the seat. And she was making these remarks all the time; like, give it to me, give it to me. At least until—well, we started being together—"

"This is late in the day for delicacy," Arthur Winner said. "You mean, until, by your various movements, it had been made possible for your penis to be inserted. If so, say so."

"Yes, sir. By then, I had it all the way in her."

"All right; go on."

Ralph drew a laborious breath. He said awkwardly: "I guess then, the next thing—well; Veronica got pretty sore. But I—"

"Angry?" Arthur Winner said. "Why should she be angry if you were doing what she wanted you to?"

"Well—" Ralph said. He cleared his throat. "You see, I guess she'd been getting me more and more excited. So as soon as I was—well, in her, then I couldn't wait any more. Right away—well, I was just too quick. So Veronica began hitting me, pounding my back with her two hands. Sort of crying; and saying: 'Oh, you can't do that to me!' "

Arthur Winner said: "What did Miss Kovacs mean by 'that'?"

Ralph said: "Well, only, I guess she could feel what happened. She meant, me being too quick—before she was ready. She could tell, I guess, that I was all through, when she wasn't. So, she got sore."

"Miss Kovacs could not have meant the act itself which you'd succeeded in completing, though she tried to stop you?"

Ralph said: "Oh, no! Not possibly, Mr. Winner! Her only trouble was, with what happened, that hadn't been enough for her yet. She only didn't want me to stop. So she wouldn't let go of me, first. And then, when I was—well, out of her, she started trying everything—you know; seeing if she could get me so I could again. She was trying quite a while—you know; with her hands; kissing me different ways."

"And did she succeed?"

"No. It wasn't any use, Mr. Winner. I couldn't," Ralph said. The look Ralph returned was, Arthur Winner realized, one perhaps often used by Ralph and one perhaps often useful—a candid-appearing gaze of calculated melancholy. "You see, I was beginning to think what I was doing—what I'd done. How it was wrong. I was thinking about Joanie. How she'd feel. Then, I couldn't do it any more."

Contemplating Ralph in silence, Arthur Winner reminded himself that the fault might be—was!—that fault of youth, the ordinary far-reaching flaws in judgment, the usual failures in discrimination. No doubt, those really had been Ralph's feelings and Ralph's thoughts. The business done with Miss Kovacs, he really might begin to think how "Joanie" would feel if she knew. In Miss Kovacs's persisting embrace of disappointment—void now of every excitant; in its ardency unshared, perhaps even repulsive—glum thoughts of virtue occurred to Ralph. While Miss Kovacs, hopeful, tried her hand, Ralph, unresponsive, cogitated his wrongdoing, deplored, now that they were dead, the appetites that had made him untrue to "Joanie." Genuinely wishing he hadn't done this, Ralph could conceive it to be contrition that now defeated Miss Kovacs in her every endeavor.

Arthur Winner said: "While I remember, I think I'd better tell you that in giving testimony, you may not testify to what you thought. You may only state the fact—what you did, or were unable to do." Frowning, Arthur Winner broke off.

He said at last: "Speaking of Miss Moore, I gather that her being here means she's willing to stand by you. How did she happen to hear about it—that you'd been arrested?"

"Helen said since I was engaged to her, and I'd told Joanie about being with Veronica, I should call her up—"

"When did you tell Miss Moore; and how did you happen to?"

Somewhat laboriously, Ralph said: "Oh, I told her the whole thing this morning. I went to see her. I had to confess it to her, I saw that."

"What exactly did you tell her? That you'd been out with Miss Kovacs the night before, and that she'd allowed you to have sexual relations with her?"

"Yes, sir. I didn't think I ought to deceive her. So we discussed it; and Joanie said she was ready to forgive me. She could see I never really meant to—well, be unfaithful to her, even. Let alone what Veronica's trying to say I did."

Arthur Winner said: "Miss Moore's attitude seems generous. If she knows the whole story, and is willing to forgive you, and to testify that she is, she'd be a help to you with any jury. What was her first reaction when you told her?"

Uncomfortably, Ralph said: "Well, she cried, of course; but she knows Veronica. I mean, she's seen her around. Joanie knows what kind of a girl Veronica is. She can understand how a girl like that, if she got a fellow out with her—why, he could lose control of himself. Of course, I admitted I never should have done it—stopped to give Veronica this lift."

Setting his finger tips together, Arthur Winner looked at

them. He said: "You felt you ought to talk to Miss Moore this morning. At that time, it wasn't in your mind that a warrant might possibly be issuing for you on Miss Kovacs's information?" He looked directly at Ralph.

Taken aback, Ralph said: "How could it be in my mind, sir? What I did with Veronica was wrong; and that was certainly in my mind. I admit I certainly had a bad conscience; and I could see that confessing it to Joanie was the only thing to do. But, Mr. Winner, how could I ever think Veronica might try to get me arrested—anything like that?"

Arthur Winner said: "Please let me ask the questions, Ralph. I'll explain my last one. People who are afraid they will be accused of something often seem to imagine they can help themselves by putting on the record somewhere their own version of what happened before the other version appears. They're quite mistaken; but sometimes they don't realize they are."

Ralph said: "Mr. Winner, I swear to God, until Mr. Breck— until this fellow asked me to come out; said he wanted to see me—showed me that warrant, it hadn't even ever crossed my mind I'd have to worry about Veronica even saying anything, let alone this. I know plenty of fellows that went with her. They all tell you: Don't worry; Veronica Kovacs keeps her mouth shut."

Arthur Winner said: "For some time, then, you'd known or believed that Miss Kovacs was willing to have sexual intercourse when boys wanted her to; and that she could be counted on to keep quiet?"

"Oh, yes, sir. Everybody knew that."

"I see. Now, let's go back to what happened last night. You said that Miss Kovacs tried to make it possible for you to repeat the act; and that she failed. Did failing anger her, or anger her again?"

With alacrity, with apparent relief, Ralph said: "Well, I suppose she was naturally disappointed, Mr. Winner. But not the way she was at first. So no; when she saw I just couldn't, no matter what she did, she'd stopped being sore."

"Was anything said?"

"Well, sir; I remember she gave this kind of laugh and said: 'Better luck next time—'; something like that. So then she got up, got out of the car to fix her clothes. She asked had I a comb. I gave her one. So then I was going to give her some money."

Arthur Winner said: "Had there been mention of money?"

Shrugging apologetically, Ralph said: "Well, no; she never asked me for any. Only, I knew she was always going out with fellows; and maybe they usually gave her something. So I didn't want her to think I was a cheap skate."

"Go on."

"So by then, Veronica had her clothes fixed; and so she found this rip in her dress—it must have caught on something while she was pulling it up. So she said, if I wanted to, I could give her something to help pay for it—getting a new dress. Because her mother took her money; so she had hardly any dresses; and where this tear was, she couldn't fix it not to show. So I had a five-dollar bill I gave her. So she said: 'You're a nice fellow, Ralphie. I'll make it up to you.' "

"What did you understand that to mean?"

"Oh," said Ralph, "you know; I could do it with her again when I wanted; I wouldn't be just out the money. So we left the pond; and I drove her down to Mechanicsville."

"Was there conversation on the way?"

"Oh, yes," Ralph said. "Veronica kept saying how if we had another date, couldn't we go some place. There was this tourist cabin place, this motel she knew near Riverside, where it was all right. Then we could have a bed; not have our clothes on."

"Miss Kovacs said in so many words that she'd be willing to go out with you again; and, specifically, have sexual intercourse with you again?"

"Oh, more than she'd be willing, Mr. Winner," Ralph said. "She was kind of taking it for granted, wanting me to promise to. Well, I didn't like to hurt her feelings, or anything; so I was saying: Yes, that was a good idea." He swallowed uneasily. "Only, I never meant it, Mr. Winner. I was certainly wishing right then that I never knew her at all! I certainly wasn't risking going out with her again! So Veronica kept saying just find some place where we could go and have plenty of time; and I wouldn't be sorry; because without our clothes on, and with a bed where there was room, not like a car, she could show me

159

what a real loving was. All I thought: I thought, when I get you out of this car, that's the last you'll ever see of me!"

Leaning back, Arthur Winner set his finger tips together again. "And then you took her home?" he said.

"Yes; I left her off at her place in Mechanicsville. It wasn't more than half past eleven."

"Were lights on in the house? Did anyone seem to be up?"

Ralph said: "Yes; there was a light. Veronica said her mother left one for her father. He works on some shift until two in the morning. I said would it be all right about the tear in her dress; and Veronica said she could say that happened any number of ways; but she wouldn't have to; because her mother and sisters would have gone to bed, be dead to the world. So I said I'd call her at the Elite—this lunch counter where she works in Brocton. But she said no, I'd better not do that; her boss gets sore when fellows call her. Why didn't I just come in when she'd be getting off tomorrow night? So I said I would if I could. So I went home—drove to Brocton."

Sitting back, pondering for a moment, Arthur Winner must conclude that this whole recount was plausible. The unpalatable lewd detail stood up; it rang with the simple nastiness of flat truth. The animal rencounter, the eager struggle to couple on the edge of the back seat might be taken as rightly recollected. Those reported suggestions by Miss Kovacs for a better-managed second date sounded in character—the experienced proposals of a girl with an itch (no doubt, some physiological abnormality) so intense that she was helpless, she had to have it satisfied. Quite believably, she importuned Ralph, she explained the, to her, well-known ways and means; she offered herself with urgence; she prompted him to make it as soon as he could—the next night, if possible. Sounding through Ralph's paraphrase, phrases that must be Veronica's could be recognized—Ralph wasn't making them up.

If, intellectually satisfied as he was that Ralph had spoken the truth, there remained in Arthur Winner's mind a sense of incompleteness, of something not quite clear, this feeling might reasonably stem from the problem posed by Miss Kovacs's sudden next move. It was of course within the range of possibility —Miss Kovacs's surely limited intelligence would put it there! —that, ardor, the overmastering itch aside, Miss Kovacs had last night another reason for making Ralph free of her. Miss Kovacs might already have been out once too often. In trouble; did she need, and so did she deliberately arrange to get, a boy to hold responsible?

The possibility, though always a real one with girls of Miss Kovacs's habits, must be dismissed. No doubt her intelligence was limited, but hardly so limited that, if her scheme was to bring an action to blackmail someone into marrying her, she would move against a father for her prospective child the very day after she had caused him to make himself eligible. No; Miss Kovacs might be better supposed to have acted her part of the compulsive strumpet with uncalculating appetite, with all good will, in all good faith. And then? Toward midnight, Ralph stopped his car in a mean Mechanicsville street. Miss Kovacs stepped to the pavement with a word and a wave. Making a certain amount of noise, the car moved away; and Miss Kovacs let herself into a hall where a light burned, into the house where everyone was supposed to be dead to the world. She went to her room. Quickly, she started to take off her clothes, on which an informed eye would very likely find evidence, traces that needed to be removed, of her evening's activities. While she stood stripped, checking on her garments and on herself, the door swung open—and who advanced on her, black with fury and suspicion? Could Veronica evade? Could she deny—look there; look at that!—what she had been doing? No, she couldn't; but in a pitch of terror, perhaps trying to dodge blows, she had a desperate, a pathetic idea. Cowering, she wept. She made gestures of the ruined maiden. This boy she was out with had forced her—

Arthur Winner said: "Incidentally, how long have you and Miss Moore been engaged?"

Ralph said: "Oh, a couple of months, I guess, Mr. Winner."

"But you didn't tell Helen until—when did you tell Helen?"

"Oh, I told her this morning. I admit I didn't tell her before because I thought she might not like it—say we were too young, or something. But it would be next week I'd have to go, if I were going to college; so—"

Arthur Winner said: "You told Helen before you saw Miss Moore?"

"Yes, sir. It was at breakfast."

Arthur Winner said: "You felt certain that you still were engaged to Miss Moore—I mean, that you would be, even after you told her what you'd been doing?"

In some confusion, Ralph said: "Well, yes, sir. I knew Joanie loved me. And if I was honest with her, and asked her to forgive me; why, I was pretty sure she would, that she'd still be willing to marry me."

"And she is still willing. Have you definite plans to get married?"

Ralph said: "Yes, we have, Mr. Winner. We discussed that, too. We decided this morning we ought to get married right away. I'd been thinking of waiting—to get a better job; things like that. But I saw now we oughtn't to wait."

"What made you see that?"

Showing some embarrassment, yet with an increase of confidence, Ralph said: "Well, actually, Mr. Winner, due to this with Veronica. Being so ashamed of what I did, I mean. It made me realize how much I loved Joanie; because I could feel how wrong letting another girl make me lose control of myself was. So I could see with Joanie and me married—well, nothing like this could have happened. But as long as we weren't married, I could see I might happen to be out with someone; and if she would happen to get me excited, I might not be strong enough to—well, remember Joanie."

Checking the reply that came first to his mind, Arthur Winner said: "Was it in connection with your plan to get married right away that you went to see Mr. Tuttle at the Union League this morning?"

Ralph flushed. "Yes, it was, Mr. Winner. I thought Mr. Tuttle might let me have a loan. I didn't know he'd be so—"

Arthur Winner said: "Under the circumstances, getting married right away wouldn't be wise. Not, certainly, while this case

162

is pending. If you feel as you say about Miss Moore, I think you should have no trouble in not 'happening' to go out with other girls. Does Helen know that you'd planned to get married right away?"

Ralph said: "No, sir. I didn't get a chance to tell her. I was going to tell her after supper; but then this fellow came—"

"How about Miss Moore? Did she tell her parents? I suppose she had to explain where she was going when you called her?"

"I don't think she could have," Ralph said. "I know her mother's away; and her father's generally at the store pretty late—"

Arthur Winner sat silent for a moment.

He said: "There's one point in your story I'd like to revert to. You told me you drove by the bus stop about half past nine and noticed Miss Kovacs waiting for the Mechanicsville bus. Now, how did you come to be passing the bus stop at that time?"

Ralph said: "Oh, I was on my way home, sir. But it was pretty early—"

"And where were you coming from? Where had you been?"

Ralph hesitated. He raised his hand and grasped his chin, frowning as though in an effort of recollection. "Oh, well; I'd been driving around," he said.

"Where?"

"Oh, no place in particular. Different places. I was just driving."

"Did you stop anywhere?"

"Well, yes," Ralph said. "Earlier, I was at Joanie's for a while. And—"

Brought to attention, Arthur Winner said: "Were you? Was Miss Moore there?"

"Oh, yes, sir," Ralph said. "She was there."

"Did you spend some time with her?"

"Oh, not so long. Half an hour, I guess. Yes."

Arthur Winner said: "What were you doing?"

"Oh, nothing," Ralph said awkwardly. "I simply went over after supper. We sat and talked some. Then, Joanie was tired—"

"Who else was there?"

"Well, nobody, right then. Mrs. Moore had taken the kids on this visit; and I think Mr. Moore was at some lodge meeting or something."

"Where did you and Miss Moore talk?"

"On the porch. We sat on the porch. It was hot, like tonight."

Arthur Winner said: "What did you talk about?"

"I don't really remember, Mr. Winner," Ralph said. He stirred uneasily. "Different things. I remember we talked about whether we'd go to this dance at Riverside tomorrow night; but Joanie said no; not when it was two-fifty just to get in. Just different things."

Arthur Winner was silent an instant. Returned to him urgently was his own phrase: a jury might infer—habitual conduct! A regular thing! He said: "In the course of this talk did you exchange any kisses or caresses?"

Ralph's shadowed face colored markedly. "Well, yes, sir," he said. "I guess, some. Like two people in love do."

Arthur Winner looked at him in silence. Speaking suddenly, he said: "You didn't have, nor attempt to have, sexual relations with Miss Moore, did you?"

"Oh, no, sir!" Ralph said. He spoke with a sound of shock. "We were out on the porch, there."

"But there was nobody at home," Arthur Winner said. "You were free to go in the house. Did you ask Miss Moore to go in the house with you?"

"No, sir."

Arthur Winner said: "You know, or if you don't, I'll tell you now, that anything I learn from you in my capacity as your attorney is a confidential communication. There's no way it can come out. Now, answer me truthfully. In the course of the talk on the porch with Miss Moore, did you suggest that you and she go in the house and have sexual relations?"

"I wouldn't, sir. I—"

"Have you, in fact, had sexual relations with Miss Moore?"

Ralph said: "Joanie isn't that kind of a girl, Mr. Winner." He moistened his lips. "She was always saying we wanted to be

164

careful we didn't go too far. She would always say not until we were married."

"If she said that, you must have given her occasion to say that. From time to time, you had, then, tried to persuade Miss Moore to have sexual intercourse. And she always refused?"

Ralph said weakly: "Joanie would say if two people really loved each other, they would love each other enough to wait."

Arthur Winner was conscious of a discomfort of pity—as though, given his unfair vantage ground of years and experience, the ease of these moves made them ugly and unkind. Ralph, the not-very-bright, and, so, helpless, youth, narrowed down on, driven by means he did not even comprehend, by a hand expert and undeflectable, into his close corner—was this very different from stepping on a worm? Arthur Winner said: "You're quite sure that Miss Moore's willingness to forgive you in this matter, and the decision to get married right away, aren't due to a need of Miss Moore's to get married?"

Held by Arthur Winner's gaze, Ralph, paralyzed, could not so much as drop his eyes. He said nothing.

Arthur Winner said: "The fact, then, is that finally Miss Moore was persuaded to let you have sexual intercourse with her. Not long ago, she came to believe she was pregnant. You were both frightened; and you agreed to marry her. When you told me you decided only this morning, that your experience with Miss Kovacs decided you, you weren't telling the truth?"

"No, sir," Ralph said. He spoke shakily; yet with the relief (always great!) of once and for all resigning a contest beyond his frightened capacities. He could abandon the exhausting struggle to keep secret some part at least of this multiplied trouble so suddenly fallen on him.

Arthur Winner said: "And when you told me you didn't suggest sexual intercourse to Miss Moore last night, that wasn't true either, was it? In fact, knowing she'd be alone in the house, that's what you went there for. You'd often done that, hadn't you? Gone over when she let you know everyone would be out, and had intercourse with her?"

"Well, no; not often, sir," Ralph said. "We did it once."

165

"You don't mean that you've had intercourse with Miss Moore only once?"

"Oh, no, sir," Ralph said. "It was only once at her house. She had it with me in the living room once—one afternoon. Usually, if we had it, it would be out somewhere—"

"You mean, in the car?"

"Well, yes, sir. Or sometimes I'd bring a blanket, and we'd have it out of the car."

"I'd like to continue with last night," Arthur Winner said. "When you went over to see Miss Moore, you expected her, in view of what had gone before, and of your agreement to marry her as soon as you could arrange to, to do what you wanted. Perhaps with some idea of regularizing her relations by not having intercourse with you again until after you were married, she refused, didn't she?"

With a look startled and fearful, as though the simple guess had struck Ralph as a miracle of second sight, the exercise of a divining power that nothing could escape, Ralph said: "Yes, sir. She said we ought not to any more until then; then I could all I wanted—"

"But you didn't agree. You'd come expecting to have intercourse; and you still wanted to. So you began to argue with her."

Weakly, Ralph said: "Well, I did ask her where was the sense in not letting me this once, after the times she'd let me before. Here, if we were going to get married, and when she says she's going to have a baby anyway, what was the harm? So if she really loved a person, she ought to prove she did by—"

The argument, in its plaintive reproachful form, as well as in its shoddy disingenuous substance, shed, Arthur Winner supposed, a good enough light on poor Miss Moore's sad, shamed predicament. You could see exactly how she got herself there. In speaking of those who "really loved," Ralph was passing the operative word. He pronounced the incantation by which chary maids were known to be turned prodigal enough. At the word's

166

bidding, Miss Moore resumed her sad self-swindle—gave way; lay down forthwith to minister to Ralph and Ralph's pleasure. Miss Moore's fatuous young hope, root of all her griefs, bloomed again. Under those fantastic leaves and flowers, she hid the plain folly of her course from herself. She blinked her clear knowledge of her lamentable mistake, the mistake that she and she alone had made, had desired to make, had disastrously succeeded in making. Still hope's fool, she stood to be undone again. If you wondered how Miss Moore came to be that fool, the oval small tear-wet face in the room across the hall might tell you. As Arthur Winner had been quick to note, Miss Moore, poor "Joanie," though she had an attractive young figure, was simply not a pretty girl.

In being disadvantaged this way, Joan Moore was, of course, hardly unique. The mean trick of nature was played on plenty of girls. The defect was, to be sure, remediless, in one sense; yet a plain girl, if she went to work, could do something for herself. She could set herself to be so agreeable or so amusing that her unattractiveness might come gradually to be overlooked—at least, by those who knew her well. She might even end by being sought after to some degree.

That Miss Moore had taken this beggars' choice, that she had elected to go to work, could be judged from her interest in high-school theatricals. Those dreary amateur efforts always had problems of supporting casts, or small parts; so a willing worker was always welcome. More than willing, Joan was no doubt actually eager. To the mean trick of nature, an unkindness of fate had just been added. Joan Moore was new in Brocton. Moving there with her parents, entering Brocton High School, she left behind whatever she might have accomplished in the way of proving that prettiness isn't everything. In Brocton, she knew no one. If a new pretty face had turned up, a week would have taken care of that—boys would feel, and would show that they felt, an immediate urge to be her friend. The girls, in self-defense, would ask her in, wanting to have her where they could keep an eye on her. For Joan Moore, nothing like this was going to happen. A glance told everyone that, as well as new, she was nobody—a thin insignificant little creature with no looks, no social standing, no money, no anything. Who would trouble to notice her further?

Unnoticed, Joan Moore, it seemed safe to guess, was not unnoticing. The unnoticed girl's ordinary solace had to be reverie; and during Miss Moore's first months, while she was trying against the terrible odds to make her way, looking for openings, weighing chances, she surely so solaced herself a good deal. In the daily life of the school, boys might ignore her; but in reverie, how different! There, she could entertain anyone she wanted—any boy she thought was good-looking, any boy whose attentions and admiration she wished she had. In view of the now-known outcome, Ralph Detweiler seemed likely to have figured prominently among such boys. In mute infatuation, "Joanie" looked for and found a practicable approach. The dramatic society would do. She could make him notice her, get on speaking terms with him. This done, she need only nerve herself to go further, to put herself in his way, to flatter him, to try to please. Before long, Ralph must be apprised of the lowly yearning regard. Because she was starving, "Joanie," the fool, for crumbs of attention—for only a word of unreal compliment, for only a look that was amiable—was ready to do almost anything. Proffered a trifle more, she would, she could be brought to, alter that "almost anything" to "anything at all."

What came next? As a rule, Arthur Winner supposed, nothing came next. The boys chosen for a neglected girl's reverie were also likely to be the boys most certain to feel boredom and embarrassment if she let her regard for them appear. They only had eyes for a quite different sort of young woman. Impatient and even annoyed—their peers might any minute start a ribbing about this "girl" of theirs—they would shake off their forlorn little worshiper the shortest way. A "Joanie" could then digest in tears the fact that nobody wanted her. Something of the sort might seem indicated here. Ralph, as Helen said, must know by now that girls commonly felt a liking for him—in short, open to him was a fairly wide choice. Girls who were pretty and popular, girls who had style and even money, would be glad of his attentions. With all this his for the going-after, why on earth, Helen asked, would Ralph be interesting himself in a waif and stray like Joan Moore? Acknowledging (with that candor of realism that surprised Arthur Winner) the primacy of Ralph's self-interest in Ralph's scheme of things, Helen answered confidently: Ralph wouldn't.

Well, the answer was wrong, was an oversimplification to be debited to Helen's temperament. Helen was far from stupid; but that fastidiously shrinking mind of hers allowed her (for all the surprising candor of realism) to look at parts only of this boy and girl business. She was not able to, she would not let herself, think below the surface, below the level of public appearance. On this level, Helen noted, accurately enough, that girls fancy a handsome boy; and that boys prefer beautiful girls. From the first, you judged that Ralph would have smooth sailing. From the second, you judged the direction in which he would want to sail. To see that neither judgment was necessarily sound, you had to know more than Helen had ever been willing to know. Arthur Winner looked closely at Ralph, at the face that Helen—reasonably—believed girls would like. In Ralph's present state of alarm and defeat, that face had a quelled and cast-down expression—perhaps truly eloquent of Ralph's trouble; just as Miss Moore's sad little face was truly eloquent of hers.

Though Helen could see (and dotingly condone) Ralph's open self-interest, could Helen see Ralph's more important, graver defect? Open self-interest was, after all, a mere matter of deportment, for most people correctable enough as soon as they realized that a show of self-interest is shortsighted. Self-interest should always be secret. Ralph's graver defect might be—almost certainly, was—one of basic personality; by definition, altogether uncorrectable. The defect's form would be a failure in initiative and energy, a lack of determined confidence so serious that even self-interest's promptings grew weak. That smooth sailing Helen imagined for him was open to Ralph; yes. The beautiful girls, looking at him, might often look invitation, exactly as Helen supposed. Ralph seemed promising. Let him make them an offer!

But suppose such female advertising for bids—the gist of opportunity to most youths; all they could ask, all they needed—

gave Ralph only pause. Suppose Ralph boggled at opportunities to sail smoothly to where work was going to be cut out for him; where rivals he must overbid would surely be found; where, however much his suit was looked on with favor, he must still assiduously sue? You asked why on earth Ralph might interest himself in Joan Moore? Your answer would hardly be Helen's. Helen's just cognizance that boys prefer beautiful girls to plain girls had here to be amended. Put bluntly: to a beautiful girl who probably wasn't a push-over, Ralph would prefer a plain girl who probably was. How this could be might go outside Helen's imaginings; but with Ralph's simple wants, was there really so much to choose between "Joanie" and the most beautiful girl in the world? When that game is afoot, discriminating indeed is the man to whom, in the dark, all cats aren't gray.

Arthur Winner said: "But Miss Moore still refused to go in the house with you. You were annoyed. You left."

"Well, Joanie said she was tired—"

Setting his fingers together, Arthur Winner said: "I'll have to suggest to you now that you didn't 'happen' to be passing the bus stop. You were, in fact, looking for Miss Kovacs. You knew her reputation; and you remembered this idea you had that she might like to go out with you. You knew where she worked, and when she got off. You kept passing the bus stop until you saw her. You were going to pick her up, buy her some drinks, and then have sexual relations with her if you could. You thought this would only serve Miss Moore right for refusing you, didn't you?"

Ralph said feebly: "I didn't think all of that. All I thought was—well, if I happened to see Veronica—"

"But what you said before wasn't true. You'll remember you said you hadn't any thought of sexual relations with Miss Kovacs until she made advances that excited you. In fact, it was all something you'd planned. You took her to this bar. You made the advances. You, not she, suggested going down to Still Pond. When you got there, you, not she, took the initiative."

"Well, no, sir," Ralph said. "Well, I admit I might have sug-

170

gested where we go. And, yes; by then I was making some advances, I guess. I mean, we were having these drinks at the Old Timbers; and Veronica was letting me put my hand on her leg —you know. So then she started fooling around with me; and I just said: 'Let's drive some.' That was only like saying I wanted to if she wanted to. And I could tell she did. I mean, a girl might let a fellow fool with her a little, and still be going to stop him. But when she begins fooling with him—it was like I said, Mr. Winner. When we got out to the car, right away Veronica was all over me, so I could hardly drive—acting crazy."

Arthur Winner said: "Listen carefully. I told you earlier what may constitute rape in the law's view. If a woman is drunk, her condition is held to make her incapable of consent, so the fact that she may not have resisted is irrelevant. You told me Miss Kovacs wasn't drunk. Think again. Was she?"

"No, sir. She wasn't."

"Be sure about that," Arthur Winner said. "If she was, you should realize that the prosecution can probably prove she was. People must have seen you at this place, and seen you leave. If her condition was anything but sober, there may be witnesses to testify to what it was. If she got home drunk, her mother may be able to swear to that. Understand me. If she was drunk, and you know she was, I have a duty as your attorney to advise you to plead guilty. By doing that, we dispose the court to leniency. The judge might go so far as to give consideration to the fact that Miss Kovacs was not a girl of good repute and her lack of consent was only technical; and you might even get a suspended sentence. If you stood trial, and a jury found you guilty, you'd be dealt with much more severely."

"No, sir. I swear to God—"

"Yes," Arthur Winner said. "If you tell your story under oath, you must be prepared to. I may say that your account of what went on at the pond satisfies me; so we needn't go over it again. Now, I think you'd better know how we handle things like this, so you'll understand what I'll be doing. There's a chance that Miss Kovacs, since she isn't telling the truth, can be broken down by cross-examination at the hearing. I may be able to make her contradict herself so seriously and so often that Mr.

Harbison will be willing to dismiss the complaint. That's possible but not probable: so we'd better assume that you'll be held. I will have arranged to have the hearing reported, so we'll have a transcript of everything she said. The object is to confront her at the trial with what she said before. By cross-examination, she'll have been made to lie so often, and in such detail, that, whether she contradicts herself at the hearing or not, at the trial she's bound to contradict herself. Once she starts, a jury can very quickly be brought to doubt her story—particularly if the jurors have formed a good impression of you. We must be careful about that."

"Yes, sir," Ralph said.

Arthur Winner said: "I want to think a little longer about this situation with Miss Moore. Since I gather there's no question of her being a girl of Miss Kovacs's reputation and habits, you seem to me right in feeling that your getting her into trouble morally obligates you to marry her. But, as I've said, marrying her right away would probably not be wise. I take it you and she are the only ones who know at present—that is, Helen knows no more than you told her this morning about being engaged; and Joan hasn't said anything to her parents?"

"No, sir," Ralph said. "We didn't want to say anything yet. We were—well, really waiting to see if she might have been wrong. Joanie said one good thing was her mother was away, off on this visit; so her mother wouldn't be noticing about her, asking her questions, maybe."

"Still," Arthur Winner said, "her parents know, of course, that you've been seeing a good deal of her?"

Ralph said: "Well, no, sir. I don't think Joanie wanted them to know she was going with one particular fellow. So she'd meet me places—say it was some girl friends she was with, or something."

Arthur Winner could be sure he must have shown the astonishment he felt, for Ralph, in slight confusion, said: "It was: Joanie said her father was kind of strict; and if he thought she was seeing a fellow, he might stop her going out at all. So it was better if I didn't meet them—they didn't see me."

The Moores had a daughter. They brought her up; they

172

clothed, fed, and they thought—her father was a "strict" man—
supervised her. Yet they did not know where she went, whom she
was with, or what she did. All summer long, Joan had, unsus-
pected by them, been going with a boy whose name they hadn't
heard, at whom they'd never had a look. This boy's whole idea
was to have sexual intercourse with their Joan; and, soon, Joan
decided she'd have to let him if she wanted to keep him; and
so she did; and (nothing remarked by them) she went on letting
him fairly regularly. There'd been an accident; and now (Mr.
and Mrs. Moore not dreaming of such a thing) she was pregnant. This moment, she sat weeping in the office of a justice of
the peace, waiting on her seducer, who was in an ugly jam,
charged with a felony; while her mother (off visiting), her father
(late at the store), thought Joan was doing—what?

Ralph said: "That was one other thing I was wondering, Mr.
Winner." He coughed as though in embarrassment. "I mean,
about when I was there last night. It was something I didn't
think of then—what the trouble could have been. I mean, she
could have found suddenly it was—well, all right. Only she
didn't like to come out and tell me the real reason why
she couldn't—well, love me just then. It might not have been
just that she didn't want to."

A stir of hope was seen brightening in Ralph. Feeling hope,
he was ready, whether consciously or unconsciously, to let go his
earlier, feebly offered "like two people in love do" fiction. He
said, almost eagerly: "Then, this morning, she was crying when
I was telling her about Veronica; and I was saying how it showed
we ought not to wait. So when I said that; she might have
thought she wouldn't tell me then either; she'd wait and make
sure we did get married before she told me she didn't have to
any more."

Did, or did not, Ralph's eager wish, his snatch at the hope
that "Joanie," the albatross justly hung around his neck, could
be got rid of, pose a nice point of morality? Could Arthur Winner say with conviction that he thought this marriage ought to
go through if Ralph's only reason for contracting a marriage
disappeared? And, whatever her wish of the moment, could it, in
the long run, be to Miss Moore's interest to have a husband who

173

didn't want to be her husband? Ralph's suspicion that "Joanie," if she lost her trump, her only card, would try to keep him from finding out might be taken as well founded—who would know better than Ralph what that folly of infatuation was able to make her do? Against that infatuation nothing had stood—not normal prudence; not common sense; not the virgin's ignorant fear, likely though that fear was to have a force almost of terror. But now, if Ralph's hope was the fact, if, no longer needing to marry him, Joan meant to hoodwink him into marrying her, the infatuation was surely pushing her past even those remarkable earlier follies.

By practicing so to deceive him, Joan would be showing that Ralph had never really deceived her. Her gained knowledge of what Ralph was like might not be much behind Helen's; yet in her, as in Helen, an utter unreason of feeling must operate. Helen saw through Ralph's amiability—he was a bluffer; he was selfish; he was weak; and she loved him. What Joan Moore thought of as Ralph's good looks might turn her bones to water; but she was not blinded. Actually, he cared nothing for her; his oaths were false; the only use he had for her was that use he had for her girl's body; so when he took her out, she knew why; she knew how she would have to settle up for every attention he paid her; and she still must have him!

Arthur Winner said: "You'd better find out about that as soon as you can. I'll give you my reasons for feeling that marrying Miss Moore while this action pends would be unwise. The prosecution would certainly hear. They'd have no trouble figuring out your reason; and neither would a jury. If the district attorney chose to ask you on the stand whether you were married, and when you got married, objections of mine wouldn't be sustained. The questions must be held legitimate, as going to your status as an individual. The court would require you to answer. A jury's logic isn't always predictable; you may be inviting them to wonder whether a man with so little control over himself that he has to marry one girl in a hurry might not have had so little control over himself that he criminally attacked another girl. On that point, their finding might turn. The risk's not one I'd be prepared to let you run."

"Well, what do we do, Mr. Winner?"

What, indeed? The intractable facts, you might say, would take care of that! You took the consequences; you went where they carried you. Arthur Winner said: "Find out first if there's anything in that notion Miss Moore now doesn't need to get married at once. That would ease matters; but even if nothing has changed, I'm afraid she'll have to wait. That, of course, is bound to make it plain that the child wasn't conceived in wedlock; but, after all, the situation's one in which a good many girls have found themselves. If Joan faces up to it, she'll find, I think, that what most people will show her is sympathy, not contempt. They understand how she feels, and few if any of them will want to rub it in; they'd rather help her live it down. I think she should see Doctor Shaw tomorrow if there's any doubt. If there's to be a child, her parents, and Helen, should be told as soon as possible."

He paused, looking at Ralph, who had paled markedly. He said: "That's something else you have to face. To get a marriage license, you'll need Helen's consent as your guardian; and Joan will have to have her parents' consent. If you put off telling them, you make things harder, not easier. Possibly it might be better, both for them, and for you and Joan, if I did the telling. There, again, I think you'll find that when they see what's done is done, they'll accept it. I think you'll find that what they want to do is help you both in any way they can."

This, of course, was almost sure to be true. They would accept, because they had no alternative. To Helen, another blow; yet Helen's mind must by now have undergone a kind of preparation. She had been already obliged to accept, and she had accepted with apparent calm of control, the fact of Ralph's confessed act with Miss Kovacs. With spirit and even indignation, she was still on Ralph's side. Her mind had handled the necessary revolting thoughts—Helen would blame, of course, Miss Kovacs. The criminal was that low girl. This was her doing; an exploit of her bad body and evil mind performed on Ralph, the victim. Ralph was a male, and nature made males with base instincts. The truth, however disgusting, was that women had the power to excite that rank animalness. This wicked girl had set herself to excite

Ralph. After Helen had admitted to herself that Ralph had yielded once, could learning that Ralph had yielded more than once have much power to shock her?

And the Moores? Not knowing Mr. Moore, never as far as he knew having seen him, Arthur Winner would have to wait to judge his reaction. Presumably he was going to be taken aback when a strange lawyer—though the chance was good that Mr. Moore, even if only a year in town, would have heard Arthur Winner's name, might be aware that his caller was a man of account in Brocton—unfolded the fact that his daughter had been ruined by a boy he didn't even know she was going out with. Conceivably, the reaction would be that of Veronica Kovacs's mother—fury at the author of, not so much perhaps Joan's, as his, shame. How dared she let fingers be pointed at her—his child; bearing his name? Could a suggestion that some blame must attach to the parents be ventured, that someone's blind inattentiveness, someone's stupidities of disregard, someone's neglects of indifference, must have been chief factors in making this predicament of Joan's possible? But, Mr. Moore might very well say: Should he have known, was he bound to expect that his daughter, a quiet, timid-acting girl was (at her age; at seventeen!) engaged in a guilty affair? Why should he think so?

Yes; why should he? Let Arthur Winner put that to himself! Arthur Winner had a daughter. Did he know all about her; or did he merely think he knew? If, a year or two from now, Ann should so choose, was it likely or unlikely that she could arrange to see a good deal of a boy without her father knowing? He did not expect such a thing? He thought he could trust Ann? Did he say to himself that Ann couldn't—a properly brought-up girl couldn't—behave that way? Yes; he did! And that, of course, would be just why Ann, if she happened to want to, would be able to. And the assumption that Ann wouldn't want to? About Ann, the child, about the Ann of today, he might have a fair idea; but how about the new person, the new Ann who was already (he had been shown) taking up her residence in that girl in the shirt and dungarees whose long-standing flirtation with Father was now hardly more than a form? Did he, did any bystander, did the Ann of this minute herself, know what, when she had fully arrived, that stranger would want? If—the picture was one he could not let himself form—the stranger wanted to encounter boys on the back seat of a parked automobile, the plain truth was that the stranger would probably find herself able to encounter them with less trouble, less scheming and lying, than Miss Moore, or even Miss Kovacs.

Appositely enough, Arthur Winner could recall an amusement of his—in part, amusement at his own start of surprise—when he began, last spring, to notice envelopes in the mail addressed by a young hand to *Miss Ann Winner*. The flap of the envelopes bore, embossed, the arms of a boys' preparatory school in New England with which Arthur Winner had every reason to be well acquainted. The school had recommended itself to Brocton people of the generation of Arthur Winner's father as somewhat select yet also wholesomely simple, and for years a certain number of boys from Brocton families in a position to send their sons away to school had been attending it. Arthur Winner had gone there himself; and so had Warren (until Warren was expelled for the offense, understandably inexpiable, of striking a master) and so had Lawrence. Arthur Winner knew of three or four Brocton boys there now.

Indulgent entertainment's first impulse had been to ask Ann who her correspondent was. Arthur Winner thought better of that immediately. The interest, proprietary and affectionate in a child's affairs, that a child might be glad of, would do obvious injury to the new status Ann had begun to establish for herself. She was busy becoming a person in her own right; and first call on a loving concern for her would be the respecting, the regarding of her accomplishment. He did not so much as mention the letters.

As it happened, he found out about them anyway from Clarissa. They were written by Russ Polhemus's youngest son, Chester; and had to do, it seemed, largely with athletic events. In several of them, added phrases protested devotion and described the devastating effect Ann had had on the writer during some Christmas vacation parties. These, Ann showed to Clarissa, remarking (though probably not unflattered) that "Chet" was *so* silly. In fact, Arthur Winner gathered, "Chet," in that normal awkward experimenting with romance, was blundering normally in his first approaches. If still inchoate, the woman in Ann could already feel real impatience with a boy so inept at the arts of gallantry that he spent three pages absorbedly exaggerating his achievements in baseball before presuming to recommend himself by writing at the end that he thought of her all the time.

One might, of course, hope that something like this would continue. Ann seemed to have formed, and she might keep, a happy habit of taking her stepmother into her confidence. Clarissa, whose understanding with Ann had always been good, might go on hearing, in the bond of femininity, about Ann's intimate concerns, from which her father, by the nature of things, must be more and more excluded. Appositely, again, Arthur Winner remembered an earlier, more brusque starting of surprise—though the surprise was, in reason, hardly warranted. The matter was no news. Clarissa, some time before, had been at pains to talk to Ann; and duly she told Arthur Winner that she had.

Noting one morning that Ann was late, her father tapped on the door of her room, which was ajar, calling to her that the station wagon that came to pick up those Roylan children who went to the Washington Hall School was even now in the drive. From the adjoining bathroom, Ann shouted that she was coming. Having opened the door, Arthur Winner observed that the room (that year, planning with Ann, Clarissa had arranged a redecorating and refurnishing into what was recognizably the chamber of a young lady, if one still on the boyish side) was in juvenile disorder—the carelessly torn-back bed; Ann's pajamas on the floor; Ann's yellow suède jacket half over a chair; Ann's schoolbooks stacked, ready to snatch up, at the corner of her writing desk. Turned low, a miniature radio had been left playing dance music. On the air hung a slight aroma of scented cologne.

With the paternal reflection that Ann must really learn to be neater, Arthur Winner glanced at the disarray of toilet articles on the little oval chintz-skirted dressing table. Clustered below the mirror stood Ann's modest, juvenile show of ornamental jars

178

and bottles: but tossed down before them rested one of those boxes that package so-called sanitary napkins. News or not, the hastily broken-open box lying there among the toilet things seemed to make definite and final the affecting truth that the long-known child was gone forever, the stranger was already arriving. In order that Ann, when she appeared, would not find him looking at her things, he drew the door closed again and went downstairs.

Ralph said, hesitating as though in distraction: "But if she's all right, Mr. Winner—well; would we have to—"

"If she's all right," Arthur Winner said, "we'll, for the present, say nothing to anyone."

SEVEN

BY JOE HARBISON'S desk, Joe, who put his glasses on again, and Bernie Breck, who hitched around his holstered revolver as he recrossed his legs, both turned their heads. Near them, Arthur Winner saw with surprise, sat Garret Hughes, one of the assistants to J. Jerome Brophy (as he signed himself), the district attorney. Garret was a thin young man with light hair combed flat on a head somewhat flat—the top of his head, at a gawky elevation (he was as tall as Arthur Winner), went back almost level from a short wide forehead, and a quaint, short, though long-nosed, face; whose expression was good humored and intelligent. For several years before his appointment as assistant district attorney, Garret Hughes had been in Dave Weintraub's office in Mechanicsville —not the worst preparation for public prosecuting, since much of Dave Weintraub's work was in criminal court. Garret said: "Good evening, Mr. Winner."

Concealing his surprise, Arthur Winner nodded. He touched Ralph Detweiler's arm and said: "Just sit down over there." Helen, he could see, was waiting with unchanged tenseness; yet her face was calm. Her gaze at Arthur Winner was direct and trustful, full of thanks. Not questioning, not wondering (she might well have wondered when she saw Garret Hughes come in; she knew who he was!), Helen continued to pay Mr. Winner her compliment of *knowing,* now he had taken this in hand, that everything would be all right. Noah Tuttle, beside her, sat with the same stony composure, the old man's heavy seat, without motion because he did not lightly undertake the work of moving himself. He looked at Arthur Winner; glanced with a grumpy, contemptuous turn of eye at Garret Hughes; and looked back, as to say: Don't miss *that!* Miss Moore was still drying those tears. Tears were now understandable enough; yet what did you learn from them? Would she, or would she not, cry so much if she were "all right"?

Surveying the Kovacses, Arthur Winner encountered from Mrs. Kovacs the same earlier glare of anger and suspicion, heightened surely by the waiting. He caught the covert shift of Miss Kovacs's eyes, sullen through her eyelashes—a good sign; he thought. Veronica was now even more apprehensive. Veronica had nerves. To arrest his unwelcome next thought—the imagination's sudden unbidden reconstruction that put the thickset ardent slut on her back, pulled up the gray dress she was wearing, pictured the hefty bare bottom, the stout thighs spread for their exercise with Ralph last night—Arthur Winner said to Joe Harbison: "Thanks very much, Joe. I'm sorry we had to be so long. What I must do now, I'm afraid, is ask you to grant us a continuance. With your permission, I'd like to have a court reporter present at the hearing."

Joe Harbison said: "Perfectly okay by me, Mr. Winner. Arrange what you want, and we can have a hearing any time you like, practically."

"Tomorrow's Saturday," Arthur Winner said. "In the morning, I'm tied up with an auditor's meeting, unfortunately. I don't like to ask a reporter to work Saturday afternoon. I'd suggest, if you think proper, whatever time's convenient for you, Monday. I know I can get a reporter then; because the grand jury will be in; and there won't be anything else in court—" He broke off; and said: "I beg your pardon, Garret! I should have asked if you were here for the prosecutrix."

Smiling, Garret Hughes said: "Why, no; Mr. Winner. Not exactly. Set your own time, thanks. Mr. Brophy just asked me to come over."

Joe Harbison, his knobby little chin looking knobbier, gave Garret, with a glint of glasses, a sharp, not-pleased stare. The fault was not Garret's; but Joe, touchy about that dignity (just in time recalled by Arthur Winner!) as a magistrate, was choosing to see a reflection on it. This matter was in Joe's jurisdiction; and if a certain party thought he was going to horn in, he thought wrong. The district attorney would get the transcript and return in due course from the clerk of quarter sessions. Until then, Joe was "judge"; he wasn't going to have Brophy, or any boy of Brophy's, interfering.

Garret's mental alertness must easily have identified that hovering of Mr. Harbison's on the edge of taking umbrage. He said: "I think it was simply someone called Mr. Brophy up, Mr. Winner. Said a warrant was being asked for; and there'd be a hearing here. Mr. Brophy wasn't free himself; so he told me to ask Mr. Harbison if I might sit in, find out any facts I could for him. Mr. Harbison was kind enough to say he had no objection. That's all I'm here for."

Arthur Winner said: "I don't mind telling you now, Garret, that, as far as the hearing goes, if Mr. Harbison, when the prosecutrix has testified and I've finished cross-examining her—" (with calculation, he allowed his eye to rest on Miss Kovacs; and he could see he was right; she might not know quite what that meant, but it frightened her!) "should still feel obliged to hold defendant, we'll be reserving the defense."

"I'll tell Mr. Brophy, sir," Garret Hughes said. "The truth is, I don't think he expected I'd get very much. I guess he just decided—" Garret smiled—"for various reasons, he'd like someone from the office to be here."

With Dave Weintraub, Garret would naturally have learned something about those "various reasons." Though so often pitted against the district attorney in courtroom struggles, Dave Weintraub was on cordial political terms with him. In Mechanicsville, Dave's feverishly active office was a sort of Republican outpost; indeed, a listening post, whose facilities were at Jerry Brophy's disposal. You could hear a lot there; so Garret Hughes would not fail to understand how it might happen that he was suddenly asked to give up an evening, for which, no doubt, he had other plans.

It might happen this way. Veronica's father, Mrs. Kovacs's husband, would be a mill hand in Mechanicsville, probably poor, perhaps barely able to speak English; of no account at all. None-

182

theless, he had paid—he had been practically compelled to pay —his dues to some social, religious, or fraternal society; and now he could be glad he had. Angered by his daughter's trumped-up story, distracted by his wife's rantings, frightened and bewildered about the law, Mr. Kovacs knew what to do. He went in haste to the clubhouse. Brought, after a suitable wait, into the presence of whoever controlled this rich society, Mr. Kovacs poured his troubles out in the blessed relief of—Hungarian, wasn't it?

You could be sure quite a show was then put on. In excesses of expressed sympathy and declared brotherhood, with easy floods of overdone Middle-European feeling, the great man behind the magnificent desk showed himself, for all his affluence and importance, the dear friend and true of every member, no matter how humble. Mr. Kovacs, offered a light for the cigar of price that had been given him, would now find out what such friendship meant. Then and there, the district attorney in Brocton was called. Mr. Kovacs could mark the friendly, familiar exchange, the greetings and statements of regard, the gradual cordial getting to business. Here was this case; a bad thing. Girl a daughter of a good friend, one of the boys. Bound to be a lot of interest in Mechanicsville; everybody wants to see her get justice. Would Jerry mind looking into it?

J. Jerome Brophy, far from minding, would be only too happy. His agreeable Irish face, lean and limber, disarmingly suggested very little of the shrewdness and resource that was his. He was a passable district attorney—which was to say, that he was better at conducting his cases (a close and dangerous cross-examiner) than at preparing them. As a politician, he was a good deal more than passable; he was gifted. If Judge Lowe and Judge McAllister sometimes criticized his indictments—Jerry Brophy favored the shotgun variety; single bills sometimes contained as many as fourteen counts—and if Judge Dealey was often acid about neglects of prosecution to subpoena the right witnesses, or failures to have exhibits in proper order, all three of them, as elected officials, knew that Jerry Brophy's name on the ticket did a good deal more than their names to continue the present county administration in office. Could *they* have held Catholic, mostly Hungarian and Polish, Mechanicsville and the lower county?

Jerry Brophy knew—that was where Dave Weintraub came in—exactly how a person like his petitioner rated, what degree of obligingness ought to be shown him. In short, how many votes he could deliver. Rated here, then, was a gesture of interest; but one of the second class; a show of extra attention, but moderate. Moreover (whatever Mr. Kovacs might have been encouraged to believe), petitioner expected nothing else. Arthur Winner supposed the essence of political influence was just that —dexterity in this type of little swindle. Mr. Kovacs had his cigar and his pats on the back and his proof apparent that the club dues exacted from him weren't thrown away; and that was all he was going to get. Mr. Kovacs's dear friend of the benevolent society had what he wanted in the affable exchange that must impress this simple member. In a county like Brocton, there never had been a possibility that Mr. Brophy, for favor, would tamper with justice. That wasn't in his power. Could he put pressure on a grand jury to find him a true bill? In no possible way! Could he bribe a traverse jury to bring in a conviction? Not by any means!

Consulting a notebook, Joe Harbison said: "Three o'clock Monday, suit you, Mr. Winner?"

"Very well, thanks," Arthur Winner said. "Now; about bail for Mr. Detweiler. To my knowledge, his sister, Miss Detweiler, owns unencumbered real estate in the borough of Brocton. So if you have a form, and will set the amount—"

Garret Hughes ran his hand over his flat hair. He said: "Mr. Winner, this information charges rape, doesn't it? Is Mr. Harbison able to take bail?"

Arthur Winner said: "I think you misunderstand, Garret. When I said I'd reserve defense, I didn't mean I was waiving a hearing. I'm asking Mr. Harbison to fix bail for Mr. Detweiler's appearance before him Monday. If, after the hearing, Mr. Harbison doesn't discharge him, we'll naturally petition Judge Lowe, or one of the judges, for a habeas corpus, and ask him to fix *that* bail."

"Oh, I understood, all right, Mr. Winner," Garret Hughes

said. "I understood that this was for a continuance. But the charge is the point, it seems to me. The statute names specifically certain felonies as not bailable by justices of the peace, or any committing magistrates. One of those named is charged here. How can Mr. Harbison set bail?"

From across the room, Noah Tuttle rumbled loudly: "Stuff and nonsense, boy! Is that something they taught you at law school? Forget it! The courts of Brocton County have held, and the mind of man runneth not to the contrary, that when a justice of the peace has due authority to investigate an offense, to commit, bind over, or to discharge a prisoner, he has full competence to take recognizances for appearances before himself. It's elementary, beyond dispute."

Smiling apologetically, Garret Hughes said: "Oh, I know they do it, Mr. Tuttle. It's just that we think it's highly irregular—"

"We? We?" Noah Tuttle said. "Who's we?"

"Well, the State District Attorneys Association, sir. Mr. Brophy and I went to the last meeting; and I remember that was brought up—"

"This is some new lawmaking body?" Noah Tuttle said.

"No, sir," Garret Hughes said, laughing. "I didn't hear anybody claim that. But I think everybody was agreed that we ought to standardize procedure in all counties; eliminate, if we could, any irregularities that might have crept into local usage—"

Joe Harbison said: "First time I ever heard anything of the kind. I know the act, maybe as well as you do, Mr. Hughes. When I send up my transcript and return, I know the proper course. This *you* say, I never heard from Mr. Brophy, since he's district attorney. Or Mr. Dickenson, before him; or Mr. Seagrist before him. Or Judge Lowe, when he was district attorney, before him. I've been squire here twenty-five years, and more; and I'll make free to tell you nobody ever sent my papers back to me for any irregularity yet."

Garret Hughes said: "I didn't mean that at all, Mr. Harbison. Anything you did, I know would be done in good faith—because, as far as you knew, you were empowered to do it. But on this point of bail, the better view now seems to be that committing magistrates never were—or, not since the passage of the act; I know they were, before that—empowered to release on bail any person charged with the felonies named. It amounts to misfeasance. In law—"

Noah Tuttle said: "I'll now instruct you a little in law, sir!" He reared his snowy head of hair angrily. "Here are basic principles for you to bear in mind, boy, when you take it on yourself to construe statutes, acts of assembly. One: constitutional right. Bail is of constitutional right. Except in capital cases, no magistrate, no judge, no justice of any court no matter how high, no one, is given discretion. Bail must be allowed. It follows that if legislators, in their wisdom, apply conditions or regulations, they must be presumed to have no intent to impair a constitutional right beyond the strict construction of their words. The words of the general act here refer to those, and only to those, duly bound over for the grand inquest. That's the strict construction. You can't extend it. All the public prosecutors in the state can't, whatever they may absurdly imagine."

Arthur Winner said: "That would be my opinion, too, Garret. The point's moot, perhaps; but until we have a current high-court ruling to the contrary, I think we should read that any powers of a magistrate the act doesn't explicitly remove remain with him as before. That his exercising them could be a misfeasance—"

"Is sheer tomfoolery!" Noah Tuttle said with fury. "The exact opposite is the case! Shall a justice of the peace arrogate to himself the right to refuse bail; at his whim or discretion, to refuse what the highest court in the state is not permitted to refuse? There would be misfeasance, if you want! Consider the status of accused! Even if the strongest sort of case had been made out against him, his right to bail would be unaffected. On application, the court of oyer and terminer and general jail delivery would fix bail immediately. Here, no case at all's made out! Lodged against him is a mere information, for all the magistrate or anyone else knows, malicious, wild, groundless, false."

Placatingly, Garret Hughes said: "Yes; that's true, sir. But that's our point, really. An accusation may be all those things; yet if the information's sworn to, a warrant issues. Of course there's a legal presumption of accused's innocence; but that doesn't prevent Mr. Breck, here, from going and attaching accused's person. Mr. Breck hasn't merely a right to do it; it's his duty. The warrant directs him to do it, and do it forthwith, and fail not. He has to compel him to come, drag him before the magistrate, if necessary."

"Don't lecture me on the obvious, if you please!" Noah Tuttle said. His incensed old face had grown crimson. His voice, full to roaring, trembled with anger. "Who questions the legality of a warrant issuing on a sworn information? Who doubts that the officer commanded to serve it may compel the person named to come before the magistrate? And who, may I ask, doubts that bail exists to deliver accused from the custody of such an officer? What nonsense is this you're talking? You sound witless!"

Garret Hughes's short pale-skinned face flushed a little. With an uncomfortable shift of his angular tall shoulders, he said mildly: "I'm sorry if that's what I sound like, Mr. Tuttle; and I didn't mean to be impertinent, if I was—"

"You were, and you are," Noah Tuttle said. "You—"

Beside him, Helen Detweiler, with an inconspicuous gesture, obviously of privilege—Arthur Winner had not seen it before; but Noah, he realized, must have asked Helen to do it—laid her slender-fingered hand on Noah's coat sleeve, gently pressing. Her mute look, fixed on Noah, was grave and supplicating.

"Then, I apologize, sir," Garret Hughes said. "I didn't intend to *tell* you, Mr. Tuttle. I was putting it to you for your opinion. The officer has a duty to arrest the accused, guilty or innocent, willing or unwilling, and carry him in custody to the magistrate. As you say, no one doubts Mr. Breck must do this; and I think no one would suggest that accused had a right, constitutional, or of any other kind, to be released from the custody Mr. Breck has him in while he's on the way to the hearing. Until a hearing's been had, isn't accused's status that of being attached without recourse? The very fact that even after the hearing you have to get a habeas corpus—"

Arthur Winner said quickly: "That's a nice argument, Garret. It might have merit; except, I think, that particular custody of Mr. Breck's in which accused must remain without recourse terminates when, produced before the magistrate, he makes his appearance and answer. However, I'll now simply ask Mr. Harbison to rule. I'm applying to him for bail and asking him to fix the amount."

Not unkindly, Joe Harbison said: "Tell you the truth, Mr. Hughes, I guess you're pretty new at this, aren't you? Like I say, this has been my business quite some time. You tell me I'm not free to set bail in my own court. Mr. Tuttle and Mr. Winner, gentlemen, like they say, learned in the law, say you're wrong; and that's what I think. Bail allowed. Seven hundred and fifty dollars too much?"

Garret Hughes smiled. "There you are, Mr. Harbison!" he said. "That would be pretty high for any offense subject to summary proceedings. For a felony like rape, it's not enough. Bail for appearance before oyer and terminer on that charge would never be less than fifteen hundred dollars."

To Helen Detweiler, Arthur Winner said: "Mr. Harbison will need your signature there, Helen. By signing, you understand you engage on penalty of forfeiture to see Ralph appears here Monday." To Garret Hughes, he said: "I don't doubt Mr. Harbison would be willing to note an objection by you in his docket; and I may say, when that's your opinion, I think your stand is a right one and I'm glad to see you make it. If your opinion's also the district attorney's, he knows, of course, his remedy's in mandamus proceedings against the magistrate—"

Noah Tuttle said: "And say to Brophy, say to him, if he opens any such ridiculous action, I will, if Mr. Harbison should wish me to, enter an appearance for him, appear without fee. And I'll fight it to the highest court, if I have to."

"Well, objection noted," Joe Harbison said. "And I appreciate that very much, Mr. Tuttle. I'd be most proud. I'll call on you, if they try to put me in jail." He chuckled. "And now the court's going to say this about what you said, Mr. Hughes. In setting bail, I give consideration to the gravity of the offense—gravity it would have if it was made out. This would be grave; so I don't put bail too low. Other hand; I give consideration to what I know about the people, if anything. I know Miss Detweiler and Mr. Winner. I don't see there's much danger accused won't appear Monday. So why should I set it as high as you say? Anyhow: defendant released on seven hundred fifty dollars' bail, and not to leave the jurisdiction, for appearance before me, justice of the peace, in and for the county of Brocton, Monday three o'clock P.M. Now, Miss Detweiler, I'll just fill in—"

Sudden and hoarse from her chair in the corner, Mrs. Kovacs, as though recovering from a stupefaction at the long incomprehensible argument, said: "I come here, mister; and I stay here since afternoon; and I still stay; and she does too—" she jerked her head toward her daughter—"until I see him put in prison!"

Bernie Breck said: "No, Mrs. Kovacs. The squire's done for tonight. Tonight, this is all. You can go."

Staring at him, Mrs. Kovacs said: "Is all? What's all? He takes my girl and—"

Looking up from his writing, Joe Harbison said: "Now, ma'am, we'll keep that for Monday. You and Miss Kovacs be here, and accused will be here, too, and the prosecutrix can make her charge. This is bail I'm taking for his appearance, so he can go until then."

Mrs. Kovacs arose suddenly. "You say you let him go? No, he don't—" She made a lumbering start toward Ralph Detweiler.

With agility surprising in so stout a man, Bernie Breck was up in time. Blocking Mrs. Kovacs, taking her arm firmly, he said: "Now, that'll do, ma'am. This is the law, here. Anybody don't behave, Mr. Harbison could put them in jail."

Nearly speechless, Mrs. Kovacs choked: "He put me in jail? So; let's see him—"

Bernie Breck gave her a gentle shake. "I'm a policeman," he said, tapping his gold captain's badge with his other hand. "Now, you don't want trouble; and I don't; and Mr. Harbison don't. So now, the best thing; you just go along home, is my advice. And never mind making any more fuss. Because no one's going to make a fuss here, that's for sure!"

Halted perhaps by the word "policeman," Mrs. Kovacs stood irresolute. Over Bernie Breck's uniformed shoulder, she screamed suddenly at Ralph Detweiler: "Dirty stinking son of a bitch, a bastard!"

Joe Harbison said: "And don't use no more of that kind of

189

language before me, ma'am! That's in contempt; and I won't have it! This case is continued, for now. Court's closed."

✦

Indirectly lighted from the streets that bounded the tree-filled grounds, the Brocton County Court House's marble mass actually assumed in the warm dark something of that majesty the architects of 1907 must have meant their edifice to have. Brighter below than above, the building came into better architectural balance. Shadow obscured most of the senseless ornamentation, both applied and structural. The porticoes, each an occasion for four Ionic columns two stories high (those at the sides were mere works of honor—not real. There was no entrance by way of them nor exit onto them), lost their overpowering effect. Half seen, they stood mysterious in the gloom, gravely monumental. The front portico's approach was by a pair of stairs of fifty steps, putting everyone who came before the court to a ceremonial climb to the high place. The cascade of solid stone, with light falling down from the main door behind the columns, was imposing. In the upper darkness, over the roofs, the small dome—like the side porches, innocent of utility; like the columns' capitals, a pure aspiring to the solemn and to the noble, to putative glories of Greece, to supposed grandeurs of Rome—mounded not unimpressive against the dim loom of the lighted town on the overcast night sky. The crowning stiff shape of that figure of Justice could just be made out.

Walking with Noah Tuttle, slowing himself to the pace of the old man's fairly spry but arthritic half-hobble, Arthur Winner had looked up at the heavy night, whose atmosphere of thunderstorms continued. The courthouse square was airless, as close as a room. Noah, headed automatically, as though in blind homing, for the Union League, was preparing himself to speak—collecting himself, Arthur Winner supposed; ordering as well as he could his new disturbance of feelings brought on when he himself had shattered that repose of law, that majestic calm of reason designed to curb all passions or enthusiasms of emotion, to put down all angers and hates of feeling. That the disturbance had been major, shaking him badly, was to be seen when, under the street light outside Joe Harbison's office, Helen stood ready to get into Ralph's car with Miss Moore. Noah advanced on her tremulously. To everyone's surprise—including, it might be, Noah's—he mumbled unhappily: "There, there!" Sudden and awkward, he inaccurately kissed Helen on the forehead.

While he and Arthur Winner crossed the street and went up the inclined walk through the courthouse grounds, rays of light touching Noah's face showed Arthur Winner the throat muscles flexing, the mute working of his jaw. Now, near the front of the courthouse, Noah said: "Bad business, Arthur! Ralph— what's he want to do a thing like that for? Look at that girl— baggage! And that woman. That kind of people! That money he was trying to get this morning. I think he wanted to buy her off."

"Well, I don't," Arthur Winner said. "He satisfied me that Miss Kovacs had been more than willing, that the complaint was a complete surprise. His wanting money had to do with marrying Miss Moore, I think. His thought, he said, was that if he got married and stopped running around with girls things like this wouldn't happen."

"Boy of eighteen!" Noah said. "Why should he have to consort with women? Other boys don't, do they?"

That, of course, was the fact. Generally, they didn't; Arthur Winner supposed. What they were likely to be doing instead might or might not be relevant. Arthur Winner said: "Much, I think, may depend on opportunity; and a good deal, perhaps, on the fact that many of them are afraid to."

In a planting of shrubbery before the courthouse steps stood a moderate-sized fountain of cast iron. Water in a thin jet climbed a yard into the night above the topmost of three superimposed circular basins. There followed a constant quiet noise of the falling splash and the steady patter of spillings-down from overbrimming basin to basin. Against the pleasant murmurous sound, plodding his way around the planting, Noah Tuttle said: "Opportunity; there's nothing but opportunity. They don't seem to care today what they do. I see them in automobiles. He's driving along. There she is, sitting squeezed

191

against him as tight as she can get. They like people to see them. Don't believe there's a virgin over fifteen in the county." That he could not very well have it both ways—Ralph not like other boys; and Ralph just like them—did not seem to occur to him. He said: "It wasn't that way when I was young—"

But in those days—sixty, seventy years ago—Willard Lowe, who liked to study old dockets, had once pointed out to Arthur Winner, every trial list was crowded with fornication and bastardy cases. The indictment was as common then as an indictment for driving under the influence of intoxicating liquor was today. That the old offense had virtually disappeared did not, of course, answer Noah's complaint that this age was given to license; to be deduced was simply the fact that the girls, in Miss Kovacs's phrase, knew how to take care of themselves now (only Miss Moore didn't seem to!). Still, you might remember that there was license in that other age, too; and records to prove it.

The truth, Arthur Winner suspected, was that, through humanity's recorded history, the proportion of girls who early lost their virtue to girls who didn't was relatively constant—the same, not very large, per cent of them always would; the same, much larger, per cent of them were afraid to, or had no desire to, and, so, wouldn't. What Noah saw with uneasy displeasure was things done differently, not different things.

As though to confirm the thought, Noah said: "That fellow, what's his name—Brophy's boy. I oughtn't ever to argue, Arthur. I know. But I didn't like that, his being there. You know why he came as well as I do. Brophy and his political friends! When Isaac Parsons was district attorney—you wouldn't even remember him—when Willard Lowe was, for that matter, no Mechanicsville politician would have called him up more than once!"

In the long-gone Mr. Parsons' case, Arthur Winner allowed himself to reflect that, for one thing, there probably wasn't a telephone in the county. Moreover, the Mechanicsville of Willard Lowe's day-in-office was still the Mechanicsville of the dead canal trade, of the moribund spoke factory where they made wagon wheels. The wire mills were still to be erected; the influx of labor, so much of it foreign, hadn't started. In fairness, you might allow that Jerry Brophy wouldn't have let himself be influenced by *that* Mechanicsville any more than Willard Lowe would. The pertinent question might be: Would Willard Lowe, though immaculately aloof from crooked politics, have rebuffed with righteous rudeness, refused to hear a word from—say, the rector of Christ Church; the chairman of the Union League; the president of the Orcutt Potteries; or some Thirty-second Degree Mason known personally to him? It seemed safe to say that young Willard Lowe would have received advice or opinion that such respectable persons might wish to offer him on a case they knew about with all attention. Where he lawfully and properly could, without doubt he would have been inclined to act as they suggested.

Arthur Winner said: "Yes; I know why Garret was there; and I don't think it's important. I'm sure the girl's lying; so there's nothing Jerry Brophy can do for her. I think I can take care of her."

Noah Tuttle said: "Yes, you can, Arthur. I know you can. You won't let anything happen to him. He's not a good boy, Arthur; but we have to think of Helen. How she'd feel if they convicted him." He brooded a moment on those sorrows sympathy esteems its own. "That girl, the other one; now! What's Ralph want to marry her for? Helen wants him to go to college."

Passing over that reason, not long ago reported to him, that Ralph gave for thinking marriage wise, Noah's question, a little muddled, presumably went to Helen's innocent point: What matrimonial advantage could possibly lie in taking to wife a Joan Moore? The statement about college, made as though to inform Arthur Winner, was somewhat disconcerting, since they had spoken of that this morning. Arthur Winner, feeling weariness, said: "Yes; I know; but Helen agrees there's no sense trying to send Ralph if Ralph doesn't want to go. At any rate, for the moment, as long as this case is pending, nothing has to be decided. Ralph couldn't go away to college even if he wanted to; while if what he wants is to marry Miss Moore, he'll have to wait."

Morosely, Noah Tuttle said: "I don't know what he wants, what any of them want—except to live without working, I suppose. I don't know! I don't know!" He cleared his throat. "This hasn't been a good day, Arthur. I didn't have to say that to your New York fellow. A Jew can't help being a Jew. I'm sorry."

Arthur Winner said: "Mr. Woolf seems willing to forget it. Tomorrow, if you wanted, I think you could—well, express regret; saying you were sorry you lost your temper would do."

"Yes; I'll tell him," Noah Tuttle said. He breathed disconsolately. With sad distraction, he moved his mop of white hair, hatless in the warm dark, from side to side. "Things were bothering me, Arthur. I don't mean only that fellow. I've handled plenty of his sort before. I'm the executor, and he'd better understand that. Just let him try citing me to account! I'll teach the smart aleck—no; no; Arthur—" For an instant, the old lion had roused; but, dispirited, he sank back. "He'll have his figures —those I found. Helen found most of them. But I didn't like having all that about poor old Mike raked up—that marriage and so on. A sad thing; a sad thing! That only happened because Mike was in over his head; and no fault of his! He'd trusted people he had reason to trust; he'd believed what he had a right to believe. I suppose you can't even remember Mike."

Perhaps naturally, with such a length of days behind him, Noah had that tendency to confuse epochs—everything past became long ago, before any youngster of fifty's time. As a matter of fact, Arthur Winner well remembered Mike McCarthy, the Mike who was in over his head. For a while, as the troubled waters were mounting, Mike was frequently at the office. Though then entitled Winner, Tuttle & Winner, the firm was actually Winner & Tuttle. Delegated to Arthur Winner Junior were various little legal jobs; but the business of his father's clients and Noah's clients was none of his. He had never known in any detail why Mike was there; and, to tell the truth, he'd been surprised to see Mike there. As Willard Lowe remarked, everybody at that time knew who Mike McCarthy was; all large local construction jobs were his; he employed a lot of people and was supposed to have a lot of money; but, even so, he wasn't exactly the type of client you'd expect Winner, Tuttle & Winner to represent.

Mike was a short ruddy-faced man, still darkly black-browed;

but the ruff of hair on his odd, somewhat potato-shaped, head was graying. On entering the office, Mike's extravagantly polite habit had been to pass around, greeting everyone individually; and when it was indicated to him that he was to go into Mr. Tuttle's room, before he went, he excused himself to everyone. Mike felt, he made plain, a humble respect for this kind of thing. He had faith in the well-appointed office, the walls of learned books, the calm omniscient sound of the dry stiff-phrased talk of those who lived always (and, well!) by their heads, never their hands. In the judgment of a man like Mr. Tuttle, Mike confided. Mike knew—everybody knew—that those who listened to Mr. Tuttle, who let themselves be guided by Mr. Tuttle, who were allowed the real (to someone like Mike) privilege of retaining Mr. Tuttle, had nothing to worry about. Now, so many years later, did Noah see the fly in all that ointment? Had the legend of Mr. Tuttle's infallibility, the general justified faith in Mr. Tuttle's judgment, the unchallenged reputation of Mr. Tuttle as the man who could always tell you the right thing to do, ended by disadjusting that judgment? Did Noah's confirmed habit of being right make Noah himself at last genuinely unable to see how he could be wrong?

Noah Tuttle said: "That business hurt a lot of people, Arthur. All of us. Your father was the only one who'd kept out; and even so, he was involved in the end. At one point, I had to go to him for money. You never knew this, Arthur; but he mortgaged everything he owned. He didn't lose—I can say that. But it was a narrow squeak—the whole of it didn't come out."

No doubt Noah was thinking of the First National's desperate situation, which Arthur Winner later learned of; but Noah was right; at the time, he had known next to nothing, he was not told anything. That money was advanced, he could guess; but he never knew how far his father had engaged himself. None of it—the progress of the anxious negotiations, the measures Noah took or proposed to take—was explained to Arthur Winner Junior. Understanding better now than he had then the essence of the partners' relationship, Arthur Winner could doubt that Noah, even with Arthur Winner Senior, had ever discussed his course, or explained, except in general or in principle, what he was doing. Noah's way was to work alone. If, at some con-juncture, Noah said he needed money, he need not say more. With skilled inconspicuousness, Arthur Winner Senior, no questions asked, tried what his credit could do, racked it even to the uttermost, and turned over the cash. Noah's reasons for needing money were Noah's business, and only Noah knew them; just as only Noah knew in any detail by what brilliant strokes of negotiation, by what expert timing in compromise, he had acted to protect and, it proved, to preserve, part, at least, of the creditors' interest. When Noah finished apportioning the money realized, and had his accounts confirmed, the matter was treated as closed. The truth was, Arthur Winner could not re-member Noah ever before so much as referring to that hurtful 'business.' "

Noah said: "Well; over the dam, over the dam! We did what we could. We picked up some pieces. Mike wasn't cleaned out. He'd been able to hold on to some land along the railroad; and though it didn't look like much then, the whole corpus of the present estate came from it. But of course Mike couldn't know that. All he knew was that he'd been a rich man; and now he was poor. He lost his confidence, Arthur; and when that was lost, for a man like Mike everything was lost. He could never be the same afterward. He'd always worked hard, done what he was supposed to do; and what had that got him? Those boys of his—they're no good; a mean pair; you can see that—I think they threw it up to him when they found how much money he'd lost. I think that was a shock to him, too—he'd never realized how mean they were. So, he got mean. I'm pretty sure one reason he married that woman was to spite them."

This, of course, could be the case. A shaken old man, bewil-dered and angered into becoming a new and different old man, might form such a plan. At any rate, you could learn that Noah hoped that was the case. The outrageous marriage being given him to explain, Noah, another old man, fastidiously chose so to explain it. He hoped to charge the aberration to urges irascible, not concupiscible. Noah, offended, determinedly rejected the ribald joke on old flesh, the suggested sexual derangement—not, as Judge Lowe remarked, uncommon in men of a certain age.

How could Noah laugh when the lean and slipper'd pantaloon (or near enough), instead of falling to his prayers, pricks his ears, pops his eyes, pants to copulate with what, fantastically, his dimmed sight takes to be a beautiful young girl?

Moreover (things were bothering Noah, indeed!), comic pursuit was this offensive jest's bare beginning. Where there had been a will, there had been a way; the cream was to come. Mike, before God and man joined to his faded slut; Mike, admitted to live with her, to be her love and all the pleasures prove; Mike, licensed to enjoy every novelty or indecency that experience like hers might equip her to afford him, did not (today's testimony was) profit much or long. A month or so, and Mike's offers were failing; thereafter he fumbled with her in vain. Within six months, the separation agreement had been drawn and that postnuptial settlement made.

Noah Tuttle said: "And Mike's insisting he was going to marry her in church—I think he did that to spite *them,* the priests. I think he thought his religion had let him down. You know how the Catholic church makes you buy everything; and he'd paid them plenty when he had money; and what did *that* get him? The thing was, the local father tried to tell him if he married her he couldn't have what the papists call a nuptial blessing. You're only supposed to get that once; and of course Mike got his at his first marriage. Well, it seems the bride said, or was able to show, that she never was what they call sacramentally married before; so, Mike found out somehow, that made her technically eligible for a blessing. So Mike went to the bishop— giving all the money very likely *did* get him somewhere there— and the bishop told the father—who knew all about her, of course; just what she was—that he had to bless her whether he wanted to or not."

The enlivening recount, the rush of recollection, transporting Noah for a moment to another part of the past, animated him. With the satisfaction usually called grim, Noah remembered how Mike (as Noah conceived it) managed to spite those no-good thankless children of his—and, to score off a no-good popish priest, too! Of the provisions nature made for sentient human existence, some, Arthur Winner must note, are merciful.

In the midst of many troubles, the feckless mind could usually produce these little distractions. A larger, an enormous, actual providence could lie in that chronic inability to look direct at one's self—see the blind beggar dance, the cripple sing! Noah was enabled to say that poor Mike McCarthy, grievously hurt, was never the same afterward. Mike was hurt, no doubt; and Noah, electing to assume an indirect responsibility for Mike's misfortunes, could name various kinds of damage Mike might have suffered; yet, what had Mike lost but a lot of money; and, perhaps, some never-warranted comfort of feeling that he was born lucky? Arthur Winner doubted if misfortune had made Mike basically any different. Mike was the simple, unlearned, same Irishman, bewildered formerly by being rich, bewildered now by being a good deal poorer.

Of course, the person really hurt, the person never again the same, was Noah himself. The wound being inward, there was, as far as Arthur Winner remembered, no general realization that Noah had received one. He was not disabled; the experience-toughened spirit, the muscular mind accustomed to reason, were by no means broken. In the weeks following the windup of the affair, Noah looked the same; he seemed to act the same. Declining to discuss the subject was, of course, Noah's ordinary way. Never a talker, he let results speak for themselves; as you would expect, Noah ignored his own extraordinary and everywhere admired success.

And, as you would expect, the person soonest aware of something more than met the eye was Arthur Winner's father. Arthur Winner Senior divined, no doubt immediately, the inward wound's existence. Not inquiring into its nature, nor admitting by so much as a word that he knew of it, he extended to his partner a silent special consideration, an unostentatious protection or shielding while the invisible hurt underwent what repair might be possible. Fixed in mind by a force of later realization, Arthur Winner could remember a trifling incident, an exchange with his father one rainy afternoon. Arthur Winner Senior, the elegantly grayed, spare figure, with its neatness of movement, its reflective, coolly percipient eye, had appeared at

198

the door of his room. Arthur Winner Junior, with a paper he wanted to ask about, was approaching, knowing Noah was alone, Noah's closed door. His father, intercepting him with a glance, said: "Not just now, Son. Let me see whatever that is. If he ought to look at it, I'll show it to him later."

The meaning in the mildly spoken words was there to be taken—just as the meaning of the closed door was there. Arthur Winner Senior was himself no talker. He omitted explanations; but, unless a client was with Noah, when had Noah's door ever been closed? Noah's ways which seemed so much the same were, then, not entirely the same. The silence about the windup of the transit company, Arthur Winner could gradually apprehend, was not related to silences of disdain to speak of a triumph. For Noah, there had been no triumph—only ashes in his mouth. They said his feat was remarkable? Perhaps, so! Noah got them out of disaster better than anyone else could have; yes! But who got them in? Who let them get in? There was the site of the wound! Who kept believing (and saying) everything was all right when everything wasn't all right? Who had been deaf to reason and blind to fact? Who had been wrong; and then, nearly twenty years, had persevered in being wrong?

Shattered here was some private assurance of Noah's, a once-proud conviction that decisions he made were not the fallible decisions of other men, a once-perfect persuasion that his own good sense was reliable—naturally, and as of course, uncommon. What real repair was possible? The tough mind, the proud spirit could and would carry on, continue in spite of hurt. Subsequent runs of success; later instances of being right again; demonstrations (as by that masterly work in redacting, to the applause of the whole state bar, the new Decedents Estates Law) of hardly to be equaled legal abilities, might comfort Noah. They could not cure him. They could not restore him whole.

There and then had been a demarcation. One year, the year before, Noah was in his manifest prime, a master among men. When another year was passed, Noah had crossed over. Step by hardly noticeable step (even to Noah, hardly noticeable; perhaps Noah saw things changing, not himself changing.

About changed things, Noah would see himself as having, quite naturally, changed feelings), Noah drew off from, grew away from, the former Noah. One day you looked at him—Arthur Winner could even remember the day; or, at least, the day's jolt of discovery—and you saw that an old man was sitting at Noah's desk.

Accepted, the instant's shock of surprise spent, Noah's state of being an old man became, of course, the natural thing—the person you knew; the person you meant when you said Noah Tuttle. Soon, too, the new state, existing through a decade and most of another, had come to seem unchangeable; yet it was not. Noah, his burst of animation gone, plodded on through the airless dark. Hopeful, he was peering ahead to where, nearby now, the steps of the clubhouse stood, well lighted by a pair of round glass globes on iron standards. Looking at him, Arthur Winner must see how Noah, hardly noticed, had been progressing again. He had left off being just old; he was very old.

Arthur Winner said: "I don't believe we'll have to be too long tomorrow. Today, I think Mr. Woolf may have been trying to give the McCarthys their money's worth. With them gone, I doubt if he'll try to drag it out. If necessary, I'll rule that whatever figures you have are sufficient as an interim accounting."

Noah Tuttle said: "Yes. I'm tired, Arthur. I may be tired tomorrow." Putting his tremulous big-jointed hand abruptly on Arthur Winner's arm, he said: "You're a good boy; you're a good boy! I know I'm a trouble to you and Julius. Maybe I was wrong about that Sutphin business. Maybe I should read that last letter again. Maybe I misunderstood—"

Disconcerted a little by the sudden change of subject, Arthur Winner said: "We think you were right. I spoke to Julius. We agree with you. I told—"

"No, don't do that," Noah Tuttle said. "Don't agree with me when you don't, Arthur. Your heads are better than mine. Only right, you and Julius should decide. I can't do the work I used to do; so I suppose I find reasons why we shouldn't take more work on. After this, I want you two to decide."

They had come to the Union League's wide steps; and Noah drew back his hand, moving away as though he feared Arthur

Winner might try to help him climb them. Slowly, with an increased noise of breathing, Noah climbed by himself.

THE ORIGINATING CAUSE OF THE UNION LEAGUE WAS
DIRE NATIONAL PERIL:
ITS INSPIRATION WAS PURE AND DISINTERESTED PATRIOTISM:
ITS FOUNDATION STONE WAS DEVOTION TO THE UNION.
THE FOUNDERS WERE THE BRAVE AND TRUE SONS
OF THE FOUNDERS OF THE NATION.
WHAT THEY LOYALLY PRESERVED,
LET ALL WHO ENTER HERE EVER MAINTAIN AND EVER CHERISH.

Through the open bronze outer doors, the tablet of white marble with the incised words, leafed with a gold once bright but dulled with dust now and partly flaked away, could be seen. The tablet was fixed above inner doors which were paned with Florentine leaded glass. The oblong foyer between was floored with tessellated tile.

That old-fashioned grandiloquence, Arthur Winner reflected, was not unmoving. That epigraph embodied a seriousness of purpose still respectable. Were people really the better for not talking like that any more? Was there any actual advantage of honesty when high-sounding terms went out? Had facts of life as life is lived been given any more practical recognition?

Beyond the inner doors with their colored glass, the spacious main hall opened. At one side stood the cubbyhole of the porter's desk and the board (neither of them now used) on which members were once pegged in and out. At the hall's center, the eye was arrested—indeed, perhaps staggered—by a great rectangular plinth of dark marble that supported a more than life size statue of Abraham Lincoln chiseled in black basalt. Near the figure's feet, and looking up with hope, crouched a basalt Negro whose shackles had been broken. To the right, and to the left, the great sliding walnut doors of the reading room and of the parlor were closed. There was no one to be seen; but, indicating that in spite of the heat of the night, people were bowling, intermittent vague rumblings and clatterings sounded from the ornate antiquated alleys downstairs. The tepid unmoved air held a mustiness of old plaster, old uphol-stery, old wood on which furniture polish had been rubbed for years.

Mingled with the mustiness, other redolences could be traced; a whiff of beer and spirits from the bar at the back; a faint sweetish pungency from cakes of deodorant in the ancient marble-lined lavatory adjoining. Also from the bar, a voice pro-ceeded, pausing, persistently resuming one of those pleased-with-its-own-sound dissertations that alcohol can sustain—the speaker, Arthur Winner recognized, was Howard Minton, a long-retired army officer. Colonel Minton's daily habit was to begin drinking at noon. He drank with solemn dignity only im-paired (and such was Colonel Minton's manner, impaired very little) by his need to find somebody to listen to him; and he continued unhurriedly drinking until the last bar in Brocton was closed. At this stage of the evening, Alfred Revere would be serving Colonel Minton himself. Alfred regarded the colo-nel with the dogged respect of some private estimate—some-thing perhaps atavistic, a feeling passed over to him from his slave forebears; an Old South concept of a largely mythical "quality" which you were, or you weren't; and when you were, any fail-ings or weaknesses unfortunately yours became quite irrelevant. Alfred trusted no one but himself with the delicate responsibility of seeing that Colonel Minton, while he was in the club, was neither refused any of the right number of drinks for him, nor accidentally served more.

Straight ahead, beyond the figure of the Great Emancipator, the wide mahogany stairs mounted in a stately arrangement of broad worn treads, low risers, and massive curved rail to an ample quarter-landing. Hung here, lighted at top and bottom, was an oil painting, five feet by ten, in the genre tradition—after Meissonier; or perhaps Julian Scott. In detail scrupulously realistic, the Eighth Pennsylvania Cavalry waited at Hazel Grove in the spring dusk of the Chancellorsville woods. The halted squadrons, men dismounted but standing to horse, merged back into obscurity. At their head, grouped in dramatic better light, were the mounted officers, sabered, gauntleted, jackbooted. Their variously bewhiskered faces, some under slouch-brim hats, some under forage caps, were painted with care in expressions of grim surmise, yet stern determination.

They were being pictured at the supposed instant when the major commanding imparted to them orders from their division's general. Horrifying intelligence had just begun to reach Hazel Grove. Jackson, surprising and turning the Union right, was even then driving the stupid and negligent Howard's Eleventh Corps in pell-mell rout back on the Union center. In the appalling, altogether unprepared-for emergency, concentrated artillery fire offered an only chance of saving the army. Time must be gained to get guns enough in battery. There was one fearful way to gain that time. If a cavalry charge (who could hope to come back?) was thrown against Jackson's van, the all-important momentary check might be effected. Those were the Eighth Pennsylvania's orders. A plate attached to the ponderous gold frame carried, as a title, the major's reputed calm response to the aide with the message: *Sir, we will do it!*

Like the inspirational inscription over the entrance, like the astonishing statue of Lincoln, this very large work of art spoke for an age; and, as it happened, not merely in being a "historical picture" of the sort no one would paint today. This picture's presence there had a history. Over the hanging, early records of the Union League could show, controversy, hot and deadly serious, had arisen. The time was 1880; so the members of the club were still mostly those who had stood for the Union in dark days; and even, in a few instances, bled for it. The Cause being sacred, that great war for the Cause was, in all particulars, sacred, too—wreaths for the living conqueror, and glory's meed for the perished! When opinion divided, men did not differ good-naturedly or debate calmly. On the issue of the donated painting, chief friends parted. People who had known each other for years ceased to speak. The vote to hang the picture occasioned at least one resignation.

Willard Lowe, turning over, in his favorite role of amateur antiquarian, old Union League papers, found minutes of several acrimonious debates. Here was a matter after Willard's own heart! In the faded lines of the long-dead recorder's copperplate script were things he liked—opportunities to re-create the past; solid problems of research; studies, to him engrossing, in vagarious human behavior. He set himself to refight the Battle of Chancellorsville. He sought out and consulted every possible source. He reached the hardly to be avoided finding of fact that those who held the painting false history were right. There had been an action that night, a brief blundering encounter in the dark with some lost Confederates: but that was all. The depicted scene was imaginary. A desperate charge, quick-wittedly ordered to purchase the time for bringing up guns, was pure invention. That division's commander (a man much given to romancing) invented the story to support his modest representation that he, and he alone, on the disastrous second of May, by seeing what to do and having it done, had saved the Army of the Potomac.

Judge Lowe enjoyed research for research's sake—the patient digging into old books; the careful comparison of old records; the poring over old maps; but such a finding of fact as this opened to him exercises of reflection and speculation even more to his taste. How did mere vaporings of a braggart come to make their way into authoritative histories by reputable writers? Why had none of them looked at the official records? The regiment's report, the brigade's report, the braggart's own report for his division, were all on file. All gave his story the lie. Willard Lowe knew an answer. These were the ways of man. This was man's incurable willful wish to believe what he preferred to believe. If a fiction pleased him more than a fact, he threw the fact away. If rumor, whispering idiots in the ear, told a story he liked, he was stubborn in crediting it.

Noah Tuttle said: "Arthur, I'll say good night. I'm not sure lights weren't left on in the office—"

Arthur Winner said: "Yes; I noticed while we were walking over. I'll put them out. There was something I wanted to look up, anyway. The rector was speaking to me about it; and I told him I'd find out before the vestry meeting Monday. I wanted to look at the terms of the Orcutt bequest. Would you know, offhand, if Christ Church as beneficiary could apply to the court to amend the trust if a change in the form of investments could be shown to be in beneficiary's best interest?"

Stopping by the stairs, Noah said: "Change? What's the fellow want to change?"

Arthur Winner said: "If we could find legal means, he'd like to see the funds deposited with the Diocesan Investment Trust. The convention was particularly asked by the bishop to consider turning, wherever possible, parish endowments into shares in the common fund. The idea seems sound to me. I felt sure you'd be glad to get it off your hands; you'd be saved a lot of work—"

"Isn't sound at all!" Noah Tuttle said. "Who knows what people like that might start doing with the money? In trusts testamentary, intent of testator's paramount. The instrument's in the general file. Spendthrift, and sole and separate provisions. Look at it, look at it, if you like! What Ezra meant to provide was income in perpetuity for the parish. The rector and his vestry may do what they like with income; but the whole intent was to hold the corpus out of reach, keep them from rushing into some scheme like this. The fellow doesn't understand money, you'll find, Arthur. They never do."

"I agree it's surprising," Arthur Winner said. "But Doctor Trowbridge gives signs of understanding money pretty well. I think you'd be impressed."

"No, I wouldn't," Noah Tuttle said. "If that's his idea, he's not practical! Wouldn't feel justified, anyway. Realizing principal couldn't be managed without some loss. Nothing to justify trustee in inflicting such loss. Only valid reason would be certainty of greater loss if he didn't. Not present here. Quite the contrary!"

"If that's what worries you, that really needn't," Arthur Winner said. "The thing's been very well planned with some features of a closed-end trust, and some of a mutual fund. You don't have to sell out to buy in—"

"No, no, no!" Noah Tuttle said. "Not sound! Not practical! Not in accord with testator's intent! You keep him from meddling, Arthur! I don't want the fellow pestering me. Let him attend to religion; that's his job. As now-incumbent, he's party beneficially-in-interest to nothing but income. That, he'll get; and that's all he'll get."

Yes; Arthur Winner and Julius Penrose were to decide from now on—except, of course, where their raw youth unfitted them to judge, where they wanted something foolish, where they proposed changes not to Noah's liking! Which was, of course, to say: any changes at all. Noah would be saved a lot of work! And you felt sure that Noah, his occupation gone, would be glad? Noah, the truth was, didn't mean to, couldn't bear to, let go, to be saved or spared, one jot or tittle of work, no matter how mechanical, no matter how unnecessary his supervision. Behind the rugged face, deep in the old mind must hide that specter of vapidity, the thought of fear: *And what would I do then?*

"I'm sorry," Arthur Winner said. He was. Like Noah, he was tired. Tired, he took too quickly the relief of supposing Noah meant it when he said he was a trouble, the relief of hoping those variances the old man's stubbornness occasioned were going to stop. That, he surely should know, was silly to suppose; and much too much to hope! He said: "I think I ought to say Doctor Trowbridge's attitude wasn't one of meddling or wanting to meddle. He was simply inquiring. He doesn't pretend to know the law. If the principal can't legally be reached—"

"Didn't say that," Noah Tuttle said. "But he won't get control while I'm alive. The trust can be struck down. Turns on vacancy in trusteeship. I'm made competent to name a succeeding trustee. If I didn't tell you before, I'll tell you now. I've named you. That's attached to the instrument. I'll show you just what to do. Then, later; you do it, if you want to. I won't know."

The words, Arthur Winner must realize, were of defeat. The old, old man, at the close of a long, long day, and nearly tired to death, peered blinking out at a world that was only waiting to go on without him. He gave up. All wishes of his, all views of his, all judgments of his—all was vanity. They would not prevail after him. The things he had done, a new age was already itching to undo. To argue was useless; he found no strength to contend. He might as well show them (sometime) how (when they were rid of him) they could get what they wanted.

"Not tonight, my boy," Noah Tuttle said. "Don't tell me any more. I'm tired. I have to go to bed. You're a good boy, Arthur. You'll wait. Good night, good night."

Turning his back, Noah Tuttle, heavy and slow, yet dogged, with a drive of purpose, began to mount the stairs. His dumpy, dark-garmented figure and the white head's measured bobbings rose toward the lighted scene of the big painting, the crowd of horses in the woods, the bright standard, the men in blue grimly conferring.

"Good night," Arthur Winner said.

He hesitated, looking after Noah in the concern of mind that such a progress naturally aroused. Would the shaky old man make it? Gaining the landing and going across, Noah saw Arthur Winner below. He gestured peremptorily—a waving-away? A beckon of farewell? In the end, must facts obtain that all man's fictions—social and economic; religious and philosophical—could not defeat? Man's tissue of make-believe was spun from hope! Noah's hopes? His hopes were gone before! From all things here, they had departed! Should he now depart?

EIGHT

I direct that the principal be held in trust perpetually for the benefit of the aforementioned Christ Church, to be invested and reinvested; and all income therefrom to be paid from time to time to the lawful, canonically constituted Wardens and Vestrymen of said Christ Church, so long as they shall adhere to and observe the doctrine, discipline and worship of the Protestant Episcopal Church in the United States of America; and by them to be expended as they may see fit, so long as it shall be for the religious or proper use and benefit of said Christ Church. . . .

Arthur Winner interrupted his professional, close but rapid passage over the formal clauses. The sound reaching him in the room's deep quiet seemed to be only that of an automobile halting on the street outside—stopped, no doubt, by the traffic light at the corner. Under handsome tole shades, the room's lights burned bright. They threw down a gentle glow on the neat gray rug. The same glow extended over the good furniture upholstered in dark green leather, passed up walls packed to the ceiling with books, gleamed off the gold frame of a portrait of Arthur Winner's father. The Arthur Winner Senior of twenty years ago sat thoughtful, caught very well in a familiar pose— he held a volume of law reports which he had just closed on a finger marking his place. Below him, centered on one of the old house's fine, much-elaborated mantelpieces, a bracket clock in a mahogany case ticked strong and solemn, unhurried but unstayed, getting toward quarter to ten.

I further direct that my trustee, said Noah Tuttle, Esquire,

208

have complete and absolute discretion in the administration of the foregoing trust; that he serve without bond; that he have power to invest and reinvest all monies of the trust however he may deem advisable and without regard for restrictions of "legal investment" as that term is now, or may later be, defined by law; that he have power to retain any investment for such length of time as he may determine; and that he have power to mortgage, to pledge, to lease, to exchange, to grant options on, and/or sell all real or personal property at private or public sale; and in whatsoever other ways, by buying or by selling, by keeping or by releasing, to take as his judgment shall dictate any and all steps by him considered. . . .

Arthur Winner smiled. If ever there were a fully empowered trustee, that trustee was Noah! And, certainly, you couldn't say the instrument didn't make testator's intent—a spendthrift trust—clear. Ezra Orcutt could be imagined—Arthur Winner had a childhood memory of the old man with his bush of white beard passing in a shiny landau behind a pair of very glossy bays. Driving him was an uncle of Alfred Revere, who wore a top hat no less glossy than the horses—issuing a summons to the fantastic castle of red brick in which he lived just west of Brocton. What Ezra said must have been, simply: "Noah, I'm going to rely on you. Carrie's to have the whole for life. Then we'll take out something to keep up Sam's church; but I want that tied. Any vestry's mostly nincompoops and nitwits; and nowadays you can't be sure the parson isn't going to be a madman." (Doctor Ives had just been installed. He irritated Ezra by speaking—no doubt, because he was born in England—as the English speak. Also, he had proposed a few High-Church practices that smelled to Ezra of popery.) "I want this money kept together; so I want you to have all the say, and them not to have any. You'll know how to see to that; and when you've seen to it, I'll know it's safe, so I won't be turning in my grave."

Well, he hadn't been wrong in thinking Noah was a man you could rely on! But, of course, empowered that way, a succeeding trustee, as Noah dejectedly saw, had only to "deem it advisable" and he could hand the whole thing to the Diocesan Investment Trust the day after Noah died. Attached to the last

209

sheet with a paper clip was the form of appointment: *I, lawful trustee of Ezra Orcutt, direct, in the event of my disability or death, that Arthur Stanton Winner Junior, Esquire* . . . Noah hadn't, in fact, bothered to tell him. The date was three years ago, with Helen Detweiler and Gladys Mills as witnesses.

Arthur Winner picked up the portfolio. Tying the ribbons, he went into the outer office where the girls worked. Gladys Mills and Mary Sheen had left their small typist's desks in good order; closed, bare, the seats set straight. On Helen Detweiler's larger desk, a number of papers had not been put away. They lay scattered; and this sight was almost startling. Helen's habit was extreme neatness. The small silver luster mug in which Helen was accustomed to keep flowers held four drooped and dead roses—they must be yesterday's. Poor Helen wouldn't have been cutting herself roses this morning! Not far from the mug, lay a used, crumpled little handkerchief chastely initialed: HD.

Arthur Winner returned the Orcutt portfolio to the document file. About to push shut the drawer and spin the combination lock, he heard, from behind him, a sound of the street door in front opening. Looking over his shoulder, he saw, astonished, a uniformed man step into the lighted reception room, and move the door back with care to stand wide open. From the visored cap and leather puttees, Arthur Winner had first taken this unknown man to be a policeman. He saw now that the uniform was a chauffeur's uniform. The man turned, and stepped out of sight. There was a moment's delay; and the screen door reopened. Holding the uniformed arm in one hand, holding in the other both his canes, while he made with vigor his difficult way up the steps, into the light advanced Julius Penrose. From the door he could see Arthur Winner. In his harsh clear voice, disdainfully made a little mincing, as though Julius intended it to mock its own grating sound, he called: "Ah, Arthur! This is a convenience I hardly expected. I didn't know where you were."

Smiling, Arthur Winner said: "And I thought *you* were still in Washington."

"I don't believe I am," Julius Penrose said. "I think I'm here."

Exertion on a hot night had somewhat reddened Julius's forehead. Under the full light falling from overhead, Julius's nearly square face looked firm and massive, without fat, but heavily muscled—a powerful mouth, a powerful jaw; broad chin and broad brow in a strong, vertical, just-not-concave alignment. He was breathing a trifle fast; but Julius's dark eyes, large; in their quality, limpid; in their expression, calmly critical, regarded Arthur Winner with a detachment and directness that any physical difficulties he might be having were not permitted to disturb. Julius wore no hat; and, under the light, his hair, dense, with a handsome wave, shone vigorously and youthfully black —the hair, you might think, of a man half his age.

Now that he had reached a level surface, Julius Penrose released his hold on the supporting arm. He grasped a cane in each hand. A developed great strength in his arms and shoulders allowed him, balancing in a practiced way, to straighten his big torso. Propped by the canes, he poised erect on the braces that stiffened his useless legs. To Arthur Winner, who had come toward him, Julius said: "This is Pettengill, who's been good enough to get me here. His kind assistance was provided, along with a motorcar of great elegance, by Mr. Marple, Bob Ingoldsby's banking friend, of whom I've spoken to you. We needed some additional papers from the file; so we arranged that I would drive up, stopping by here to get them. They took a plane to New York, where I'm going on to meet them—we'd hoped, by midnight; but we were a little late starting; and Pettengill's had nothing to eat."

Transferring the cane from his right hand to be held with the cane in his left, Julius Penrose dipped into a pocket and came out with a folded five-dollar bill which he must have put there, ready. He said: "Halfway down the street, where you see a horseshoe in neon tubing, is a fairly clean and commodious— er—pub, Pettengill. Get yourself some refreshment. And take your time. This is my partner, Mr. Winner; and I'll be a little while talking to him."

"Very good, sir. Thank you, sir. If you won't be needing me immediately, I believe I'll first give the dog a walk again."

"Pray, do!" Julius Penrose said.

Alone with Arthur Winner, he said: "As a traveling companion, we have a cultivated-looking poodle bitch of Marple's named Valentine. She sits in front and takes turns with the driving. Or, even if she does not, I've no doubt she easily could. Unfortunately, in spite of her intellectual gifts, she seems to suffer from the chronic female complaint of constipation. The state of her bowels causes Pettengill much anxiety. You observe, he would rather see to that than eat."

Arthur Winner said: "And what about you? You can't have had anything to eat either. Julius, why don't I call the Union League? Alfred's still there. He'd fix something for you quickly and send a boy over."

"I'm fed," Julius Penrose said. "I ate in transit. I caused the hotel to put up some sandwiches and a Thermos of tea. So much simpler than stopping somewhere. The sympathetic interest strangers always take in me when I make an appearance among them I try to appreciate; yet even after all these years I can't seem really to relish sympathy, let alone interest. For the same reason, I prefer not to descend at service stations. My remaining pride is Montaigne's; I can hold my water eight hours; yet, in Pettengill's sense, I'll take myself for a walk, here."

He began with efficiency to transport himself toward the lavatory at the back of the hall. Pulling up near the door, he said: "I won't delay to say that things have turned out very well. Don't count our chickens until I've finished hatching them all; but after I called you this morning, Beckert called me. He said he and the commissioner had studied the précis I made for them of the applicable law as I saw the thing—I left that with them after the conference. The commissioner's view seemed to be the same as Beckert's; and he'd been directed to prepare a formal opinion and recommendation—the gist: that we could proceed along the lines I proposed with fair assurance of no additional tax liability. Much of the detail was interesting. For one thing; they were ready to concede that redemption of the bonds was not a distribution, or the essential equivalent of a distribution, of income. You remember that point?"

"I do," Arthur Winner said. "I felt sure you were right.

Julius, I'm delighted! I don't see what more the Ingoldsbys could ask. You really must have done a job."

Julius Penrose said: "Yes, I did. I think I did well. I'll treat myself to admitting that." He moved; and halted again. "Also, I think I did a job on Beckert. I told you, didn't I, that I later found out he was Lawrence's boss—his chief of section? I didn't know that until I had dinner with Lawrence and his wife—they seem well and happy, incidentally. Yesterday, I got a chance to mention Lawrence to him; and Beckert spoke of him very highly —in fact, though he was properly cagey about the matter, I got the impression that if he leaves Internal Revenue he expects Lawrence to go with him. You may hear more soon." Putting himself in motion, he said: "At any rate, the plan is, in effect, approved; and for once, at least, the job's a remunerable one, not an intellectual exercise for free. Nor are they going to be confused about whose the plan was. To my considerable surprise—and pleasure, be sure!—the idea of incorporating 'thin' seemed never to have occurred to Marple, and him a banker! I had to spell out the tax advantages for him—draw him up a couple of contrasting balance sheets." Julius Penrose smiled. "Marple looked what I can only call nonplused. Pretty clearly, he hadn't expected the country boy even to know what a balance sheet was. Since they all see how much they're being saved, I reflect with satisfaction that good stiff fees are going to be in order."

Transferring his cane again, he opened the lavatory door and snapped the light on. "Yes, I'm very pleased, Arthur," he said. "Perhaps I ought not to let myself be so far swayed by small triumphs. Still, I feel good. I feel, if only for a moment, and perhaps mistakenly, that the struggle does avail. You do learn; you do improve yourself. Ten years ago, though then—and this is of the essence—I might not have realized it, I wouldn't have known enough to be able to show those people a thing or two. *Ergo,* I still ripe and ripe! This, believe me, your father, or Noah when he was really Noah, wouldn't have been ashamed of." Passing himself in, not without deftness, he said: "My unbecoming boasting you must lay to my sad disability. Compensa-

213

tory! Even I realize that. When a man's physically crippled, his character's soon crippled, too. I'm now in fettle fine enough to declare what I've long known but usually think it unadvisable to say: Never believe that afflictions improve character, enlarge the understanding, or teach you charitable thoughts! The man not afflicted, the easy, open fortunate man is the likable man, the kindly man, the considerate man—in short, the man who may have time and inclination to think of someone besides himself. Be virtuous, and you'll be happy? Nonsense! Be happy and you'll begin to be virtuous."

Julius Penrose shut the door.

Julius Penrose said: "A full day, a full day! I can see that! I'm glad I wasn't here."

Arthur Winner said: "Well, one feels sorry for Helen."

"Yes; one might," Julius Penrose said. "But refusal to face the verities, though not without immediate satisfactions, carries penalties. There's a Fool Killer, personifying the ancient principle; whom the gods would destroy, in this world; and he has a list; and that's a good way to put yourself on it. Then, the question's just one of time, of how soon he'll get around to you. Still, Ralph seems a misfortune that perhaps shouldn't happen to anyone. A simple unaffected lowness about that story engages the misanthropist in me. Boys, off in a corner, will be boys! And girls? Give me an ounce of civet, good apothecary! Have one yourself!"

Sitting erect in the green leather barrel chair by Arthur Winner's desk, Julius Penrose had arranged his wasted legs, outthrust in their braces, at an angle. Since they had been reduced to not much more than stilts of bone, the cloth of his trousers hung from them in loose folds. Taking up the cane that rested against the chair arm near his right hand, he raised it, pointing it, sighting along it reflectively, at the empty fireplace. "So much for moral indignation!" he said. "One practical thought occurs to me. Has the wench's ogress mother taken her to a doctor?"

"I don't know," Arthur Winner said. "Since we're not denying Ralph had connection with her—"

"Nevertheless, I'd investigate that," Julius Penrose said. "Those societies generally offer medical benefits. To provide them as cheaply as possible, they're apt to have a quack or two more or less in their pay. You've seen them yourself in personal injury cases. If I were you, I'd make that my first business tomorrow. If she hasn't been to a doctor; all right. If she has—you could get Garret Hughes to find out for you—I'd make a formal demand on her that she submit, and without delay, to another examination, by somebody like Reggie Shaw."

"Well, there's no way we can compel—"

"No, there isn't—if she refuses. But you'd at least establish the fact of refusal. You should. You might need it. Your theory is she's a loose young woman; and you plan to plead consent. What happens to that plea if J. Jerome calls a physician, qualifies him in that he says he went to school and it can't be shown he's lost his license yet, and then gets him to put on the record his professional opinion that the state of the prosecutrix's pudenda, seen the day following the alleged assault, was that of the freshly ravished maiden? Not good at all! Unfailingly, thoughts of an intact virgin being deflowered by a brute excite a juror's sympathies—or, could it be, just excite him? In any event, he's more than likely to hold her innocent of consent until she's proved guilty beyond a reasonable doubt. Hard! You've allowed the burden to fall on defendant. I've an instinct in these sordid matters, Arthur."

Lowering his cane, Julius Penrose tapped the floor. He said: "When I was doing criminal trial work, I used to find my instinct invaluable. Something, I cannot say what—a distrustful nature; an unamiable habit of suspicion; perhaps, actually, a nice nose for hanky-panky got from knowing what *I* would be doing if I meant to pull a fast one—had a way of warning me. I soon found I neglected those intimations at my peril. I'm this minute being insistently informed by one of them that, if Brophy indicts the brat and he's put on trial, more will be involved than the mere issue of whether she let him or didn't let him. Instinct says to me: Watch out!"

Smiling, Arthur Winner said: "You couldn't ask instinct to be a little more explicit, could you?"

215

"No, I could not," Julius Penrose said. "Instinct doesn't like work. Instinct doesn't bother to explain. Instinct just indicates where I ought to look. I'm supposed, then, to use my head. Here, instinct seems to want me to look at this interest J. Jerome is taking."

"I didn't find that very puzzling," Arthur Winner said. "Someone Jerry knows in Mechanicsville must have got in touch with him. Noah didn't like it; but I couldn't see how it mattered. I can't see any reason for Jerry to have a serious interest."

"Well, there's the use of instinct," Julius Penrose said. "Instinct comes in when you need to know, but you can't see. Let us take my instinct's word for it that Brophy *is* interested. Now, we use the head. Why is he? Well, getting a conviction might please people he has a political interest in pleasing. Is that all? I think not. J. Jerome, in case you don't know, though often so practical, has never, or not for some time, been merely practical. The first occasion was indeed a surprise; but on several occasions now I've seen him grasp at intangibles, amazingly disinclined to take cash and let the credit go. Detweiler's a pretty good Brocton name. J. Jerome did not come from Greenwood Avenue. His father kept a low saloon on Water Street. Could this humble origin ever have caused people who did come from Greenwood Avenue to treat him, though of course with all politeness, as not quite one of them? Might there be something not displeasing in getting a son of George Detweiler convicted of an infamous crime and sent to the reformatory? I think so!"

Arthur Winner said: "I see the possibility; but—"

"No," Julius Penrose said, "I don't suggest that he'd fabricate evidence himself; but I'd expect him to accept without too-close inspection anything that might help convict. I'd be prepared to see him play to a jury. I'd be careful about that jury. I'd study the panel. In selecting jurors, I'd use my challenges with the general idea of keeping off, as far as I could, anyone with a foreign name and anyone I'd learned was a Roman Catholic. The precaution seems to you extreme?"

"Yes," Arthur Winner said. "I can't feel religion needs to be brought in. To suppose, because Jerry's a Catholic, Catholics would try to find for him, seems to me a view of prejudice."

216

"I merit the reproof, no doubt," Julius Penrose said. "I can't say instinct is silenced; but I, perhaps, ought to be! Perhaps I should not glance at Mr. Brophy's religion. First; prejudice is in itself held censurable; an evil thing. So I'm anti-Catholic, am I? Still, in passing, I'll confess I wonder, as one of them, why the only people who may be openly criticized, found fault with, and spoken ill of, are those of white, Protestant, and more or less Nordic extraction. I, it seems, am game and fair game for every-body—a kind of *caput lupinum*. Nobody writes the papers threateningly when I'm decried or disparaged. I don't say this is unreasonable. I myself have no wish to abridge any man's right not to like me if he so chooses. Only, in my bewildered way, I keep thinking there ought to be a turnabout. There isn't! Not only may each bumptious Catholic freely rate and abuse me if I reflect in the least on his faith; but each self-pitying Jew, each sulking Negro, need only holler that he's caught me not loving him as much as he loves himself, and a rabble of pro-fessional friends of man, social-worker liberals, and practitioners of universal brotherhood—the whole national horde of nuts and queers—will come at a run to hang me by the neck until I learn to love."

A muscular remote smile passed on Julius Penrose's face. "Well, here, *in propria persona,* I stand—or, rather, sit; since I find sitting easier nowadays. And, of course, there's that other very good reason why glancing at Mr. Brophy's religion isn't, for me, quite the thing, right now. What I wished to speak to you about, if you don't mind, is Marjorie. We stopped by Roylan and I saw her for a moment, to say I wouldn't be home until sometime Sunday. Our colloquy was brief; but she told me she'd called you; and that you'd kindly agreed to let her discuss her religious problem with you."

In some embarrassment, Arthur Winner said: "She seemed disturbed, Julius. She seemed to have the idea that I could, I can't think in what way, help her. When I didn't hear any more, I imagined she'd changed her mind."

Resting on Arthur Winner a gaze into which he seemed to put both sympathy and irony, Julius Penrose said: "She might hope you could afford her the help of listening. Anyone can see

217

you are an understanding sort of person. Moreover, there's her subject matter. She observes that you're by way of being a religious man—"

Arthur Winner said: "I don't think I could really claim—"

"Perhaps not, perhaps not," Julius Penrose said. "What a man's religious beliefs really are should never be inquired into. And, of course, still less, why he holds them. On the point of why; belief or professed belief in a supernatural religion speaks for itself. Though believers will give you a good deal of prose on the subject, the subject's always touchy, fruitful of offense and anger; because the awkward truth usually is that they have no reason, they just feel like believing. At any rate, you attend Christ Church. To boot, you're a member of the vestry there. I can imagine Marjorie entertaining, perhaps not aware that she does, some very faint hope that there might be an alternative—"

"In that event, I think she ought to talk to our rector—"

"Do you?" Julius Penrose said. "I somehow doubt if talking to that, I must say personable, young man would meet her need. I don't believe she'd be in her present emotional predicament if good-mannered piety, or gentlemanlike spiritual guidance, or assisting at well-bred devotions were what she wanted. They don't take enough of the responsibility from her. Not able to discipline herself, she craves to be disciplined."

"If that's the problem," Arthur Winner said, "I don't see how she could hope discussing things with me would help her—"

"Who knows?" Julius Penrose said. "There are disciplines and disciplines. More properly, since all disciplines are arrangements of reward and punishment, there are rewards and rewards, and punishments and punishments. She might hope, by talking, to get the reward of your understanding approval. To confide in you, and at length, would be the first step. How, in the classic phrase, does she know what she thinks until she hears what she says? By common consent, I'm a hard man, insensitive to finer shades of feeling, easily put out of patience. Would I be likely to support with understanding that seemingly necessary talking around and around?"

That Julius had such a picture of himself, and that many people who knew Julius Penrose slightly thought of him as a hard man, were both doubtless true; yet an acquaintance of years inclined Arthur Winner to say that both Julius and common consent erred, too easily taken in by harshnesses of manner and sharpnesses of speech which, in fact, manifested that Julius was a sensitive man, not an insensitive. Julius might see himself soured by affliction; by his physical crippling, slowly or quickly crippled in other ways; but what evinced it? Under the first shock, when the cruel misfortune of his paralysis fell on him ten years ago; through the bitter, long (indeed, endless, since he would never be quit of it) job of fair recovery—at least he was not wholly helpless; at least he was able to go on with his work—had Arthur Winner ever found occasion to excuse in Julius, to call explainable, those not-to-be-mistaken strikings-out of someone brought to recompense himself for his hurts by hurting others? Could Arthur Winner pick from his recollection one instance of the self-denominated hard man acting (though he might often seem to speak it) a hard man's regardless, ruthless part?

Julius Penrose said: "As for why you didn't hear any more this week, Marjorie's Polly, this Mrs. Pratt, seems to have been away. Marjorie only had a card today saying she was back. The point, you'll have perceived, is that she and Marjorie have concluded (for some reason!) that I feel an antipathy toward Mrs. Pratt. Meetings must be managed when the field's clear. Thus, Marjorie was dismayed to see me tonight."

"Well, I think Clarissa had told her—"

"Yes. She'd been thinking I'd be back tomorrow, so she couldn't have Polly. Then Clarissa said that you said that I said —so, she supposed tomorrow was clear, and called Polly, who is coming. I soothed her. Tomorrow was still clear. Mr. Marple, as a further kindness, was planning to have Pettengill drive me back here Sunday morning. I offered to extend my absence, if she liked. She appeared moved by my willingness to accommodate her; but she said tomorrow would give her and Polly time enough."

Arthur Winner said: "I don't think I'm quite clear about Mrs. Pratt's part—what Marjorie wanted her down for."

Taking up a cane, pointing again at the fireplace, Julius Penrose said: "I wondered myself. I made free to ask. Marjorie's plan seems to be to talk with you; and then to tell Polly what you said—to see what Polly says to that. It suggested to me Marjorie's possible hope against hope. Something you said by way of advice; or, maybe, something she said by way of explanation, might raise new issues of fact or feeling. She wanted to be able to take them immediately to Polly—who, one gathers, is to hang around in the offing, ready and waiting. The arrangement has an ineptness, an involvement, that, I'm afraid, sufficiently identifies the author."

Julius let the leveled cane drop. He said: "Well! She wanted to get word to you. She called the lake, and they told her you'd had to go down to Brocton. I said I'd find you. Her situation: she assumes, she wishes to assume, that you're willing to see her tomorrow. Her suggestion: would I ask you to let her know if you weren't willing." He made a faint grimace. "Do I flinch a little? Alas, could anyone but Marjorie be speaking? These trifling left-handednesses come naturally to her. She's preordained to fumble; she's fated always to confound confusion. With solemnity, I told her I'd known you for a long time. If you engaged yourself to do a thing, you would do that thing without fail. Will you?"

"Of course I'll see her," Arthur Winner said. "I'm afraid I can't say just when. I don't know how much of the morning our Mr. Woolf means to take; but I'll find time."

"Good," Julius Penrose said. "Or, is it? I'd be deceiving myself if I didn't recognize that this, while more talk, amounts to action. I confess I hoped the matter would never leave the stage of shilly-shally. The hope seemed reasonable—by not deciding, Marjorie protracted the emotional titillations. She must talk and talk again with Polly and with Polly's monsignor. She must even talk, or try to talk, with me. There's a recent sudden change. I fear her hand's being forced. I suspect an ecclesiastical ultimatum has been handed her—in substance: piss or get off the pot! Among the apparent terms or conditions is one that's far from agreeable to me. A contingent or reserve hope of mine had been that, if anything did come to be done, Polly and Polly's pet monsignor would manage the doing in the seclusion of Polly's private chapel. The latest is: that's out! She'll have to go to Father Albright, at Our Lady of Mount Carmel, here. This being sent home has points of interest. I think you've met Polly—Mrs. Pratt?"

"I believe I did, a year or so ago."

"Yes; that was when she made her last open visit to Marjorie. They were college acquaintances. If you remember Mrs. Pratt at all, you'll remember she's a large overdressed woman exuberant in manner, of less than average intelligence and somewhat sheeplike appearance. She and Marjorie had not seen each other for twenty years or more; yet I believe Mrs. Pratt never once failed to send Marjorie a Christmas card. My informing instinct soon told me the story. During their college years, the now Mrs. Pratt had harbored a consuming crush on Marjorie; though Marjorie, my instinct assured me, had not returned the feeling. Did she even know? I feel certain that Marjorie's taste in love was early and uncompromisingly oriented to males. Women's-college affairs, whether short or not short of active tribadism, weren't likely to have hit the spot with her at all. Moreover, at eighteen or nineteen, Marjorie, never of an independent mind, and no leader, would unfailingly have accepted her social attitudes from those around her. At any good woman's college, Polly's faith must have made her something of an outsider—one of that handful of not quite, quite girls who by special arrangement went somewhere for mass Sunday mornings. The others would have no particular reason to get to know any of them."

Raising his eyebrows, Julius Penrose looked at Arthur Winner. "Nasty little snobs!" he said. "However, there's that, warm and uncritical, in Marjorie's nature to give her kindly impulses. Without meaning anything by them, she'd be always, in effect, blundering into kindnesses or civilities. In the weak unwillingness to hurt, she'd say something cordial or do something friendly. A word or smile of the kind, given just because it was easier, probably started Polly dreaming. A few more such accidents, and Polly was probably a goner. I expect she never dared push the matter—something would probably warn her where Marjorie's interests lay; and, so, that any girl-to-girl courtship would be a mistake. I imagine she just dreamed on, feasting silent and from a distance on Marjorie's hair of gold, on Mar-

221

jorie's adorable face, on the sweet disorder, the pretty confusion of Marjorie's ways. At a venture, one dream had to do with Marjorie somehow turning Catholic; losing all her friends, but not minding, as she twined arms with Polly and they wandered off into the sunset. You follow me?"

"So far," Arthur Winner said. "But time passes, and—"

"I was coming to that," Julius Penrose said. "Twenty years pass. The two of them lead separate lives. There are only the cards at Christmas; yet those, at last, pay off. Year after year, Marjorie, if she should ever want to, knows where to find Polly. Meanwhile, on Marjorie various factors are working. Her life has been mostly a discontented one. Now, to aggravate the accumulated disappointment and regret, come the moods of the menopause; and the rationalist's poor recourse of grin-and-bear-it fails her. Desperate for relief, she remembers, by one of the ordinary ironies of our life, Polly; and how Polly stood apart and aside at college—not, in this retrospect, because nobody invited her in, but because a light of faith, a truth of certainty kept her out. Polly's kingdom was never the pinchbeck one of this world that Marjorie's finding more and more uninhabitable. She writes Polly. Polly instantly comes. Time has worked on them both. Both, I would presume, got some shocks; but one thing hadn't changed. The college crush—I wonder, in passing, what Mr. Pratt, whoever he may have been, found living with her like. He doesn't seem to have lived long—was unabated. Polly was still in love."

By an effort, putting down his elbows on the chair arms, Julius Penrose lifted his hips. With a grunt, he was able to shift his inert legs to a new angle. He said: "And now, bliss of blisses, the advances are Marjorie's. Marjorie doubts, she fears, she asks to be saved. Is she too late? Bursting with joy, Mrs. Pratt cries: 'No, no; there's time yet! You can still get in on the ground floor.' Indeed, I myself recall from Sunday school that you may give the heat of the day a miss; the eleventh hour will do. Every man one cent is the way of the other world."

Breaking off, Julius Penrose shook his head. He said: "I must try to remember that Marjorie is in distress. Making fun of her ill becomes me—and, furthermore, what am I thinking of? The

222

joke, so much on me, is most unfunny. Marjorie is being, or is about to be, converted. Well, I'd, of course, noticed recently an upsurge of primitive religious belief. I give you my word, I've had it from Dave Weintraub that he and his family reverted not long ago to the Jewish dietary law, known, I believe, as kashruth. If they divide the hoof, they have to chew the cud. No kids seethed in their mother's milk. Separate sets of utensils—don't get the plates mixed up. Dave reports that, now he's a practicing Jew again, he feels one hundred per cent better."

Arthur Winner said: "I see how that could be."

"Oh, so do I," Julius Penrose said. "I just thought it was an unusual example. Marjorie's project certainly isn't. In the newspapers, conversion to Rome appears to be the fashion, a phenomenon of the day. I confess I hadn't paid much attention—I suppose, because so many of the news-making converts fell in categories to me naturally suspect. A fancy or high-brow author or two. Sentimental newspaper columnists. Inmates of the theater. Figures of flamboyance in politics. Quondam leading Reds or professional atheists. Uneasy Episcopalian ministers. In short, men and women who must long have been ill-balanced."

Arthur Winner smiled.

"Yes," Julius Penrose said, "jokes should be amusing! By hitting them off that way, I clearly mean to make light of them. Still, what I noted, I noted. Not a few of the male converts, for instance, have to me the look of former homosexuals; not a few of the females, the look of former alcoholics. I'm trying to say that what they *were* before their newsworthy conversions strikes me as often suggestive. Doctor Johnson, I believe, once said: To drive out a passion, reason is helpless; you need another passion. The more it changes, the more it's the same thing? I think so! However, this was idle; general reflection on a topic of the times. I only sat up and took real notice when I saw Marjorie might be serious about Romanism. I remembered Lord Macaulay's pronouncement that there is not, and there never was on this earth, a work of human policy so well deserving of examination. High time I examined it!"

Turning his head, he glanced at the bracket clock on the mantel. "The subject's no small one," he said. "I asked a bookstore to inquire. After a little delay—for secular persons to want such books seems unheard-of—I was provided with a standard four-volume study of moral and pastoral theology by a learned Jesuit; an admirably concise treatise on apologetics and doctrine by an Australian—*quod ubique*, I suppose!—archbishop; and the code of the canon law. All, I've perused with much interest and some instruction. I've a better idea of what Marjorie would be comforted to believe than I had before. But I wasn't won over to their way of thinking. I've never asked you. Are you interested in theology, Arthur?"

"I suppose not," Arthur Winner said, "or I'd know more about it than I do."

"Then I won't belabor you with my personal conclusions at any length. My final reflection, I'm afraid, was that if hypocrisy can be said to be the homage vice pays to virtue, theology could be said to be a homage nonsense tries to pay to sense. The forms are learned and serious. Of the substance, a good idea may be had from an expounding of the now dogma of the Assumption that I followed with attention. The Saviour, the incarnate deity, is defined to be without sin. However, his human nature derived from his human mother—where else could he get any? Now, what does this tell us? Why, naturally, that the nature of the Blessed Virgin must have been without sin. More centuries than I would have thought necessary were given to thinking the thing through; but, in the end, it became of faith that the Blessed Virgin was immaculately conceived; meaning that, at the instant of her conception, the original sin in all human nature was miraculously removed from her. What now follows? Obvious! Lots less time is needed here! Death is the wages of sin. No sin, no death. The Blessed Virgin had no sin, so she could not possibly have died. Yet, she is not on earth. The explanation? In logic, there can be only one. Her human body was translated to heaven, and is there now. Irrefragable reasoning!"

"I see," Arthur Winner said. "But you are not persuaded?"

"Logicians though they may be," Julius Penrose said, "I question if they fully grasp the fact that no number of succeeding syllogisms, though each unassailable in its formal validity, can

224

cure even one unestablished premise, even one absurd postulate. And, indeed, I'll do them the fairness of suspecting they feel free to offer argument of this sort only because they don't actually rely on it. My archepiscopal apologist introduces all his expositions of the more critical and difficult dogmas with the proem or caveat I soon got by heart: 'For a Catholic, it is sufficient to know that the infallible church teaches the above doctrine; the following proofs, therefore, are not necessary; but they are useful as giving a knowledge of sacred scripture and ecclesiastical tradition.' Having read that a few times, I couldn't but realize we had nothing, they and I, to discuss on the rational level, the only one I can reach. Let us return to Marjorie. Where was I?"

"You said, I think, that she was being pressed to take some action."

"Yes. There seems at long last to have been a cracking-down or getting-tough policy. Polly's pet monsignor is not proving quite as pet as expected. Indeed, why should he? He has produced quite a number of more or less maudlin best-selling books; he is a radio and television performer; he has a lot to do. Also, he must know a good deal about the use and abuse of emotions, and possible variations on the religious sentiment. His experience probably said: Let business be got down to! This Mrs. Penrose is married. She lives in something called Brocton, out in the sticks. Her parish is there. Polly may be very rich and very pious, but there are limits. Polly can be her sponsor, yes; but the reception will not take place intimately with happy mists of tears in that private chapel, probably to have been banked with lilies. Mrs. Penrose will get her formal instruction from the local priest in Brocton, and be received there by him. Do you know Father Albright?"

"Not really," Arthur Winner said. "I've met him. I even had one fairly long talk with him last year. He came to me about the board of education's plan to show those so-called sex education films to the high-school children. I couldn't agree with him; but—"

"I'll say it for you," Julius Penrose said. "I've observed him, and heard him speak, on several public occasions. His theme is usually the menace of atheistic communism; and since none of his hearers, whether through ordinary wisdom or plain dumbness, is in the remotest danger of embracing a nonsense too stupid for the intelligent and too complicated for the stupid, he can, not unadroitly, urge the scarcely less nonsensical identification of what he calls 'Americanism' with, of all things, Catholicism. Still, he appears to be a worthy enough fellow, of virtuous, I'm sure, habits; sincere in his peculiar professions; and, as men go, a good man rather than a bad one. You agree?"

"Yes, I do. He seemed earnest and honest."

Julius Penrose said: "Though probably both, the significant, and, so, painful, point to me is that he's also quite common. Of course, when Marjorie's preparing to swallow a camel, to strain at gnats would be silly. It's disagreeable of me, it may be trifling of me; yet I ask myself, with a kind of dismay, how can anyone go, for any sort of 'instruction,' to a person who, when he means 'modern,' says 'modren'; and when he means 'interesting,' says 'inneresting.' I don't, of course, suggest that every Roman cleric is in this case; Polly's Catholic circle I'd judge to be quite a cultural cut above these priests of the people—the least little bit cheap, perhaps (I have monsignor in mind); but I speak as one of his readers only. Meeting him, I daresay you hardly notice, you hardly notice! However, the particular cleric I must consider is Father Albright; and I'm given pause to know that Marjorie's new emotional needs are so imperative that they transcend all fastidiousness as well as all reason. Tell me about your talk with him."

Arthur Winner said: "It didn't end very satisfactorily. He managed to drop a pretty strong hint that one reason I might not care what went on at Brocton High School was that I didn't send my daughter there, I sent her out to Washington Hall. By then, of course, he'd realized nothing he could say would change my attitude—I'd told him at once that I'd seen the films, along with the rest of the board, and considered them in no way objectionable. I daresay he felt that, being an Episcopalian, I wouldn't know any reason why immorality shouldn't be promoted in schools. I could hardly blame him for being put out."

"And just why couldn't you?"

In the tone of blunt inquiry, in the casual pause for answer, Arthur Winner must feel, always glad of it, the force of long-established habit. Over the years, what hours had he and Julius passed in quiet converse, alone together, talking to each other! On evenings when they worked late and the office was, as now, empty; on afternoons while the law delayed and one or another of them waited on a jury, or on the court in recess, sitting together at counsels' table below the bench, or in seats taken at random up near the door; on winter Sundays with snow on the ground at Roylan, by Julius's smoldering fire, or his; on fore-noons of late spring week ends at the lake, looking out from the terrace, beneath the great oak beginning finally to burst its vires-cent buds of leaves, over the warming water's sunny shimmer —how many discussions had engaged them! In exchange of un-hurried thought, in give-and-take of comment, they proceeded to how many meetings of mind!

As a rule, these two minds could meet quickly in agreement; but in disagreement, a conclusion of reticent understanding could be reached, after so much practice, quite as well. Not by talkative openings of the heart, but by a silent long-held knowl-edge of each other, a basic like-mindedness, they could enjoy a mutual unspoken comprehension. That comprehension respected the privacy, or even secrecy, which alone, at some points, digni-fies a man; yet each, after all, had had a share in shaping the other's thoughts—amused, Arthur Winner could notice some-times phrases of his in Julius's mouth; or, perhaps more often, phrases of Julius's in his. Ceremony between them would be absurd. They were free to differ, if in the end they did, with no loss of concord.

Arthur Winner said: "Father Albright had a grievance. His argument seemed to be that since his church wasn't financially able to maintain a high school in Brocton, parochial-school chil-dren *had* to go, through no choice of his or theirs, to the public high school. I think at first he may have thought I just hadn't realized, hadn't the moral training to know, that what I was vot-ing for was gravely wrong. Now that he'd told me, now that I did know, my duty was plain. I wasn't doing it. I was still set on contributing to the moral delinquency of Catholic minors. Of course, I told him we weren't planning to force any child to see the films. Those whose parents wanted them excused would be excused. I'm afraid I was put out a little myself when he treated that as more of my ignorance. He said that wouldn't do at all. That would work a discrimination, make an issue of a child's faith. Because Catholic parents couldn't, on pain of sin, expose them to what the church regarded as dangerous to their morals, Catholic children were to be singled out in an open and invidious way. I think he thought our only right course was to do as he wanted—not show the films to anyone."

"You may be sure he felt exactly that," Julius Penrose said. "And I've no doubt his irritation was extreme. What must be the chagrin and frustration of a man, the emolument and solace of whose celibate, hard-working life is power—*alter Christus,* he can actually say of himself—when he finds again, except with his own parishioners, he has only the velvet glove? Where's the iron hand that ought to be in it? Instead of you, a heretic, being haled before him, and told what to do, and warned on pain of, not just sin, but of fire, to do it, his pitiful only expedient is to come and ask you to please be fair! Yes, I think the bad temper of one who suffers such humiliation is explainable; though I'm not very sympathetic. I know no better than John Locke knew why those who do not, and morally cannot—against truth, error has no rights; and they, and every doma, doctrine, and practice of theirs is truth; and you, my friend, are error—tolerate should themselves be tolerated."

Shrugging, Julius Penrose breathed wearily. He made a movement of discomfort, reminding Arthur Winner that this, too, differentiated Julius from more fortunate men. To them, pain was passing and occasional; Julius lived with pain—not acute; but never in his waking hours wholly relieved. Julius said: "Yet, of course, the intolerance is a necessity; that exercise—the firm use of power, the rigid requirement of submission—is a true *sine qua non.* Games, to be any good, must have rules. People won't value what doesn't cost them anything. All the slightly troublesome, perpetually recurring, obligations of worship; all the arbitrarily imposed, slightly irksome fasts or abstinences: that, for instance, tails-you-lose-heads-I-win disciplinary stand on contraception, help the players feel this game is real. The same, with the constant exactions of cash; the masses and candles at a price, the tables of the money-changers in their church doors. A wise utilization of great psychological truths, a wise manipulation of the sense of values, enables, if I may repair to Locke again, the priest to offer the more-wanted pennyworth. When all's done and all's paid, the faithful, like Dave Weintraub, feel one hundred per cent better."

Julius's muscular remote smile showed itself an instant. He said: "Yes, I confess to more than a mere temperamental distaste. As a free man, I have to fear that canny practice, that patient know-how, those vibrant God-love-yous—all *that* alarms me. Here, today, Father Albright is still only able to ask you to be fair; you are still free to hold that he's as much entitled to his opinion as you are to yours. But tomorrow? Who may then be beseeching whom to be fair; and who—ho ho! ha ha!—is going to hold that you're as much entitled to your opinion as he is to his? Oh, I know that in Maryland, once their Maryland, a land speculator and political lord of their faith did solemnly declare a resolve, I think sincere, that the weak were never to oppress the strong: so would I could believe I was simply a bigot, merely moved by what the newspapers name bias. Yet does any free man, without grief, without shame, without fear, see names so proud a hundred years ago in their birthright of liberty as New Hampshire, Massachusetts, Rhode Island, Connecticut, little by little in the last fifty years degraded to designate virtual papal states?"

Julius Penrose shook his head. "Yes; there was a trade; messes of pottage were chosen; and stuck with that trade we are! To make a fast buck, our great-grandfathers' grandfathers used their shipping to bring over the black man who could be worked in the South for no wage. Today, hamstrung by our humanitarian principles, what wouldn't we, North or South, happily pay once and for all to be rid of him? To make a later fast buck, the shipowners' canal-and-railroad-building, their mill-operating, descendants raked, for cheap labor, every area of Europe where, life being wretched, superstition was rife. In consequence, fastened on us—and probably, as Macaulay suspected, forever—we have Rome! Let us now praise famous men! Our God is jealous and visits the sins of fathers on children! Our gods are just, and of our pleasant vices make instruments to plague us." Julius Penrose laughed aloud. "I feel better!" he said.

His expression somber again, Julius sat silent a moment. He said: "I must hurry this up. Pettengill and Valentine will be waiting. I must let them get on. And you. You're going back to the lake tonight?"

Arthur Winner shook his head. "It was just a day's party for the children. Everyone's coming down this evening."

"The children, yes!" Julius Penrose said. "All, today, must be for them. Is this well considered? I hear rumors that my daughter and yours find having an automobile essential. How unkind to deprive them of any pleasure costing only a few hundred dollars! The philoprogenitive instinct, brooding on the brats, is tickled to do them service—the more, the merrier! It's poor Helen again! But, how about the brats? Could we prepare them better for life if we arranged things so that instead of being ministered to all the time, they were soundly cuffed into ministering a little to their elders? Looking at my own offspring, I wonder. Priscilla's been encouraged to play, a gross miscasting, the lass with the delicate air. Indulged, Stewart, no fool, takes a leaf from that young man in Holy Writ who said: 'Sir, I go'; and went not. What's to be done with human beings? What can be done for them? The question puts itself about Marjorie."

Aiming a cane at the left shoe, locked in his leg brace, Julius looked along it, frowning. He said: "I think I should tell you what I believe to be wrong with Marjorie. My instinct identifies the trouble. She's afraid. What frightens her? She is afraid of herself. She feels that she is, and always has been, helpless in the hands of herself. This, an ordinary human situation, is not news to the reflective; but reflective is the last thing Marjorie's fitted to be. She never had any clear grasp of the human situation. Late in time, some sense of that situation intrudes. She can't stand it—and, indeed, the sight's one to shake stouter nerves than hers. She sees a system by which such grasping is made unnecessary. Seek and ye shall find; knock and it shall be opened to you! That means, I learn from the system's loquacious apologists: stop saying; *if* you see, then you'll believe. Believe, and *then* you'll see! There's some smell of charlatanry, to be sure; but charlatans can show wonderful cures. As it has respect either to the understanding or the senses, happiness, Jonathan Swift admonishes me, is a perpetual possession of being well-deceived. Let her be happy. I'd no more argue with her than I'd take, or try to take, a blindman's coppers. This, assure her, is how I *really* feel."

He looked intently at Arthur Winner.

He said: "Of course, Marjorie could have found out by asking me. But, my forbidding air quite aside, I'm afraid that would have been too easy. She needs—a requirement of her nature—to do things in roundabout ways. A paradox: but making things intricate and dramatic is Marjorie's means of falsifying into simplicity the frightening complications of life. So she'll tell you her story; and you'll tell me as much as you think I ought to know. You're to persuade me that, God helping her, she can do no other. What, she'll ask you, is the best thing? She can't bear to hurt me; and she knows how I hate the idea of her being a Catholic."

He shrugged patiently. He said: "Dramatic, you see. I *hate* it! The accurate statement would be that I don't like it. I don't like it, because, to me, it seems a futile little ignominy, a peace-at-any-price panic. Silliness in Marjorie isn't new; but this is servile silliness, mean submissiveness. This has the sheer vulgarity of all frightened acts—the cringe of face, the whine aloud for mercy."

Julius Penrose shook his head. "Like it, I cannot! But all that actually, in her term, 'hurts' me is seeing a human being so lowered. Hers isn't the situation of what I find is called a Cradle Catholic—not, born; babies, you might say, are all born protestants—who guesses the priest must know something about religion and leaves all that to him. This is personal. What, Marjorie hears in terror, doth it profit a man if he gains the whole world and suffers the loss of his own soul? Of course, not she alone! This type of terror, though of a womanish cast, is available to men, appears in fact to be true religion's gist. I seem to

231

recall that one celebrated pietist of the seventeenth century—a time that was the term, I suppose, of serious attention to such subjects on the part of any man of really first-rate intelligence—reduced by his atrocious anxiety over that dear, dear soul of his, proposed gambling as a figure—belief is the best bet, a wager which a man is mad not to make. Since, when less than utterly distraught, the mind he records is of often interesting perceptiveness, he was naturally obliged to own that this feeling was unreasonable. However, shivering in his shoes, he wanted to be safe, cost reason what reason might be cost—he couldn't face the dreadful chance that the mumbo jumbo would work, and he'd miss out, be damned eternally. Not pretty!"

Julius Penrose shook his head again. "No; be it Marjorie, be it Blaise Pascal, I don't like to think of anyone cowed that way, whimpering on the knees before some Father Albright: O God, I am heartily sorry that I have offended thee. I'll do anything, anything, if only you'll let me live forever. I want it! I want it! Please, please, don't make me just die; grant me eternal life, and let perpetual light shine upon me! Please, please believe I *am* heartily sorry—"

He broke off, shrugging once more. "Well, one must remember Marjorie's choice isn't free; to this, she's being driven. Circumstances have combined against her until she breaks—she must quit, give over, cut and run. Circumstances, I say, combine to drive her; and here *I* come in. This is to some degree my doing. Here, I'm in *pari delicto*, I'm afraid. Granted that Marjorie, or Marjorie's nature, was always apt to make her life an unhappy one. Granted that the self Marjorie fears, she fears with cause. Yet, that's not the whole story of her unhappiness. By nature, she's unable to do without men; and she has been unfortunate with men. She's found them deceivers ever. She might, of course, be said consistently to have mistaken their promises to her. At any rate, what she took them to be promising, they did not perform. And, of course, here, too, she had her sad share in bringing about whatever happened to her. Even in the case of her first husband, I think there was a complicity. I don't know whether you remember Carl Osborne?"

"I never met him," Arthur Winner said. "I remember him

around, when they had that place out at Oakdale. What became of him?"

Julius Penrose said: "I wanted to know that myself. My recent studies in canon law revealed to me that if he was still living, the Roman view, in which Marjorie must of course acquiesce, was that no marriage ever subsisted between her and me—nor, could one; unless I wished to venture the considerable sums required to represent before the Curia in Rome that defects in consent had made invalid the union between Mr. Osborne and so-called Mrs. Osborne under canon ten eighty-three or canon ten eighty-six, which can plainly be read to void, if grace so directs the court—*stare decisis* is a principle, I discovered, unknown to their advocates—virtually any marriage at all; so the Roman rule on divorce is not nearly so oppressive at least, for the well-to-do, as non-Romanists may suppose. At any rate, I recently had Osborne traced. He's in an institution—which came as no great surprise to me. When Edmund Lauderdale read the notes of testimony in Marjorie's divorce, he impounded them in a hurry. Still, of that part—the remarkable list of duly substantiated indignities to the person—too much needn't be made. Females have resilient persons; and Marjorie's unpleasant experiences didn't create in her a revulsion against men."

Julius Penrose looked steadily at Arthur Winner for a moment. "Not even temporarily," he said. "A month or so after she left Osborne and retained me to start divorce proceedings, she was induced with no great difficulty to have an affair with me. Though we imagined it to be secret, I daresay it was known. In a lawyer-client relationship, I must unhesitatingly pronounce any such proceeding as the height of impropriety and imprudence."

"For one, I didn't know," Arthur Winner said. "This business disturbs you, I see."

"To a degree," Julius Penrose said. "To a degree! But don't lay that disclosure—not, I admit, in the best of taste—to overwrought feelings. I'm led by Marjorie's present plight to review as well as I can Marjorie's emotional history. The history's that of one who has been the dupe of designing persons. What made her so? Manifestly, the fact that her feelings, whether those

233

known or unknown to her, need only be reached. Reached, they unman her. You then take a firm line, and she'll do whatever you want."

A faint wince of pain—the partly wasted muscles in his hips or thighs must have cramped—passed on Julius's face. Impatiently, he lowered his elbows and, by a powerful heave, changed again the angle at which his legs rested. He said: "How, for instance, did Marjorie come to marry Osborne? Well; she'd probably say she doesn't know; at the time, she just felt she had to. She'd never think of asking herself why she felt she had to. Knowing her as I do, I could tell her. She felt she had to because he'd told her she had to. Indeed, since he often made the threat later, I think he may have said he'd kill himself if she didn't marry him. Very potent, with a natural-born dupe of the kindhearted kind! Could she bear to think of him being so unhappy, when all she had to do was say yes? Then, too; the affecting fact that he was crazy! Leaving college, Marjorie, determined to be a Career Woman, and actually imagining she had literary abilities (how typical that she could so mistake her bent or aptitudes!), went to work for a news magazine. I've often wondered how she could have got the job. She says she just went in and asked. Osborne was on the editorial staff. As nearly as I can judge, everyone who worked there was at least a little crazy; but he was more so."

Julius Penrose moved his head impatiently. "You have to think of the facts of the case as seen, all of them, through this daze of Marjorie's reached feelings. Does she observe that he's something of a drunk? Her heart's touched. She'll cherish him by drinking with him, by becoming something of a drunk, too. Does she discover—as she quickly did; he, of course, seduced her almost at once—that he's affected from time to time with what amounts to satyriasis, and that when the fit is on him, his tastes are likely to be sadistic? Marjorie finds that no impediment to marrying him. She may wring her hands; but if that's what he wants, she feels she must accommodate him."

Julius was silent, seeming to hesitate. He said: "I'd better be a little more specific, I think. 'Accommodate' is a vague term; you could form too tame or normal an idea of what was involved. During the last year of their life together, Osborne's whim was, on one occasion, to insist that Marjorie watch while he had intercourse with another woman, a house guest of theirs. Then, in more, perhaps, than fair exchange, he once brought home two men he'd met at a bar, and Marjorie was required to have intercourse with them, while *he* watched. Admittedly these were single episodes, and involved drunkenness. By that time, the Oakdale place had come to be known familiarly in the village as Alcoholic Hill. No doubt, as I say, Marjorie began drinking out of sympathy; but soon enough she was drinking out of what she conceived to be necessity. She early learned to read the signs; so when the signs told her tonight was the night, or this week end was the week end, she'd start getting as tight as she could. She didn't seem to see anything else to do. I'm not sure she'd ever have seen anything else to do if Osborne hadn't, at last, made a serious attempt—there was no doubt about it; he'd have been indicted if Marjorie hadn't refused to testify— to get rid of her by poisoning her."

"That, I never knew," Arthur Winner said. "How really shocking, Julius!"

"Yes, yes," Julius Penrose said. "What, for all we know, or trouble to imagine, any person may have behind him or her is nothing short of amazing. I thought that if you heard some of this, Marjorie, as seen over the years, would be clearer—or more explicable. Remember, to Marjorie, things are a perpetual surprise. She has the childish, almost animal, innocence that hardly connects cause and effect. Deeply discontented, she might feel she was not getting the things she needed; but why she wasn't getting them would always be beyond her. What did she need? Difficult to define; for the good reason that, being a joinder of incompatibles, the needed thing could not, in this life, exist."

Julius Penrose looked at the cane he held. He studied it a moment. He said: "Her need, I believe, was always dual—two needs, or types of needs; and, as I say, in their nature blindly antagonizing together. Most of the time, the need uppermost, the need in charge of the conscious Marjorie, was manifest in Marjorie's little-girl exterior—little-girl needs; pettings; treats; playtime; the story hour. Meeting these, if these were all, would present no problem—except perhaps of patience. But these were far from all. Inside the little girl, not showing most of the time, something quite other, with quite other needs, was implanted —a very part of her, too."

Dispassionate, he looked at Arthur Winner. He said: "We could call this, I think, the principle of passion. At first sight, the idea that such a principle would reside in someone like Marjorie must seem ridiculous. It resides in her notwithstanding. This principle neither trifles, nor is to be trifled with. When its times come, it simply takes over. The little girl's away for a while. Into her place steals, I think, something like a maenad. On a small scale, Marjorie has actually become that Fatal Woman of story and history. What, one asks one's self, is the secret of such disastrous power? The stories neglect to say. They only relate the thing accomplished. One sees Circe; one sees swine. What was in that cup?"

Thrusting his cane at a slant against the brace below his knee, Julius, with an expert twitch, levered his legs a little more to the right. He said: "Personally, I've no doubt that an incidence in these uncommon women of the true classic *furor uterinus,* an oestrual rage, is what does the job. Lying deep, it will usually lie, as well as hidden, quiescent. What discovers it? In some celebrated cases I have a poet to tell me that Anthony comes to supper, and for his ordinary pays his heart; Romeo gate-crashes a ball, and touching Juliet's, makes blessed his rude hand. In Marjorie's humbler case, discovery may be less startling. I conclude that a special, in one way or another, intimate, relationship develops first. The course of the relationship works Marjorie to some pitch of nervous emotion—what emotion, hardly matters; the reaching, penetrating of her feelings is all that counts. Her feelings sufficiently penetrated, the principle of passion, the interior rage—without its hostess's intention; maybe, without even her knowledge—is made to stir. The stir is electrifying. The unsuspecting, very probably astounded, male, in sudden erotic rapport with her, is beside himself. Seizing on him, rage answers rage. I venture to assert that when this gadfly's sting is fairly driven in, when this indefeasible urge of the flesh presses them, few men of normal potency prove able to refrain their foot from that path."

Tightening his fingers on the raised cane, studying the start-out of strong muscle in the back of his hand, Julius Penrose said: "I speak, of course, for and of myself; but I think, also, of Osborne. He being half-mad, his rage, his not-refraining, took half-mad forms. Thinking of those, one thinks first of Marjorie as his victim. If he is to accomplish an act of love, she has to be caused mental or physical anguish. Yet I must wonder if, and in a way quite fatal to him, he was not actually her victim. You see how?"

"You're, perhaps, ironic?" Arthur Winner said.

"No, I'm not," Julius Penrose said. "When I'm ironic you may be sure I mean to say this thing is nonsense. I can't so consider Osborne's plight. Marjorie, by being helpless and hapless, lured him on. He may be guessed to have found her practice of drunken submission insupportably exciting. Such a year-in, year-out round of excitements as Marjorie provided was debilitating to a damaged mind. Osborne, orginally half-mad, ended wholly mad. By comparison, Marjorie could, I suppose, be said to have got off unscathed. There, I'm, perhaps, ironic."

Arthur Winner said: "And, if he looks as if he might have money on him, a man becomes guilty of being hit on the head and robbed, if he is?"

"Indeed, I think him guilty, if he takes that look of money where hittings-on-the-head and robbings are accepted means of livelihood," Julius Penrose said. "But I find no parallel, because I think the drinking and submitting deserves a closer look. I feel sure that, as far as Marjorie knew, she didn't like what Osborne made her do, or did to her. How could she like these things? Often, they'd be physically painful; mentally, or if you like, spiritually, they were abominable—revolting debasements; studied outrages; systematic violations of all the sensibilities. Who but the maniac forcing her to them could desire them? My considered answer: Marjorie, though all unknowing, could! She could see such a punishment as condign. She had to submit, because in an anguished way, she craved to have done to her

237

what she was persuaded she deserved to have done to her."

He gazed an instant at Arthur Winner. "You find this far-fetched?" he said. "Yes; we who are so normal are reluctant to entertain such ideas; yet that, I believe, was the true why of it. Identifying anything so far removed from consciousness is guess-work. I make the obvious guess—she harbors a consuming sense of guilt. Knowing the principle of passion residing in her, aware of how the maenad could be made to materialize, she gets no rest from that guilt. She must do something in propitiation. For her pleasure, the pleasure that the maenad cannot be denied, she must pay in pain. The situation then becomes this: A mad-man, as perhaps only a madman could, divines her true state. He perceives her principle of passion, and the potentialities, to him exciting, of Marjorie's guilt about it. At the same time, that guilt of Marjorie's, though Marjorie is quite unconscious of anything but powerful feelings that she 'has' to 'love' the madman, perceives *his* potentialities—by him, every pleasure will be properly punished. She is led to throw herself at Osborne. People, I think, are to be pitied! You consider this too complicated?"

Arthur Winner said: "Perhaps not. But I've often wondered how far anyone can see into what goes on in someone else. I've read somewhere that it would pose the acutest head to draw forth and discover what is lodged in the heart."

Julius Penrose said: "Yes: good! No; I don't insist that these goings on were exactly, in every particular, as stated. Dichoto-mies of the sort are seldom clear-cut. The parts of a person's mind merge; they change; those once dominant may be superceded; some seem to die; others are born. In Marjorie's case, her final fear for her life served, I think, to relieve her specific guilt. The guilt sense has little use for logic; a last supreme fear may have ended the need that kept her with Osborne. I don't know. At least, at last, she was able to break with him. Next time, she was not to be so lucky."

He looked once more at Arthur Winner. "Yes," he said, "I, too, was a deceiver. For compelling the still-Mrs. Osborne to an affair with me, I'll excuse myself. I don't consider that I wronged or harmed her—the contrary, rather! I think, since she did not know the real reason for her experiences, that secret wish of hers to have them, she imagined there might be something wrong with her as a woman that made normal acts of love impossible. When she found, through me, that this was not the case, I think she regarded me with gratitude. I mean to say, I reached her feelings."

He paused an instant. "No," he said, "I was never the man that I allowed—even, led—her reached feelings to see me as. I was not the man to meet any of her conflicting needs. I had a nature detached and analytical. What Marjorie would take to be my scornfulness and my cynicism were bound to make their appearance, and bound to hurt her. Here was no nice little boy for a little girl to play house with! On the other hand, neither was I a fit instrument for the visiting maenad. The passion I protested was, in a sense, not really mine—not the natural-born sexual athlete's spontaneous expression. It was a temporary response to novelty that the rage in her provoked. Novelty gone, the normally moderate man would too soon lapse into moderation. His analytical mind must, too soon, remind him that this pleasure is, after all, brief; and this position is, after all, ridiculous. Loss of interest may be expected."

Julius Penrose smiled sharply at Arthur Winner. He said: "Of course, the interest's a renewable one. Some regular recurrence could be counted on—quite enough to content most little girls, where a little girl is all there is to content. Here it was different; though I think I could say that Marjorie as maenad was served no worse by me than she would have been by most men. Our known national ordering of habit and convenience that makes, for millions, Saturday night connubial love night—or, not to overornament what must be the fact in more bedrooms than not, the scheduled time for discharge of the seminal vesicle —certifies as much to me."

Raising his hand, Julius Penrose yawned. "The plea's a poor one," he said. "I don't enter it. That defendant's no different from many other men is immaterial. *I* fell down on a job I asked for, I insisted on taking, I engaged to do. Marjorie didn't expect her seduction to lead to marriage. She was, in fact, most reluctant to be made an honest woman of. Though not able to

239

phrase her reluctance, she felt the unwisdom of what I proposed; and, for that moment, I now see, she was far ahead of me in intuitive understanding. But she was also weak; and I'm the man for a firm line. She couldn't bear to wound me with a rejection. So when her decree was made absolute, I directed her to present herself with me before your friend of this evening, Joe Harbison. She, of course, obeyed. We were united. For this, I must answer! I exercised undue influence. For this, I can invent no good excuses. I perpetrated a fraud. Here, I *did* wrong her; here, I harmed her."

Taking the arms of his chair in both hands, Julius Penrose made to rise. Seeing him move, Arthur Winner had risen immediately. "Yes," Julius Penrose said, "if you please! I always like to try. I keep having the fatuous notion that I'll suddenly find I can. All I ever find is that once really well down, I can't. I must get the Ingoldsby folder."

Bending to give Julius a purchase on his arm, Arthur Winner said: "I'll get it for you." Straightening himself, he brought them both erect; and Julius neatly swung his canes in place. "If you please!" he said again. A darkness of anger entered his face. "Hell and death, I tire of this, sometimes! I think I'm reasonable. At my age, I wouldn't ask to run the hundred yards in ten seconds. I'd ask only the privilege of moving around a room like anyone else, of walking with my feet, not my hands."

"And, very little to ask," Arthur Winner said.

Julius Penrose said: "Forgive me, Arthur! Since, yourself, you do nothing stupid and say nothing silly, in my place, I think you'd not waste breath in vain repinings. You are kind to overlook mine. And that, on top of sitting silent while I talk and talk! One perceives you see it's, indeed, compensatory! I can do little; so I say much. I suppose such feats of comprehending are why I love you. Yes; fetch the folder; and be quick, since you're able to be!"

Making his laborious but practiced way after Arthur Winner into the outer office, Julius Penrose said suddenly: "Where did you think of seeing Marjorie?"

Arthur Winner pulled out a drawer of the correspondence

file. While he flicked over the index tabs, he said: "I'd thought of calling her in the morning when I got back from the court-house and asking if she could come down here."

Julius Penrose said: "If by any means you could manage to, I'd just as soon you met her—or them—at Roylan. Mrs. Pratt, the truth is, attracts attention. She has a car quite as large and costly as Mr. Marple's; and the one I saw last was the color of a daffodil. I shrink somewhat to think of Brocton gapers observing her and Marjorie drawing up outside here. Not that I mightn't be wise to accustom myself, as soon as possible, to Marjorie being stared at. She will, I suppose, soon be taking the station wagon, and for the period of a mass, leaving it parked with that dismayingly endless Sunday morning range of cars one sees crowding the curbs around the new Our Lady of Mount Carmel. Well, no help; so, no matter! Yet, meanwhile—" He broke off; and said abruptly: "Clarissa wouldn't like the idea of this talk? She doesn't like the idea?"

Arthur Winner said: "She knows Marjorie wanted to talk to me. She felt, and I must admit I agreed with her, that it wasn't likely anything would be accomplished; and that, in fact, you might not thank me for interfering. She thought I ought, per-haps, to tell Marjorie that I simply couldn't go into it with her."

"Good advice!" Julius Penrose said. "Sound sense! One should be wary when people try to make their business yours. I'd not ask so much of you, Arthur, if it weren't that I feel (I would!) that the situation is a special one—the sort of thing you might be of help in. Who knows? Your manner of reasonableness might restore a balance. I withdraw the Roylan suggestion. See them here."

Arthur Winner said: "I can see them there. I'd thought, I sup-pose, of arranging things so I could remark that I'd talked to Marjorie—instead of announcing that I was going to talk to her. But since—"

"Yes; but since!" Julius Penrose said. "I, too, think seeing her and saying nothing would be ill-considered. How very strange that you said nothing! Down that road, there's always trouble. Could you put it to Clarissa that you were seeing Marjorie only because I asked you to? Would that be sufficiently near the truth? I think so. Put it to her."

"I'll do that, if you don't mind," Arthur Winner said.

Carrying the file folder, he came into the hall with Julius and opened the screen door on the front steps. Out in the hot night, in the pale flood of street lighting, he gave Julius his arm; and, supporting his weight, went down the steps with him. From the long black car, the chauffeur started with alacrity, swinging open the rear door. Arthur Winner could see, in the shadowed front seat, the shape of the poodle, head alertly turned.

Preparing himself to make the toilsome transfer from the pavement to the car's interior, Julius Penrose said: "Ah, Pettengill; thank you! Ah, Valentine!"

Hearing her name directed at her, the dog lifted her muzzle. She uttered one clear short bark.

"What enchanting intelligence! What a ravishing creature!" Julius Penrose said. "Were I younger, sound, and a single man, I'd ask her to marry me."

NINE

Arthur Winner's car stood in the narrow parking space paved with concrete, shut in by the backs of buildings, behind the office. The office lights put out, the doors locked, he had gone to it through the rear entrance. While he stood in the sultry dark, feeling a damp of sweat on his face, searching his pockets for the car keys, to his ears came an expected sound; dull; at first hardly to be heard; then, growing gradually, momentarily prolonging itself; then, dying in heavy stillness—the unmistakable mutter, the menacing ruffle far off of thunder slowly falling on thunder. From aloft in the thick night, the courthouse clock across the street spoke profound and unhurried—the sombrous strokes of eleven.

Arthur Winner started the car. Moving carefully along the path of radiance with which his headlights filled the narrow alley to Court Street, Arthur Winner halted to look right and left. At the lower corner, near the First National Bank, a group of people, several of them women, sauntered together. A street light cast their long shadows ahead of them. Someone called out something, and they all laughed boisterously. Looking the other way, Arthur Winner saw, through the corner of the courthouse grounds, the still-lighted steps of the Union League. A lone figure descended them. By soldierly erectness, as well as by slight, controlled tiltings off the perpendicular, this could be recognized as Colonel Minton. His time had come to proceed to what would be the last bar of his evening. Down from that corner, the headlights of a single car approached. Arthur Winner waited. The car, driven in a leisurely way, slid through the

243

shafts of Arthur Winner's headlights, gleaming bright scarlet. It was Rodney Revere. In the manner disapproved of by Noah Tuttle, a colored girl, smiling and prettily dressed, rested in affectionate repose against Rodney. With a grand sweep, Rodney curved into Federal Street.

As though to meet Rodney, another single car, sedate and dark, was coming up Federal Street; and, indeed, at the sudden wave of Rodney's arm, an arm appeared in answer, waving back. The car was Judge Lowe's, which Rodney's cousin Harcourt drove for the judge. Slowing, it went to the curb before the Federal House—Mr. Woolf was being delivered to his lodging. On an impulse, in some freak of tiredness disinclined to drive past, by any chance to be seen, Arthur Winner turned right on Court Street, heading in the other direction. He could go the slightly longer way out Greenwood Avenue to the Oakdale road, down that, crossing the river by the upper bridge, and so gaining the highway.

As he entered Greenwood Avenue, Arthur Winner's headlights swept through the deserted stone close of Christ Church—he must remember to speak to Doctor Trowbridge tomorrow. He must tell him why bringing up the question of the Orcutt bequest and the Diocesan Trust at the vestry meeting Monday wasn't advisable. Presumably the rector would be disappointed; and there'd be no reason not to tell him who was named succeeding trustee. Doctor Trowbridge could have at least the hopeful thought that his wish might not go too many years unrealized, that Mr. Tuttle was old, that he could not live forever.

Down the night-bound avenue, spaced street lights were shrouded by the overarch of big trees. No one was to be seen on the sidewalks. No cars moved. Looking ahead to his mother's house, Arthur Winner saw windows still bright—in the living room on the ground floor; and, to his surprise, two others, shining through the tree branches, higher up. He identified them at once as windows in that round tower built into the corner of the house—a piece of Victorian ostentation studying to please an age that looked at ostentation with respect. The tower room had been called the "den"—a term that, today, must prompt the same smile that the tower prompted.

Fitted in part as a workshop, in part as a study, the "den" had been Arthur Winner Senior's retreat, a place where he was not to be disturbed. It was exempt from all housecleaning routines. Lining the walls were the books that really interested him—on gardening; on fly-casting; on antiques—as opposed to formal sets displayed downstairs in the "library." Tables and little workbenches held the equipment he needed for the smaller sort of fixing jobs—clockmaker's and jewelers' tools and lenses; little lathes; little vises. The battered articles of furniture were not of the kind that Arthur Winner Senior, with so much taste and judgment, brought home for use in other rooms. Here, he kept an old tufted couch, an adjustable graceless Morris chair; an ugly roll-top desk. The Man of Reason, sensitive to both, did not confuse beauty with utility.

Passing the house, Arthur Winner looked up the lawn. Through those front windows that went to the floor, he was able to see deep into the lighted living room. At a small Sheraton card table—one of his father's early prizes—his mother and his Aunt Maud faced each other. Both sat motionless; both looked lost in thought. On the table between them would be, Arthur Winner knew, the card spread of a teasingly complicated form of double solitaire. Since this was after bedtime, the game tonight must have proved unusually difficult, refusing to come out. Arthur Winner looked again at the mysterious lit windows high in the house. His mother, or his Aunt Maud, had gone to the never-used room, put a light on; and then, leaving, left the light. Forgotten, it shone inscrutable. What could possibly have been wanted there? Ought Arthur Winner to stop? Unless he came in, told them, and went up and turned it off for them, the light would burn all night—well, let it burn all night!

He was past. He could make out the obscure mass of the Tuttle house next—closed; boarded up; knee-high weeds and long grass were now the lawn. Rusted padlocks secured the iron gates of the carriage drive. Fifty years ago, residents of Greenwood Avenue, shocked at such a blight on their "nice" street, would have called it an eyesore. Today, who noticed? Nobody wanted those old oversized houses; uncared-for vacancy was their natural state. The drifting, forlorn thoughts of disuse and decay returned

Arthur Winner to that lonely unexplained upstairs light in his mother's house. Less than serious, vague, sad, nonsensical notions proposed themselves to the melancholy mind. The card players downstairs all unaware, could another hand, a hand that knew just where to find the switch, have reached and put that light on? Would that hand, when what was looked for had been found or not found, reach and turn the light off? No; never! Mummied, shrunk on the bones, that dexterous hand was recumbent in Christ Church cemetery. Mindless, obedient agent, that hand had served its onetime master faithfully and well. Better and more faithfully, you might conclude—with sinking spirits, Arthur Winner could feel true experience's malaise: Ye shall know the truth; and the truth shall make you sick!—than mind, the master's more regarded servant. Mind made the Man of Reason duly reasonable; the thinking reed duly thought. Too good for this world, good sense had its comeuppance!

In the cool and calm of the Man of Reason's mind no place was found for fusses over nothing. That dry, rational self-command was almost absolute—no admission to the weak man's ignominious worrying about himself, his coward alarm over trifles. Thus, the Man of Reason did not hurry to bring trifling symptoms—especially, when the chief trifle was ignoble, undignified, half-comic; no more than stubborn constipation—to a physician's attention. The physician to whose attention he casually, when occasion happened to offer, did bring his symptoms was old Doctor Albert Shaw, Reggie Shaw's not-yet-retired father. Old Doctor Shaw was a physician of ripe experience. He palpated the Man of Reason's abdomen. He found no cause for concern. As people aged (the doctor himself was seventy), functions altered. Arthur Winner Senior was sixty-six; that was the answer. Let him try some changes in diet. To the Man of Reason, this sounded reasonable; to the inconveniences of aging, philosophy's tranquilizing consolations must be opposed. It was Reggie Shaw, seeing patients of his father's while the old doctor was on a fishing trip, who thought otherwise. His concern was instant and active. Medicine is an inexact science; and this, of

246

course, was months later. Earlier, Reggie might very well have been unconcerned, too.

The heavy story needed no going over. To the height of this great argument, to justify to men these ways of nature, no tongue or pen ever successfully asserted anything—that was impossible. As of course, nature's inhumanity to man passed even man's to man. With tremorless calm, Arthur Winner Senior accepted the quickly reached decision. To assurances that the outlook was not unfavorable, he gave courteous assent. The Man of Reason, Arthur Winner supposed, knew better; but if his reassurers were cheered to think they were cheering him, why not help them think that? The operation was a success. Skill and science, in wonder-working union, paraded some of their then latest amazing resources. Only a few years before, this patient must have died; but not now. Or, at least; now, he need not die right away. He could serve his hospital term, clothe himself in his clothing, and be brought home.

What was this, if not success, if not recovery? Yet, soon apparent became the truth that the physical organism, so miraculously left viable, was not young enough to readjust, to survive the terrible mutilation of its "cure." More than that—an aspect of the known truth that memory made every effort to throw out, that the secrecy clause of the Hippocratic oath went to: the doctor must keep this quiet; no one must tell!—things had happened to more than the Man of Reason's body. Far from the separate, superior entity he seemed, plainly he had been part and parcel of the mutilated organism, a mere quick coal of mortal fire. A colostomy had been resorted to; and this somewhat disgusting method of relief seemed to shock further a nervous system already wrecked by shock. The failing nerves, the radically resected gut, the wasting frame, lacked means to support such extras as humor and courage. The Man of Reason had to go. Actually, he died at the hospital. Many weeks later, at home, Arthur Winner Senior died, too.

Past the corner of Magnolia Street, Arthur Winner went by

the Detweiler house—another large house; but the outmoded architecture was that of the early nineteen hundreds; unnecessary steep expanses of slanting roof; oversized graceless verandas of no practical use. In point of physical appearance, the earlier Greenwood Avenue would not have seen it as an eyesore. Helen's tidiness put her to the considerable expense of keeping things up. Yet, being in bald fact a boarding house, what a social blemish, what an affront to the select old street's high respectability!

Windows of the Detweiler house were all dark. Most of Helen's boarders—an elderly assistant manager of the Brocton Potteries; a young chemist working in the Ingoldsby Mills laboratory; and two woman schoolteachers—must be in bed. Colonel Minton, who had a room there, was, of course, still out. Helen, exhausted by her day on the rack of emotion, presumably slept. Ralph, exhausted by his frightening evening, presumably slept, too. Or, did both of them lie awake, sickening themselves with worry? Light from the street showed Arthur Winner Ralph's car standing in the drive. A contention of the court's juvenile officers was that the automobile got today's kids into Ralph's kind of trouble; and Arthur Winner supposed they might be right. Ralph and the foolish "Joanie" made the living-room sofa serve their turn; but how often? Didn't Ralph, probably telling the truth, say—once? True; those fornication and bastardy records from the old dockets appeared to prove that the Miss Kovacses of another day, females of ardor, were little hampered by lack of modern transportation. With the buggy and the haymow they made do very well; but a question could remain whether, given the restricting inconveniences of those days, the Miss Moores, the ones who really didn't want to, who asked why if two people loved each other they couldn't love each other enough to wait, weren't better able to keep to their preferred course of virtue.

This likelihood granted, opportunity's enormous guilt conceded, ought one to go further? Arthur Winner thought again of that call on him he had told Julius Penrose about, of the plumpish priest's more and more incensed remonstrances. Was Rome, in its generation, always wiser than the self-supposed

248

children of light? Did Father Albright, red with vexation, have a point? Was his recipe of: see no sex, hear no sex, speak no sex, the best one? Whatever a cleric's presumptive personal in-experience with this passion; however limited he might be in intelligence and perception by those traits of character he was required to give proof of before he could be allowed to have a "vocation," he was schooled (leaving him with no real need to experience; nor even any special need to think or perceive) to pronounce the preserved instruction of centuries.

Here, that instruction seemed to be that carnal thoughts, im-ages of lust, were of their own devilish motion unendingly ready to insert themselves in every human consciousness. To plan, intentionally and deliberately, to agitate, to raise the sub-ject, to invite adolescents to morose delectation—what folly! What wickedness! That you did the raising in a form (you thought!) sober and wholesome was altogether irrelevant. It was not what you thought; it was what they thought. Among the young unmarried, this subject was never safely raised. The very saints in their self-accusations bore witness that it polluted the holiest minds. As for other minds; did you presume to for-get of what nature were the frequent meditations of your own heart?

A last street light hung above Greenwood Avenue's termina-tion on the Oakdale road. The village of Oakdale, a few houses gathered on either side of the road, lay four miles north. On a rise not far beyond, along what was called the Ridge Road, was the "farm" Carl Osborne once owned—Alcoholic Hill! The name was not, in fact, applied specifically to the Osborne place. Osborne's was one of several such "farms." City people with no local connections or interests had bought them and provided them with drilled wells, plumbing, and inevitably, swimming pools. They were places of week-end retirement, far off and se-cluded, from the standpoint of their owners. All these owners, like Osborne, came from New York; like him, they all seemed to be mixed up with one or the other of the arts or trades of self-expression; like him, they had a way of life the villagers regarded as riotous.

What went on at the Osbornes'—those ordeals of Marjorie's

249

—could not have been widely known; and of course there was no reason to presume that similar dark secrets lurked in other places. Of record, glimpsed by spying yokels or reported by hired "help," were, however, drunken antics and crazy escapades. At one party, a decision was reached to burn the old barn; and the blaze was a spectacular success. The local fire company, arriving unsummoned, had been reassured, invited to stay and watch; and the volunteers got home, most of them, drunk. There had been occasions when the singing and the shouting on the ridge lasted all night. Arthur Winner understood that some of the original revelers still lived there, or still came out there summers; but age must have made them more circumspect. Time and perhaps the ill-health of excess had reformed them. Did they gain wisdom; or did they lose spirit? At any rate, the revels, silly or scandalous, now were ended.

Arthur Winner turned south, away from Oakdale, toward the river bridge. Through the night-bound fields and bits of black woodland he drove faster, intent on getting home. He was tired; yet, watching the tarred road surface extend progressively down the tunnel of light that the car pushed swiftly ahead, a habit of thought—of, you might say, settling things for the night, brought him back to consider Ralph Detweiler again —one last, professional, short check (on which he would sleep) of the case at law. Ought Julius Penrose's idea about Brophy's possible interest of malice be taken under serious advisement? Even if it became by any chance, or by any means, in Jerry's power to ensure by some manipulation of evidence, a guilty verdict, would making the attempt be in character?

Arthur Winner thought not. Perhaps Jerry occasionally (such a surprise!) grasped, as Julius said, at intangibles. Those intangibles would surely have something for Jerry in them. Jerry's constant obliging effort was to do anybody any favor that, as district attorney, he legally could. The chance he never seemed to miss was profiting himself by making a friend. Unless he had an immediate important object—say: teaching someone that injuring Jerry didn't pay—would Jerry waste present time on things past? When opposing counsel was a lawyer of Arthur Winner's experience, Jerry would know he couldn't hope to conceal his unusual maneuvers to convict, or his play to a jury, for very long. Would gratified malice be worth not only all the trouble of cooking the case, but the perfect certainty that for the rest of his professional life he would have against him, hostile to him, a man not good to have against you, a man of the first influence among members of the bar?

Or was this comfortable conclusion the old ordinary error of letting yourself suppose men to be all of a piece; of assigning them, from your scraps of observation, "characters" in which (for your convenience and readier comprehension) they were always to act? What Julius suggested was, after all, no more than the rule of experience—the practical, profit-minded, friend-hunting, politician usually animating Jerry Brophy, not only could have, but almost certainly, must have, his hours, perhaps his whole days, off. Arthur Winner thought: Yes, I'd better see if I can arrange for Reggie to examine Miss Kovacs.

The road before Arthur Winner began to rise, bending to the approach of the short but high-set iron truss frame by which the upper bridge spanned the narrow river. On the glare-lit macadam appeared suddenly, with a sluggish scurry, a small frantic animal—an opossum, Arthur Winner saw. Whether blinded, whether horrified, the opossum pulled up. He wavered on his handlike feet; his scaly snake tail gave a twitch of terror; his little shining eyes stared in despair. He made to go back. He made to go on. The car, too close to be stopped or slowed, swept at him. Mercy's idiot impulse—to swerve, certainly crashing the guardrail, and spare the innocent creature—was corrected in an instant. Driving straight on, Arthur Winner felt the gentle jar of the left rear wheel passing over the plump furred body. Riding smooth again, the car, with an easy swift rumble, took its tonnage onto the bridge's plank flooring.

✦

Arthur Winner was home. He drove in his own gate; and the soft scrunch of the raked gravel sounded under him. The house's lighted lower hall showed through the front door, left standing open on the hot night; and, as he proceeded, he saw

251

upstairs the bright windows of Clarissa's room. Between the syc-amores' big trunks, his headlights passed across the gently roll-ing, smoothly mowed long stretches of grass. Swinging farther, on their way to shaft into the garage, whose ranged overhead doors were up, the headlights reached and lit for a moment, deep in the little wood along the brook, an octagonal summer house. The once white-frosted, wedding-cake fanciness of scroll-work and lattice had a nearly paintless, ghostlike look of neg-lect; and indeed it was neglected, never now made use of. It was a relic of those very much more extensive works of garden-ing to which, for so many years, Hope enthusiastically devoted herself—a passionate interest more fully shared, the truth was, with Arthur Winner's father than with Arthur Winner.

Over there, toward the brook, in the little wood, Hope and her father-in-law had delightedly planned and developed—though neither knew it, this was to be the last of many such engrossing projects—a "wild" garden, a collection of native plants in natural settings. To people who were not gardeners, that might sound simple. In fact, the undertaking was of ex-traordinary difficulty; for experts only. The material, the shy plants, the charming and delicate small flowers, lacked the adaptability of cultivated hybrids. Each and every exacting de-mand of varying soil condition and surroundings must be met if you were to succeed with them. Sagaciously and happily, Hope and her father-in-law caused them to be met. With infinite patience, they coaxed patches of trailing arbutus to spread. Clumps of the small wild columbine were established. Down in a spot that was damp enough, they persuaded fringed gentians to grow. Ferns in remarkable variety, their tastes for sun or shade suited, crowded the path. Not interested in gardening as a youth, Arthur Winner Junior, living in Roylan after his mar-riage, had been brought to find an interest in the simpler mat-ter of growing roses. Before long, he was even competent to admire these higher horticultural exploits—the way to the sum-mer house, winding through the wild garden, seemed to him very pleasant. He appreciated the art in concealing art that made such plantings—not to say, the art, inspired and open, that set the lacy, airy, altogether artificial summer house to be come upon in a contrast with the seeming natural that must amuse and delight. Yet, left to him, these works of yesterday disappeared. Plainly, his had never been that engrossed interest, that real enthusiasm, stirring in those happy co-workers, the eager girl, his wife; the elderly man, his father.

How pleasant the picture of that serene relationship! As Arthur Winner's mother remarked, her husband, though busy with so many things, was an unhurried man. He liked to have tea in the afternoon; and so did his daughter-in-law. On nice days in spring and summer, he would often find time to drive out to Roylan. Arthur Winner could see again, on afternoons late in May, or early in June, his father—the figure, graying, gracefully spare; the composed face with the dry but warm smile —getting with neatness, but with the care of those no longer young, from his car, halted here by the garage. The arrival had been witnessed. Hope, working in some part of her perennial borders, would drop her trowel. Like a girl, she came scampering, out of breath. The delicate thin-skinned face shielded from sun by a floppy-brimmed gardening hat might this day glow with jubilation. Today, she had something to show "Father Winner." Pulling her loose gloves off, seizing him by the hand, she led him down a brilliant afternoon to the wood of the wild garden. Here was a triumph—their triumph! *Cypripedium acaule,* the pink lady's-slipper, satisfied with the homelike setting so painstakingly provided, was embarked at last on its mysterious process of reproduction. Where three had been before, there were going to be ten! On her knees, looking up ecstatic at her father-in-law, Hope showed him the tiny first leaves appearing at random over the sloped bank of dry old pine needles. Oh, wasn't it wonderful!

There were other things, strolling around together (in this, how good they could not know, his final spring) that he was anxious to see, and she was anxious to show him while they waited for tea to be brought to that charming summer house. The summer house, as you would expect, had been found by Arthur Winner Senior. Originally, the so-called "kiosk" stood among the too many pretentious, tastelessly placed, lawn furnishings of the "gentleman's country seat" created soon after the Civil War for

Ezra Orcutt out of those fine profits the Brocton Potteries were realizing from their early patent water-closet bowls. At the auction settling Ezra's estate—the "seat" was being torn down to make way for a building development—Arthur Winner Senior bid in the summer house for next to nothing (the moving did cost something, however!). That selective glance, unconfused, unimpressed by what at any moment might be fashionable or popular, could pick unfailingly from the thousand abominations produced by such jigsaw work and senseless ornament, the one example—perhaps, the only one in the world—that, in a miracle or accident of perfect frivolous means to a perfect frivolous end, instead of offending, charmed the sensitive eye.

Continuing with his thought, necessarily saddened, of how people who were now dead had once been happy, Arthur Winner remembered the circumstances of the summer house's arrival. Long secure in the knowledge that his selective taste was also Hope's, Arthur Winner Senior had the amusing, delightful structure trucked to Roylan, placed to best advantage in the little wood, and freshly painted, during Hope's absence. The work went on while Hope was at the hospital when Ann was born. On her home-coming, wan though she was, Hope, at sight of her present, flushed with pleasure. Did she like it? Weak though she was, Hope clapped her hands. With rapture, she turned and kissed her husband's father.

Arthur Winner ran the car into the garage. Drawing down the overhead doors, he heard through the hot dark, that sound of thunder again. The sound was fainter and duller; the storm was in the hills—going, not coming. A fairly steady low on-and-off flicker of lightning let him see by recurring illumination, the mass of the house, the great still trees, the surface of the drive, the long lawns. In such uncertain dimness, he was a moment making out—at first, he thought he must be mistaken—something that moved, a figure approaching. The figure's shape seemed small and short—a boy, perhaps, wearing what appeared to be white trousers, walking ghostlike from the direction of the summer house.

254

Astounded, standing still, Arthur Winner said: "Ann?" A somewhat stronger flare on the verge of the horizon showed him Marjorie Penrose.

Moving quicker, coming close, she said in a low voice: "It's me, Arthur. I was up there." In obscure movement, her head nodded back to indicate the summer house. "I was sitting there. Oh, don't worry!" Her voice broke with a sound like an unhappy laugh. "You needn't worry. I'm all right, Arthur. I'm not being crazy again. I'm not going to do anything crazy." In renewed weak light reflected from the heavy sky, Arthur Winner saw that she had on slacks and a sweater—the costume of the morning that Clarissa spoke of, he supposed. The scent she was using—heliotrope?—reached him. Though it was quite strong, mingled with it, definitely discernible, was another scent— whisky. Marjorie said: "Julius saw you?"

"Yes. I was at the office. I saw him there. The car took him on to New York."

Marjorie said: "Yes." She prolonged a pause which the fading thunder, rolling fainter, more remote, filled. "I didn't know whether you'd want me to talk to you, Arthur. I've no right to ask it, really. So I thought I'd come and wait here. And if you don't want to; tell me."

Arthur Winner said: "Marjorie, if there's anything I can do, I'll be glad to do it. But hadn't we better talk tomorrow?"

"Yes, tomorrow," Marjorie said.

The lightning flared weakly; the night returned to darkness. On Arthur Winner's arm she laid a hand; but instantly she withdrew it; and Arthur Winner realized that he must have started. She said: "I'm sorry." In a new waver, ever dimmer, of the lightning he made out her face, the lips darkened with lipstick twisting to a sad smile. She said: "There's so much I need to say. Things I have to explain—things I want to explain to you."

Disturbed, Arthur Winner could smell the whisky again; but she spoke clearly. "Julius will listen to you; and you're the only person he listens to. It's because he thinks almost everybody's a fool. He thinks I am; and, oh, I am! But I know he loves me, too." Her obscure motion was that of her hands brought up and clasped together tight to her breast. "It's a love I'm not worthy of—" She choked a little; she seemed to falter into incoherence. "And, well, things that happened have always been my fault, never his, never anyone else's. I've wanted to say that, have you know I know. I'm the trouble—"

Clarissa probably heard the car coming in. Soon she would wonder what kept him. Arthur Winner must suppose Marjorie could guess his thought, for she said quickly: "I know, Arthur. I'm going in a minute. While I waited there in the summer house—"

Arthur Winner said: "Marjorie, I don't think Julius feels—"

"No, I'm the trouble." She spoke with patient pain. "I understand that, now. You see, I've come to realize your sins will find you out—they must; they do; and then you know whose they are. Yours and only yours." The least lighting of the thick dark showed her parted lips repeating the sad smile. "Sometimes, soon; sometimes, later; and sometimes they find you out in ways you might not think of. I'm not saying what I mean, Arthur; but I know what I mean. I mean, perhaps people can never find out exactly what you did, unless you tell them, confess to them. But whether you tell them or not, sooner or later, something you do or say tells them you did something. They feel it; and then they can't like you. Nobody wants anything to do with you."

Made uncomfortable by an awareness that, though this pain of Marjorie's was real, and hurt her, she still found in it (Julius was not wrong!) some sort of harrowing enjoyment, Arthur Winner said: "Marjorie, I think you imagine—"

She said: "No. Ask Clarissa. You see, she meant to be friends with me. Because of you and Julius; and she knew what friends Hope and I had been." In her voice was a sudden sound of tears. "Be sure of that always, Arthur! I adored Hope. Hope was everything I would have wished to be. Her death—something in me died, too."

A play of lightning, so faint and far off as possibly to be the last from the storm that had not come, paled the heavy dark long enough for Arthur Winner, looking down, to see the faint shine of wetness on Marjorie's cheeks, the tears wrung from her. Like the pain, they were real; a fact; yet what evoked them,

Arthur Winner must remember, was half or more a fiction. Hope, gentle to everyone, had not failed to be gentle to, to put up with, Marjorie; but that picture of what friends they had been was one of later emotional fancy. Marjorie said: "How I used to feel about Hope, I know now, was almost the only good thing in me. But because I, the rest of me, wasn't good, nothing good could stay with me; because I'd do something bad with it. You see, I said a dreadful thing to Clarissa once."

Now that no relief of rain was coming, the still heat of the night seemed to increase. The darkness was so deep that Arthur Winner could hardly see the face before him. He said: "Marjorie, this is a little hysterical—"

She said: "Please, Arthur! I have to tell you. I'd been drinking. I know now that was all part of it. I wasn't to be allowed to have Clarissa for a friend; so I had to be made to say what I said. If I was drinking, I'd be sure to say it; so I had to drink. What I told her was that she needn't imagine she could ever be to you what Hope had been. You hadn't been married long then; and I knew Clarissa would be thinking sometimes—she'd have to—of how here she was where Hope used to be; and you'd lived with Hope for years; and you'd only lived with her a few months. And—"

Arthur Winner said: "Marjorie, Clarissa would see how you happened to say it; she wouldn't seriously—"

"I said more, too—that she was just a thing you had for going to bed with. You see, I could tell that, up till then, she'd never been to bed with a man; and that she was liking it; and that whether she ought to so much, whether you'd think she ought to, was worrying her. Clarissa knew I knew. She knew I meant to hurt her where I saw I could; and so she knew what I was. I'd been made to show her." She began, not quite silently, to cry again. "I'd have gone on my bended knees to take that back as soon as I'd said it; but, of course, I'd had to say something that couldn't ever be taken back. That was how I had to pay. Good night, Arthur, dear."

Marjorie Penrose turned, a motion sensed as much as seen. Yet in the dark, she seemed to have something of a cat's sight that let her move quickly away, down the drive without uncertainty, toward home. While Marjorie had been speaking, another passage of lightning, hardly to be discerned, had shown itself. Now, sometime after, followed thunder, a thudding, dying fall that barely reached the ear, a murmur fading into heavy silence.

"Good night, Marjorie," Arthur Winner said. He stood a moment, disturbed. Only then, when she was gone, and he turned toward the house, did he remember that no arrangement had been made about tomorrow.

✦

Arthur Winner said: "So that's how we stand. If we come to trial, I expect to be able to get him off. Of course, the Moore girl's another matter. He isn't obliged to marry her; and he may, as you told Fred, be too young to marry; but he doesn't seem to be too young to get her with child—"

"What a nasty boy!" Clarissa said. In her nightgown, she was sitting with a pillow behind her on her turned-down bed. From the bed's head, a reading lamp focused, in the otherwise shadowed room, a glow past her shoulder to a book in her lap. Reflecting up, the glow gilded her clear features. Her head was bound in a blue scarf—she had washed her hair. As she listened, she had been frowning a little; and now she frowned more. "And girls are such fools!" she said. "I admit I can't help feeling most of it's their fault. If they weren't such fools, the boys might have to behave themselves!"

She spoke with energy; and Arthur Winner could guess that, for an instant, she had recovered earlier feelings of her own—the onetime Clarissa Henderson's mettle; her spirit, fierce for whatever hidden reasons, of engaging independence. She disdained fool girls and their silliness. She scorned and despised the oafish boys who might or might not meditate putting their hands on her, working their nastinesses on her. She looked indignantly at Arthur Winner. Laughing, she said: "Well, they are, *too,* fools!"

"No doubt," Arthur Winner said. "But how many sensible and intelligent boys do you find? Perhaps they're made for each other." He moved through the open door connecting his bedroom with hers. Clarissa laughed again. "Are we going to have a storm?" she said. "A bad one seemed to be coming at the lake; I thought it would catch us before we got home. But nothing happened."

"That, or another, now seems to have moved off," Arthur Winner said. "I think there are several around. We may get one later."

"Well, I suppose we could use rain."

"I closed things up downstairs, just in case."

Sitting on the blanket chest at the foot of his bed, Arthur Winner, bending to take off his shoes, could see Clarissa through the door. Covering a yawn, she put the book she had been holding on the bedside table. He said: "After Ralph's business, I went back to the office for a few minutes; and Julius, to my surprise, suddenly turned up. He'd changed his plans. He was being driven on to New York, where Ingoldsby and the others had some things to do tomorrow. He'll be back Sunday. From what he said, the Washington trip was a great success."

"Oh; good!"

"He'd stopped out here and spoken to Marjorie; and it seems she told him about that talk she wanted to have with me. I didn't know it until tonight, but her ideas are no news to Julius. I don't know just when, but some time ago, he began to take her trouble seriously enough to look into various Roman Catholic teachings—which is, of course, like him. He never mentioned it, which is, of course, like him, too; but he seems to have made quite a study. I daresay he thought Marjorie would be bound to be all mixed up; so he'd better find out for himself what she was going to believe. He sounds resigned; but also, disturbed; and he said he wished I *would* let her talk to me."

Clarissa, changing the position of her pillow, had been about to lie down. Instead, she sat up straight. "Oh, dear!" she said. "Well, I suppose if he wants you to, you'll have to; but, darling, I still wish you could get out of it. Did Marjorie ask him to ask you?"

"I don't think she asked him to say that he wanted me to. She asked him to ask me if I'd be willing to, tomorrow. And you were right, it was this Mrs. Pratt she was going to call. Mrs. Pratt's coming tomorrow. I don't know whether Marjorie has some sort of general consultation in mind—I won't be free until tomorrow afternoon, anyway; with Mr. Woolf in the morning and some things I want to see to about Ralph. I'd thought of having her come down to the office; but Julius, because of Mrs. Pratt—one of the things that seemed to show he was disturbed —said he'd like it better if I talked to Marjorie, or them, out here. I gather Mrs. Pratt attracts attention."

"Yes," Clarissa said. "See them here. Have them over here. Em's brother Harold came to the lake with a truck after supper; and he'll stay with Em to close up tomorrow. I ought to go and see how they're getting on sometime; so I can be out of the way." She hesitated. "Darling, what worried me when you told me this afternoon was that I could see Marjorie working up a situation. I thought her idea was to talk to you without telling Julius—preferably, have a number of secret meetings with you. This is better; still I don't like it. She wants to get you involved."

"My dear, I really don't see how she can," Arthur Winner said. "I'm not being asked to take sides. I'm certainly not going to try to tell her or Mrs. Pratt what to do. Of course, she's making a situation; that was almost the first thing Julius said. He understands her perfectly—that she can't do things simply. And, of course, too, the situation's rather pointless. I mean, Julius doesn't need me or anyone else to 'explain' anything to him. He regards what she does as entirely up to her. If she feels this is what she must do, he thinks he would be—his word was, inhuman, to oppose her. One must admire him. Fred Dealey happened to say something about that. He put the point: Could *you* do it? Julius wouldn't like the term; but Christian charity seems to be his attitude. He wants her to be happy, if possible."

"Then, what disturbs him?"

"Just the general idea, I suppose," Arthur Winner said. "He doesn't seem to care for Catholic usages—they demean you, he seems to think. There are also a few practical difficulties—some, perhaps, about the children, if Marjorie has to bring them up Catholics. That's only a guess; Julius didn't mention that. He did mention one difficulty. In the Catholic view, he and Marjorie are, and always have been, living in sin—not married; since her first husband's still alive. It follows, of course, that any physical relations between them are immoral—but, the truth is, I don't know, since Julius has never said, whether that's a problem or not—"

With an abstracted frown, almost absently, Clarissa said: "Well, I think it's not; not in any ordinary—" Coloring, she bit her lip. "No; how can I say—"

Arthur Winner said: "Julius is of a reticent nature in personal matters. I take it Marjorie isn't. However—"

"Yes; but I know now she's also the most outrageous liar. You can never be sure what's true and what's not. She used to come over and tell me things—I think, hoping to shock me. She insisted on telling me about her and Julius—" Clarissa colored more. "Well; what she said they did, what they—he, had to do. But, as I say, I know now she can't help lying. Something makes her say things; and I think all the time, even while she's saying them, she's sorry. She knows they're lies, and she can see you know they're lies; but she can't stop. And, of course, she has an absolute obsession with sex—the most fantastic ideas. I could tell you more; but I won't. Well; yes, I will! I'll give you a mild example. She asked me once if Reggie Shaw had ever made a pass at me. Then she said: 'Well, he may. I want to warn you. If he ever tells you to get undressed, and there isn't a nurse there; don't!'" Clarissa spread her hands. "I can't claim to know all about Reg's habits; but if you're a woman, you usually feel things like that. And I'm prepared to swear Reg would be the last doctor in the world to make a pass at a patient. I think she's always thinking of things like that; and the unlikelier they are, the better. Oh, I could tell you a lot more! But I've been bitchy enough. And in fairness, I ought to say this isn't recent. She saw I wasn't going to listen; so she hasn't tried to tell me anything for a long time. And I know she can't help it; and I try to be sorry for her; but, believe me, she's dangerous, Arthur."

She paused, looking at him gravely. "And, yes," she said. "Here's more of the bitch in me. If you and she had a lot of meetings and confidences, what's to stop her from making up a few stories about you? So, there! Good night, darling. I know you'll have to talk to her; but talk to her as little as possible, will you?"

Out of a confusion of dreaming and waking, not immediately sure which was which, Arthur Winner roused himself. He had been approaching the summer house. He saw the long-unpainted wood, the old screens that had holes in them. Probably he had approached to take shelter, for a black storm impended. About to step in, he recoiled. On the floor of the summer house, bent double, lay Marjorie Penrose. She had been frightfully injured. Her clothing—a kind of house dress—had been ripped off her. Her arms must have been broken. They angled behind her like a doll's arms. Her torn face ran with blood. At once, the storm broke. The slant white glare of lightning that severed the gloom; the splitting crash of thunder that came with horrid fury on top of the gruesome sight filled Arthur Winner with a confounding nausea of fear. Rising from the death of sleep, dazedly gaining full consciousness, he perceived then that the thunder was no dream; a clap of thunder broke with cracking force on his awakened ears. The storm, the rush of wind, the noise of the big treetops walking—these were real. The dial of his clock, luminous, said: one fifteen. He had been asleep a little over an hour.

The dream, though fading, though identifying itself as such, had left the inexplicable shocking picture in his mind. Still shaken, Arthur Winner got out of bed. Rain drove at his half-open window. He closed it. In Clarissa's room, he found her stirring, sleepily lifting her head. She murmured: "What?"

Arthur Winner said: "Just a thunderstorm, my dear. We're getting one, after all." He drew her windows down. "I'd better see about Ann."

Passing back through his room, he went into the hall and snapped the light on. Blinking in the brightness of this undisturbed indoor calm, he went down to Ann's room. In darkness made intermittent by the fast lightning flashes, Ann lay asleep.

262

Her slight pajama-clad form was partly covered by a rumpled sheet. Her fluffy dark hair was displayed loosely over the pillow that she embraced and burrowed her face into. Neither flares of light, nor replications of thunder, nor the vehemence of wind, nor the opening door could break that deep sleep. Not unaffected —Defend, O Lord, this thy child!—Arthur Winner looked down a moment on the young sleeper, on the concernless slumber of the young. Might not such quiet of trust without question—this was home; what danger, what hurt, could ever reach her here?— such innocence of unalarm be seen as peace attending Ann? Around her breathed, you might very well say, a pure and holy feeling all through a night. He pushed the windows almost closed. Ann did not know. Unknown to Ann, he returned to the door and shut it after him.

Clarissa had come into the hall. Uncertain in drowsiness, a hand on the rail by the stairhead to guide her, her other hand raised dazedly to her forehead and half-closed eyes, she said: "Is everything all right?" She turned her head toward the lash of rain on the tall window above the stairs.

Coming toward her, Arthur Winner said: "Yes. I don't think this will last long. I think most of it's passing north."

The clear face under the blue scarf's turban-like binding looked blank with sleep. Clarissa's long nightgown of white crepe clung to her, a hem of lace dropping on her slippered feet. One lace-edged strap, ready in unheeded disarray to slip off her shoulder, made the narrow lace yoke hang uneven. Beyond the hall window's wet panes there was a brighter flash, and a shock of thunder from which the very stone walls of the house seemed to take a tremor. Arthur Winner came up to her; and, lifting her arms, Clarissa drowsily put them around his neck. She turned her turbaned head and laid her cheek against his chin. She murmured: "I want to come in until it stops."

Arthur Winner said: "All right, my dear; come on."

She leaned against him, and he led her, his arm around her waist, into his bedroom. When he paused at the door, she moved ahead to sit on the bed's edge. She dropped the slippers from her feet. "Leave this open?" he said.

Clarissa shook her head. Moving sideways, lifting her knees, she lay down. Coming to the bed in the darkness, lying down beside her, Arthur Winner could see in the next short flare of lightning, that her eyes were open. He said: "Do you want the sheet over you?"

She said: "No."

"Everything's all right," he said. He slipped an arm under her; and she moved, turning on her side to face him. There was another, brighter flash, a heavy topple of instant thunder. Clarissa lifted her left hand vaguely, finding his shoulder, his right arm, his hand, on which she closed her hand.

"Everything's all right," Arthur Winner said again.

Letting his hand go, Clarissa's fingers passed up his forearm, slipping under the sleeve of his pajama jacket. Turning more, she let herself rest closer against him. Moments passed. Withdrawn from his arm, her hand, in shy seeking, found and moved his hand toward her. The room lit with a wavering glow; and Arthur Winner saw her closed eyes.

Lightning continued in frequent flashes. Heavy, often jarring, thunder followed. Rain beat the glass; wind rushed among the trees; but Arthur Winner now gave them little heed. First prickings of the blood, first low throbs, inchoate and not of his volition, had been uncertain. He waited to know if they were to proceed, or if they were to be put down. Clearly signaled to, becoming certain, they surged in force. To shiverings of the senses, to thrilling thuds of the heart sent faster, delighted anticipation swelled, rose pent. The upstaring flesh made haste, made head, stiffened and pulsative, made hard to brook the little delays of readying and getting ready—the disposings of accustomed practice, the preparations of purpose and consent; the familiar mute movements of furtherance.

By flickering passages of light, Arthur Winner had his eyes' tender knowledge of the bound-up head backed against the pillow, of the rapt, half-lit face's smile of transport, of the tense seen mouth whose lips were open for breathing. Through moments of dark, by searching contacts of discovery, by successfully pressed explorations, he had his body's speechless cognizance of

264

her body, the rigid member's trembling knowledge of the mouth unseen, the central hairy diadem, whose lips prepared to open. Regardless of time—a run-by of unrecorded moments; regardless of place—a room now partly dark, now partly light; the field unfenced of a bed's dim expanse, Arthur Winner, mastering yet overmastered, gathered all in, cried **Oh**, and mounted; made all one with him.

His as much as hers, the supple and undulous back hollowing at the pull of his hands to a compliant curve; his as much as hers, her occupied participative hips, her obediently divided embracing knees, her parts in moist manipulative reception. Then, hers as much as his, the breath got hastily in common; the thumping, one on another, of the hurried two hearts, the mutual heat of pumped bloods, the start of their uniting sweats. Grown, growing, gaining scope, hers then no less than his, the thoroughgoing, deepening, widening work of their connection; and his then no less than hers, the tempo slowed in concert to engineer a tremulous joint containment and continuance. Then, then, caution gone, compulsion in control, his—and hers, as well!—the pace unreined, raised, redoubled, all measurable measure lost. And, the incontinent instant brought to pass, no sooner his the very article, his uttermost, the stand-and-deliver of the undone flesh, the tottered senses' outgiving of astoundment, than—put beside themselves, hit at their secret quick, provoked by that sudden touch beyond any bearing—the deep muscle groups, come to their vertex, were in a flash convulsed; in spasms unstayably succeeding spasms, contracting on contraction on contraction—hers! Hers, too; hers, hers, hers!

The storm was moving away. Rumbles of thunder, though they still sounded, were dull. The fast flashes of lightning were dimmer, scarcely lifting the dark. In the trees the wind was dying. Drowsily, at intervals, Clarissa's lips touched his cheek. The clinging arms, lax, enclosed Arthur Winner in rest, a resting together, sleepy.

"Arthur—" Clarissa said.

Lifting his head, Arthur Winner saw that the hall door had opened. Against the hall's low light, Ann's juvenile, narrow-legged figure stood in its loose pajamas.

"Father!" she said. "I thought I'd better wake you up. There's a terrible storm coming, I think. Maybe we'd better—"

Ann broke off. "Oh!" she said, startled. "Oh; I'm frightfully sorry, Hendy! I thought—" She groped for the door handle, missed, groped again; and, stepping back, drew the door closed.

Freeing herself, Clarissa sat up. She put her feet to the floor, reaching for her nightgown. Standing, she raised the nightgown, and let it drop around her. She bent to find her slippers. She said: "I'll just see she's all right. Good night again, darling."

PART TWO

A NOISE OF HUNTERS HEARD

ONE

At half past eight, over the low hill of Brocton, through streets full of morning sun, a brisk breeze blew. Arthur Winner, crossing from Court Street to pass the granite front of the First National Bank, came on Roger Bartlett, the bank's president, about to put his key in the lock of the bronze and glass outer doors. He said: "Arthur; get your notice about the special directors' meeting?"

Arthur Winner said: "Next Thursday? Yes."

"Well, several people didn't. I don't know what happened. The thing was, Harry thought we might as well wait until Judge McAllister got back from his vacation; he understood, Monday. So I sent notices last week giving the new date; but Ewell didn't get one; and neither did Bert Brown. Between you and me, I don't believe either of them had much else to do; but they acted as if they did when they came in and found there wasn't any meeting yesterday. I think they're going to move to fire the whole lot of us."

"Well, I got my notice," Arthur Winner said. "So I'll move the motion be tabled."

"Do that!" Roger Bartlett said, grinning. "See you!"

The traffic light at the corner changed. On the other curb of Federal Street was Edna Keating. Coming toward him, she said: "Good morning, Mr. Winner. Do you know where you're going to be, later? Judge Lowe wants to see you."

"I'm going into the Federal House for a minute," Arthur Winner said. "I've an appointment at the office at nine. I'll be over at the courthouse at ten."

She said: "I'll tell him."

Passing on, Arthur Winner went up the Federal House steps under the recently installed new copy of the original sign—a ferocious spread eagle with ribband in his beak and arrows in his talons. Recently, too, the lobby had been refurbished by a decorating job that cleaned out what was merely old and replaced it with what was, or what affected to be, much older— a few genuine antiques; a good many reproductions, authentic at least in style. The effect could be called refined.

Mrs. Lambert, at the cashier's desk by the entrance to the lunch counter; known as the coffee shop, said: "Good morning, Mr. Winner."

Earl Michels, who was a barkeep when the bar was open, but who was not above running a dust mop around the lobby, said: "Morning, Mr. Winner."

Across the lobby's end stretched an extensive reproduction break-front china closet. The many shelves were filled with fine early blue Canton, perfectly authentic, having been discovered in barrels in the attic, with the original invoices to show that it was ordered for the old Federal House in 1818. Why the service had never been used, no one could now say. The numerous doors of the closet stood open, and Paul Atkin, proprietor of the Federal House (himself not above doing a little dusting where he would not trust anyone else to do it), was tenderly wiping one of a row of hot-water beefsteak dishes with a cloth. He said: "Hello, Arthur. Nice day again."

Fingering the dish's lemon-peel glaze with pleasure, he returned it cautiously to its place. "Looking for your New York fellow?" he said. "I know he was down to breakfast. I think he went upstairs a minute."

"Yes; I did want to see him, thanks. I'll wait."

With a gingerly movement, Paul Atkin reached into the cabinet. From the crowded array, the rows of pieces large and small, whose massed gleam of figured living blue the indirect north morning light from across the lobby seemed to intensify, he selected a helmet pitcher of graceful shape. Wiping it admiringly, he said: "Ever see anything prettier than that? I always remember it was your dad, Arthur, who found all this stuff.

That was just before I bought the place from Willoughby. Somebody opened one of the barrels—showed him a piece. Said was it any good. Truth is, though I knew what *he* said, I didn't think too much of it until that decorator said we ought to have this thing, put it in it. A man, an antique dealer, told me he was from Philadelphia, driving through last week, offered me five thousand dollars for the lot, here. Not for sale, I told him; but I could see your father was right."

Putting the pitcher back and closing the door, he said: "Arthur, have you happened to hear what they're going to do in court about that girl who killed her baby? I mean, is there going to be a murder trial? I'd just like to know if I'm going to have to put up a jury next week—with a couple of alternates, and two tipstaves, that's sixteen. Of course you can't tell how many rooms they really need until you see how many women jurors they pick; but I wish I could find out whether they're going to need any."

Arthur Winner said: "I don't think they're planning to try her, Paul. I believe they're taking a plea, or arranging to, today. I know Judge Lowe had the girl in chambers yesterday with her counsel. Why don't you call Jerry Brophy? He'd know."

Lowering his voice, Paul Atkin said: "I wouldn't ask that bastard the time of day!" His flat-cheeked face assumed a look of incensement. "Brophy was down in the bar the other evening with some Mechanicsville people; and one of them got pretty loud; and Earl, there—" he nodded toward Earl Michels, over by the closed dining-room doors with his mop—"said he'd have to ask him to be a little quieter. So the fellow took offense. Started saying everyone knew how stuck-up we were here; but he was just as good as anyone else; and he had as much right here as anybody; and did Earl want to make something out of it."

Paul Atkin give his head a jerk. "I don't know who he was— one of those Hunkies, I guess. In politics, I suppose, if Brophy was buying him drinks. Earl said everyone was welcome here, except patrons who disturbed other patrons. So Brophy said: 'Forget it, Earl! Nobody's being disturbed. Give us all another drink.' So Earl said he was sorry, he couldn't serve them another. So Brophy got mad, and asked if he was trying to imply he, Brophy, was drunk. Earl said: 'No, Mr. Brophy, you're not, and maybe your friend isn't; but in my judgment he's had enough; so I won't serve him.' So Brophy started giving him hell—told him he'd damn well be out of a job. I can tell Brophy, Earl damn well won't! And I could tell him some other things about what I think of a fellow—district attorney, so I guess he knows the law about serving intoxicated persons—who threatens a man because he's obeying the law. Brophy and his political friends can go somewhere else. They won't get service here—"

From the cashier's desk, Mrs. Lambert called: "Excuse me, Mr. Winner! Your office. Miss Detweiler says someone's trying to get you— Yes," she said to the telephone she held, "I'll tell him. It's Harold Revere, at Hancock, Mr. Winner. Should she ask the operator to put it on our pay-booth phone?"

"Yes; if she will."

Mrs. Lambert said: "Mr. Winner says yes."

Paul Atkin said: "Harold Revere? What's Harold doing now?"

Arthur Winner said: "As little as possible, I expect. His sister Em gets him to help her sometimes. I can't think why he'd be calling from Hancock."

"Well, I know he doesn't work too hard," Paul Atkin said. "But he was here, a while; and I'd be glad to have him back. Earl's nice about helping out; but cleaning up's not his job—"

The bell in the booth rang. Stepping in, Arthur Winner took down the receiver. With a certain eagerness of excitement, Harold Revere's voice proved to be saying: "That you, Mr. Winner? Em said we better call you as soon as we could. Reason I'm down at Hancock is, we don't have any telephone from the lake. In that storm last night, that big tree, Mr. Winner, that oak tree out there, got hit. This big lightning flash hit it something awful."

"You and Em all right?"

"Except, we were sure scared! I never want one that close again, Mr. Winner! Funny thing was, this storm hadn't been so bad. I and Em hardly thought anything of it; it looked about over, when suddenly there was this light like it was daylight; and this splitting sound, so loud it was like it was in your head; and the whole ground kind of jumped—we'd set up these cots in the hall to sleep on; and even inside, it about knocked us out of them. Everything looked on fire; it seemed a whole minute; and I thought the lodge had caught; but, don't worry, it didn't! We don't have any electricity; and the telephone don't work; but everything else is all right. We weren't hurt."

"Well, I'm glad of that. What happened to the tree?"

"It was hit something awful, Mr. Winner. Right then, we couldn't see so good—I didn't even want to go near it. Em was saying I should call you right away; but I said—this was late; half past one—you'd be asleep; and anyway what were you going to do that time of night? So she found then the telephone didn't work. Another thing; I said we didn't even know it was the tree was hit. But it was. That tree, this morning; it's ripped right open, from way up this big branch to the top, down. So Em says, now I got to take the truck right away, get a telephone in Hancock; because she knows you certainly liked that tree; and how could I tell if those tree people, or somebody, if they got here quick, couldn't do something. Only, I think it's killed, Mr. Winner. In the trunk, it's got this split you can put your whole arm into."

Arthur Winner said: "I'll get somebody to look at it. The main thing is, you and Em weren't hurt. Mrs. Winner's planning to drive up this afternoon—"

"Yes, she told me, Mr. Winner. I called Roylan first. I didn't know had you left yet. So I told Mrs. Winner; and she said she was certainly sorry, too. She said: 'Oh, that wonderful tree!' So then she said ring you at the office, and you'd say what to do."

"Yes. Thanks for letting me know, Harold. I'll try to get a tree man up today."

Through the open door of the telephone booth he could see a woman coming—trippingly, would describe it—downstairs. The woman was Miss Cummins. Her plain small face was animated. She had on a brown smocklike garment; and on her arm she carried a shining new pail in which were a scrubbing brush, some rags, and a box of cleaning powder. Arthur Winner dared-say he showed astonishment; for, noticing him as he stepped from the booth, she gave him a smile of grave gaiety, and said at once: "I know it looks funny, Mr. Winner; but we found they'd finished the work in the kitchen at the rectory yesterday. So I'm going over this morning to get it good and clean." More earnestly, looking up at him, she said: "Everything's so awfully nice, Mr. Winner. The vestry was so nice to be willing to have all that done for us. Whit and I do appreciate it!"

"We want you to be comfortable," Arthur Winner said. "Is Whit going to be there this morning?"

"He'd better be! I'm going to make him help."

"There was something he wanted me to find out for him. I'd like to talk to him. Would you tell him I'll stop by sometime around noon?"

"Gladly, Mr. Winner." She turned, paused; and said; "Oh—good morning—er—Mr. Woolf."

Arthur Winner turned, too. Descending the stairs, Mr. Woolf had halted formally at the bottom to bow to Miss Cummins. Smiling, she gave him a gracious nod. Tripping still, she passed across the lobby and out the front door.

Transferring his melancholy, pleased smile to Arthur Winner, Mr. Woolf said: "Nice young lady, Mr. Winner! Mrs. Trowbridge, the rector's mother, told me that he and Miss Cummins were to be married the week after next. I certainly congratulate them both." In his hand, Mr. Woolf held some folded yellow telegram forms, and an opened letter. Silent, he extended the letter, which was on the stationery of the Union League of Brocton.

Arthur Winner read: *Dear Sir: I hope you will accept my earnest and unfeigned apology for the gross discourtesies I offered you today. Any seeming insinuations of mine reflecting on your professional honor, I freely and fully retract. I regret certain remarks I made of an offensive personal nature. Yrs. sincerely, N. Tuttle.*

Mr. Woolf said: "Now, *that* I feel really bad about, Mr. Winner!" He shook his head regretfully. "I don't like to think of the old gentleman supposing he had to write that—distressing himself; imagining I'd take any serious offense from things he said when anyone could see he was angry. This was here at the hotel when I got back last night. A boy brought it over, they said. I thought of calling this club, to speak to him; but then I didn't know whether that was where he lived or not."

Arthur Winner said: "I saw him during the evening; and I know it was on his mind that he hadn't been fair, Mr. Woolf. He means what he wrote. He's sorry he lost his temper. He'd be distressed about that; but apologizing, where he decides an apology's owed, wouldn't distress him. When he recognizes he's been in the wrong, he'll always say so."

Admiringly, Mr. Woolf said: "That attitude you certainly have to respect! That takes a lot of character; and I know now what the judge meant yesterday—Mr. Tuttle has a lot. And, speaking of apologies, I've got some to make, too. I'd like to tell Mr. Tuttle—I will—that I'm sorry about how I acted. I can see that, speaking of discourtesies, my proposing to cite him to account was pretty discourteous. What I'd done was notice your act provided you could cite after six months; I'd mentioned the provision to Mr. Polhemus; and he said, yes, that was the provision. But he didn't happen to tell me that you never do it that way." Mr. Woolf's mournful smile faintly lit his swarthy pallor. "I guess he didn't mind my not knowing. I admit I don't like it too much either, when my client brings in additional counsel in a matter I thought was in my hands. I might feel: If this fellow's supposed to be so smart; why, just let him go ahead and show how smart he is!"

Arthur Winner was obliged to answer the smile. He said: "Our court, as I suppose you've gathered, more or less adheres to a rule of its own about accounting. Since we don't, I'm afraid, feel that the provision to cite is either necessary or wise, we don't invoke it. In fact, our attorneys advise all executors or administrators against filing their accounts, and certainly against any distribution, until a year runs. We see that as a proper routine precaution. In this jurisdiction, the waiting protects you from any claims—except, of course, the Federal government's—that might, unknown to a personal representative, be outstanding. If notice of them hasn't been given within twelve months after the grant of letters testamentary or of administration, they're taken care of; they're debarred. So our local practice is to wait. But I don't think anyone could expect you to know that."

With gravity, Mr. Woolf tapped his chest. He said: "I could expect myself to know it, Mr. Winner. Just as I ought to have known about your arrangement for this kind of hearing or meeting. I took the liberty of going over your rules of court when I was in your office yesterday. If, to start with, I'd been sure about the auditor's functions, as I should have been, I wouldn't have needed to look foolish trying to except to you the way I did. It's a lesson to me, Mr. Winner. Because there wasn't any really big money involved, and I happened to be pretty busy, I didn't look up your law myself. I just sent one of our young men to our library and had him abstract from the relevant acts. That's how you get careless! Yes, sir; I guess I thought I'd just go down and teach those people a thing or two about probate. So, what happened was, you taught me a thing or two!" With unexpected joviality, he gave Arthur Winner's arm a light slap.

Somewhat uncomfortable, Arthur Winner let himself laugh. "I think there's a good deal you could teach us," he said. "I'm not sure we attach enough importance to procedure—some of ours is pretty casual. Still, I think you'll find the court's not casual about law. And I feel I can safely reassure you about our accountings—they aren't casual either. As I said, we're accustomed to wait a year, so Noah saw no reason to hurry— and, of course, when appointment of an auditor to hear matters going to the validity of the will was petitioned for, he'd see even less reason to hurry. There'd have to be meetings, a transcript of testimony, a report to the court, and the court's eventual decree before distribution could even be considered. Noah has his own ways of working, but when the account's filed there'll be no question about what happened to this or that item of the inventory."

Mr. Woolf smiled again. He said: "I regret those questions of mine, Mr. Winner. They were really just a little piece of idle curiosity on my part, which I couldn't even claim was relevant to any issues of fact before you. Simply, the executor was there; and I'd been looking at the inventory. I know now this isn't the time for that; so I'll ask nothing further. As far as I'm con-

cerned, you won't have to sit more than ten minutes this morning, and I'm sorry you have to sit at all—leave your lovely home
and come in here on a Saturday."

Again a little uncomfortable, Arthur Winner said: "I'm appointed for the accommodation of all parties in interest, Mr.
Woolf, and I'd try to accommodate any of them in any way I
could. But as it happens, I'd have had to be in. I've a client to
see. I came over to say I'd be tied up for a little while before
the meeting; but if you have work to do, any telephoning,
anything of that kind, I can put an office at your disposal again."

Mr. Woolf said: "That's very kind indeed, very kind indeed,
Mr. Winner; but I did my telephoning yesterday. Incidentally,
I asked the operator for the charges on them, and gave your
girl—Miss Mills, I think—the money. I was very much obliged."
Smiling more broadly, he tapped the folded telegrams he held.
"I'll tell you what these are, Mr. Winner. You remember, I happened to ask Mr. Tuttle the whereabouts of those government
bonds; and he said they were in a safe-deposit box. As I mentioned; what led me to ask him was looking at the inventory
after he gave an approximate figure for cash on hand. I didn't
see how he could have that much; so I felt this idle curiosity."
He smiled deprecatingly. "It wasn't right for me to press him,
Mr. Winner. As you say, why should he have cast his accounts
yet, strike any balance? And we all know older people can forget
things."

Arthur Winner said: "That was a perfectly legitimate question. You could properly want to know the form in which the
assets of the estate were being held—"

"Yes," Mr. Woolf said. "But when I asked: 'Where are those
bonds at present?' I should have seen he didn't know—I mean,
that minute, he couldn't remember exactly about them. But
he didn't want to say he couldn't—I've seen older people do that
before—so he said they were in a box. He wasn't going to say:
'I forget what I did with them.' " Mr. Woolf's smile saddened,
the amusement shading into plain compassion. "So that was just
a guess, the box. I'm sure, by now, he remembers; but I'm not
even going to ask him again. You see, I found out what happened to them."

Arthur Winner supposed that the look he gave Mr. Woolf was baffled; for Mr. Woolf, now with the joking smile of a man about to answer a riddle, said: "Easiest thing in the world, Mr. Winner! There was all that cash he said, to the best of his belief, he had. Of course, I saw he might not be right about the amount; but I had another idea. I just made a note from the inventory of the serial numbers of those bonds. If you give them the numbers, the Bureau of Public Debt, I'm sure you know, will check for you. So I telephoned Chicago from your office, and asked them to wire me collect the status of those securities." He tapped the telegrams again. Bright-eyed, he gently poked Arthur Winner's arm. He said: "The thing Mr. Tuttle couldn't remember right that minute, that made him confused, was that he redeemed them all about two months back—July twentieth, to be exact. That's how he came to have the cash. See?"

"Yes," Arthur Winner said. "I see." Indeed he could, and with virtual certainty, see more than Mr. Woolf saw. Mr. Woolf, showing how smart he was (and no mistake!), was still quite mistaken; he misplaced his kindly understanding, he wasted his compassion. Old men could forget—yes; this or that uninteresting trifle might slip Noah's mind (Ann? Who's Ann?); but Mr. Woolf didn't know Noah. You had only to think of Noah's care to the last detail, his jealous eye on such portfolios as the Orcutt bequest to guess whether he'd forget that he'd decided to have the bonds redeemed. He was asked the "whereabouts" of these securities. The impertinence filled him with fury. So pestered with a popinjay, Noah deliberately balked, angrily answered he knew not what (nor cared!); in substance: Where would you expect to find securities? Now, be off, or I'll kick you downstairs! Arthur Winner said: "I daresay they were Series G bonds in deceased's name. If they're held more than six months after death, the interest stops."

His gravity returning, Mr. Woolf said: "Right you are! That was it. Right thing to do! Well, you see I had all I wanted. Those items weren't mislaid, or anything; so I said to myself: 'Why not drop it?' I wouldn't want to embarrass the old gentleman by showing him my telegrams, or bringing up the matter in any way. All I plan this morning is to put on the record that on behalf of my clients I'm satisfied with the information I now possess, and will not ask the executor to account further, pending the auditor's report on the other issues, which I presume will contain his findings of fact and conclusions of law."

"Yes; that's what the court expects from me," Arthur Winner said. "Our rule requires fifteen days' notice of the auditor's intention to file. You get, of course, a full opportunity to examine the report and enter exceptions. About the other, I'll say I think your attitude's very considerate, Mr. Woolf. But there's no reason to debar yourself from asking any questions you may wish to ask, and that the executor may reasonably be supposed able to answer."

"No, no," Mr. Woolf said. "Placet! Placet!" He gave Arthur Winner's arm a friendly squeeze. "Mum's the word!"

✦

It was nine o'clock. From Ralph Detweiler's state of nerves last night, Arthur Winner would have expected him to be early, rather than late, at the office; but Ralph had not appeared. Mary Sheen, though her opened typewriter showed she was in, was not at her desk. Gladys Mills, at her desk, sat touching up one of her painted fingernails with a little brush from a little bottle. He did not see Helen Detweiler.

Gladys said at once: "Mr. Winner, there was a call from Mrs. Penrose. Just, would you call her back when you could?"

"All right, thanks," Arthur Winner said. "Gladys, ring those Excelsior tree people and see if anybody's there yet. I'd like to talk to the manager."

"Yes, Mr. Winner."

Helen Detweiler came out of Noah Tuttle's room. Arthur Winner said: "He's not in yet, is he?"

Helen said: "No, he isn't, Mr. Winner." Coming closer, lowering her voice, she said: "Mrs. Jennings is there."

"Aunt Maud?" Arthur Winner said. "Oh, Lord! Well, I'd better speak to her. Helen, do you happen to remember Mr. Tuttle making a deposit in the McCarthy Estate account—say, twenty thousand dollars, after the middle of July?"

"I'm afraid I don't, Mr. Winner. I'll look."

"It's not important," Arthur Winner said. "In a minute, I'd like to speak to you for a minute."

"Yes, Mr. Winner."

Crossing to the door of Noah Tuttle's room, Arthur Winner said: "Good morning, Aunt Maud."

His Aunt Maud, her dumpy black-clad bulk solidly seated in one of Noah's ancient black leather chairs, was looking at a copy of the Brocton *Morning Advertizer,* held at arm's length. Letting the paper down in her lap, she blinked, removed her spectacles, and said: "The morning's as it may be, Arthur. Now, trying to talk me out of this won't do any good. I'm going to see Noah; and since it doesn't please me to wait in halls, I'm waiting here."

"By all means," Arthur Winner said. "Though describing our commodious and expensively appointed reception room as a hall isn't very kind of you."

"Doors are at both ends, and people walk through," his Aunt Maud said. "Not that *this* is particularly pleasant!" She wrinkled her nose. "This place wants cleaning. It even smells."

That was true. The shadowed morning air held a definite faint odor—old cigar smoke. The smell had to be old, for Noah gave up smoking some time ago. Coming to plague the old man in one of his surviving pleasures, a catarrhal condition developed. Doctor Shaw said: "No more cigars." This smell was ghostly, then! Hour after hour, day after day, year after year, innumerable cigars gave off their smoke here—cigars of friends stopping by with a good story; cigars of clients coming out long-windedly with what bothered them; cigars borne in by Arthur Winner Senior entering from his room for one of the partners' laconic but unhurried discussions. The slow fumes had suffused the very walls, penetrated the furnishings, seeped into the leather bindings of the never now disturbed ranges of old books, permeated their foxing paper. The smoke stayed longer than the smokers. Except for Noah, forbidden to smoke, those cigar-enjoyers of yesterday were—Willard Lowe had said it—dead, every man Jack of them!

"Some airing would be possible," Arthur Winner said, starting toward the windows.

"No; there'll be a draft," his Aunt Maud said. "Arthur, I've decided Noah will give me five thousand dollars. He started something when he said I was getting senile. He's right! From now on, I mean to be no more of a fool than I can help. I've had enough of being careful with my money. And to what end? To leave a few thousands to children who won't need money then half as much as I need money today."

Arthur Winner said: "Well, I think—"

"Then, just think to yourself for a minute! I've things to say. I've really been very good to my children. I've never put Sutton, who's as tightfisted as his excellent father ever was, to the pain of having to allot me money that that wife of his would want to spend on herself. I've never suggested that Dorothea and her nitwit husband provide me with a home with them in California—of course, I'd rather be dead than 'given a home'; but that just happens; that's nothing a child has a right to count on. I'm perfectly aware that what I want to do may lose money, not make money—but that's a risk Sutton and Dorothea will have to join me in. I'm going to send Sally King five thousand dollars, as she suggests, and ask her to have her friend invest the money for me."

Arthur Winner said: "May I stop thinking to myself now?"

"You may! Though, of course, I know what you're going to say."

Arthur Winner said: "I'm not sure you do, Aunt Maud. If you were asking my advice, I couldn't in conscience tell you anything but what I told you yesterday afternoon. I'd have to point out to you that in speculation there's only one sound principle. Speculate when you have more money than you need; never, when you need more money than you have. But you're not asking my advice; you're telling me what you've decided. So, I've only to satisfy myself that you understand, as you seem to, what you're doing—I mean, that you're risking the money. You still want to do it. All right! About Cousin Dorothea and Cousin Sutton, I think you're sensible. Let Dorothea's husband

281

make provision for her. Sutton, being a man of my age, strikes me as old enough to make provision for himself. Your money's yours to use. You can't get me to say I approve of this use; but I think you have an absolute right to do with it what you want. So go ahead."

His Aunt Maud said: "Well, thank you for that!" Drawing her fan from under the folded newspaper in her lap, she snapped it open and began to fan herself. Her color had mounted somewhat. "Being an old woman's not enjoyable, Arthur. Everyone tries to run you. Everyone thinks he knows what you want better than you do." She paused in her fanning, while her other hand found a handkerchief in her bag. To Arthur Winner's astonishment, she dabbed at tears in her eyes.

Careful to gaze away from her, Arthur Winner said: "Yes; you might as well expect Noah to object; but if he sees you're serious, he'll have to give you the money whether he likes the idea or not. Only, this morning, we're having a meeting at the courthouse at ten; and I'm not sure he'll come here first. I could call him at the Union League; but—"

"No, don't!" she said. "Right now, he's probably struggling to get his withered bowels to move."

By her sardonic grunt, she showed that she had effected a recovery. Wary though she was, the unmitigable woes of age had surprised her for a minute; overcome, she felt the vain wishes of the sighing heart—the wish, say, that she could remember Sutton's excellent father, Ambrose Jennings, as less the curmudgeon, and more the loving helpmate; the wish, say, that tightfisted Sutton and his disliked wife, heard from seldom in New York, and Dorothea and her nitwit husband, remote in California, might be (instead of what they were) her dear children, all the four; and all gathered, devoted, around her. To her rescue, she now rushed up her part, consciously played, of Holy Terror, her posture of defense. The Holy Terror opened her mouth and dealt out roundly the tonic remark—something that shaved coarseness to take care of anyone who dared to think she was a nice namby-pamby old lady; something rebuffingly rude to take care of anyone who was pitying a meek little widow woman. She'd rock them back!

Herself again, his Aunt Maud said: "Then, I'll not wait." She came to her feet with ostentatious energy. "I'm not going to be left cooling my heels in this rat's nest." Though there was a shamble in her gait, the shamble was vigorous. Halting by the door, she said: "I really wanted the pleasure of telling the old fuddy-duddy in person; but I suppose he'd be bound to have a tantrum, and perhaps end in a fit or a stroke, which would be on my head—"

"I'll tell him," Arthur Winner said.

"That's Hattie's good boy!" she said. "No; don't come traipsing to the front door with me. I'm not a cripple." While Gladys Mills, and Mary Sheen, back at her desk, observed amazed and amused (though sidewise and with lowered eyes) the progress, his Aunt Maud sailed across to the reception room, and out.

Helen Detweiler, who had been in the files, said: "Now, Mr. Winner?"

"Yes; come in," Arthur Winner said.

Mary Sheen said: "Oh, Mr. Winner; the district attorney's office called while you were out. Mr. Brophy said if you were coming back, could you spare him a minute if he stopped by?"

"Tell him; yes," Arthur Winner said.

In his room, he looked at the clock and said to Helen: "Ralph understood he was to see me this morning, didn't he?"

Helen, too, looked at the clock. "Yes, he did, Mr. Winner. He said you said nine. He should be here—he went down to speak to Joan Moore; but—"

The buzzer of the telephone on Arthur Winner's desk sounded. He took it up. Mary Sheen said: "Doctor Trowbridge, Mr. Winner."

Replacing Mary's, Doctor Trowbridge's voice said: "Er—Arthur? Whit Trowbridge. Good morning! Midge gave me your message. I just wanted to say; any time that suits you. I'll be here all morning—either in the church office or the rectory."

Arthur Winner said: "Good. About half past eleven, I hope, Whit. There are points I thought we'd better discuss before the vestry meeting."

"By all means," Doctor Trowbridge said. "Since it's really my

283

first full vestry meeting, I must depend a great deal on your advice, Arthur. Oh, incidentally, I've been looking around the church—I thought I ought to familiarize myself with the whole building—and in the belfry I noticed a condition that I thought might be unsafe. In the mounting of the big bell, in the suspending beam, I don't know the exact term, there are many cracks. I asked Mr. Revere if he'd noticed." He laughed kindly. "A little tactless of me, I saw then. At his age, poor man, I don't think he does much climbing to belfries! He said he'd go right up; but I told him not to bother. What I wondered was whether you'd care to look at it with me and see if you thought we ought to have an architect, or builder, or someone—"

"I'd be glad to," Arthur Winner said. "Some of Harry Minieri's men are still working in the rectory, aren't they? I believe he pays them off at noon, Saturdays; so he'll be around; and we can get an opinion at once."

"Splendid!" Doctor Trowbridge said. "The bell appears to be very heavy; and one wouldn't like to think there was any chance of its falling. I was interested to read the inscription; but surely this can't be *that* bell—the original?"

"No," Arthur Winner said. "They recast it—larger; with the bell metal of the original in it, and the old inscription, as the bourdon bell of a chime hung when the present church was built. The other bells were afterward removed."

"I guessed as much," Doctor Trowbridge said. "Most interesting! Well, I mustn't keep you, Arthur. I'll see you later, then."

Arthur Winner said: "Sorry, Helen, I—"

She had turned her head to look through the open door. She said: "I think Ralph's here, now, Mr. Winner. Yes; he is."

"We won't be long," Arthur Winner said. "I'd like to go over one or two things with him." Looking at the strained thin face under the tightly drawn-back, fair, shining hair, he said: "Helen, I hope you'll try not to worry. Ralph satisfied me that he's telling the truth about what happened with Miss Kovacs; and I think we'll clear him."

Helen said: "I knew he couldn't have done what that girl said; and when you were willing to appear for him, Mr. Winner, I knew he'd be all right. I'm really not worrying about his—well,

284

having to go to prison or anything." She smiled painfully. "Things are funny! Yesterday, I was so worried about his not wanting to go to college. I thought nothing could worry me more than that; and then *this* happened; and *that* stopped mattering. I thought: If only he can get out of this, that's all I'd ever ask! Then I could see, after you talked to him, that you believed him; and that meant you'd get him out—"

Helen hesitated; but the called-for word of caution, the wry byword of the attorneys' room: *you never know with a jury!* would have to be reserved. Arthur Winner said: "Yes; I believe him, Helen. So that tells me Miss Kovacs's story is a lie; and since I know that, I can reasonably expect to shake her before I finish with her."

Hardly heeding, Helen said: "Yes; so I ought to be satisfied. But, now, I can't help feeling: If only he wouldn't marry that wretched little Joan! And if only we didn't have to have a trial —have everything in court and in the paper—" Her voice, which she tried to keep steady, to hold on the things-are-funny level, shook with an agitation of fear; as though, knowing herself, she did not know what to do about herself. Wretched little Joan meant the utter, unmistakable ruin of all her long, long fantasies on Ralph's future. A trial meant the detailed development in open court of what Ralph could stoop to do. The newspaper, though bowdlerizing the few paragraphs in obedience to small-town ideas of what was decent, would not fail to publish the six-thousand-times reduplicated declaration that Ralph Detweiler admitted to "intimacy" with a low slut who had haled him into court, charging that he attacked her.

Arthur Winner said: "Of course, I mean to do everything I can to keep it from going to trial." Helen, he saw, though working in a law office, knew no more about criminal law than Ralph. "There's a possibility that I can make Miss Kovacs, at Mr. Harbison's hearing, admit she's not telling the truth; but that's only a possibility. The district attorney's office sometimes gets permission to nol-pros a transcript and return, because the charge is ridiculous and they know about the person bringing it. That could be what Mr. Brophy wants to speak to me about—they may have found out enough about Miss Kovacs to make them doubtful. And, of course, there's the last chance that the grand jury will decide she's a liar and not find a true bill. I'm afraid that expecting any of these things to happen isn't realistic. I think we must be prepared to go to trial."

Helen said: "Yes, I know, Mr. Winner." She breathed deeply. "And I know, in one way, Ralph has himself to thank. She's only able to accuse him of what he didn't do because of what he did do—go out with her. And she's so awful, Mr. Winner! I just don't understand—I mean, how he could. And, of course, I see that's the trouble—I don't understand. It's like the college thing. It's something I didn't do right. Father would have—well, I don't know what he would have done; but I just know this never could have happened if he'd been alive."

Arthur Winner said: "I think you should remember that what happened is something that, given certain circumstances, can happen to almost any—and, perhaps, any—young man. That's not to condone it; but there's no one who can be sure he won't make this sort of mistake—"

The sudden thought came to him that here might be an exception, standing before his eyes. Had Helen ever, would Helen ever, make in that meaning, a "mistake"? Could you imagine her ever feeling a troublesome physical appetite? That mind could not even conceive the principal truth about what she didn't "understand"—that what she blenched at, that what was "awful" to her in Miss Kovacs—the low sensuality; the gross lust—was often honey to male flies.

Arthur Winner said: "I think Ralph's very sorry indeed for what he did. That's the way one learns. If he knows now that he'd better avoid girls like Miss Kovacs, that he can't trust himself in certain situations, he isn't a loser from all this—in the long run, he's a gainer."

Helen regarded him earnestly; but the steady blue eyes held still a darkness of untouched trouble—the heart's internecine struggle with the head! She said: "Mr. Winner, is there any chance that girl would take money?"

The little jolt of surprise was gone as soon as come. Arthur Winner must recognize and accept a quirk that was integral to most female minds—seeing a so-much-wanted end, no means

286

could ever be unjustified. As gently as he could, Arthur Winner said: "I know how you feel, Helen. But even if she'd take money, which I doubt, because I think her mother's making her bring the charge, I couldn't consider that."

Helen flushed. She said: "Mr. Winner, I'd never ask you to! I wasn't thinking of involving you. I know it's wrong; but I don't care. I just wondered if I went to her and offered her—"

"My dear," Arthur Winner said, "that amounts to subornation. You must not even think of it. I've been in this business a long time; and the longer I'm in it, the surer I am that honesty's not merely the best, it's the only possible policy. Everything you do must be perfectly straight. No other way works; and there aren't any exceptions. This case is a good example. The point of ethics aside, doing something not straight would be also extremely foolish. We're in the right; Ralph, we know, is innocent. We have, or will have, positive means of defense. That's what I meant. Since Miss Kovacs is telling lies, there's no chance that, having to tell them all twice, she can keep them all straight. A jury will very soon be shown she can't be believed; and then acquittal's a virtual certainty."

Taking her hands, holding them firmly a minute, he said: "Helen, I can tell you something else. These things pass. None of this will be easy; but all of this will soon be over. And remember, if you can, that what probably distresses you most is something that doesn't even exist, something you're only imagining. What comes out at a trial, what a paper prints, seems important to you because it's about Ralph. But people in general aren't in the least concerned about Ralph; to them, it's an item in the news—nothing at all! Those who know the name may pay a moment's attention because they know the name. When they see the thing's disagreeable, they'll—most of them—be sorry for a moment. But that's all; Ralph really doesn't matter to them; so they won't waste on him time they need for their own concerns. They'll think no more about it. And much sooner than you suppose, you'll think no more about it. A year from now, it won't matter at all."

Would he patch grief with proverbs? Helen said: "I know, Mr. Winner. I try to tell myself things like that. Only, now's not next year." She raised a wretched smile to him. "And I wish I hadn't said that about offering her money. I just suddenly thought I'd give anything—"

Holding her hands tighter a moment, Arthur Winner let them go. "I wish there were some way, too," he said. "But neither of us would really want that way. Why don't you go out and get some coffee?"

Helen said: "I will, Mr. Winner. Shall I send Ralph in? Oh— I checked all Mr. Tuttle's July deposits. There weren't any large ones in the McCarthy Estate account; but on July twentieth there was a twenty-thousand-eight-hundred-dollar deposit in his general account. Would that be the one? I suppose that could have been McCarthy money."

"It would be the one, thanks," Arthur Winner said. "I'm sorry. I didn't mean you to go to all that trouble."

"It was no trouble, Mr. Winner."

No trouble? Alone, Arthur Winner, dismayed and exasperated, must reflect that something really would have to be done. Specifically, he was thinking, he supposed, of Mr. Woolf (or someone like him) discovering these offhand procedures—from Helen's comment, you had to see, a constant or ordinary practice. To say, to know, that such monies were in no way interverted, that the old man by his own methods and in his own good time, would account to the last penny, was all very well; but these procedures were indefensible; and trying to explain how they came about didn't better the business. Noah had always done things that way? All the worse! Noah knew who was due what and didn't purpose to bother with a lot of technical forms? Those forms were provided by law! Noah might never know what had nearly happened to him here; but Arthur Winner must consider it. He considered it with consternation.

Mr. Woolf had turned good-humored. Mr. Woolf was not going to press the matter of the redeemed bonds. But could one reasonably have expected this? Suppose, in the line of his duty, and in the line of his attitude yesterday, Mr. Woolf had chosen to press? Suppose he demanded bank statements, actual evidence of that cash Noah claimed he held, and that Mr. Woolf was in a position to prove he had received? Did the executor mean to say that this money rested in his own account? And had been there since July twentieth? Mr. Woolf never in his life heard of such a thing! There was a blunt word for that in law—mingling! The law forbade it. Could a man of the executor's legal experience pretend he didn't know such conduct was actionable—a statutory offense?

Arthur Winner thought suddenly of that concerned exclamation of Clarissa's—"Arthur, he's really *too* old!" With pain of mind, he thought: So he is! I'll have to take this up with Julius. We'll have to find a way to keep an eye on these things.

And who, Julius might inquire, bells the cat? Of course there was Helen; but things of this kind could not, unfortunately, be left to her alone. Though wonderful at figures, Helen, you soon realized, saw them as abstract patterns, bare exercises in arithmetic. Presented with figures, she was expert in what to do with them, how to arrange them, where they ought to go. That the arranged figures then formed a picture or told a story seemed not to occur to her. She felt no curiosity about their meaning; they were where they were and what they were because Mr. Tuttle had provided her with them. As long as his noted receipts and noted disbursements in the end balanced, Helen simply would not know whether interim money transctions had been in order or out of order.

Well, if Helen herself couldn't manage an effective supervision, could one be managed by means of Helen? Helen knew—no one better; since she must baby him through them—that some days Mr. Tuttle was a little vague. Loyalty to her employer had never allowed her to mention it; and he and Julius had never mentioned it to her; but why not now ask her to join them in facing the fact? Let them agree that, for Mr. Tuttle's protection, some track ought to be kept of what he was doing. No one wanted to affront or wound the old man with such a suggestion; and such a suggestion wouldn't be necessary if Helen would simply do this. She saw all deposits, or withdrawals, or transfers between accounts. When Mr. Tuttle told her to make one involving any large sum of money, would she, before she did anything, show to him or Julius whatever it was? That way, a serious mistake was fairly sure to be caught before harm was done.

And if, and when, they came to catch a mistake? If, no harm yet done, they held up the transaction; with tact, pointed his obvious error out to Noah? Yes; how then? Who but Helen could have known what was proposed? Who but Helen was pry, spy, secret reporter?

Occupied with his worried thoughts, Arthur Winner had been a moment in noticing Ralph's hesitant entry. From Ralph's expression, Arthur Winner could now learn that his own expression had been one of set sternness; and that Ralph had not failed to connect this with Ralph's own, to him all-absorbing, trouble. He visibly quailed. He said feebly: "Excuse me, Mr. Winner. Helen told me I was to—"

Rousing himself, making himself smile, Arthur Winner said: "Yes. Shut the door, Ralph; and sit down."

Watching Ralph, while Ralph in an agitated way did what he was told, Arthur Winner could see him with some sympathy. The facts of the case, the stupid or ugly shifts, the slippery little nastinesses, that he had heard Ralph recount, were moving back in time, becoming past history. The power to repel, so strong at first hearing, lost freshness. Losing that, those facts no longer stood in the way of a simple present fact—not a fact of the case; a fact apart from the case; and now, properly, less and less colored by the case—of the unhappy youth in his unhappy situation. This youth, as even Helen saw, still had himself to thank for being there; but today his human plight could begin to put its subtle *ad captandum* appeal, dependence's best, surest call on humanity. He was frightened. He didn't know what to do. He needed help. Arthur Winner, at competent calm ease, well able to help, must (by the habit of man's nature) grow more kindly disposed. The helper's invariable (and often, overabounding) benevolence toward the helped would presently take command.

Arthur Winner said: "I think we have your part of this in good-enough shape, for the moment. As I said, I'll reserve our defense Monday, so there's nothing we need to prepare now. After the hearing, I'll want to spend some time with you on the transcript of Miss Kovacs's testimony. We must check her story in detail against your recollection of what really happened; so when I have her on the stand, I'll be able to press her where she's likeliest to contradict herself. I think we've nothing to worry about there—she'll be in trouble very soon. I haven't yet seen the district attorney; but I'm expecting to this morning. When I've seen him, we'll consider any other steps we may need to take. What did you find out from Miss Moore?"

Observing the instant change in Ralph's expression, Arthur Winner reminded himself that this highly readable face of Ralph's might be a trial factor of weight. In the course of hardly more than a minute, Ralph's feelings had passed—in plain sight of anyone watching him—from fright when he imagined Arthur Winner's show of sternness was for him; to relief, when he got a smile; to confidence (risen too high) as he guessed how formidable an ally he had, as he foresaw Miss Kovacs demolished. Now he came down to earth; and with a bump. He slumped in too-easy dejection, distracted and dismayed. Obviously, the trial tactic would be to go slow, to begin direct examination by beating about the bush. Jurors ought to be given ample time to accustom themselves to that play of the unstable face before anything that could be thought to involve the issue of guilt or innocence was touched on.

Ralph said: "Well, she says she's pregnant, Mr. Winner. She says she isn't all right."

"Did you suggest that she see a doctor?"

"Well, Joanie doesn't want to. She says she won't. She doesn't want anyone to know until we're married."

"But she understands, because of this case, you're not in a position to marry her immediately?"

His distraction growing desperate, Ralph said: "Well, that's the thing, Mr. Winner. Joanie just won't be reasonable. She wants us to get married right away; and when I said we'd have to wait, she said: 'No, we can't wait.' So then I told her what you said. So she said we could get married and not tell anyone until later. She was crying and everything; so finally I had to say I'd ask you if that would be all right—I mean, if we kept it a secret."

Arthur Winner said: "She forgets that marriage licenses are a matter of public record. Anyone interested can look them up.

You couldn't keep it secret; and the fact that you tried to would only do you more harm."

With increased agitation, Ralph said: "Well, that's what I thought, Mr. Winner. But saying what you told me made her see I must have told you about her having a baby. So then she was practically yelling at me; and said I hadn't any right to. And if I was telling people, if everybody knew she was having a baby, why I ought to know she could make me marry her. She was even saying I took advantage of her; and I was going to marry her; and if she had to, she'd make the law make me marry her. I don't know what to do with her, Mr. Winner. Joanie wasn't ever like this before."

The obvious rejoinder might be that, before, "Joanie" had never found occasion to be like this. About women, a two-sided sex, Ralph was now starting to learn an important truth. When she is good she may be very, very good: but when she's bad, she's horrid! Ralph had accepted with pleasure his mistress in her aspects of amenability or adoring meekness. He let himself make the mistake of concluding this manageable "Joanie" was the only possible "Joanie." The night before last, he came, amazed, on other aspects. A new, quite different "Joanie" showed herself. Though the house was empty, though the living-room sofa had served their turn once before, and was only waiting to serve it again, she faced him with a flat and obstinate refusal. No plea to be reasonable, no declaration of right, budged her. Ralph, as indignation succeeded incredulity, could do nothing. Nothing; except, think of Miss Kovacs, who might be used to get even; and leave, aggrieved, to range around until, unluckily for him, he located Miss Kovacs, and duly got even!

Now, just when Ralph thought *that* disastrous episode had been adjusted as far as "Joanie" went, and he looked to see the old amenability restored, more aspects of "Joanie," the obstinate refuser, presented themselves. These went beyond the merely aggrieving; they were downright frightening. One might judge that the perspicacious she (instinct in every girl child) had realized (and told "Joanie") how good a hold on him Ralph's weaknesses of fear gave her. That minute, "Joanie" was in the saddle, ready with inherent female know-how, to sit her caught male with address. This manège had many devices. Obey he must! When he was no more than a little restive, gentling could be feasible. By pattings and makings-much of him, by seasonable portionings-out of physical gratification, the adept equestrienne might keep him obeying for the sake of his pleasure. On the other hand, if he began to buck, some savaging could become necessary. With her whip of tears and tantrums, with her spur of threats and reproaches, she might have to harry, plague, and bedevil the bridled brute until he obeyed for the sake of his peace.

Arthur Winner said: "Miss Moore's mistaken about the law. We'll agree that in this situation you're obligated to marry her; but the obligation's moral, not legal. An enforceable legal obligation exists only in the matter of a child—her expenses in having it; and its support—"

On Arthur Winner's desk, the telephone buzzer sounded. Mary Sheen said: "A Mrs. Pratt would like to speak to you, Mr. Winner."

"Pratt?" Arthur Winner said. "I'm afraid I don't place her. Just say I'm engaged with a client. Try to find out what she wants; and, if necessary, I'll call her back." To Ralph, he said: "Whether born in or out of wedlock, a child has an enforceable claim on its father for support. The child's mother can get a court order on him for regular payments, which he must continue as long as the child's a minor. Being a court order, an attachment can issue and he may be jailed for contempt if he fails to keep up the payments. But the court won't order—the court has no power in law to order—anyone to marry anyone. I think I'd better see Miss Moore. Do you know where she is now?"

"Well, I suppose she's home," Ralph said.

"She hasn't yet told her parents?"

"No," Ralph said. "But her mother's coming back this afternoon; and that was another thing she said. Unless I married her right away, she was going to tell her mother."

"I think she would be wise to. I've no doubt I can make her parents, when they understand the situation, see why we have to wait. Go and have another talk with her. You might try to per-

293

suade her to come here with you about eleven. I expect to be back from the courthouse by then. I think I can explain to her so she'll understand, what it is we want to avoid—"

The telephone buzzer sounded again. Mary Sheen said: "Mr. Brophy is here, Mr. Winner."

"Tell him I'll be with him in a moment."

"Oh; Mr. Winner, that Mrs. Pratt was calling from Mrs. Penrose's. She said it was a personal matter—could she talk to you when you were free."

But, of course! "That Mrs. Pratt" was Marjorie's friend Polly. She must have arrived; and since Marjorie hadn't heard —Arthur Winner said: "Please call her back and ask if it would be convenient for her and Mrs. Penrose to see me about one thirty at Roylan." To Ralph, he said: "I don't want to keep Mr. Brophy waiting. Yes; tell Joan I think she should tell her mother; and that I'd like to see her before she does—but if the idea of seeing me upsets her, don't press her. Just tell her what I told you—that it might be easier for me to put it to her mother than for her to. Anyway, let me know what she says."

Arthur Winner paused a moment. He had been about to tell Ralph he could leave by the back—not encounter the district attorney. On second thought, he arose, went and opened the door to the outer office, gesturing to Ralph to come with him.

In the outer office, J. Jerome Brophy, a man tall enough and spare enough in flesh to have an angular look, stood at ease near the middle of the room. On his limber, long, somewhat pale face, the skin was firmly drawn, yet flexibly hung in shallow narrow folds down the cheeks from the high narrow forehead. Jerry Brophy's eyes were, in their color, an unusual near-golden brown, in their quality, a little feline, at once sharp and somnolent. His straight thin hair was a dusty but dark-toned blond. At the moment, an effective and engaging look of friendliness that Jerry often wore warmed his face. Arthur Winner could see that he had not wasted the few minutes of waiting. All affability, he was passing the time of day with Mary Sheen and Gladys Mills—both, he did not forget, voters. Helen Detweiler was not in sight—she wouldn't, Arthur Winner recognized, wish to face, nor even to see, the man who would be prosecuting Ralph.

With a movement of his head, prompt yet unhasty, that took leave of the girls, yet avoided any brusqueness of dismissal, Jerry Brophy transferred the friendly look to Arthur Winner. He said: "Good morning, Art. Hope I'm not interrupting?"

"Not at all, Jerry," Arthur Winner said. "We'd just finished. This is Mr. Detweiler."

"Yes; I've seen him around," Jerry Brophy said. He gave Ralph a direct, attentive glance, his face more serious. He said: "I'm sorry to hear about your difficulty, Ralph. But, with Mr. Winner, you're in good hands. You're fortunate, young man."

Appraising Ralph's clear inability to answer, he went on, not smiling, yet not unkindly: "You'll understand our office has its duty; and when a case comes to us, we do whatever our duty is. Chiefly, we feel our duty is to get the facts. If they convict, it's true; we say—fine! But if the facts acquit; we say—fine, too! Fair enough?"

Ralph Detweiler managed to say: "Yes, sir."

His purpose accomplished—Ralph had been given at least a look at what he would be up against—Arthur Winner said to him: "All right; I'll see you later."

Wordless, with numb embarrassment, Ralph nodded. He made his way quickly out to the reception room.

✦

With Jerry Brophy seated by his desk, Arthur Winner said: "I don't know how far you've gone into this thing of Ralph's, Jerry. You wouldn't have heard, for instance, if a physician saw the girl?"

Jerry Brophy said: "I really wouldn't know, Art. The office had a call—just saying this girl claimed she'd been attacked; and an information was being filed at Joe's. There's a good chance she didn't go to a doctor—they're pretty ignorant people, most of those Hunkies. Afraid of doctors, as a matter of fact."

"Would you have any objection, if she's willing, to Doctor Shaw's examining her?"

"Not if *he* is—well, I guess you could take care of that! You know he doesn't like having to give evidence. We had to slap a subpoena on him to bring him in this morning on the Dummer girl business. He wasn't a bit happy. Too busy, I guess."

"If he's going to be in court, I can probably get a chance to speak to him. Frankly, I want to be able to put in evidence the fact that she refused, if she does."

"Good idea," Jerry Brophy said. "Well, Art, you know I meant what I told your young man. We're never out to prove anyone guilty; we just want to establish whether he is, or not. I won't ask what your defense is; I suppose, consent. I haven't heard what these circumstances were, but I guess we all know that if the girl's conscious and kicking, and not scared into letting him, there had to be some consent, or he couldn't have done it. What I mean, Art, is: we may have to prosecute the charge; but that doesn't say for a minute I'm assuming rape. Especially not, when Garret tells me that keeping her legs crossed is something the prosecutrix never seems to have been good at. Still, we also all know a prostitute can be raped just as much as a nun; and the girl's entitled to have her story looked into."

"We ask nothing more—or better," Arthur Winner said, smiling. Not unwary, not (for instance) missing the offhandedness in Jerry's mention of "a call" (which, you could infer if you wished, was not person-to-person in any sense, but just one of those tiresome pesterings of "the office" that you had to expect and put up with from some among the many thousand taxpayer and voter masters that a public servant had, by definition, undertaken to serve), Arthur Winner could nonetheless conclude that Jerry, here, and now, and for whatever reason, meant (as he declared) what he said. He was making an offer, which might or might not be a large one; which might or might not include a passing-up of some minor political haymaking; which might or might not involve swallowing down personal feelings that

Julius thought were Jerry's. Maintaining a smile, Arthur Winner waited.

Soberly smiling back, Jerry Brophy said: "Art, what I came over about is this. We hear definitely from Harry Burnett that we're getting the fourth judge for this district. The assembly won't be able to act until December—so the usual interim appointment will be coming up. But I don't see any contest. We can expect whoever's appointed to be named on both tickets next year."

"Good," Arthur Winner said. "We certainly need another judge. When the court has to sit Saturdays, it's time something was done."

"Yes. There's too much work for three men. I think the appointment can be made before Christmas, all right; and I know who a good many people would like to see appointed. I know who I would; and there'd be no question about unanimous endorsement by the bar association in a recommendation to the governor. Art, are you interested? Would you be willing to have some of us circularize the membership, saying you were our choice, and would they support us?"

Taken aback, Arthur Winner said: "That's kind of you, Jerry. And I appreciate the compliment—" He spoke with a sense of throwing phrases into the gap, the open unfilled space between the words of proposal and Jerry's still-ungrasped intent or object. Perplexed—Jerry must know he hadn't any such ambition —he said: "But I'm afraid I can't see myself as a good choice."

Looking steadily at him, Jerry Brophy said: "We're convinced you are, Art. Everybody's thought so for a long time. Of course we understand, with a practice like you have, there'd be some financial sacrifice; and, in that way, we know we're asking a good deal. And I know you've been asked before. But we wonder if you might not feel, this time, that you had a duty? I think we're all proud of our bench; and we want only men of the highest caliber there. So when that's what somebody is, ought he to go on shutting his mind to the thing?"

The effusive, if complicated, compliment had been brought out with earnestness—so much so, that Arthur Winner (aware that he was hardly fair) found his perplexity taking specific form. What interest of Jerry's could possibly be served if Arthur Winner—a man never active in politics, and so of only indirect weight there; a man obviously (he hoped!) no more to be reached by influence than those judges now sitting—were to be successfully persuaded of a duty to go on the bench? Sparing him an immediate need to decide, the telephone buzzer sounded.

Mary Sheen said: "Excuse me, Mr. Winner. I've kept trying to get those tree people; and I just did. Mr. Shields *was* in; and he ought to be back. The girl says could you leave a message?"

"Yes," Arthur Winner said. "Tell her to tell Mr. Shields I wish he'd go up and look at the big oak on the terrace at the lake—"

But if Jerry's interest was perplexing, not plain to see, what *was* plain to see (though perplexing, too) could be considered—something a little inept, not thought-out, in the phrasing of the earnest, unexpected proposal. Jerry spoke understandingly of financial sacrifice (which of course made a doing of duty only more commendable). Did Jerry in fact credit men with this potential of pure altruism? Or was he setting forward a screen of high purpose that he thought Arthur Winner might wish to use; while, all the time, Jerry, unfooled, looked to his politician's knowledge of men—certain that Arthur Winner was no freer than the rest from the hidden hankerings of vanity? Arthur Winner might have put the crown by once; but, for all that, would he fain have had it?

Bread to eat in secret—the sound, not ungrateful, of "your Honor" in his ears; the agreeableness of wearing, on the bench, a secure if modest power, of wearing everywhere a secure if modest dignity! So far, so good; that weakness was strong, that weakness was reliable; but hadn't Jerry forgotten something? Would a hankerer after them, a man of pride of place to whom these vanities could be breath and life, find acceptable a last place on the bench? Would the vain man happily sit junior to a younger judge, junior to Fred Dealey, who had begun as the vain man's junior, and in the vain man's own office? To the telephone, Arthur Winner said: "Tell him he'll find lightning hit it last night. I want to know if he thinks the tree can be saved. And how much it would cost."

"Yes, Mr. Winner. Oh; Mr. Winner; Mrs. Pratt said to tell you one thirty will be convenient."

To Jerry Brophy, Arthur Winner said: "Sorry!" He pushed the telephone away. He said: "I'll agree that members of the bar, when they're fitted, and when they're needed, have a duty to serve on the bench. But a good many things go into making a man fitted. One of them, I feel more and more, is the point of age. Being a good judge takes experience; and I don't think a man should be in his fifties when he starts. By then, a man's less teachable, more settled in habits of practice. And, of course, the community stands to get a longer period, very likely a whole additional term, of experienced and competent service when the new judge is forty instead of fifty. Feeling this way, you'll see I couldn't, at my age, presume to think I had any 'duty.' Unless there were no younger men. But we've plenty. Lew Studdiford, for instance—"

Jerry Brophy said quickly: "Well, I can't pretend I didn't know you felt that, Art. I know that was why you supported Fred—when, of course, just as now, the bar would certainly have endorsed you unanimously, if you'd let them. But people can change their minds; and I wanted to find out if by any chance you'd reconsidered; or if we could somehow get you to. It's definite that we can't?"

With a sudden accession of light, Arthur Winner said: "I'm sensible of the honor, Jerry; but I'm afraid it is definite."

From his pocket, Jerry Brophy brought a key ring. Dropping the ring on his forefinger, he circled the finger slowly, spinning the bright keys around. Watching them, he said: "I wish it wasn't; because I think you're the best man we could get. But if we can't have you, we'll have to find somebody else."

He paused, allowing the keys to rest quiet in the palm of his hand. He said: "You may know there's been a movement—without my permission, and rather embarrassing to me at this stage—to suggest that I be appointed. Dave Weintraub may have started it. Of course, like you, I feel complimented. I take it as an honor that Dave, and any others, should think of me. And I don't say that, if the bar proved to be relatively unanimous, I wouldn't gladly accept the honor. But I feel I'd have to

299

be sure about that. Naturally, I can't expect to please every-body; but if there seemed to be going to be a serious division, I'd want to stop this movement before it started. I know some people are opposed to me. I have to see that I have some draw-backs." He paused again. "Art, if you're out of this yourself, would you give me your advice on whether I ought to try for the appointment?"

Arthur Winner said: "Jerry, I don't think I'm the right per-son to advise you. For the simple reason that I've never held, nor run for, any public office—unless you call being on the board of education a public office."

Jerry Brophy smiled. He said: "I guess you don't run for that. They just chase you until they catch you! What I meant was, Art, as far as the bar went, you'd be in a good position to have some idea of the general sentiment—"

Arthur Winner said: "To tell you the truth, Jerry, I haven't any idea at all. Since everyone has known we were trying to get an additional judge, and probably would, I suppose some mem-bers of the bar have thought of it—have someone in mind. Per-haps, themselves! But I don't know who they are; or who's favored by anyone. You'd be a lot better able than I am to say what a given person's chances were."

Jerry Brophy said gravely: "I'm not so sure. As I said, the question's how serious a division there might be. I know, in my own case, some members of the bar wouldn't like to see me a judge; but I don't know how many. I suppose a few think I'm just not up to the job—haven't the abilities. Well, I don't claim to be a great legal mind; but I think I know enough law not to do the bench any discredit that way. Then, some may say I've been a politician. So I have. I'm not ashamed of that. But they may think I'm too much of a politician—that a judge ought to be, or seem to be, clear of politics."

Arthur Winner said: "As long as judges have to run for office, I don't see how they can ever be entirely clear. We may expect them not to show political bias on the bench; but, off the bench, the fact that a man's a good vote getter could hardly be held against him."

Jerry Brophy smiled. Moving his finger in a circle, he started the key ring twirling again. He said: "It so happens that it can be so held—by some people. Just as some people don't like my religion. They'll tell you you can't trust a Catholic."

Arthur Winner said: "I wouldn't imagine that, nowadays, that was a serious issue with enough people to make any difference."

"I just mention it," Jerry Brophy said. "I'm a Catholic because that's what my father and mother were—what I was brought up. As an issue, I don't say it's too serious; but there are people who'd feel a lot easier about me if my parents had gone to your Christ Church, and Episcopalian had been what I was brought up. And, of course, then my old dad wouldn't have been running a saloon either. I guess there never was an Episcopalian saloonkeeper. Well, as I say, the point, one point, is how many people are against me; why they are, doesn't matter. Then there's the point: just who are they? That would have something to do with how many would be too many. I have friends, like Dave Weintraub; and he carries a lot of weight in Mechanicsville—none more! I think, as an attorney with a big practice, he carries some weight with the bar association, too. But I wouldn't say he was one of the men who carry most weight there; would you?"

Arthur Winner said: "Jerry, in the sense you mean, I wonder if anyone carries much weight there. This is a pretty individualistic profession. I've never seen even a bar association entertainment committee that was willing to take its lead from any one member. They meet to find out how many of them have coinciding opinions that the annual dinner should be at the Federal House instead of the Brookside. Nobody speaks for anybody else."

Steadily twirling the key ring, Jerry Brophy renewed his smile. The tenseness in it was barely perceptible; but tenseness was there—Greek, Arthur Winner thought, is meeting Greek! Could I be, to Jerry's mind, the better fencer, the Greeker of the two?

Jerry Brophy said: "Well, are you willing to speak for yourself, Art?" He laughed, not quite easily. "I don't have any

301

right to ask you; and to tell you the truth, anyone else, I wouldn't *be* asking. Because I know he'd just say anything he felt like saying, whether he meant it or not."

Looking at the ring of keys, Jerry Brophy closed his fingers over them, holding them tight. Speaking quickly, he said: "I don't ask: Will you support me, Art; I know you don't go in for that. I mean, I know Fred Dealey was a special case. He was qualified; and he was a friend of yours, had been in your office; and he was your brother-in-law. You'd have to come out for him. Not taking sides would amount to being against him. I'm just saying: Are you willing to tell me whether or not you're going to oppose me?"

The speed of thought was too slow. The allotted time of a conversational pause was too short; the ground that thought's trip-of-a-moment ought to cover had the extent of a continent—the whole range of man's relation to man. Here was the offer in full—the honest-enough trade, the open-enough deal, the earnest pathetic terms of the proposed contract. I engage to be reasonable; and in evidence of my good faith, I showed you just how reasonable. Like the law itself, I'll bend backward to hold your young man innocent until he's proved guilty beyond a reasonable doubt. Will you do as much for me? Will you be fair? Will you far enough put down your "not liking" to see me—the practicing politician, the untrusted Catholic, the unvalued saloonkeeper's son—rise to the bench and sit level with my betters? Will you do me ordinary justice? I'm not unqualified. I have as much law as the next man—and more than some! As long-time district attorney, I have—and you can't deny it; Judge Lowe was district attorney; Judge McAllister was district attorney!—an additional important qualification that no other member of the present bar can match. I'm also a man of the age you think is right. So how about it? Will you trade? Is it a deal?

To Jerry Brophy, the moment, though so trying, must have seemed too short, too. That practical politician in him, inspecting what he'd just said—blurted out?—perhaps gave him a jog, showed him how close the direct question came to breaking sound politics' most essential rule: Never so state your position that you

302

can't afterward compromise; never force the other man to so state *his* position that *he* can't compromise. He said: "I won't try to rush you into answering, Art. I've got to get over to court for that plea. But let me say this, if I may. I'm not going to ask your reasons if you feel you have to oppose me. If you feel that some-one like—well, Lew Studdiford, is better fitted, I'll respect your opinion. I can't say I won't be disappointed; but I can say there'll be no hard feelings; because if you're against me, tell-ing me now does me the biggest favor you could possibly do me."

He smiled. "You could let us go ahead with this without say-ing anything, and when I was committed as a candidate, pull the rug out by proposing someone else. That would mean a con-test, people taking sides about the endorsement; and because I'd divided the bar, I wouldn't be the one who got it. That would cook me. I'd tried; and I'd failed. I couldn't expect an-other chance. But if I never announced as a candidate, I'd only have to wait. Four years from now, when Judge Lowe's term ends, and I know he'll retire, I *would* have another chance; there'd be nothing standing against me; I'd be eligible—"

Here, before your eyes, was opened the reposeless, anxiety-blighted world, the bleak slave state, of the ambitious; and you might ask yourself how any man could will to live there! People said they pitied the wretch in bondage to lusts of the flesh, yet compared to ambition's bondage, how easy was the yoke of those appetites, how light their burden! They were self-limiting; their demands were intermittent; you met them in your spare time. The resolve to rise permitted no intermissions; ambition was never sated, there was no limit to what might be exacted of you.

You sat, forcing yourself to affect an easiness, while that por-trait of Arthur Winner Senior, his painted face forever with-drawn in cool reflection, in his painted book, the just-read re-ported case forever marked, watched you, while you watched with fearful care the dead man's son—another of the same politely contemptuous stamp. Straining every nerve, you pro-duced the dumb-show gestures of comity. Acting friends with him, you spoke your hollow part of friendly regard. Fine friends, these! Could you persuade this remote fellow not to dash your hopes, not to do your hopes the fatal injury that your circumspective anxiety saw to be in his power? Would he, could he, have what amounted to the mercy not to spoil the chance that was much to you, but nothing to him? The petition was before him. *And your petitioner shall ever pray* . . . The black Protestant, only the name of friendship between them, was now thinking. He'd have to see; he'd have to see! Maybe, yes; maybe, no!

Not unmoved by the bitter predicament of all such petitioners, Arthur Winner said: "I won't oppose you, Jerry. I think your experience sufficiently qualifies you; and since you're qualified, your services seem to me to entitle you to the appointment. If I'm asked, that's what I'll say."

TWO

With wheezings, with irritable wags of the head that made the mop of white hair shake, Noah Tuttle moved in short steps—a shuffle that seemed more than usually infirm. Coming close to the door that led from the back hall where the conference rooms were, to the main courtroom, he began to speak. "No; no use, Arthur!" he said. "Can't abide that kind of fellow. Give him an inch, he takes a yard. No manners. Try to praise a person to his face! No gentleman! All that lickspittle stuff about respecting me. No taste! Does he think I was born yesterday? Well, let's hope we've seen the last of him. And I think we have. I know what made him change his mind—not bother with the account any further. Too little money involved—fees wouldn't come to enough. That's all he'd have any regard for!"

There was nothing to answer. Though, in form, Arthur Winner was addressed, in fact, Noah held ruminative colloquy with himself. To Noah's own mind, nowadays so often, perhaps, surprised by the doings and sayings of this old man in which it housed, Noah tried to explain how the old man felt—perfectly reasonable feelings! Not pausing, Noah reached familiarly and found the handle of the great paneled door. With a quickness, which might show that fear that Arthur Winner would try to help him, he tugged the door open, shuffling forward, his head determinedly down, to cross the well of the court. A double row of chairs, placed for the convenience of waiting attorneys, was in his way. Plodding forward, Noah avoided them, made to pass behind them. He veered, head still down, toward the center aisle that mounted at a moderate incline to the main entrance doors that gave on the front part of the building. Some glimpse or sound of movement reached him then; for he stopped dead, blinking. To Arthur Winner, he said loudly: "Court sitting? Today's Saturday."

"They arranged to take a plea," Arthur Winner said. "That's why I wanted to come in. Willard asked me to see him; and I thought I'd catch him when he came off the bench. I don't think this will take long."

Having said it, Arthur Winner must immediately wonder if he was right. Sitting back in the witness stand was Reggie Shaw; and medical evidence would presumably be the prosecution's. Below the bench, a handful of people were distributed—at their railed-in desks, Mrs. Langley, the deputy clerk of quarter sessions; the crier in his jacket; and Bob Ferris, one of the court reporters, his poised fingers touching the keys of his stenographic machine. At the prosecution's table, Garret Hughes sat patiently alone. The Dummer girl and Lew Studdiford were side by side at defense's table. Lew's massive form and big solid face had set themselves, immobile, in full attention to the witness. Mobile, in full inattention, Caroline's innocent moron face was pleased-looking under the yellow hair, still stiff with that tight fancy curling Mrs. Morton had so kindly provided yesterday. Caroline's stubby-fingered hands lay on the table. From one to the other, she tossed, contentedly playing with it, a little beaded purse.

Outside the rail of the bar, in the first row of seats by the aisle, a thickset man with a stupid, stupefied expression, surly yet mournful, and a woman, fat and faded, whose moony face, an older version of Caroline's, identified these spectators as the girl's parents, sat together. No one else was in the courtroom. Across the ascending rows of empty seats fell successive bright oblongs of sunlight. They shafted, a little hazed by motes of dust, from the tall windows rising between tall pilasters whose elaborate capitals with gilded volutes and helices purported to support the cofferwork (in the recesses, also enriched with gilt) of the great ceiling.

Elevated by the bench's ample mound of carved mahogany, Willard Lowe and Fred Dealey occupied two of the three

306

judges' chairs. The opening of the rear door, and Noah's entrance, Noah's unheeding, shuffling march out onto the floor, had produced a pause. Seeing Noah, pulled up, blinking in surprise toward them, both judges gravely bowed. Turning where he stood near the witness stand, Jerry Brophy, smiling, inclined his head, too.

"Here!" Noah said to Arthur Winner. "I'll sit down a minute." Going to the front row of attorneys' chairs, he put himself in one. "What's this?"

Sitting down behind him, Arthur Winner said: "The girl, there."

Facing his witness again, tilting his head back, Jerry Brophy said: "But you say you could tell nothing from your observations, Doctor?"

Reggie Shaw lounged sideways, one leg crossed over the other. His long-fingered hands, clasped together, rested on the rail of the stand. He had the unmistakable impatient manner of a man who hasn't time for this, can't stay long. He said: "Not 'nothing,' Mr. Brophy. Just; not what you ask."

From the bench, Fred Dealey, seated nearest the stand, leaned forward on his black-robed elbows and said: "In other words, Doctor, your examination wouldn't indicate whether the child born was a fully developed, living one; or whether it was in a more fetal stage, and not living—a miscarriage, in short?"

Turning his tired sunken eyes briefly on Judge Dealey, Reggie Shaw said: "The extensive tear in the vagina suggested to me that a fairly large object must have passed from the uterus —probably, if you want guesses, a full-term infant, or near that. And, more likely than not, living. Unless through some external injury to the carrier, a fetus that had gone nearly full term wouldn't be apt to die in the uterus at the last minute."

Nodding, Fred Dealey made a note on his pad.

Jerry Brophy, tipping his solemn face up, said: "And nothing indicated to you in what manner the baby was born? That is —I mean by that—whether it came out headfirst, or feet first?"

Making plain his thought that the question was silly, Doctor Shaw said: "I couldn't possibly tell that from examining the young woman. Don't ask *me!* Doctor Duncan may have an opinion. He saw the dead infant—did the autopsy. I never saw it."

Doctor Duncan, the county coroner, who was sitting within the rail on the other side, next to Mrs. Morton, half stood up. He said apologetically: "There was nothing I saw that would signify in that connection, Doctor. Defendant's statement—the one you read, Mr. Brophy—seemed to be describing a breech birth; but that's the only evidence for it I know of."

Noah Tuttle's turned head showed Arthur Winner, sidelong, the heavy old face somber and brooding, the lips pouted in moody distaste. Made to hear some facts of our flesh, obliged by them to ponder a while the ugly and agonizing origination of a human being, the way, revolting as it was cruel, that every one came into the world, Noah perhaps felt a need of respite. Turning his head more, inclining his head back toward Arthur Winner, he said suddenly: "Had a letter from Lawrence. Did you?"

"No," Arthur Winner said, bending forward toward the old man's ear. "But Julius told me he'd seen him."

Noah Tuttle grunted to himself. He moved away his head. Brooding again, he stared through the tops of his glasses at Doctor Shaw.

Studiously unruffled, Jerry Brophy said: "Thank you, Doctor Duncan. I should have put that question to you on the stand. One more question in connection with your examination of defendant, Doctor Shaw. I believe you said you asked her several times whether she'd had a baby, and she persisted in denying it?"

"That is right," Doctor Shaw said. "I asked her what she'd done with the child; and she said there wasn't any. Certainly it wasn't there; and her mother knew, or said she knew, nothing about it. I had no time to look for it. I cleaned her up a little, packed her, and got her to a hospital. That's all I could do." More impatient, he crossed his legs the other way. "I can't tell you anything further."

"Well, just let me ask this, Doctor. Did you come to any opinion as to why she was denying it?"

Doctor Shaw said: "Why she denied it was none of my business. The only opinion I came to was that she lied. Couldn't be anything but a lie. The lower abdomen, the perineum, the whole genital tract, showed every *post-partum* sign. She'd been in labor within the last four or five hours, no matter what she said."

From the bench, Judge Lowe said: "Of course, you'd never treated this defendant professionally before, Doctor?"

"Didn't know her from—well, Eve," Doctor Shaw said. He uttered a harsh laugh. At the poor joke, the unexpected flippancy, made scornful by Reggie Shaw's unsmiling mouth and haggard eyes, Judge Lowe almost started. At the sound of the laugh, a shadow of displeasure crossed his face. Reggie must have seen it; for he added quickly, as though explaining, rather than apologizing: "I hadn't been even told her name, your Honor. I don't practice in that part of the county. I just happened to be up that way; and I'd stopped for gas at a service station. While I was there, the mother came panting in—very excited; wanting to telephone. Get a doctor! Hurry, hurry; daughter dying. So I went back with her—just across the road. That's how I happened to get mixed up in it." He passed his hand wearily over his cropped, grizzled reddish hair. His expression stated clearly that, if this was going to be the result, another time he'd think twice before he acknowledged his professional obligation to act in an emergency.

Jerry Brophy said, his tone ingratiating: "I know you're a busy man, sir. I'll try to be—and I'm sure Mr. Studdiford will, too—as brief as possible."

Lew Studdiford said: "I don't plan to ask any questions—so far!"

Noah, inclining back his head again, said: "Haven't the letter with me. Seems he wants to borrow money. Loan at interest."

In some left-handed way, Arthur Winner's surprised look clearly pleased Noah. Lawrence, excluding his father, not telling him anything, made application to his grandfather. Lawrence's father, if he hoped to know how his son came to need money, would now have to make application, too. Noah savored his private knowledge for an instant. He said then: "He wants to quit the job—with some fellow, chief of his department, I think he said. Set up a practice there. Between them, he seems to think they now know enough to show clients how you swindle the government legally."

From the bench, Judge Dealey's voice came sharp, saying: "And I don't understand either, Mr. District Attorney! Surely you can phrase your question better than that."

A least tinge of color showed on the vertical folds of Jerry Brophy's cheeks; but he said, his voice unflustered: "I agree with you, your Honor! Let me try again, Doctor. I'm aware that you never saw the dead baby. What I meant was: Will you be so good as to give the court your expert's opinion as to the more probable means or causes for the death of a baby under the circumstances? What, for instance, might be one sufficient cause for a baby, had by a woman by herself, who was ignorant of what to do, and was without professional medical assistance, dying?"

Judge Dealey frowned faintly; but he said nothing. Doctor Shaw said: "There might be twenty reasons." He moved his shoulders in a weary shrug. "Well; one—if you want it—ought to be obvious to you. I heard the coroner say the umbilical cord hadn't been tied. That, taken with his other statement about the small quantity of blood in the body, certainly suggests the baby died of a hemorrhage."

"Then, to save an infant's life, the first thing that must be done is tie the cord. What next? I mean what do you do after that?"

Doctor Shaw stared at him. "Well, do you want me to describe —well, after ligature and division of the cord, you need to clean the infant off—sebaceous matter, blood, mucus, and so on—just what do you want to know? What's this got to do with anything?"

Judge Dealey said: "What has it, Mr. District Attorney?"

"Very well, your Honor; I'll let it go. Now, Doctor, where the umbilical cord is severed by any means, and not properly tied, how long would a newborn child live?"

Doctor Shaw drew a weary breath. He said: "That would depend on just when the cord was severed. Severed immediately, before pulsation stopped, and left untied, the infant would die, exsanguinated, in a matter of thirty or forty seconds—because what was functionally an artery would be bleeding. If, after pulsation had stopped—say, after about a minute and a half—the cord was severed and not tied, the infant might live some time, still bleeding—but the bleeding would be venous—much slower."

"That's to say, if the cord was severed, torn apart, and not tied at the moment of delivery, the probability is?"

"That the infant wouldn't live longer than a minute."

Noah Tuttle said: "I suppose they think they have to have some kind of fancy setup—impress the sort of people they'd be dealing with, and don't expect to make the price of it at first. I suppose they'd be debarred from a good deal of stuff for a while because they'd been the government's attorneys in earlier actions. Lawrence thinks they need twenty thousand dollars. Other fellow can put up ten; he wants to put up ten. Don't suppose Lawrence ever saves anything. He must think I'm made of money!"

Some such thought was not unlikely, Arthur Winner could tell himself. Lawrence, casting about, might very well have decided his grandfather could find the money more easily than his father. Lawrence might even be showing delicacy—he had help from his father to supplement his salary. He might hesitate to ask for a large loan on top of that.

Jerry Brophy said: "And is it also possible, Doctor, for a child in an—did you call it breeched birth?—to be in the process of birth asphyxiated by the cord, so it would be delivered dead?"

With a movement of smothered impatience, Reggie Shaw said: "Whatever the presentation, if the cord is wound tight enough to be flattened, closed, and if it remains so, asphyxiation results."

"But death by asphyxiation is a greater danger in a breeched birth?"

"Breech!" Doctor Shaw said. "Breech! A buttock presentation! Generally, the danger is greater; yes."

Noah Tuttle said: "I don't know. In my day, a young man

311

did things for himself; he didn't have to have everything done for him. He didn't have to do things before he could afford to do them."

That, by all accounts, was, used to be, true—though the "day" had surely been less Noah's than Noah's father's. Noah's father framed the terms; and Noah complied with them, whether he really liked them or not. Noah, the young man clerking in a law office, was working to earn his law learning while he was getting it. Admitted to the bar, he was supposed to be ready, with what he had learned, to make a living. If his income was slender to start; then, to start, he must limit his expenses. Incredible as today might find the fact, these terms, Noah's youthful lean times, were not of real economic necessity. Principle, not poverty, imposed them.

The Tuttles, when Noah was born, were well off. Owned and shrewdly operated by Noah's father was a busy, money-making waterpower gristmill—those walls that still stood at Roylan. Noah's mother's grandfather, one Asa Warren, had acquired the mill put up there in the early eighteenth century. Noah's mother's father enlarged, improved, and in the end, devised the good business to his daughter and her husband—in testator's opinion, stated with old-fashioned candor and bluntness, the only *man* in the whole lot of visible heirs and possible assigns. The estimate was just. Noah's father kept the Roylan mill prospering—it shut down, its day done, only in the 1890's. For their home, the family had the respectable house on the square in Brocton. True, Noah's father, when his milling needed active supervision, never hesitated to don an apron and use his dusty hands; but he put on, leaving the establishment, the stovepipe hat of a gentleman of the sixties. Servants served him. He kept a carriage.

Such relative affluence, which continued and even increased during Noah's boyhood, was seen as having no bearing (or not much) on the natural—really, the religious—obligation of every young male (unless physically handicapped) to strive for himself, in the sweat of his face to eat bread. Young Noah's "advantage" (and, to the thinking of all right-thinking men, a great one; quite enough for him!) was that he needn't, nothing else considered, proceed from school into the milling business. The prosperous father was able to, the good father was glad to, bestow on his son the munificent boon of freedom to choose how he would earn a living.

The goodness of miller Tuttle hadn't, moreover, stopped there. Noah was of an age when young men may fairly be required to support themselves; but, electing the law, Noah, while he read, was allowed to live at home, receiving his board and lodging for nothing. Even that was not the end. The inexpensive simple clothes suitable for his daily wear, he was, of course, expected to provide himself with from the small sum of money he received, along with his instruction, for sweeping out his preceptor's office and copying papers—if he shopped wisely for them, and took care of his clothes, he ought to be able to. But an understanding parent understood the outlay, however modest, might leave a young man little to spare. Every month, therefore, he was presented (his cup ran over) with a dollar for pocket money.

Arthur Winner said: "I know Lawrence spoke to Julius. Julius did say he had more to tell me about Lawrence's plans; but we got off on something else. I'll say this for Lawrence. I'm sure everything's been carefully considered; and if he thinks now's the moment, he's probably right. I imagine he does know Washington pretty well by now; and with an older man, who knows it, too—"

Noah Tuttle gave another grunt.

At defense's table, Lew Studdiford had heaved himself deliberately to his feet. While Caroline Dummer, the game with her purse interrupted, turned up at him a vacant stare of wonder, he said: "If the court please! I don't know that I have any actual objection; but may I respectfully suggest that the district attorney, as well as examining, now appears to be cross-examining his own witness? If I follow him, he seeks to offer in evidence expert opinion tending to show the offense charged was not committed. It would seem rather for me, than for him, to do this. A little more, and I must say to him that I'll feel entitled, when he closes, to ask leave to demur to the evidence. Frankly, since I never had this experience before, I don't know

313

whether that motion's admissible in the hearing of a guilty plea. Perhaps I should petition the court to direct that my plea be withdrawn. But surely if prosecution's case, instead of going to establish the degree of the crime charged, goes to cast doubt on the corpus delicti itself—"

Jerry Brophy said: "As far as we're concerned, Mr. Studdiford, we aren't pressing for, and I don't think the court is considering, a finding of any offenses comprised in the bill of indictment over and above involuntary manslaughter. And, of course, concealing the death of a bastard child—count two."

Lew Studdiford said: "Well, for heaven's sake, your Honors! May I now have leave to demur to the indictment? If the prosecution is offering to show involuntary manslaughter—"

Judge Dealey said: "Yes. How is that possible, Mr. District Attorney?" Hitching up his robe, he turned a cool, annoyed glance down from the bench. "We undertook to accept a plea of guilty to the general charge of murder. As provided by the act of twenty-four June nineteen thirty-nine, we sit to determine, by examination of witnesses, the degree of the offense, and to give sentence accordingly. Need I tell you that involuntary manslaughter isn't a degree of the offense, and couldn't possibly be comprised in the counts of your indictment?"

Flushing, his eyes starting from somnolence, opaque with chagrined anger, Jerry Brophy said: "I beg the court's pardon! I meant, voluntary manslaughter, of course. I think your Honor might have recognized 'involuntary' as a slip of the tongue."

"That's not up to us," Judge Dealey said. "We've no charter to assume that what you say isn't what you mean—especially in light of the seeming effort to show by this witness that death might have been caused involuntarily or accidentally. I agree with Mr. Studdiford. Your questions amount to cross-examination. The witness says he's told us all he knows about the young woman's condition. I don't see the sense of these hypotheses you're putting to him."

At the prosecution's table, Garret Hughes, looked down with a slight wincing movement. Guardedly, he rolled his eyes.

Judge Lowe cleared his throat. He said: "Voluntary manslaughter. Yes, Mr. Brophy, I'm sure you had no thought of anything else. We're agreed, I believe that that—off the record, please, Mr. Ferris!—should be our finding. We have the reports of Doctor Arsavage of the state hospital staff; and he advises us that defendant is rational, in the sense that she's not too confused to relate what happened—her experiences." He looked toward a very tall thin man Arthur Winner had not been able to place, who sat by himself behind the jury box. "That is a fair summary, Doctor Arsavage?"

"It is, your Honor."

"In defendant's signed statement, she declares that after the baby was born, she observed movements of the hands and feet. We've no reason to doubt her; so we've no reason to believe the infant was born dead, however quickly it may have died. I'm afraid we must conclude that defendant's taking it and putting it in the clump of bushes, and her subsequent refusal to admit its existence, were voluntary acts—"

Lew Studdiford, reaching for the bound sheets of a transcript on the defense's table, said: "If your Honor please—I have it right here. I ask leave, in that connection, to call to the court's attention, in view of the court's statement that we have no reason to doubt her—yes; here it is. In the course of Doctor Arsavage's study of defendant, his conversation with her—page seventeen—in response to the question: 'Suppose, Caroline, that you had thought this child was living, not dead. What would you have done?' Answer: 'I would have taken it in the house.' "

He tossed down the transcript. "I submit that we have reason to accept this, too, as a true statement—that, so she would have! I submit that a strong presumption exists that the parent-child relationship will be in most cases what common experience shows us it usually is. A powerful instinct, rarely or never lacking, compels parents to cherish and protect, not reject and harm, the child. I submit that we are bound to presume the child this girl brought forth in sorrow was dear to her. If, through helplessness of ignorance and ineptitude—"

"Yes, yes, Mr. Studdiford," Judge Dealey said. His sharp glance had a glint—icy; crystal—of humor. "But I see no jury in the box! As for the court, we don't conceive that malice in the legal—or for that matter in any other—meaning was involved. As Judge Lowe tells you, we aren't contemplating a finding of murder in either the first or second degree. We will, if you wish, take judicial notice that a parent is apt to cherish a child. We conceive, then: such could have been the case here. It's still surplusage, if not entirely irrelevant; for the child is dead. Whatever defendant's thought or intention, and allowing, as we may, that ignorance and ineptitude could or did largely relieve her from actual moral guilt in the death, we don't see her relieved of legal responsibility. I'm afraid we can't properly admit any doctrine of *mens rea*. Let's not confuse the issue. Though committed with the best intentions in the world, or though committed by accident, error, or complete inability to avoid the commission, what is by statute a crime remains a crime. That's well established. Innocence of purpose no more excuses a statutory offender than ignorance of the law excuses him."

Noah Tuttle said: "I don't have the money right now. I don't know that I want to borrow."

"Well, perhaps I can do something," Arthur Winner said. In Noah's pouched eyes, swimming large through the thick lenses of his spectacles, Arthur Winner could see again the faint light of that odd triumph—Arthur Winner hadn't been asked to do anything! Arthur Winner said: "Julius may be able to tell me more when he gets back tomorrow. If the opportunity's a good one, and has to be taken now, I wouldn't want Lawrence to have to miss it. I'd find him the money. Part now, perhaps; and—"

Noah said: "Didn't say *I* wouldn't. But it's whether anybody should find it. Like this nonsense Maud Jennings was talking—wants the means to make a fool of herself! I know about schemes like Lawrence's. Work with cheaters! Not really law. You're peddling influence, or pretending to. Your business is bribery in one form or another—"

Arthur Winner said: "I don't think so. I'm sure what they plan to peddle is simply special legal knowledge. The fact they need money seems pretty good proof there's nothing irregular. I'm sure money wouldn't be a problem if they were in a position to, and planned to, peddle influence, get people favors."

"Well, if you like to see it that way, I suppose you can," Noah Tuttle said. "He's your boy."

Judicial notice was taken that a parent is apt to cherish his child! And—significantly, of course—a lot more apt to cherish the child than the child was to cherish the parent! If the old man made himself useful, he might be thought of not unkindly; he might even be shown something of that affection the domestic dog, or to a less degree, the domestic cat, shows for its self-styled master, the great, good, food-giver. Jumpings-up on you, purring rubs against you, were gestures of hope, the proverbial importunity of the horseleech's daughters. Lew Studdiford's "powerful instinct" seemed to be a one-way obligation.

Arthur Winner turned his head enough to look at Caroline Dummer's parents—the distressed, resentfully mournful, disconsolately baffled, two faces over beyond the rail of the bar. Of their daughter's feelings about them, her actions might be taken to speak. Could you imagine that thoughts of mom and dad (where thoughts of Jesus, and social diseases, and the danger of having a child, didn't) ever weighed with her? Caroline's limited intelligence naturally spent itself on immediate worries of Caroline's. If, in her half-wit amorous play with various lovers amid the dirty laundry, she gave the authors of her being a thought, it could only be to fear that they would beat her if they caught her.

And what of them, the mother and father in their resentful, surly sorrowings? Unintelligible to them would be the law, proceeding step by solemn step against their daughter—a lawyer submitted some presumptions; a judge rejected the doctrine of *mens rea*—yet the painful sum of the steps must be intelligible enough. Caroline at the table there—now playing with her little purse again—had done them grievous indignity and injury, had put shame and disgrace on them. In the midst of pain, were they still the helpless subjects of some force compelling them to love her who did the wrong? Behind those slow-minded peerings of sullen anxiety did dumb unreasonable surges of love swell—a pain separate, a suffering purely for Caroline, distinct and different from the acute pains of their wounded self-esteem?

Yes; what about these visitings of the sins of the children

317

upon the fathers? Thinking last night of the parents of Ralph's "Joanie," those Moores, all unsuspecting, whose "shame" or "disgrace" of the same kind (if more decent in degree) stood accomplished, waiting merely to be discovered to them, Arthur Winner had felt able to prefigure, following the first horrified anger, the distraught recriminations, the general fury of family woe, a bitter necessary acceptance. But could you believe the real quick thus soon to be cut to, the springs of their impending distress, would be loving—they loved their little girl so much? Thinking further; Helen Detweiler, at fervent, selfless labor *in loco parentis,* might be thought of. If Ralph, her fondling, went by mischance to prison—what? Why, first and most certain, Helen would never hold her head up again!

That said, was all said—reduced, simplified, but true; the entire actual truth? What did the cherishers in fact cherish? Must the "powerful instinct" and all its myriad shapes of earnest devotion and eager sacrifice be, to a psychologist, suspect? Subject of so much piety and praise, did this great paternal tenderness's every exercise boil down (alas, alas!) to: *I love me?*

His head held up, his chin raised, Arthur Winner looked reflectively away. In the middle distance, low against the sunken veined-marble panels, thirty feet high, of the courtroom's back wall, his eye fell on, caught on, the silken flag draping motionless folds around the erect staff held in a stand behind the carved high backs of the judges' chairs. In an ordinary tactic of evasion, his mind, seeking to get off the course of a disturbing line of thought, seized any random irrelevancy. Arthur Winner noted the flag's sharp clean colors, and how like they were (being, indeed, the same as) those of that uncased standard (butt set in a stirrup socket; staff closed in a trooper's gauntlet; and so, held similarly erect) shining bright through the fateful chiaroscuro twilight, the carefully brushed-in forest of the night where the cavalry waited in the Union League's huge military work of art above the stair landing. This distraction, hopefully offered, was too weak. Arthur Winner's thought returned. He answered: No;

that's not the truth. I don't believe it. There *must* be disinterested affections. There *must* be loves purely loving—

He was obliged to smile. His skeptical psychologist doubtless smiled with him. From so unhandsome a world, this thinker recoiled. He did not want the decent cover lifted—his mother had said: "You are like your father." Was he also like *her?* Like her, did he determinedly protect himself against unwelcome and disturbing thoughts, determinedly choose not to see beneath the surface shows of parent-and-child love, the brazen forehead of self-seeking, self-interest's sly picking and stealing, self-regard's incessant preenings at its glass? Such ugly concepts outraged him. They threatened his equanimity. He said: Let them not be! One firm exercise of disbelief—and there they weren't!

Arthur Winner thought: Lawrence, for old times' sake, distrusts me a little. Which is to say, he fears me a little; he sees me as somehow posing a threat to him. Which is to say, he cannot really like me. For this, I have to be to blame. If I had been able to present myself to him as reliably wise and kind, I could not have occasioned distrust. Therefore, I—like Helen!—did things wrong. Can I now say what things, and what made them wrong? I—like Helen!—spent time enough trying to think what would be right, what would be best. I believe Lawrence, once grown up, may have seen this—understood, in a puzzled way, that after all I meant well, I just lacked imagination. Unlike Warren (who, I know now, I brought to despise me), Lawrence I brought (he often showed it) in many ways to respect me—his distrust or dislike is, I think, quite respectful. From that, do I learn anything?

In a disturbance of self-questioning, in the vagueness of regretful uncertainty, Arthur Winner's gaze moved from the bright flag. Not far off, he came on Willard Lowe's grave old face. Clearly, there was a repose that, with years, could be arrived at. The judge's features rested in convincing calm, a calm of thoughtful eye, a calm of closed lips—by all indications, a calm of mind, too. Willard sat stalwart, seemingly undisturbable; seemingly, on his old man's broad bottom, solid as the mahogany over which his wide black-robed shoulders showed.

319

What bred this calm? What guessable factors of his experience, what known circumstances of his life (if any!) made contributions to it?

There was, for instance, the sufficiently remarkable circumstance that Willard Lowe had never married. In his time (and still) very much a man, robust, nearly plethoric, he was not the person you would expect to choose celibacy. Reasons for the choice he must have had; but Arthur Winner doubted if anyone ever ventured the impertinence of inquiring about them. They were not, evidently, connected with aversion to females as such. Willard Lowe had an eye for a good-looking woman; and, with cheerful courtliness, he could make all the public motions of a squire of dames—as Ruth Shaw said last night with a laugh, dancing girls were something Willard wouldn't mind seeing a few of! There was, of course, the sometimes-told story that Judge Lowe, when he was young, suffered disappointment in love. A girl (not a Brocton girl, or more would have been known) was supposed, at a dramatic last minute, to have jilted him to marry someone else. Arthur Winner dared say there might exist a foundation of fact—one fact! An engagement might have been broken; but the storybook notion of Willard Lowe, to some faithless loved one faithful unto death, lay marvelously cross to the common experience of mankind.

In real life, effects of such a disappointment are observed to be unenduring. An irreplaceable she was, in ordinary practice, replaced with almost ludicrous ease and dispatch. When his serious object was matrimony, a man was never long in perceiving there were still good-enough fish in the sea, and plenty of them. If Willard Lowe remained a bachelor all his days, what reason did he need but that he preferred to? Had he regrets? He showed none. He gave no sign, if now, too late, he wished he had accepted the stake and tether of most men, he wished he had not foregone, deprived himself of, the felicities of connubial love, the joys of fatherhood.

Arthur Winner thought: To Warren I was never a threat—only a sort of unshakable minor nuisance. Warren was the bad boy; by definition (what "bad" meant, here) Warren was safe from the danger of repression. There was not the faintest chance that Father would ever shape, influence, or manage him. Lawrence was the good boy; by definition (the true sense of "good," here) tractable, brought readily by reasonings and mild admonitions to do what Father said was best. Since Lawrence respected reason and heeded admonition, you would rightly conclude that he was levelheaded by nature. Even as a child, he had an orderly mind. Diligent to learn, Lawrence stowed his child's findings with neatness—a place for everything; and everything in its place. Just where, in this harmonious construction, was he to put the things learned year by year about, or in connection with, Warren, his brother?

Warren was disobedient; Warren neglected his duties at home and his studies at school. Things Warren did displeased Father; and even made Mother cry. The orderly mind saw that this behavior was not right and not reasonable. How ill-advised of Warren to do the things he did; he would be sorry! As Lawrence, awed and alarmed, foresaw, upbraidings and reproachings of Warren ensued. Lawrence knew of them, even if he did not hear them. He observed how Warren (as Warren had been warned he would be) was solemnly punished—all in order; all confirming the important thesis that if you wish to be happy, you must be good.

Yet the orderly mind might mark other discordant, and, so, confusing facts. On Warren, penalties and pains had no apparent effect. They impelled him to no amendment; they wrung from him no sign of grief. Where they did have an effect—the world was turned quite upside down—was on Father. Instead of Warren, who deserved to feel it, Father felt grief he could not quite conceal when Warren was punished. Father, not Warren, was sorry for what Warren had done. By his disobedience and his wrongdoing, Warren of course attached to himself a surface disesteem or disfavor; but Lawrence was not deceived. What being bad really did for Warren was win him an intensity of anxious attention, a depth of ceaseless concern, not to be found in routine tokens of approval that came Lawrence's way.

Amazement once digested, Lawrence, with his neat little mind's discursive reasonings, should perhaps have been prepared (certainly, he soon came to be prepared) for what followed.

When Warren was bad, Warren got all the attention; and when Warren was not bad, or less bad? Like the prodigal son's brother, that other son who was out in the field, Lawrence time and again drew nigh. He heard the music and dancing. He smelled roast fatted calf. Need he ask why? The scapegrace, the riotous liver, was back. Was Warren even penitent? Had he been required to declare himself unworthy? It seemed not! Warren, bold as ever, heedless as ever, came home on what amounted to his own terms. Warren's defiant face, his intrepid eye, signed with a contemptuous cheerful smile his willingness to, his offer —take it or leave it—to, suspend hostilities.

Father snatched at the offer; he tumbled all over himself to accept. Surely Father knew better? Surely Father knew that Warren engaged to nothing; Warren just allowed his neck to be fallen on. In Lawrence, the stage of incredulity would be short. The level head resigned itself to what *was*—the melancholy, confidence-killing fact. Father could not help it; it was Father's weakness. Father's feelings, overcoming reason, overcoming right, made a fool of Father. Lamely, nearly wheedling, untrustable Father excused his foolishness to Lawrence; emotionally, he explained his unfairness: *This thy brother was dead, and is alive again; and was lost, and is found.*

Noah Tuttle said: "I'm a poor man. People don't know how poor. Iniquitous taxes! You can't lay anything by."

With faint amusement, Arthur Winner reflected that Noah and Mr. Woolf, if nowhere else, were in agreement here. He said: "That's what seems to me to make a project like Lawrence's feasible. When there may be so much at stake, expert advice is worth buying. Lawrence isn't impulsive or careless. I imagine he and his friend know exactly where the business is coming from; and I'm quite ready to believe that, a few years from now, so many people may be wanting to retain them, it will seem a sort of joke that they once had trouble finding ten thousand dollars."

From the bench, Fred Dealey, his hand cupping his chin, his elbow rested on the desk, said: "May we take your case to be concluded, Mr. District Attorney?"

Jerry Brophy said: "I have nothing more, your Honor."

"Then we'll excuse Doctor Shaw. Thank you, Doctor."

Reggie Shaw gave him an ungracious nod. He got with alacrity out of the witness stand, cutting across the open floor before the bench with a fast stride, heading for the back door. Coming near Noah and Arthur Winner, he said: "Damn lot of foolishness. How do you lawyers stand it?"

"I'm not sure we do," Arthur Winner said. "Reg, would you have time, any time today, if I can arrange it with her, to look at a girl who says she's been raped, and see what you think? The boy says she consented; and we believe she's done a lot of consenting. Could you tell?"

"I could probably tell if somebody'd been there—yes." Reggie Shaw looked down at him derisively. "And if he'd been rough about it, that might show." Aware, perhaps of the puritanical strain in Noah which, even then, was taking the occasion of this language to put on a disapproving look, a stern censorious stare, Doctor Shaw said more harshly: "But if you mean, for God's sake, can I tell how often she's been screwed, I can't. You don't miss a slice off a cut loaf, you know! Give me a ring later, if you want. I'll be in the office." He walked on.

Stony in his silence, not without dignity, Noah Tuttle said nothing.

On the bench, Fred Dealey, leaning over, had approached his head to Willard Lowe's. Turning then, sitting back in his chair, he said: "I think we're in agreement, Mr. Studdiford, that no useful purpose would be served by subjecting defendant to direct or cross-examination. Since her statement is incorporated in the record, we feel it will be sufficient if she identifies that statement, declares she gave it of her own free will, and that it's a true statement. Therefore, she need not go on the stand. Let her come before the court, and be sworn. Since we have agreed to accept her statement in evidence, Judge Lowe joins me in feeling we should waive determination of whether she understands the nature of an oath, which might otherwise be incumbent on us. And let Mr. Dummer and Mrs. Dummer come up with her. We'll hear them, if they have anything they'd like to say before we pass sentence."

Judge Lowe had been looking at his notes. Lifting off his

glasses, he said: "Yes. But if I may ask you to wait one moment, Mr. Studdiford. I've a question or two I wish to put to Doctor Arsavage—bearing on defendant's mental condition. You may answer from where you are, Doctor. On the record, Mr. Ferris; this will be redirect examination. Doctor, I think you stated that while defendant's physical age is twenty, her mental age is eight?"

"About eight, sir." Beyond the jury box, Doctor Arsavage had erected himself awkwardly, his tall thin frame in nervous movement.

"And I believe you said, Doctor, in reference to the state of her education, that you were doubtful about the validity of intelligence tests that involved reading, because her reading ability did not extend beyond the simplest words?"

"I did, sir. In grading her, we had to rely mostly on performance tests—no reading involved."

"And these tests led you to classify her mentally as, I believe you said, a moron."

"Well, sir, she tested in the low fifties." Doctor Arsavage restlessly clasped and unclasped his thin hands. "By the commonly accepted scale, a subject testing twenty-five to fifty is classified as an imbecile. One testing fifty to seventy is in the moronic range. A testing in the fifties, then, indicates a low-grade moron."

"Yes. I don't think we asked the direct question before. We will put it to you now. My understanding is that while some morons are to be regarded as dangerous and, like imbeciles, should not be at large, some aren't. What is your opinion, on this point, as to defendant?"

"I'd expect her to be entirely harmless, your Honor."

"Then you do not consider confinement or restraint in an institution essential either for the protection of society, or for her own well-being?"

Doctor Arsavage lifted his high thin shoulders jerkily. "Well, sir; not for the protection of society, no." He paused, grimacing nervously.

To Arthur Winner, Noah said: "Ought to be in an asylum himself! Don't know why; but just notice that! All these institution people—not one in ten, who isn't a little crazy too."

324

Doctor Arsavage said: "I would consider significant the fact that this trouble she got into did not occur until she was twenty. With her mental capacity, this or the equivalent might have been expected much earlier—five or more years ago. Therefore, she's probably not devoid of all judgment and all self-restraint. Of course, if there were unlimited, or even remotely adequate, institutional facilities the story would be different. I might then feel that custodial care was desirable. We could do so much more for her than could be done at home—occupational therapy; special training; regular psychiatric treatment. We could probably help her make better adjustments—even, possibly, prepare her to, enable her to, in time go out and lead a nearly normal life—"

"But, for the moment," Judge Dealey said, "you haven't the room. So you'll leave her at large and hope for the best."

Doctor Arsavage smiled thinly. "Well, not quite as bad as that, sir. From a careful study of her, my considered opinion is—well, I see no reason why she shouldn't be all right at home. Especially, if her parents are acquainted with, and accept, her limitations. Realize that she—well, *does* need to be watched a little. And if they're willing to show her—well, extra patience."

He coughed, and let his eyes go across a moment to Caroline's mother and father. He said: "I'd suggest, if I may, that the court remind them—the parents—that, like anyone else, a mentally deficient individual responds to kindness. In that respect, the deficiency doesn't make him or her any different from other children—Caroline, of course, must be treated like the child, mentally aged about eight, that she is. At that age, no child has the capacity to understand always why he must or must not do things. The parents will need to be firm with her; but firm in a kind way. They must try to help her understand that rules, restraints, are for her own good. They won't find this easy—"

With a sardonic glint of his swift eye, Fred Dealey, in his turn, could be seen to glance from the bench for a moment at the Dummers. Doctor Arsavage said: "They may need to work on their own mental attitude. They should try to understand that they have more to do than order, threaten, or punish. They should try to realize that the only dependable obedience is that, not of the child who is afraid, but of the child who seeks to please. If they so comport themselves that Caroline is brought, out of feelings of affection for them, to want to please them, I would expect all, or almost all, their difficulties with her to disappear."

From glancing at the Dummers, Fred Dealey had turned his eye, still with its sardonic glint, back to Doctor Arsavage. On this expert's innocence, on his learned unknowing, Fred allowed himself the comment of a repressed smile. The good counsel of the men of theory—the psychologist; the philosopher; the doctor of divinity—seldom failed to contain some stuff of farce; the labored long expatiation to the grand invalidating suppositive; the stipulated condition comically contrary to fact; the serious call naïvely exhorting to that which, a glance at the exhorted assured you, could never be accomplished.

But, after all, they meant no mischief. Simply, these sapient sirs were strangers in a world not theirs. This world was the law's, the literal world of human acts and human beings, where you were foolish at your peril. None of them was prepared for such a contingency. At home, in his own world (all of words) the man of theory found foolishness perfectly feasible. Having there no special ill-consequence, foolishness was not penalized. When, unwarned, unwary, he strayed out here, who had the heart to be hard on him? Perhaps he (like anyone else) was susceptible to kindness!

Fred Dealey said: "I think we follow you, Doctor. You recommend that the court direct Caroline's parents to induce Caroline to love them." Not unkindly, his smile sympathetic rather than superior, he gave Doctor Arsavage a humorous, marveling look. He said: "Doctor, would that one could! Would that we were empowered to make orders to that effect; and to compel faithful compliance with them!"

"Right now, I wouldn't know where to turn," Noah said. "Everyone wants money, whether it's due them or not. I've been paying accounts out of my own pocket. Lucky for them I'm trustee, not a bank. A bank would be charging them interest. I don't. It'll be the ruin of me." As though Noah even now envisaged bankruptcy, he sat somberly brooding, gloomily contemplating his penniless self, plodding, as likely as not, over the hill to the poorhouse.

The complaint was old; the gloomy view a regular thing. Neither, Arthur Winner knew, needed to be noticed. Noah said, glooming on: "I suppose I might get rid of the Greenwood Avenue place. I haven't anything else to sell. But who wants that?" He broke off abruptly.

Arthur Winner had seen Jerry Brophy speaking to Garret Hughes at the prosecution's table. Garret had arisen, crossed over, and now came up to him and Noah. Garret stood still, civilly waiting for Noah to finish what he was saying. For his pains, he got a stare that seemed to mean Noah thought he was an eavesdropper. Undeterred, Garret said: "Good morning, Mr. Tuttle. D'you mind if I speak to Mr. Winner a moment?"

"Mind?" Noah said. "Mind? What do I have to do with it? Speak to anyone you like!"

"Very well, sir," Garret said, "I will, if I may. Mr. Winner, I'm going now to see Miss Kovacs. If she'll consent to a physical examination, how would you want it done?"

"I'd like to have Doctor Shaw do it; and I'd like it done today," Arthur Winner said. "I've spoken to him. If she agrees, will you call him? Arranging an appointment might be simpler that way, than if you called me and I called him. I'm sorry we're putting you to this trouble, Garret."

Garret Hughes smiled. He said: "Mr. Brophy's willing to have Miss Kovacs, or her mother, told that without medical evidence, we're doubtful if we have enough to indict on. Of course, it's a little delicate, saying what we'll do or won't do, when it's still before Mr. Harbison." He paused. "This occurred to me, Mr. Winner. Feeling as he seems to, Mr. Harbison himself might —I mean, if he happened to think of it—be ready to rule that satisfying the magistrate a prima-facie case existed was pretty much on the prosecutrix; and that as long as she refused to let herself be examined, he'd remain not so satisfied."

Smiling in return, Arthur Winner said: "Thanks. If she refuses, that's what I intended to see Joe had a chance to think of. I'd have expected you to oppose me. I believe you could effec-

327

tively argue that where the offense charged is one committed with no witness but defendant, a sworn information must make a prima-facie case, and what was or what wasn't sufficient evidence would be for a jury."

"Well, there *is* that, sir," Garret Hughes said. He laughed. "But if Mr. Brophy has me at the hearing, and that's the situation, I wouldn't oppose a motion to dismiss, if you wanted to make one; and I know Mr. Brophy wouldn't feel I should, because he just said he wouldn't. I'll let you know as soon as I can, sir." Bowing politely to Noah Tuttle, he went over to the aisle, and up it.

"Humph!" Noah said. "Changed his tune! What's that mean?"

"I hope, that we're not going to have too much trouble," Arthur Winner said. "I talked with Jerry this morning and I don't think he wants to prosecute this very much."

"Never trusted him," Noah said.

Jerry Brophy, rising from the table where he had been getting his papers together, stepped forward to the bar. Staring at Jerry's narrow back, Noah said: "Ambitious! He's always looking out for himself. If it paid him to, he'd tell you one thing and do another." Noah looked around him with an unease of general gloomy suspicion, his stare stopping on Caroline's parents, the Dummers. Pushing each other, telling each other that Lew Studdiford, by his signaling gesture, meant that they were to come, they were leaving their seats. They came clumsily, with skittish uncertain movements of their dumb-brute bodies. Their expressions were both abashed and alarmed, as though they thought that, exposed in the well of the court, they might be pounced on and dragged off to prison.

From the bench, Judge Dealey watched them, too. In his sharp eyes, the humorous if rueful light of that not-unkind mockery with which he answered Doctor Arsavage was fading. What Fred mocked was no particular person, but the fantasy of human hopes—which was to say, all persons, everyone, himself not by any means excluded. Now, time was come to implement folly; now, for the futile forms, the performance of the vain act! The girl, the outright idiot, the parents, the near idiots, were to be recommended to each other, shown the paths of wisdom and right. What waste of breath! If you had eyes to see, and if affection was the condition of Caroline's obedience, that those parents would not get obedience was foregone; it was not in them to know how to get affection. Caroline, her movements coy, her expression simpering while she made her way to the bar with Lew Studdiford, observed the approach of her father and mother with shrinking little scowls of aversion. Sage advice, good counsel were surely coming (as when didn't they?) late in the day!

When it gets to where you come in—well, it's bound to be pretty late in the day! Not excluding himself when he repressed that smile, Fred might be presumed to remember, to mean also to comment on, what Arthur Winner, too, remembered—Fred engaged in his own broodings, half serious, half jeering, about the nature of things (another world of words!) on the boathouse path last night at sunset. *Afterward, you can say: If only I'd known that; if only I'd done this. . . .* Yes; would one could have known, could have done, differently! Would there was a court empowered to make, as well as orders that ye love one another, orders in repair of the past, returns in time to points at which you might now be wise—instead of after, before the event!

And where would such a point be? At what point in the babyhood or girlhood of poor Caroline could (supposing them by some far fetch of the imagination to have been capable of such a thing) these Dummers have intervened with effective understanding, found means of clear communication with that impaired brain; inclined wisely, firm in a kind way, the twig? Caroline being Caroline, they being they, one perceived the impossibility—at no time! There was no such point—not with those handicaps.

And without them? Given parents of good intelligence, surely capable of understanding, seemingly well able to be firm in kind ways; given their sound, their fine healthy infant; must communication be better, must understanding be surer? Nameless until then, a small sentient creature (having formally undertaken, using the mouths of his sponsors in baptism, George

Detweiler, and his Great-Uncle Herbert Carstairs, and his mother's good friend Betty Polhemus, to renounce the devil and all his works, the vain pomp and glory of the world with all covetous desires of the same, and the sinful desires of the flesh) was aspersed with water drops. While their fall on him made the little Gothic alcove where the font stood in Christ Church echo to his indignant wails, he—it!—infant of the Winners, was pronounced to be (syllables sounding in retrospect so heavy with calamity!) Asa Warren.

One could not, naturally, expect to establish communication at three months. The inutility of responding to the squawls of the mindless creature-in-arms with an explanation that the marking with water was to his great benefit, making him a member of Christ, the child of God, and an inheritor of the kingdom of heaven, was apparent. And when somewhat more graspable concepts were to be conveyed to what had the semblance at least of a mind, at three years? In the silver mug rolling across the floor (answer, in Warren's way, to the good counsel that all the milk should be drunk if Warren hoped to be a big strong boy), did you observe an improvement in communication? Or, at ten years? *Warren, you've been told repeatedly that you must not* . . . Was understanding gaining? Or at sixteen years? *My dear Mr. Winner: It is with deep distress that I write you to say that the best interests of the school leave us no alternative but to request that you withdraw Warren. . . .* Or, at twenty, when the years ran out? *I regret to inform you your son 2nd Lt Asa W Winner killed airplane accident here this date please wire your desires details follow Willcox Commanding General.*

Had there been any time when any effort could have changed this course, any point at which a saving understanding would have been possible; any means, other or different, by which you could have broken into that fastness—unreachable; uninfluenceable; really, unknown—where Asa Warren Winner lived his self-sufficing, venturesome, strife-filled short life? Warren being Warren, Father being Father, and each to that circumstance being prisoner, one perceived the everlasting impossibility. In the acorn was the oak—the fig tree is in its seed, the thistle in its.

Had Father, though anxiously acting as if he didn't, long known this to be true?

Arthur Winner could believe that Father, that person who was himself (yet not any longer, not quite, his present self), had known. He could believe so; for he had not forgotten the unfolding of that last telegram—the strips of pasted tape printed by teletype; the letters, by the breaks in their progression, freezing into intelligibility: *I regret to inform* . . . No more need be read! The falling, heart-stopping sensation, though in effect perhaps like them, was not, could not be, any horror of amazement, any sickness of surprise, any incredulous stun of sorrow. Rather, a long-standing incipient conscious state burst across consciousness's threshold, became a simple clarity of recognition. This had always been going to happen. This had been years in the preparing; every necessary arrangement was made. Immediately, before he heard them, Father found himself knowing exactly what, in their character, those promised "details" would be like. The essence of the clarity of recognition was that Warren's life, the life of the bad, disobedient, and fearless boy, had all along been pointing to, leading to, foreordaining, a manner of death. The event, the befalling, was, then, anything but casual or fortuitous; anything but an undesigned, not-to-be-foreseen mere occurrence. Except in some short-term view, limited and, so, ignorant, *accident here this date* was just what Warren's death hadn't been.

Arthur Winner was aware of Noah's nearby breathing, the measured asthmatic wheeze. The old man's pouched eyes stared steadily out from the stony, craggy old face as though attracted and held. Was Noah able (wise with years) to find eternal significances in the scene, in the line of ill-assorted figures at the rail below the judgment seat—the district attorney, with no part to play but that of being present, standing patient; defense counsel in his decorous, earnestly concerned professional stance of being for his client yet not against the court; his client next to him, slouched limply, spinelessly, in her prison dress, hanging her foolish head; her mother, next to her, sneaking apprehensive, comprehensionless looks right and left?

331

At the end of the line, Caroline's father stood talking. This must be his reply to something (unheard by Arthur Winner) that Judge Lowe had said to him. He was not so inarticulate as he looked; with defensive sounds of excuse and explanation, he was even voluble. He was saying: ". . . so when she done that, why I, I says to the wife: Nobody can do nothing with her. . . ."

Gravely, Willard Lowe gazed down at him. Fred Dealey gazed down at him coldly. Did Noah ponder this problem of separate beings, of separate minds, each with care bolted and barred not only against every foe, but also against every friend? Arthur Winner saw that Noah's heavy eyelids had sunk. Not moving, not nodding, Noah had dozed off—an involuntary little nap of age.

Never explain (they said); *never apologize!* The measure was strategy's—the most serviceable tactic when you had laid yourself open to criticism. The measure was much neglected. Instinct was dead against it. Instinct's immediate urge was to throw the shield of words around the exposed position. Might not a shut mouth be taken as saying there was nothing to be said? Present conclusions about past states of mind were always questionable (how you thought now might largely shape the idea you adopted of how you once thought); but Arthur Winner felt no doubt that, in the state of his mind during the hours—even, days —after that telegram about Warren came, instinct's urge prevailed. Like Mr. Dummer, he was driven to an uneasy defense of himself.

Today he was not quite sure (and maybe he hadn't been then either) of what he was defending himself against. The sudden fatal conviction that this had always been going to happen, that things could not possibly have happened otherwise, ought to rule out any assignment of blame—unless, of course, in some rage of bitterness one dared the contumacious thought that "accidents," if they are not of chance, must be planned or permitted, and the great Planner or Permitter might have something to answer for. That kind of exculpation did not, Arthur Winner seemed to remember, do much to cure the confusing distracting feeling that nevertheless he remained blamable. He, the father incapable of establishing communication, was, however unwitting, an important factor in the design, an essential contributor to the end that destiny might be thought to have proposed. It was such a feeling as, perhaps, underlay the ancient common-law concept of the deodand—the instrument occasioning death, though inanimate, in no way a deliberate agent, was guilty—was forfeit as a thing of blood.

To what might be called this problem of himself was naturally added the problem of Hope. If Hope had not been his first thought, she had been his second. The very coming of the telegram, when he had read the message, spoke to him of Hope. Though addressed to Roylan, the telegram arrived at his office. As the brisk message was printing itself out on the tape, somebody at the receiving instrument had made a decision. He had shown a swift thoughtfulness, a simple considerateness which Arthur Winner, even in that numb moment, was able to find moving. The disinterested somebody's decision (how could you say man had no choice in what man did? Choices like this lay within his power!) was that the telegram would be delivered to Mr. Winner's law offices in Brocton, not to his home, where Mrs. Winner might open it. Men were supposed to be better able than women to support the initial shock of bad news. Let Mr. Winner find out first. Give him a chance to prepare his wife, to break it to her gently.

The supposition that the man could support such tidings better than the woman was, here, true indeed. Not in Hope would it be, reading that Warren was dead, to prop herself up with reflections that this thing was fated, that she had always known this was going to happen. Resignation's arguments of reason— that cause had been, and here of necessity was, effect; that this falling-out of things was, alas, condign; that Warren had got only what Warren was always asking for—would never suggest themselves to Hope.

The truth had been that Hope's nature, the ethereal mold's native gentle passionlessness, gave, in an understandable way, the utmost force, allowed the fullest power to, that particular "powerful instinct" of Lew Studdiford's. Hope could see, even with anxiety and sorrow agree, that Warren was often "bad"; yet to that instinct, misdemeanors and disobediences were no more than figments of the reason, never the realities of feeling. Hope's woman's capacity for the persisting wish, for patient expecting of the impossible, for knowing a thing to be true while simultaneously not believing it, had little trouble providing that what Warren *did* should never be confused with what Warren *was*. Principles of reason, or even justice—that point of just deserts—were altogether inadmissible to Hope's heart. To irrelevancies of that kind, Hope with a fierceness of unexpended (being in other ways unexpendable) passion, returned one fully sufficient answer: *Hadst thou groaned for him as I have done* . . . Yes; try breaking the news gently to Hope!

That restless sense of being himself at fault, that helpless sense of no means to comfort Hope, joined, Arthur Winner supposed, in hurrying him to act. The intuitive realization that, right now, he could help Hope most by leaving her alone, that Hope's feeling about Warren was something between Hope and herself, only to be handled by herself, made feasible the doing of what his sad perfect certainty that the end Warren had come to would prove to have been a violent, troubled, "bad" end prompted him to do. If, instead of wiring his desires, he telephoned at once to say he was coming down, he thought he saw a way (practicable or not, he didn't really know) to intercept, to forestall the sending of, those details to follow. If he presented himself to this Willcox Commanding General, he thought (the seasoned lawyer was scheming) he might manage to prevent anything from being put in a form that would exist to be seen, and that he would want (the one thing he might be able to do for Hope) to keep Hope from seeing. If not in actual words, in acts, he would propose a compromise settlement; he would attempt an explanation, he would offer an apology.

As it developed, Arthur Winner was to find explanation superfluous and apology unavailing; but, thanks precisely to his rightness about Warren's end, his project was practicable. The Willcox of the telegram, a short and slight, a neat, sober, graying brigadier general, received Arthur Winner with civility, sitting at his desk before his stand of colors in a Florida air base office where the continuous multiple rising and fading thunder of airplane engines carried from the blazing, brilliant morning outside. They were alone. There was, the general said at once, a security angle; so nothing about the accident had been or would be released to the press. Except for personnel at the air base, nobody knew what had happened. He paused significantly, conveying well enough what he meant—that Arthur Winner would not only be allowed to, he would be expected to, keep the details quiet, hush them up. In short, then and there the bereaved father had what he came for. Hope need never know.

However, the general said, he understood that Mr. Winner was a lawyer; and, involved were certain—er—legal aspects, a matter of army regulations. In order to avoid later misunderstandings, he would like to make these clear now. The presumption in military law was that a person who dies in the active military service dies in line of duty, and not as a result of his own misconduct. To rebut this presumption, substantial evidence was always necessary. The special investigating board, appointed by him, had found an abundance of such substantial evidence. Lieutenant Winner had met his death in direct disobedience of orders the most explicit possible; and as a result of his indefensible conduct, other men had died, and great damage and injury had been done the air force. Therefore, the status of Mr. Winner's son was not, and could not be, that of a pilot killed in an accident of the ordinary sort. By his indubitable misconduct, Lieutenant Winner forfeited all rights and benefits of the service, and had to be regarded, in effect, as dishonorably discharged.

"Mr. Winner!"

The low voice behind Arthur Winner startled him. Mary Sheen, painstakingly unobtrusive, must have slipped through the rear door, and, keeping herself inconspicuous, come on tiptoes to where he sat. Apologetically poised, bending to whisper, she said: "Mr. Winner, there's a message from Ralph Detweiler. He said to tell you he wouldn't be in later this morning, so not to wait for him. He said he tried; but he couldn't do what you wanted."

335

To suppose that the slight overtone of impudence was not Ralph's seemed reasonable. Ralph, seeking to inform Mr. Winner that (probably) "Joanie" had balked, refused to come with him; and Ralph had then done as he was told—not pressed her, but seeking also to keep Mary Sheen as much in the dark as possible, must have had trouble stating the case. Mary, duly uncomprehending, relayed the ambiguous message as well as she could.

Arthur Winner said: "He didn't speak to Helen?"

Mary Sheen whispered: "Helen went out, Mr. Winner. She wasn't back. So Gladys and I decided I should tell you—" (Plainly, little pitchers had big ears; Ralph's caution was vain; they probably knew all or almost all!) Mary said: "It was about twenty minutes ago, Ralph called."

"Good; thanks. I won't be back to the office this morning, then. But tell Helen, if she hears from Ralph later, that I expect to be at Roylan all afternoon, and if he has anything he wants to tell me he can reach me there."

"Yes, Mr. Winner."

Moving his head with a jerk, Noah Tuttle said: "What is it? What is it? What about Ralph?" He turned enough to see Mary Sheen slipping modestly toward the door. "What's she want?"

"There were some things I asked Ralph to do. He telephoned the office. It's not important."

"Nothing's important, until you find it is," Noah said. He spoke thickly, struggling out of the drowsiness that his minutes of sleep had left him. "That boy worries me, Arthur. He's weak. No discipline. Won't come to a good end. He'll kill Helen before he's through."

Arthur Winner said: "I had a talk with her this morning. I think you'll find she feels better today."

"He'll do other things," Noah said. "And no telling what! You can't understand them. You just know they'll do something. Try talking to them, and pretty soon you see you aren't speaking the same language. Used to be like that with Warren, I remember. He's like Warren."

Disconcerted—two young men could hardly have appeared

336

more unlike—Arthur Winner said: "I wouldn't have thought so."

"You don't know what they want, what they're trying to do," Noah said. "You can't tell what they are—or I can't! Maybe somebody can. And what they are, is why they're in trouble. Here; I'm going! I'll see Helen."

Arthur Winner said: "I don't know that I'd say anything like that to her. I think she's convinced now that we can get Ralph clear. I think we can. And I don't know that we need to expect he'll do other things. I think he's had a bad scare; and I've heard that's the beginning of wisdom."

"No," Noah Tuttle said. "When someone's scared's when you really can't trust him."

Those bright blocks of sunlight fallen across the ranges of empty seats must be bothering Judge Lowe's eyes. At his gesture, a tipstaff had gone up the side aisle, and, one after another, was letting down the long Venetian blinds. Before the bench, Mr. Dummer still talked, still explained. Finding himself so patiently listened to, he had become confident, illustrating his remarks with his hands. He seemed to have seen an opportunity to save face. This public shame of his daughter's disgraced him, yes; but undeservedly! He was a good man, meriting the court's applause. As proof, he was protesting, not his willingness only, but his eagerness, to do good, to lavish on poor Caroline a father's affectionate care. Arthur Winner, left alone, sat motionless, hardly hearing.

Noah was not wrong about the root of bafflement—you needed to know what they wanted, what they were trying to do. The lamb's good is not the lion's good! You needed to be able to tell what they were! Brought back to that wartime morning in the office of General Willcox, to the general speaking with blunt economy of words against the incessant superhuman noise of airplane engines, Arthur Winner could remember how, unsurprised, he soon detected in the flat tones of detachment the note that he expected. Arthur Winner was unsurprised, because

337

he had heard that note before, when those who sat, of right and duty, in judgment on Warren sought to sum up. They could, of course, find nothing at all to be said for what Warren had done; yet, in the doing, Warren would oftener than not be found to have compelled, exacted from them, an exasperated secret approbation, a reluctant unconfessable respect. Without reproach, Warren definitely wasn't (and they blamed him); but, seemingly, Warren was (as every man wishes *he* were) without fear.

General Willcox, flyer and soldier, was perhaps even better equipped than earlier judges to appreciate this recognition. Though in manner so neat, sober, and mild, he had eyes and mouth of a shape or look that declared his whole military life had not been that of a desk officer. Arthur Winner did not think the general was a man of too much imagination; but in the narrow field of his own experience and capability he was probably perceptive. He could be presumed to have reached a quick, to him exciting, understanding of Warren. Warren was a brash, unruly youth who had dishonorably discharged himself; but, even in anger and indignation of command responsibility, even as he smarted from the reprimand that the responsibility had surely brought on him, General Willcox must have been unable to disallow the thing he recognized. Warren was a born flyer, a born—rarer far than mere soldier!—warrior.

Disguised by the mussed eight-point-twos and crushed garrison cap, by the sunburned boyish face and the boyish cropped curly hair of bronzed-brown color, what, in Warren, climbed into a cockpit, was in its potential no more nor less than the true heathen berserker of the skins and tusks, the dreadful champion of Nordic myth. He was indifferent to iron and fire. For others and for himself he was uncaring. He was outside all law. He counted no costs. He brooked no equal, and admitted no superior. With stern joy, Willcox, soldier and flyer, must see this foeman to the foe, worthy of anyone's steel, swim into his limited ken, into his very command. Lions littered in one day, danger and Warren looked eye to eye; and Second Lieutenant Asa W. Winner outlooked danger. Danger knew full well that Warren was more dangerous than he.

Strictly disciplined, so long schooled both in obeying and

being obeyed, the general (though he had not wholly hidden) had put down, covered up, any improper back-of-the-mind lament for the temerarious dead Siegfried. Here, soldierly duty was to subscribe to all that Army Regulation 600-550 provided in cases like this of deceased officer. Inflexible, the general proceeded with his duty. When Mr. Winner knew the circumstances he would be able to see how section four, paragraph eighteen applied.

The circumstances were simple. Lieutenant Winner had undertaken to do what they called "buzz"—make fighter passes at —a bomber cruising over the air base. The bomber was not just any bomber. This was a test prototype of the Very Heavy Bomber then almost ready to come into production. The so-designated XB-29 in question had every available space crammed with congeries of not-readily-replaceable special instruments. In addition to the flying crew, civilian technical personnel, still less readily replaceable, were on board. For a week the top-secret flying laboratory had been taking off from and returning to the base daily; and air space to be given the plainly marked, and, anyway unmistakable, great craft was specified in special orders —keep one full mile away! No plane had thought of disobeying —none, that is, until on the seventh day, a high-flying P-51 spotted the huge shining ship on its monotonous back-and-forth cruise. The P-51 belonged to a squadron recently equipped with these new fighters. The pilots were undergoing advanced tactical exercises to familiarize them with their planes before they proceeded to an overseas staging area. This particular P-51 displayed on the forward fuselage the freshly painted red figure of a meat ax, and the red words, daubed as though in dripping blood: *Butcher Boy*. The plane was Lieutenant Winner's. Handled with a special dash, with that vernacular daring of Warren's, *Butcher Boy* had been much noticed in flight, was well known to the entire base.

From a position four miles up, close to the sun, ringed with the azure world, Lieutenant Winner, finishing, with his wingman's plane, a high-altitude exercise, must suddenly have marked the forbidden XB-29 above the field, creeping far beneath. Apparently the sight had been too much for him. From the cloud walls of his mountain of air, he watched a moment. Orders or no orders, he then tipped into a power dive; and like a thunderbolt he fell. At the base, the descending snarl was heard and a hundred people lifted their faces. *Butcher Boy* was seen to swerve left to pass the quarry abeam, fifty yards off, severely rocking the big four-engined wings. Breakaway was down and forward. Contemptuously barrel-rolling, *Butcher Boy* drove ahead. Half a mile in front, Warren lost enough speed to turn. He turned one hundred and eighty degrees, and came back. His mock attack this time was delivered at what they called twelve o'clock level.

Lieutenant Winner's sportive intention had no doubt been to pass under at the last minute. Possibly Warren's estimate of the closing rate was at fault. Possibly (even probably! The born-flyer's inerrant eye and instinct had been amazing instructors since Warren's primary training days) the pilot of the bomber, incensed and nervous, made at that same last minute the error—fatal, with his unwieldy monster—of trying to evade. *Butcher Boy* did not pass under. At full throttle, Warren met the XB-29 head on. He lit the day with flame. He went down, and nine men (two, aeronautical engineers of no little importance) with him, in a commingled mass of metal junk, a mid-air pyre dropped aslant the sky, trailing volumes of black smoke five thousand feet to earth.

Judge Lowe said slowly: "Caroline, you have done something very wrong and very serious. We hope you understand that. We hope you see that you need guidance. You must let yourself be guided by the judgment of those who care for you, love you. Now, you told Doctor Arsavage that you got cross at your father because he was so strict with you. Do you remember that?"

With a smile, Caroline tilted her head to one side in a movement that could be either a nodding or a shaking. Judge Lowe said: "If you do, Caroline, say 'yes'—so Mr. Ferris, the man there, can write it down."

Caroline said: "He was mean to me."

"But he intended what was right for you," Judge Lowe said.

"He knew better than you did. He was afraid that what did happen, would happen. Now, you want to go home again, don't you? You don't want to have to stay in prison?"

"I don't want to." She shook her head violently.

"Then, you must promise us, the court, that you will obey your father and mother."

Clutching the skirt of her prison dress, Caroline began abruptly to cry. She said: "I want to stay here!"

Judge Dealey uttered a sharp little laugh. To Judge Lowe, he said: "Well, I told you! Now, what do we do? Sentence her to her home for an indeterminate term?"

THREE

DOCTOR TROWBRIDGE swung
open the narrow door in the ogival arch at the left inside corner
of the narthex. "I believe Mr. Minieri and a man will be up
there now, Arthur," he said. Standing back, he held the door for
Miss Cummins.

Miss Cummins, her hands in the pockets of her smock, glanced
at the tight steep winding of the circular stairs' stone steps. She
grinned and said: "I don't think you're too practiced a gallant,
Whit! There *are* occasions when ladies prefer not to be first. I've
read somewhere: Always let the gentleman precede you over the
stile. You and Mr. Winner go ahead. I'll take my place of modesty behind."

Doctor Trowbridge laughed. With a touch of color, he said:
"I never thought of that."

"And never thinking of that is very godly, righteous, and sober
of you, sweet! Women have baser minds. Lead on!"

Doctor Trowbridge set a good pace; in the recurring light of
the slit windows, mounting with energy. Conscious of Miss Cummins following, Arthur Winner found himself somewhat winded
as he emerged through the laid-open trap in the floor of the bell
loft.

Doctor Trowbridge said: "One hundred and two steps—quite
a climb!" But he gave no sign of having just finished it—the
difference, Arthur Winner would have to allow, between being
thirty-odd and fifty-odd. Miss Cummins, he was glad to see,
breathed faster, her face becomingly flushed.

Massive and motionless, the metal shape of bell hung in the twilight of the slanted stone louvers, screened to keep out nesting pigeons. On the round sweep of the bell's side, letters of the inscription rose embossed: VIVOS VOCI MORTUOS PLANGO WHEN I DO RING GODS PRAISES SING WHEN I DO TOULE PRAY HEART AND SOULE.

Gazing with amazement, Miss Cummins said: "Goodness, it's big!"

Harry Minieri, short and stout, turned, striking dust off his hands. To the man with him, who was up on the cross timber, he said: "Okay, Tony! Hello—er—Reverend; hello, Mr. Winner. Well, everything's all right. Don't worry."

Doctor Trowbridge said: "Midge, this is Mr. Minieri, whose men have been doing so much to make us comfortable in the rectory. This is Miss Cummins, my fiancée."

Awkward, not looking at Miss Cummins, Harry said: "Pleased to meet you, ma'am." With understandable slight confusion, he shifted his eye from Doctor Trowbridge's clerical collar and cleared his big throat. "Yes," he said, "that there suspension beam's seasoned oak—er—Reverend. Those little cracks don't mean a thing. We been over it all; made sure it's seated good on the torsels. Out of weather, that kind of beam lasts longer than it was steel. Ought to be here, no different, two-three hundred years when we're all gone. You never need to worry about *that* breaking!"

At the uneasy appellation "Reverend," Miss Cummins had thrown Doctor Trowbridge a faint mischievous smile. Changing the smile to one of pleasure or interest, she said: "What are those funny things up there, Mr. Minieri?"

"Oh, them?" Harry did look at her—a quick peek at what a Protestant in priest's clothing was apparently going to marry. Caught—as people, Arthur Winner judged, must usually be—by the smile and the interest, he said, becoming easy: "They're the speakers your chimes comes out—like loud-speakers. They're electric, ma'am. They don't have nothing to do with the bell. Got a lot of power! We hear them way down on Water Street. Nice!"

"Well, I'm sure we're greatly obliged to you, Mr. Minieri,"

Doctor Trowbridge said. "I'm sorry to bring you and Tony all the way up here for nothing—"

"Any time!" Harry said with warmth. "I appreciated Mr. Winner giving us the remodeling contract—" He hesitated in an obvious little diffidence of doubt—was this new "priest" the boss (he knew who was boss at Our Lady of Mount Carmel!); or was it still Mr. Winner? "We try to do everything right," he said. "We want you to be suited; and anything not right, we make right. So any time there's anything, I hope you let us give estimates. We got a motto, maybe you seen it on the trucks: No job too large or too small."

✦

"The difference is technical," Arthur Winner said. "There, the civil code has, among the general statutes, a title on religious bodies, with chapters for each of the principal denominations. They deal, of course, only with administrative organization and church property. That's to say, those parts of the Episcopal diocese's constitution and canons that define the authority of bishops, or rectors, or vestries, and rights of tenure, or use of church-held funds or real property, are written into law, given the force of civil law. Anything done in defiance of them is actionable directly—just as, say, a breach of commercial contract is."

From the rector's office in the parish house, a wide and high oriel window looked on the close of Christ Church. The many mullioned sections were glazed with an intricate amber-colored paning, relieved at random by decorative stained-glass escutcheons emblazoned with sacred emblems—the tetramorph, alpha and omega, the fish, the anchor, the dove, the lamb. Through this merely translucent medium, the brightness of the fine September morning came subdued, but in mellow tints, designedly dim and religious, a sober, rich gloom suited to the weighty dark wood appointments, all of conscious ecclesiastical temper. Behind his desk, against the back of his monumental desk chair whose shape was very Gothic, Doctor Trowbridge appeared both slim and youthful. He sat forward, while his narrow fingers, unattended, filled a pipe slowly.

344

"I see," Doctor Trowbridge said. "I'm ashamed to confess, Arthur, that I never knew any of that—how the church actually stood in law. Of course, there, I wasn't the rector; so I suppose I simply never gave it thought. You'll find me shockingly ignorant about a number of things I know I should know; but I mean to acquaint myself as quickly as I can with them—not put off on others responsibilities that are properly mine. Yes; these are just the sorts of things I need to understand. I must not interrupt you."

"The difference here," Arthur Winner said, "is that we have no direct legislation on religious bodies. A good many years ago, the assembly passed an act to require title of property of all religious bodies, if the property was to be tax exempt, to be vested in the congregations. There was a feeling at the time that the privilege was being abused; that groups, describing themselves as religious, but really operated for the private profit of a few people running them, ought not to enjoy the exemption. The act seemed to offer an easy way of making sure a church really was a church."

"It seems quite reasonable," Doctor Trowbridge said.

"Yes. Since most religious groups already met the requirement, they felt no inconvenience—here, at Christ Church, a title in the vestry, the chosen representatives of the congregation, was proper under the act. But those who framed and passed the act weren't long in discovering what they appeared to have forgotten—the Roman Catholic church. There, the act was entirely unacceptable. The Catholic church was unalterably opposed. Catholic congregations have no rights in church property, and the church hadn't the faintest intention of giving them any. Of course, nobody wanted to stand up and be counted on that issue—shall Catholic churches be made to pay taxes on their property."

Doctor Trowbridge laughed. "I wouldn't have thought of that. But, I see! You'd be oppressing a minority—"

"I'm afraid this wasn't entirely that kind of tenderness," Arthur Winner said. "Catholics may be a minority; but they're always a loud one, and, at least to elected officials who may only have won office by a few thousand votes, a dangerous one. The

courts found some construing-to-nullify expedient; and enough
pressure was finally put on enough legislators to repeal the act.
Our present position results."

Doctor Trowbridge was looking at him, silent and apparently
perturbed. The thought came to Arthur Winner that here, hands
washed in innocency, might be a mind not quite able to imagine
how a man (let alone, numbers of men) sworn to public faith
and duty could stoop to consult expedience instead of principle,
could set office above honor; could so crawl to keep a political
plum, could go—in what perfect literalness!—to this ignoble
little latter-day Canossa.

Arthur Winner said: "The law's present position is that organized churches may hold property and maintain internal discipline according to their own rules. That's to say, while no rule
of any church is law, the courts will treat conformity to rule as
the test of who's entitled to use, or benefit by, any particular
church's property. Those who don't conform may not hold the
property; and if they try to, an action in replevin will lie against
them. Equity actions, petitions for injunctions, are also admissible. I'm afraid the point has more legal than general interest."

"But I am most interested!" Doctor Trowbridge said. He was
glad, perhaps, to get past that unpleasant notion of a moment
ago. "Do I follow? Our vestry has title to this property; but only
while acting in conformity with the charter of the parish and the
constitution and canons of the diocese—"

"You follow," Arthur Winner said. "If we, the vestry, try to
apply church property to other than church uses, or vote to join
the Methodists or Presbyterians, or refuse the rector some canonical right of his, like access to the church, the test fails, and the
courts will admit an action against us. We lose the title. On the
same basis, in the case of the Roman church, the courts would
not admit an action brought by Catholic laymen to compel a
bishop to account for monies, because the church holds all collected monies the bishop's to do as he sees fit with. On the other
hand, because Catholic congregations aren't given power or right
by the church to select their own priest, the courts *would* move
against, eject, any priest who tried to officiate in, or act as rector

346

of, any parish to which the bishop hadn't appointed him, even if he were the congregation's choice."

"I see, I see!" Doctor Trowbridge said. "I think I see perfectly, thank you!" He laughed. "That last," he said, "I don't think that happens often! Rome has the advantage over us of an exacted full obedience. And the advantage's disadvantage!" He became serious. "With their sort of sacerdotalism, their error of clericalism, the laity, I'm afraid, tends just to pay its money and take its faith. They have, of course, any number of saintly, spiritually vigorous individuals; and I would not wish to speak uncharitably; but the rank and file do give one an impression of passively buying magic, rather than actively practicing religion. That is why I cannot but feel the Anglican communion has the better, wiser—and, yes, more blessed; and, so, holier—approach."

If the enthusiasm of conviction in Doctor Trowbridge's voice surprised him, Arthur Winner supposed it was because old Doctor Ives was the pattern of a clergyman to which he had grown accustomed. That Doctor Ives had felt the same conviction, and quite as strongly, was hardly to be doubted; but religious belief (Doctor Ives's ordinary manner made plain) was too serious or solemn a subject to be bandied about in general conversation or done the disparagement of being discussed like any other topic. In scores of meetings of the vestry during Doctor Ives's incumbency Arthur Winner could not remember the old rector ever introducing amid the proper business of expenses and receipts, of improvements or repairs, so much as a reference to faith and doctrine. He reserved faith and doctrine for the altar and the pulpit, for the appointed hours of divine service. Sacred subjects belonged in church, where sanctity of atmosphere and setting ensured the reverence that was their due. Out of church, all Christians (as far as in them lay) were of course bound to follow the teaching of Our Lord; but to go around talking about religion was almost sacrilegious.

Doctor Trowbridge laid down his filled pipe, forgetting it. He smiled. "But, you may say, this is talk, these are fine phrases. How to be doers of the word? That lies in individual congregations; and their first step must be self-examination. Are they realizing in terms of today the purposes for which they are joined together? Is their worship alive and active?"

Smiling again, Doctor Trowbridge broke off. He said: "You'll realize I'm in the course of preparing a series of more or less catechetical sermons on the worship of the church. Not, of course, departing from the essential rites and ceremonial principles that the Book of Common Prayer sets forth; but involving very definite changes in form, in the order of worship—" He laughed outright. He said: "Oh, I've no thought but to make haste slowly, Arthur! I see I've disturbed you! Let me say that my whole feeling about changes of this kind is that they must be wanted. They must be at the desire of the congregation, or there's no health in them! I'll do nothing until I'm sure I see that desire."

Surprised again, Arthur Winner would have to allow that, slight and young-appearing though he might be, Doctor Trowbridge could—he did!—assume with all naturalness the mien of pastoral authority, the good shepherd's confident fatherly manner. He was the rector; he was not for a moment forgetting it. Arthur Winner, this big, balding, middle-aged man before him, however much his senior, however much his superior in such wisdoms of the children of this world as business and law, was a parishioner of his, one of his flock.

"My dear Arthur," Doctor Trowbridge said. Bending forward, he put out a hand and laid it gently on Arthur Winner's sleeve. "Understand me. On points of what to do, I have the instruction of my own conscience, the conviction of clear duty arrived at through much study and prayer. But on how to do the thing to do, when there are various possible ways, and none wrongful, I've no such instruction, no such conviction. When you earlier told me about the situation with Mr. Tuttle and the Orcutt bequest, I hope you didn't doubt me when I said I was most grateful. I believe as much as ever that great benefit would accrue to the church in this diocese if the Diocesan Fund were made the repository for every parish's endowments. But after what you said of Mr. Tuttle's scruple about the benefactor's intent, I wouldn't for worlds argue with him. There seems to be no fault of any kind—quite the contrary!—to be found with Mr. Tuttle's management. There'd be neither reason nor justice in pressing a good steward to give up his charge. No moral principle is involved. There's a great difference between what is necessary, being of right; and what is, being of opinion, merely desirable! I wish to be and will be entirely guided by your experience in matters of this kind. Now, does *that* satisfy you?"

"Where I can be of use, I hope you'll use me," Arthur Winner said, laughing. "About what you tell the vestry of your plans; I'll venture to suggest you say no more now than that you mean to preach on the services of the church. The vestry's part of the congregation. They'll hear the sermons. To tell them you want to make changes; and then to promise them you won't until they agree, could, I think, only unsettle them. They're led to ask themselves: What terrible changes are these which we're foreseen to be, perhaps, against?"

"How right you are!" Doctor Trowbridge said. "How very right!" He looked at Arthur Winner with admiration. "One sees at once that one would plant entirely needless doubts, prepare them in advance to be on the lookout for things to dislike. Yes; let us make haste slowly!" He spoke with firmness, as though admonishing himself, determinedly sobering himself out of a too-exhilarating consciousness (as he surveyed his new domain with enlivened, energetic eye) of tide in the affairs of men, of the urgent temptation to take it at the flood; to press in; and with the head-swimming succeedings of success, out of much to make, while the making was good, more.

Glancing at a scratch-pad on his desk, he said mildly: "With that in mind, I daresay I can advise myself about the one other point I thought of raising Monday night. The composition of the vestry; rules of election. There, too, I'd like to see changes— though I know they would involve amending the charter of the parish. An increasing practice in this and other dioceses has been to set up rotating plans, with vestrymen ineligible to succeed themselves. The purpose, of course, is to bring more men to share in the responsibilities of directing parish affairs—" He laughed. "Yes; you *have* been a great help to me. I *can* advise myself! Would I want it to be supposed that, in the interest of innovations, I was arranging to pack the vestry? Yet, a change of so much proved usefulness I think we should, in time, give earnest consideration to."

Doctor Trowbridge's expression was, in fact, earnest. He said: "Not, you may be sure, that I want to rotate you, Arthur! I trust I've made it plain to you that, in the event of Judge Lowe resigning, my very great hope and wish is that you'll let me appoint you senior warden in his place. I know, both from the parish records, and from a most pleasant conversation I had with your charming mother when I called on her, how long and well your father served in that capacity. I've looked over the vestry minutes of past years, so I know what your father's contribution was. One recognizes, as well as practical churchmanship, the kind of active faith our world stands in such sore need of. His memory must be a great gratification to you."

"It is," Arthur Winner said. "And you're quite right about his wish to serve the parish, his attachment to Christ Church."

If the response was a little difficult to phrase, and also a little disingenuous, the response was in no real way untrue. The record of the Man of Reason, uncontestable, remained in the minutes of the vestry for Doctor Trowbridge, the Man of Faith, to read. The Man of Reason had seen fit to practice, with his usual effectiveness, "practical churchmanship." The record said nothing more. That the Man of Reason's detached, dispassionate, well-tempered mind had seriously received the begged questions, the circular arguments, the false analogies, commonly cited as "proofs" of a Divine Creator's existence, was hard to suppose. Nor, under that keen inquiry, would substitute pleas of special revelation, nor the contentions of mystical double talk, the voluminous rhapsodical maunderings (whether new or old) about supernal illumination or the fruition of states of grace be apt to stand up. Their demonstrations were not in accord with scientific method; their data being all doubtful, their inferences must be all unjustified; and their similarities in image and argument must suggest, not so much that these things could be true, as that all mystics of report had been typically deranged.

350

In short, did the Man of Reason ever accept the story of the incarnate godhead, or the story of the risen Christ, for what his rector and his friend, Doctor Ives, liked to call them in the pulpit—the one; the central fact in human history; the other; the best-attested historical event of all time? The Man of Reason had done the reading of his day; and what was this he was being told but the very stuff of myth—the woman got with child by the deity in time to bear an infant savior at the winter solstice; the grievous formal murder of the theanthropos whose earth-breaking return from the dead must occur near the vernal equinox. Could the Man of Reason credit the dreadful drama's orthodox accounting-for? Could ethical assent ever be given by him to all that the shocking, the really monstrous, dogma of the atonement implied? What was here but allegorical fantasy, a laborious attempt in symbols to relate the finite known to the infinite unknown? You received such stories, not as shedding light on, but as admitting, the mystery, awesome and permanent, of life.

However, the stuff of this myth had long been the sacred fiction of the Man of Reason's people, his race. A fable so venerated, around which their civilization, for century on century, had formed itself, had a vested right. Were such established uses of piety to be lightly scouted? Raised, in the first place, were considerations of decorum, of mere manners. The man who is reasonable takes with civil accommodation reasonable account of his fellows, of the feelings and beliefs that comfort or calm the great majority of minds neither detached, dispassionate, nor tempered well. Very meet, right, and his bounden duty, at all times and in all places, was a profession of respect for reverenced forms, a public observing of the order generally observed. Private judgment's obtrusion, unasked for, uncalled for, would be an act of unthinkable insult and scandal. Shows of doubt had the offensive smack of *hubris*. Professed skepticism was a vulgar sin against taste. Whether or not any given doctrine was true, any particular rite efficacious, any specific rule of conduct divinely ordained, didn't matter, was not of moment. Of moment, could be only the simple question of what was seemly and what was unseemly.

The Man of Reason made himself, with decent devoutness, a regular communicant. In the collection plate, he cast such generous gifts of money as were proper for a person of his means. Freely, he spent his valuable time ensuring sound management of the vestry's business. When, at the end, Doctor Ives (tears in his old eyes) came to the fresh grave (while his senior warden's scientifically mutilated, wasted remains were made ready to be laid into the earth) and commenced, the old voice breaking: *Man that is born of woman hath but a short time to live* . . . the appropriateness of that then-concluding ceremony, and of those manifested sentiments, surely stood unquestioned.

"The matter's one for thought and for prayer," Doctor Trowbridge said. "I'm glad to see you regard it as I do—not to be lightly entered into. Think. Pray. And when you have, Arthur —" his smile took on a light and lively youthfulness—"I'd bet a good sum what answer you'll receive. And I'll receive! Talents aren't meant to be buried; and, by the grace of Our Lord, they aren't allowed to be!"

Where his experience lay, Doctor Trowbridge was experienced enough. He could be seen to recognize with understanding, even with indulgence, the to-be-expected shy slight shamefacedness of the average no-matter-how-good churchman when his pastor took him from temporal activities and functions of the church to articles of belief, to holy thoughts. These God-shy people need not be thought the worse of for their embarrassment; and aggravating embarrassment unnecessarily would be neither politic nor kind. Still, for their soul's sake, they mustn't get away with it altogether! Seasonably, Doctor Trowbridge eased the religious atmosphere with the secular whimsy of betting. Seasonably, emphatically, he called the spiritual back for a moment by his swift reversion in so many words to Our Lord.

Arthur Winner said: "I'd like to do that, if I may, Whit. Among other things, I must ask myself if I'm as well fitted as, say, my father was. Whether other men might not have more to contribute."

The response sounded lame, for the good reason that it was lame. Arthur Winner felt the steady, gentle but earnest pressure of the other mind against his. The feeling was familiar. Such pressures were the working tactics of attorneys at law, the very process of their engagements. A veteran of legal engagements, not used to being found unready or fumbling in response, Arthur Winner had no trouble determining his difficulty. The difficulty was that of putting himself where he put himself with ease when the opposing mind was of opposing counsel—in the other's place. Just imagining that he was transposed, his position in space exchanged, for Doctor Trowbridge's—Arthur Winner seated in the ugly tall Gothic chair, Arthur Winner with a reversed collar and light jacket of clerical cut—would not serve. To see things as "Whit" saw them, a transposition of temperament was needed, an exchange almost beyond imagination's power.

A man's temperament might, perhaps, be defined as the mode or modes of a man's feeling, the struck balance of his ruling desires, the worked-out sum of his habitual predispositions. In themselves, these elements were inscrutable. There were usually too many of them; they were often of irreducible complexity; you could observe only results. Useless, to ask yourself what specific turn of his temperament would first incline, and then equip "Whit" to be unshakably sure that he saw the unseen and knew the unknown. Simply to be observed, was that sure, he was. He stood perfectly persuaded that the Lord God was a sun and a shield. And in no mere abstraction of theory! The to-be-observed result was a total way of life. As far as the natural self-divisions in a human being would allow, this simple theocentric view, this way of life, conditioned all knowledge, all emotion, all action.

When "Whit" faced personal problems of choice or decision, his recourse (he had indicated) was to go on his knees in some convenient place and humbly to enter a petition to a Presence he confidently felt to be ever present that he be shown how to settle the matter. A sane proposal! The Presence being assumed to, being stipulated to, knew all devices and desires of the heart, knew not only those that a man might be concealing from his fellow men, but also those he might not know himself. Nothing less than omniscience heard your suffrages; and what was handed down, however unforeseen by your limitary mind, however counter to your ignorant hopes, could not be error. Receiving that word, you had but to act on it. Anguishes of indecision eased; you were refreshed. That intimation of the material man, sad and wearisome, sometimes despairing—that everything was up to you; you must think things out; you must find a way, or make one, you must do it all—no longer weighed on you. The everyday sore puzzle of the spiritual man: What was of the world, and what was of the spirit? Which, Caesar's things? Which, God's?—stood, every day, resolved.

Miss Cummins, smiling, gently joking, admired an innocence which had never thought of ways to see the legs of a woman; and could Arthur Winner doubt that that same innocence had unhesitatingly brought questions of legs, questions of women, to the Presence in prayer? Reverently, "Whit" (it was as good as certain) had inquired on bended knee whether making provision for certain recurring physical needs would be well for him; or ought he to subdue such impulses—Arthur Winner thought of his mother's phrase: "interests not appropriate to his calling." Duly, the signification must have come: *He shall take a wife in her virginity. A widow, or a divorced woman, or profane, or an harlot, these he shall not take; but he shall take a virgin of his own people to wife.* To the humble petition, Miss Cummins was the plain right answer. Once their union—holy; approved above—was solemnized, "Midge" could be well imagined (they having first side by side knelt to say their night prayers) affording with affection but also modesty (no needless showing of legs on her part; no needless looking at them on his) just those soberly managed, temperately used, measures of relief that the divine sanction might be thought to have contemplated.

"There!" Doctor Trowbridge said. "I've kept you much too long; but I'm most grateful for your most helpful advice." He stood up. "And, speaking of duties, I know Midge is going to

354

feel I'm shirking some of mine! I was to report to the kitchen with no unnecessary delay. There are things that need to be taken down, and things that need to be put up. We can't persuade you to stay for what potluck there is with us? Usually we've been lunching with my mother at the hotel; but Mother had to go to town today, so Midge thought it would be fun to see what she could fix here—well, maybe you're wise not to risk it!"

Smiling, Arthur Winner said: "I'd risk it with pleasure; but I told Clarissa I'd be out to Roylan before she left—"

An abrupt, ear-filling clamor interrupted him. Poured down in the outdoor quiet of the church close, surging through the indoor quiet of this room's tinted light, the electric pealings, the slow and mighty simulated bell notes of Christ Church's carillon, began to pronounce from the high tower: *Abide with me, fast falls the eventide . . .*

Doctor Trowbridge's startled expression had gone into a wince of distress, humorous, but not wholly humorous. He stood stiffly for an instant, like a man who might be counting to ten, while the clangorous melody, rung out so much rounder, stronger, and truer than any real bells could ever ring it, proceeded: *When other helpers fail, and comforts flee; Help of the helpless, O . . .*

Doctor Trowbridge's lips now tightened with determination. He said, raising his voice: "This is really most exasperating! In one way, it seems making much of a small matter; that's why one hardly knows what to do. But, do something, I will! If Mr. Abbott chose to come into the church and play the organ at odd hours; that would be one thing. I'd see no objection. But, as Mr. Minieri remarked, this can be heard all over Brocton. Heard without rhyme or reason. No! I can't, and I won't, allow that." He crossed to the office door.

Out in the stone, fan-vaulted, hall with him, Arthur Winner said: "Would you like me to speak to Mr. Abbott, Whit?"

Doctor Trowbridge said: "Well, Arthur, you did speak to him once, didn't you? I shouldn't have asked you to! I see I was evading the issue. The church buildings are in my official custody and I must direct the uses of them." He looked up at Arthur Winner with an easy, composed purposefulness, a calm of decision. "I'm

355

aware that Mr. Abbott has given his services for years to Christ Church—incidentally, an arrangement never well advised, I think, Arthur—and I'm sorry to have to speak this way; but if he will not do as I direct, Mr. Abbott may not continue as organist and choirmaster." He paused. "I will, of course, explain my reasons, put it as a request, before I put it as an order; but nothing is to be gained by delay. I must act now." He nodded toward the notice board near the entrance. "I saw on Miss Hartzel's schedule that you and Judge Lowe were tomorrow's ushers; so I'll see you in the morning." He turned and walked toward the arch of the corridor that led to the choir room and sacristy, and so into the church.

✦

With noon at hand, the morning had grown warm; but unlike yesterday's, today's warm air was light, not heavy. Unhazed, sparklingly, the quality of June was in the September sunlight. Without ceasing, the steady breeze stirred the leaves of the big trees out of which the courthouse dome emerged. Small and sunny, Justice's effigy stood against the stainless sky.

Stepping into this fine day from the end of the cloister before the parish house to cross the church close, Arthur Winner was still smiling at the near abruptness of his dismissal. Doctor Trowbridge might never be Christ Church's boss in quite the sense Harry Minieri meant, in the autocratic, unprotestable way that Father Albright (his bishop permitting!) bossed Our Lady of Mount Carmel; but (you might say) who was going to wear the pants, "Whit" made plain enough. Christ Church's carillon had fallen silent. Elmer Abbott, a man of Arthur Winner's age, gentle, even effeminate in his manner, would be receiving, no doubt a little dazed, the law—what he was to do, and what he was not to do; and he'd better read, mark, learn, and inwardly digest!

Arthur Winner, walking the flagged walk, was near the High Street gate when a voice behind him said: "Mr. Winner!"

After him came Alfred Revere. Alfred, probably in the sexton's room, must have heard talking in the hall. Allowing Doctor

356

Trowbridge time to go into the church, Alfred must then have followed Mr. Winner quickly, trying to overtake him. Concerned to see Alfred hurrying, Arthur Winner stopped, turned, went to meet him.

Alfred Revere said: "I don't know whether you spoke to Judge Lowe, Mr. Winner." He stood quiet, his spare frame held straight. He was bareheaded; and tight dense frizzles of light gray hair clung like wool to his narrow skull. His bony, intelligent black face, in which, too, Arthur Winner seemed to see a cast of gray, was grave.

"Yes, I did," Arthur Winner said. "I was extremely sorry to hear about it."

Alfred Revere drew a breath. He moved his eyes to meet Arthur Winner's reluctantly, as though they were lingering with pangs of regret on the sunlit day. He said: "I wonder if you happen to have told the rector."

"No," Arthur Winner said. "Judge Lowe asked me not to say anything to anyone."

"Yes; I was just going to ask you, if you hadn't, not to, Mr. Winner. I asked the judge would he tell *you*, but that's all. I don't have my mind made up yet what I'll do. Just in case anything happened, I wanted the judge and you to have known that it could happen."

Arthur Winner said: "From what Judge Lowe told me, I think there's only one thing to do, Alfred. You must take care of yourself. You must do whatever the doctor says. Who was he; and what exactly did he say?"

"Well, he's this specialist in the city," Alfred Revere said. "So he said he'd make these tests—he's a colored man; but I think he's as well-educated as a white doctor. He puts these things on me that make this machine make a graph or something on a paper. That was the first time. So when I came back, he did it again. So then he looked at them together; and he said: 'Can you afford to stop working?' So I said: 'Yes, I have provision made that way.' So he said: 'Stop; you got to have absolute rest. You can't keep straining that heart of yours. I don't like to frighten you; but my professional duty is to let you know that if you do anything but rest, with this condition, any moment

357

could be your last. Whatever you're doing is too hard for your heart. I'm not saying it couldn't stand up quite some time still; I don't know. But I *am* saying, you go on abusing it, and one day it just stops. That's sure.' "

"Then, I think what you must do is clear," Arthur Winner said. "Your first obligation's to yourself, to your health—"

Alfred Revere said: "Oh, I see that, Mr. Winner. If I was dead, I couldn't do my jobs either. But I look at him; and he's saying here are these pills I got to carry with me all the time so I can take one if I feel this coming on; and that's all *he* can do for me. This condition, I'm the only one can treat." Alfred Revere smiled thinly. "But, hearing him talk, sort of shifting what he's saying around, I see what he isn't saying. This condition, nobody can treat! Nothing's going to cure it; it can only get worse. He advises me, rest; and if I want to think I'm treating it, good! I won't know I'm wrong more than one second before I don't know anything."

Arthur Winner said: "He wouldn't necessarily think that, Alfred. Plenty of people with heart trouble, by simply being careful, live comfortably for years. I think it's much more likely that he believes you could, too. He doesn't, as he said, like to frighten a patient; but I think he meant to frighten you; because, if he could only make you do what he said, he probably felt you had a good chance."

With a nod that seemed to be of thanks, a polite acknowledgment of this lip comfort, Alfred Revere said: "Yes; he frightened me some. I don't say I'm not frightened. But I keep thinking of a funny picture I saw once. This man, he'd fallen off this high skyscraper; and there he was, falling through the air; and about halfway down, he was passing this window with these scared-looking people seeing him; so he calls out: 'Don't worry! All right so far!' I guess that's for all of us, Mr. Winner. When we get born, we fell off something; and just we wait, and we'll find out how all right we are! At my age, the ground's got to be getting pretty close, no matter what I do. So do I want to be resting the rest of the way; or do I want to be working? I mean, suppose this doctor did say the real truth, that I could treat this condition so I live longer. What would I be doing with myself, besides being careful?"

From the hopeless tone, Alfred plainly saw (with more imagination than Arthur Winner would have given him credit for) that the alternatives were both fearful, loss of life hardly more so than loss of occupation. Farewell, the tranquil mind; and farewell, too, those usefulnesses, those small importances, which were the sum of human happiness. What was Alfred without the just and quiet satisfactions of his ceremonial power and authority? After all, he, in practice, owned Christ Church, the familiar stone fabric of the buildings rising around him here. The church was his charge; he oversaw it. At his direction (since he decided what should be called to their attention), the rector and vestry did what was needful for care and repair. He owned the Union League. By his authority, that old building, too, was kept up; he determined who worked there and what was done; he ordered the supplies and paid for them; the club members were his guests. These great possessions was he to cast away for a shadow's shadow, a breath, an uncertain little length of empty extra existence?

Alfred Revere said: "Of course, there's others I got to think of. When I know what I know, I couldn't just not say nothing, pretend nothing was wrong, have the club not know they might not have any steward tomorrow; or, here, they might not have any sexton tomorrow. I have to let them be able to take steps, look around for somebody. Before I stopped, I'd have to make arrangements, find them somebody they could trust—"

Brought to resume his accustomed role of the general manager, of the confident lawgiver, Alfred could be seen for a moment forgetting that he was so sorrowful, so scant of hope. He said: "Sexton wouldn't be too hard; I think Harcourt could learn to do that, if I showed him. But I don't know who could run the club, I surely don't! There's no one in my family—for a while, I was thinking of Harold; but he can't do anything without Em tells him. Those that could, they don't have any interest. It's like Rodney. I had him in, had him bus boy when he was twelve. He had sense; you could teach him. But pretty soon, he says: 'Uncle Al, I'm not aiming to be a waiter; I'm going to be a dentist.' So, I said: 'You think you study hard enough to be that?' He said: 'Yes, sir, I do.' So I asked Aaron to let me look at Rodney's report cards; and they were all A's. Same with Marigold's Morgan. I don't mean he ever got A's—he failed his first year high school. But he started in this garage—they fix automobile bodies—on Water Street; and he saved his money; and pretty soon he got the bank to give him a loan, and he bought it. He's the boss, now. Today, that's what they want— unless they're one of the shiftless few you couldn't set to doing anything."

A fond, amused smile showed on Alfred Revere's face. "Blaming them's the last thing I'm doing; I'm proud of them. I just remember how I thought it wonderful, when I was first working at the Union League, and after a while, my grandaddy said to me—I was checking in the storeroom: 'Boy, you'll do! You go on like you're going, not lay down on the job, and there's no reason you can't be steward here someday.' That isn't what they think's wonderful now. It's different now."

But the amused lapse into reminiscence had not been fortunate, Arthur Winner saw. Yes, now, how different! Where now, that earnest, pleased, bright youth in the storeroom, by old Paul Revere (the born slave, who knew the difference between involuntary servitude's shame, and the freeman's dignity of choosing to serve) solemnly approved, promised such a great reward, such a golden future? That youth was this old man, gray-headed, worn with his decades of work; now, with weary depressed visage, brought to stand here on the last edge of life. Alfred, or his body for him, had suddenly recalled his state, his "condition." Like Montaigne's condemned prisoner, who found no delight in even the most beautiful and interesting sights along the way as they carried him to the headsman's block, Alfred perceived that all is vain. He stopped speaking.

Arthur Winner said: "I don't know how anybody could take your place either, Alfred. But I'm sure we're all agreed your health comes first. Judge Lowe spoke of various possibilities. As far as the sexton's work, here, goes, I wonder if you couldn't, as you suggested, show Harcourt what to do—that is, you'd still

360

be in charge; but you wouldn't have to do anything active. At the club, I think it's time we considered closing the dining room and kitchens. They've been operating at a loss for years now; and we know that's the only way we can operate them. If we stopped serving meals, managing the club ought to be so much easier I don't see why someone like Harold couldn't handle the rest—for the time being. I mean, you'd only have to come in for a few minutes now and then to check up on him. As a matter of fact, Judge Lowe proposed something of the kind."

As a matter of fact, Judge Lowe had proposed a good deal more than that. Leaving the bench after he had sentenced poor Caroline Dummer (that "indeterminate term" at home!), he had beckoned to Arthur Winner. Going into his chambers, sitting down still in his robe, Willard Lowe said: "Arthur, here's what I wanted to talk to you about. Alfred Revere has bad news. The doctors tell him—"

Though speaking with regret really felt, a personal sorrow, Willard Lowe spoke also with the longanimous resignation of the sensible man of seventy who must find sad news about still another person he has known for years no news. "So that's how things stand," Willard Lowe said. "Arthur, I wonder if we shouldn't perhaps take this as a sign. You know and I know the Union League's moribund. Only two things have kept us going. One; Alfred. The place couldn't have been run without him —no one else could even have found a staff. Two; the endowment. If, any time in the last twenty years, our dues had to pay our costs, we'd have been shut in a month. True; that was what Sam Orcutt left the money for—younger men who might have smaller means were to be able to belong, to enjoy the privileges of membership. And, do they? Not so as you'd notice! The truth is, we've lost our purpose. You can't count twenty members who really use the club. Who'd miss it? Perhaps a few old men like me, who aren't going to be around much longer anyway. When that's the case, continuing the organization can't be justified."

Sitting there, heavy, hunched a little in his folds of somewhat worn black silk, Willard Lowe, dispassionate, laid out his demonstration. Does this make sense? With that detachment which had so surprised Mr. Woolf on the subject of confiscatory taxes, Willard Lowe didn't admit to consideration such an irrelevancy as the feelings of old men who might miss old things. One more loss; but what did you expect? The charge was uselessness; and, in this trial by time, the burden was on defendant. The club was no longer used? Then, the club must go; it must go the way of the Ponemah Association, the summer night singing around the fire; of the buckboards and the horses that drew them up the old valley road; of those fine speeding trolley cars that passed Shelby's, that rocked with a rush and glitter down from Eatontown— and the way of so many, many friends, now among the dead. For a new scene: *Time:* Today, the stage had to be cleared.

Willard Lowe said: "Roger Bartlett told me something I'll ask you to treat as a confidence. The committee on membership settled a few weeks ago on several people to approach; and there was one Roger felt pretty sure of. You'll perhaps understand why; but Roger was wrong. Jerry Brophy. Jerry simply said that, thanks, he didn't want to belong. No close friends of his were members; there'd be no benefit to him; and the truth was, in Mechanicsville, the lower county, he might even be hurt—people might think he was putting on airs. He very kindly said he didn't want to leave Roger in the position of being publicly turned down, so if Roger would allow him to decline privately—"

In Willard Lowe's eyes, the hint of a wry smile appeared—his unspoken invitation to Arthur Winner to share the joke of the turned tables, the possible serving-right of this declining, falling, now only so-called, Union League for the presumption of palmier days, when what chairman of what committee on membership would ever have dreamed of asking a J. Jerome Brophy to join the gentlemen in the parlor?

Willard Lowe said: "For many reasons, then, I think we should seriously ask ourselves whether it ought to be moved at the December meeting that the board of governors put the question to the membership—a resolution for an aye or no vote. I think we must recognize the time is ripe. If Alfred has to

362

stop, so does the club! I see no special legal difficulties in wind-ing up. I don't think the court need hesitate to hold that the original purposes of incorporation are no longer realized; and that funds and property lawfully may, and they should, be put to some present use agreed on by the governors as consonant with those original purposes—promoting good citizenship would perhaps define them. That would give us wide field."

Arthur Winner said: "In point of statutory law, there may be no difficulties, Willard. But, in point of procedure, a difficulty occurs to me. Who's going to do this so-holding? Lowe, Presi-dent Judge? McAllister, Judge? Dealey, Judge? All members of the petitioning organization. All interested parties."

Willard Lowe said: "Been a bear, would have bit me!" He let himself snort with laughter. "Never once thought of that!" He laughed again. "There's your father in you, Arthur! That sounded just like him! Start scorching off in all directions, and he was the man to put a spoke in your wheel!" Willard Lowe paused a moment, nodding several times; as though that old friend's shade, recollected, pleased him. He said: "Yes; we'd need to arrange to have someone specially presiding. We could get Hollis over from the eleventh district, I imagine." His voice was quite cheerful.

Alfred Revere said: "I hope that won't have to happen, Mr. Winner. I wouldn't feel good, having you do that just because of me. We lose money, yes; but nobody saw that a reason to stop before. Anyway, I hope doing anything could wait. I'd like to think some, if I could."

"Of course!" Arthur Winner said. "Take your time—"

Alfred Revere smiled faintly. Another "funny picture"? He said: "Then there's something else I'd like to ask you, Mr. Win-ner. I never made a will. I wonder if I could consult you on that—have you write it for me? I mean, come to your office, a regular client, and pay you." He held his chin up gravely.

With answering gravity, Arthur Winner said: "Yes; I'd be very glad to draw a will for you, Alfred. Let's arrange an ap-pointment. The best thing, I think, would be for you to make a list of everything you own and bring that with you. By estimating the values and phrasing the clauses properly, estate taxes can often be minimized. Then, if you intend naming more than one legatee or beneficiary, by devising specific items—saying who is to get what—you avoid any chance of loss in more or less forced sales. You might give that thought."

"Yes," Alfred Revere said. "That's it! That's what I wouldn't have any way of knowing myself. Things like that. I want to get myself good advice." But you could see again the unhappy transition. For a brief space, Alfred achieved self-forgetfulness. He spoke, enlivened by his gratified feeling of consequence, his agreeable feeling of the propertied man, in this making of business arrangements with a lawyer. Now he remembered why he was making them. He said: "Maybe I better not leave it too long, Mr. Winner. Could it be Monday?"

"Monday at nine, if you like," Arthur Winner said. "When I know what your wishes are, we'll put them in shape right away, draw the instrument, so you can sign before you go."

Alfred Revere moistened his lips. He looked at Arthur Winner with an instant's hypnotized blankness of eye, the blankness of a mind nauseated by animal despair. Not without a responding qualm, Arthur Winner remembered the opossum on the upper bridge road last night—the frozen poising of the little pointed head, the paralysis of the plump furry body, while on the poor creature swept the hideous, night-born (never to be accounted for by any opossum!) monster, the fast-coming juggernaut that blinded him with light, lit him like day for a second or two before, disinterestedly, it mashed him dead.

Arthur Winner said: "About what the doctor told you, Alfred. I think it's wise, where there's a condition that may be serious, to have more than one opinion. Why don't you let Doctor Shaw examine you?"

Alfred Revere brought his eyes to focus. He smiled sadly. He said: "I saw Doctor Shaw, Mr. Winner. That is, I went there. He said come about suppertime and he'd be able to examine me. But—" Alfred paused delicately—"I think he wasn't feeling well himself, right then. He'd have to make these tests, too, he said. He was going to; and then he said no, he couldn't

364

do them now. He had this blood pressure thing on my arm; and I could see he couldn't get to read it right. He said he'd call me; but then he didn't. So I thought I'd better see someone else if I was going to. So I got an opinion; and I don't too much want to do all that again—"

Looking past Arthur Winner, Alfred Revere suddenly roused himself. "Well, thank you," he said. "I'll be there Monday with that list. I guess I'd better be at the club, now." He inclined his head politely and walked away.

Looking where Alfred had looked, Arthur Winner could see Alfred's reason for thinking he'd better be at the club now. Coming through the church close in a short cut from the Greenwood Avenue gate there had appeared and was approaching—with care, unhurried; with care, erect—the tall figure of Howard Minton. Under a Panama hat dingy with age, the ravaged long face's pallor was relieved by slight hectic stains of color on the upper cheeks. The nearly livid lips were compressed with a stiffness of suffering. From the glazed, yellowish whites of the large eyes, dazed pupils of dark brown stared fixedly to the front. Howard Minton wore a starched collar and a black knit tie knotted precisely. His herringbone tweed jacket had been (how many years ago?) expensively tailored. It was buttoned and neat; but everywhere—at collar, at elbow, at cuff—the cloth showed threadbare. Just as much worn, his black trousers were nonetheless freshly pressed; the ancient good shoes were freshly polished. Coming near Arthur Winner, observing with a start that he was observed, Howard Minton tipped up his scarred, silver-topped Malacca stick in jerky salute. There was a crapulous trembling of lips and cheeks, as though he willed (for a moment, in vain) his tongue to speak.

Arthur Winner said: "Good morning, Colonel."

Howard Minton got his lips open. He said: "Mr. Winner! Good day, sir!"

He passed, the upright wreck of a man, moving as though mechanically drawn, making his noon beeline for the Union League bar. Arrived there, his foot planted on the brass rail, he would stand stoically waiting, while Alfred Revere with deference prepared the only medicine that now could mend him—

the drink poured out, placed ready in front of Colonel Minton, for the stroke of the hour that signaled the trembling hand to raise the glass, that set Colonel Minton free to down a short convulsive swallow—the first today!

Himself moving on, Arthur Winner went through the gate. This block of High Street was posted with NO PARKING signs; so he had put his car in the service drive that ran to the back of the parish house. To get there, he must walk around behind the rectory.

Clear of the church close, the breeze up the street blew pleasantly in his face, the sparkling sun poured down on Arthur Winner; yet the slight shadow of those facts, these ends of men's roads, fell across the fine day, the day's bright look of June (false; since summer was over). *How dies the wise man?* said the far-from-jesting Preacher—and stayed him for his answer. *As the fool!* Like Alfred Revere's, Howard Minton's other helpers failed, his comforts fled. Swift to its close ebbs out life's little day! Colonel Minton was well along in his particular form of that ruination to which, for which, men were born. But Colonel Minton's wound, you wished to object, was self-inflicted? You could say that. The hand directed now against this old soldier was clearly his own hand.

Farewell, the neighing steed and the shrill trump—or the now equivalents (Arthur Winner heard again, in General Willcox's Florida office, the rising and falling thunder of the two-thousand-horsepower engines); farewell, whatever prides and pomps the age's wars of offices and machines once held for Colonel Minton! Some decisive defeat in life had been inflicted on him. The victor, his vanquisher, was, of course, the vanquisher of all men, those forces, ever victorious, of circumstance.

What the special circumstance or circumstances had been—what single sorrow or sum of sorrows; what faults of others or of his own; what breakings-down of mind or body—need not be inquired into. Perhaps there had been enough to defeat any man; perhaps some, perhaps most, men would not have been defeated—never mind that! The force had been sufficient to defeat Howard Minton. The fact was accomplished and the fact spoke. For Howard Minton (the fact told you), events had somehow so fallen out that the past was only painful. He could not, with pride or satisfaction, live in *I was*. In *I will be* he found, for whatever reason, no longer any relish of hope. Ahead, he saw nothing good. Nothing he could look forward to was worth a price of present effort. What remained but *I am*? There, acknowledging no past, expecting no future, Colonel Minton had decided (the fact told you) to live.

With order (those pressed old trousers; those polished old shoes!), with control (from the body of the morning's death, delivery waited on high noon), Howard Minton had devised himself a way of life. The careful budgeting of his pension money, never a penny wasted on nonessentials; the studied arranging of his affairs (his simple prescription was to eliminate in the interests of drinking all other businesses or activities) made possible the spending of most of Colonel Minton's waking hours in *I am*'s grateful numb bemusement. Arriving soon after noon, he stayed in *I am* until two o'clock the next morning. At two o'clock, often drunk indeed but never disorderly, he emerged, as they were turning out the lights, from his last place of refreshment. Waiting at the curb would be a cab marked: *Supreme Taxi*. With a respectful greeting, with (when needed) some tactful, inconspicuously offered assistance, Alfred Revere's younger (though now far from young) brother Arnold, owner of the cab, saw Colonel Minton safely shut in, and drove him out Greenwood Avenue to his room at Helen Detweiler's. The long day's task was done; the old soldier must sleep.

Unwilling to, unable not to, Arthur Winner let the dismaying picture occupy his mind a moment. Dismay was reasonable. Only an occasional man, an always-potential alcoholic, might find imposed on him terms for the ending of his days that circumstance imposed on Howard Minton; yet Howard remained *exempli gratia,* a proposition illustrated in an instance. What man, you were asked to ask, ever ended his days on his own terms, free to the end, at liberty mentally and physically, competent in mind and body, to choose his course of greatest wisdom or his course of greatest good? As he grew weary, as he grew weak, opportunities to choose departed from him (he could elect to do only what he was able to do). Of the fewer and fewer choices left, more and more (it seemed safe to guess) would be made between what he wanted to do very little, and what he wanted to do even less. With a vain wish that things were ordered otherwise, with a discomfort of increased compunction (not uncolored by self-concern) for the human predicament, Arthur Winner turned in the service drive.

Beside him, the high back wall of the rectory rose bare and mostly blank. This masonry was no less solidly laid than any of the rest, but the lavishness of Gothic trim, the sparing-of-no-expense that overornamented elevations facing the church close and High Street extended only to the corner. This was a building's backside, the part to which no polite eye looked. Where show would be without profit, there was no show. Farther along, coming on the kitchen wing, you found an associated line of thinking. Kitchens being where menials toiled, the wing was so placed in relation to the grander rooms, where masters and mistresses were waited on, as to get little direct sunlight. The wing's lower stonework, like the strip of ground between the wall and the cinder drive, was dank with areas of moss. Passing a window sun would never reach, Arthur Winner could see that, inside, the lights were on—a light from flourescent tubes in newly installed modern fixtures, a light of artificial noon, really quite as good as nature's.

This indoor day, flooding the spotless renovated walls and all the gleaming last-word in functional fittings and equipment, showed Arthur Winner Doctor Trowbridge and Miss Cummins. They sat, as though they were children, side by side on the edge of a large enamel-topped table in the center of the room. It was to be observed that Doctor Trowbridge had his arm around her; and she was looking up at him, her sober small face pleasantly radiant. With gravity, Doctor Trowbridge bent his head and kissed her.

✦

High in the sycamores, a breeze kept clutches of coarse large leaves gently heaving and waving against the parti-colored big

368

boughs and shining blue sky behind them. Gently the breeze, the wandering airs, moved over the lawns. Down farther slopes of wood and field that encompassed steeply the little hollow of Roylan, the sun at half past twelve struck broad and direct, suffusing even the air in the shade with brightness.

Arthur Winner, past the house, bringing his car around the bend toward the garage, was obliged to put his brakes on with some abruptness. Out the first of the row of raised overhead doors, the station wagon was in the act of backing. At the wheel, Clarissa, with a casual yet careful glance across her shoulder, swung in an arc, swift and decisive, on the raked gravel of the turning space. Arthur Winner watched, admiring that always-admirable handling of things. A response of pleasure, the starting of a smile, saw the sightly, right, unconscious motions, the effortless efficient sequence that put Clarissa's hands, gloved in white mesh, inevitably where they ought to be. A response of tenderness, the little twist of the heart, saw such grace ingenuous (the more affecting, since this was no longer a girl) as of unspent youth, the tranquil vitality that informed the clear face and the clear look. In simple naturalness perfectly complementing look and face were the fitted garments of fresh linen that Clarissa liked to wear in warm weather.

Yet the response of pleasure had been interrupted. On the agreeable, admiring amusement, on the bemused tenderness, on the warmed heart, how cold a hand laid itself! The hand was doubt's, was dread's, was death's—could this be mine to keep? Ah, no; this is beyond mortal man's deserving. Such knowledge is too wonderful for me; it is high, I cannot attain unto it. The chill was returned dismay's. Those warnings of the morning had come back—Noah's craggy yet broken-down old face; the stertorous laugh of Willard Lowe's resignation; Alfred Revere's despairful calm; Colonel Minton's dazed, glazed eye. They were the successive notes, heavy tolled, of going, going, gone. They were the daily falling, falling of this life, gist of that grisly joke: *All right—so far!* They were the indirect but inescapable sad evidences of that truth, well known, well said: *Time shall rifle every youthful grace!* Anguished—ah, let this last!— the heart could yearn to stop the thief, to stay the flight, to

369

hold one magic instant motionless, its hour at half past noon, in this momentary similitude, breezy and sunny, of the enviable isles—through storms you reached them, and from storms were free! Arthur Winner waited; and, for a moment, time, too, seemed to wait.

Catching sight of him and the stopped car, Clarissa lifted a hand; and, the waiting moment gone, Arthur Winner let his car move, driving forward. Clarissa neatly cut the station wagon around so that she came abreast, and pulled up. She said: "Darling, we'll have lunch as soon as you're ready. I wanted to bring the car down because, for various reasons, I'd like to get away after we've eaten. Priscilla and Stewart are here. I'm taking them out to the lake, too."

Answering his look of inquiry, she said: "Things are in a state of moderate confusion. Marjorie's Mrs. Pratt arrived, all right— I guess you know, since she said you'd made an appointment with them. But, after that, she had to come over to see me. Marjorie, it seemed, wasn't feeling, in Mrs. Pratt's phrase, very well—in fact, so little well, that I could suppose the truth was she'd passed out, or at least was making no sense, and couldn't be expected to make any very soon. So Mrs. Pratt's thought was that she'd see you alone, if that would be all right. Is it?"

Arthur Winner said: "Well, really, it's not. But I don't know what I can do. Did she say why she wanted to see me?"

Clarissa said: "Perhaps she did. Much of what she said I couldn't quite follow. She was as friendly as possible—in fact, even friendlier, I guess; seeing we'd only met once briefly. I'm afraid she repels me a little. She keeps giving you these smiling —well, clinging looks; and all I can say is she soon had me feeling somewhat sticky. I don't want to do her wrong; but she gave me the impression that she finds this quite exciting—a chance to exercise loving kindness or something even better than she hoped. Fending her off as well as I could, I suggested that the children come over here, and I'd take them with us for the afternoon. She said I was wonderfully understanding. No doubt I am! But I want to get away before she comes back."

"Very well, my dear," Arthur Winner said. "I'll be right in."

"Some people called. Somebody who said he was Garret

Hughes. He seemed rather confused to find you weren't here; so I asked him if I could take a message. I hope I have it straight. He said would I tell you that complainant (I think that was the word) hadn't been to a doctor, and wouldn't agree to go to one; and so he hadn't telephoned to make the appointment you asked him to make. Oh; and he'd let Mr. Brophy know. Is that intelligible?"

"Perfectly," Arthur Winner said, smiling. "Complainant's this girl of Ralph's—the one bringing the charge. That's fine. I was really afraid she might co-operate. This way, we've only her uncorroborated statement to deal with."

"Yes; well, then Helen Detweiler called. She didn't say what she wanted; but she had such a distraught sound, I could guess, something about this business. I didn't know whether I was supposed to have heard; and since acting as though I hadn't was a lot easier, I so acted. I told her I thought you'd be home very soon; and she said she'd call again. Find the girls, will you, dear? I think they're behind the garage with Patsy. Patsy, poor dog, proved most unexpectedly to be in heat this morning, so we shut her up. I only trust, in time." The station wagon moved on, passing down to the house.

Halting his car on the wide cement floor of the garage, Arthur Winner got out. A small door at the back stood open; and, in the silence, he could hear Ann saying: "No, not tomorrow, darn it! In the morning, Father's sure to want me to go to church— I mean, because of Doctor Trowbridge being new, and all that. And in the afternoon, tomorrow's the Sunday we have to have tea at Grandmother Winner's—she's so terribly old, we have to do that every other Sunday. We might go after school, Monday —no, not Monday; there'll be registration and everything. Tuesday. Tuesday we could not go home in the bus—"

Priscilla Penrose's voice said eagerly: "Ann! I just thought! If Rodney's still around, why don't we see if we can get him to pick us up—he's awfully nice; I think he would—and take us there? And then he could talk to the man, too—"

A silent moment passed; and Ann said: "Inside, sugar; it's raining!" Her tone was of mock shock; and from the inflection more than from the enigmatic words, Arthur Winner could take

371

the sense of this new-to-him idiom in their foreign language: *Beware! You're heedlessly endangering yourself!* Ann immediately confirmed it. With (you could feel sure) her eye-closing, hair-swinging pantomime of being exhausted by her endless struggle against human folly and the mad world, she said: "Oh, don't mistake me! As far as I'm concerned, I'd think nothing of it. Not a thing on earth! But, you infant, he *is* colored. And if somebody like Mrs. Farquhar, or even Old Nosey, happened to be looking out, and saw what the lift we were getting was—oh, happy days at Washington Hall!"

Reaching the door, Arthur Winner could see the girls. They had let themselves into the enclosure of wire net that fenced a narrow ten-yard runway extending from the back of the garage. Ann knelt by the doghouse in the shade. Priscilla stood beside her, right hand supporting her chin, left hand holding her right elbow. The pert vivacity of the poses, the air both had, even while doing nothing, of ready excess energy, was that of children; yet in Ann's turn of her dark head and knowledgeable lift of chin, in Priscilla's questioning tilt of her blonde head, woman's ways were visible, femininity without age, the same in a girl as in an old crone.

Ann said: "Ah, there she is! Here, Patsy, here!"

Out the little low arched entrance of the doghouse a brown cocker spaniel was emerging slowly and reluctantly. Her movement was a feeble wriggling grovel. The stub of her tail twitched spasmodically. To Ann's hands she gave a listless lick or two. "Ah, Pat, Patsy!" Ann said. "Mother's sorry to shut you up in this nasty run! But, sweet, you might have the most awful puppies; think of that!" The dog, worming closer, pressed her back against Ann's knees. "Yes; Mother knows just how you feel!" Ann said. "There, Patsy, there! I know! You feel just *mean,* don't you?"

"Lunch, I think, ladies," Arthur Winner said.

Coming in the front door, blinking in the shadow of the cool hall, Arthur Winner saw the stiff thin figure of Stewart Penrose. Stewart stood on one foot by the hall table where the mail was put. He held a magazine, which Arthur Winner now saw was a new copy of the *Journal of the American Judicature Society*. The boy's amusing look of stern critical inquiry made Arthur Winner (immediately sorry that he had said it) say: "Do you find that interesting, Stewart?"

Stewart gave him a defiant stare. He said: "No. What's in it?"

"Just articles on legal matters," Arthur Winner said. "I hear you're having lunch with us. The girls are getting washed. I think we ought to have it pretty soon."

"Yes," Stewart said coldly. "I guess Mother's drunk again."

FOUR

IF NOT TRAGEDY'S, Helen was unhappiness's own child! Some fatal sign must be on her—what Julius Penrose suggested; what Julius meant about that list the Fool Killer kept. By means of the sign, misfortune could always find her; seeing the sign, mistake and misadventure knew whom to dog.

Before he thought, speaking his mind, put-out, Arthur Winner said: "That wasn't wise, Helen."

He had expected a call from Helen, of course; but he had expected it earlier, and the fact was the call now took him by surprise. When the telephone rang, he had been in the act of escorting Mrs. Pratt through the hall toward the porch, or, more properly, the terrace, roofed, screened-in, and stone-flagged at the back of the house. From the library, where Arthur Winner stood with the extension telephone, he could see Mrs. Pratt's costly car—a sports model in delicate light yellow—waiting in the drive. The car, Mrs. Pratt's electing to use a car to come so short a distance, had, for a moment, been a matter of wonder to him. Reconsidering, he could see that she might have a reason. The sound of wheels on the drive gave formal notice of her coming. Drawing up before the house and stepping out, she arrived in good style—not, or not intentionally, with show or pretentiousness, but with a manner of ease hardly to be got from just walking over.

Helen said: "I know I shouldn't have, Mr. Winner. But I wasn't going to do what you said not to—I mean, I wasn't going to say anything about money. I just thought if I could appeal

374

to her, if I asked her, if she knew her story wasn't true, would she please not go on with this, not do this—"

Giving in to vain wishing, how fatuous could you get! The scared, sullen slut, Miss Kovacs, to save (no doubt, literally, since she had a mother who might be just as moronic as, and evidently was far more savage than, poor Caroline Dummer's mother) her own skin, had found herself obliged to swear a false information. If you, Ralph's sister, went to her (as woman to woman?) and asked her please, if the charge weren't true, would she forget, never mind about, those considerations of self that had frightened her into acting, did you seriously conceive that she might oblige you?

Arthur Winner said: "Perhaps I should have made the point clearer, Helen. Passing money, though that would go to the point, isn't the point. The point is the common-law offense of dissuading, hindering, or preventing a witness from testifying. Whether you use money, or appeals, or threats, doesn't matter—"

But would anything be served by spelling out the legal situation for Helen; by explaining to her that what was charged on Ralph, once a warrant issued, was an alleged offense against the peace and dignity of the state; that Miss Kovacs was simply a witness offered to prove the offense; that, to the state, not to Miss Kovacs, Ralph must answer? Obviously, no! Explaining might allay a lawyer's exasperation at the foolish and dangerous intermeddlings always to be expected in those unlearned in law, but what other good would be done?

In a wretched voice, Helen said: "I'm terribly sorry, Mr. Winner. I don't know why I did it. I just thought I'd walk down and see if she was at that diner. I just felt I had to do something. I just couldn't help it."

A startling statement? Here speaking was the Helen Detweiler who permitted herself to ask of life nothing in the way of personal comfort or easy living. Speaking, was the pitilessly self-driven Helen of the office, who (by what stern application; by what relentless resolve!) had taught herself to handle, with no sense of their significance yet with never an error, reams of complicated figures; who had trained herself to draw neatly and swiftly, letter-perfect in terms she did not exactly grasp, the complicated legal instruments whose actual purpose she could not have explained. Speaking, was the Helen whose whole existence appeared one unbroken act of making herself do what she determined to do. She felt she *had* to; she had to do what her feelings pressed her to do! Possessed by her feelings, she couldn't help it! On the real nature of the human will, on all vaunted self-control, on all admired self-discipline, were those words the last word?

Gazing out at the bright day, at Mrs. Pratt's splendid waiting car—and on the terrace, Mrs. Pratt waited, too—Arthur Winner let pity subdue the pulsing of exasperation. He said: "No, you shouldn't have gone to see her, tried anything like that, Helen. But I'm glad you told me; and I'm sure no real harm's been done—particularly if, as you say, she wasn't willing to listen to you. I've heard from Garret Hughes, who went to see her, too—" (Helen, unknowing, might, Arthur Winner must admit, have performed a service of sorts; annoyed by Helen's foolish visit, Miss Kovacs was probably in no mood to listen to Garret) "and she refused to let a doctor examine her. That weakens her case—we may even hope, fatally. At present, neither Garret nor Mr. Brophy's inclined to believe her; and if *we* make no mistakes—"

"Yes, I see," Helen said. "Mr. Winner, you haven't seen Ralph, heard from him, have you?"

"Yes. I had a message this morning. Mary Sheen talked to him—"

"I meant, since then," Helen said. "He said he was going out to Roylan to talk to you."

"Yes. I'll be here all afternoon. I told him that."

"Well, he'll probably ask you. He was home for lunch, though he really didn't eat anything; and the thing was, he wants to go up to Eatontown to see a boy he knows, a boy named Stanley Brown." She paused. "He used to live here, go to high school here; and he was supposed to be Ralph's best friend. I don't know whether Ralph ought to do that. I mean, may he? And I don't like Stanley. He always seemed to have a lot of money, I mean, more than you'd expect a boy his age to have—"

376

Arthur Winner said: "I think I know who he is. His father's Bert Brown, who has a number of electrical-appliance shops around the county. He's a director of the bank, here. I imagine he's pretty well off. As far as the terms of recognizance go, Mr. Harbison said not to leave the jurisdiction, which would mean the state; so I think Ralph would be free to go to Eatontown— particularly if he lets you, as bailor, know where he goes, and gets back, of course, before Monday. Did he say why he wanted to see the Brown boy?"

"I think he thinks Stanley might be able to help him get a job. Yes; that's Stanley's father; so I suppose he might be able to give Ralph something." She spoke with a sad flatness of voice. "I think the real thing was, Stanley called him this morning and asked him to some sort of a party; and Ralph wanted to go —" She broke off. "It might mean he'd stay there overnight. Would that be all right, too? I wasn't sure—I didn't like to say he couldn't go. I mean, at first I was feeling so badly about it all, I really wasn't thinking about him—that he was feeling pretty badly too; I mean, he was frightened, he was awfully unhappy. And, if it would make him feel any better—"

Helen spoke, it was plain, in that peacelessness of a love whose loving is a necessity, a loving that cannot be lived without. Accustomed by the passage of a night and a morning to those first feelings she mentioned, to the sorrow brought *her* by Ralph, Helen was now ready for the sorrow succeeding that sorrow, a sorrow on Ralph's behalf, a sickness at heart that he should be frightened, that he should be awfully unhappy. Moreover, this heavy succession was direct, passed into without pause, without that respite, in normal pathognomy, of anger at the hurt done her, of those fiercenesses of hate or hating without which the loving heart can hardly survive its injuries, without which love's livable balance of I and thou (*But when I hate you, it's 'cause I love you . . .*) fails. Helen said: "I suppose he saw Joan this morning."

Arthur Winner said: "He had a talk with her. I asked him to. I know how you feel about that, Helen. But—" (he remembered Fred Dealey, sharp, assertive, and not impossibly right, rallying

Clarissa on the boathouse porch last night) "Ralph with responsibilities might be a good deal better off than Ralph without them."

Helen said: "He has to marry her, doesn't he, Mr. Winner?"

With a certain smart of mind, a certain wryness, Arthur Winner thought: *Confidential communication! Privileged!* He said: "Yes; that's the size of it, Helen. You'd have to know sooner or later, so you might as well know now. I want them to wait until this is settled; then, I think they ought to be married as soon as possible. From what I saw myself, and from what Ralph tells me, I'm satisfied that Joan's a perfectly decent girl. I feel sure she never had an experience like this before. She lost her head over Ralph. They're both young; they made a mistake. Mistake though we'll agree it was, we ought to remember the mistake's one a good many girls have made—"

"Yes," Helen said. "Well, I suppose I really knew. There had to be some reason. I knew Ralph couldn't—well, be in love with her, couldn't really want to marry her—"

Arthur Winner said: "I think we should look at it this way. Ralph hasn't really known what he wants—very few young men do know. He feels, and I feel, too, that, married to Joan, he'll settle down, accept, as I said, responsibilities. There's the baby; and—"

Almost absently, Helen said: "But he must have known about that, about Joan, when he went out with this other girl—"

"Yes," Arthur Winner said. "But what he thinks, and what I think, too, is that if he'd been married to, living with, Joan, there couldn't have been this trouble." (Would Helen be able to grasp the gross thought, and so, see the proposition as sound? Indeed, was it sound? Well, perhaps! Marrying a girl Ralph didn't want to marry might be unlikely to bind the spirit; but if, married to "Joanie," Ralph, in the words of her stated promise, "could all he wanted," such simplicity and convenience of unlimited access might conceivably conduce to a binding of the flesh; for a time at least, might regulate Ralph's life by leaving him neither appetite nor energy for outside adventures.) Arthur Winner said: "There's nothing here to change what I

378

said before, Helen. We learn from our mistakes. If Ralph learns from his, he can't be a loser—in the long run he's a gainer. What will happen tomorrow, none of us can know. Assuming things will turn out well is always unwarranted; but no more so than assuming things will turn out badly. It's no good exercising ourselves over what might have been; the question always is: What's now the reasonable thing to do? I think the reasonable thing is to do all we can to help Ralph and Joan work this out. So, yes, if Ralph thinks his friend can get him a job, tell him to go ahead—were you expecting to see him again before he left?"

"I think he'll come back. He had some brushes he said he had to deliver. I don't think he meant to go to Eatontown until later. I don't know quite what to do. Ought I to tell him I know about Joan?" Her voice wavered a little.

"Not if you don't want to, now. I'll tell him, if you like. Try not to worry, my dear. I think things are going to be all right."

"Yes," Helen said. "I will try, Mr. Winner."

✦

"Roses!" Mrs. Pratt cried. "Ah, roses! How I love them! Could we go and look at them, Arthur?"

From the terrace at the back of the house, the walled garden had been laid out to descend in three stages. Only the second, containing the rose beds to which Mrs. Pratt had looked, was still really a garden. On the high level, nearest the terrace, had once been serpentine herbaceous borders with backgrounds of shrubbery. These borders were gone. Perennial in no more than name, without Hope Winner's devoted tending and watchful planned replacing, delphinium and digitalis, aquilegia, dicentra, and phlox, disappeared. In a few years, the shrubs, self-sufficient, grew out; and gradually grass grew in toward them. Up here now were no flowers, merely an open-ended oval of mowed lawn, down which, to steps, the straight path, aiming at a miniature round point on the level below, passed. Centered there at the point stood a sundial, an armillary sphere's loops and rings of aged bronze, resting on an old millstone. In orderly groupings, the many roses surrounded it.

Indicating the revived September display with a gesture, Mrs. Pratt, as if out of eagerness to go down and be among loved flowers, had started up. Though she wore a suit, a jacket and skirt almost mannish in cut, the suit's material—a pelt cashmere tweed of such thinness, fineness, and softness that there could be no doubt about its expensiveness—in a shade of yellow to harmonize with her automobile, worked against attempted severities of tailoring. Mrs. Pratt's good-sized figure worked against those severities, too. Her soft members, that seemed all preternaturally rounded, achieved, mannish suit or no mannish suit, effects of excessive muliebrity seldom seen outside Victorian paintings of the so-called Pre-Raphaelite school—the upthrust, rather high, apparently girdleless full globular abdominal curve (Thy navel is like a round goblet which wanteth not liquor; thy belly is like a heap of wheat set about with lilies); the ripe, half-melon breasts supported in their hidden slings of cloth to fill the shirtwaist near to overflowing; the elongated curving swell of columnar thighs that started, ripplingly tweed-draped, through the clinging skirt. In spite of modern dress, Dante, observing her beside the Arno, might well have recognized Beatrice.

In keeping with her figure, Mrs. Pratt's face was also good-sized. Her big brown eyes were soft; her large lips were set softly in curves of sweetness; but any single features were dominated by the conformation of the whole in a slightly disconcerting resemblance which, Arthur Winner realized, Julius had hit off exactly—sheeplike, somewhat sheeplike! At least suggested, was the countenance (protruding a good deal, if in a blunted way; and, if narrow, big), was the muzzle, of an eager and earnest, of an amiable, sheep. On her head Mrs. Pratt wore a large pale blue beret that flopped softly sideways as far as the left ear's ear-ring-hung lobe. From the band of the beret escaped, to the right, vigorous curls of wiry dark hair. Julius, Arthur Winner remembered, had remarked that Mrs. Pratt attracted, or might attract, a certain amount of attention. Julius, as Julius's custom was, had understated it.

Not entirely at ease, Arthur Winner opened the screen door. He said: "I'd be glad to show them to you, if roses interest you. I'm ashamed to say you'll find them rather neglected. We've had a long spell of humid weather; and I didn't get around to dusting them as often as I should have; so there's a good deal of black spot—"

With an extravagant movement, Mrs. Pratt, flopping the beret, tossed her head back (she was a little in front of him) to survey him searchingly. Parting, the collar of the shirtwaist showed Arthur Winner the cylindrical roll of her long, perhaps swanlike, neck. Below, at a low point, an ornamental pin kept together the fine linen that stretched across those round fullnesses of bosom. The pin was a gold crown of thorns enclosing a gold cross, both encrusted with small amethysts. She said warmly: "I can see that's like you, Arthur. Modest! I know from Marjorie that no one grows such roses. Oh, how pretty they are!" She trotted down the steps to them. "What are these?"

"That's Gruss an Teplitz," Arthur Winner said. "An old variety; but one I've always liked. It's an early hybrid on the original China, or Bengal, rose—"

"What heavenly fragrance!" With a supple enough, smooth-membered swaying forward, all those ripe curvatures of form dropping pendent in their wrappings, Mrs. Pratt buried her nose in a blossom. She gave Arthur Winner, over it, a liquid ecstatic up-glance. Swaying erect again, she said: "And what's down there?"

"Nothing, now, I'm afraid," Arthur Winner said. "We used to have a lily pond—"

"But what a darling little statue! Oh, let's look at it!" Passing around the armillary sphere, she went through the rose beds to the lower steps.

The onetime pool's shallow, wide, empty tank, whose molded rim was overhung with vines, whose bottom was matted with leaves, grew a shag of hardy weeds. Beyond, stood a marble pedestal, chipped and cracked. The pedestal supported, before an arched recess in the old brick wall, a figure about half life-size. Worked on by perhaps a hundred years of sun and frost and rain, the statue, now less a statue than the remains of one, might be judged to have originated as some not-very-gifted cemetery monument stonecutter's copying of a copy of the Medici Venus. The poor-quality marble's long attrition made the face almost featureless. That mannered pose, a goddess's modest quail of pudency, was quite uncalled-for. The pocked and pitted hands, poised in such coy alarm of nakedness surprised, had almost nothing to screen—above, bumps of stone breasts wasted too far to be worth notice; below, the retiring pubes worn blankly neuter, all sexual definition lost.

No need to ask what questing eye lighted one day on this object of art in a corner of Jake Hyman's junk yard; nor whose private smile had acknowledged charms of wistfulness in the figure's absurdity, charms of melancholy in that decay of weathering. No need to ask who made Jake an acceptable offer, who provided for the dispatching, pedestal and all, in Jake's wagon, who showed some husky laborers where to wrestle the statue into place in what was still little more than a field—the selected site of a new daughter-in-law's new garden. Arthur Winner looked back at a windy April day, the standing wagon, the thin sunshine on scattered clumpings of just-planted, meager-looking shrubs, on unfinished trenches which were to be footings for the brick walls, on stakes and string that outlined beds and paths.

Mrs. Pratt cried: "Oh, I love this!" She moved her hand in a happy inclusive gesture. "There's something so old-timey about it—like the ghost of a garden! Could we stay here? Shall we sit over there, a while?"

The semicircular stone bench that Mrs. Pratt indicated was one of a pair that faced each other on the cross axis of a vanished formal parterre. Both now stood deep in leafy grottoes. That not-so-long-ago wilderness of an open field was again something of a wilderness; but today (you could hardly believe it) of gross overgrowth. Those poor sticks of new bushes, forlornly spaced apart, had come together in dense great thickets. Cotoneasters, rampant, crowded out past the bench on one side. On the other, abelia mounded up—in blossom, but sparsely; because there had come to be too much shade. Thrust low overhead, thickly branched, crooked, twiggy boughs of two flowering crabs extended. They were designed to make a spring contrast—one, white; one, pink. They had grown out of all bounds.

382

Approaching the bench with Mrs. Pratt, Arthur Winner said: "That's not very clean, I'm afraid." Stooping to avoid the overhang of branches, he took a handkerchief and brushed twigs and dry bird droppings from enough of the stone seat and stone back for her to sit down. The earlier breeze had died. The shade was grateful; and, in the shade, an odor of ripening small crab apples hung pleasantly. "Delicious!" Mrs. Pratt said. She breathed with rapture. "Oh, how nice!"

The bench's curve brought Mrs. Pratt to half face Arthur Winner. Sinking down, she had arranged herself in a pose of ease. She sat with her head lifted enough to stretch smooth the swanlike neck. One arm, one tailored sleeve, lay indolent along the bench's stone back. She was silent a moment, the big brown eyes luminously soft, gazing away past the hanging flop of the beret; and, noting the trancelike look, Arthur Winner was troubled again by a resemblance—not, this time, in features or lineaments; not that recognized face of the amiable or friendly sheep. The resemblance was of expression—a bemused look of absent happiness; a look he had somewhere, sometime, seen on some other face, a face he could not place. The look altered, and Mrs. Pratt said suddenly: "You're wondering why I wanted to see you, Arthur. You're wondering what we have to say to each other."

Mrs. Pratt spoke with sober intensity; but she also spoke dramatically, as if she thought to dismay Arthur Winner. Her overtone was of gentle triumph, of gay, almost mischievous confidence. The significance of the overtone must be that she saw herself as mistress of this little field. That she could so see herself must, in turn, signify. Not missing, she had misconstrucd Arthur Winner's constraint. She was ascribing it to anything but its actual cause—the mild embarrassment caused him by her appearance and emotional manner; the discomfort that comes from seeing anyone (all unawares, and all assurance) act the fool; the practical, easily anticipated concern over difficulties in dealing with a Mrs. Pratt. Instead, Mrs. Pratt must be taking his stiffnesses of manner, his rejoinders of made conversation about recent weather conditions, roses, and the cleanness of benches, as token of a gruff helplessness of male bewilderment assailed by superior female wits. She *did* know what she wanted to see him for; she *did* know what there might be for them to say to each other. He, poor embarrassed dolt, waiting to hear, was bound to hesitate, shuffle, wonder. By keeping him off balance, she planned to handle him. Where she led, he was to find himself willy-nilly following.

Arthur Winner could not forbear to smile. He said: "Yes; but I suppose you're going to tell me."

The brief answer could not have been the response, nor the sort of response, Mrs. Pratt looked for. Visibly, she checked. Incredulous, she seemed to require a moment to realize he had finished, made all the reply he intended to make. Jaunty enough, the would-be leader stepped out; but, looking back, she saw no one following. The hesitating now had to be hers. The upper hand lost, she must attempt a rally of forces. The attempt was not without success.

Slow and deliberate, denying her moment's confusion, she answered his smile with a smile of her own. Intense, tender-voiced, she said: "I like your directness, Arthur. I've heard so much about you that I expected it. I know you'd never say anything that you didn't mean. I can see that's why people turn to you, why they respect you so much, and trust you." She hinted a pause; but his unmoved professional gaze must have warned her he was too old a bird to be caught with chaff. She went on: "You know, of course, why Marjorie couldn't come over. She's drunk."

"Is she?" Arthur Winner said. "I haven't seen her today."

"I could tell this morning that Mrs. Winner knew what the trouble was. So I suppose it happens fairly often. Arthur, we must help her; mustn't we?"

Bright chirping of sparrows sounded through the shady thickets. Beyond the shade, sunlit butterflies, in passage to the scant flowering of a few long shoots of buddleia that persisted, despite every neglect, against the garden wall, continually wafted themselves across, drifting by. Arthur Winner said: "About that, I've nothing to suggest. Getting drunk's something Marjorie does from time to time—I wouldn't say fairly often. I don't think she could be called an alcoholic. I mean, I don't think there's any physiological basis, for which treatment of one kind or another might be possible. She seems to drink only when—" he remembered Julius's phrase: *a situation again defeated her* —"she reaches a certain degree of emotional disturbance. Then, she decides to get drunk; she makes a choice. I don't know how you can help, there. In my experience, you can't make other people's choices for them."

Smiling mysteriously, Mrs. Pratt said: "There *is* a way to help, Arthur. Not by making other people's choices for them; oh, no! Naturally, a man as wise as you would see that! Perhaps, if you have power over them, you can sometimes stop people from making a choice they want to make; but you can't stop them from wanting to make it. You haven't helped them; they're unchanged. But people *can* be changed, Arthur; and, when they change, their choices can change too. You follow me?"

Arthur Winner said: "If you mean that circumstances have been known to alter cases, I believe I do."

"It's naughty of you to tease me, Arthur," Mrs. Pratt said indulgently. "But say that, if you like. In Marjorie's case—we'll agree, won't we?—the choice is unhappiness's choice; happiness would never make it. There's only one true happiness in this life, Arthur—peace of soul. And we gain peace of soul only one way. That way is love—in practice, loving others. But, by God's grace, by loving others we work much more than our own single happiness. Love's law is that love answers love. By your love, by sheer love, you create, you bring into existence, a return of love. You make others loving; and, being made loving, they, too, know happiness. Your peace of soul you have brought to them. That is how Marjorie can be helped."

With inward amazement—his amazement, felt often enough to be familiar, yet always fresh, was amazement at the infinite capacity of our human minds to hypnotize themselves with words—Arthur Winner could see that Mrs. Pratt, having pronounced a rigmarole, was fully persuaded that she had said something. Her look, still softly, steadily mysterious, was inviting him to admire the higher wisdom, the deeper insight, demonstrated in this assemblage of phrases that had no exact significance, of tautological terms, of proofless postulations. These, in themselves, could have no meaning. They said nothing (except, perhaps, that an abstraction denominated "love" was lovely); but, of course, the fervent saying of this kind of nothing did have meaning. What, here, spoke of love? Victorious ever, love here spoke of love. Love proposed the truth undoubted, the truth observed, true with its old force of universal explanation: lovely love, the wonderful, wonderful what-is-it, through love's incomparable delectations (in her peace of soul, in her happiness of loving, Mrs. Pratt half swooned with bliss) conquered all!

Ah, how wise, how sure, how right, was that genius of the language whose instinct detected in the manifold manifestings of the amative appetite (however different-seeming; however apparently opposed) the one same urgent unreason, the one same eager let's-pretend, and so, wisely consented, so, for convenience covenanted, to name all with one same name! Explaining, sweet unreason excused; excusing, sweet let's-pretend explained. The young heart, indentured (O wearisome conditions of humanity!) to reason, pined, starved on the bare bitter diet of thinking. One fine day, that heart (most hearts) must bolt. That heart would be off (could you blame it?) to Loveland, to feeling's feasts.

And what a table, in the presence of his immediately impotent enemies, was prepared before the runaway! What abundance, what choice of viands, what profusion of delicacies! Here were lovings of the higher sort (one or more forms of which presumably possessed a Mrs. Pratt); religious ecstasies plain or fancy; rarities of immortal longings; enormous exploding loves to fill up all the mighty void of sense; as, for the Eternal, or for the whole of Mankind. Farther down the groaning board, less sublime but still reverenced, stretched the enticing spread, the square meal, of individual littler lovings—of the blood relation, or of friend for friend (here came possessions like Helen Detweiler's, by one form or another of which, presumably, no one was left unpossessed). Here, for the run of people to help themselves, were set out all nonsensual cherishings, all glad gushings of pure tenderness toward dear persons; all joyful, generous agitations about this or that one-and-only; and (never an insipid moment) all the pains of pleasure and pleasures of pain thereto inuring—heavy tears; as, for Absalom, my son, my son; light tears (Jesu Maria, what a deal of brine!); as, for a physically unobtainable sole panted-for she, some Rosaline or other.

And even now, at the table's foot, down finally to earth (with Rosalines, the rear brought up) sweet unreason's devices, sweet let's-pretend's resources, were not exhausted. Here, well below the salt, Rosalines *did* become obtainable. The fare was coarser; yet let's-pretend had tricks of seasoning. Over the everyday crude commerce of the sexes, unreason waved her wand. Before your eyes, the moment-ago's plain piece of tail sea-changed, metamorphosed into something rich and strange. Where an itch had been, was now—a thing heroic and classic; a thing of general awe— Grand Passion. While Tristan, warbling tenor, set himself to mount Isolde; while Paolo, in *terza rima,* set himself to mount Francesca, Grand Passion prepared to gild the tumble and fumble, to ennoble the bump of bellies, to elevate with its timely pinch of pity and terror the crisis of connection—and the world well lost! In Loveland, how various, how beautiful, how new, could be the life—the many available lives!

Mrs. Pratt sat waiting, studying Arthur Winner earnestly; and if she were again letting herself imagine she had him not knowing what to say, this time, he must grant, she was right. The juncture was one at which experienced tacticians prefer to say nothing. Silent, saying nothing, Arthur Winner, too, waited, amiably studying her in return.

With a forgiving smile, yet with a sigh, Mrs. Pratt at last said: "I know I can't expect you to completely understand me, Arthur. There's a point at which we have to part company, because you aren't able to believe many things we Catholics believe. For instance, if I were to say we can't really love anyone else unless we first love God; if I were to say freedom is submission to the will of God—we're the slaves of ourselves until then, you'd have trouble understanding me unless you understood, had as your own, a Catholic conception of God, and lived in a Catholic's relation to God—which is to put the whole of oneself and one's desires and experiences, good and bad, into God's hands, and talk to God about them."

"Where there are differences in religion," Arthur Winner said, "I think it generally wiser not to discuss them."

"Oh, I don't mean to!" Mrs. Pratt said. "I just don't want you to be—well, suspicious of me, Arthur. I know many Protestants imagine Catholics are always trying to convert people. But, of course, it's not any human being, it's God who converts; so we feel we can leave a little of the work to Him! And I know you've heard we Catholics believe there's no salvation outside the church. Yes, we do. But we don't limit what God may know to what *we* know, or what appears to us to be the case. God, and only God, can say who is outside His Church and who is in it. To God, many Protestants may mystically be members; while some pious-appearing Catholics may not be!" She uttered a comradely laugh, showing a mouthful of big well-shaped teeth. "So, don't imagine I'm sitting here thinking you *have* to go to hell, Arthur, because you aren't a Catholic!"

"Suspicious" was not the word Arthur Winner would have applied to himself in this connection—for one thing, he felt nothing so active; he hadn't that much interest. Yet he couldn't doubt that, however passive or indifferent, something was there for Mrs. Pratt to feel—an antagonism or enmity of mind, residue of the abhorrence and distrust by ten generations of forefathers passed down to him; the reformer's recoil from the Whore of Babylon's idolatrous pomp and circumstance; the Puritan's warlike wariness, become now mostly disdain, yet never really lulled. Today, he might not be dangerous; he might try to be (as Julius noted) "modren" and "American"; yet look at Giant Pope's hands. Old Protestant blood caked them—*if they shall desire to have some gunpowder for the shortening of their torment I see not but you may grant it!*

This, of course, was what Father Albright felt at the opening of that interview, spoken about to Julius last night. Recoil was what the priest had expected, had come prepared for. A fairly young priest, Father Albright probably hoped, by man-to-man heartiness of address, by cheery reassuring looks, by civilities that protested good will, to dissipate once and for all Arthur Winner's

388

benighted fear of the bogy, Rome. At any rate, with his pathetic, no doubt seminary-taught confidence, he did persist in the effort of cordiality until almost the end, until he realized he had no chance of succeeding, that the refusal (obstinate as it was polite; wicked as it was obstinate) to give Rome, Rome's way was, in fact, final. Then, understandably enough, he lost his temper—and also, perhaps, some of that stopgap tolerance, that generous theological uncertainty about who would go to hell and who wouldn't!

Sobering, Mrs. Pratt said: "And, of course, Catholics must not offend against charity; we may not think uncharitable thoughts even of those who appear to hate us and to hate the church. Scripture warns us: Do not judge, that you may not be judged."

The wording, so flatly wrong-sounding, the jar on the ear as of misquotation, meant, Arthur Winner recognized, that this was (which of course it would be) the Douay, or whatever the present Catholic, version's version. A prejudicing trifle; yet ample, Arthur Winner, half-amused, must admit, for a hostile mind's purposes of distrust. What impertinence! Testy, the mind, the jarred ear, made correction: *Judge not, that ye be not judged!* What else? What else? What was this presuming, obtuse and alien, that mouthed the word-established over, that defiled a well of English? But, then, more what. What of the effrontery (just now recalled) of a Father Albright demanding, insistent if weak, that his and only his wishes be consulted? Yes; Julius was right! Regard that overweening hierarchy; above those mostly poor-boy bishops, elated by their local power, those impudent princes of the church—this plump, canting pudge of an eminence here; this malapert, threatening ignoramus of an eminence there! Regard that state within a state which, flown with insolence, could arrogate to itself (if covertly; still daring hardly more than whisper of blackmail to nervous newspapers, to nervous advertisers, to nervous politicians) a privilege of foreigners to tamper with laws of the land, to abrogate an act of assembly duly made and provided, to exempt itself and its property from regulations all good citizens saw as reasonable, to refuse those rights of the governed in their government on which our free society rested.

Arthur Winner said: "I'm sure that controlling, as far as we can, our prejudices becomes us all. But I feel, as I've said, that where differences are fundamental, discussing them never helps. All discussion can do is show us how foolish and stubborn people not of our opinion are. The charitable thing seems to be also the wise thing—not to judge." He smiled. "Not to consign each other to some sort of hell because we don't agree. Are we getting a little away from our subject?"

Mrs. Pratt smiled in return. "You might think that, Arthur," she said. "But we're not. It concerns Marjorie, poor dear. Very much so! You see, a great deal's demanded of you if you are to be a Catholic. We don't, for instance, smile at hell. We can't. You see, a Catholic's required to believe intelligently. A Catholic never can commit the absurdity of private judgment, of picking and choosing parts of an indivisible truth that please him, and believing only them. Now, eternal punishment is a dogmatic fact, demonstrable by reason. A fact can't be blinked merely because it's a terrifying fact. I suppose all this sounds very strange to you, Arthur?"

"No; not very," Arthur Winner said. "I notice that people are usually inclined to think whatever they believe is necessarily true, and only reasonable."

"Yes," Mrs. Pratt said. "You answer well, Arthur! But, to my very point! For people to be inclined to believe what they find easy and comfortable to believe is quite usual, isn't it? With Catholics, that's not the case. Catholics have to face facts. Revelation and the teaching authority of the church clearly establish that, after this life, those who are burdened with grave guilt must receive from God a judgment and an execution of penalty, which is everlasting torment."

She smiled. "You look dismayed, Arthur! Shall I dismay you more? Yes! This dreadful judgment isn't something God couldn't change if He wanted to. In the next life, quite as well as in this, God, if He chose, could remit punishment, give souls another chance; everything depends on His free will. But we must not cling to that straw! We know He does not choose; and that He never will. We must believe, too, that this divine disposition is in no way contrary to the perfection of any of God's attributes

390

—neither His justice nor His wisdom; neither His mercy nor His goodness. Does *that,* perhaps, sound strange to you?"

Rousing himself, Arthur Winner said: "If you mean, do I find an idea of that sort strange—yes. If you mean, do I find it strange that people are able to believe such things, my answer's the same as before—no."

Arthur Winner had needed to collect himself, for what Mrs. Pratt described as a look of dismay had been, in fact, an outward sign—apparently surprised from him; he had not been conscious of giving any sign—of a minor inward relaxation of mental relief. He had it! That troublesome question of resemblance—where, not long ago, he had seen a look like Mrs. Pratt's—troubled him no more. The abstracted, rapt expression, the face's bemused blank happiness, the innocent absence of all solemn thought, the saint's mute serenity (Thou liest in Abraham's bosom all the year!) while the busy tongue, reciting of itself, with no one really there, prattled on of reason and revelation, of justice and mercy, of wisdom and goodness—this was Caroline Dummer, at play at counsel's table with her little purse.

Quite unconcerned, happy and unheeding, Caroline had withdrawn from life, from the world. She had given up the effort, so much too much for her, to understand, to decide, to choose for herself. Caroline was where, unknown to her, Caroline had always wanted to be. In that lovely jail, the wicked (or, rather, the "mean") ceased molesting and the weary were at rest. They laid out a neat, clean prison dress, which she liked very much, for her to wear. If Caroline was a good girl, a good child, she need not fear everlasting torment. If she made her bed, swept her cell, scrubbed the cell's beautiful flush toilet which was just for her, a kind Mrs. Morton, with maternal pats and encouraging smiles, dressed Caroline's hair like a picture in a magazine; and often Caroline could have ice cream for supper. Such, and of such, the kingdom of heaven!

Mrs. Pratt was regarding him with an air of sorrowful sympathy that clouded, though no doubt only in passing, that basic inner light, that shine of thoughtless happiness. She sighed (clearly, for him, not for her), but sighs (one perceived) she found enjoyable, too. She said with tender regret: "You can't understand, can you, Arthur? You don't understand, do you?"

With some stiffness, Arthur Winner said: "I'm able to understand that you wanted to show me an example of the kind, or perhaps type, of belief a Catholic's expected to have. From what you said last, I suppose you meant that no matter how hard a thing might be to believe, people can believe it if they want to enough. What I'm afraid I don't yet understand—"

"Is, why I bore you with all this!" Mrs. Pratt gave him a brilliant smile. "I'll tell you, Arthur. Before we spoke of what might be done for Marjorie, I needed to know a little about how you think, to find out how far I could expect you to follow me if I brought up a Catholic's principles of action. I know now what I need to. You've shown me, for instance, that what I mean by sin probably isn't, probably couldn't be, what you would mean. And, you see, that's important; because Marjorie's chief troubles are those of sin and guilt."

Julius Penrose had said: *For her pleasure, she must pay in pain.* That Mrs. Pratt would see that truth, too, would so easily identify Marjorie's need to hurt herself, ought not, Arthur Winner supposed, surprise him. While he was showing Mrs. Pratt whatever he had shown her, she had been showing him that her perception—when intuitive, not formulated by thought—was good. Half concealed by the smatter of pseudo-reasoning, the silly relish in mystification, the talkative zest in repeating the (probably standard) rationalizing of those submissions of faith, some wordless discernment of hers, some natural sense, did indeed seem to divine attitudes and feelings, seize on the things thought but not said, the things known but not mentioned—a point to bear in mind! Arthur Winner said gravely: "I'm glad if you've grasped some of my limitations."

Bending forward, stretching a quick hand to reach his arm, Mrs. Pratt said: "Arthur, you're offended! You mustn't be! All I meant was—well, what you said a moment ago was a little bit sarcastic, wasn't it—about what a person could believe? Oh, don't think I mind, Arthur! You couldn't offend me. I've said I've found out what I need to know. I've found out what you don't or can't believe, what we can't hope to agree on. But much, much remains! I've also found out that you're wise, and that you're kind—"

Arthur Winner said: "I don't think you could offend me either. All *I* meant was that many abstract concepts are a good deal beyond me; and discussing things I'm unable to understand would only waste our time. In the case of what you call Marjorie's chief troubles, I'd understand sin to be a term for wrongdoing, and guilt to be a distress of mind about it. I'm afraid all of us must admit that from time to time we've done wrong; and I think most of us have regrets. Someone of Marjorie's temperament would perhaps feel more strongly—"

Looking at him with earnestness, Mrs. Pratt said: "Yes; people are weak, Arthur. That's what original sin means. Of course, we'll sin; of course! We have to! We're all born to a state of sin. And sin is hateful to God—oh, dear, I forgot! I mustn't talk about God to you, must I?" She grimaced comically. "Yes; Marjorie's temperament makes her feel whatever she feels very strongly. She feels that she's sinned greatly—even, that some of her sins are inexpiable. That's one stumbling block. Because, of course, the fact of the Atonement makes such an idea impious—no; don't be alarmed, Arthur! I'm not going to read you the catechism! It's just that what she feels about sin, as opposed to forgiveness, she feels rightly. She *has* sinned greatly. I know, because she's not kept anything from me. I've heard all a confessor would hear—"

Arthur Winner said: "I'm sure I needn't tell you that Marjorie, in certain states, doesn't always distinguish between fact and fancy. You must be prepared to find that a good deal of what she says isn't actually true."

"Yes, I know." Mrs. Pratt smiled kindly. "Poor lamb, she sometimes can't help exaggerating. But whether *she* always can, or not, those who love her and understand her can distinguish, can tell when what she says is true. The things that are really on her conscience I'm sure aren't invented; because, given her nature, they're likely things. For instance, it's no fancy that Marjorie's sex impulses, her sexual appetites, are very intense—much more intense than the average woman's; and so sexual sins she accuses herself of—do I shock you, Arthur?" She laughed indulgently. "You mustn't expect me to be prudish. Only Protestants think that prudishness is part of religion."

She gave him a mischievous smile. "I don't mean they all do," she said. "But, you see, with us, the church, wherever marriage makes it licit, very far from frowning on physical passion, commends it. Indeed—perhaps you wouldn't know—the church really commands it, forbids abstaining except by mutual consent. That is, unless the demand's altogether unreasonable—made, say, an extraordinary number of times in one night—any refusal of either spouse freely and fully to satisfy the other is held a sin. So married Catholics can't very well be shamefaced about their sexual relations. We don't, like some non-Catholics, look on the physical side of married love as so indecent that we must try to pretend there isn't any such thing!"

Bemused, yet intent, as though searching him narrowly for signs of embarrassment, Mrs. Pratt's large soft eyes fixed themselves on Arthur Winner's face. She said: "Don't imagine I'm without experience, Arthur. When I was younger, I had a number of years of married life. My husband was physically very passionate; so to meet in conscience my marriage debt required a great deal of me; and there's not much I didn't learn about how men are with women; or how, when they're aroused, their sexual need may become so urgent they're hardly able, whether it's licit or illicit, to help what they do. Under the circumstances, I had to say good-by pretty quickly to any shyness or false modesty I might have felt at first. So, you see, once and for all, I did."

Pausing again, still fastening on Arthur Winner that gaze bemused but intent, with now a smile, faint, strangely enigmatic, reappearing, Mrs. Pratt resumed her earlier statuesque pose, resting against the stone back of the bench with her arm langorously extended on it. She said: "Telling you these things is unconventional, I know, Arthur. But I felt I must set you right. I mean, before I said more, I wanted you to see that there's no reason why we shouldn't speak frankly of Marjorie's problems— that you've no need to be embarrassed by some idea you might have that certain things couldn't be mentioned; that I'd think them terribly improper; or that I wouldn't have the personal experience to understand them."

That wine scent of the ripe small crab apples seemed to hang stronger on the leafily shadowed air. Beyond the green cavern of shade, the sunlight seemed to fall hotter on the extent of grass and the empty sunken lily tank. Through increased heat, the continual slow passage of the butterflies seemed slower, more languid. In the overgrowths of thicket, the chorus of bird-chirping had hushed. These, the details of his surroundings, the incidentals of a fine mid-September day, of a midafternoon hour, Arthur Winner observed abstractedly. His face, he could be confident, still wore his professional, unmoved mask, the front of an impassivity that would have been perfectly genuine in the presence of the kind of minor embarrassment that Mrs. Pratt (how superfluously!) urged him not to feel—the silly social awkwardness aroused in those easy to fuss by unconventional mention of the normally not-mentioned.

This embarrassment, mounting while Mrs. Pratt talked, was major. Original trifling unease, felt on Mrs. Pratt's account, felt on behalf of a manifest fool, had been, by new disturbances, compounded into a whole greater surely than its sum of parts. Individually, the disturbances were keyed low—feelings of mildly exasperating entanglement, of faint distaste, of half-baffled incredulity, of vague consternation. These feelings came less from anything Mrs. Pratt had so far said than from a trend of thought or of emotion transpired to him through means he did not know, from his more and more uncomfortable awareness of possible unconscious motive and potential conscious purpose, from strange workings (with or without Mrs. Pratt's formal consent) in this mind over against his.

Since this mind was shaped and fitted to understand what Arthur Winner (Mrs. Pratt rightly told him!) couldn't and didn't understand, strange workings, to him often incalculable, were only to be expected, weren't they? Arthur Winner's inclination had been to accept the curiosities shown him as facts that must rest unexplained, simply to be taken as so, and dismissed as of no practical consequence—as to say, what he didn't know wouldn't hurt him. The procedure was perfectly practicable with a Doctor Trowbridge, where the unexplained seemed to have a tranquilizing directness and lucidity, a well-bred simplicity and (if you liked) reasonableness. He and "Whit," in mutual agreement on matters a good deal more fundamental than articles of faith, could speak of other things. Encountering Mrs. Pratt in her creed's emotional murk of mysteries and dramas, was he right to be so sure that what he didn't know—those yet undefined, but now disturbingly adumbrated shapes of motive and purpose— wouldn't want watching? Had he been too quick to dismiss the vaporings as no possible concern of his? He had not forborne to smile at Mrs. Pratt's simpleton's offer of wits play. In the dark of his ununderstanding, had he smiled too soon?

Mrs. Pratt stood earnestly, eagerly committed to her system of heady make-believe—yes! But here was no Helen Detweiler (poor frightened girl on the moonlit landing at the lake; poor frightened grown-up woman) single-handed, in single strictness, fighting off reality, fleeing the nature of things. Here was no Marjorie Penrose (poor lamb) in her sad hankering to be properly punished, worrying her weak flesh, plaguing her not-un-educated little brain with a last desperate effort to find peace through magic. Helen, though always near exhaustion, gallantly plodded on, a solitary forlorn fugitive; Marjorie, the world being too much with her, faltered, halted, slumped down to drink facts out of mind; but Mrs. Pratt, going in the same general direction, made part of the column of a well-organized expedition. Formidable (as Julius saw them) in their antlike numbers, under effective and experienced leadership, with angels' bread well victualed, and with a train of proved sufficiency to meet any and all of the journey's carefully ascertained hazards of let and hindrance, the meek happy pilgrims of this progress to a land of let's-pretend need suffer no serious misgiving. If they obeyed orders and kept in line, they were absolutely sure to get there.

Of course, some of the sureness might be laid to a judicious limiting of objectives. Doctrine and dogma could remain what first they were—unto the Greeks, foolishness—but nothing was foolish about the practice or the discipline. Conductors of the

396

expedition had, and never forgot they had, human beings and human nature to deal with. Flight from physical self, as Helen and Marjorie, in their different ways, could witness, was futile. Volitations of that kind were, for the expedition's rank and file at least, neither afforded nor countenanced. In matters of opinion, claims somewhat contrary to fact might be encouraged ("There's only one true happiness in this life, Arthur"), little white-lie aids to doubt-beset minds might be offered ("You see, a Catholic's required to believe intelligently"); but in matters of human fact, fact was indeed faced ("Of course we'll sin, of course!"). Openly and realistically, ample account was taken of—name it yourself. The fact faced was that original sin, man's baser nature, the subconscious (named as you chose) kept unkilled, stirring and convoluting as in a crowded, fairly well-secured snake pit, many unholy gross urges, many wicked dumb longings, many frustrate mean impulses, many unavowable dark desires. Only fairly well secured, never quite subdued by grace, strays were now and then bound to escape their subterrane. Creeping above ground, insinuating themselves where nature had fallen, they could strenuously work for a while their unclean wills.

But among the forewarned, forearmed faithful, such escapes were no occasion for panic, nor even for agitation. The strays were the devil's—bad; they worked evil; they spread confusion among pious or sacred thoughts and intentions; but what would you? Evil's energies must flag, too; and when they flagged, means to recapture and recommit the unclean spirits had been appointed. Grace, failing to confine, still enabled contrition; mercy saved the contrite—just keep your shirt on! Meanwhile, nature must take nature's course.

Was this, then, the substance of that mysterious, disturbing transpiration? Without a doubt! In among those brisk bustlings of religiosity, those blanked-out spells of mystic bliss, those recurring, substantively mindless serenities of a saint (or of a Caroline Dummer) pushed suddenly the stray let loose, the unavowable dark urge, the terrestrial serpent. By subtle slidings, by way of the laugh indulgent, the smile mischievous, the sly pull of the prudish Protestant's leg; by way of the general, of statements of what Holy Church held (in pastoral theology could be no scan-

397

dal) to be licit, the marital employments of Catholic spouse by Catholic spouse prescribed practically ad libitum, the denizen of the snake pit with adroitness approached its end, triumphed, turned Mrs. Pratt's fallen nature to its unsanctified purpose.

This sensual urge, delicately, insidiously, then immediately dissembling ("I felt I must set you right") had got where it wanted to be; the general, left for the particular. Arthur Winner had been invited—no, willed!—to turn his mind's eye on this ultimately named one particular one of those the-busier-the-blesseder marriage beds. Mrs. Pratt's claimed knowledgeableness of how men were must give her ground to hope that this man would willy-nilly think upon the (you might gather, incessant) conjugal rites that were performed there, that had engaged there (in nature's state) certain specific (and not at the moment far from him) soft sizable round members, certain buxom areas curving their way through nearby drapings. On this strange delectation—not in venery itself; but in venery at a remove—Mrs. Pratt waited, guiltily helpless, guiltily obedient, while, for the miscreant urge's pleasure, she pictured picturings, imagined imaginings, clingingly looked and looked on the invited onlooker. In the speculatory, enigmatic soft eyes, in the delectation-at-a-remove still visibly aquiver, was that which suggested the superintendent urge, still lickerish, had not finished with Mrs. Pratt—nor, Arthur Winner must see, with Arthur Winner.

So seeing, Arthur Winner could feel, in that compounded whole of major embarrassment, a heavy added dismay. Having identified the urge's occupation, knowing now the meat that must be found for it and fed to it, Arthur Winner could hardly doubt where (incredible as the idea might have seemed to him half an hour ago) this amazing conversation trended, what Mrs. Pratt would next bring up, next seek to linger on. The dismay, he must admit, was not unlike that dismay of a respondent in equity, safe to a point in the other party's ignorance or mere indefinite suspicion, who now conceives that a bill of discovery is about to lie, an enforceable demand for the truth of circumstances that will constitute the case against him.

Arthur Winner said: "Not to be frank would be foolish of us. But I must tell you that I don't, and I could not, feel free to discuss private affairs of Marjorie's with anyone. I know of some unhappy episodes in the past. There may well be others I don't know of. I can see that they might have a bearing on, have something to do with, creating present problems. But, since they're past, there's nothing to be done about them; and so, I think, there's nothing to be said about them. Possibly we should get to what can be done now, what Marjorie wants, what you think I can do for her."

By speaking with an edge of sternness, by the magisterial saying, in so many words, that he was unwilling to discuss past history, by directing Mrs. Pratt, in so many more words, to state now the one admissible business she might have, Arthur Winner's idea had been to challenge her—on the chance that her hint of cards she held was bluff, to call her. Yet an act of challenge must, to those thoughtless good perceptions of Mrs. Pratt's, make his consternation clear. Could the device of the stern manner, the curt directions, be expected to deceive? The odds were to the contrary. He advertised his wish, and, so, his need, to evade. He had been alerted; and, alerted, he was alarmed. Those occupations of the dark urge, that feeding-on-thoughts by the vicarious enjoyer, the voyeur, shook him. He manned defenses; he stood to arms. Not such, the peaceable aplomb of blamelessness! The man of no secrets does not mind being viewed. The man of no dereliction fears no visitor. Tracking pleasures for her urge, Mrs. Pratt would not miss so promising a scent. This supposedly intrepid Arthur Winner (his represented strength being as the strength of ten) shrank from truth, also. He, also, the man of candor, had things he needed to conceal. He, also, fled facts; he, also, wished he could pretend away, if not an unliked here and now, an unliked there and then.

The second apprehension was correct. Mrs. Pratt had not been deceived, nor had her flair failed her. In pleased tones, with a calm of knowledge confirmed, she said: "Very well, Arthur. You ask what Marjorie wants; and what I think you could do for her? She wants you to forgive her. I think you could do that."

Last night in the deep darkness, Marjorie said: *Nothing was anybody's fault but mine.* . . . This, then, was Marjorie's story, and Marjorie stuck to it. Did Mrs. Pratt, hearing it, believe it?

Seemingly, she did. In mechanical reply (vain pretense!), Arthur Winner said: "Forgive her? What possible—"

Mrs. Pratt, so easily victor, smiled with sympathy. "Yes; forgive her, Arthur. You see, she knows now she once did you a very great wrong; and she can't be easy. She's afraid you hate her for it." The big eyes clung to his face with concerned interest. Under the dark urge's management, that softness of mind became formidable. Pressed, the softness would gently give; but Mrs. Pratt still closed in, enveloping, even smothering. Like the eyes, viscous, softly clinging, she would not let you go. Mrs. Pratt said: "I know. And, Arthur, you mustn't mind. When I said Marjorie told me everything, of course I meant *everything*."

To Ralph Detweiler, found out, sitting in paralysis, Arthur Winner said: *The fact, then, is that finally Miss Moore was persuaded. . . .* The burden of pretense, when you saw pretense to be vain, was grievous. The sheer wearisomeness of a long lie weighed on you. How to traverse an allegation that was true? These things tired Ralph. They could tire anyone. Arthur Winner said: "If you've been told what I must suppose you've been told, you'll recognize one of Marjorie's fantasies. If you know what happened, you know that a wrong could only have been done to her, not by her."

Mrs. Pratt said: "Oh, I admire you, Arthur! You never say what isn't true, do you? Such constancy! Oh, how many men would answer that they didn't know what I was talking about! And, of course, being just, you look for your own possible faults before you look for other people's."

Mrs. Pratt spoke with warmth; and the warmth was the unfeignable warmth of inner exhilaration. Though oriented on sex, though sex was the matter of the eager imaginings, the urge perhaps found chief relish in manner, in novelties of approach. The wanted, and now achieved, occasion for acts of passion to be thought of and talked of was no ordinary occasion. What rich emotions might here be developed, what somber intricacies, what wars between passion and virtue, what dramas of temptings and fallings, what ensuing sad excitements of remorse or regret! The urge, perhaps, never had it so good.

Mrs. Pratt said: "But in this case, you're wrong, Arthur. Yours isn't the great fault. You don't know the whole story. You'll remember what you said about Marjorie's drinking. She doesn't drink because she can't help it. She decides to, you said, and does. I agree. So you should be able to see how, in other matters, decisions could be deliberately made—apparent accidents being anything but accidental. They could have been planned. There's evidence that they were planned."

Certain foolish responses that he might make occurred to Arthur Winner. Should he say, pompous: "Is discussing this really necessary, Mrs. Pratt?" Should he say, the scathing lawyer: "What you call evidence can be nothing but hearsay, madam. You're competent only on what you did yourself, or what you saw done. In the ordinary rule, what you're told is never evidence. You weren't there. You don't know." He said nothing.

Mrs. Pratt said: "Then, you'll let me tell you. You see, it wasn't what you might have thought, Arthur. Not sudden impulse. No doubt, *your* impulse was sudden; yes! But you did only what you were meant to do. The time, the place, all the circumstances were arranged so that you could and you would. For a long, long while Marjorie had been working, watching her chances—oh; only after the death of your first wife, Arthur! That should be said. Marjorie assures me of that. Knowing her, I believe her. She says she and—Hope, wasn't it?—were very close. So close, in fact, that I think, unknown to Marjorie, the great grief she felt affected her—caused her to have the other feelings she began to have. Perhaps you wouldn't know; perhaps this sounds shocking to you; but such things happen. In the weakness of our nature, from the purest feelings there's only a step to the impurest."

This fresh deviation into sense caught Arthur Winner again unprepared. He would have thought Mrs. Pratt the one who might not know, Mrs. Pratt the one who might find this shocking.

The dog, the horse, the rat had life; but no breath there! Thou'lt come no more—four times never! In the empty house— the day was Thursday, the helps' day out; and though, with Mrs. Winner taken to the hospital last night, Em and her then husband had offered to stay in, no good reason could be seen to upset their plans—Arthur Winner stood first at loss, blankly reliving the morning's progression, the grotesquenesses as of dreaming, the necessary incredible things done. Notified, the undertaker, adept at the sober suavities of dealing with "bereavement," went smoothly into action. His practiced routine, in familiar conjunction with the hospital people (cheerful good mornings; friendly casual exchanges) could be counted on to see to Hope, to (why not say it?) dispose of Hope.

There had been Ann. Ann could do nothing; yet letting her, untold, finish an ordinary school day was patently unthinkable. He must send for her; and she'd better go to his mother's. Similarly, Lawrence, in his last year at law school, needed notifying. A telegram must be written. Things like these taken care of, the natural next thing would be to go to his mother's, too. Why drive out to Roylan? What errand had Arthur Winner in his empty home?

Outside, snow kept falling. Steady but not thick, a slow downdrift of rather large flakes was no more than lightly whitening the landscape of lawn and garden. Without conscious decision —prompted, maybe, by his promise to Hope when the ambulance came last night that, for the few days she might have to stay at the hospital, he would not forget them—Arthur Winner soon went into the well-tended little conservatory off the living room to see what plants of Hope's might need watering. He stood, in his hand a two-quart brass pot which he could fill at the ornamental tap above the lavabo, a shell-basin in the wall. Moist warmth surrounded him; and, around him, the shapes and scents of flowers—*herself a fairer flower, by gloomy Dis . . .* He put aside the pot. He went upstairs, experiencing as he climbed a weakness in the legs, a reaction of deadly weariness. In the bedroom, he sat down on the nearer bed—Hope's. Then, slipping his shoes off, he lay down. He could not stay; he must get back to Brocton, to his mother's; yet the need to consider his state, the chaos of this situation, held him. He must take stock of a heartsickness in which, subrogating grief, was (could that be? Yes! The tremor of nausea was identifiable) fear—to unhinge the nerves, monitions of dread.

402

Clammier than thoughts of the mortal, hundred and ten or so pounds of Hope committed to licensed hands, descended by service elevator through the hospital, wheeled quickly out the back door, quickly lifted and slid to rest in the waiting vehicle; colder than thoughts of how now to live in the ruins, the wreckage of a house of life, was the great thought of undistinctive death that grew from this, death's latest illustration of death's outrage, of death's vile designs on every man. Since, for men, for him, unfailing death had in store a snowy sunless morning, his own day of mortal sickness, his own morning of overwhelming misery, what warmth, what wellness could avail against that knowledge? His father, growing old with foreseen efficiency, with grace, with (to a point) the Man of Reason's calm, had not been allowed to continue, to go on in so admirable a beginning. To the skull's steady bony grin, the intelligent dry smile must give way. Warren, the bad son; Warren, danger's incorrigible brother, looked insult in the eye of death one moment too long. He died young. And what time was left the middle man, the thought-stricken body down on the made bed, this living Arthur Winner—no matter! In the calendar of days, his very day, his trysting day's unknown but certain date, waited. Perhaps despair, stuporous, deadened all his senses. There must have been sounds in the silent house; but he had not heard them. He simply saw Marjorie Penrose at the room's open door.

A coat was thrown about Marjorie; and on the coat's camel's hair, and on her tousled hair, she had brought in a few still unmelted snowflakes. Her contorted face gleamed with tears. "Arthur!" she said. "Arthur!" She moved, running, dropping the coat, coming to the bed. Though impelled to rise, to sit up, Arthur Winner seemed muscleless. Those stupefacients, loss, sorrow, fear, had done their work. She took his face between her shaking cold hands. She began to sob. Lying suddenly down, she pulled his head against her breast, clasping him to her. She said: "Oh, what shall we do? What shall we do?"

Arthur Winner did not seem able to feel even surprise—as though the calamities, the grotesque dreamings of the morning, had taken away all further power of the implausible or the impossible to impress him. Whatever was, became only to be expected. With desperate motions, Marjorie's hands left his head and went to her dress. She opened the buttoned front. On her bared breasts, on the warmth of skin, on the softness of flesh, she despairingly pillowed his face. She held him as though rocking a child. Beyond the bedroom, in Hope's upstairs sitting room, an extension telephone began to ring.

Prodded to self-awareness by the hard ordinary sound of the mechanical bell, Arthur Winner said: "I must answer that." Perhaps brought to herself by the sound, too, Marjorie let him go. Sitting up, crying quietly, she began to adjust her dress. Arthur Winner, in his stocking feet, walked to the other room. The telephone's voice was that of old Doctor Ives, each ecclesiastical intonation vibrantly deepened. "My dear boy, my poor boy—" Doctor Ives, after all, remembered this man at Sunday school. "I don't know how to express to you my sorrow at the tragic news! Call on me in any way—" There would, of course, be funeral services to arrange.

So the episode, whatever you would call it, was (might he not have dreamed the whole?) over. The brief madhouse scene, the dumb byplay of the theroid idiots, the demented two sorrowers —the passive sorrower stupid and incurious; the active sorrower frantic for means to comfort—was no sooner begun than ended. Yet the scene remained among the broken-up but sharp memories of that ugly day (no dream); and attached, bound to the scene remained, too, harrowings of knowledge hardly to be acknowledged. The successive, earthquake-like throwing-over of a counted-on years-old stable state of things had opened fissures. Through one of them, Arthur Winner stared a giddying, horrifying moment down unplumbed, unnamed abysses in himself. He might later deny the cognition, put thoughts of the discovered country away, seek to lose the memory; yet the heart's mute halt at every occasional, accidental recollection of those gulfs admitted their existence, confessed his fearful close shave.

No telephone ringing, time passing, the two bodies left to lie together; and (he knew what he knew) Marjorie's rumpled, unbuttoned dress was going to be drawn up around her. No least opposition or resistance would have been offered (he knew what he knew); and so, almost before he realized, yet in full responsible intention, in an overcarrying idiot potency of sudden-found passion, there and then, on Hope's bed, on the morning of Hope's death, a death that must be laid to his account, the desolated, collapsed uxoricide, with his already started (he remembered what he remembered), slow, incredible erection, would have been found (whatever was, was only to be expected) presently coupling with, fully engaged in coition with, his sobbing all-acquiescent comforter, his close friend's wife.

True, the telephone rang. True, by admitting (if guardedly and never completely) that the unthinkable *was* thinkable, the power of himself to surprise himself might be thought of as diminished. He had the salutary scare of the thanked-God-for near escape. He had the profound, the unutterable relief of retained innocence, to which could be attached the important cautionary subauditur that he retained innocence thanks to luck. He was warned against himself; he knew he *could* have been in a kind of trouble he would have thought no Arthur Winner, no man of his habits and principles, could ever possibly be in. (To Helen Detweiler, he had pronounced this morning that Ralph, if he learns a lesson, isn't a loser from all this—in the long run, he's a gainer.) Yes; he'd been well warned! To see that nothing further developed with Marjorie would be easy enough—far from coveting his neighbor's wife, he rather disliked her, found her more unattractive than not. He'd have no trouble taking care that, thenceforward, occasions for intimacy with Marjorie never arose—indeed, with Hope gone, with the Roylan house closed, what occasions could arise? How often would he be likely even to see Marjorie? As of then, the probable significance of the much-too-much protesting was (to the best of Arthur Winner's recollection) lost on him.

Arthur Winner said: "Things happen as they happen; yes. We agree that everybody makes mistakes; and I think we should agree, too, that our mistakes are always our own. Saying somebody else led us to make them, even if true, leaves them just as much ours as ever. They don't need to be investigated with the idea of assigning responsibility. That's assigned already."

Mrs. Pratt almost smiled. "You aren't able to say 'sin,' are you, Arthur? It's easier when you can; because there are degrees of sin. People may do wrong things because of circumstances—some situation catches them, and they have a weak moment. That's not the same as deliberately proposing to sin. The others do wrong; but not to the degree of a person who thinks a sin all out, plans sin; who may say, months and months earlier: 'In July I'll do it. Almost everybody will be away then. He'll be coming out evenings to work in the garden. Going over to talk to him would be perfectly natural. Even if someone saw me, nothing would be thought.' That's deliberate proposing."

Arthur Winner said: "I very much doubt if anything was deliberately proposed. All that, I think, would be just something imagined afterward." He spoke again with sharpness and dryness; but, again, against the yielding envelopment, the viscid softness, the givings-way which ended by only drawing him nearer to be surrounded more easily and fully, all effort to fight free was failing. What preposterous suggestibility, what laming of the mind and sapping of the will, put him in this leechlike prattler's power? A little maudlin, Marjorie whimpered: *Sometimes it's soon; and sometimes it's later; and sometimes they find you out in ways you might not think of. . . .* Mrs. Pratt herself said: *You aren't able to say "sin," are you? . . .* The copybook said (word sufficient to the wise?): *Conscience does make cowards of us all.*

Mrs. Pratt shook her head. "No, Arthur. Not this time. Marjorie didn't imagine this. You might doubt a story you couldn't test; but here, facts bear her out. You see, steps had to be taken in advance. They were taken. For instance, there was the long, long business of getting Julius to go to that place and try those special treatments. That was hard to arrange; because, you may remember, your doctor, your local doctor, didn't recommend them, didn't think they'd do any good. But Marjorie insisted. She knew she had to have Julius away. Can you think why? She wasn't worried about Julius following her around, spying on her, anything like that. But with you and Julius seeing each other every day in the office, she knew she'd never manage, you'd never give in. Julius would simply have to go away, so she'd be sure, for six weeks, you wouldn't see him."

That inner exhilaration of Mrs. Pratt's, that excitement from the alternation of contrary thoughts or feelings, had revived, Arthur Winner could observe, as this eager little demonstration of a scheme of sin, of sin's astute sly painstakings, was outlined. One moment, Mrs. Pratt might, with creepings of painful pleasure, allow herself to dwell on the sin's object, the piercing prick of the carnal goad, the luxury pell-mell. The next moment, she might (you could see: vertiginously, she did!) feel, with shudders of thrilling dread, a heat of hell's flames fanned up to that edge of the pit where the furious enjoyments took place.

Breathing deeply, Mrs. Pratt said: "Oh, she planned so carefully, Arthur! You see, she'd need a number of weeks, because she couldn't risk hurrying. Until she got you ready, you mustn't realize what she meant you to do, or you'd be frightened off. She had to go slow, keep you from noticing anything. She'd watch you, so when she saw you'd done about all you were going to do in the garden, she could come over. There were little friendly familiarities she could get you used to. Hardly saying anything, being brave, she could make you think she was lonely and unhappy. She told me that took almost two weeks, and she was getting frantic; because, you see, she knew this was now or never. That was the worst thing—her knowing that."

Mrs. Pratt gazed at him with a lively sorrow, a tragic vivacity. "Yes; then, or never! She'd known early in the spring that it would have to be now, this year; probably, before the summer was over, or not at all. That's why this aspect was the worst—the grave wickedness of consciously contriving for another to sin. You see, Marjorie, I think because she really was in love with you, knew, was able to realize, two things you didn't know, or, at least, weren't yet admitting to yourself. You wanted to get married again. You'd been living alone almost two years and you'd begun, whether you realized you had or not, looking for someone. Then, though you really didn't know yet, she knew that you'd found someone—the present Mrs. Winner, of course. She's so charming, Arthur! I must congratulate you. But perhaps you can see what the realization meant to Marjorie. It told her, first and most important, that you were in a mood for, had a definite, probably growing want and need for, physical relations with a woman—" Mrs. Pratt broke off.

Putting out the quick hand again, she reached and touched his arm. She said: "Oh, please don't imagine I think that was all, Arthur. Or that, with *you*, that came first. I meant, it was most important to Marjorie. Marjorie saw it as definitely giving her a chance. That is, though she was in love with you, she never thought for a moment she could make you fall in love with her. Her situation was that she knew you needed, wanted a woman; but at any minute, what was also known to her—that you were going to marry again—might become known to you. Once that happened, the chance was over. Until that happened, she might very well hope the chance was good. You, feeling the strain of not having a woman, and she being one, she might hope, by playing her cards right, to induce you, if only for a little while, to have her. So she set about managing it; she set about, step by step, preparing you, arousing you, so that a moment might come when, in literal truth, you wouldn't be able to help having her. And you think things just happened! Oh, Arthur, men are such innocents, sometimes!"

Of those images of memory, his several gone selves, a man in his time playing many parts, Arthur Winner had surely forgotten much; yet, bafflingly, that late one, the summer evening gardener with his eventual guilty secret, was one of the ones he seemed to know least about. He could distinctly remember thoughts (and even feel again certain feelings) of the boy who, in the great Ponemah oak—last night blasted, after many a summer!—climbed and swung. Thoughts and feeling of the gangling bridegroom at Christ Church's flower-fragrant altar whom Hope Tuttle took to be her husband—and her widower!—were, some of them at least, recoverable. He recollected easily, recalled clearly, much of what he had thought and felt as the older, settled, married man, the one who marked, in the bevy of child-women across a dance floor, "Hendy," Brocton's shining teen-aged tennis star, and agreed, disinterested: yes; too bad she had to be so tall.

About that lost, that strange gardener, Mrs. Pratt's supposed innocent, a few facts could of course be stated. He was a man still unsettled in his mind—he could not seem to make his mind up. He and Ann were living with his mother in Brocton. Were they going to go on doing that? If so, why didn't he get rid of the Roylan place? The gardener, moreover, was gardening not for pleasure, not for love of horticulture, but for unclear, inconclusive reasons—part, no doubt, of the same halfhearted indecisiveness. Exercise was supposed to be good for you, so he was exercising. Then, Hope's gardens had meant so much to Hope that a continued care seemed, in some not-very-reasonable piety of mourning, imposed on him. Lingering broodings about himself as the actual, if remote, cause (Fred Dealey judged correctly; the thought was, for long, distressing to live with) of Hope's death, perhaps helped to exact these amends of sorrow, to make him submit himself to the sights of Roylan—Hope's house, once always open to the summer airs, shut up, unlived-in; her last projects of planting left unfinished; another year's growth of flowers, sadly still-persisting, that those deft hands would never tend again.

Yes, Arthur Winner remembered well enough what was outward in that stranger who had been himself. At early evening he could watch his man driving in, driving past the house, past the great sweep of lawn—now, lawn no longer, really; Doctor Shaw's farmer came with a tractor and sickle bar a couple of times a summer to mow the high grass and collect hay for the doctor's cows—to the garage. Upstairs, in one of the several bedrooms once occupied by servants, that man put on his working clothes. He came down. He got his tools, and progressed methodically from place to place, weeding and cultivating until dark. And if he wished, he was, of course, also able to see (too well, too well!) precise physical circumstances, details of sense impression, connected with the acts of eventuated guilt. What he could not see, what he did not now know, nor seem able now even to imagine, was what passed in that man's mind, what unremembered thoughts prompted and accounted for the painfully remembered actions. Things must have been thought, just as things must have been said. He could not think what they were; things done were all he had to go on.

Well, then, what of things done? Did remembered actions suppose a dumb innocent, a dazed sufferer from the blow of his world's shattering, then as earlier surcharged with stuporous melancholy, hardly conscious of, not in control of, his situation? Or did they suppose a man (not such an innocent!) recovering from the debilitation of grief, the image of his late-espoused saint so dimmed she could no longer look reproach; a man ready now for that to which he had always (his thanked-God-for escape in the madhouse scene not actually wanted; and, so, only seeming, only imaginary) been committed? When Marjorie began coming over those July evenings did the gardener really suspect nothing? While snares (if snares they were) were being set, did he see nothing? While Marjorie, with or without plan, insistently proffered herself, did he never think of such a thing? And, at the come moment, when he was (right enough!) not able to help having the woman who (no need to doubt!) wanted him to have her, had he been prepared only unconsciously? Today's Arthur Winner simply could not say.

All he could say was that, just before one evening's darkness fell, a thunderstorm passed short and sharp somewhat north of Roylan. Marjorie, as (yes!) she took to doing after Julius went away, had walked over. She was there. She had been telling him (yes; with her husband gone and the children at camp, she seemed sad and lonely!) what she heard from Julius. A pattering heavy fall of rain from the edge of the storm sent them into the summer house. They sat together, watching the lightning, very bright beyond the great treetops, but ten or so miles away. They heard, between rolls of thunder, the water-trickle that dripped from the quaint conical roof above them. Through the fancy diapered lattices, they felt stirrings of moist cooler air. Arthur Winner did not remember anything said; and that might be chargeable to the same default of memory that kept thoughts the gardener must have had from him; yet that, also, might have been fact. The heart, the nerves, the stimulant glands have no special use for speech. Speechless, neither the man nor the

410

woman required to be told by the other that their moment was come. The ebbing, the departing, storm; the new stillness; the secret drip of rain, conjoined, made imperative, the sudden kisses; the briefly resisted next moves; the ended resistance.

Shades of night hid all, hid the evening gardener from himself, hid him from his visiting friend, his friend's wife. Thick darkness hid the fact of their answering anguished excitements, the fact of the uneven matchboard of the damp floor, the soon fact of strangled oh-oh-oh's gasped past his ear. Because of night, because of darkness, these two need have no faces and no names —simply, some woman was in her paroxysms of pleasure; and, surmounting her, some man was in his. Was not darkness that opportunity whose guilt is great? Did not darkness palliate all that was culpable, soften wrong to mere accident? Two people, not themselves, encountering of a sudden, not even seeing each other well—surely they were entitled to forget what they did there, to be uncertain whether any such thing had ever happened. Let them pick themselves up presently; say, if they liked, good night; and hereafter—tomorrow; forever—hold their peace!

Ah, but it had not been that way, it was not to be that way. The poor argument of accident with mitigation of darkness might serve once—but; alas, alas! Grant that Mrs. Pratt was right, that Marjorie, before that evening in the summer house, had done some planning. Who afterward did some? Arthur Winner must behold his mystery man, his incredible, unfathomable gardener—oh, yes; the fellow was mad!—the very next day back to garden again. Observing that he had come, his last night's visitor (if, until then, anxious; certainly, then, exultant) would guess why. Since he had not taken care to stay away, one accident was not to be one accident only; they would (if she liked) make this a practice. From now on, the deed that had been done by darkness was (if he liked) to be done by daylight. Immediately sure, the visitor did not delay to visit. She came purposefully across the road and opened the garden gate.

No defaults of memory here! With pain of amazement, with

smarting of mind, Arthur Winner could present to himself the pictures of that practice. The order of those July evenings at Roylan came to involve little waste of time. Quietly the garden gate opened; the mute expectant looks exchanged themselves. The man stopped what he was only pretending to be doing. He spoke and heard some few unmeaning words. He walked with her, hidden by the garden wall, to the side door of the garage. That man opened the door for her, already in full excitement, already quaking in foretaste of the high-seasoned known near orgy, which, neither questioning, they were (helpless; as though in spite of themselves) accepting the commitment to re-enact, accepting the vassalage of re-enacting. Hasty, stealthy without need (they were all alone; the bolt was shot behind them), they gained the hushed, the heated, upstairs twilight. These window blinds, shutting out the last sunlight, had not been raised for months. Along the narrow, unaired, undusted hall, careful not to touch each other, they tiptoed to that room at the end whose door stood ajar. They were now arrived at the appointed place of execution. An old iron bedstead underpropped a worn mattress, terrain of their engagements.

Beneath the printed cloth of the house dress she was accustomed to wear, Marjorie never had anything on. A pull of a fastener, and at once she was unrobed, the shed dress dropping to lie on the floor. She stood bare in the warm air. She waited by the bedstead's edge while he put off his garments. Surveying him, her slant eyes more slant, she seemed unseeing. Yet, she saw; she looked. At sight of how ready he was for her, she started to tremble. At his advance, a patent fury, a torment, of inner vellications that would not admit of delay made her encounter of him instant. Hardly down on the mattress, the mucid encompassment took place, he was invested by her. To the multisonous harsh music of stretched springs, she, seized of him, hied him on, forcing a pace (she usually in the lead) which must, with something of her fury got into him, in some impetus, some plunge of venereal urgence long unfelt—no; never felt!—soon terminate the violent to-and-fro, let the giving springs be still, leave the prostrated mattress-mates spent, exhausted of motion. That was all—for the time being.

For the time being! Ah, there was the crux of the revulsive, today inscrutable, vexed, vexatious question that those ugly souvenirs, now winced at, kept posing. The business done upstairs in the garage, life's other businesses would, must, go on. In all (had, having, and in quest to have), here passed at most, at best, only a trifling fraction of a day's time. How did that man spend the remainder—the long parts before, the long parts after? Could the rest of a day proceed, detached from, unconcerned about, those occasions (past and future) of the athlete of the swaying bedstead? Could thoughts and feelings of other hours come and go forgetful of the uncleanly exploits of the worn mattress's careering courser? (With a spasm of recoil, Arthur Winner had to remember that he afterward took care to destroy that mattress. Seen in a good light some months later, the many semen stains left him no choice but to bundle it secretly down to the incinerator behind the garage, make a fire, and burn it.)

Yes; what of those several other (and how different!) Arthur Winners who had been obliged, while this went on, to allow that clandestine lecher with his sullies and spots to be numbered among them? For example; the one who politely breakfasted, more or less the model son of riper years, with his mother (Ann was up at the lake at Miss Henderson's camp; Lawrence, as a reward for passing his bar examination—that he didn't mean to practice in Brocton still known only to Lawrence —was in Europe with two law-school classmates). For example; the man who entered his office, spoke, with no difference of affable manner, his good mornings to Helen Detweiler and the girls; who got efficiently busy at his desk, or, Noah having waddled in without ceremony, listened, attentive, to the old man's long-winded but worth-listening-to declamation on some point of law. For example; the man who publicly, in open court, taking his turn among colleagues of the bar, few or none of whom failed to regard him with high respect and friendly liking, arose with calm of use to ordinary business: *May it please the court; in the court of common pleas, I have here the final decree in an action to quiet title.* . . . How did these coexisting characters come to tolerate their low companion's turpitude? All, all honorable men, couldn't they find means to rule, or at least to check a little, the furtive fornicator, the base meddler with a valued friend-and-partner's wife?

No; they could not! Men of honor, men of principle, men of integrity, they must have acted if they could have acted. This underhand fellow, sprung up importune among them, defied the only restraints they knew, the restraining theorem that had always seemed so sufficient. Whatsoever things are false, whatsoever things are not honest, whatsoever things are unjust, whatsoever things are impure, whatsoever things are ugly, whatsoever things are of bad report—why, one simply didn't do them! Perhaps they—innocents indeed, if you liked!—were in fact too far dumbfounded, as the incredible development proceeded, to know how to act. Thrown in deep water, men drown who never had opportunity or occasion to learn to swim.

So when the afternoon latened and the day drew toward a close, the one Arthur Winner exempt by the unheard-of very nature of such conduct from the jurisdiction of decency, the direction of those innocent other Arthur Winners, would be driving out in his car to his ostensible gardening in the cool of the evening. Deaf as yesterday to all representations of right, he purposed further perfidy, once more pawning his honor to obtain his lust. Deaf as yesterday to all remonstrances of reason, he purposed to sell himself over again to buy venery's disappearing dross—some moments of transient dallying with eye or hand, to which untied impatience quickly set a term; some impassioned moments of the now engendered beast of two backs, of that acting androgyne whose he-half was excitedly prodding and probing, whose she-half was excitingly prodded and probed. The little life span of the beast soon sped, its death was died. At the she-half's flings-about in her extremity, the he-half's spoonful of phrenetic sensation was tweaked to spend itself—and, there! There was the buy, the bargain, the prize, the pearl of price! All possible gain now realized; and, in sum, but loss, would the fallen rider, fallen steed still under him, contract another time for such a run? Yes (if flesh could); a hundred times! In proof, was the truth of fact that, until a day or two before Julius was due home, the indoor turfman had his sport

414

as often as opportunity (his mount was much of one week men-
struating) could be afforded him.

On that, on the end of the episode, all along (it seemed) had
been between them a perfect understanding. By silent mutual
agreement, by settled common consent, an evening was to come
when the signal of the arriving car would go unanswered, no
Marjorie appearing. To both, the meaning would be known—
time to call a halt! As though nothing had happened, the gardener (at long last) gardened outdoors again. With open show
of honest toil, he resumed his former fit-to-be-seen labors,
his guiltless occupations of weeding and cultivating.

Was something wanted to round out their shame? These slippery lovers supplied it! Excused, they never could have been;
but, by this piece of prudence, not even the trumpery explanations that might try to cite nature's weakness or plead passion's strength were left them. Here went no star-crossed pair,
hearts lost to each other, gently to be judged. Here, making off
to hide, were a couple of cheap sneaks, greedy in stolen use as
long as use was safe, adept at snatching easy chances; but wanting no trouble, ready to run no smallest risk. Surely, surely, those
two, such a two, never could have done such things! Done them,
that same transgressing two indubitably had. Who could explain
this, who could say how this had been possible? Not Mrs. Pratt's
reluctant vis-à-vis of now, the present's confounded Arthur Winner; never, the man of little more than six years later, today's
man of not a word to say, seated across from his penance of Mrs.
Pratt!

Mrs. Pratt said: "So you know now how the whole thing was
done, Arthur—who was really responsible. You look away! Yes,
of course, your consent had to be given. Of course, a man of
your straightforwardness, your honest instincts, can't see himself
as blameless; and—" She broke off with a startled gasp. Faintly,
she said: "Oh, Arthur; there's a snake."

"Yes, I just saw it," Arthur Winner said.

Whitening, sharply trembling, Mrs. Pratt said: "Oh, I can't
bear snakes. They frighten me so." Her agitated voice failed her

a moment. She swallowed, and said: "I know you're going to tell me it's perfectly harmless; but I don't want to stay here, Arthur. I can't stay here—"

Astonished, Arthur Winner said: "There's absolutely no danger. The snake sees us. That's why it doesn't move. It won't come any nearer; all it wants to do now is get away. But I'm afraid I can't say it's perfectly harmless. That happens to be a fair-sized copperhead. We don't know where they breed; but every now and then one turns up in the hollow, here. Just walk to the steps—"

Paler still, Mrs. Pratt said: "Oh, Arthur, I don't dare—"

With continued astonishment, Arthur Winner regarded the astonishing transformation. That was no affected fear! The mantle of the confident preceptress had fallen from Mrs. Pratt in midsentence. Mrs. Pratt's very fibers of being declared an uncontrollable horror of aversion, an aversion of such paralyzing power as, draining the brain of blood, to work a near syncope. This lapse into female foible, though surely ludicrous, might also be seen as pitiable. You wished to laugh; but could you? In the face of one solid sense perception—the true, tangible (if not very big) hideous serpent in the garden—where was that serenity of the simpleton saints? When you thought about it, how sad a taking of the wind out of those full theological sails; how unhappy an exploding of the spiritual bubble! What pathetic forgetfulness of that situation of safety in the eternal arms, in those divine hands where, Mrs. Pratt so feelingly said, she had put the whole of herself, her desires and experiences, good and bad! The spirit only was willing; the weak flesh voted no confidence. Omniscience and omnipotence might, or might not, be on the job today. This wasn't the time to put your trust in moonshine!

"You've nothing to be afraid of, I promise you," Arthur Winner said. "Just stand up; and you'll see."

"Oh, no; I can't—"

At sight of human beings on the bench, the snake, which must have got through a drain tile under the wall somewhere in the recess of shrubbery, had frozen motionless on the open grass

416

not far from the empty lily tank. Nothing stirred but the slight flicker of the delicate tongue sampling the odor-laden air as to chances of not being noticed, of not having been observed. Judging that she spoke the truth, that Mrs. Pratt, sagging in shock on the bench, really could not, Arthur Winner himself stood up. At his movement, the snake, too, moved, flashed into movement. The dull-banded body whipped away in a gliding dart, reached in an instant the stone rim of the tank, sinuously slid over, down into the weed tangle at the bottom, and vanished.

"Good!" Arthur Winner said. "He may stay there for a while. Because of the children, we try to kill them when we see them. I think I left a hoe near one of the rose beds. If you'll come up with me, and go on to the house, I'll get it and kill this one—if he'll be kind enough to wait."

"Oh, yes; I'd rather be in the house," Mrs. Pratt said. She gave him a dazed look, unhelped by his smile. She came totteringly to her feet. She said: "Oh, Arthur, I hope I'm not going to faint." She made a faltering step.

Taking her arm firmly, moving with her, Arthur Winner said: "Of course you're not! That's all over. You won't see him again. Neither will I, probably. But there's a chance he'll think he's safe down there; and I'd like to dispose of him if I can."

Gaining the steps, and, so, perhaps feeling escape assured, Mrs. Pratt seemed to gain, too, a little strength or confidence. She said: "But if he's poisonous, aren't you afraid he'll bite you? You're so brave."

"The contest I propose isn't going to be very equal," Arthur Winner said. "Don't worry. No bravery's required. With a hoe I can reach him and take his head off from a distance at which he can't even begin to reach me. He'll be more or less cornered in the tank there; and I shouldn't be long. Yes; there's the hoe. Would you like to sit down by the sundial a moment?"

"No, I can walk up," Mrs. Pratt said. "May I sit inside on the terrace? I'm sorry to be so cowardly, Arthur. I just can't help it."

"By all means," Arthur Winner said. "I'll come up presently and get you some whisky."

417

"Oh; I don't drink alcohol, Arthur," she said. "I've seen too much of what it can do."

Though no bravery was required of him, Arthur Winner, approaching the lily tank quietly, hoe in hand, needed a certain resolution. To be overcome, along with a disinclination to violence and a distaste for, a slight squeamishness about, acts of blood, was reluctance, ingenuous and absurd, born of no match, no equal contest. He was the deliberate aggressor; the snake wanted nothing but to live and let live, to go in peace. The approaching man projected not a fight, but a murder, to which he advanced with all unfair advantage—the man's designing mind, and the man's amazing prehensile hand that wielded by the safe long handle the edged steel blade; against the crawling creature, mindless, handless, with his little pair of fangs his only resource, ineffective in this situation, his sack of venom useless. Tightening his lips, Arthur Winner suppressed the ridiculous qualm.

His selected victim, a close look showed Arthur Winner, was still there. One or another snake sense must have supplied warning of the enemy's return to the neighborhood. Perhaps hoping again to be overlooked, the snake had taken refuge in a corner (just what the enemy would have wished, if a snake had only known!). Half hidden by burdock leaves, he had assumed a combative posture. He waited, coils gathered, small wedge-head couched, ready for trouble not of his seeking—even, it might be (conscious of means-to-kill in his mouth) conceiving himself able to give better than he got.

Marking the snake's position, moving up, gauging distance carefully, Arthur Winner feinted down toward the burdock leaves with his hoe. Like a spring uncoiling, swift as sight, the wedge-head leaped, striking up, little jaws yawning open, at the poised blade. The recoil of recovery, though far from slow, was not fast enough. Arthur Winner drove down the blade with force. Hitting an inch behind the recoiling head, the hard blow dashed the body against the leaf-littered tank bottom. Barely checked by the tougher spine, the steel edge sliced on through, decapitating the creature. Turning, with a new qualm, from this quick taking-off's immediately ensuing convulsive thrash of muscular reflex, the violent castings-about, as though the beheaded body continued a separate agonized life among the swaying weeds, Arthur Winner wiped on the grass blood traces from his hoe. He laid the hoe down. He would return and dispose of the corpse later.

Walking slowly in the hot sunlight, still—or again—qualmish over his fast, easy, neat achievement, Arthur Winner went up the steps and passed around the sundial. He could see the light color of Mrs. Pratt's garments beyond the tall screens of the terrace. To his surprise, she was not sitting down, she was standing; and in a way that, even from a distance, looked dazed, as though she had suffered, for no reason he could imagine, new alarm or fresh dismay. He was close enough then to see that she was not alone. Confronting Mrs. Pratt in a pose of apparent belligerence, wearing brown trousers and a dark blue sport shirt, was a short chunky man Arthur Winner did not know, had never seen before.

FIVE

MRS. PRATT SAID: "Oh, Arthur; this man—I don't know what he wants—" By her helpless gesture, she both appealed to Arthur Winner, and indicated him to the stranger.

The man said: "You Mr. Winner?"

Closing the screen door behind him, Arthur Winner said: "I am Arthur Winner."

He had been right about the pose of belligerence. Turning from Mrs. Pratt, the short figure was lifting to him a wrathful countenance—a round red angry face with protuberant small round angry dark eyes; a bitter-looking round small mouth; an insignificant round snub nose.

At the blunt question, at the turn of the threatening face, Arthur Winner was taken aback to feel an answering anger—proof, if he needed any, of extensive damage done him by Mrs. Pratt's garrulous suggestive soft pressings; of equanimity, usually his, disabled by the hurts self-criticism inflicted on self-esteem; of nerves strained by the bafflement of a mind called on in vain to account for the fact of that file of dirty pictures, that indisputable evidence of onetime acts demented and disgraceful, of things simply not done, done over and over.

Arthur Winner said: "But I don't seem to know who you are; nor why you're in my house. You'd better tell me."

The man said: "Who I am, I'm Mr. Moore—Joanie Moore's father. So what I want is: Where is he? You got the son of a bitch here some place?"

Arthur Winner said: "There's no one here but this lady, a

guest of mine, whom you seem to have been disturbing. And I don't think she likes your language any better than I do."

"I'll call him what he is," Mr. Moore said. "The dirty, sneaking little skunk! So he does this to Joanie, has his fun with her, and then he thinks he'll just forget about her, huh? He runs to a lawyer—you! You'll get him out of it—you think! He gives Joanie this story you won't let him marry her. He says you say he don't have to; there's no law he has to! We'll see about that! You and me are going to have a talk, mister!"

To help him quell his own start of anger, Arthur Winner had this spectacle of a man angry—anger's ridiculousness, anger's uselessness, anger's absurdities of huff and puff. Like men dosed with strong drink, Mr. Moore, dosed with anger, could be seen to have attained the temporary illusion that he really was what, vainly, he always wanted to be. Anger's fumes of error went to that weak head; he felt full of courage. All judgment lost, he churned up rage, he lashed himself to fury, attempting the part of the effective, commanding, dangerous man, the mouse made lion.

Arthur Winner said: "Yes; I was intending to have a talk with you, Mr. Moore. I thought I'd have to explain your daughter's situation to you. I see I don't have to. You're mistaken if you think I'm opposed to Ralph's marrying her. Either Joan misunderstood him, or you misunderstood her. It's true that, in law, he can't be made to marry her; but I feel he ought to, and he feels he ought to; so we have only ways and means to discuss. This isn't the time or place to discuss them. I'm engaged at the moment; and this is my home. I do business in my office. You can have an appointment there sometime Monday. Incidentally, if Mrs. Moore doesn't know, you'd better tell her. I'd like her to come with you. I'd like to be able to talk to you together."

"Oh, no, you don't!" Mr. Moore said. By speaking louder and more angrily, blowing anger up, he showed that he recognized the one greatest danger to his illusion of strength—reason, reasonableness. Admit any of that, and the lion would in a minute be mouse again. At the threat of reason, he looked hate and fear. That bitter little mouth had, of course, a history. Readable there, was a lengthening record of defeats and disappointments —do mice dare to demand, dare to be angry, dare to play the man? In those unconfident surly dark eyes was registered the long hard-luck story of the incompetent. Mutely his eyes protested the continual wrongs fortune did him; they declared his weak smolder of resentment at how he never had a chance, how people no better than he was got the breaks, how the fault was always someone else's.

Mr. Moore said: "I don't need no Monday appointment. We got to discuss! Yeah, I know you lawyers! Discuss, hell! You and him discuss, if you want. What I got to say, I'm saying now, not Monday. Ways and means, hell! He takes her to a justice, whatever you call them, and marries her; but quick! That's his ways and means! If he don't; I give him fair warning, and I give you fair warning; I'll kill the sneaking bastard!"

Mrs. Pratt, as though overcome by cumulative shock, made a frightened sound, touched the arm of a nearby chair and sank down.

Arthur Winner said: "I spoke to you before about those expressions. Don't let me hear any more of them." But when you had sized Mr. Moore up as what he clearly was—a loud-mouthed little vulgarian, a weak blusterer, surely incompetent in life and probably incapable in business, had you ruled out all capacity to suffer real and deep pain, all right to protest the hurt to his wronged child? Arthur Winner must remember those personal thoughts of his own last night. What *did* one do under these circumstances? Who would have daughters! Imagining himself in Mr. Moore's place for a moment, he felt the plummet of the heart as Ann (such a thing never remotely suspected by him; such a possibility never really considered!), frightened and tearful (how unlike Ann!), finding herself obliged to, forcing herself to, tell him her trouble—

He said: "You'd be wiser, Mr. Moore, to treat me as someone who's willing to help you, and whose help you may need. Since you can't seriously suppose that getting yourself indicted for murder would solve any of Joan's problems, I won't take what you said last as seriously meant. The ways and means we need to discuss are what arrangements would best serve Joan's interests as well as Ralph's. That's what I'm willing to help you with. Ralph's sister is his legal guardian; and, as he's not of age, he must of course have her consent—"

At the relentless advance of reasonableness, Mr. Moore looked his hate and fear again. He uttered a sound that might almost be gnashing of teeth. He said: "So never mind her! I seen her already. I found out she worked for you, see; so I found out where she lived. So I fixed things with her, all right. Don't think I didn't!"

Arthur Winner said: "What things did you fix?"

"What things do you think?" Mr. Moore said. The pot-valiancy of anger became a little more truculent. "I told her what I told you. I told her I don't care what happens to her brother; he's nothing but a sneaking tail-chaser—look at this other girl Joanie says there is! But if Joanie's going to have a baby, the baby's going to have a name!" With loud triumph, he glared at Mrs. Pratt, as though, extending his audience; he was inviting her, too, to admire so telling a statement of his high purpose. "So what I said; once Joanie gets her marriage license, we're through with him—see? And I hope he does go to jail; and when the baby's born, he gives her a divorce—see? But if he don't marry her, I'll kill him, I said. And don't worry, she consents, all right! She's too scared to make any fuss, or anything."

Arthur Winner said: "I can't consider scaring women much to a man's credit, Mr. Moore. I wouldn't boast about it, if I were you." At least, Helen had not been wholly unwarned—no policy like honesty, after all!—but at the thought of poor truebred Helen, appalled by the hectoring shouts, horrified by the scurrilous yellings, a return of anger filled him. Mr. Moore, being Mr. Moore, knew not, you might argue, what he did; but if, brute and boor, he couldn't draw a line, could no lines be drawn for him?

Arthur Winner said: "Don't, for any reason, go near Miss Detweiler again. I'll see about getting her consent when the time comes. I'm prepared to make some allowance for the state of your feelings; but you'd better know that neither your feel-

423

ings, nor the fact you may not mean what you say, can excuse repeated threats to kill. Any more of them, and you're likely to find yourself in very serious—"

"So I don't mean what I say, huh?" Mr. Moore scowled. "If he don't marry her, he'll find out whether I mean it or not! I got something here." He patted his trouser pocket significantly.

"What have you got there?" Arthur Winner said.

From the pocket, Mr. Moore produced, for Arthur Winner to see, the butt of what appeared to be a thirty-two-caliber revolver. Mrs. Pratt, seeing, too, gasped: "Oh!"

Arthur Winner said: "Can you show me a pistol permit from the sheriff's office? I don't think you can. I think you took that from your store manager's cash drawer, or safe. Put it back there as soon as possible; or I'll be obliged to report you to the police. You'll get a five-hundred-dollar fine, or a year in jail; or since you've been threatening to use it, I'd expect, in our court, both."

Mr. Moore had reddened more, as though angered more; and this moment, Arthur Winner must realize, had dangers. Ringing hard in Mr. Moore's ears was the level, hateful voice of that part of the superior practical world which would always have been his master and his enemy, which was forever brushing him impatiently aside, or beating him casually down. That voice regularly pronounced sentence on him, assigned him his usual pains of disappointment, his accustomed penalties of failure. Beside himself, furibund, the ridiculous frenzied mouse, the frantic weak virtual half-wit whose chief impediment must always have been that he owned no judgment, that he never could count costs or weigh consequences, might, in throes of his despair—

His eye deliberately menacing, his face formidable, Arthur Winner said: "Be very careful! Return the gun; and meanwhile, show it to no one else. Don't take it out of your pocket; and don't consider pointing it. Pointing a deadly weapon is a separate indictable offense, and would get you an additional fine, and an additional jail term."

The libration of a perhaps never-doubtful balance, the moment of possible danger, had ended. Some muttering noises came from Mr. Moore. Arthur Winner heard them not without relief; yet, freed by relief's reassurance, sympathy tinged relief —the mouse was safely mouse again, back in the ordinary degrading predicament of mice-men, of most men in their frailty: *I would—but I can't; I dare not; I don't know how!* Wishes aren't horses; beggars aren't going to ride!

Putting, by his tone, that moment of possible peril behind them both, Arthur Winner said: "I suggest you go home and talk to Mrs. Moore. Tell your wife you have my definite word that Ralph intends to marry Joan; so she needn't be uneasy about that. Tell her I hope she'll come to my office with you about one o'clock Monday—it's on Court Street, nearly opposite the courthouse; you'll see my name by the door—and we'll go into the necessary arrangements, work them out together—"

Sullen, Mr. Moore said: "I can't get off Mondays, not afternoons—"

"If some evening would be more convenient," Arthur Winner said, "I'll come back to Brocton and see you then. I won't be free Monday evening; but Tuesday, if you like."

"Well—" Mr. Moore said. His voice was bitter. Visibly he made an effort, if a feeble one, to raise a little of the lost bluster, to cover the retreat. He scowled pettishly. He said: "Just don't try to arrange no buts or ifs, is all I say. What we arrange is, he marries her. And I want proof he will. You got to prove he won't duck out on her."

"You needn't worry about that," Arthur Winner said. "You forget that, because of the other matter, Ralph couldn't go anywhere. He's under a legal restraint; so he wouldn't be allowed to; and if he tried, he'd be picked up at once." He paused. He said: "Like you, I wish this hadn't happened, Mr. Moore. I'm sorry about it; but my experience is that once we accept what we can't change, a little patience and good will can make most unhappy situations much less unhappy. Remember, you don't know Ralph; but you know Joan. I've seen her, and she doesn't look to me to be the sort of girl who'd do what she did with just anyone. I think we can agree that she must have cared a great deal for Ralph—and, had reason to believe he cared for her. I think this gives us grounds to hope that—" And what were the believings of a poor Joan worth? Except for her desperate foolish wanting to, what reason could she ever have had to believe Ralph cared for her?

Mr. Moore gestured with distraction, a movement of fending off the words that were always besting him, the defeating talk which had first frightened him out of the anger that was his only strength and now spoke smooth things, prophesied deceits. His small round eyes darkened with impotence. Thwartedly, his small mouth quivered. "Hope, hell!" he muttered.

He turned in eloquent inarticulateness, walked from the terrace through the hall door; and, his gait quickening, down the hall. A moment later, the front screen door closed after him with a slam.

Mrs. Pratt, still looking dazed, sat in an apparent anguish of deep unease or continued alarm, a breathlessness of persisting tonic distress which seemed to say that she found recovery from the irruptions into her fancy's world—a venomous snake in the overgrown old garden; in the house, in the pleasant shadows of the roofed terrace, an angry runt of an armed moron—of the unlovely world-as-it-is to be hard work. With a sharp rap or two, reality would seem to have shattered her crystal sphere of loving and believing, where, harmonious in diversity (concepts of one Divine Mind), room could be made for First and Last things, for supernal grace, for sacraments and sacramentals; but also for roses and the scent of crab apples, for costly gleaming motorcars and finest pelt cashmeres; but also for sexual musings, for thoughts a little sinful.

In this, her visional world, a fit entertainment and elegant had been projected. There was to have been a delicious drawn-out causerie, a conversation piece set against the golden slow hours of an afternoon in September, voices low in intimacy. With looks that traded delicate meaning, with subtleties of implication, with allusive fleeting smiles and not-unhappy sighs of significance—all would have come at length to who-could-say-what understanding of thoughts too rare for words, or even too deep for tears.

426

The entertainment was over, of necessity discontinued. After these breakings and enterings by fact, after the mischiefs fact was sure to have perpetrated on the premises, making the house of fancy habitable again would be, Arthur Winner was glad to guess, no work of a moment. With her fancy homeless, Mrs. Pratt was incapacitated. The result might be (happy thought!) to dispose of her as a present problem, in the same way that Mr. Moore's browbeaten swift wilting disposed of him. His part no longer playable, his fanciful notion of himself as the puissant angry man dispelled, there remained nothing for Mr. Moore to do but, muttering discontents, go home. Her part no longer playable, her fanciful notion of herself as the sage counselor, the wise spiritual mentor, the superior female of poise and wit dispelled, would there be anything for Mrs. Pratt to do but, perhaps faltering apologies, go home?

Arthur Winner trusted not; yet, as he felt a second easing of relief, he could feel relief tinged again with that same sympathy which (how much against his interests!) must regret all defeats of human hope—the sillier the hope, the sadder, in a sense, the dashing. The sadness was of the vain attempt, the sadness that turned irony's edge, that checked the earlier first inclination to laugh. Of course, a laugh, as well as unkind, would be unreasonable. The test the true believer had just flunked was only that often-flunked test of little things—*what, could ye not watch with me one hour?* No call was made on the religious feeling's sources of strength. For that reason, here, if nowhere else, *unfaithful in great things* did not follow from *unfaithful in little things.* To taunt Mrs. Pratt with her weakness of a fear she was silly to feel, with her foolishnesses of posturing, with her little lapses of delectation in off-color musings or smutty imaginings, would be the bootless business of taunting her with her humanity. This same humanity, when worked-on feelings had sufficiently inflamed the willing spirit, when emotional excitement anesthetized the weak flesh, could meet, the report was, uttering joy, the tyrant's brandished steel, the lion's gory mane.

Arthur Winner said: "I'm sorry you had to listen to all that. These situations don't submit themselves to—"

The forehead of the dazed sheep-face reddened around the coquettish curls. That tonic distress now entered Mrs. Pratt's large limpid eyes. Distress shook her voice a little. She said: "Arthur, is there a bathroom here I could use?"

Disconcerted—the distresses he had been supposing hers were only mental or spiritual—Arthur Winner said: "Why, yes. Of course—"

But this was really too bad of fact! At fact's surely unkindest prank of all, Arthur Winner must protest, generously indignant. Fact had right and license to punish fancy and to dash silly hope; but fact was always going too far, fact stooped too low! By any humane means, Arthur Winner was agreeable to being got out of more uncomfortable converse with Mrs. Pratt; but he had in mind her orderly withdrawal only, not a rout. For rout this was! Here, fact had the fact-shrinker by the short hairs. Mrs. Pratt held with being frank about physical love, yes; she found "sexual needs" easily mentionable, yes; but for the obvious good reason that fancy's transfigurations, the techniques of let's-pretend, could partly cope with, could to a degree dress up, arts and facts of love. Not fully, not entirely; since the Author of our beings (to assist to chastity, no doubt) had been pleased to provide, in the injurious patristic phrase, that these our lusts and those our filths should lodge together; yet, even so, a good deal of topical glossing could be achieved.

To love's eye, eager and appreciative, warm with appetite, *this* really could seem something like a vale of lilies; *that*—O, my America, my Newfoundland!—might offer convincing configurations of, and in trial prove genuinely to be, bliss's bower. For many such matters of fact, delightful terms were hit on without too great trouble. But how in the world of fancy did you put delightfully the human circumstance whose undressed substance was that Celia, Celia, Celia shits—or, even, that Mrs. Pratt most urgently requires to piss? Who, nurtured in fancy's world, ever kept the forthright face, the saving ordinary sense, to say: *So, what?*

Arthur Winner said: "Right in here." Moving promptly down the hall, he opened the door of the lavatory under the stairs and switched the lights on. "There you are," he said. "If

428

you don't mind, I've a telephone call I'd like to make. I'll be in the library."

In far Cathay, they were going on a journey—clearly, the Grand Panjandrum's progress, with shoulder-borne fancy litters and curtained palanquins; with troops of horse, bowmen in front, spearmen behind; with long lacy-edged slim banderoles flying. As their way passed above humped bridges, below walled compounds and pagodas with rising roof corners, under trees burgeoning fantastic foliage, the people of the procession were looked up to from glades of grass, from shallow streams, from miniature boats in deeper ponds, by a scattered quaint assortment of saucer-hatted peasants, wallowing water buffalo, and poling boatmen.

Looked at hundreds of times, familiar in every detail, the exotic scene which stretched across the closed lower doors of a small secretary-cabinet in gold and black lacquers went usually unnoticed by Arthur Winner. His eye was taken now. Some transmarginal apperception, puzzling on the infinite variety of human ideas and happenings, might have found, might have wished to call to his notice, a correspondence (some similar lack of any reasonable relation to ordinary life, to the trivial round, the common task?) between that remote painted never-never land of fantasy and this afternoon's so-recent acted fantasy—Mrs. Pratt's lusciousness of appearance and talk; his own troublous memories of lust; a murdered snake; an angry Mr. Moore.

The black lacquer's onetime shining jet was reduced to velvety duskiness by a gloom of misting. The lines of once-bright gold, though still distinct and fine, were delicately faint. Clarissa, like Hope before her, made use of the line of pigeonholes revealed by the let-down writing flap to store receipted bills, bank statements, and miscellaneous household papers. Nearby, drawn up beside a matching chair with decorated turnery and caned triangular seat, was the telephone stand.

Arthur Winner felt a fatigue of sorts, but that chair's elegant light construction, the delicate mortises and tenons, the old glu-

ing, was not for sitters of his size—a swift sad vista of memory
opened to show him Hope, just the slight right size, perched
there characteristically. In earnest attention, Hope tipped her
dark red head to the side. As a child might, she held the lifted
instrument to her face with both slender hands. Those lips of
charming shape, whose affectionate cool kisses were familiar to
Arthur Winner, poised themselves, parted, ready to respond.
After a moment, a not-forgotten voice, perhaps sympathetic,
perhaps mirthful, would break the silence of listening; speak,
lucid, into the mouthpiece. Standing, as his habit was, Arthur
Winner picked up the telephone.

Marigold Revere answered. Her voice, by reason of her growing deafness, loud and suspicious-sounding, said: "Who that?"

Loud in return, Arthur Winner said: "Mr. Winner, Marigold."

"Mister who? Wait, while I turn my aid on! Now."

"Winner."

"Oh, Mr. Winner; yes. Yes, sir! Miss Helen's up in her room.
I don't think she feels very good. She's taking a rest, I think.
You want to talk to her? This man came here; I think he's a
crazy man—"

"I know about the man," Arthur Winner said. "Don't disturb
Miss Helen if she's resting. Just tell her when she comes down
that I've seen Mr. Moore, and that's taken care of. There'll be
no more trouble with him. Is Ralph home?"

"No, he's not, Mr. Winner."

"Miss Helen said he was going to deliver some brushes.
When he comes back, would you please ask him to call me. I'm
at Roylan."

"Oh, he did that, Mr. Winner. He came back. It was only a
little while after that man left. Miss Helen was upstairs by then.
Ralph, what he said, I think he might be going out to see you,
sir. He took his car. I guess he thought he better see you. I
told him look out. I was telling him this man had been to look
for him, pretty mad. That's all I said; but after a while I saw
from the kitchen window his car go—"

Marigold, to her own mind privileged by faithful service that
went back to when Miss Helen was a baby, and assiduously all

430

eyes, and all, if now somewhat deaf ones, ears, wouldn't be long in peeping out any happenings at the Detweilers'. With her concern of well-intentioned curiosity, her inquisitiveness of anxiety, she must by now have put together most of what there was to know. A loyal discretion required her to maintain formal and official ignorance, since she had not been formally and officially apprised; but that didn't mean she couldn't dispense justice. Ralph, angel child though once he might have been, more recently was observed to be making Miss Helen worries. Look how he grieved her! Carrying on with girls, and all! Let *him* worry some!

Marigold said: "Only, about Miss Helen, you want me to stay to tell her, Mr. Winner? I was going out today; Miss Helen said I should; Mr. Ralph wasn't going to be in for supper, he was going to Eatontown, I don't know why; and she wasn't going to be in. It's Miss Keating's birthday, today; and they're giving a surprise party, having dinner at that Brookside restaurant, some of the ladies." (Poor Helen, Arthur Winner thought, must have needed to lie down; she couldn't be feeling much like parties.) "So I was to just go when I got ready, she said—"

Along with duties to which the attachment of years, and of her wages, bound her, Marigold had rights about which she was no less firm. Smiling, Arthur Winner said: "Oh, no; just leave a note for Miss Helen, if you will. Just say I talked to Mr. Moore after she saw him, and he won't make any more trouble. Say I'll be at Roylan, if she wants to call me. You said Ralph told you he was coming out here? When was that?"

"That was around half past two, Mr. Winner."

"I expect he'll be along pretty soon. In fact, I think I hear a car now—"

"Mr. Winner talk to Mr.—"

Arthur Winner spelled it for her.

"Yes, sir. I have it written. Good-by."

Arthur Winner put the telephone down. From the hall, faint and muffled, the discreet rush of sanitary waters in the lavatory reached him. Stepping to the window, he saw that he had been right; a car approached the house—but not Ralph Detweiler's.

431

Fred Dealey was driving in. Driving fast, Fred swept with impatient accuracy around Mrs. Pratt's car, giving it a stare as he went, and pulled to a sudden halt beyond. Getting out of the car, Fred proved to be wearing a loose gray sweat shirt and a pair of old army chino trousers that had on them partly laundered-out splashes of green paint. He took a file folder of papers from the car seat and knocked the door closed with a slam. Giving, his sharp chin up, a second stare to Mrs. Pratt's car, he strode toward the house.

Arthur Winner said: "Mrs. Pratt, this is Judge Dealey, of our county court—"

The afternoon, begun with so much enjoyment, must, for Mrs. Pratt, too, be ending in a discomfit of the fantastic—an unlimited fantasy of the not-foreseen, the improbable, the grotesque, the embarrassing. Emerging now from her retirement, she found the state of fantasy still in effect. Bewildered, she made a doubtful motion of her head to acknowledge the introduction. Her expression seemed to say that everyone knew a judge was an old man in a robe which he probably even wore to bed. Was this person with his trim, wiry, youthful appearance, his worn sweat shirt and paint-daubed pants some sort of imposter, for some mad reason now to be foisted on her? She supplemented the doubtful nod with an indistinguishable, almost protesting murmur. Swallowing to recover her voice, speaking with strain, she said to Arthur Winner: "I must go. I—could I see you alone for a minute?"

"Here!" Fred Dealey said. He moved his glance of cool astonishment from Mrs. Pratt. "I won't interrupt. I just brought over an opinion I was doing, Arthur. I didn't know you were busy. I'll leave it. Some other time—"

"Oh, please!" said Mrs. Pratt. "I have to go. I'm going—"

Inspecting her agitation with continued astonishment, Fred Dealey said: "First come, first serve! Simple as that! This is the end, I trust, of the Smillie estate. I'm going to have to hold against Noah, which he won't like; and I'd appreciate your

432

looking at it. I'm not handing down until the week after next—"

Arthur Winner said (not without haste!): "Wait, Fred. I'll be glad to look at it. I'll go out to Mrs. Pratt's car with her for a few minutes."

"Oh, thank you!" Mrs. Pratt said. Seemingly giddied to fatuousness by her relief, her eagerness to be elsewhere, she added vacantly: "I'm very pleased to have met you, Judge. I—"

What Fred had been doing was his never-too-good best to repress his contempt of astonishment, to stretch his limited patience. At this last straw of inaneness, he could no more! "Likewise, likewise!" he said, his tones as breathless as hers. "Your obedient servant, madam!"

Out of the house, moving down the path to the drive through the shadow play of the high sycamore leaves, renewed wind talking in them, Mrs. Pratt drew a breath. Perhaps, by Judge Dealey's short way with fools jolted into collecting herself; perhaps, on the other hand, having heard nothing more than a sound of speech from the imposter in the sweat shirt, she said composedly enough: "I oughtn't to have come, Arthur. I see now I've done harm, not good. You'll have to forgive me as well as Marjorie." Her smile was rueful. "I'm not prudent. I've never been. I talk too much."

The meek confession was disarming—though of course in humbly accusing herself, Mrs. Pratt half excused herself. The circumstance of being Mrs. Pratt was regrettable; but there you were! She, too, just couldn't help it, if, for a whim of no actually practical or exactly discernible purpose, a whim of what came down to relish of racy gossip, of intimate, delicately done scandalmongering, she was always being driven to make other people's business her business.

Arthur Winner said: "Good's been done if I've persuaded you Marjorie's quite wrong about feelings you say she imagines I have. I don't have them. Everything's long over. Let's agree, if she likes, that we were both to blame, and—" He had been about to go on: *say no more.*

Indeed, indeed, by him a consummation very devoutly to be

433

wished! Who, besides Mrs. Pratt, was never prudent? Who, as well as Mrs. Pratt, talked too much? What more, what next, might Marjorie's tumultuary pitch of religious—if it was—passion, her yearning to abase herself, her craving to be punished, compel her to?

Arthur Winner said: "Of course, I'm far from sure she ever could, in rightness or fairness, really be held to blame. Perhaps she planned; but how did she happen to plan? I think that's only more evidence of how little she was a free agent, how completely compulsions she hasn't the means to resist can take charge of her and keep charge of her—"

Turning the sheep-face, so singularly unmeaning, yet so full of expression, and now suddenly lighted, on him, Mrs. Pratt said: "Ah, Arthur, you understand that, I see! That's the bondage of sin we were born into. We aren't, of our own effort or will, able to extirpate what's part of us. To imagine that we are, insults God by saying we needed no redemption, by denying the justice of evil in our fallen state. God justly permits evil; but perhaps you see how mercy provides that even evil may be a good thing. By bringing unhappiness to us, evil teaches us to abandon ourselves to God. That's what's happening to Marjorie."

Mrs. Pratt had revived; and here, be it allowed, you saw a working, if in trifles, of a wonder, a little day of Pentecost. Mrs. Pratt's lips, able to move again with facility as the spirit gave her utterance, made haste to rehearse her formulas of solace. You watched a healing transformation perhaps analogous to those abrupt transformations brought about by antibiotics in physical medicine—at first, the doctors didn't believe their eyes! Medicine for our fitful fever, for that malady this life, had been given Mrs. Pratt; and the subjective response was nothing short of magical. She heard what comfortable words her Saviour Christ said unto all who truly turn to him. Ecstatic, she twittered: yes-yes; and mountains prepared themselves to be moved. The mere weak frightened longing of a moment back, the timid doubtful bare hope, in a jiffy became eternal imprescriptible truth. The young disease (that was to have subdued at length) appeared to check; the but-one-only miserable age-old upshot of

434

every man's story underwent revision, was immediately returned to read: Triumphing over death, and chance, and thee, O Time.

Not to wish a recovered spirit joy would be ungenerous; but renewed speaking in tongues could, if Arthur Winner didn't watch out, get them back to where they started, the weary empty debate on things unseen, beginning instead of ending. He'd better make an end; and if, before he did, he meant to try to do practical business, he'd better boggle no more and get to the point. He said: "I very earnestly hope that whatever's happening can mean for Marjorie a real solution, a way out of her emotional troubles. I gather the process is one of stages, meeting successive difficulties. I don't know whether you know, whether Marjorie said anything; but I talked to her a little while last night—"

Mrs. Pratt said: "Yes, she told me, Arthur. That was what made her so unhappy. Oh, not that you weren't kind; but she said she saw from what you said that you couldn't forgive her. She thought you thought she had no right to ask you—that's what started her drinking."

Arthur Winner almost said: *But she'd been drinking before she talked to me.* He said: "I can only repeat, she's quite wrong—"

Mrs. Pratt said: "Oh, I believe you, Arthur. You've shown me that she's wrong. That much I can do for her. I can tell her, reassure her. I will. And you're right about the stages, the difficulties—the labyrinthine ways, the poet said. They come from—"

Firmly interposing, Arthur Winner said: "I wanted to say that the stage at which she seems to be now, the stage at which she seemed to be last night, this blaming of herself, struck me, I'm afraid, as showing she was under one of those compulsions of hers. I'm a little concerned about how far the compulsion may carry her. I won't say I think her deranged; but I can imagine her, in her present state, doing—"

Mrs. Pratt said quickly: "Doing something to herself, taking her own life? There's no danger, Arthur. I'll tell you why; though I know you can't accept the idea. You see, what works in her is grace. Grace knows her needs. Grace may purge her,

435

even with fire; but grace will also always stand between her and the sin, despair—you'll see."

Arthur Winner said: "I hadn't thought of her killing herself. That, I think, isn't at all likely. A psychiatrist who'd come to testify in a case of mine once told me—and what I've seen since makes me think he wasn't wrong—that suicides, where they aren't acts of intelligent persons who may more or less reasonably prefer not to live incurably ill or financially ruined, are mostly committed by people who have emotions they can't express; or, what amounts to the same thing, who lose an emotional outlet they've become accustomed to and can't replace. So, yes; I can accept your idea in principle at least. I mean, whatever works in Marjorie provides the outlet—"

But this instructive reply, Arthur Winner must admit, was so much procrastinating. Being interrupted, he had been relieved; he found himself with half a mind to let the misunderstanding stand, to abandon a project, perhaps after all unnecessary, perhaps after all useless, and (no perhaps!) more than a little demeaning, more than a little humiliating, with such a smack of craven self-interest that any principal purpose other than self-interest's was hardly to be believed—even by himself, with his own knowledge of the nature of his own feeling. The distressed vibrating of the mind between the counsel to proceed as planned and that more comfortable counsel to drop the plan was almost immediately resolved—no doubt as his temperament dictated! Comfort was out of luck.

He said: "What I meant I could imagine was that Marjorie might do more than you, or the church, really required her to do. In her present state, she might feel, for instance, that she had to go to everyone she sees herself as having injured and confess what she did. I don't know how much of that sort of thing your beliefs may make necessary; but I'd be glad if she didn't have to, wasn't compelled to—let us say; ask Julius to forgive her. Unless, for reasons you and your church think good, she's expected to do that, by stopping her from doing it, you could, I think, avoid a great unkindness. We'll agree that the time to consider Julius was then, not now. But quite simply, I'm afraid that hearing about Marjorie and me would be a

436

severe blow to him. Of course, for my own sake I'd rather he didn't know; but I'd like to say, and I think I truthfully may, that I'd rather he didn't for his sake, too. Since Julius has always held people aren't to be trusted and only fools trust them, I'm sure he'd take it with composure, neither greatly shocked, nor even angry. Still, finding out he was right again would in this case probably hurt him a good deal. I would hope he needn't know. I believe both he and I would be glad if he didn't have to discover that what may very well be the one remaining person he continues to trust was really just like all the rest."

"And you want me to tell Marjorie that Julius needn't, mustn't know. You want me to keep her from going out of the way to do something that could only hurt him?"

"Yes," Arthur Winner said. "If your scheme of things makes that morally permissible, I do."

With a tender shine of the big soft eyes, Mrs. Pratt gave her head a gentle, incredulous shake. She said: "Poor Arthur! That's quite quaint of you; that's ever so likable of you!" She paused in an enjoyment clearly innocent, without malice or derision. She said: "It *is* hard for you to understand, isn't it?" She laughed indulgently. "You're thinking: Anyone who turns Catholic must really be out of her mind—why, she might do anything!"

Presented with what—in fact, if in simplified form—he did indeed think, would Arthur Winner deny that the laugh was only her due—well-timed; much called-for! So; privately he pooh-poohed as colored water Mrs. Pratt's marvelous nostrum! This peace of God, he said, passed all understanding. Was the implied reproach good? He alleged, perhaps, fraud and misrepresentation? What else had Mrs. Pratt and her upcast eyes ever said; the nostrum was plainly so labeled. And who was he? What prevented him from conceiving with Mrs. Pratt's entire success that he owned an immortal soul, or had an unbegotten Heavenly Father who could be pleasured into saving souls if sufficiently magnified, praised fulsomely enough, and propitiated with plenty of that cringing obedience Julius mentioned? A wiser head and sounder sense; or the accident of an unbelieving

437

temperament, questing and questioning? By his lights, he might be given reasonably to think Mrs. Pratt's grounds of action foolish, her world chimerical; but what gave him reasonably to think himself undeluded, his grounds of action, truth, whole truth, nothing but truth? Laughter was surely a good comment! And had somebody spoken of fraud and misrepresentation?

Perceiving that—if not, how—she had scored, that she had made him think again, or think twice, Mrs. Pratt pushed on happily. She said: "Oh, I know our faith must look mad to you, Arthur; but you'll find our practice quite, quite sane. You truly will!"

If only, in that magistral nostrum, this effusive unction weren't ingredient! If only, surprised by joy of man's desiring, the nostrum's imbibers weren't driven babblingly to share the transport! Must she, in her spiritual tipsiness, God-besotted, throw her generous arm around you? Though rejoicing with joy unspeakable and full of glory in her Caroline Dummer bliss, couldn't she keep from giggling to herself? No! How hard, then, to do her the justice her simplicity, her unthinking, her unmalice, entitled her to! Exuberant to teach, Mrs. Pratt went on—alas, you saw, could not help going on: "Where reparation's in one's power, one must make reparation, of course; and that would generally mean, or amount to, telling a person you'd wronged him. In penitence, you're bound to repair injury if you can— say, give back what you stole. But here there's no repair possible. Penitence can only see that the injury isn't repeated. Could an act of disclosure benefiting no one and hurting someone be a sane requirement? Our practice, Arthur, is almost the last sanity left in the world, you know."

How true, that you first found your faith and then your faith found you—*certum est, quia impossible est*—your arguments! *They* offered themselves not because *He* needed to receive; but —how true!—because *they* needed to give. Gently exhorting, Mrs. Pratt said: "Don't you see that charity—not to do hurt—is what, as a Catholic, Marjorie becomes first, and most, obligated to? Oh, dear; because she confessed to me, and tried to confess to you, have you been afraid she'd also be telling Julius? Only one situation could obligate her to tell him. What the chance of that is, you'll judge better than I could. Knowing Julius as you do, is he very likely, or very unlikely, to say someday to Marjorie: Were you at one time unfaithful to me with Arthur, my friend?"

Slipping a sudden hand into his, Mrs. Pratt closed her fingers, pressing his hand an instant. Turning, she opened the car door, and seated herself. She let the door click solidly closed. Almost silent, the big engine awoke. Mrs. Pratt, with a toss of her beret, said: "I'm going to pray for you, too, Arthur. Bless you—God bless you!"

Hardly making a sound, the car drew away. The final management, the exit line, Arthur Winner must allow, was not ineffective.

✦

Fred Dealey said: "Now, what in the name of God was that?" With a copy of yesterday's *Wall Street Journal* held open, he had been fixing a critical stare on the box of a Digest of Earnings Reports. He said: "Wish I'd bought steel when Roger Bartlett said to. Only, using what for money?" He tossed the paper down and looked at Arthur Winner.

"That was a friend of Marjorie Penrose's who wants to help," Arthur Winner said.

"Oh; *her!*" Fred Dealey said. "That one! Del met her once. The help is to be from heaven, I gather."

"Yes. And Marjorie being Marjorie, I think helping her that way may be feasible."

"And what are you supposed to do? This? Explain, when need arises, how feasible it is?" Fred Dealey shook his head. "You're really a kind of universal fall guy, Arthur! They all come to you." He frowned almost angrily. "And greatly to your credit, greatly! Philosophy and religion assure me that 'fall guy' is the righteous man's other name. I wish I had the knack. As things are, I tell myself—courtesy of Edmund Burke—I was not made for a minion or a tool. Meekness—that's the stuff! Who sells it? I'd really like to be nicer to more people—the stupid bastards! I really know they can't help the way they are. What do you do first?"

439

Arthur Winner laughed. "First," he said, "I think you have to want *them* to be nicer to *you*. Do you?"

"No," Fred Dealey said. He, too, laughed. "I'd know the damned hypocrites didn't mean a word they said. How could they?" He moved restlessly. "Anyone older than fifteen must have learned you can't change people—least of all, yourself. If you try, you get nowhere fast. So why not stop worrying? I don't know! I've spent most of the day worrying every few minutes about that idiot girl this morning. We certainly got nowhere fast with her! And quite rightly, quite rightly! That's the thing to do about things. Let them slide. Hope for the best. Maybe it'll turn out all right."

Fred Dealey jerked his chin up. "What do I suppose I'm being—ironic? Sagest counsel ever given! Del, I'm pleased to report, is enjoying the most thoroughgoing cramps today; and, believe it or not, after all, she doesn't mind—very cheery in her discomfort. She was only having me on with that darling little baby girl project. In short, cross your bridges when you come to them. Haste makes waste. Only suckers worry. Will I ever learn? Now I think of it—" he tapped the file folder he had laid on the table—"why am I worrying about this? I'm worrying because Noah's balled up on a trust question. But he couldn't be, you say. But he is. The rule against perpetuities excludes a specific, but not a general, appointment. Any second-year law-school man could tell you. And as if that weren't enough, two of his cases cited—Hogg's Estate, which is certainly ruling now; and another—hold exactly the opposite of what he's arguing—"

He broke off, staring at Arthur Winner. "Trying times, Arthur?" he said.

"A little," Arthur Winner said. "That can happen from the way Noah works. You probably remember. He notes his citations on different slips; and sometimes he mixes them up. For a while there hasn't been much Julius or I could do; but I think, from some things Noah said last night, he's beginning to realize himself, now—"

Bitterly, Fred Dealey said: "What fun that must be for him!"

"Yes; I thought of that," Arthur Winner said. "But I've come to wonder. That's putting yourself in his place. Things I've seen make me doubt if anyone but an old man can really put himself in an old man's place. Values seem to be different—I suppose; less and less matters to you. I hope so."

Fred Dealey said: "He taught me all the law I know. Well, the Learned Court's going to hand down. We're going to opine that Mr. Tuttle's amended argument is still without merit; and order that the prayer of within petition be granted and the rule issued thereon be made absolute—fall, chips, where they may! This is a very bright opinion by Dealey, J.; a very bright boy. Why am I trying to make you read it? Don't I know whether I'm right or not? Haven't you anything else to do?"

"No, I haven't," Arthur Winner said. "Except, Ralph Detweiler may stop by for a few minutes. I may as well tell you he got himself into trouble of sorts. A girl's charging him with attacking her. If you wondered, that's why I went down to Brocton last night. I won't go into it, since it could come before you; but I'll say I don't expect the charge to be made out. You'll hear about it soon enough."

"I *have* heard about it," Fred Dealey said. "Brophy told me. Your expectation seems to be his."

"Then I can say I expect to have ample evidence that the prosecutrix's reputation for chastity is bad; and Ralph's story stands up circumstantially, so, if it came to trial, I'd hope to be able to show that she consented. I'm sure she did."

"Brophy thinks she did, too," Fred Dealey said. "An outgiving of some interest to me, since he'd heard nothing but hearsay, and hadn't seen the prosecutrix. Deraignment by intuition, I guess! His attitude struck me as—well, novel. I gather the girl comes from down the county—Pole; Hungarian; or something. Admirable opportunity, I would have thought, for J. Jerome to make time with his large following there."

"How did Jerry happen to speak to you?"

"You know," Fred Dealey said, "I *thought* you'd ask that sooner or later! He needed, he averred, advice on a point of procedure. Brother, how right he was! Good thing he spoke to me—though, after our little tiff this morning, I was surprised he did—instead of Willard. Willard thinks people ought to know what they're doing, even when not in the men's room. I doubt if he'd have bothered to be as nice as I was. Anyway, this will make agreeable hearing for you. Brophy's problem, in brief; how to get Ralph's case dismissed."

Fred Dealey looked at Arthur Winner. "Yes," he said. "I'm aware that to deliver the innocent is as much the duty of a public prosecutor as to incarcerate the guilty. Has Ralph, by some chance, powerful political influence with the young reformatory set down at the Old Timbers Tavern? What the *quid* is, I don't pretend to know; but the *quo* was: did I see any objection to telling Squire Harbison that he, Harbison, might as well discharge accused—you can imagine how that pompous little squirt would react—because he, the district attorney, had investigated, and the complaint was groundless. The girl was just lying; so any return of Harbison's would simply be nol-prossed. Of course, entering a nolle prosequi required the so-called approbation of the court; Brophy did know that much. In view of his feeling there was no case, how would I like to approbate?"

"Well—" said Arthur Winner.

"Yes; well!" Fred Dealey said. "So I spelled the thing out for him. In the first place, nothing was before *me* et cetera, et cetera. In the second place, a committing magistrate was an independent judicial officer. If a man attempted to influence a magistrate's determinations by means other than testimony offered at a hearing, that was embracery; and his being district attorney made him no different from any person so attempting, et cetera. A statutory charge brought in proper form pended before competent authority. Failing voluntary withdrawal, the charge could in no way be dropped, dismissed, quashed, nol-prossed, or otherwise got rid of unheard. Had he, I didn't ask, lost his reason? This kind of thing, I didn't say, wearies me."

Arthur Winner said: "Well, I can see how the point might never have come up before—as far as Jerry went. I suppose it's only in homicide cases that he ever has any occasion to work with justices of the peace; and there he knows he's expected to get in as soon as he can and more or less take over. A magistrate being what he usually is, I don't doubt Jerry's in the habit of telling him what to do—who'll be heard; what he wants in the transcript and return; and so on."

442

"A generous view," Fred Dealey said.

"Well, he might argue that if he has the responsibility and right, because he'll be prosecuting, to get himself what he'll need in one case, why hasn't he the right to decide he hasn't got what he needs in another? If he concludes he hasn't, why not so advise Joe Harbison and save everybody a lot of time and trouble. I'll agree that deciding that with no hearing's improper; but I don't know that the idea's very unreasonable."

"A Daniel come to judgment!" Fred Dealey gave him a grin. "My first duty as an attorney is to my client!" he said, rolling his eyes as though in recitation. "If there's a charge lodged against him, and someone's trying to get the charge dismissed, you bet your life I don't know that the idea's unreasonable! If the scheme afoot was one I thought would work, I doubt if I'd even know it was improper. In the line of duty, a counselor at law may excusably not know a good deal. On the bench, I can't excusably not know anything that's knowable. The state's peace and dignity's my client; and while I'm retained, I must put that interest first. And if I really did, I'm not sure I shouldn't be causing friend Brophy to be proceeded against for mis-, mal-, and nonfeasance: to wit; posing as learned in the law in order wrongfully to enjoy emoluments of an elective office."

Arthur Winner laughed. "Jerry strikes me as a good-enough prosecutor. Small points trip him sometimes, I know; but I haven't heard any complaint about delays in the district attorney's office; and he also seems to get a lot of convictions. I don't think more than two defendants were acquitted by juries last term, were they? I'd say that almost had to mean he can prepare a case and knows what he's doing when he presents it. Of course, I've never been up against him, I mean in a criminal action, because, except for a couple of guilty pleas, I haven't taken any criminal cases since he's been district attorney; but I've watched him occasionally—"

"I've had the obligation to watch him plenty, woe is me!" Fred Dealey said. "Perhaps he *can* try a case; and when defendant's guilty as hell, as he usually is, get him convicted—though you might remember that Garret Hughes and Phil Larkin between them prosecute a good deal more than half of every list.

That doesn't take too much law. The law's for the court; Brophy only has to repeat the facts, overstating them a little, and remember not to do or say a few things that might get a juror withdrawn. But, knowing what he's doing is exactly what it doesn't mean—he just plays a kind of game he taught himself. Things like this show you. I don't say he ought to know every word of every statute—who does? We all have to look the law up. But the thing about Brophy, the thing that stops me about him, is that he's always showing you he doesn't even understand the principles—he doesn't know, he has no idea, he has to ask, what's proper and what's improper."

"Well, at least, he *does* ask," Arthur Winner said.

"Yes; mighty white of him!" Fred Dealey said. "I'll now tell you what you may not know yet. Lawman Brophy's been busy for a week—since the word about a fourth judge came through —looking for strings to pull, and burrowing around the bar association to line up people to recommend him for the interim appointment. Top that, if you can, for sheer damned impudence! Judge Brophy! I'd admire to hear him rule! He could be trusted to work more reversible error in half an hour— I tell you, Arthur, if we're going to have political judges, bring politics to the bench, I won't sit. And I'm sure that would go for Mac McAllister, too. Willard's been saying he wanted to retire for a long time; so I know he wouldn't stay. If that's the kind of court that's shaping up, let Brophy stack it to suit him."

Arthur Winner said: "Well, now, I thought your Honor's client was the state's peace and dignity. If a man you think isn't competent comes on the bench, do you see it as serviceable for those who *are* competent to leave?"

"That was a lot of crap, of course—that peace and dignity speech," Fred Dealey said moodily. "And, I guess; so's the I-quit speech. But has he one damn single qualification you can see?"

"Yes; I see one," Arthur Winner said. "He talked to me. He wants to be a judge. He wants to be a judge very much. He has a reason."

"His reasons wouldn't exactly bewilder me," Fred Dealey said. "Just tell me what the wants of a graduated ward heeler have to do with qualification."

444

"In this case, a good deal," Arthur Winner said. "It was before your time, but I suppose you know Jerry's father kept a saloon on Water Street."

"Seems likely," Fred Dealey said. "Ah; I get the point! Liquor and law! Both begin with 'l.'"

The poor sarcasm, the glancing gibe, were recognizable to Arthur Winner. They broke from Fred against his intention, manifesting the syndrome in him of angered pity whose component symptoms—he'd really like to be nicer to people!—were reactions entirely automatic. Impatience to find that fools must still be suffered provoked him; indignation at the unfairness of the fact (could they help it?) that fools must still suffer provoked him. While Fred's tongue, turned bitter, spoke to any such point, his bitter eye shone bright in an irate general denouncement. He found angry fault with the intractability of circumstances, the random brute works of mischance, the callous uncaring of whatever superintendent force might be supposed to rule the world. Let whoever arranged it, go to hell! Let whatever originated it, take this creation and shove it—the vitriolic passion of outrage quickly reaching the level where Fred's sharp mind must detect and reject its excess of unreason, Fred, as was his practice, stopped short. His eye veiled with embarrassment, with the chagrin of having to agree that this was a damned silly way to talk—or, to think! Now what fool, simultaneously suffering and insufferable, had allowed feeling once again to make a fool of him?

Arthur Winner said: "Yes; I daresay that was exactly it—just that; that's all the two did have in common. He was going to get away from Water Street. He wasn't exactly a poor boy. His father was in a position to let him go to law school, put him through law school, though I don't think his father ever understood Jerry's idea. A saloon—at that time it was a speak-easy—could turn up a lot of business for a lawyer, so why not have one in the family? Anyway, Jerry must have seen very soon that a law degree, being admitted to the bar, hadn't got him where he wanted to go. Representing saloon patrons of his father's up for assault and battery wasn't the idea at all. He'd try politics, get into public office, and they'd have to respect him. Of

445

course he was a born politician. The chairman of the county committee then was Nelson Eubank—you remember him. *He* wasn't a politician; he lasted at the job only as long as there really weren't any Democrats anyway; but he had just sense enough to know a politician when he saw one—"

"Yes, yes," Fred Dealey said. "Like me. I don't know how it's done—I suppose, because I don't want to—but demonstrably, J. Jerome can do the necessary. And I know somebody has to do it; and, whoever he is, very likely he has to be the least little bit of a crook—nothing serious, of course. Nobody ever catches you with your hand in the till—nothing obvious. In short, since I know who keeps me elected, hollering: stop, thief! would ill beseem me. I should not denigrate the ox who's treading out the corn. I grant that Brophy's labor may be what leaves me so free to keep my nose nice and clean. Let him labor on; but, damn it, we don't have to make him a judge, too. This bench has standards. Think back! Lauderdale; Taylor; White; Gammack—perhaps they weren't all legal giants; perhaps *all* the present incumbents aren't, either. But they damn well knew their law; and they damn well knew their dignity; and they damn well kept judicial office out of politics."

Arthur Winner said: "You're not getting the idea, Fred—well, I didn't myself until Jerry let me see what he had in mind. The one thing you can be perfectly certain of, that I'd even undertake to promise you, is that Jerry won't bring any politics on the bench. He'll be the least political judge who ever sat."

"And may I ask why in God's name you imagine that? Has he ever done anything that wasn't political?"

Arthur Winner said patiently: "I don't imagine it, I know it. Because he *has* to get away from Water Street. He's tried everything else; so the saloonkeeper's boy *has* to be a judge. And I mean, and he means, a judge; not what you call the least little bit of a crook in judicial office. This is an obsession, one of those things that take a person over. You aren't free to choose. If I understand what a religious vocation is, I suppose this is something like that."

"A religious—for Jesus' sake!" Fred Dealey said. "Excuse me! I must start reforming my language, stop blaspheming. I let slip

446

an expression last night your rector had to reprove me for. Wait while I check this. J. Jerome is going to be a judge for religious reasons—"

"No," Arthur Winner said. "He's going to be a judge because he *has* to be a judge. You and everybody else may find it incredible; it may not be in character; it may not make sense—" He hesitated.

And Mrs. Pratt *had* to be a babbling believer, and so became one? And Helen, poor girl, *had* to be to Ralph—where was that brat, anyway?—a more-than-mother, and so made herself one? And (let's hush it up!) Arthur Winner, for all his temperate reflective airs, for all his aptness at moderation in thought and speech, *had* to be a onetime adulterer, and so (not in character; not making sense!) was? Exactly—of necessity, and so of choice; the choice of no choice! He said: "When that's the case with you, you can't help yourself; you can't stop. And usually, I think, you can't be stopped; because the opposition's opposition will seldom or never amount to an obsession, too. To get that appointment, there's nothing Jerry hasn't done, or isn't doing, or won't do. People who don't like the idea of him as a judge aren't going to work that hard."

"Make me understand," Fred Dealey said. "Why? Why? He *has* to be a judge. And not because he thinks he could play politics better. Then, why? What else could he want? Do you know?"

"Yes, I believe I do," Arthur Winner said. "It's all Water Street. He has to prove something. Julius was speaking of that last night when I told him about Ralph's business. Julius thought, like you, that Jerry might be expected to go all out to get a conviction, though not because of the Mechanicsville vote. He suggested Jerry might like to get even with certain people in Brocton, that sending someone named Detweiler to jail might be a real pleasure to him."

"I can see that, all right," Fred Dealey said.

"Yes; there would have been the day when, as a boy, he found out what so-called respectable people, as opposed to the saloon customers, really thought of his father and his father's business. When you're hurt that way, several responses are possible—for instance; who cares what they think?—but Jerry's response was

447

that he'd show them. So he left Water Street and went to law school; but, from time to time, he must have kept finding out what the same sort of people kept thinking, or kept taking for granted, about him. He was a lawyer, an educated man, yes; but since lawyers can be shysters, they naturally presumed he was a shyster. All right, he'd get political power, and make them respect him. Only that wasn't how it worked. Instead of respecting him, they simply, while asking him to use his power for them, held him cheap for having it."

Fred Dealey said: "I didn't say my attitude was admirable. Using him and at the same time being unpleasant to him isn't nice. I guess that's something I *have* to do. I richly deserve it, if he hates my guts. I wouldn't expect him not to try to get even with me if he could."

Arthur Winner said: "Well, granted he might be moved to try to get even with a number of people, there's the point of how he'd get even. Send Ralph to jail? Last night, I thought Julius might be right; but I didn't know then some things I know now. You have to realize, as I didn't, that Jerry knows anyone like Julius *would* think that. If Jerry 'got even' that way, what would he be? Just what they always said he was—a cheap little shyster trying to get back at his betters. No; the saloonkeeper's boy will show them yet! How will he show them? He'll get out of politics. He'll be a judge, whether they want him or not; and what's more, he'll be as good a judge as any on the bench. If he needs to know more law, he'll learn more law. He'll work like a dog. His judicial conduct will be beyond reproach, his integrity will be above suspicion. He's no friend of people like you, or Willard, or Mac McAllister; and he doesn't expect his fellow judges to be friends of his. This is strictly emulous. He doesn't want to join you; he wants to lick you. If it's the last thing he does, he's going to make you take back what you may not have said, but what he knows you think. That's all; that's why."

"Forgive me if I can't believe that's all, or why," Fred Dealey said. "I *could* believe he might think being called your Honor would be fine—the sap! I *could* believe he—or more likely that wife of his—wants to go social or something; yes. Have you thought of that?"

"I have," Arthur Winner said. "But I happen to know it won't do. I've been told in confidence that Jerry was approached not long ago about joining the Union League. He turned down the bid. He explained that joining might hurt him politically in the lower county. This was to Roger Bartlett; who, of course, isn't too quick; and, anyway, wouldn't have dreamed Jerry was making fun of him. Having talked to Jerry, I know that that's just what Jerry was doing. He didn't care to give his real reason; so he amused himself by telling Roger the sort of thing people like Roger were always ready to believe." Arthur Winner smiled. "It showed more of a sense of humor than I thought Jerry had. I think it showed at the same time he wasn't interested in, as you say, going social."

"Well—" Fred Dealey said. He paused rebelliously. "That could also show he knows the Union League's dead on its feet. Joining costs money; and what do you get?"

"No," Arthur Winner said. "The real reason went to the point of his joke—what people were ready to believe about him. Roger, probably bumbling along, was saying: We know a Water Street boy would like to get in here. We'll overlook the fact you don't belong and we don't want you, though naturally we never would overlook that if the membership wasn't dropping and we didn't need more dues-payers. So, we've agreed to let you say you're a member of the Union League. Jerry, of course, understood him perfectly. The chance was pretty ignominious, but what Water Street boy wouldn't jump at it—proving, of course, that he *was* a Water Street boy. Since Jerry's out to prove exactly the opposite, there'd never been the faintest chance he'd consider joining. He has to be the real thing, or nothing. That's why, if he can get the appointment—and you'll find he can—he's going to drop his political connections and he's going to be a working judge; and as good a one as work can make him. And you, as I say, are going to have to admit it, much as you'll hate to. That's how he's going to get even."

"Or," Fred Dealey said, "if I'm such a stuck-up bastard I

449

won't admit it, I'll have to know at least that I'm also a dirty bastard, and an unfair one."

"Very well put," Arthur Winner said.

Fred Dealey sighed. "The order's large," he said. "I'll see what I can do." He paused. "You believe all that, don't you, Arthur? Well, everybody says you're kind. Everybody says you're wise, too. And damned if I'm not persuaded you're both! Do you realize what, I regret to say, crossed my mind when you started explaining about Brophy?"

"I don't believe so," Arthur Winner said.

"Then, I sure as hell won't ever let you find out," Fred Dealey said. "Look, there's a car. Is that our young fornicator?"

Moving to the windows, Arthur Winner said: "The car's certainly not Ralph's. It looks like—well, it is, Elmer Abbott. Oh, Lord, I know what this means! Could I be so tied up with you I can't see him right now? I suppose not. He's going to tell me about some differences he's having with the rector."

"Of course he is," Fred Dealey said. "Of course he is! Proceed, fall guy; get caught in the middle again! I'll yield the floor. May I leave my opinion? If you get a chance to look at it between now and Monday, I wish you would. The points from Noah's brief deemed crucial by me are quoted—with emphasis supplied." He smiled thinly. "I'm satisfied that Noah's just as wrong as hell—er—as *heck;* but I'd be glad to have you agree before I hand down. Here; I'll sneak out the back. Nances and I don't get on."

"Elmer's not really that," Arthur Winner said. "That was gone into once very thoroughly. Some people thought he was paying too much attention to his choirboys. I happened to be one of the ones who investigated, and there was nothing to it. He was perfectly innocent—a perfectly reasonable attention to boys he thought promising, and hoped to interest in musical careers. He has unfortunate mannerisms—"

"I'll say he has!" Fred Dealey said.

SIX

"Aʀᴛʜᴜʀ," Elmer Abbott said, "I've really never been spoken to that way in my life! I'm terribly upset!"

As the case so often was when an excitement of feeling possessed him, Elmer Abbott's voice rose toward a tremulous falsetto. As the case so often was, he writhed with a sort of frustrate impotence. He wobbled his head to toss from his high white brow that lock of his too-long, now graying hair that had a habit of falling forward. He displayed his slender-fingered but plump-palmed hands as though about to wring them.

With the Fred Dealeys of this world, men not unfair, not unjust, in their determinings; but knowing the world's ways, and seldom long-suffering, an Elmer Abbott understandably couldn't win. Were those "unfortunate mannerisms" only excesses of affectation? An intelligent man had no patience with that kind of nonsense. Were they, to the contrary, quite unaffected, the natural and all-too-suggestive demonstrations of the incorrectness of a nature with which Elmer Abbott had been born and must live? A manly man then liked them still less. His hostile eye surveyed that weak wilting stance, that unrobust yet fleshy physique. He observed that walk, that sinuous carriage that twitched the full buttocks now right a little, now left a little. He noted the girlish animation of gesture. He heard that far-from-virile voice dramatizing its mannered rushes of my-dear-too-too talk by unexpected suspensive pauses and sudden intense emphasizings. The goddamn fairy! He had half a mind, just on general principles—

Elmer Abbott said: "After all, one's a gentleman; and one expects those one associates with to be gentlemen."

Yes; after all! Elmer's mother was an Orcutt; and to Elmer had, in due course, descended his portion of that patent water-closet bowl wealth. By profits, one was created gentleman. They entitled an Orcutt to stand first in what good society Brocton could show; just as in metropolitan society those who bore once-lowly names of a scow-boatman or a pedlar with a pack, dubbed gentle by profits even greater, had their warrant to queen or king it over their special subjects, the four hundred or so people proposed as fit for them to know.

Elmer Abbott said: "Certainly I think one has the right to expect one's rector to be a gentleman. He's supposed to come of very good people. His mother seems to be a lady. I can't understand it. No person of breeding would speak that way—ordering me around like a servant!"

Arthur Winner said: "I don't believe Doctor Trowbridge intended that at all—"

"So much the worse!" Elmer Abbott said. "After all, we know a gentleman's been defined as a person who's never rude unintentionally. I'm really very much upset, Arthur. I've given myself time to think about it, making what allowances I could, and I'm still upset. It isn't that I question his right as rector to give directions. I object to his manner. I feel some consideration is owed me for my services at Christ Church—for which, after all, I've never accepted a penny. Quite the opposite! At my own expense, I've had the organ kept in condition. I've furnished our musical library with many, many scores and parts for the choir. I've been glad to. I'm not asking for thanks—"

Arthur Winner said: "I think Doctor Trowbridge does appreciate that, Elmer. He was talking to me just before he went in to talk to you this morning; and I know he meant to do nothing but tell you what his wishes were about the use of the carillon. He felt, as he must have told you, that the hour should be fixed. Since that's really not unreasonable—I mean, when it's heard at odd times, as this morning, people don't know what to make of it—I, frankly, feel his wishes should be deferred to."

Elmer Abbott said: "I offered to explain that, Arthur. That was part of his unexampled rudeness. As a matter of fact, I

452

was ringing the carillon for a very good reason. There'd been trouble with a circuit breaker, and I'd had an electrician check it. I was merely making certain that the carillon manual was functioning properly. He chose not to hear any explanation. He said, in effect, my reason didn't matter; he simply required me not to do it again. No; I'm not deceived, Arthur. He didn't berate me the way he did merely because I was trying the carillon briefly. It's quite plain. He hopes, by being unpleasant to me, to get rid of me; and I suppose in the end, he'll succeed." He spoke with a sad fatality. "Of course, we all know why."

"I don't," Arthur Winner said. "Unless you and he really find you can't agree, and I see no reason for you to find that—"

"Well, you *do* know why, Arthur—none better! It's the same thing." With a not-unimpressive gravity of stoicism Elmer's voice grew firmer. "And I know. I know I'm not like other men. I'd be very silly if I tried to be, wouldn't I? I know what people are likely to think. That's my misfortune. But he might do me the fairness of not judging me out of hand, without trying to find out whether there's any truth in what he may think. I consider it most uncharitable of him, most unfitting his cloth, to assume with absolutely no proof, that because I'm different I'm also immoral. Oh, I'm used to that, of course. After all, you aren't likely to have forgotten that time under Doctor Ives when those slanderous rumors were spread about me; and you may be sure I haven't. I know I owed it to you that I was allowed any sort of hearing. No matter how falsely he's accused, a man's usually not permitted to defend himself. There are always some intolerant people who get a pleasure out of persecuting him, even with physical violence—when they haven't any evidence, they'll even tell boys what to accuse him of; trump up evidence—"

Elmer Abbott's voice wavered a little. Though no such things had happened to *him*, he had, no doubt, a fascinated frightened interest in anything he read or heard of such persecutions. Brought to blurt out these known ugly, hateful possibilities, hearing his own words with his own ears, Elmer Abbott could be seen to lose that somewhat unexpected brief dignity of stoicism.

453

He panicked faintly, swallowing against flutters of womanish near hysteria as he thought of fate's wholesale unfairness to him—those ever-possible actual perils, the brutal persecutors, the punishing blows; the never-relieved apprehensions he must in consequence wake up to every morning; the daily weary weight of the not-often-expressed, yet seldom absent, vilipending of hostility or contempt in almost all his fellow men; and, perhaps, the (for all Arthur Winner could tell, harder to support) occasional disturbing advances to him in that freemasonry of knowing, natural companions, which Elmer, whether, as he implied, out of moral scruple, whether, as Arthur Winner thought just as possible, out of a paralyzing timidity combined with maiden distaste for the physical, was obliged to reject.

Counting over these cruelties and harassments so wantonly visited on one who sought, as Elmer himself would say, to live only for music, the tears of an unhappiness of self-pity welled in Elmer's pale eyes. And even there, in the music he lived for, his remaining refuge, could Elmer know secretly (could he help knowing?) of another of fate's unfairnesses, a final refinement of fate's unkindness? No musician himself, Arthur Winner ventured no personal opinion, but he knew the opinion of those who were musicians and competent to judge was unanimously that Elmer was not much of a musician—a mechanically adequate but altogether mediocre performer, with a taste so limited or aesthetically uncomprehending that (Arthur Winner remembered the overheard remark) any hymn tune was as much music to Elmer as the Ninth Symphony.

Elmer Abbott said: "Arthur, you can't imagine how unfair people are! The measure of it's that there's not one other person in Brocton, not one, I could come to for any understanding but you. They wouldn't listen to me; they wouldn't help me if they could. I know Doctor Trowbridge is going on with this, unless someone will take my part. And I know that once others grasp his attitude, they'll start talking—just the way it was before; and then he'll say he can't have people talking, that people are saying: Where there's smoke, there's fire. I've never known who started the talk that other time; but someone who

454

always wants to believe the worst must have passed on what he liked to believe as though he knew it was true—"

But, there, Elmer Abbott was mistaken. That person, never known to Elmer, was very far from always, or even ever, wanting to believe the worst. Belief, not liked but hated, and not invented, not imagined, had forced itself on that person. Arthur Winner could say so with conviction, for the person, to Elmer forever to be unknown, who first worried about Elmer Abbott and his choirboys, or at any rate, who first definitely voiced the suspicion that led, really drove, Arthur Winner and others—his father; Willard Lowe; Russ Polhemus; Doctor Ives—to make the thorough investigation of Elmer, his life and his habits, happened to be Hope Winner.

Now, as then, the idea of Hope being the one to become persuaded that Elmer Abbott was impairing the morals of minors, the one to denounce him to her husband, was startling. Hope would surely be the last person in the world to suspect somebody of sodomy. To form this suspicion you required (didn't you?) a good working knowledge of certain indecent—indeed, to the virtuous, vile!—acts and practices; what exactly they consisted in; how they were performed and under what conditions they were most likely to be performed. They were acts and practices that Hope, it seemed safe to say, could only know of in the sense that once or twice she might have *heard* of them vaguely. She would have heard of them with so much shrinking, with so much vestal aversion, that, the odds were, she would never quite let herself believe men actually *did* such things.

Yet, of course, considered another way, a somewhat ironic way, Hope's being the one was perfectly natural. The absurd, if also painful, comedy of errors to be played depended on that very innocence of Hope's, Hope's shocked aversion which would not look too close, Hope's retained ignorance of the world sensual, the world sexual, the world vile. With many other women —with, say, Betty Polhemus as a pertinent example—that par-

455

ticular comedy couldn't have been played. Hope *had* to be the one. The example of Betty Polhemus was pertinent because Elmer Abbott's evil habits, if any, must concern her for the same reason that they concerned Hope. At that time, like Lawrence Winner, Betty's son Martin sang in the choir. Like Lawrence, he was one of the boys frequently invited to Mr. Abbott's house, where Mr. Abbott lavished refreshments on them. These enjoyable feeds, held in Mr. Abbott's artistically furnished living room, were lighted by large candles. While his guests stuffed themselves, Mr. Abbott played records for them, burned incense; and presided in an elaborate Japanese kimono, a treasure he had brought back from Nagasaki, port of call on a world cruise he once took. About these gatherings there was nothing concealed or clandestine—Martin unhesitatingly described them to his mother; who, in turn, had often laughed about them to Hope. In short, Betty saw them simply as harmless, la-di-da expressions of Mr. Abbott's well-known Artistic Temperament. She thought nothing of them.

A Betty Polhemus's instinct, Arthur Winner was to reflect afterward—another trifle accreting to the sum of results observed that sometimes *does* make older men wiser—could safely have been relied on. Betty, a hefty, hearty girl whose vigorous acceptance of life had no nonsense about it; Betty, a woman a great deal earthier and saltier than Hope—Betty was known to like a dirty story; though, of course, only if it was *really* funny—would have tumbled in no time to what was going on, if anything were. Instinct could be observed to have told Betty with all definiteness not to worry. The somewhat question-raising trappings, the candles, incense, fancy dress, were here significant merely in making Mr. Abbott out a sissy. Betty was satisfied that they did not make him out a pederast—or, at least, not a conscious, designing, practicing one.

The latest of these spreads reported by Martin to his mother had been no different in most respects from any of the others; but Martin did happen to say that the guests, numbered, as well as Lawrence Winner, Lawrence's brother, Warren. This circumstance might be thought remarkable for several reasons. True, Warren was a onetime member of the choir; but, even before his voice changed, Warren had (naturally) proved himself unamenable to Mr. Abbott's fussy small rules and regulations. Finding occasion to tell Mr. Abbott to go to hell, Warren was told in return that he was through. That, of course, was several years back; and, no longer personally responsible for Warren, Mr. Abbott might consider bygones bygones and feel perfectly friendly. But the question of why Warren, older than the others, and set apart from them by the fact he was now away at school, only home for the spring vacation, would consent to attend such a contemptible little-boy social function was hard to answer.

By some casual chance, Betty had mentioned Warren's presence at the party to Hope; and to Hope that question no doubt posed itself—she hadn't known Warren was there; and it certainly didn't seem like Warren; but since complaints about Warren's behavior weren't involved, Hope might have been ready to leave it at that, the question forever unresolved, but for the accident that, a couple of days later, this party was again brought to Hope's attention. What brought it to her attention was a clearvoiced comment of Martin Polhemus's, made to Lawrence Winner while Martin, out at Roylan for a wet Saturday, was looking at lead soldiers in Lawrence's room. The party must somehow have come up. There was a certain amount of exclaiming and chortling as this or that was remembered. Martin Polhemus then said with animation: *And did you see the way Abby was sucking up to him, kissing Warren's ass!*

Yes; the joke-to-be, the imminent comedy of errors had a good joke's virtue of simplicity. Such figures of speech were naturally not familiar to Hope; but even the nicest mind had to know what "ass" was a vulgar term for. Nice minds could (Hope made plain) go further; could, from some assignment of confused, only half-understood yet privately comprehended connotations, take a dreadful meaning from that "sucking up," take the statement in the word-by-word, literal, primary, unidiomatic, horrible sense. That sense taken, recoil as she might, Hope, with maternal fierceness to defend her young, saw what must be done. Greatly distraught, she conveyed in shaking paraphrase what she had learned about Elmer Abbott—his kissing boys; it was too horrid

457

to talk about! Warren was one of them—to her husband as soon as he came home that evening. He must do something drastic right away!

Of course a man must! Was Elmer's self-pitying complaint about the unfairness of prejudice, the unfairness of people, well founded, or not well founded? Need a distraught Hope develop her unpleasant subject more specifically? Hope need not! Had the reflective, careful lawyer objected that all this was hearsay, of no evidential value? No! In what Elmer Abbott looked and sounded like, he conceived that he had, and had long had, a full substantiation of the charge. Of course! He should have known. Habits of professional consideration caused him to say equitably enough: *Before doing anything else we must make sure this is true.* Certainly, as Elmer said, he purposed to let Elmer have a hearing; but was Arthur Winner's mind, at that moment, really open? At that moment, did he so much as remotely consider the possibility of Hope's being mistaken, of Hope's having misunderstood? He did not! He got around to that only after ten days had passed, and much had happened—most of it going to exculpate Elmer; and so, of course, in one way good; yet, in another, not unembarrassing to the prudent investigators. Relieved, but also baffled, Arthur Winner thought to come back to where he started. Pressed, told the importance, Hope at last repeated, in the exact words, what she had heard.

There had been prudent investigators (plural) because Arthur Winner suspected (and, again; what evidence had he? He simply went by the cases occasionally coming into court) this thing might be widespread, with many boys involved; and he concluded against proceeding alone. Arthur Winner spoke to his father, who agreed that Russ Polhemus ought to be told. Willard Lowe would be a good man to admit to any discussions about what to do. The four of them then decided, perhaps unfortunately, that the rector must be informed. Doctor Ives, while in general trusty and prudent enough, maintained that, in righteousness, Elmer Abbott should not be moved against secretly, unwarned that he was a subject of investigation. The first thing to do, as the others saw it, was question boys involved or possibly involved. Doctor Ives was adamant. *First,* Mr. Abbott must be told these charges had been made. He must be asked whether they were true. Doctor Ives went personally to Elmer, and came back with what Arthur Winner judged to have been a tearful, even hysterical, denial.

Now to question some of the boys. Russ would talk to Martin. To his sons, Arthur Winner spoke separately. Lawrence, well taught to tell the truth, was not ten minutes in convincing his father that he couldn't have been involved; he didn't so much as understand what his father was getting at. The talk with Warren, not to Arthur Winner's surprise, went less easily. Warren, in his customary self-contained indifference to authority, paternal or other, answered with scornful bare civility—a half-shrugged yes; a half-shrugged no. Why had he gone to Mr. Abbott's? He went for a free feed; Mr. Abbott met him on the street and asked him. No; Mr. Abbott never was out of the room with any of the boys. No; he didn't see Mr. Abbott touch any of them. Yes; he stayed a while after the others left. Mr. Abbott was showing him a book. What book? A book of pictures of ships. No; Mr. Abbott didn't put his arm around him. Had Mr. Abbott ever kissed him? Giving his father a look, Warren said: *I'd like to see him!*

Right; Warren would! Here *was* surprise; at that look, those words, the mind rocked with revelation, with the falling of things into place and pattern. *Ex pede Herculem*—the shock was recognition's shock. With consternation, deeply jolted, Arthur Winner had been given, in the space of that answer, to know the whole plan of that young savage, his son. Indeed, the consternation was complete—in Warren, in a schoolboy, in yesterday's no more than naughty, disobedient child, you could glimpse a well-grown unmoral ruthlessness—yes, a depravity; yes, a competent calm villainy (enter a murderer!) beside which slips of sexual misconduct must amount to nothing worse than misdemeanors. Why did Warren go to Mr. Abbott's house? At school, Warren must have heard about Elmer Abbotts; and he remembered he knew one at home. Warren planned to see if Mr. Abbott could be lured into making advances. Warren then planned to beat this soft, despised adult into as near a pulp as possible. That Warren, tough-muscled, hard-fisted, even at fif-

459

teen an athlete to be reckoned with by astonished older boys, could have done it seemed indicated when, less than a year later, Warren struck the master at school and was expelled. Warren, seen slapping away a smaller youth foolhardy enough to have gotten "fresh," had answered the master's sarcastic observation in penalizing Warren that Warren might try hitting someone his own size, by a couple of blows that broke the unfortunate man's jaw.

However, here, in Mr. Abbott's case, Warren must grudgingly admit—Warren's was never the lying malice of the weak; Warren's malice was straightforward, unconcernedly open and truthful—that he'd failed. Not even by staying afterward had he been able to tempt Mr. Abbott to do what he hoped Mr. Abbott would do. Though put in so many words by neither Warren nor his aghast father, that was the size of it! Both were anxious to end the interview. No; Warren didn't know any more, nor anything else. So; could he go now?

Arthur Winner, the truth was, had then and there been satisfied about Elmer Abbott. Whether Elmer had native impulses that were unnatural, or whether he didn't, hardly mattered. If he did have them, he was clearly incapable of acting on them; too timid to make advances, he was even too timid to accept invitations. Arthur Winner was prepared to believe that Elmer's feelings, though so copious when aroused, were feeble and tepid, sentimental rather than erotic. The proved fact that no woman could stir effective desire in him (at the young Elmer Abbott, regarded as handsome in his refined way, and of family, and of means, to make him as good a catch as Brocton had to offer, a succession of suitable girls threw themselves, or were thrown by their parents—alas, in vain!) was very likely complemented by the saving probable fact that no man stirred anything effective either—at least, in the sense that desires, if he occasionally felt them, whether to have some man for a husband, whether to take some boy for a wife, were so weak, so vague, so enfeebled by fear, that they couldn't oblige Elmer to obey. In saying that Mr. Abbott had never solicited them, the boys could reasonably be supposed to have told the truth— Elmer was innocent of overt acts. Therefore, he was innocent.

Led by Arthur Winner, Elmer's prudent, his fair, four judges agreed to acquit him. There had been smoke—or, incense—yes; but no fire. For mental anguish Elmer might have been caused, regrets were expressed. Elmer wept. Perhaps because a principal responsibility—his tongue devised this mischief—lay on him, Arthur Winner had found, he remembered, the scene of acquittal as disturbingly piteous as it was hard to stomach. Could absence of manhood go further? Here was Elmer Abbott, an Orcutt, a well-off man (with all that meant in the way of perfect freedom to quit himself like a man) so tame, so pridelessly relieved at the withdrawal of a false charge, at the permission to continue his namby-pamby round, keep his piffling post, his unpaid job's clung-to prerogative of inflicting on a captive audience his mediocre music, that he cried!

Elmer Abbott said: "Arthur, I don't know what to ask you to do. Perhaps you're tired of doing things for me. Perhaps you feel that if I have to keep having this kind of trouble, you don't want to be bothered any more. I wouldn't blame you. But when I saw Doctor Trowbridge, that *person,* looking at me that way—so vindictive! And those rude, rude things he said—Arthur, it *is* so unfair!"

A sound from within the house was reaching the terrace where they stood. Arthur Winner heard it not without relief. He said: "Sit down, Elmer. That's the telephone, a call I was expecting. If you don't mind, I'll answer it. Then, we'll talk about what to do."

"Oh, yes, Arthur," Elmer Abbott said. "By all means answer. I will sit down. I will try to calm myself."

From the lifted telephone, a voice said: "Brocton Borough Police calling. Mr. Winner? Just one second, sir. Captain Breck—" A new voice cutting in, said: "Bernie Breck." Bernie cleared his throat elaborately. "Something I wanted to ask you, Mr. Winner. About that thing last night—Mr. Detweiler. You know where he is—Ralph's whereabouts?"

"I was expecting him here. I had word he was driving out."

"Uh-huh. But you haven't seen him? Well, we've come on something kind of funny—might be! Far as you know, there wasn't any place else he was going—away from Brocton?"

Speaking carefully, Arthur Winner said: "After he saw me, I understood he thought of going to see a friend in Eatontown about a job he hoped to get. We felt there'd be no objection to his leaving Brocton, or the county, as long as he didn't leave the state, and was back tomorrow, as I understand he plans to be. What did you want him for?"

"Well, Mr. Winner, I'll tell you what we happened to find out—was told us. There's this car comes into Clifford's, that service center out by the bus station on the highway. Driver asks Cliff to give it a grease job, see. Says he'll get something to eat at the lunch counter in the bus station, wait for the car. Cliff said he'd seen the fellow before, but he didn't know him, know his name; so he says: Sure; they'd hurry it up. So pretty soon this through bus, Washington and New York, Boston, too, I guess, pulls in. They stop a few minutes, you know, in case people want to go to the rest rooms. The bus fellow comes over to see if Cliff has a little piece of friction tape he wants for something, and goes back with it—how Cliff happened to be looking at the bus, looking that way. So just before the doors closed, he suddenly sees this driver, the one who brought the Chevy in, come out and get on the bus. Of course, it could be none of his business, he's got the car; but he thinks it's funny. So he walks over to the station, says to the girl at the ticket window, he knows her: 'Where was that blond fellow going, you notice?' She says: 'New York.' Cliff says: 'Don't know who he is, do you?' She says: 'It so happens I do. Not to speak to; but I see him sometimes down at the Old Timbers. I think they call him Ralphie—Detweiler, I think his other name is.' Cliff says: 'Well, he left this car I got on the hoist. You sure his ticket was New York?' She says: 'Yes. Because I knew he lived around here, I asked him didn't he want a return. But he says: No, he didn't.'"

"That girl might have been mistaken, I think," Arthur Winner said. The reply was, of course, counsel's—my client's interests come first! The old hand at law made the rejoinder-automatic not only conceding nothing, but instantly insinuating doubt. Yet, could there be any doubt? Would such lack of common sense be like or unlike Ralph?

Bernie Breck said: "I thought of that, Mr. Winner. That's why I called, in case you *did* know where he was. Might still be some mistake, I thought. You see, what happened: right after, a prowl car of ours, Jack Olsen was driving, comes in to make a turn there. So Cliff flags him down, mentions this to him—kind of funny, he can't help thinking. He tells Jack what Eloise— the ticket girl—said. So Jack says: 'Hell, we can settle that quick. Read me the car registration number. We can put in on the owner; ask them flash us right back. Don't take ten minutes.' So he calls from the car, gives the desk the number; and we put through. Comes back: owner, Helen Detweiler, Brocton. Now, of course, somebody else could have swiped the car and dropped it there. But, the way Cliff described him, that was Ralph, all right. What I saw of him, he's a kind of nervous fellow, Mr. Winner; and I think he got this idea to do something foolish."

"I see," Arthur Winner said. With a swift rise of annoyance, with a slower burning of irritation, he did! Had that story about Bert Brown's boy and Eatontown been all a bluff; a thin story, but with Helen unfailingly prepared to believe her young liar, good enough, good for a clear twenty-four hours or so before she wondered, or anyone started to look for him? Possibly! But more probably this was the censorious Marigold's unwitting work. Marigold thought some worry would serve Ralph right. Warned, surely with no grimness lost in Marigold's cryptic relation, that somebody was after him, Ralph panicked. In Ralph kept, as well as the weak planless fool, the coward; and now the coward took over, informed the fool with the coward's desperate purpose, the coward's frantic resolve. For his friend the coward, the fool huddled up a fool's plan; for his friend the fool, the coward sped it into action.

Bernie Breck said: "Cliff happened to write the bus number down; so we got that. And I don't think we need to figure on Ralph doing anything very smart; he don't seem to have thought any of this out too good, if you see what I mean." Bernie spoke almost commiseratingly, as though the very poorness

463

of the plan—the weak-headed failure of imagination, the incompetence of thinking which could overlook such ever-present facts of small-town life as a "Cliff" with his sharp eye for the kind-of-funny, as a It-so-happens-I-do girl—who could seriously suppose, living in a place the size of Brocton, he could pass anywhere without being identified by someone?—made Bernie a little sorry for Ralph. Bernie said: "So probably *he* figures now nobody knows where he is, so he'll just stay on the bus until he gets to New York. So what I thought; we might give him time to cross the state line—" Bernie coughed. He said: "Of course, technically I guess the bailor arrests on bailpiece. Perhaps you think I ought to check with Miss Detweiler—"

"No; please don't do that," Arthur Winner said. "I don't think we need to stand on technicalities. If you think he can be picked up, I'd rather she didn't know anything about it until we got him back."

"Well, like I say, Mr. Winner, we got the bus number. We only have to put on the teletype a two- or three-state alarm, special attention highway patrols, to stop the bus and apprehend passenger answering Ralph's description charged with felony and wanted for breaching terms of bail. They'd find him and take him off quick enough—a private car, they possibly could miss; but they couldn't miss a bus. Only thing is, when we ought to do it."

"The sooner the better. Why not now?"

With something of reproach, Bernie Breck said: "Well, Mr. Winner, I don't have this of my own knowledge, or my officer's own knowledge. We never saw anyone buy any ticket to New York and get on any bus. So I don't know we can arrest him on, as if it was, view. But, of course, once the bus leaves the state, the jurisdiction, with him, we aren't only acting on suspicion, we *know* he's committed an offense; we can ask they stop him and hold him—well, I just didn't want to do anything someone might call us on later."

At another time, the legal nicety might have amused Arthur Winner—word was around, to whom it might concern; with Mr. Winner, be careful! Do what the book says! Let him find you took any little short cuts; and when he has you on the stand, saying you meant all right won't help you; you got troubles! Arthur Winner said: "Taking the bus sufficiently shows an unlawful intent, I think. Personally, I'd expect you to arrest him whenever and wherever you're able to. I mean to raise no questions. Technically, you're right, of course; to apprehend and, if bailor so chooses, to hand over is bailor's privilege or business. I'm prepared to act for bailor. Once he's been picked up, I'll assume custody; so you won't have to charge him, put him in jail, do anything that might give occasion for question."

Bernie Breck said: "That's good enough for you, that's plenty good enough for me, Mr. Winner." Earnestly, with the comfortable aplomb of a man about to say a few words that he feels (and justly) are going to do him credit, Bernie cleared his throat. "Like I said; Ralph's being nervous is why he got this idea to do something foolish—" The repeated phrase plainly appealed to Bernie, a handy little summing up of a distinction he benevolently held between misdeeds that might be unlawful, but weren't vicious in their nature, nor professional in their performance; and the true criminal act which was always one or the other and often both. "He didn't think this out; he's mixed up. My only idea: don't hold him, don't charge him; give a kid like that a chance to get things straight, give him a helping hand." With gravity, with satisfaction disarmingly open, Bernie could be seen to consider the spectacle, to him (and indeed to everyone) not unengaging, of the long-time policeman, the competent cop (and he could be a tough cop when toughness was needed, and don't you forget it!) as guide, pragmatic philosopher, and friend—but, of course, nobody's fool. He remained experience's pupil, apt and sage, over whose eyes you couldn't pull wool.

He said: "No; nervous is all, Mr. Winner. He don't have anything real to run away from. That girl last night; he never attacked her. I knew that right away. I been Joe, she couldn't even have got me to let a warrant issue. Nobody ever raped her! What I hear around, you can't; she's raping you before you get the chance. Jack! Thing I wrote there; that Special Attention;

take that in and put it on the tape, will you. I'll let you know, Mr. Winner. Any luck, we ought to have him inside an hour."

Doest thou well to be angry? Surely not! Could anger at the stupid, at those many thousands who, no matter why, cannot discern between their right hand and their left hand, be a reasonable anger? Bernie, the philosophic policeman, explained Ralph's behavior fairly—nervous, is all! His unexcited cop's estimate of the situation was right—machinery once set in motion, picking Ralph up should be no great trouble, so no great harm had been worked. What but the spite of annoyance informed Arthur Winner's wish (like Marigold's) to visit some trouble on the troublesome, entertaining if only tentatively the, in Elmer Abbott's word, vindictive, peevish thought that, Ralph being apprehended, bailor's option to surrender Ralph to proper authority might be exercised, Ralph might be enabled to enjoy a day or two in jail? To what purpose but exasperation's? Was Ralph a wily and determined fugitive from justice who required to be kept in custody? Even spleen had to smile! Let Arthur Winner, like Elmer Abbott, try to calm himself!

Elmer Abbott's gaze was mute, meek, and beseeching. Elmer, while alone, did seem to have become calmer; but manifestly this was no true calm, it was a quiet of spent spirit. Elmer's agitation had exhausted him; he no longer had the energy to be agitated; he came forlornly to rest. Though only by his own broodings, Elmer was defeated. He sank back into his ineffective self, much as Mr. Moore, by a drastic taking in hand, by some cutting words emasculated of his anger, subsided helplessly in his old familiar impotence. Elmer said: "After all, what can you do, Arthur? I know you won't want to go to him, bring up the subject, ask him for some assurance that he doesn't mean to force me out—"

There, then, was Elmer's woefully contrived poor proposal, what Elmer weakly wished done for him—and, of course (the brooder brooded), Arthur Winner wouldn't care to do it. Complaint fell to plaint. What help could Elmer expect? What hope had he? Arthur Winner said: "No, I wouldn't want to do that,

466

Elmer. The point's one of policy. Never defend what isn't being attacked. If anything of the kind is to be brought up, I'd rather have it put to me. By bringing it up myself, I've conceded that a doubt could very well exist. I may even plant a doubt. I say, in effect, I know what you must think. If it hasn't been thought of already, it certainly will be then—"

Elmer Abbott said: "But he *has* brought it up, Arthur. Oh, not in so many words; but you had only to hear him. He wasn't making any secret of how he felt about me—"

Arthur Winner said patiently: "Elmer, you're reading into whatever he said something I'm sure he didn't in the least mean. As I said, I was in the parish house with him when you began to play the carillon this morning. He was annoyed; because he understood you'd been told he'd prefer it to be heard at a fixed time every day and only then. I think he felt you were deliberately disregarding his wishes—"

"Yes, he said that. But I wasn't deceived, Arthur. You see, if that had been his real reason, he had only to listen to my explanation to realize the case wasn't that at all. But, no! He said I must understand that what powers and authority I had were delegated to me, were ex officio his, and he must resume them if he felt they were being used improperly. Oh, no; that was just pretext. What he meant was he'd decided I must go—"

Arthur Winner said: "I think your first thought, to try to make allowances, was the right one, Elmer. This is a time of some strain for Doctor Trowbridge. He's a new man; he never had a parish of his own before. To feel a little uncertain would be only human; but of course he realizes he mustn't let that be seen. He's probably been told that now, at the start, is the critical moment. If he hopes to be an effective rector, he mustn't delay to establish his authority. He must show at once that he knows his canonical rights and means to exercise them. Because, to him, the moment *is* critical, his sense of proportion may sometimes be affected. He may put things more strongly than he needs to—but that's simply inexperience. I think we might also remember he's quite young."

Elmer Abbott swallowed doubtfully; but, less listless, his eye brightened, he tossed back his lock of hair with a faint revival of animation. The altered picture was of course to his liking—himself, the wiser older man invited to show his magnanimity; the rector, a boy with much to learn, excited and arbitrary, because he was unsure. Elmer said: "Yes; I must try to remember that—"

Arthur Winner said: "For the time being at least, that's the fairest attitude, I think. I think it's fair; because, as a person, he impresses me favorably. I'm quite satisfied that making much of trifles, or getting angry over what doesn't matter, isn't natural to him. I'm also satisfied that he's perfectly open and straightforward. We've discussed parish affairs pretty fully. He mentioned certain changes he wants to propose to the vestry. If, for any reason, he felt he must ask you to resign, I know he would have told me."

"Well, he might not, Arthur," Elmer Abbott said. "You don't know how prejudice affects people. Secretly they want to hurt you; they try to trap you—so underhanded! That other time, you know, Doctor Ives, out of a clear sky, never having let me know what he was thinking, simply came one day and told me he must ask me whether what boys were reported to have said about me was true—"

Heard distantly through the house, another sound, repeated after a pause, had been reaching Arthur Winner. He said: "Elmer, I'm sorry; I think that's the front door—" Ralph, after all? Back here, you seldom heard cars come in. "Let me just see who it is."

Though Elmer plainly made some effort not to, he looked hurt—he wasn't, his fallen face said, blaming Arthur Winner; he was, Arthur Winner supposed, blaming life, the persecution by circumstance so unfeelingly thoroughgoing that even in the mere telling of his troubles he was frustrated and interrupted. It did seem hard! He might at least be given a reasonable chance to make Arthur understand—he said dolefully: "I know how busy you are, Arthur. I know I shouldn't be taking your time. But I haven't anyone I can talk to; and I did want to finish—"

"And I want you to," Arthur Winner said. "Sit still. Whoever's here will have to wait."

468

But, Arthur Winner could realize at once, whoever was here was not Ralph. The figure, seen down the length of the hall, beyond the screen door at the other end, was one he didn't recognize. The figure was of a man, spare and tall. Something in the posture (a slight defensive diffidence in the carriage of the shoulders; a young man's artificial resolve of hope, but of hope so often deferred as to be hardly hopeful at all?) seemed to suggest that, though not Ralph, like Ralph this seldom-welcomed type of caller had come with brushes, or vacuum cleaners, or who knew what, to sell. Arthur Winner, advancing with purpose, making ready by some hardening of the heart to stop the usually pathetic sales talk before it started, saw then that this young man was not a salesman, he was Garret Hughes.

The police teletype! But, no; that wouldn't be possible. Not enough time for word to get to the district attorney's office— closed this afternoon, anyway!—and then for Garret to drive to Roylan. Arthur Winner said: "I'm sorry, Garret. Did you knock before? I was talking to Mr. Abbott on the terrace; I only just heard you. I got your message this morning, thanks. If you'd like to go over the situation with me, come in and wait in the library, won't you?"

Garret Hughes said: "Thank you, no; Mr. Winner. I won't come in. I won't keep you. I have Agatha in the car. Mr. Brophy wanted me to stop by and let you know that the charge against Ralph Detweiler is being withdrawn—that is, won't be pressed."

Opening the screen door, Arthur Winner came out on the front steps of stone. In a car not far off, a slight fair girl was sitting with a baby in her lap—he'd never, Arthur Winner realized, had occasion to meet Garret's wife of a couple of years. His passing glance discovered that the young woman, curious, had been quick to look at the eminent Mr. Winner. Mrs. Hughes, "Agatha," she now made evident, had been given a lecture on Mr. Winner as a man of moment—the thing, perhaps, her husband might in time hope to be; a leading lawyer, a lawyer of good name, and—how wonderful; virtue's reward didn't have to be only virtue!—quite a rich lawyer, too. Abashed to be caught looking, clearly not knowing just what to do, Mrs.

Hughes performed a flustered little bow, and then ingenuously
blushed. Arthur Winner bowed in return. He said: "That's very
kind of you, Garret. I'm glad to know. Is this from Joe Harbison?"

"No, sir," Garret Hughes said. "There's that point, Mr. Winner. Mr. Harbison doesn't know yet. Of course, I'd told Mr.
Brophy about the prosecutrix's attitude; and he thought he'd
better make some inquiries, so he went to Mechanicsville for
lunch. He talked it over with some people there who knew Miss
Kovacs's father—they explained to Mr. Kovacs, I suppose, that
it would be better to drop the charge; and he decided to. Mr.
Brophy got word about a half an hour ago."

Garret Hughes hesitated, passing his hand over his flat hair.
"Mr. Brophy said, if you don't mind, he'd like to handle the
thing with Mr. Harbison this way. He wanted you to know as
soon as possible; but he'd appreciate it if, for the moment, you'd
say nothing to anyone. At the hearing Monday, the prosecutrix
simply won't appear. When Mr. Harbison finds she isn't there, I
suppose he may be willing on his own motion to discharge
accused. If he doesn't seem to be, I'll suggest that he continue
the hearing until Tuesday; and our office will be glad to investigate for him. We can notify him Tuesday that we learn the
prosecutrix has changed her mind, refuses to testify. That would
free you to make a motion for discharge." He looked at Arthur
Winner directly and earnestly; but with a slightest reticent ill-
ease of anxiety. "Would you have any objection to that, sir?"

If, as Fred bitterly asserted, Jerry Brophy was unlearned in
the law, allow, at least, that he was teachable! Curtly taught by
Judge Dealey that there was one and only one way to get rid of,
to strike from a docket, a case in continuance and not yet heard,
Jerry with impressive promptitude used his new knowledge.
The charge must be withdrawn? Very well; the charge would be
withdrawn.

In Mechanicsville (as where not in the county?) all persons
of importance or influence were known to Jerry Brophy; and
very few of them weren't—never mind why—beholden to him.

470

To one or another such person, nearly anybody you could name would in turn be found beholden—or, if not beholden, adequately bound by friendship, interest, or fear. A simple matter! That call to Jerry's office obviated even the delay of needing to ask around, of having to find out who could do what Jerry wanted done. Jerry already knew. When you knew that, you simply ran down to Mechanicsville and had a bite of lunch.

Soon after lunch, a bewildered Mr. Kovacs, conveniently not yet gone on his mill shift, made, at summons, a second trip to the clubhouse. Along with another cigar of price, he received a word, amply sufficient, *from* the wise, a word to make Mr. Kovacs wise. The hidden, half-feudal pressures of the benevolent society's powerful machinery were turned on. Confused, Mr. Kovacs perhaps started to protest; but he was soon made to realize what was best for him. Obedient, he would plod home. Virago, ogress, Mrs. Kovacs, with her blows and bellows, might be a terror to her tear-stained slut of a daughter; but she would have kept the handed-down, old-country knowledge of her appointed peasant place under the Man. (If she showed the least sign of forgetting, her lord the male could have blows, as needed, for *her*). Muttering, but not loud enough to do any good (or any harm), Mrs. Kovacs must resentfully obey, too, must gloweringly agree that for reasons none of her business, Veronica wasn't going back to the "trial" by the "judge" up there. Mission accomplished; and no doubt the district attorney was much obliged to His Honor. Judge Dealey said what to do; Jerry knew how to do it; so everything was in order.

Or, was it? That look of Garret's meant, of course, that Garret, now that his message had been given in its entirety, was not comfortable. Arthur Winner's first guess about the man at the door hadn't been altogether wrong. The then anonymous figure's strained hunch of shoulders declared in fact the unwilling salesman's conflict—his whipped-up resolve to do the business he came to do, wrestling with his hearty wish that he were somewhere else, doing something else. Waiting for his knock to be answered, Garret had been inwardly worried, wondering how Mr. Winner would like these wares with which Garret had been sent out, and of which he himself felt faintly ashamed.

Garret must, then, have double trouble; on top, most immediate, the uncertainty about Mr. Winner—would Mr. Winner regard everything as in order?—underneath, and maybe more troublesome (being not just of this moment, but probably of lifelong persistence in Garret), some uncertainty about himself —whatever Mr. Winner thought; did, could he, Garret, regard everything as in order? As for Mr. Winner, would Mr. Winner fail to see what was so plain to Garret—the palpable design on Mr. Winner? Even if never directly told, Garret must be aware of his boss's ambitious present project. Garret was in a position to mark how wide and how firm a foundation Mr. Brophy was scrambling to lay. Where this astonishingly energetic intervention in the Detweiler case might strengthen the underpinnings, Garret saw very well; he understood the alacrity that hadn't lost a day, an hour—no; not to make a formal deal—that would never do with a man like Mr. Winner—but, subtly, insinuatingly, to oblige with great obligingness (*That's very kind of you, Garret . . .*); by cordial willingness to co-operate, by freely taken trouble, to nurture good will where good will might be a great help.

As for himself, Garret, seeing all this, might, of course, retort: Well, what's wrong with willingness to co-operate, with taking some trouble to stop an unjust and vexatious prosecution? The district attorney, fully satisfied (and so was Garret) that a criminal information had been false, acted nothing if not laudably when he caused those trying to press the charge to be advised to drop it. Could the fact that the result might relieve and please Mr. Winner make corrupt in intent and felonious in fact what was, until then, unobjectionable? All true, all true; only, plain to see, Garret still felt, could not stop feeling, that without a law being broken, law was done impudent despite, held light, some slipping around law deliberately and knowingly effected, something shady pulled off. What but something shady did this, Mr. Brophy's chosen form of reporting his success, suggest? Notice that nothing was put on paper, nothing even said on the telephone. The magistrate who had jurisdiction was neither consulted nor informed; all he would ever know was that the prosecutrix didn't show up, failed to press the charge. His disingenuous arrangement made, the district attorney with elaborate casualness took care to enter himself into no contact of a kind to hint collusion with accused's counsel. He asked Garret if Garret would mind just stopping by Mr. Winner's home and saying that Mr. Winner might like to know—

Yes; know what? Would Mr. Winner know, and if he did know, would he like knowing, that the "word" received by Mr. Brophy about a half an hour ago had come of neither free choice nor of chance, that something more than "explaining the situation" had been involved; that somebody had been something more than "advised"; that, in short, Mr. Brophy, self-interest his guide, had decided that this was going to happen, and then seen that it did happen? Would Mr. Winner, man of well-known honor, apprised that Garret bore from his boss not just news, but gifts, a gift-wrapped bid for favor, an unasked affrontive offering begot in guile and tendered in guile, now pack both gifts and bearer coldly off? Deferential, with something of his young wife's abashment of respect, Garret stood restraining an impulse to shift his feet. Modestly, he could be seen asking himself, waiting anxiously to hear, what standards of conduct that Garret (abashment said so) privately thought the highest possible would proceed to find on these artful, extralegal, and, as Garret himself saw them, if not definitely dishonest, perhaps dishonorable goings-on.

The sweeping voiceless compliment, the silent, single-minded expression of so real a respect (surely real, being silent, being supposed private) could not but gratify; yet, to most people, pause must also be brought—pause, both on one's own behalf (to protest self-consciously: not so! would be a gross gawkishness; while the grave acceptance of no comment must amount to, be the next thing to, the nod complacent, to oneself proclaiming: *I am not as other men are, extortioners, unjust, adulterers . . .*); and on behalf of the single-minded complimenter (not a high look only, but a high aspiration, is apt to go before a fall). Such scrupling might be magnificent; but was it business, was it law, was it life? In practical matters, wouldn't a more temperate virtue be a wiser virtue? Wouldn't a young man's safer, surer course be the sufficiently straight if less narrow path of intelligent caution, of plain prudence—thou shalt not (explicitly) steal; thou shalt not (explicitly) bear false witness—rather than aiming at more, rather than arguing stubbornly against much evidence (Garret had been in Dave Weintraub's office!) that more must be possible, rather than pinning a probably close-to-last hope on some Arthur Winner as your living proof that more *was* possible?

Duly made to pause, Arthur Winner could reflect that he had now, at any rate, a new reading of Garret's surprising, even a little bumptious-seeming, scrupulosity Friday night on a point of procedure, the dogged if vain intervention on the arguable point of Ralph's bail. It might look like—enraging Noah—a smart aleck's quibble of maneuver; but—remember the even-handed civility, the modest patient reasonings, the judicious bowing, though of the same opinion still, to the combination against him—clearly had not been. Garret took a quiet stand for what, being law, he thought right, and what, being right, he thought law. At once, with this illumination, Arthur Winner had also the plain answer to a question, an idle query of curiosity, last year presented to him when he read in the Brocton County *Law Reporter* of Garret's appointment as an assistant district attorney. The note under "Bar Association News" might look unnotable, but few members of the bar would fail to pull up, read again. The known fact was that young lawyers could as a rule be induced to serve as assistant district attorneys—work that was demanding; and poorly paid—only so long as beginning practices afforded them no more than a scatter of minimum fees and left them with plenty of free time. Whoever heard of resigning from a firm like Dave Weintraub's to be an assistant district attorney? A job with Dave was what you went to, when the chance came; not what you quit.

The attorneys' room said with a laugh, but not a laugh of disbelief, that if you had the misfortune to get into trouble with the criminal law in Brocton County, you would, if you were smart, make just two statements. One: I have nothing to say. Two: Mr. Weintraub is my counsel. Unless your trouble was such that no human possibility of getting you out existed, you could, if you'd kept your mouth shut, and had the cash to pay Dave to defend you, stop worrying. On Dave's past performance, the odds that you would be acquitted were approximately ten to one. Single fees of the size that Tuttle, Winner & Penrose, or Polhemus & Studdiford, sometimes commanded might not come Dave's way; but his income, year in and year out, very likely averaged as much as, or more than, theirs.

This was certain: the Weintraub office never lacked for clients; and any young man admitted to work there, and working there to Dave's satisfaction, was in the money—he need feel no misgivings about his financial future. Relieved on that score, most sensible young men would (wouldn't they?) take, tempering virtue with discretion, that safer surer course. They would see, either at once or very soon, the inutility, the impracticality, the overniceness of entertaining misgivings on other possible scores.

That there was nothing, that great care was taken there should be nothing, to hide in Dave's offices went without saying. You'd find, naturally, silences, keepings of confidences, in which all lawyers were privileged, and to which all were bound; but anything that the police, or the board of censors of the bar association, or even an honest young man working for Dave, could consider something, you would not find. As a matter of fact, men of Dave Weintraub's brains would rarely be so empty of effective expedients as to need to fall back on doing the outright unlawful—that is, doing anything by which they were made actually liable to indictment. Even if such need arose, a man of Dave's brains would have the sense not to try anything unless he knew (and when Dave *knew* things, those things were so!) it could under no circumstances be brought home to him. Yes; search all you liked, you wouldn't uncover a scrap of evidence to substantiate accusations of irregularity against Dave. The office was wide open to any and all; look in all you liked! If, looking in, you happened to see a Garret Hughes, attentive to his duties, earnestly at work on cases of Dave's, could Dave help it if you jumped to favorable conclusions?

475

That, Arthur Winner never doubted, had been Dave's real reason for offering Garret a job. Dave would, of course, have looked into Garret's law-school standing, made sure that Garret hadn't shown himself a complete fool; but Garret's qualifications—what Dave had wanted Garret for—had nothing to do with law-school scholarship, or Garret's legal abilities (at this stage, you could be sure, nonexistent). In blunt terms (Dave did not mind bluntness; he took realistic views), Garret had one qualification in not being Jewish. No unreasoned anti-Semitism on Dave's part was reflected; simply, Dave *was* Jewish, and Dave already had in the office a smart young man, also Jewish. Two was company; three could be a crowd.

As well as the qualification of what he wasn't, Garret had to offer, in Dave's always-clear calculatings, what he was. Garret came of farm people rooted in the lower county since the Revolutionary War. Those farms that once surrounded Mechanicsville were mostly gone. On some of their former fields, factories had risen. Where the unpretentious, but spacious and sound, built-to-last stone farmhouses used to stand, "developments" often extended, serried ranks of new houses, for the moment spic and span, but far from spacious, and in construction and material unsound, built not to last. Another generation would be unable to remember the countryfolk of the long past who lived on these farms; but today, right now, many, and particularly the more substantial, citizens of Mechanicsville (and Brocton, too) remembered them well, knew the old names.

Though they could be called just farmers, meaning real hand-to-the-plow farmers, dirt farmers, too hard working to have time to be cultivated or refined, people like the Hugheses were very well thought of. Their education would ordinarily amount to no more than what a one-room school could provide; but native good sense abounded in them. They were temperate and self-respecting, and if parsimonious, also provident. They were God-fearing in that, after their grave unemotional fashion, they were strongly religious; and anyone who knew them could tell you they'd starve before they stole. Garret's father was Henry Hughes of Lower Makepeace Township, whose produce often took first prizes at the state fair. Garret's grandfather had been

Enoch Hughes. As well as a farmer, old Enoch was the last horseshoeing blacksmith in the county, wore a beard that covered his whole chest, and was reputed to be able to lift a thousand pounds. The boy Garret proved a smart one at his books, and Henry encouraged him, had him go on, get an education; and Garret was in the law; but, even so, you could be sure he was all right. No Lower Makepeace Hughes ever needed watching. For five generations the word of any of them had been as good as his bond; and in that time, to none of them attached a known shame or scandal.

In short, Dave had figured out a good way to attract and inspire with confidence clients of a type or class that often had profitable legal work, but heretofore hadn't thought of bringing any to the Weintraub office. Dave Weintraub, naturally, made no public disclosure of the terms of the offer that Garret, just out of law school, just admitted to the bar, received; but doubtless they were terms such as to surprise and elate him. Dave Weintraub was not only, in his private life, a generous man, a man of many unpublished charities; in his business life he was too practical a man to pinch pennies where, having decided on what he wanted, he believed what he wanted would be worth paying for.

All, then, must have been well to start. Garret, Arthur Winner had heard, did not fail to prove quite as useful as Dave could wish; such things take time, but new business, business in addition to Dave's regular business, had undoubtedly been turned up. As far as Dave went, Garret was fine. As far as Garret went, you could be certain Dave had never at any time directed him to act improperly; and, moreover, that any parts of Dave's regular business inexpedient for Garret to see would never have been seen by him. What, then, got into Garret? More than satisfying Dave, making if anything more money than he could reasonably ask, why must Garret leave?

Though fantastic, the fact, Arthur Winner felt prepared to guess, was that Garret, joining issue with his bread and butter, served papers not on Dave, but on himself. The case was of contract, and in contract Garret must demand of Garret specific performance. What had Garret freely, and even elatedly, undertaken? He had struck hands with a person, engaged for very good and valuable consideration to be that person's man. His duty was loyalty, which meant the ready, willing, and unreserved serving and advancing of his employer's interests—told where to go, what to say, Garret had just now driven out to Roylan; just now, to the best of his ability, followed with faithfulness instructions he didn't like! Plainly, to rest easy with himself, Garret had to be conscious that he was so acting, serving any employer he might have wholly and undividedly, in the spirit as well as in the letter.

In the spirit? On the air-conditioned air of those ceaselessly busy Mechanicsville rooms, very modern in their *décor*, expensively sleek and functional, well swept, well garnished, did Garret's long and evidently fastidious nose persist in detecting a slight odor? Not—by no means!—a fetor like that of stealing or forswearing; only, unventilated, never quite filtered away, passing faint whiffs of slick practice. (Those accident cases, taken on contingency, that Dave was so good at winning in court, or out of court so successful in settling high; that sort of confounding medical testimony—doctors can disagree, can't they?—that Julius Penrose commented on last night). For a year or so, Garret must have been sniffing with indecision this faintest, never exactly identified, perhaps only imagined, taint. He did not want to, really couldn't afford to, be a fool; but, at the same time, since Garret was Garret, he did not want to, could not submit to, as well as being not a fool, being in that phrase of Fred Dealey's, the least little bit of a crook—which was to mean here: not a person chargeable with a share in slick practices, nor even one who knowing of them winked at them; but a person self-convicted of taking Dave's money without the entire fidelity of an unreserved readiness also to take, not in some things but in everything, Dave's part.

At last, and not long last, that indecision had been naturally resolved—a Lower Makepeace Township resolving, you might say; and this was surely a good joke on Dave. Dave knew about smart young men. To most of them, that wiser course of practicality and utility, of being not too good for this world, is bound to seem—the very measure of their smartness—the better

478

course, and so the only course. Garret being smart, Dave could look with confidence for Garret to do the smart thing. The joke was one that Dave might be expected to be the first to see, and even, with the good nature of a man whose count of successes is so long that he can, unperturbed, write off to experience a slip-up now and then, wryly to relish. If Dave complained, his complaint must be the funniest ever heard. Garret, the green boy, had fooled the old (or, at least, fully mature) fox. How? Simply, by being everything in fact that Garret's background and appearance purported him to be. This was the genuine article, in all respects the article that Dave, seeing how he could use it, had shrewdly bargained for and paid high for—a plain honest son of those plain honest farmer-fathers. Garret's meticulous views of right and wrong could be trusted; anything he did would have to be honest; anything he said would have to be so.

Meticulous was, of course, the word for those views; and might all fathers of sons, might the father of a Warren and a Lawrence Winner, well ponder the word? Around Roylan, one or two farmers of the stamp of Garret's father still farmed, and Arthur Winner knew something of their family life. In the sense that those fathers were religiously God-fearing, those sons showed themselves religiously father-fearing. Rudimentary instruction in right and wrong, in father's pleasure and God's, had been commenced as soon as they could lisp and toddle. What is learned in the cradle lasts to the grave! The little cate-chumen grew up, inclined as he was firmly bent; at the back of his mind, or at levels below his consciousness, believing forever after in that father almighty, maker of a child's heaven and earth, and of all things visible and invisible. Do wrong; and father's infinite wisdom always found you out; father turned on you his wrathful countenance. Something known as strap oil was kept in the woodshed for transgressing boys. After a few applyings, which consciences schooled to quake must wretchedly admit had been nothing but righteous retribution, nothing but your due, your desert, you were stupid indeed if you continued to doubt that only fools make a mock at sin, if you hadn't learned, once and for all, which way lay happiness, lay peace of mind. Be not deceived; never be deceived! Those stern, just,

479

eyes that saw you (you did not know how) in the corn patch
or the wagon shed, saw you in the offices of David Weintraub, Esq., Counselor at Law; saw you at Joe Harbison's last
night; saw you an hour ago with the district attorney; saw you
now on the steps of Mr. Winner's Roylan home. Any moment,
that serious voice might pronounce: *Son, is there something you
haven't told me?*

Arthur Winner said: "No, I wouldn't have any objection to
that, Garret. If Mr. Brophy prefers to do it that way, I see no
reason why he shouldn't. I think we're entitled to assume the
prosecutrix was coerced into swearing the information. I'd regard
any steps taken to end coercion, to leave her a free agent, as
proper, as not the same as dissuading her from testifying to
what she knows or believes is the truth. I wouldn't feel that we,
the defense, could ethically make such representations; but if
an informed party, without interest in the cause, felt representations should be made, I see nothing to stop him."

With a controlled but evident brightening of relief, Garret
returned Arthur Winner's look almost gratefully. Not unmoved,
Arthur Winner said: "I don't see that we interfere in any jurisdiction properly Mr. Harbison's either. Since the charge is one
in which he's not competent to determine guilt or innocence,
he enters into a hearing only as a committing magistrate. That's
the essence of his jurisdiction, and I'd say it doesn't vest until
there's something before him; that is, until complainant has
appeared and, in the presence of accused, concluded sworn testimony to substantiate the complaint. Swearing the information
empowers a compelling of accused to come before him, but no
one else. So, I think Mr. Brophy is right—Mr. Harbison needn't,
for the present, know anything his own record doesn't show
him."

Garret said: "Oh, I agree, sir! I expect I made my ideas about
a committing magistrate being a committing magistrate, and
that's all, a lot clearer than Mr. Tuttle thought I needed to last
night." Much easier, he smiled. Was uncertainty resolved? Seem-

ingly so! Modest, Garret accepted instruction in these recondite points of legal ethics; and the resulting relief, when you thought about it, might be no small one. At considerable cost—and not to himself alone; there was that girl over there in the car, and that baby which must have been at least in prospect—Garret had made his decision, had purchased a supposed freedom. Taking this job, he had taken this job to be a job in the fresh, the really open, air. That the man who tendered it, the man who awarded it to him was, as well as district attorney, a practicing politician, had naturally been known to him. Life with Dave Weintraub must naturally have enlightened him enough for him to suspect that law might not always be divorced from politics, that Mr. Brophy would always have political irons in the fire, that to some of Mr. Brophy's activities (like some of Mr. Weintraub's) there might be more than met the eye.

Yet, surely (Garret must have felt) a difference that was important, that looked sufficient, existed. Mr. Brophy's political activities in no way involved Garret. In no capacity but that of public prosecutor had Mr. Brophy a contract with Garret. The work of the district attorney's office was the work of the court; and in Brocton County, who ever had questioned, who could question, the court's integrity? The Honorable the Judges there sitting were not so in name only. Under them, that part of the court's mechanism, the attorney for this judicial district, the public prosecutor, whatever his outside activities, would be able to set himself no end but justice. The prosecution sought only fact; the prosecution had no hope of fees for perplexing and dashing counsels, for making the worse appear the better reason. Rising before a jury, an assistant district attorney's one care need be for truth, whole truth, and nothing but truth. Yes; Garret would take a crust and liberty! He had taken it. The crust had been real enough—Garret and his Agatha very likely moved to a cheaper house, cut every possible expense. That car, somehow pitiful in contrast to Elmer Abbott's nearby Cadillac, must be ten years old. But, liberty? Had there been, this afternoon, a chill of doubt? There had been! Mr. Winner, who would certainly know, now viva voce resolved doubt! Gar-

481

ret breathed his uncontaminated air. He said happily: "Well, that was all, sir. Then, I'll tell Mr. Brophy you're willing to do that—have nothing said until the hearing."

"Yes," Arthur Winner said. "I see no need to keep Mr. Harbison informed—nonappearance can't concern him until it's a fact. Even in the case of accused, whose appearance Mr. Harbison may compel, nonappearance isn't established until, duly called, he doesn't appear. Since Ralph won't be called until Monday, I have, of course, seen no reason to tell Mr. Harbison what I now think right to tell you, for your information and Mr. Brophy's. Ralph ran away this afternoon."

"Golly!" Garret said. At his exclamation's involuntary boyishness, Garret blushed. He said: "Excuse me, sir! It's just—well, you know, sir, the funny thing is—I hope you won't mind my saying so—I thought last night he might do that—oh, not as going to presumption of guilt, or anything! It was more because of that girl who was crying. I could see she wouldn't have been there unless she was—well, his regular girl. I guessed he wasn't denying he'd been out with Miss Kovacs; so even if he wasn't guilty as charged, he'd have a lot of explaining to do to his girl, and probably to Miss Detweiler, too. And—well, anyway; looking at him, I just suddenly thought: That kid's going to skip."

"I could wish I'd thought of it," Arthur Winner said. "Not that we expect to have much trouble finding him. Fortunately he was seen leaving, and the police know where he meant to go, so they hope to pick him up pretty soon. I daresay your office wouldn't be hearing about it until Monday, when we ought to have him back; but since Mr. Brophy's been good enough to be open with me about having the charge dropped, I'd want to be open with him. In that connection, I would have wanted, if Mr. Brophy didn't mind, to let Miss Detweiler know as soon as possible that the prosecutrix wouldn't appear—I could answer for her saying nothing; and since she's been greatly upset, it would seem kind to let her know. However, I won't ask for that permission right now. She doesn't know Ralph's gone. I couldn't very well tell her one without the other, so I'd rather not tell her anything until we get Ralph back. Still, if you're seeing Mr. Brophy, you might ask if he'd object if I told her then."

Garret said: "I'm pretty sure he wouldn't mind that, sir. I'll check and let you know. Well, sir; thank you."

"Thank *you*," Arthur Winner said.

✦

Clarissa said: "And are there to be more talks?"

Arthur Winner said: "I think not. I think everything Mrs. Pratt found sayable was said, even if she hadn't perhaps finished. We were sitting in the garden; and by what I guess was my good fortune, she saw a snake that frightened her. So she left fairly precipitately, helped a little by an appearance of Mr. Moore, the father, I learned, of Ralph's Joan Moore, who expressed himself as determined to have Ralph marry her; and of Fred Dealey, who stopped by with an opinion he's writing. I expect Mrs. Pratt got the impression I was a busy man. I was. Before Fred left, Elmer Abbott turned up, hurt because he thought Doctor Trowbridge had been impolite to him. Before he left—"

"But Mrs. Pratt never really did say what she wanted?"

"I'm not sure she wanted anything but a chance to look me over."

"Yes; she would want that," Clarissa said. "That was plain this morning." Though spoken composedly, a faint acidulous feminine note was not altogether absent. "You can be sure Marjorie had given her plenty of the kind of talk I told you about last night—you know, that she, Marjorie, had always had a hopeless passion for you; that you were—well, her secret if platonic love. Did Mrs. Pratt ask you to do anything?"

"She seemed to believe that Marjorie had been made unhappy by the thought that I disliked her. If that were the case, Mrs. Pratt asked me, in effect, not to. I told her I did not dislike Marjorie. She also seemed to want me to understand her religion, parts of which she tried to explain to me. That was rather long. She was kind enough to say she'd pray for me when she left."

483

"Good!" Clarissa said. "At least, I hope that means what that sounds like—that she saw she wasn't getting anywhere with mixing you up in this. I told you she was quite mad."

"Well, she's quite emotional, at any rate," Arthur Winner said. "But I think her sentiments are genuine; and I think she's by nature very kindhearted."

Clarissa said: "You also think Marjorie's kindhearted—remember? I'm always surprised, Arthur, because I never expect to be able to tell you anything—I mean, I'm flabbergasted all the time, in my limited dumb way, to find you really know almost everything about almost everything. But, as I've said before, and just because I'm female, I suppose, there *are* some things I do believe you need me to tell you. Kindhearted is what emotional people, particularly if they're women, really never are. They're always so busy playing with their own feelings they haven't any time for your feelings—or, at least, they haven't unless they want to use yours to build up theirs. I found that out long ago—not because I'm intelligent, or could ever think it out; but because that bitch you sometimes notice in me just *knows*."

Smiling, Arthur Winner said: "You're quite right; there are indeed things I need to be told. And I don't want you to suppose I'm dissatisfied with your description of what I know— almost everything about almost everything, would seem to cover as much ground as anyone ought to claim; but, right here, I think your surprise may be due to confusion in our terms. Terms of that sort, as I use them, aren't meant to be absolute. When I say I think a person's kindhearted, I by no means mean I've decided he—or she—is all compact of loving-kindness, and nothing but loving-kindness. I only aim to state that this person impresses me as disinclined, rather than inclined, to do heartless or cruel things. I mean, I see no sign of a temperament that could take pleasure in doing them. Which is to say, I would expect him to do them only if some very important interest of his own required him to. What you mean by kindheartedness—"

Clarissa said: "What I mean by kindheartedness is something you can depend on in a person, something that you know will always make him try to help you, because that's the way he—

and I'm really afraid it usually is 'he'—is. You're kindhearted, my darling, if you want an example. That's why you sometimes need someone like me to see you're not imposed on."

"Then I must hope I'll always have you."

"Oh, you will!" Clarissa said. "You've absolutely no chance of getting away. Any fancies of that kind are just idle. Because of your one rash act in marrying me, you'll find you have to please and provide for me all the rest of your life. That reminds me; I must invite you to take me out to dinner tonight. I told Em we wouldn't be eating in. I didn't know whether you'd hate going out or not—and if you do, I can fix something; but I didn't want Em to have to. I told her she could just get herself fed and go to bed. I didn't know where you were when we came in—"

"I was engaged in removing the corpse of the snake I mentioned and giving him a decent burial. It was a copperhead, again; though it's the first I've seen in several years. So I killed it. We'll have dinner wherever you like."

"Well, the thing was, Em had a hard day; and I don't believe they got much sleep last night, because of the storm— Oh, the oak! I won't even try to tell you about it; it was just split from top to bottom; I don't blame Em and Harold for being scared almost to death. Anyway, your treeman came up, a very learned young fellow in riding pants, and went over it, part of the time with a magnifying glass."

"What did he think?"

"Well, as I say, he was very learned. I gather it could be worse, even if I didn't see how. I mean, he explained that it was usually worse if it happened during the spring or early summer. Because there's more water in it then; which, I think he said, a lightning bolt generally vaporizes to steam, which may be at such a pressure that the tree really blows up all over. And that may so injure the inner bark layer, I forget what he called it, that it amounts to girdling the tree. He says you can't immediately tell whether that happened or not—yes, I know, darling! You want to hear what he finally said. He suggests that he trim and spray the furrow—it's the most terrible split—with some preservative or something, and wait and see. Next spring, if it leafs out fairly strongly, it could be permanently repaired and saved. Meanwhile, he thinks the spraying and cleaning up—there's an enormous limb down on the terrace—would be about a hundred and fifty dollars. With, he was careful to say, no guarantee that, in the spring, the tree won't be dead. Ought that much to be spent? And, of course, really repairing it would cost a lot more."

"Let us venture the money," Arthur Winner said. "I'll tell him to go ahead."

"Well, I hoped you would. I hate to think of it gone. I suppose, because I remember it as a child. We used to climb around in it."

"So did we," Arthur Winner said. "Did you and Ann decide where you want to have dinner? There's a call I've been expecting, and I'd like to be able to tell the telephone operator where I could be reached, if it doesn't come before we leave."

"We could go to the Brookside, I suppose. Oh; and part of the reason I thought we might eat out was that Ann wasn't going to be home for dinner. I forgot to tell you. She has a date. There's a barbecue at the Updykes, and Chet Polhemus is coming for her. She's dressing. I must see how she's getting on. She's wearing something rather special; and I said I'd help her do her hair."

"Haven't I heard that she thought young Mr. Polhemus was silly?"

"Arthur, you must understand that a date is a date. We poor females have to have them, because we have to make men notice us. It's quite simple. The fact that she may not think much of Chet's intelligence hasn't any bearing whatever on the really important fact that if Ann lets him take her to the party, every boy there observes that another boy, and one of some distinction, since he's now allowed the use of a car, sees something in Ann."

"The stratagem, I perceive, is masterly," Arthur Winner said. "I can't say I altogether like the car part of it; but I'll comfort myself with reflecting that I know Russ Polhemus well enough to be sure he'd see that any car he let Chet take was in good order, and that Chet was able to handle it. My feeling that sixteen—and, I guess, a half—is far too young for car-driving isn't entirely dissipated. But I gather no one else thinks sixteen too young, and since the state's prepared formally to license such children, I see how the unsafeness may be all in my own aging mind."

"I'm sure Chet would be a careful driver," Clarissa said. "You can tell by looking at him. He's rather a solemn youth, and I don't believe he has much enterprise—which is good. I mean, for this purpose. In many ways, Ann's definitely more grown up than he is—she'll let him be a little silly about her, if he wants; but she won't be silly about him, you can be certain. Moreover, and another good point; with Chet, there's no danger of any going, as they say, steady; because he'll be away at school again, beginning the week after next."

"Goodness!" Arthur Winner said. "Thought has certainly been given this."

"Of course!" Clarissa said. "That's why I don't think you ought to object, or need to be uneasy, Arthur. Chet will do very well; he's a quiet boy and he has good manners. You understand, don't you, that this is really quite important to Ann? You see, it amounts to her first date—that is, going to a party with a boy, as opposed to going, probably with some other girls, and meeting the boys there; and I want things to start right." Clarissa blushed faintly. "I know it's important, because at around Ann's age I was 'off' boys; I didn't let anyone date me; I was really afraid of them. It wasn't right, it wasn't normal, and it easily could have spoiled my whole life. I want Ann to begin now having occasional dates; so she'll learn about boys and how to be natural with them. I think the party tonight plans to dance somewhere afterward. I said that, if the others went, Ann might go; but I told her, and I'll also tell Chet, that she must be home by eleven o'clock. Is that all right?"

"My dear," Arthur Winner said, "let me admit the reprehensible truth that, without you to say, I wouldn't know. You'll manage these things far better than I could. I don't know what Ann and I would do without you."

Her color coming again, Clarissa said: "Ann's a very nice girl; and we're going to keep her that way; and we're going to make

487

a nice young woman, and a happy one, too, out of her. You'll see. I'll go up. She must have had her bath by now, and we can start some primping."

The observations of ;he undersigned in his former opinion at page 226 of 15 Brocton County L. Rep. remain applicable. The amended language of the supplemental brief is prolix in form and indefinite in content, so that plaintiff's preliminary objections numbered 5, 6, and 7, being motions for a more specific pleading as to the various parts of paragraph 2 of the new matter must all be sustained. . . .

Raising his eyes from the typed page of Fred Dealey's opinion, Arthur Winner smiled.

Ann said: "You might tell me I look nice, Father."

"You do, indeed. You took me by surprise. Ought you to be downstairs before your escort arrives? In my day, we were often made to wait half an hour, and I think it was quite good for us."

Putting out a hand, Ann touched his cheek. She giggled. She said: "Oh, I'm going upstairs again, don't you worry! But Hendy said to show you how nice I look. When Chet comes I'm only to have eyes for him; so you have to say it now."

"I did. I will again. You look charming."

"Don't I, just!" Ann said. "Hendy has me all dolled up. You see, Dick Updyke and Chet are taking Lucy Bartlett and me, and maybe some others will go too, dancing afterward." The blue eyes shone engagingly with volatile eagerness. "There's this place where Saturday nights they have a real gone band, everyone says."

"A real gone band?" Arthur Winner said. "I believe I grasp your meaning. Clearly, a place good to know. Where is it?"

"Oh, it's called the Old Timbers Tavern. It's down toward Mechanicsville—not far."

"Yes; I've heard of it," Arthur Winner said. "And I'm afraid, whatever the reputed quality of the band, I must ask you not to go there."

"Oh, Father!"

"I'm sorry, Ann; but I'm also serious. That place has the lowest possible reputation; and I know that the man and his wife who run it will shortly be in trouble with the law. I'm glad you told me; because I can tell you definitely you wouldn't like anything about it. You wouldn't find it fun."

"Oh, Father, you just heard that somewhere; you don't know that. Somebody's always saying that about any place that isn't dead and buried. Lots of people go there. It's perfectly all right. Hendy said I could go dancing."

"But I don't believe you mentioned where you planned to go, did you? There must be other places you can dance. That the Old Timbers would be a good place is something I think *you* just heard somewhere." He smiled. "I don't think you'll find anyone you know has ever been there."

"Chet has."

"Then, in suggesting he and Dick take you and Lucy, he shows extremely poor judgment. He must have seen what sort of boy goes there, and the sort of girl he brings with him. He must know there's a lot of drinking by minors—and other things."

"What sort of girl?" Ann said. "What other things?" In instant alteration her face had darkened with sullenness. Scorn or resentment sounded suddenly in her voice. "I know the stork doesn't bring them. I'm really not exactly a child. And Chet and Dick don't drink."

Almost obliged to smile, Arthur Winner said: "I'm glad to hear that. I'd think it a pity if they were developing the habit at their age."

"And Chet doesn't do 'other things,' either."

Arthur Winner said: "My dear, don't imagine there's any question in my mind about how you and Chet would act. I'm sure that if you went there, Chet, as you say, wouldn't drink, and that neither of you would do anything else you'd have any reason to be ashamed of. The point is, that won't be true of most of the people around you. The boys are there because they know they can have drinks served them; and since, I'll agree, you're really not exactly a child, I don't have to tell you what the girls with them are ready to have the drinking lead to. Boys of that kind and girls of that kind would see at once that you didn't belong there; and I don't think you'd be welcome. To go where you don't belong and aren't welcome is to ask for something unpleasant to happen."

"What could happen to me?" Ann said. "Would I be ruined if a Fallen Woman was in the same room with me? What am I? So pure and holy I'm too good for her? All of us are just human, I guess."

Heightened, resentment turned Ann's face a heated dusky red. Her voice trembled disdainfully. Too angry to look at her father, she looked down and away. Could those flung-out last words, that scorn-strained voice, mean anything but one thing? The sting of injury drove Ann to speak, to answer back, to retaliate. By the slanted light from the hall, to the rumble of an ending summer storm, that indignantly averted young glance must, retrospective, be seeing again the semidark bedroom's dim disordered bed where, joltingly, two grown-up bodies, bare together, were discovered at their turn of love. Stark naked, the woman's body lay still extended in the position of its rendering. Stark naked, having just done you-know-what, the man's brute big body still half covered hers. And this stripped-for-action man of late last night was—who? The man, the very same, sitting here of early this evening, sedately clothed as though he always wore clothes, the very votary of right with his unctuous words. Reproving, he frowned, censorious, he shook the head at awful "things" that (he warned) roadhouse drinking, given a boy and a bad girl, might "lead to"!

Arthur Winner said: "All of us are, indeed, just human, Ann. We should never imagine otherwise. We ought to remember that people have their human reasons for acting as they act, and that if we had the same reasons, we might very well act the same way. So; no, I don't consider you, and you're right in not considering yourself, too—if you wish—pure and holy, for girls who may be doing what they do because they've had difficulties you never had, or found that they must make choices that never faced you."

Fred Dealey said: *You get nowhere fast*. To allay her disappointment, Ann was urged to contemplate concepts of charity

490

and humility. In place of an exciting planned party, she was offered good counsel. Come, let us reason together. . . . Arthur Winner said: "Ann, look at me. Can you say you really believe I'm objecting to your going to this place because I like to disappoint you, because I don't want you to have a good time?"

Ann let him see her accusing eyes a moment. She said unsteadily: "How do I know what you want? You spoil everything; and then you say—" She broke off, biting her lip—plainly in order not to cry, not to inflict on herself the ultimate ignominy of tears.

"Listen carefully, Ann," Arthur Winner said. "My concern isn't at all about what you and Chet might do. And it isn't that I think being on the same dance floor with girls who are more or less promiscuous would contaminate you. I told you what concerned me. Whether they know it or not, if Chet and Dick, boys less than seventeen, take two even younger girls to a place like that, they ask for trouble. A number of very tough young men, several with criminal records, spend most of their time there. Seeing what they would consider a party of kids walk in, they might decide to amuse themselves, and to teach you not to go where you aren't wanted. They might, for instance, invite themselves to join you. If they insisted that you and Lucy dance with them, I don't believe Chet and Dick would prove much protection—and nobody else would help you. Everyone would say, since you had no business being there, anything that happened served you right. That's why I couldn't be easy about your going to the Old Timbers. That's why I must ask you to tell Chet, if he suggests going, that you're not allowed to."

A tremor of rebellion moved Ann's lips. Committed to contend, the angered child's unthinking impulse was to go on; childlike, to hug to her the sore mood of resentment; childlike, to persist in her retaliation of being contrary. (*So what? Maybe I want to dance with someone tough!*) Then, no less childlike, Ann could be seen to falter. Her attention had been directed to the, in fact, unknown; to dangers, because indefinite, infinite. Making out the grim doubtful shapes, the child in Ann retreated, at heart quite as alarmed for herself as ever Father could be alarmed for her. Brought to this pass, Ann stood for the comic, the affecting, moment in her child's quandary. Her nervous hands smoothed her frock's full skirt, and that tactile sensation, the hint of frills and furbelows, was perhaps decisive. Help of a kind no child could give was called for, and in Ann the coexisting woman stirred, roused, answered, faster than thought went to the rescue. On the instant, touched as with a wand, Ann was endowed with the talisman of woman's wisdom, made over to woman's attitudes—a woman's disinclination to cry for the moon; a woman's sagacity about true interest (why ask for what you don't really want? You might get it); a woman's reliable sense of where substance is and where shadow is.

The woman now swept with a critical eye the leavings of the deposed child. The child's smolder of anger served no purpose of hers—away with anger! On the same puff, anger's creature, the whim to be contrary, dissolved in air. With the child who had broodingly entertained them gone, what further use could be found for the child's corrosive thoughts about the passage of love of last night's man and woman surprised? Matter-of-factly, Ann packed them all off to their proper place out of mind, the place of safe deposit where in normal balance the normal woman kept the less good, the too true, the unbeautiful —not locked away and never, never (poor Helen Detweiler!) to be brought to mind; but shelved tidily. At need, or even just in vacant or in pensive mood, they might be secretly examined or mulled over; but meanwhile they remained out of the way of, at a distance from, woman's daily comings and goings, her busy made work of clothes, of cosmetics, of chatter; her energetic humdrum of little enterprises and little interests—not to say, her sometimes demanding servitudes of cooking, children, and, when the fashion was, church.

To instate the woman, to tidy up after the child, had taken Ann no time at all. That dusky red in her face gone as quickly as come, her eyes composedly cleared, she regarded Arthur Winner directly, with an ease of assurance—even with playful condescension; even, with affectionate teasing. She said: "Oh, Father, I wasn't really serious—"

Ah, yes; catch, ere she change, the Cynthia of this minute!

Ann was in good earnest; she not only said that, she believed that. By her woman's fiat, what she was not now, she never had been; what she didn't now mean, she never meant. Won by the grace of its exercise, Arthur Winner must concede the woman's prerogative. He must observe with wonder that uttermost of confidence, that complacence of femininity (ageless, their wise little heads tilted, Priscilla and Ann intimately planned together in the wired dog run before lunch). He must allow that taking charm, strong and good, that efficacious power. Some man might act, in limited, temporary overlordship, as Ann's father; some other man might come to act as her husband (and on his lawful occasions, the recurring business of the bed might give her from time to time an appearance of being—and often gladly; and often with delight—subject to him), but in her belly was the womb. There it hung, little as a pack of cards; yet the fruit of it was this our race. That thewy capsule's few cubic centimeters were life's font and origin, and woman the custodian. What had any man to set against it? Potentially mother of men, Ann, though she might not yet, though she might not ever, consciously know why, felt the dignity and authority of high office, felt an easy motherliness toward the male.

Ann said: "Oh, Chet was just talking about different places where they had good orchestras. He said *that* was supposed to be the best. But I knew he was just talking—" Ann repressed a reflective, conspiratorial smile. "I'm pretty sure he wouldn't have enough money to take us there. Hendy says: Be careful about that—when you aren't sure they can afford to, always say right away you don't want to."

✦

From the room to the left of the door where members of dinner parties arriving at the Brookside restaurant could gather before they went to their table, a sound of singing loudly issued, a female chorus that just now reached its conclusion in an obstreperous gay hubbub of screams, shrieks, and jocund squeals. "Happy birthday, dear Edna," they had been chanting, "Happy birthday to you—"

493

"Heavens!" Clarissa said. "What are we getting into?"

"We aren't," Arthur Winner said. "That's a party for Edna Keating. As you may have gathered, today's her birthday. The girls are surprising her. Helen Detweiler was supposed to come. If you don't mind, I'd like to see if she's here. Let me order you a drink."

"I'll wait, darling. I forgot to ask you how that business of Ralph's was. Not too bad, I suppose, if Helen feels like a party."

Arthur Winner said: "I know she didn't feel much like one earlier; so she may not have come. Ralph's business is a little complicated—that call, just before we left, was Garret Hughes to say Jerry Brophy had no objection to my telling Helen what Garret told me—the girl, I think very wisely, isn't going on with the case."

"Well, that should be a relief! Not that I can bring myself to care much about Ralph; but I really am glad—for Helen."

"Yes; but as luck, and bad luck, would have it, there's a stupid little complication I'll tell you about. Until that's cleared up, I thought it better not to say anything to Helen. That's why I wanted the operator to know where I could be reached. If I get word it's all right, I can tell Helen—if she's here."

Crossing the low-beamed entrance hall whose walls were crammed with a collection of early lithographs, framed samplers, warming pans, trivets, and other colonial utensils—Mrs. Pratt, Arthur Winner thought suddenly, would perhaps describe the effect as old-timey—he paused at the room's open door. A dressed-up little throng half filled it, clustering with animation around Edna Keating, who wore what was clearly a creation of pale blue lace—which, taken with Edna's head of elaborate gray curls, might suggest that the party had not, perhaps, been a total "surprise." Those present were mostly the courthouse "girls"—Mrs. Morton, taking an evening off from the jail, and looking, Arthur Winner must say, quite surprisingly smart; Miss Foutz, an assistant probation officer, who, though big, placid, and sleepy-faced, was the shrewdest possible investigator of family "conditions" of the more sordid sort; Miss Jordan, the slight, wiry, weathered-appearing juvenile officer for girls; Mrs. Langley, the white-headed deputy clerk of quarter sessions; Mrs.

494

Appleton, the recorder of deeds. They were also, mostly, of a certain age, at which, alas, not one woman in ten can fail to grieve the eye and hurt the ear. Providentially unconscious of this depressing fact, they made merry, giggling, babbling, trending toward a table at the room's end where a waiter in a white coat was lining up what Arthur Winner judged to be one Manhattan cocktail apiece.

Helen Detweiler was not to be seen. Most of the backs were toward Arthur Winner in the movement, with its exclamations, jollity, and general slight air of devilishness, to help themselves to drinks; but Miss Jordan, turning, had glanced at the door. She gave Arthur Winner a friendly, if startled, little wave; and, as though apologizing for them all, a swift wry smile.

Arthur Winner said: "Lillian, can I speak to you a moment?"

She came quickly, her alert eyes lifted to his. She wore trimly, but with traces of the stiffness of unpractice, something made of black crepe with elbow-length sleeves—that coarse skin of Lillian's!—and a pink silk collar covered with rhinestone embroidery.

He said: "Helen's not here?"

Miss Jordan moved her head enough to see behind her. Finding no one near, she said: "Helen called Bella Langley this afternoon, Mr. Winner, and said she didn't think she could come; she knew Edna would understand." Her voice fell in that habit of discretion her work often required. "I'm awfully worried about her, Mr. Winner. I heard about Ralph. Really, *too* bad of him; but Edna told me the girl's name; and I looked— I thought so—and our office has material on her, some reports mention her. Of course, she's not a juvenile, and I never saw her; but she seems to go around with several boys who're on probation, and I believe Dot Foutz knows quite a little about her, if you think it would be of any use to you. I mean, whatever happened, I'd feel pretty sure the girl must have been more responsible than he was."

"It's kind of you to tell me," Arthur Winner said. "Yes; we do know her reputation's not good."

"Well, that's all right, then. I was going to call Helen; but Bella said Helen said she was going out—"

"Did Helen say where?"

"I don't think so, Mr. Winner. Bella thought probably Helen meant, go to a movie or something. I suppose she didn't want to just sit there. I think she did go out, because I decided I'd call anyway, in case she hadn't gone yet; and nobody answered. Do you have to find her? Would you like me to see if Bella knows any more—I mean, about where Helen went?"

"No, don't bother Bella," Arthur Winner said. "I'll try calling Helen at home later. I didn't want anything, except to see how she was. This has been pretty hard on her."

"Oh, it has!" Miss Jordan said. "Really, poor Helen—I mean, she's so nice. I mean, she just doesn't know about these things. I honestly can't imagine what she'd do if she had to spend a few days in our office—I mean, had any idea of what kids today are up to, or may be up to. Oh, here she is! Bella, Mr. Winner was looking for Helen, and I was telling him—"

"I thought he might be," Mrs. Langley said. Her serious, once-pretty, now fleshy and folded face showed sympathy. "Why, I saw Helen about five o'clock, Mr. Winner, and she was all right. Of course, we're all worried about her. She looked awfully tired; but she was perfectly—well, calm. I'd come back to the courthouse this afternoon—because of that Dummer girl's case this morning, we didn't get much done, and there were some things Mr. Brophy had to have for the grand jury Monday. They'd locked the courthouse; but my window was open, and Helen called up. So I went down and let her in. That was right after I spoke to you, Lillian. What she wanted was, could I cash a check for her—"

"A check?" Arthur Winner said.

"Well, of course, today's Saturday so she couldn't go to the bank; and Helen knows we generally have money in our safe. So she gave me her check for a hundred dollars—"

"Did she say why she wanted money?"

"Yes, she did, Mr. Winner. She said Colonel Minton needed some money. He'd lost some, or something—" Since Arthur Winner naturally knew what everyone knew about Colonel Minton's unfortunate failing, she passed on with delicacy. "So I took the check and let her have the money—I hope you won't tell on me! But, really, it made me feel better about Helen—I mean, of course you could see she was under a strain; but I think she—well, had sort of accepted it. I mean, she wasn't just moping around worrying—I mean, taking that trouble for Colonel Minton was perfectly natural, just like her, always doing things for people. I said again—I guess Lillian told you Helen called me before about not coming to the party—why didn't she go to a movie, it would be cool. She said yes, that was a good idea; she'd get something to eat early, and do that. So I just wanted to tell you, so you wouldn't worry about her."

Behind him, a voice said: "Mr. Arthur Winner please? The telephone, sir."

Clarissa said: "How annoying!"

Arthur Winner said: "Yes; but annoying's really all it is. When it got to be seven o'clock I began to half expect something of the kind. The bus would have reached New York by then, so I guessed that something must have, as Bernie says, slipped. Bernie's annoyed, all right. He'd explained to me that highway patrols couldn't miss a bus. I think he has some offended suspicion that the only reason they did miss this one was that they saw the teletype message was from the police chief in a one-horse town, so they didn't bother a great deal."

"So that means Ralph got away?"

"Oh, no. That's what he may think, but he can't get far," Arthur Winner said. "Bernie didn't call me until now because he treated himself to talking direct to New York. It may take a little while, but they're bound to pick him up—Ralph wouldn't know how to hide out."

"Really, that boy! I suppose poor Helen loses her money—the bail."

The abruptly spoken first thought, womanlike both in its taking off at a tangent, and in being first—a going instantly to a material, practical point—made Arthur Winner smile. He said: "No; we won't forfeit bail. I can take care of that; though I may need to do a little maneuvering, since Joe's not to know the charge won't be pressed until he finds out for himself. If

497

Ralph's still gone, I'd come before Joe Monday with Garret and ask, on one or another of the standard pretexts, to continue. Garret and I would then have to put on an act of sorts— I mean, waiting with Joe for the prosecutrix to appear and be told the hearing's put off. When she's not there by ten o'clock, say, Garret can simply do what Jerry Brophy was going to have him do anyway—offer to investigate for Joe. Then, Tuesday, Garret comes back and formally reports their office learns Miss Kovacs changed her mind, won't go on. There aren't any other witnesses; so that's that; and I've no doubt Joe will call me and say he's striking it from the docket on his own motion. So whether we're in fact able to produce Ralph or not won't matter a great deal."

"Well, I see you're not worried. Good."

"No, I'm not. My capacity for worry diminishes," Arthur Winner said. "A benefit of age, I expect. Experience is a great teacher. I suppose anyone after he's heard 'wolf, wolf!' a certain number of times and come running only to find there wasn't any wolf feels more and more inclined to keep his seat."

That, of course, was true. Age, experience could quiet you down, bring you moments at least—even, in middle life, a whole season, of gained balance; yet experience's lesson certainly couldn't be that worrying was needless, uncalled-for. There was that "funny picture" of Alfred Revere's! *All right so far* was, indeed, the most you could hope for; the whole, complete in little, of the comfort or reassurance that fact, as opposed to some adopted faith, could warrant. Merely by experience; almost, you were persuaded never to worry. In a careful review of worries of their lives, most men's finding must be, neither that there was nothing to worry about, nor that worry couldn't be on occasion, a valuable, profitable exercise; but that all or nearly all those fervid past anxieties of doubt or anticipation had been to no purpose. You so seldom worried about the right things. Over evil that never happened the heart had sunk most often and the spirit sickened. Evils actually come to pass, evils that a timely worry (it was conceivable) could have prevented or eased, befell you as a rule without warning, not bargained for, as a sudden dirty surprise.

Reaching across the table, Clarissa touched his hand. She said: "Not age, whatever it is. And, good again—if true."

Arthur Winner smiled. He said: "Well, I might be somewhat worried about Helen; but, as I say, she fortunately thinks Ralph went to Eatontown, and since he said he might, she'll suppose he stayed overnight when he doesn't come in later. On the whole, I believe I'll leave it at that. Bella Langley's probably right; Helen's probably adjusted herself, pretty well accepted the idea of the hearing Monday. She may be anxious, but I think not very; because I think she also accepts the idea that I'm going to get Ralph off. That being the case, and Helen being Helen, I'm afraid she'd be more upset to hear Ralph's run away than relieved to know he won't be prosecuted. Tomorrow I'd have to tell her—but by tomorrow there's the not-bad chance they'll have picked Ralph up—"

"Yes," Clarissa said. "I see what you mean. You couldn't tell her one without the other?"

Arthur Winner said: "I'd prefer not to. The situation's a whole—you can't divide it. Telling only part amounts to a form of half-truth, which is meant to be, and is in effect, a form of lie. And the fact is, if getting older's taught me anything, it's taught me that there's no such thing as a wise lie—that is, a lie that in the end will prove to have been a kind one, or to have worked some good. When you're not asked, tell nothing, if you like. When you are asked, and don't see fit to answer, don't answer, if you like. But if you do answer, if you elect to tell something, tell the whole truth." He heard suddenly Mrs. Pratt's deliberately dulcet, archly encouraging tones: *Only one situation could obligate her . . . is he very likely, or very unlikely, to say someday . . .* He said: "Whenever you don't tell all the truth, you may expect to regret it."

"Oh, dear!" Clarissa said. "Isn't that very hard, sometimes? What were you thinking about then?"

"About that," Arthur Winner said. "Yes; there may sometimes be a hard moment; but when that moment's past, it's past. The other way, you're likely to have coming any number, hours together, of hard moments. So when I tell Helen, I'll tell her all I know, you may be sure. And, of course, I'll tell her if she asks me. But, as I said, I think Bella's idea's right—Helen isn't too upset, so I don't expect her to call me tonight, to ask me. Since she didn't call this afternoon, I'm sure she got my message about Mr. Moore, the only other thing that might be seriously disturbing her. No; I'm sure she's all right—" He paused.

"And now what are you thinking about?"

"Nothing, really. Or nothing very relevant. About Howard Minton, actually. For no reason, I keep trying to imagine why he'd need to ask Helen to get him some money."

"Well, darling, I've always heard that drinks *do* cost money. In fact, I notice that the cocktails here now cost ninety-five cents, which I think is outrageous."

"But why go to Helen? It's true, he wouldn't be able to write a check of his own. I happen to know he has no bank account— he brings in his pension checks and the bank gives him cash for them. But I don't see him drinking himself out of money unex-pectedly. His habits, however bad for him, are perfectly regular —he always, I understand, drinks the same amount, so he knows how much money to have with him. Moreover, why a hundred dollars? I don't see him getting into a sudden scrape. He's never disorderly; he never quarrels. By the same token, sober or not sober, the colonel's a remarkably courteous and considerate man. So I particularly don't see him, even if he must have a hundred dollars right away, asking anyone, let alone a woman, to go to all the trouble Helen had to go to to get him the money. It is *not* in character—"

Clarissa said: "Arthur, your capacity for worry is supposed to be diminishing; remember? And even I find this quite simple. There's been a death in the family. Colonel Minton was at the Union League quietly soaking when a telegram saying Aunt Eunice had just died, please come at once, was handed him. Much saddened, he hurried back to Helen's to pack a bag. Then he happened to discover he hadn't enough cash on him. His being so courteous and considerate made it awfully em-barrassing, but—so Helen, of course, said: Yes, of course. She knew where she could get money—"

Laughing, Arthur Winner said: "Only Howard, poor fellow, has no family left, you know."

PART THREE

WITHIN THE TENT OF BRUTUS

WITHIN THE TENT OF BRUTUS

ONE

FROM THE PEACE of sleep,
Arthur Winner (he could understand) must just have stirred;
even, started. To himself, with deep inquietude, with tense anxiety, he was actively repeating: *I must keep calm; I must reason
this out.* . . . The admonition clearly had to do with the progress of a dream which his coming to consciousness now suspended, left pending—broken into only; not broken up. Though
the waking mind clutched at its relief of recognizing the dream
as such—not really real, not really happening, not really re-
quiring such an anguished effort to grasp and to explain—the
dreaming mind with desperate hypnagogic attachment would not
let go, leave off. A running engine of phantasmogenesis, power-
fully engaged again, pressed him to dream on; and, little as life,
Dunky (could that man be still alive?) angrily, excitedly, confronted him.

Dunky was, of course, wearing one of his two funny-looking,
European-made suits. He was as cadaverous as ever; his extraor-
dinarily prominent Adam's apple moving up and down in his
skinny throat. Dunky was saying: *This is unheard of, Winner;
this is impossible.* . . . His voice was reduced to a hissing whisper. He kept rolling his eyes apprehensively as though to see
behind him in case someone came up the ill-lit bare brick
hall (this place was known perfectly to Arthur Winner; but
where, but when?); in case any of the long range of doors
opened. He hissed on: *I am proctor; I have duties.* . . .

In grateful release, suddenly unblocked, the effort to think
succeeded—this was the monastery-like, plain, long second-floor

503

corridor of Perkins Hall. The two of them were facing each other near the closed door of the room Arthur Winner had occupied his last year at law school. And Dunky was being a little crazy, as usual. Relief immeasurable! In the full clear flood of recognition, Arthur Winner could almost have laughed. Yes, the proctor was indeed supposed to see that university rules were observed; and the obligation was what kept Dunky a little crazy. Dunky, a physics instructor, a friendless foreigner who was a political exile, was very poor. As proctor, he had his own accommodations free. Perhaps reasonably, he was in a panic over the idea of any scandal, which, transpiring, he might be blamed for and lose his post. His obsession was that graduate students in his nominal charge were entertaining women in their rooms—and he did not mean relatives, a mother, a sister, who, with permission, could come to tea.

Dunky's resulting antics were, if exasperating, a settled joke. As far as Arthur Winner knew, the thing Dunky suspected had never been done, nor even attempted, nor even, perhaps, thought of. Perkins Hall residents were grave and studious. That there was a loose-liver in the lot was doubtful; it was certain that the last place you'd logically look for him would be among the toilful men of the law school. Most of them only after midnight put, exhausted, their books aside; and, as often as not, arose in the five-o'clock cold of morning and, breakfastless, set themselves to get what more they could of their enormous assignments done before their first lectures. He stood a moment, living that life, at the time, so long, so permanent-seeming; now, lost and gone, now, dead. Sarcastically, he said: *As a matter of fact, Dunklemann*—he stressed the point that he did not feel friendly, would not call him Dunky. Yes, he was tired of this nonsense. He had a right to be sarcastic—*the lady you ask about is my wife.* . . .

Exasperation filled Arthur Winner. As well as untrue, the statement was unnecessary. Thus detained, his sleeve grasped by a crazy man, in his anxiety, his sense of needing to hurry, Arthur Winner seemed to have lost all judgment. Exasperation became real anger. Thanks to Dunky's intolerable pestering, he would

504

now have to stick to his own absurd falsehood—but, wait! Perhaps this way was best—an assertion inspired. To explain everything—that he had not for years lived here, nor been in Dunklemann's charge; that there was no possible occasion of scandal; that Helen Detweiler worked in his office; and so on, and so on, would take an interminable time. Helen would not know, did not think of, the university rules. In all innocence, and being desperate, she naturally sought him out. Later, he'd better tell her that coming here wasn't wise—for her own sake; because of Dunky's—and, indeed, not only Dunky's—possible misinterpretation. He said (but why did he have to?): *She has come to me in great trouble. . . .*

And that at least was so. With a freezing of apprehension he reminded himself of, he saw again Helen's appearance, as startlingly, she had opened the door, presenting herself. Her trouble must be terrible. Under the shining hair drawn tight, her face was deathly pale, her eyes closed. She might also, he saw, need medical attention. Her lips articulated with difficulty: *Everything frightens me. . . .* Agitated—he ought not to have left her alone so long—Arthur Winner rapped on his closed door. He seemed to hear vague sounds of movement. Indistinct, from within, a voice, not Helen's, said: *In a minute.* A man's voice! Meantime, while he was delayed, had a physician been called? To himself, he said: *There is something wrong; I must go in. . . .*

The room was very dark; yet not so dark that, confused anew, back to where he started, back to utter perplexity, he could know at once the room was never his room. He must have mistaken the door. The drawn window blinds seemed to mean this room was a vacant room. Dimly to be made out, the only article of furniture was an iron bedstead—against the little light, he could see the tracery of the framework, painted white, at the head and foot; and see, too, where those vague sounds of movement originated; and, brought to a halt, see why the voice said: *In a minute.* Of the fact that they were no longer alone, the man and the woman in their obscure struggling effort together took no notice. Her husky voice whispered: *Now, can't you, honey; now, can't you?* . . . As though himself addressed, Arthur Winner, recoiling, said: *No; not here; not now. . . .* With horror, he knew then that he *had* been addressed; he had been all along himself engaged there on the bed. The husky whisper went past his ear; he was joined in that struggle to loosen further the hampering clothing; appalled, he felt the closer touch, the physical warmth, the physical moistness. With sudden dreadful suspicion, he said: *Sue-Anne?*

At the edge of an illimitable parade ground—or was it, airfield?—off which blew a hot stale hard wind, Warren, holding her arm, said: *This is Sue-Anne. . . .* How affected, how, in fact, vulgar a name, Arthur Winner thought. On Warren's bold heartless face, Warren's smile was frank—amused; disdainful. Warren did not care in the least what they thought. She was a tawny-haired Texas girl—very young; too young. She stood small, straight, and jaunty. Smiling, she looked past Arthur Winner. To Clarissa, she said: *I'm so pleased meeting you, Mrs. Winner. . . .*

With a jump of the thankful heart, with a relieved slowdown of the heart's pounding, Arthur Winner detected the error, the saving absurdity, among so much exact, undoubtable detail of experience, the interpolated falsity, sure token that he only dreamed. This picture was wrong; this was not a real happening. Then, the dark room, the bed, the obscure figure clasping him, the almost accomplished carnal connection, had been no more real. In Texas, not Clarissa, but Hope was with him to see Warren get his wings. Not to Clarissa, but to Hope, the thin girl spoke and smiled. It was Hope, puzzled a little, but ununderstanding as only Hope could be, who smiled trustingly back at her son's Texas friend.

Arthur Winner observed the neat star on each shoulder of General Willcox's blouse. Stiffly polite, the general said: *No one will disturb you here. . . .* The door closed, and, standing alone, Arthur Winner saw the bare deal table. Among the mute piles of Warren's things in orderly arrangement was the packet of letters, the lavender-colored envelopes addressed in a slanting, young, unfinished script. With a sad pang of self-reproach, with the not-unmoving thought of who knows anything about anyone, he looked at them. The last envelope had never been opened—had he better see what it said? Yes; he ought to! Who could tell? Who could tell?

To read the other letters would not, he knew at once, be necessary. Warren's father could be sure they were the same, the same rambling obscene relations, the same dirty words; just as he could be sure this was Warren's calm ruthless work more than hers—something that Warren with easy natural unfeeling, almost innocently brutal, had pleasure in teaching her to do, an abjection required of her. On these terms he would let her kiss, on these terms Warren would hold the cheek. *Do you miss me? Ah, Lover, I miss you so! How I wish you were here now to fuck*—the handwriting, ill formed, yet in its frailness almost delicate, repeated the eye-jarring word seven times—*your lonely, lonely Sue-Anne.*

Quietly Helen Detweiler had come in. Seeing him busy, she was waiting. At his glance, she said: *Do you want me for anything, Mr. Winner? . . .* Arthur Winner shook his head. With casualness, he moved his hand, covering the letter, so Helen would not by accident read what was written. Strains of music began to reach him—a band. He remembered this was a military post—some units must be parading. But surely, strange for a military band, the music was religious—a hymn tune. Perhaps something to do with Sunday services? The far-off plangency of brass and drums continued . . . *like him with pardon on his tongue in midst of mortal pain. . . .* Helen had still her exhausted, utterly spent look, yet now without fear; in keeping with the strange music, strangely calm, strangely peaceful. He said to her: *No; there's nothing more you can do. I'll take care of things. Go and rest. . . .* Over Arthur Winner, too, a peace had come. *Rest,* he said, *rest. . . .* As though the very word lulled him, he sank bemused. With a fading of anxiety, a drowsy surcease of sadness, a release of uncaring, he felt sleep deepen to cover him, the voices silencing, the martial strange music, farther and fainter, moving away.

✦

Seating himself on the step of the millstone base that supported the armillary sphere's weathered metal in the rose garden, Arthur Winner took off his gloves. The morning shadow of the yellow-wood tree up by the house, over whose top the sun was only now beginning to slant, had kept the garden shaded, and the stone on which he sat was cool—through the worn seat of his working trousers, he could feel the cool granite surface; while, with absent motions, he filled from a tobacco pouch the pipe he occasionally smoked. In a content of work done—three beds of the rose bushes had been inspected with care, any black-spot-touched leaves removed, and dust applied—he allowed himself, idle and reflective, to be aware of the pleasure of the day; the faint haze of evaporating dew on the still air, the diffused drifting tea-rose scents, the repeated run of bird notes, clear in the Sabbath quiet.

Beyond the garden walls, the same calm of hazed brightness and fresh shade filled the hollow of Roylan. Over the wall, between big trees across the road—one of them was an ash, and Arthur Winner now observed that suddenly (overnight?) the early-turning foliage, despite the summer-like day, presented its portent of close-approaching autumn, the green going, or gone, to delicate pastel shades, hues of smoky lemon, yellowish orange, pale rose, pale brownish purple—sunlight lay on part of the slate roof of Julius Penrose's house. Beyond the hollow, beyond the enclosing tree-covered rises, the same serene flood of sun would pour on the long straight concrete line of the highway—at this time, with an occasional car, only; by afternoon, there would be a solid procession. Beyond the highway, the well-known farmlands sunned themselves, in a patchwork of wood lots, of fields where grains had been cut or where uncut tall corn for silage still stood; of fenced pastures with brooks and willows where dairy herds, milked earlier and turned out, moved or paused, grazing in groups; the countryside unfolded in flattened hills and gentle dales to the narrow Brocton River five miles away.

Over the river, Brocton's streets and houses, displayed in familiar vista, all calm, all bright, would mount the moderate slope in succeeding rows of roofs interspersed with many treetops, to little high points lifted against the fair sky—the court-house dome with its tiny crowning effigy; Christ Church's square pinnacled tower. In keeping with the calm hush, the bright lull, six or seven thousand inhabitants of Brocton were, some, still asleep; some, eating unhurried breakfasts; some, turning pages of Sunday papers; some, without haste, tinkering with or polishing their automobiles, mowing oblongs of lawn in their front or back yards, or weeding garden strips of full-grown zinnias or asters; some, dressing in their best to go to churches of their persuasion.

Out from Brocton, across the entire county, across county after county, across state after state, across woods and templed hills, across waterways and railways, across beaches, bays, and capes, across the corporate limits of towns large and small, across great cities spreading for square miles, across the enormous panorama of the whole eastern seaboard, the same shining morning, the same serene radiance, might confidently be figured to lie.

From the house, Em's distant but penetrating voice, plainly raised to call upstairs, came to Arthur Winner: "Miss Ann! Everyone's eaten but you. You come right down, now. Your breakfast's spoiling!"

Above the garden, the screen door to the terrace slammed. Clarissa, who must have finished her coffee, came out in a dressing gown. She stood a moment, looking to see where Arthur Winner was. Idling along, a cigarette in her hand, she moved down the path, approaching the steps. She said: "Darling; half past nine. If you're ushering today, hadn't you better stop and get dressed? Marjorie telephoned. She wanted to know whether you knew when Julius expected to be here. I said I'd call her if you did."

"I don't," Arthur Winner said. "Just, sometime. Is she all right?"

"I suppose so. I rather think she may have gone to Brocton to mass with Mrs. Pratt. I saw that car coming back, half an hour ago. Priscilla, on the other hand, wants to go to church with

Ann. Of course, she does, now and then; but I couldn't help wondering if, poor child, she wasn't, this morning, making as much of a point of it as she could—you know; lodging a protest, letting her mother, and Mrs. Pratt, too, see how she felt—if they cared! I'm sure Priscilla knew perfectly well what the trouble was yesterday."

"I daresay. Stewart knew, all right. He told me."

"Oh, dear!" Clarissa said. "How nice if everybody would just be normal."

"Hardly possible," Arthur Winner said. "Everyone, I've heard, is queer but thee and me; and sometimes thee is—"

"Oh, you have a point there!" Clarissa said. "When you take my history, I'm, indeed, one to talk! Still, I notice most women don't have to drink until they pass out; or imagine every man they meet is trying to make them; or turn Catholic all of a sudden. Why can't she behave like other people? Did I hear the telephone, earlier?"

"Yes. Bernie Breck. I thought it was nice of him to have our business on his mind. Sunday or not, he was down at the police station to see if anything came in during the night. The night man reported no; but Bernie said he hadn't counted on that much. Ralph would have to sleep somewhere, and the chance to pick him up wouldn't come until he went out in the morning."

"I don't see how, in a city the size of New York, they'd ever find anybody."

"They have their methods. They can narrow down. For instance; the number of people who arrived yesterday, while perhaps large, wasn't infinite. Then, as Bernie points out, Ralph has to sleep; and, not knowing anyone would be looking for him yet, he probably wouldn't go very far from the bus terminal to find a place. All the patrolmen and traffic police around there will have him as a wanted person. But, of course, that doesn't mean they'll necessarily get him this morning, nor even this afternoon."

"Then you'll have to tell Helen?"

"I think so. I think it *was* best not to worry her last night; but the Eatontown story won't do much longer. She may be at church. Yes; I'll go up. How was Ann's evening? I heard her talking to you."

510

"Quite a triumph for Ann, I think. And, for me. After all, she *was* home at exactly eleven. If she hadn't been, some sort of fuss would need to be made, which I didn't look forward to. Of course, this may not have been a real test—they didn't go anywhere, it seems. They just stayed at the Updykes' and danced to a record machine. Chet apparently tried to get them to go to that dreadful Old Timbers dive; but Ann says she told him there'd be a lot of people there they didn't know, and since Mr. Updyke would let them use the rumpus room, wouldn't that be more fun? I think she must have managed rather well—you know; letting him think he was deciding. As I told you, I didn't want us, or even me, to be downstairs formally watching the clock; but I'm afraid, when I heard the car, I went and eavesdropped a little at the hall window. Chet was escorting her ceremoniously to the door; and I could hear him saying in a fairly moony way—which, remembering the letters Ann showed me, wasn't a surprise—that it had been swell; but no attempt at anything more demonstrative. He's probably still a little too young, and a little too bashful for *that* to need managing—"

Arthur Winner said: "I can only repeat; against these cynical and polished plotters, what chance does a young man have?"

"Arthur, there's nothing cynical about it!" Clarissa said. "And you shouldn't think of it as funny. A girl has to learn how to behave; and to do that, she has to practice; and she's wise to practice where she doesn't really care. Then, when she finds suddenly she does really care, she knows already just what to do—she doesn't make a fool of herself, or blunder around, perhaps boring him, or even scaring him off. Ann did very well—as I hoped and expected, a good deal more grown up than Chet. She thanked him nicely—just the right tone. He could guess, if he wanted to, that she much admired his looks, his raiment, his dancing, his manners, and his brains—making her, from his standpoint, a very interesting and desirable girl. There'd been progress; and Ann wasn't saying there might not be more, if he proved himself worthy. He then, I daresay, went home and dreamed about her —which is, of course, the whole idea."

✦

THE CARILLON OF THIS CHURCH
RINGS TO THE GLORY OF GOD
AND IN LOVING MEMORY
OF HOPE TUTTLE WINNER

On the stone north side of the narthex, in one member of the short emphatically Gothic arcature with which the wall was enriched, the cast-bronze tablet crowned by a little cross could be read. Standing alone for the moment, Arthur Winner, thoughtful, read it, while a hundred feet above him in Christ Church's tower, from those loud-speakers, from those efficient magnifying stentors, the wonderfully various, wonderfully powerful bellsounds poured out on the sunny, near-eleven-o'clock air, ringing to that glory and that memory. With not unamused indulgence, Arthur Winner could concede that they also rang a melodious testimony to an at-last triumphing purpose in Jonathan Ives, D.D., of this church the eleventh rector. The project of such a chime had been dear to Doctor Ives; achieving it, no doubt he died the happier.

Not that Sam Orcutt, planning and appointing his "cathedral" with so lavish a hand, had left bells out. To the rising tower, a chime of an octave and a half had been trucked by many straining horses uphill from the railroad depot, and, with much even more interesting labor, hoisted, bell by bell, into place. A very cumbersome system of trappings and springs, of weights and counterbalances, connected the hung bells with what looked like a row of long wooden pump handles in a ringing room halfway down the tower. To play the chime, a strong back, but no knowledge of music, was needed. Such simplified hymns as the chime's range could compass were, on large cards, translated into numbers, showing you in what order to push the pump handles down. Note after separate note, somewhat harsh, somewhat stiff, somewhat hesitant (the tempo was that of a tune picked out on the piano with one finger) could be made, a tonous and a reverbrating clangor, to utter over the courthouse square, for instance: *Love divine, all love excelling.*

Not at any time in his forty-year rectorship had Doctor Ives been content with this awkward and presently antiquated arrangement. Of course nothing was to be said, nor so much as hinted, as long as the old Orcutts, old Sam, old Ezra, persisted in staying alive; but Doctor Ives could privately interest himself in what advances technology was making in these matters. With even Ezra buried at last, the rector moved less circumspectly, openly ascertained how chimes powered by electricity could be installed, what such systems cost, and who supplied the best ones. In patience, he then possessed himself, watching for what might be called his opportunity—a proper occasion for a proper (meaning; able, if he chose, to afford the gift) person to provide for a departed loved one a proper memorial.

These points of propriety finally coming together, Doctor Ives was not the man to neglect his duty, his cure, by failing to convey to the indicated individual what would be fitting in and for him. He never purposed, and he would never practice, anything so crude as soliciting. With genteel tact, but also with perfect firmness, this proper person would, instead, be brought by sober homiletic indirection, to realize that he wished to give Christ Church modern bells. When Hope Winner's sad death occurred, the rector, though so truly sympathetic, must spiritually have rubbed his hands. Avoiding indecent haste, but with no unnecessary delay, he went into action; with whole sincerity, proposing not Christ Church's good alone. Though other comforts fled the bereaved (in Doctor Ives's eyes, young) husband, comforts of piety, of knowing he had provided for Hope's reverent remembrance, could be afforded him, could always be his.

Ah, well! Ah, well! Were you to say such projected goods, such serious kind gestures, such ingenuous—yes!—comforts were ill-considered, did no service, served no turn, merely because in some larger sense, in the terminations, the comings-about of time, under that aspect of eternity, they might prove, like everything that man endeavored, ephemerals, vanities of vanity? The bell-sounds, themselves made suddenly part of the past, vanished from the air; and Willard Lowe's solemn tread on the stone paving approached. Willard was returning from the now well-filled nave. He moved not without a stateliness of presence, a still upstanding, and, so, still entirely dignified bearing. His port and person were distinguished by his formal morning coat, his pin-striped trousers, his Ascot tie. He reached a halt, his erect uncovered head (distinguished of itself) not far from the dedicatory tablet on the wall.

Head turned, as though looking through the door after those vanished bell-sounds, Willard Lowe said: "This quiet I find a boon. The admission's ungracious to you, Arthur; but what's the truth? I've never stopped missing the old chime. Of course, I realize these fancy noises are probably much better. Of course, I realize that all I actually have against this is just that it's modern. Nothing modern, with the possible exception of the electric heating pad, seems to suit me. Of course, I realize—"

Coming up the steps with obvious awareness of being late, passing the door, Roger Bartlett and his wife appeared. Together, hushed, they said good morning as they went by.

"Good morning," Arthur Winner said.

Willard Lowe said: "Yes, good morning! Of course, I realize the rejection, in most cases, isn't reason's. That's the human defect. We feel first; and then with the advice and consent of whatever the feeling is, we think or think we think. I say think we think because I can't but observe the thinking's seldom more than an inventing of arguments in favor of the feeling. I say to myself: Back in Sam Orcutt's day, things were real. Bells were bells, not electric switches. I say to myself: There's no honesty and no quality in anything today—everything's done by short cut, by shirking work. Soon, there'll be nothing that's not an imitation, a substitute, a fraud. At that point, I retain just sense enough to say to myself: Oh, be still, you tiresome old windbag!"

Laughing, Arthur Winner said: "Did you get our visitors straightened out?"

"They consented to move," Willard Lowe said. "Obviously, it was new to them—they'd never heard of rented pews, pewholders. Thus, as well as not Brocton people, I'm satisfied they're not church people. One's led to ask oneself what brought them. Curiosity? The power of advertising? Had they been reading those hortatory billboards that commerce, apparently making character, slips into the run of Pepsi-Cola hits the spot? You know: Attend—the imperative—the church of your choice *this* Sunday! Be that as it may; with one hand coldly plucking them out of the Bartletts' pew, with the other I warmly welcomed them to Christ Church. Alfred get here? I see that he did."

To the left, the wide paving of the narthex extended into an area recessed under the tower and used as the baptistry. Through a hole opened in the corner of the stone vaulting above the font the rope of that great bourdon bell, all that survived of Sam Orcutt's chime, dropped down. There, Alfred Revere had stationed himself. Over Alfred's thin shoulders, open on his decent dark suit, hung an English verger's gown. Being English, the excellent worsted, lovingly cared-for, was still sound and whole; yet time had given the folds of black fabric a least tinge of green, the slanting velvet bars on the full sleeves, a least tinge of gray. The garment, in fact, dated to decades ago, when Doctor Ives personally procured it for old Paul Revere—ostensibly in appreciation of a faithful sexton's services; but also, in result and real intent, one more step (another of the "frills" at which the aged Ezra Orcutt fumed) of those stubbornly taken steps by the then new rector toward approximating the mother church's stricter, if not faith, order; toward correcting religious manners and usages of America, of Brocton, which he considered altogether too off-hand for a House of God.

Alfred saw that Willard Lowe had seen him.

"Good morning, Judge," he said, his voice soberly cheerful; but his turn of countenance was almost sad, his eyes almost sheepish, his slight bow and smile almost shamed. Beside Alfred (also in a decent dark suit, and with a look of special grooming; also inclining his head with civility to Willard Lowe), stood Rodney Revere. The bell rope had been unhooked and swung down, and Rodney's big well-shaped hands grasped it. Mutely, his duty paid, Alfred Revere looked away, looked at Rodney's hands, looked at the gold watch his own hand held.

To Arthur Winner, Willard Lowe said: "You've talked to him?"

Arthur Winner said: "I have. He wanted a will drawn. We're going to do that tomorrow."

Alfred Revere, eyes fixed on his watch, gave a nod. Rodney hunched his muscular shoulders, drew hard on the rope, let go, and at the sudden mighty metallic bong of the single bidding note in the tower, with deft strength caught the rope again, bringing its movement to a stop. In answer of custom, over the square, the courthouse clock began to strike.

From the chancel, flooding the nave, covering the rustle of the rising congregation, a great surge of sound swelled out of the organ. Taking a voluntary as already provided by the carillon, Elmer Abbott blew prefatory, prompting jets of music from his pipes, prephrasing the hymn, modulating to key and tempo. Turning, Arthur Winner could see, a little above the heads of standing people, the processional cross, advanced at a pace of ceremony into the north transept, shining gold, jeweled with big semiprecious stones. This morning, Arthur Winner observed, the crucifer was Chet Polhemus (arisen from dreams of Ann?).

Behind the cross came the singing choir. Since most of his singers were still distant, Elmer, in support, was opening the distincter stops, diapasons and flutes sweetly voluming. First into the transept, and alone for that moment, altos broke on the ear—a dozen scrubbed, starched-collared small boys piping up, pure and neuter. (*The church's one foundation is Jesus Christ her lord . . .*) Now, four square-capped sopranos could be heard to have entered. At once that clean thin soar of children's voices was merged, swelled, warmed, unmistakably colored with sex. (*She is his new creation by water and the word . . .*) On the heels of the women, men were passing the door of the choir room. A not-bad tenor and three by-courtesy baritones joined in with loud firmness, pulling down the high chant toward male levels of solidity or strength. (*From heaven he came and sought her to be his holy bride . . .*) Two basses, marching big and sedate in their cottas, immediately re-enforced the sound, heartily roaring together in their barrel chests. (*With his own blood he bought her and for her life he died . . .*)

Behind, separated by a few steps, in cassock, surplice, and the green stole of the Trinity season, his hands laid formally together, his good-looking face prayerfully turned up a little, his lips moving, either in singing or in simulation of singing, Whit-

516

more Trowbridge, with unostentatious movement, followed after them, came, at the end of the procession, to the crossing.

Doctor Ives's rule—or, rather (of course), indicated wish—had always been that the ushers of the day, when the service started, would remain at the door until the absolution that followed the general confession was given. The congregation's attention was not to be distracted by people entering while those solemn and important offices were in progress. Late-comers would have to wait.

Side by side, midway between the open great doors and the stone tracery screen whose glazed arches divided the narthex from the nave, Arthur Winner and Willard Lowe gravely stood guard. At the top of the outside steps, framed by the elaborate portal's pillar clusters and upswept multiple-molded high archivolt, Alfred Revere had been dismissing Rodney, nodding a measured approbation; on Rodney's hefty shoulder, laying the accolade of a pat, a touch of thanks or affection. None of the Reveres but Paul, and Alfred after him, ever had attended services at Christ Church. This rule was old Paul's. A gathering of his extensive clan at Christ Church would not be right; Christ Church was for those who had always gone there—none of them, colored. For colored people their own church was provided—they attended the church of their choice! Specifically; the African Methodist Church on Water Street. Whatever a new generation might decide to think, in Paul's view—and Alfred's—this was no humiliating exclusion, no enforced abasement. Just as Paul held himself high, Alfred held himself high. The rule, to them, was a natural rule of self-respect.

What self-respect could that man have who tried to intrude where, he saw at a glance, he did not belong; who was so lacking in delicacy and decency, in all proper pride, that he would enter where he was not invited, that he would persist in going where no one welcomed him and no one wanted him? For the sexton of Christ Church to be a communicant was proper, was needful; but at celebrations of Holy Communion, Paul then, and Alfred now, with the delicacy, the politeness self-respect required of them came last to the altar rail. The good, the just, man had consideration for others. By delaying, he took care that members of the congregation need never hesitate to receive the blood of Our Lord Jesus Christ because a cup from which a Negro had drunk contained it.

But those possible hesitaters were unchristian and unworthy, were undeserving of any consideration, were, by a Christian, to be discountenanced instead of accommodated? That was not for Paul to say, as Paul saw it—nor, Arthur Winner suspected, for Doctor Ives, as he saw it, to say either. Doctor Ives observed the observable inequality of men in every known human society. Yes; they were equal before God; but that equality was no more nor less than the equality of flesh—every man was born naked and imbecile; he must eat and he must excrete; and he must die. In those things men had been created equal, and in those things alone he would remain equal. If you wished to further predicate, you must not venture beyond the particular affirmative, the particular negative: *Some men are/are not* . . . whatever your experience persuaded you to report them as being or not being. Some men were wise, some men were stupid; some men were rich, some men were poor; some men were black, some men were white. Their ultramundane Creator, because He had so willed, had so ordered. Was this His resolved servant, Jonathan Ives, to make light, to make nothing, of divinely appointed differences, to dispute them, to find fault with them? On all sorts and conditions, God's great enjoinment was only charity, love of one another; the kingdom not of this world's motto was never stated to be: liberty, equality, fraternity.

Alfred Revere, quietly coming from the door, quietly passed them, moving, inconspicuous, into a back pew. His eyes following Alfred, Willard Lowe said: "Noah is not feeling well this morning. Forgot to tell you. Had a bad dream, he says. Don't think there's a great deal wrong with him. He may be eighty and more; but he's got the constitution of an ox. Anyhow, he said he wasn't coming to church. Not that he does come much, now he's older."

Willard Lowe paused. He said: "Often wonder what, if anything, he still believes. Last night I happened to be reading something written by a supposed ancestor of mine; Quaker; contemporary of William Penn's—Thomas Loe. There is a faith that overcomes the world; and a faith that is overcome by the world. About the size of it, I suppose. A man may gradually grow to feel there's not much in it for him. What's the point of it all—" He cleared his throat sharply. He must have realized how close, by inadvertence, by some absence in brown study, he had been to letting fall an admission unbeseeming, unconsonant, most indecorous in him, out of the question for a man of his position. Covering the near slip, he frowned weightily; he glanced past Arthur Winner again, looking toward the nave, affecting a routine check of the progress there.

But the ulterior, the ultimate query that Willard, in good enough order, backed away from, stayed as wonderingly stated —the point of it all! Standing in his practiced, unfidgeting repose, erect and motionless, his hands clasped (at parade rest?) behind his back, Arthur Winner was aware of a trifling but appreciable tightness in the morning coat that he, too, wore, in the snug encasement of his neck by stiff collar and complicatedly tied tie. Used only a few times each year, these articles of apparel were slow to wear out. Perhaps they wore better than that younger, thinner man for whom they had been made, the man who year after year gravely donned in his scheduled turn the fancy dress; who got older, got a little heavier; who grew gradually to feel—what?

Looking where Willard had looked, seeing along the lofty nave in the stained-glass dusk the couple of hundred inscrutable backs of heads, the hats of women, haired skulls of bareheaded men, both enclosing brains, could you attempt to say what was, in any one of them, felt; what was, in any one of them, believed? Some heads of those couple of hundred were older, wiser heads. Did age and wisdom help or hinder a joining without reservation in this practice? How many of them had that faith that overcame the world undamaged by practical considerations, free of the fretful thinking that went round and round—truth can (or cannot?) be indemonstrable and yet existent? It can? To what evident foolishness you have opened wide the door! How right (or, how wrong?), that certain claimed subjective "experiences," certain asserted "revelations," should (alone in all one's small range of knowable things) be exempted from objectivity's everyday tests of true or false. How right? How hard to take! Blessed are they that have not seen, and yet have believed. A bit thick?

Adding emphasis to indicate his coming conclusion, Doctor Trowbridge's voice carried distinctly from the chancel. Little to his taste in worship as this too-protestant office, this Morning Prayer, might be, "Whit" contrived to convey not neat diction only, but urgent feeling. He pronounced: "Wherefore I pray and beseech you, as many as are here present, to accompany me with a pure heart, and humble voice, unto the throne of the heavenly grace, saying—"

At his organ, Elmer Abbott blew out a single soft note, reverently dropped in the key of E, where he would sustain the murmurous recitation not quite synchronized with the rector's continuing firm voice: "Almighty and most merciful Father; We have erred and strayed from thy ways. . . ."

To Arthur Winner's arm in the time-tightened sleeve of the morning coat, Willard Lowe approached his own abruptly, jogging him. Willard, his thoughts whatever they were, had turned to resume that watch of custom they supposedly stood. He was looking through the great portal's shaded arch to the bright morning of the church close. In tones unaffectedly astounded, he said: "Do my eyes deceive me? My eyes do not! He looks as if—oh, Lord, he *is* coming here. Can't possibly be sober. You deal with it, Arthur. Better stop him out there. Get him to go home—"

Crossing the close, coming from the direction of Greenwood Avenue, striding with an air of agitated unsteadiness, with an air almost unseeing, but of purpose, the gaunt tall figure of Howard Minton was headed for the church. Generally speaking, Howard seemed dressed as usual—the threadbare but exactly buttoned jacket, the infinitely worn but carefully polished shoes; yet Arthur Winner at once observed two, though so small, startling—Willard must be right!—differences. Colonel Minton, who always carried one, carried no stick. Colonel Minton, who always wore one, wore no hat. Even at a distance, the hectically marked face could be seen to have a higher, apoplectic color. The pouched eyes stared. Through parted pale lips, Howard was breathing fast.

Arthur Winner moved. He came to the portal and briskly descended the steps. He came—calmly, he hoped, and unhurried-appearing—to intercept Howard where the walk from the close joined the walk to the door. Howard Minton did not stop; but, at sight of Arthur Winner, he slowed his pace. He brought up a bony, shaky hand and pressed his chest. Closing his mouth, he made to get his breath.

Though in so shaking a state, Howard not only *could* possibly be, at close hand, he was, completely sober. With an unlooked-for but now-instant and searching chill of precognition, Arthur Winner said: "Good morning, Colonel. Is something wrong?"

Howard Minton's mouth went on working. The wrecked, discolored face quivered. Howard's pallid tongue appeared, applying itself with difficulty to his lips. He said: "Mr. Winner. Good morning. There has been an accident. I summoned Doctor Shaw, who is there. He suggested I would find you at church; and if you would be good enough to come—"

"An accident—" Arthur Winner said. "Where?"

Howard Minton said: "Miss Detweiler has had an accident. At home."

✦

Fear no more the heat of the sun—yes, Arthur Winner must allow, all that was to be said, for what all that might be worth. *Their pleasures here are past; so is their pain.* True, true; thank you kindly! By us, nothing further can be done; she is beyond our help. So acknowledging, the sorry heart might venture a *requiescat,* some final, uncertainly directed prayer, some last benevolence of fancy's pitiful wishing—*no exorciser harm thee, nor no witchcraft charm thee; ghost unlaid forbear thee, nothing ill come near thee. . . .*

Noah Tuttle was wretchedly muttering: "Poor thing, poor thing. . . ." Those habitual wags of the head twitched that snowy unkempt mop of hair. The fingers of Noah's large-knuckled old man's hands distractedly opened and closed. Getting out of bed, he had not forgotten to put slippers on his old man's gnarled feet. Unable, seemingly, to sit itself down, or even to stand still, Noah's lumpy nightshirted old man's body padded the big faded wall-to-wall carpet, moving back and forth from the big Morris chair and the bars of sunlight fallen near the windows to the big bed whose disturbed coverlet was left strewn with his morning's means of pastime—the tray of breakfast scarcely touched that had been brought up to him; the scattered sections of Sunday papers; a volume of the annotated statutes taken from the office; a couple of paper-bound mystery stories with scenes of colored violence on their covers. Adding to the slept-in, undressed look of the room, the cavernous closet's door stood open, revealing the hanging row of numerous dark and outmoded garments. Some drawers were not shut in the immense chest of drawers on whose top stood in no alignment a few framed photographs—his dead wife, Hope; his dead daughter, Hope; his dead son, Noah Junior, wearing the absurd high-buttoned military uniform of 1917.

Pausing in his padding, with a sudden energy of anger Noah said: "Boy ought to be shot!" He swallowed twice. The energy failing, he mumbled: "She was his guardian. Now, I guess I'll have to be. Willard can appoint me. Speak to him. I'm too old. Well, he'll only be a minor three more years. I might live that long, I suppose. Of course, there're those cousins in Eatontown. I don't know. I don't know. Find me her will, Arthur. It's in the document file of the big safe. I want to see her account file, too."

"Yes. I'll have them out. Monday, we can—"

"I want them now. I want to see—"

"All right," Arthur Winner said. "I'll bring them here. Why don't you get in bed again?"

"No. Can't do that. You go, Arthur; and I'll get dressed. I won't come over; but I'll get dressed." A paroxysm of little shakes seized him. "Who found her?"

"Colonel Minton," Arthur Winner said.

While they walked in their awkward press of haste—Arthur Winner had not taken time to get his car from behind the parish house—up Greenwood Avenue's leafy tunnel, high and wide, of tree branches, Howard Minton had been panting lightly, breathing a staleness of chronically disturbed metabolism, the faintly foul aftermath of yesterday's alcohol. He said: "Then, I noticed her door wasn't quite closed. You see, I was waiting for a chance to speak to her. I saw her yesterday afternoon. I had returned to my room for some money; and I found I—er—was missing a certain sum. Once or twice before, I thought I missed a little; but this time I knew I could not be mistaken—the amount was a hundred dollars. I'm afraid I thought that possibly Marigold—I did not like to suggest that; but I felt I must tell Miss Detweiler. I don't know whether I was right, whether she somehow recovered it from Marigold; but the money was in an envelope on my bureau when I returned late in the evening—"

Of course, of course!

Enlightenment must be instant; the picture, the afternoon's once-mysterious pattern of events, came clear. Of course, Howard had occasionally missed a little before! That natural sneak, Ralph, would have found out that Colonel Minton kept cash in his bureau. Ralph, with sneaky smartness, might easily guess that a man of the colonel's habits would not always be sure how much was there. Why not put him under regular contribution of a couple of dollars? So yesterday afternoon, Ralph, regarding himself as in a hopeless jam, perhaps in danger of death, certainly in danger of marriage, made his witless decision to "disappear." He needed journey money, and he knew where money would be found. As Marigold reported, Ralph came in; and when he went out to abandon the car and take the bus, he had his hundred dollars. And Helen? Of course, Helen, too, had instantly known. Marigold? Marigold would never touch anything. Ralph lied about Eatontown; Ralph intended all along to run away. Her heart irreparably rent, Helen could now know that, on the old, doubtless long-accepted, lapses of frequent lying, on new lapses of getting an unwed girl with child and whoring on the side, Ralph had superimposed, extending his undone state, thievery and—what could she say to Mr. Winner? —bail-jumping. . . .

523

Howard Minton said: "So at last, when I knew she would ordinarily be up—Marigold comes late on Sundays; but Miss Detweiler always prepares coffee quite early and leaves it on the electric range for anyone who wants it. So when I saw she hadn't done that, and the time was well after ten o'clock—I may say that both Mr. Rose and young Mr. Holland happen this week end to be away, and Miss Falk and Mrs. McGolrick were, I knew, at the shore for ten days; and Ralph, as I ascertained, was not at home either; so I was alone in the house. At any rate, I finally tapped on Miss Detweiler's door; and, receiving no answer, I took the liberty, since, as I say, it was ajar, of opening it farther; and I was indescribably shocked to see Miss Detweiler lying near the bed—"

Arthur Winner said: "He went at once and called Reggie Shaw; and Reggie—"

"That ruffian!" A quick energy of anger caused Noah to revive. Explosively spoken, the stilted, the bookish, the obsolescent epithet itself almost came alive, sounded almost natural—the one right term to tell Noah's indignation at this thought. Noah had not forgotten, nor forgiven—nor, being Noah, ever would forgive—the manner and gross matter of those remarks, profaning the very penetralia of Noah's carefully kept late nineteenth-century temple of convention, that Reggie let drop, for Noah to hear, in the courtroom yesterday. "Fellow like that oughtn't to be allowed near a decent woman. Ought to be reported to the medical association. Don't know what's come over him. Man's gone mad, if you ask me."

Doctor Shaw, downstairs, was discovered at the telephone. To Arthur Winner and Howard Minton he turned, with that manner Noah had in mind, a look both baleful and contemptuous.

His breathing still more labored, Colonel Minton said: "I think, if there's nothing more I can do, I'll go up and rest a little while—"

Laying his hand over the mouthpiece of the telephone, Reggie Shaw said: "Yeah; you'd better. I'll leave something for you." The tone of his voice cleared his words of any concern or consideration. To Arthur Winner, he said: "So you're here. All dressed up, huh? Well, sit down a minute, sit down. This is out of my hands. I'm trying to get Duncan—his wife says he's around somewhere; she's looking for him. You never can get the coroner when you need him. Your law seems to make out that a *felo-de-se* has committed a criminal act, so I'm supposed to notify the authorities. Fine; let 'em have it!"

"There's no doubt that—"

"Yeah, the colonel had some idea about an accident. I can't report it that way, so don't ask me to. This isn't the well-known overdose of barbiturates taken by the well-known mistake. Nobody ever swallowed half a bottle of this stuff by a mistake. I don't know how in hell she managed. It's certainly doing it the hard way." His cold stare seemed meant to call Arthur Winner to account. "What in God's name made her? You know?" To the telephone, he said: "Duncan? Yes; Shaw. I'm at Helen Detweiler's on Greenwood Avenue. And this is for you, I guess. Yes; dead. Drank one of those cleaning fluids—phenol compound. I finally found the bottle; but I could pretty well establish it anyway. Smell. State of the mucous membrane. Drew some urine with a catheter—smoky, greenish; characteristic. I don't see what more an autopsy could get you; but I read that notice or whatever it was your office sent out about different kinds of so-called homicides, so I suppose you may have to go through the motions of posting the body—"

Arthur Winner said: "Not unless the cause of death can't otherwise be definitely determined."

"Yeah," Reggie Shaw said. "Mr. Winner's here. He's giving me legal advice. No; no other significant traumata. The face is pretty bad—slopping that stuff around doesn't improve your appearance. Oh; I did observe some minor contusions on the head—right cheek, and left temple. I'd explain them by saying she must have fallen down a couple of times. She seems to have taken it in the kitchen, and somehow—it's beyond me, Doctor; generally, even if only a little's ingested, you can expect a very quick paralytic effect, I don't have to tell you—she got upstairs to her room. I think she must have been alive, in a coma probably, for an hour or two. I'd fix time of death as shortly after midnight—"

Yes, it had been poor planning; but Helen had no use for, no interest in, studying out the quickest way, the easiest way. Events devoiding her of hope, she felt immortal longings in her. With unflinchingness, this mortal house she'd ruin. Any way at all would do. What means were open to her—ah; she could swallow fire! The label said: Poison. The label said: Induce vomiting. The label said: Summon physician immediately. That was good enough, explicit enough, in its promise that, this grateful cordial quaffed, there'd be no more living for her.

Reggie Shaw said: "Anything else you want to know?" He listened a moment. He said: "I notified them. They say they're sending a police ambulance. I thought you'd rather look at her at the morgue. Couldn't see any reason to leave her there on the floor, any possible reason for photographs, or anything; so I put her on the bed and wrapped a sheet around her. They don't like it, they can lump it! My certificate's ready. I'll leave it for them with Mr. Winner. I can't stay; I have to get to the hospital. So that's that."

That, how true, was that. For the sheeted body deposited on the bed, for the explanatory certificate, the police would soon come; we others have businesses to be about; we cannot stay. Though firmly willed to composure, Arthur Winner, from the corner of his mind's eye must watch the break of day, of the dawn's early light, silent light, holy light, growing on the western world. He thought of the great beauty of today's morning—his cool garden, and outside his garden walls, a gold-lit peace; wide countryside at rest, a whole continental coast all radiant; all radiant, far-off Atlantic seas beyond the horizon. Through these beautiful hours, Helen, not yet discovered, lay quietly dead. And so had lain since the fixed time; since, comatose, slowly, surely dying, she shortly after midnight died? Since—since the time (the same) that, released to leave there, exhausted, her eyes sealed, she paid—forever and forever farewell!—some blind last calls? Silently translated, without a sound

526

entering the dreamer's dream, diffident about disturbing him yet bidden by duty's habit, she inquired gently: *Do you want me for anything?* But, what nonsense, what nonsense!

"And, look, Doctor," Reggie Shaw was saying, "if proceedings have to be held before you, for God's sake try not to subpoena me. I can't add anything. I seem to spend my whole damn time testifying in courts." He hung up. He pushed the telephone sharply away. His hollow eyes moved to Arthur Winner. "They say you're crazy," he said. "Or, they say you're cowardly. Well, the average chinless wonder probably does have to say something. He'd never dare do it; so it gives him quite a turn when he sees somebody who does dare. What's the pitch, here? Or, aren't you telling? Or, don't you know? She didn't happen to have got herself knocked up, I suppose? No; I know she wasn't that. Well, I don't care. Nothing to me. When they don't like it, let 'em leave. I'm no lawyer. I'm no policeman. I just pronounce them dead."

Anger—Noah's anger; as Noah would see it, from this madman's violation, chastity wasn't safe even in death!—had filled Arthur Winner. He had actually opened his mouth to say what he thought of that question about Helen. Closing his mouth (did he mean to let a—well, ruffian, provoke him; did he propose to brawl at Helen's obsequies?) Arthur Winner waited a moment. Reggie Shaw said: "Incidentally, take my advice; don't go up and look at her. Not nice. You wouldn't like it."

His tone made casual, Arthur Winner said: "I hadn't thought of looking at her. Just one thing, Reggie. What's wrong with you nowadays? Can I, can anyone, help you?"

"Me? I'm right as rain," Reggie Shaw said. He spoke with loud derision, a stony defiant mockery; but, even while they mocked, Reggie's eyes—what was that darkness: fear? pain? weariness only?—had wavered, lost some of the stoniness. "Sure," he said, his voice kept gruff with great effort. "I need a rest. Why don't you say that? Ruth keeps yammering about it. What the hell would rest get me?"

Ah—simple, this unriddling! Here was no more than that opposite truth behind most tough talk—a panicky, impotent little Mr. Moore yelled at himself, with the blustering threat,

527

the loud vaunt, the viperous tongue, hied himself on. Did he sound tough enough? Would someone suspect? Better, perhaps, go further? Better shout louder? Fruitless the effort! The note was ever false. So Reggie meant you to know he was hard as nails? True callousness, cold and contained, true heartlessness, seldom saw occasion to raise the voice. To cry: *I don't care* would never cross uncaring's mind; uncaring didn't labor the obvious. Sneers, insults, taunts—the voluble bitter tongue's many inventions—were found by feeling, not by unfeeling.

Arthur Winner stood silenced, silently appalled, since he must understand how catastrophic—here, now, and for Reggie—was the simple unriddling's purport. A riven heart that wished to beat no more, the torture of the dreadful drink, the poor corpse (unhappiness's own child!) by the examining physician lifted to the bed—*nothing to me!* Once upon a time, would this physician have said that? No; once upon a time, in the sense of any pitying personal involvement, that could have gone without saying. Once upon a time, Reggie (with civil expressions of a regret no doubt real, but soon dismissed, fleeting soon, as his load of work reoccupied him) had, in fact, as of course, just pronounced them dead.

Brought, together, to a pause, they faced each other, look unwillingly engaged by look, the discoverer and the discovered. No, no; of comfort no man speak! Not here, the easy stare of contempt, the impetuous accents of a young Fred Dealey rousing to lay with a will his lash on those asses (himself included), men. Men's follies and ineptitudes exasperated Fred, yes; but discouraged by them he wasn't. He'd drive the asses, yet! Not here, the open, illusionless steady gaze, the precise ironic accents, of a Julius Penrose separated, in the rare solitude of an adult mind, from most human beings; with his equipoise of facts envisaged and veracities recognized, ready for whatever might come next. Try as hard, or try as long, as you liked: asses don't drive! Sooner or later, you're going to have to take asses as asses are—and life as life is. In virtual freedom from every foolish hope, Julius spoke out the stoic's cheerless—but firm; but manful—word. Now with matter-of-fact grim insight, now with a jest; in scorn of fortune almost impassible, so mostly imperturbable; neither fearing nor favoring; seldom complaining, and when he did, soon silencing himself, he freely said his say. One with hope, one unhoping, those two took strength from true experience (bitter or not) and might be expected to go on taking strength. What terrible, different case was this of Reggie's?

As with a Howard Minton, material in which originating cause might be read was not given; given, was only the result of a result. Calamitously lost (you read in the result's result) was some once-saving carapace of a mind detached, which (you easily saw) the man whose practice was physic could not dispense with. Dropped off piece by piece (you might read) had been the armor so long proof to any day's professional doings—to all severings of limbs and manglings of flesh, all fluxes of purulence or excrement, all bloody splits and tears of parturition; to the hydrocephalic baby with its bird cries and pulpy veined great head mass; to the boy by accident made eyeless; to the young man with his shattered spine; to the tormented old man with his not-to-be-helped, often disgusting, failures of function; to the terrified old woman with her not-to-be-helped, often stinking, proliferation of neoplasm.

What in particular played this late-come havoc? Something complex? Something simple? Something that was both at once, being merely cumulative—one Tom Henderson too many dead on a float? One surgically butchered Arthur Winner Senior too many? One too many irrecoverably hemorrhaging Hope Winner? No matter, no matter; univocal was result's result. With a palliative, alcohol (or, looking in dark and desperate eyes, Arthur Winner thought for the first time, a drug?), Reggie evidently doctored his vital wound; and to what avail? For that wound, what drug was vulnerary, in that pain, what poppy would medicine him again to a student's, an intern's, a once-boyish Reginald Shaw, M.D.'s sweet sleep of scientific attitude?

A minute passed. Perhaps acknowledging himself found out (a soldier, and afeared!), Reggie Shaw shrugged, ended the engagement of eyes. He looked sharply away. He said: "Here." Pulling his bag to him, he took a bottle and a small envelope. Into the envelope he spilled pills. "Minton better have some of these. He isn't up to this kind of thing." Uncapping a pen, he scrawled a few words on the envelope. "When they come, there's their certificate—there." Breaking off, looking at Arthur Winner angrily, he said: "What's wrong with *you?* Aren't you up to it either? You need a rest, too?"

"Possibly," Arthur Winner said. He was aware that, absorbed by this shock of new knowledge and inwardly not unshaken, he had also given an outward start. Collecting himself, he said: "Did you hear a curious noise?" He turned to look up the hall. The noise, now distinctly heard, was a sound like low muffled wailing, punctuated by weakly struck or uncertain thuds, as of poundings on wood.

"Somebody trying to get out of a coffin?" Reggie Shaw said. He uttered a bark of laughter. "That's the redoubtable Marigold starting again. She got tired before; and I forgot about her. She's locked in the kitchen storeroom."

"She's locked—"

Reggie Shaw repeated the bark of laughter. "That's what I said. I locked her up. She came in just after Minton went for you. I told her what happened; so she lets out a howl, starts throwing her arms around, tearing her hair, trying to rush upstairs." With a certain savage cheerfulness, Reggie Shaw nodded. "I wasn't going to have any of that. I was still looking for the bottle. I didn't need any hysterical moron bothering me; and she didn't need to see Helen. I noticed there was a key in that door, so I just shoved her in and locked it. I think you might be smart to leave her there until they take the body away. Suit yourself."

"Reggie, you really can't—"

"Illegal, isn't it?" Reggie Shaw said. "Well, Arthur, you can always advise her to sue me. Good-by."

"That boy, that boy!" Noah Tuttle said. "All his fault! She couldn't go through with it, I suppose. May never find him. What'll you do about Monday?"

"They'll find him," Arthur Winner said. "But Monday will be all right. That's taken care of. There isn't going to be a hearing. The girl's decided to withdraw, or at any rate, drop, her charge—"

"Oh, no . . ." Noah Tuttle said. He stopped dead. He said again, his voice shattered: "Oh, no!" On his chest, his gnarled hand clutched folds of his nightshirt as though they were his heart. The rheumy eyes had overbrimmed; but he swallowed loudly. Then, stolidly enough, he croaked: "Well, go along, Arthur; go along."

TWO

Picking up the telephone on his desk, he said: "Arthur Winner."

"Oh, oh, darling!" Clarissa said. "How unspeakably awful! Willard told us as soon as church was over. I've been trying to get you; I didn't know where you were. Can I do anything? And Doctor Trowbridge—I'm calling from the rectory—asks me to ask you if there's anything he can do."

"No, my dear; you can't do anything. And, thank him; but neither, at the moment, can he. I'll call him later—" Checked by sudden unexpected recollection, he wondered if the old prayer book rubric about those who have laid violent hands upon themselves still stood in the present revision. The truth was, he hadn't the faintest idea. "If I may," he said. By the bracket clock, it was five minutes of one. "I think you and Ann should go home and have dinner. Em will begin to be worried."

"Oh, I called Roylan. I thought maybe you'd gone out for something. Em expects us to be late. Willard said you were going to the club to tell Noah. Did you?"

"I did. Everything considered, he took it fairly well—better than I'd been able to hope. I'm just here getting some things to bring back to him—"

"But, Arthur, you must eat—"

Arthur Winner said: "At the moment, I don't feel a great deal like eating—" Noah's quavering *Oh, no . . .* sounded in his ears—the dazed old mind's shocked, feeble protest against, repudiation of, the supposed comedy of awful error, the brutal as-luck-would-have-it joke. His wits recovered, time taken for

532

the bitter, slow mulling-it-over, was the old man going to say: *You mean you knew Ralph was clear yesterday? You mean you might have told her; but you didn't?* Answer: *Yes, I might have; but, no, I didn't. I decided not to, for some interesting and involved reasons; to wit* . . . He said: "When I go back, I'll have a sandwich at the club. They brought Helen to the police morgue; and I want to go down there—see the coroner, see what arrangements I can make."

"Darling, I know how dreadful all this must be for you; but please do eat something. What about this afternoon? Will we go to Mother Winner's?"

"Yes. We'll have to," Arthur Winner said. "By evening everyone in Brocton's going to have heard—poor Marigold will see to that—" On the desk, a letter tray covered in green finely gold-tooled morocco held several papers, looking like legal forms, which he had not before noticed. The uppermost, presumably some affidavit or other, Helen had notarized. He looked at her carefully impressed seal, her name neatly signed. *My commission expires* . . . Rubbing his forehead, he said: "So Mother will have to be told. She was always fond of Helen; and I'm afraid it will, as she'd say, agitate her. Suppose I meet you there about four?"

"Arthur, why don't you let me tell her? Ann and I can come a little early. That way, she'd know before she sees you. I think that would be better—I mean, I think it might be easier for her to hear it from someone else—not you."

Yes; of course it would! Arrested, Arthur Winner must—as so often he must—mark marvelingly, in contrast to his own mind's pedestrian movements, his laborious careful considerings of what would be the best thing, sensibility's winged divinations, this perceiving prescience of the feelings which saw at once what other feelings would be; and so, instantly and certainly, never stopping, never stooping to think, could just *know* the best thing. He said: "You're quite right. She'd very much prefer to hear it from you. She'd get a chance to adjust herself a little. How nice of you! How did you know?"

Clarissa said: "I've told you about that. We're women, you see."

533

"My dear!"

"Yes; I seem to be crying. Isn't it absurd? I don't know why —so unlike me. Now, I've stopped. Good-by, darling."

Make me to know mine end, and the measure of my days, what it is. . . . The simple, inevitable moment, with those counsels of gravity and recollection, better and better known to Arthur Winner as the years went, was again arrived at. It was a moment made sober, made sobering, by the very absence of all ceremony, by the plain-dealing ordinariness of the observances. The double doors of the big wall safe were opened. In a narrow document drawer the right envelope of those numerous open-ended envelopes would be looked for and found. Arthur Winner would remove it. He brought it to his desk. He sat down. He put on his reading glasses. Withdrawing the folded stiff sheet or sheets, he unfolded, flattened on his blotting pad, another last will and testament. Gravely greeting his comprehensive first glance might be this or that flourish of ancient form: *In the name of God, Amen. I—; Be it remembered, that I—; Know all men by these presents—*. At once, he skipped on, passed to the end in automatic professional check—date; proper signature; proper attestation of subscribing witnesses; executor or executors named. Turning back, such points of validity all seen to, a businesslike brisk reading could be begun; an attentive scanning that took in, ticked off, paragraph after paragraph, item after item, this now-corpse's imperious orderings, this now graspless hand's devisings and bequeathings, a scanning that also considered, that critically assessed, the frequent surplusages of fussy direction, the sometimes intricate rewarding or punishing provisions of bestowal. Food for thought, they often suggested that testator, in his Soul-thou-hast-much-goods self-importance, in his plans to continue to rule his heirs and assigns, to bend future time to this will, grasped no better than most men that, in order for his orders to be operative, his will to be done, all scheming and planning of his must first (*huddled in dirt the reasoning engine lies*) have an end, that he was to be dispossessed of all possessions,

534

that the "my death" this instrument so unexcitedly mentioned was to involve actual dying—no more of him.

When the telephone rang Arthur Winner had been at the wall safe. The safe was open by then, but opening it took him a few minutes. Helen always opened the safe. Since he last used the combination, several years had probably passed; he was not sure of the numbers. He had found the envelope quickly enough, and at the buzz of the little switchboard across the office, he was able to carry Helen's will in with him to his desk. The telephone put aside, he took the envelope. To facilitate finding it in the file, *Helen Detweiler* had been penciled—by Helen herself, he saw—at the top. The envelope was without bulk—no self-importance would puff up this testator; a couple of paragraphs could take care of all Helen had and all she might intend. What reason would there be for Noah to think he needed to see it? Of course, there was no reason; Noah had no need to. In stupefaction confounded, Noah said a mechanical something for the sake of saying something. When a person died and you knew a will existed, you always asked to see the will; you always went through the form of reading it before the executors offered it for probate.

No name of God here; no importunings to remember; but, flourishless: *I, Helen Everitt Detweiler . . .* His glasses on, Arthur Winner had given the sheet its comprehensive glance; yet he got no futher forward. Executors, he had seen, were Fred Dealey and the First National Bank of Brocton; but there he stuck. Though this was not Noah's incapacitating stupefaction, nor anything near it, a certain thickness or numbness of mind interfered with his efforts to put thought in order—indeed, resisted thought, persisted in what was not thought at all, but only feeling's idiot asseveration, renewed and renewed, that this that was true *couldn't* be true.

From the frame above the mantel, mature face intent and thoughtful, finger forever marking his place in the bound volume of reports held by the competent hand, the competent mind forever pondering its point of law, Arthur Winner Senior, forever unknowing, forever unaware of various later happenings, gazed down at Arthur Winner Junior, father surveying son. Fixed in his moment of time, that year of his life when he sat to the portraitist, Father was, in age, being approached, overtaken; would presently be passed—the man of the portrait quite soon now (how strange the thought) become a younger man than his son. Proceeding to live longer, might the son, being now the senior, sometime come to have learned more, actually (incredible!) know more, than the very paragon of learning, sense, wisdom, whose unpedantic dry instruction for years had gone to teach a young man (in all three relatively lacking) points of learning, points of observing, points of thinking; whose stored sayings were in fact still a bible at the back of the mind, without recourse to which, even today, few days ever passed—for apposite example, what of that favorite half-serious maxim on will-drawing? *Always remember, Son, to provide for the thing you think can't happen; because that's going to be what does happen. . . .*

Yes; exactly! Consider how, here, under his hand, a course of events laughed at the judgment of another day. For Noah to have named himself executor of this will would have been absurd. Already an old man, he couldn't possibly outlive Helen, a girl just come of legal age. Little more likely to survive her were men then past their youth like Arthur Winner Junior and Julius Penrose. The odds, of course, were also against Fred Dealey's surviving her; but disparity of age being less, Fred being young—just entering the office, not yet a partner— they could put his name in for the time being. When Fred came to see himself as too old, he could so advise Helen, help her select someone else. Helen, anyone who knew Helen must feel certain, would still be there, devoted and faithful still to a work and life that suited her so well; white-headed, perhaps, but active and alert, the absolutely dependable, in the field of her duties completely competent, indispensable then as now, manager of the office, as long as he had one, of what would be in her series of aging employers, the last old man. What would he do without Helen? Helen would never leave him!

But tomorrow, Helen, who was always to be here, would not

be here. Monday she would not be in. Intruding among the afflictive thoughts of original incredulity, an incredulity of horror that pushed away the idea of Helen, the poor girl, the tormented young woman, dead in despair by her own hand, were now those different thoughts, unconsonant with the decencies of pity, with grief incongruous; yet thoughts pressingly relevant, the thoughts of business that brought along a different incredulity, an incredulous, vexatious foreseeing of a dozen petty practical problems. Why, Helen was always in; she had to be in. Helen opened the office every day. At eight thirty on the dot, she admitted herself with her key. She hung up her hat and coat, perhaps went to the lavatory for a minute, and then, without delay, to her desk. She would have collected the morning mail, fallen through the front-door slot on the floor, and she quickly sorted it. Carefully, so no time would be wasted, she planned, laid out, a day's work for the girls—what, when they came in, she would give Mary, what she would give Gladys. To each of the partner's desks, she brought, with his mail a little list of appointments, of things he must remember to do today. The office now in readiness, in order, waiting for the day to begin, Helen, in her own quiet of readiness and order—the clean tight-drawn shining hair, the unpainted immaculate face, the thin hands whose perfectly manicured nails had never worn polish, the neat, simple, well-fitted, well-cared-for clothes—waited too.

Waiting, Helen kept busy, of course. Those first things done, she would have spun the dial, pushed back the wall safe's doors. There, revealed in the much-compartmented interior, ranged her special charge—those rows of journals and ledgers, Noah's years of fiduciary accounting, Noah's work of a lifetime. Not a few of these records, though never thrown away by Noah, were of accounts long closed, the decree made final, the trust terminated; but many more were live, a formidable continuing task of bookkeeping, almost a whole-time job for anyone. Those endless entries in form of charge and discharge; the patient postings from journal to ledger; the debitings of inventory and creditings of estate, this to corpus, that to interest; the often numerous schedules carefully to be kept separate in a single account—for the last five or six years Helen had really been doing it all. Noah's part, nowadays, was no more than supplying Helen with scratch-pad memos for this account or that, jumbles of figures with cryptic abbreviations well understood between them, but which, you might be sure, neither Gladys Mills nor Mary Sheen —nor, for that matter, Arthur Winner himself—would be able to make head or tail of. Only Helen, never wasting a minute, could do it. Tomorrow, the week beginning, eight thirty would draw near, would come, would go; and no Helen.

But, of course, tomorrow they would close the office. In that vacant but anxious bemusement, that slightly stunned slowness of mind, even the obvious could come as a surprise. Arthur Winner hadn't thought of that. Gladys and Mary must be told. And what else was there tomorrow? Alfred Revere—well, Alfred, at church when the service was over, would have heard, would know, would guess that Mr. Winner's Monday appointments were now canceled, and that Alfred (if wait he could) would have to wait. The same for any other business. Monday, no one could expect Tuttle, Winner & Penrose to be open as usual— Noah was unlikely to have any appointments; with Julius not certain last week that he would be back from Washington, none would have been made for him. The time, Arthur Winner saw, was twenty minutes past one. He must stop this; he must not just sit here.

He read: *1. I direct my just debts and funeral expenses to be fully paid and satisfied. 2. I give and bequeath to Marigold Revere Parsons, if she survive me, the sum of one thousand dollars.* . . . No more, surely, than an affectionate or grateful gesture; like those possible executors that age had disqualified, Marigold, admitting to fifty and probably nearer sixty, could have no real hope of taking—but, but: *that's going to be what does happen!* Ralph, then, took the rest, Arthur Winner saw. Actually, he didn't know just what Helen died seised of. The Greenwood Avenue house; funds to some amount in trust with Noah—that money to put Ralph through college; oh, yes; and a secondhand car, now in custody of the police. A small checking account; perhaps a small savings account. Certainly, safeguarding little Ralph, some life insurance—with, perhaps, a suicide exception?

538

Arthur Winner thought (the thought's vain spite surprised him): *Well, I hope so. . . .*

Through his open door, Arthur Winner heard the new buzz at the switchboard; immediately on his plugged-in line, the green light winked. Holding his hand a moment—with whom would he have to deal now? Did he want to?—Arthur Winner then lifted the receiver. He said: "Arthur Winner."

"Arthur, Arthur—" Noah's stammer was at a pitch of anxiety. "I tried to get you—the line was busy—"

"Everything's all right," Arthur Winner said. "I'll be over presently. I was just looking at the will. It's in order. I'll get out the account file—"

"No," Noah said. "No! Don't bring anything, Arthur. Don't want to see them. Don't feel like seeing them. Leave everything alone. Account file may be in my room. You can't find it—don't touch anything on my desk—just get things out of order. I'll see to it."

Now the old fool would; now the old fool wouldn't! Well, he himself, Arthur Winner must allow, was little better off—he was tired, even though this was only midday or shortly after; he was probably hungry, even if he didn't feel hungry. A moment ago, remember, he was feeling that spiteful hope that Ralph would be paid no insurance money. He said: "All right. Really, I think tomorrow would be better. Today, I think we're all—"

"Yes; don't want anything now. Don't touch anything. Who's executor? Fred? I'll get the will to him. And speak to Willard. He'll have to appoint me that boy's guardian. Don't come back here, Arthur. Don't want to talk about it; don't want people to bother me; not this afternoon—"

Exasperation must subside in compunction. The old man could be seen to have thought things over, testing perhaps his own shaky reactions. He had fallen into worse shakings; the distracted old mind said: No, no—he couldn't face it. The sound was pettish, but the mind's inefficacy could be actual fear—who knew? The weights of grief and dismay might, if increased, stop the laboring old heart. Frightened, he fended off even his serving boy, Arthur—not now, not now!

"Very well," Arthur Winner said. "I'll see you aren't disturbed.

539

If you do happen to want anything, I'll be at Mother's later this afternoon. We'll close the office tomorrow. Julius plans to be back today sometime; so if you feel like it then, we can go over things—"

"Yes; you're a good boy, Arthur. Tomorrow. Tomorrow."

. . . *just get things out of order!* Conceivably, that was so. In the crowded, the yearly increasing, disorder which Noah, pondering, planning, working, surrounded himself with, order of a sort there might be. Perfectly true that, peering about, padding about, the old man quite soon put his hand on whatever he wanted. Demonstrably, the books and papers that covered in piles every flat surface were not piled at random; they constituted a filing system of Noah's own. Still, Aunt Maud was not far wrong—the place looked like a rat's nest. Going into Noah's room, to lay the will now returned to its envelope, on Noah's desk, Arthur Winner could hardly find a clear place to put it down.

The door had been closed, and on the unventilated air were those traces of mustiness, that ghost of cigar smoke, to intensify the feeling of things past—upholstered furniture in old, old cracked leather; on the paneled walls in need of paint, old, old tarnished gold picture frames containing old, old engravings that nobody would hang today—Sir Edward Coke, in ruff and skullcap; Sir William Blackstone, robed and bewigged. In one thronged large scene, King Charles the First was come before President Bradshaw and the regicides soon-to-be; in another, Webster was risen to reply to Hayne. Above a side table deep under books, displayed on a mahogany mounting, was an enormous stuffed trout caught by Noah in 1909. Above Noah's chair hung the enlarged photograph of a gun dog, a pointer named Boy who had died in the nineteen twenties. Packing the high wide bookcases were undusted sets of legal reference works so outdated—Wait's *Law and Procedure;* Parsons on Contract; Kent's *Commentaries*—that no one would now think of consulting them; and, in runs of ten or even twenty years, bound volumes of law journals or financial periodicals no longer published. In the empty hearth under the fireplace's fine mantel—another part of Noah's filing system—were tottering stacks of newsprint, of what must be roughly the last hundred issues, on the left, of *Barron's Weekly,* on the right, of the *Financial World.* The wide window ledges were deep with accumulated layers of this year's, last year's, and even the year before last's, plain or fancy, interim or annual, reports of dozens of corporations.

In the center of the littered desk, placed on a closed file folder were seven or eight checks—drawn by Helen and put there for Noah to sign. To the one on top a note in pencil had been attached with a paper clip: *Mr. T. this will be an overdraft*—yes, that was the sort of thing you could count on Helen for; the reason for these transactions she might not know, but the result she had always at her finger tips. The checks were lying loose, already a little disturbed, scattered; and bringing them together, Arthur Winner had been about to lay Helen's will on them; yet he hesitated—something too grim about that, too pointed; though pointing to what he could not say. He opened the file folder to lay the checks in there—or would Noah then never find them? In the folder was a long legal-sized sheet headed in Noah's handwriting *Schedule of current indebtedness*—he remembered suddenly the old man moping in the courtroom yesterday—*everybody thinks I'm made of money. . . .*

Arthur Winner smiled. The sheet was covered with what seemed to be notations of money due—dates; what were probably account numbers—yes, he saw: S204 was an account against which one of these checks was drawn. By this confusing record, did Noah, on some system of his own, keep track of his informal, his private transactions—cash advanced, as he glumly said, out of his own pocket? Over the months, constant emendations or corrections had been made—items canceled; items inserted. As nearly as Arthur Winner's casual glance could puzzle them out, the original notations were of amounts in debit, canceled when they were paid. At sight of that long, long array of fussy, grubby figurings, of meticulously kept calculatings, so eloquent of the worried old man's worryings—*I'm a poor man. People don't know how poor*—some brief grief of pity must stir. Closing the folder's cover on the account sheet and the checks to sign, Arthur Winner drew a depressed breath, took a step away. He stopped.

Stopped no less short, even more sharply arrested, the mind held again before its eye the worked and reworked sheet. So seen, did method show in layout of dates and figures, of sums noted as drawn, of sums then paid, or not yet paid? Could a pattern be thought to have appeared? Arthur Winner stood stock still, aware of pricking sensations, a creeping of unease, an increasing coldness as though of a draft on him. *Schedule of current indebtedness* . . . Look again? No, no; no business of his. Private figures, figures not meant for him to see, figures that only by this impossible, this hideous chance—Helen must first die—he ever came to see. *Look again?* Those dates? But *that* was when Christ Church's quarterly money was paid. And from an account numbered S204, and an account numbered S98, Noah withdrew—in an instantaneous fitting-together, a falling into place, the pattern was established. The staggered, the stunned mind must take a meaning. Those accounts uncanceled, left showing money owed (and by token of this continuing, changing record, at any time, at all times, some of Noah's accounts), were short. Which was to say? Which was to say no more nor no less than that Noah Tuttle, this paragon of honesty, this soul of all honor, blameless of life and pure of crime (. . . *a man of complete probity, Mr. Woolf!*) had—for years?—been helping himself to, now repaying, now taking again, money that was not his.

Arthur Winner stood in his continued chill, in a stunned sense of solitariness, as though the early Sunday afternoon world around him had, more than merely stopped, come to a halt, to an end, had dissolved, had withdrawn in space, leaving him on a point of rock, the last living man. He said aloud: "I am a man alone." The silly words, the stilted, sententious sound, jarred him. From the silence no response could be expected; yet, dazedly, he became aware of silence broken—something moving, something moved; a delayed click-closed of a door toward the back; a progress of difficulty—a wounded man dragging himself? A dead man being dragged? His cold was horror's. Slowly, stiffly, Arthur Winner made himself turn, look through the open door.

Coming from the back of the reception room into the outer office with a deliberate practiced plying of his canes was Julius Penrose.

✦

Not moving, Arthur Winner said: "Julius!"

"Yes; I've heard," Julius Penrose said. "And though I never thought the day would come when I would need to say it: you must compose yourself, Arthur. Let us go into your room."

"How did you get here?"

"I have transportation," Julius Penrose said. "Marjorie brought me down. She seems in a mood of penitence. I gather she was not herself yesterday; and the subduing aftereffects—I saw you wondering the other night whether I knew that Marjorie's drinking was not absolutely or altogether a thing of the past. I did. I do—conduce to deeds of what I expect she feels is Christian charity. Moreover, Marjorie not being herself, Mrs. Pratt, I understand, was inflicted on you. I agree you're owed an apology; but I find Marjorie is ashamed, would prefer not to see you just now. Having no doubt you'd much prefer not being apologized to, I had her bring the car around the back where I would not need any help with steps. By a little such planning, help is often made something I can take or leave alone. Perhaps I should say that Mrs. Pratt, before she fled my coming, seems to have reported herself more than satisfied with you, your conversation, your courtesy, your kindness—now let us consider this other matter. Sit down, Arthur."

Letting himself carefully into the chair in Arthur Winner's room, Julius Penrose arranged his legs, laying his canes across his lap.

Arthur Winner said: "How did you come to hear?"

Julius Penrose said: "By a set of curious chances. Barely had I been delivered home, when the telephone rang. It was Clarissa. It was about Priscilla, who had, I learned, happened this morning to go to church with her and Ann. Clarissa, getting her news about Helen from Willard Lowe, who got the news, I gather, from you—"

543

"Yes. I told him. The service wasn't over; but I felt I had to go and see Noah—"

"I concede the necessity. At any rate, Clarissa hadn't been able to find you, and she didn't want to come out to Roylan until she'd talked to you. Therefore, Priscilla would be delayed. Marjorie might worry. Surprised, but also relieved, I think, to find me answering the phone, she told me all she could. Yet—will you believe it?—I knew already."

With steady scrutiny, the dark observant eyes rested on Arthur Winner's face as though they meant to offer him, to carry to him, their calm of preciseness, of impassivity. Julius Penrose said: "More chance: but also, what a commentary on our age! As merrily we rolled along, almost, the good Pettengill and I, arrived at Roylan, he asked my permission to put on what he calls the wireless. The next thing I knew, I was hearing, appended to a news broadcast, an appeal to one Ralph Detweiler, or anyone who knew his whereabouts. Would he come home; there had been a death in the family. A death? In the family? Would Ralph come home? I was indeed taken aback; in part, by the instant intelligence, since I knew Ralph's situation, conveyed. Not very surprisingly, Ralph had lost his nerve, had run; not very surprisingly, Helen, distracted, found this too bad to bear. I grasped all."

"Perhaps not quite all," Arthur Winner said. "She found out that, in order to run away, Ralph had stolen some money."

"Ah, yes. That Fool Killer's touch!" He studied Arthur Winner. "Our actors are all ham—a point not unrelated to the commentary I spoke of—the incident of the—er—wireless. Those things, police doings, I suppose, I'd heard of; but never actually heard—the ear, possibly, of millions taken to ask—solemn moment; death in family—one unsignifying brat to please come home."

With steadiness, with unmoved strength of calm, he studied Arthur Winner again. He said: "Yes; the spirit of the age! We're in an age pre-eminently of capital F Feeling—a century of the gulp, the lump in the throat, the good cry. We can't be said to have invented sentimentality; but in other ages sentimentality seems to have been mostly peripheral, a despised pleasure of the

544

underwitted. We've made sentimentality of the respected essence. If I believe my eyes and ears, and I do, sentimentality is now nearly everyone's at least private indulgence. The grave and learned are no whit behind the cheap and stupid in their love of it. Snuffling after every trace, eagerly rooting everywhere, the newspapers stop their presses, the broadcasters interrupt their broadcasts, so it may be more immediately available. In professional entertainment, in plays and motion pictures, it is the whole mode. In much of what I'm told is our most seriously regarded contemporary literature, I find it, scarcely disguised, standing in puddles. The houses of congress, the state halls of legislature, drop everything to make and provide it whenever they can. There are judges who even try in their courts to fit the law to it—"

Julius Penrose broke off. He said: "I see my artful indirection does not work. I see this chitchat doesn't divert you. I see you will not be talked out of it, Arthur. Well, we must try other means. Let us be direct. Clarissa is concerned on two counts. Easily enlisting my sympathies, she asked me to find out about them. First: she conceives, because last night Helen seemed to have you worried, that you may be telling yourself this wouldn't have happened if you'd spoken to her." He paused. "Privately, I thought that concern unfounded. I've never seen you act without adequate consideration. One may very well, one may often, wish one had done differently; but when a man has used his best judgment, done his best, the result though disappointing, though disastrous even, can't be a reproach to him. He did all any man could do. Regrets of that kind are unreasonable, unrealistic. *It might have been*—not so much the saddest as the silliest words of tongue or pen! Let us face it. What happens to people is simply what was always going to happen to them. To think otherwise is vain visioning. That's not really your trouble now, is it?"

No; not really! Troubles are relative; problems differ in degree, tasks in difficulty. Poor Helen put it well. *Things are funny. Yesterday I was so worried about his not wanting to go to college. . . .* How trifling the troubles, how simple the problems, how easy the tasks of only yesterday! Yesterday morning, the trouble was no more than to determine the best steps to take (which came naturally to him) in a commonplace criminal action where, everything considered, his cause was in good shape, the defense hopeful. His problems were what to answer to a Jerry Brophy's humble petition, and whether he could in conscience (in interest!) go along with a "Whit" Trowbridge's pastoral exhortings, with his rector's good-natured determination to name him senior warden. His tasks were to sustain the embarrassments, the not-undeserved chagrins put on him by an enraptured friendly fool of a Mrs. Pratt; to quell a negligible Mr. Moore; to soothe an alarmed Elmer Abbott; to instruct an agreeably co-operative policeman about that ass Ralph; to accept, in the slight awkwardness of a young Garret Hughes's too-plain apotheosis of him, the gratuities of the district attorney. Indeed; how trifling the troubles, how simple the problems of only an hour ago! Arthur Winner said: "No; that's not my trouble now."

Julius Penrose said: "Second concern: Clarissa conceives you've had nothing to eat. Neither have I. In my cabinet you'll find, as usual, a decanter of sherry and a tin of biscuits. Allow me to offer you some refreshment; though I won't offer to get it. You get it."

Accepting the filled sherry glass, Julius Penrose took a swallow. "This unhappy event has several unhappy aspects," he said. "Well, we owe nature a death, I'm told. By our choosing to be born, we contracted for death. Recision would be inequitable and unjust. Let me hear no more complaining! The terms of payment? Not exorbitant, I think. What could be more generous? If we pay this year, we won't have to pay next year." He took another sip of sherry. "Regarding the dead, our pious rule is nothing if not good. Ralph, let us agree, is a little bastard; and you won't suppose I mean by the term that Alice Detweiler could have ever had the appetite, let alone the imagination, to play George false. Helen is known to have been faithful and true, good and self-sacrificing, and, perhaps not so relevant, but they are qualities in the main admired, chaste and pure. She is, therefore, virtue; Ralph is vice. Because of all this virtue, Helen's sorrows, her sufferings, the last full measure of her rash act, put her publicly, in terms of public opinion, unassailably in the right. Everybody must feel that."

Julius Penrose took a sip of sherry. "Yes; I too feel it; but do I think it? An entrance is won to the heart; but to the head? Passion and reason, self-division's cause! I'm afraid I think that this gentle and unspotted soul was and is, has been and now always will be, very much in the wrong. On people as people, I try never to pass judgment—we can seldom know what the real truth about them is. Yet on acts, acts of theirs, I see no reason to hesitate in passing judgment—this is good; this is bad; this is mean; this is kind. On such points, I'm competent, as every man is. Like the common law, we secular moralists aren't interested in the why; we observe the what. Here, the what that gives me pause is this. Ralph's a little bastard; yes. Something ought to have been done to and about him, I'd think preferably with a horsewhip, if nowadays one could be found. Be good, or I'll beat you! That's in order. That's fair warning and fair play. Could the same be said of a verbal threat to do a thing like this— Ralph must be good, or Helen will kill herself? And how much less, if, for mere threat, performance is substituted? No; there is a want of principle, which is to say, too much feeling. I pronounce this bad. I pronounce this mean. The sentence, of course, is on the act, not the person. I pity the person; I take her to be mad, possessed by love. Her feelings acted. Here is simply more of feeling's comic or tragic, yet, to the feeler, always juicy, fruits. I quote: 'A warmth within the breast would melt the freezing reason's colder part. And like a man in wrath, the heart stood up and answered: I have felt!' Let us pass on. Your refection is spread; take some."

"I'm not hungry," Arthur Winner said. "Julius, how long have you known that Noah's accounts were short?"

"Ah!" Julius Penrose said. "Well, I'm not sorry to have you ask! Yes; that's where I was putting off getting; and I may say that how long *you* could continue *not* to know has been a recurring slight anxiety of mine. Sometimes I even wondered if you *did* know; but each time, I decided no, you didn't. At this juncture—to tell you the truth, it's why I'm here; why I directed Marjorie to get out a car; why I had no lunch—I saw that you'd

547

better know, that there was the possibility of our finding ourselves in a situation of sorts—one of those unhappy aspects of
this unhappy event."

"How long have you known?" Arthur Winner said.

"How long?" Julius Penrose said. "Well, let me see. It was, I
think, thirteen years ago last July that your father asked me if
I'd be interested in joining my practice with Winner, Tuttle
and Winner's, coming in as a partner. I would, indeed! Though
no longer a boy, nor without experience, I was always one to look
to the improvement of my mind. There was his reputation; there
was Noah's. My legal acquirements were not too meager; but
working with the best minds of our bar would infallibly give
them polish. There was the circumstance that you and I had long
been friends; and that Noah had no living son. This first-rate
heritage we stood to inherit."

His strong teeth bit a biscuit in half. Thoughtfully, Julius Penrose chewed. "Yes; I meant to improve myself by grasping, particularly in fiduciary matters, what I could of the methods of a
man of Mr. Tuttle's abilities. My turn of mind, while not I
think inquisitive, was and is investigative. Old Mrs. Hunt was
still in the office; and Helen, all earnestness, was being, in effect,
broken in. To Helen, the figure work had to be explained. I
took occasion both to listen, and, the books being out, to look. I
am good at figures. Though seemingly satisfactory to her, and to
Helen, Mrs. Hunt's explanation of some parts of the accounting
process left me perplexed. *This,* I kept hearing, *is how Mr. Tuttle
wants us to do it. . . . But why?* I kept asking—myself, not
them! *But why?* I needed, if I remember, a number of months—
a couple of quarter days would have had to pass before my data
became complete enough for me to draw a firm conclusion. So
how long have I known? Well, let's say, twelve years, give or
take a month or two."

"And you said nothing? Julius, I think that's indefensible."

"Do you? To be able to know and still say nothing often seems
to me the most creditable of human accomplishments. King
Midas has ass's ears! Whisper it, if only to the reeds, most people
must! For overcoming this common weakness, I give myself good
marks. What purpose but mischief, and what result but more

mischief, could my saying something have? From my standpoint, the business was strictly Noah's; and he was, I soon came to see, handling it ably. I confess that before adopting this disinterested view, I made a careful check of my own legal position. You'll recognize it. Incoming partner. How, then, could saying something be my business?"

"When you know this and say nothing, you're an accessory after the fact. Julius, how could you?"

"I've just explained how I could," Julius Penrose said. "Here was the then situation as I put it together. The greater part of the Orcutt money simply wasn't there—except, you might say, on paper. I don't know whether you ever troubled to read the instrument. Principal is put in Noah's absolute control. The books showed the trust as holding various securities, mortgages, and so on, from which interest was duly entered. Those holdings were imaginary. The so-entered interest was of course real; money has to be. Fortunately, under Noah's almost as absolute control were other trusts, other funds. At bottom, the process is merely robbing Peter to pay Paul. But with improvements, refinements. When the time comes to pay Paul, Peter, unknown to Peter, is caused to lend you some of his money and Paul's paid. And when the time comes to pay Peter; Tom, Dick, or Harry, unknown to him, may be caused to lend you some of *his* money. Of course, you have to look alive, watch your step, exercise foresight and judgment—"

"Julius, I still cannot believe—"

"I fear you're going to have to. Impracticably complicated? Yes; for many people; but to a man of Noah's parts—and also, of course, to a man to whom no least question, no faintest suspicion ever attached—the procedure of lawfully receiving into his possession and unlawfully appropriating money was simplicity itself; even, quite safe. As you very well know, the only circumstance under which the accounts he was tampering with could become subject to audit was if *cestui qui trust,* not getting his money, applied to the court. The circumstance never arises. Income is always paid when due. To keep accounts in any way he wanted them kept, he had, first, Mrs. Hunt; and, then, Helen, both of them practiced with figures, both of them quite incapable of interpreting figures, and both accepting as gospel anything Noah told them—"

"What I can't believe is that you'd knowingly stand by—"

"But I fear you're going to have to," Julius Penrose said. "That's just what I did. I tried to tell you why—"

"As you've said, why, doesn't matter, Julius. What, as you say, is what matters. In this case, it still amounts to compounding a felony."

"I wonder," Julius Penrose said. "A felony is something I must be found guilty of by a jury of my peers. Before that finding, where is the felony? I ask myself how you compound that which does not yet exist. But, yes; *what* is, indeed, what matters. My whole regard was for what. My eye was on the certain results, the fruits. True, that had been done which ought not to be done. I saw that conversion, embezzlement, must have been practiced for some time—and, I confess, the 'some time' seemed to me not unimportant. Who, so far, complained? Nobody. Everyone was perfectly happy. True, the embezzlement was on no small scale. By a fairly easy calculation—given the interest—that is, what I computed to be the sum of Noah's quarterly 'borrowings'—to find the principal. I judged the Orcutt funds short, holding dummy or imaginary securities, to the amount of about two hundred thousand dollars."

Arthur Winner could suppose that the color must have left his face; for, interrupting himself, Julius said: "Yes; when I finished figuring, my wind, too, was rather knocked out. Don't imagine I regarded my discovery as funny. For the younger, rawer man I was then, I cannot but claim my feat in saying nothing and showing nothing was really remarkable. I, let me tell you, was scared. My practice had not happened to turn up anything like this. For the act of one of them, what, if any, limits were there on the liability of other partners? I've seldom applied myself with such intensity of attention to the statutes and to the reported cases. However, as I say, I was soon relieved. There weren't two opinions. The time of the original conversion, which subsequent conversions had been to cover, was what counted. If I had not been a partner when that took place, no action to recover from me personally could lie."

550

Portentous, despairing, those empty words: *I am a man alone* . . . recurred to Arthur Winner. He said: "So, seeing yourself safe—"

"Yes; just so!" Julius Penrose's voice, though calm as ever, though precise as ever, allowed itself a tone of mild reproach. "Yes; I scare easy; but recovering from my scare, I found myself rational, able to look at this from all sides. I was free to dismiss self-interest, to do right and fear no man. Whether I'm morally obligated to be my brother's keeper always seemed to me moot. However, my brother's ruiner and destroyer, and for no earthly reason, and for no personal necessity or profit—*that* I surely have no moral obligation to be. If I'd elected to take the upstanding stand you seem consternated to hear I didn't take; if I'd blabbed my not-exactly-stumbled-on yet unintentionally discovered secret; if righteously horrified, I'd pressed for a C.P.A. audit, the beneficiaries of the Orcutt bequests would have been awarded every cent your father had and every cent you had— your innocence of the smallest wrongdoing, as you know, notwithstanding. Seeing myself, in your word, safe, I, no longer scared, naturally did not so much as consider such a dastardly act."

Aware of a sinking in his voice that reflected faithfully a felt sinking of the mind, a vortical faintness, Arthur Winner said: "My father would not have thought that way. He'd have pressed, himself, for an audit—" He put out a hand, took up his glass of sherry and drank it all.

"I'm sure he would have," Julius Penrose said. "Therefore, he had to know nothing. That was not too hard. He had every confidence in Noah, and, happily, a disability of confidence is always that you see what you look for, what you expect to see—"

That sinking of mind was a disturbance so great that no ordering of thoughts was possible—blindly, the mind groped around. Arthur Winner said: "But why would he need to? How could it happen? Yes—I've read the terms of the Orcutt instrument—I know he could do or buy anything he wanted. Yes; bad investments can be made—but not on that scale, not by Noah—"

Julius Penrose said: "I've heard he made a bad investment once. There was the Brocton Rapid Transit Company—"

"No Orcutt money was ever put in that, I know," Arthur Winner said. His responses, labored, seemed to be automatically supplied by some other speaker, aberrant, unconnected with him. "He did put some in before, when they were trying to save the company; but I know where he got that. He borrowed it from my father. You might not remember, but by the time the Orcutt trusts were operative, Brocton Transit was out of business. The creditors chose Noah, and the Federal District Court had appointed him trustee in bankruptcy. There was no more question of investment there—"

"Yes," Julius Penrose said. "That liquidation was interesting. I've tried, without the least success, to learn the particular circumstances. I thought Noah might be willing, by way of giving me a point or two, to tell me what he did. I found that he was not willing."

"I don't think he wanted to think about it," Arthur Winner said heavily. There was that feeling of nothing to hold onto— no, nothing! What did Alfred Revere say? *It's like this funny picture.* . . . "I mean, though he had no legal responsibility, he felt a personal, private responsibility which he took very hard."

"Yes, I've heard that, too," Julius Penrose said. Lifting a cane, he leveled it carefully at the fireplace. "Indeed, I venture to suggest that supposed responsibility might even have deranged him a little. I mean, of course, emotionally. I hear everywhere that his handling of the business was as astute as possible, a masterpiece of management. I, of course, searched out what was of public record. The scrutiny was uninformative; but, forever buried there, I'm irresistibly led to guess, may be something unique in financial history. My guess: the trustee in bankruptcy paid out to the creditors—other than himself—some hundreds of thousands of dollars not received, not realized from assets. I see easily how this could be possible, how it might not be remarked. You've had experience with our Federal referees. You'd look a long way before you found one who knew anything except that good old Senator Joe Blow was a friend of his. He might stir himself if trustee reported in receipts much less than the manifest market value of assets; but, more—well; God bless you, my boy! In short, I think a timely use of Orcutt money saved the financial lives of a number of people like your Mike McCarthy. I say: I think. But the more I think, the surer I am."

"But he'd have to be crazy," Arthur Winner said. "He'd have to see that in the end—"

"Not necessarily, not necessarily!" Julius Penrose said. "Emotionally deranged was my preferred term. He would betray himself, sacrifice himself, before he let down, sacrificed, those who had put faith in him. An emotional idea. Ah, what a mess these possessions by feeling may make of lives! But I think he also hoped, and had some reason to hope, that, given time, he could restore the money. If a man is shrewd—and also lucky, which is usually the same thing—about investments; if a man is frugal and careful—yes; and if a man is brave; not a little may be done. I like to think how trifling, lived with so long, the unending anxiety must by now have come to seem to Noah. But he *has* supported it, lived with it, years and years. Think of that! There's self-command, if you like. There's stoutheartedness; there's prudence; there's a masterpiece of management! I have, as you may imagine, kept what I think I'm justified in calling a quiet eye on this matter. By my latest estimate, he's short now not above a hundred and twenty thousand dollars—maybe less. In July, he made quite a quiet killing with some common stock warrants, you know—or did you? Of course, the debit balance is still not peanuts, not to modestly monied men like you and me; but I do believe the old boy may pull out yet."

Arthur Winner said: "Julius, what you seem to be suggesting just isn't possible. There's an honest course; and a course that isn't honest. If you take the course that isn't honest, you're in trouble immediately—"

"Affirmed as stated," Julius Penrose said. "Honesty's always the easiest policy. Could that be why men so often call it the best? Weaving tangled webs is really work, very demanding."

"No, Julius. It's no good. I cannot be party to doing what's dishonest."

"But you *could* be party to causing to be laid before our Mr. Brophy such evidence of embezzlement as would require him to prosecute Noah? Hm! Specific acts must number hundreds. I see no practicable defense. Offered a plea of guilty—or, as I personally would recommend, since civil action pended, *nolo contendere*—to one indictment, the court, I imagine, would consent to dismiss the others. Five years, and five thousand dollars? In consideration of the plea, we might hope, I think, for two years —with time off for good behavior. I doubt if even Brophy would feel that more of an example than that ought to be made of so old a man, and a man heretofore so generally revered."

Julius Penrose stirred to ease himself. He breathed as though he summoned strength, an extra supply to meet, imposed on the pain in which he lived, this wearying pain of exposition. He said: "And you could also be not only party to, but principal in, taking immediate steps to assign all your property toward restituting and restoring the corpus of the Orcutt bequests? I've a fair idea of your current commitments. I imagine you're doing something for your mother. I know you're helping Lawrence— who, incidentally, is, I came to suspect, on the verge of asking you if you'd be able to advance him what he'll need in the way of capital for this projected venture with his boss. The expense of maintaining a place at Roylan is well known to me. You have a daughter to educate; you have a wife who—again, incidentally —has, I suspect, the indefatigable hope of providing you with more children. You'd be sorry, I'm sure, to see either without proper provision. Yet, by the time you'd made your partner's stealings good, I don't think there'd be a great deal left."

"Julius, I can't understand you—"

Soberly, Julius Penrose said: "Well, perhaps I'm hard to understand. There are times when I myself wonder whether not-as-other-men is what I am. I'm told, for example, that we may forgive those who injure us, but never those we've injured. As far as I go, poppycock! In lines, mostly of business, I've deemed it from time to time necessary or convenient to injure a number of people. I bear none of them the least ill will. Unless they try to retaliate—indeed, unless they succeed in retaliating, my feelings remain entirely cordial; I haven't a thing in the world against them. Then, I'm told that men excuse in themselves what they don't excuse in others. Applied to me, totally untrue! I readily excuse in others what I'd consider inexcusable in myself. What

554

would you? They are only they; but I am I! However, here, in the instant case, on this point, I'd have imagined myself altogether understandable. These are preliminary objections in the nature of a motion to strike. The case for a fine upstanding stand seems to me not made out. Insufficient averment—mere indecisive and unfounded technicalities are being pleaded. Too costly, too."

"The cost needn't worry you," Arthur Winner said. "I agree with your view that you can't be held liable."

"The law is clear. There is no other view," Julius Penrose said. "But I, also, am human, am not without human weaknesses of vanity and self-regard. I have an—er—honor—" he grimaced— "of my own to pet. I wouldn't, I warn you, feel able to dissociate myself, legally liable or not. If you persist in this quixotism, if you're resolved to ruin yourself, I'll have to join you. Yes; I think I can arrange that. I promise you that if you denounce Noah and do not agree to let me share and share alike in the consequences, I'll have to, *nunc pro tunc,* denounce my guilty long knowledge of these peculations. Whether it would be enough to get me prosecuted, I don't know; it would assuredly lose me my means of livelihood by getting me disbarred."

"Julius, that's ridiculous—"

"I think so, too. Neither alternative appeals to me in the least. The first—since I'm sure you'd admit me to the first, rather than force me to the second—would cost me a great deal of money. For this loss, hearing on every hand how nobly we behaved would not really recompense me. I am a cripple; I am getting old. Were I neither, it might be different, of course. The easier way, the easiest policy, could then be a calculated risk—possibly worth taking. Given more life expectancy, I might chance it. Honesty, integrity, honor so well advertised, could pay off. Like Job's, my patience might prove worthwhile. I might end up with more flocks, more herds—and even, were I at that age or stage, more sons and daughters—than I had to start with. But such expectancy isn't mine. I'm on the downgrade. Therefore, I ask you not to do this thing to me, Arthur."

"Julius, after what you said earlier, you can't seriously—"

"Some want of principle, yes," Julius Penrose said. "But I am not joking."

Julius Penrose's look was compassionate. He said: "Yes, yes; think of an octogenarian cast in prison; think of your unfeeling disservice to those near and dear—hard to kick against the pricks, isn't it? So stop! Or, as a wise old man once said to me: Boy, never try to piss up the wind. Principle must sometimes be shelved. Let us face the fact. In this life we cannot do everything we might like to do, nor have for ourselves everything we might like to have. We must recognize what the law calls factual situations. The paradox is that once fact's assented to, accepted, and we stop directing our effort where effort is wasted, we usually *can* do quite a number of things, to a faint heart, impossible." He dropped one cane to the floor and neatly levered his legs a little to the left. "Did I ever tell you how I retaught myself to walk— or, would the juster term be: get around?"

Arthur Winner could feel light creepings of sweat on his forehead; the stand-up collar, the thick folds of formal tie constricted his throat; the slight tightness of the morning coat bound his shoulders.

Julius Penrose, in tone chatty, almost humorous, said: "At the beginning, I must admit I didn't take my, as I hear people say, misfortune, well. I was impressed by the wanton unfairness of this thing, in those days still generally known as infantile paralysis. Exactly! An affliction reserved for children. An adult, a man past his youth, coming down with it was almost unheard of. Then; why, of all men, me? For my sins? They were many, yes; but look at others I could name to whom this didn't happen. Why should I alone get the dirty end of the stick? All those who find themselves out of luck are, I imagine, subject to such thoughts. We feel very hardly used—and, of course, so we are, so we are! Our resentment's reasonable and legitimate, if that's any help to us. A help to us is, however, just what resentment isn't."

To his son, watching wordless beside that bed, that in fact deathbed of many weeks, Arthur Winner Senior, a wasted shape under a blanket, had, on a silent Sunday afternoon, suddenly

556

smiled, had suddenly said: *I've been among the luckiest of men.*
. . . Most of the time mindless, massively drugged, the Man of
Reason was briefly revisited by mind; comprehending for a moment interrupted uncomprehending. *Maybe one in a thousand
has had it happen to him. Close calls, sometimes; sometimes, I
saw that in a minute I might not be able to help myself; but I
don't remember ever once having to do what I would have preferred not to do.* . . . While the skin-and-bone face, the too-
bright eyes were lighted for a minute or more with this vague
thankfulness, Arthur Winner Junior, shaken both by the startling
announcement, and by his own mind's quick comment: *except
this, this?* saw, only mystified, the smile; heard, only mystified,
the words, the voice of wonder. Against the sound of Julius Penrose's voice, the measured sentences' light mocking of fate,
illumination flared, one more clap of knowledge came: *And now,
all these years later, I know at last what he was talking about.
The thrusts of fate! Yes; lucky the man* . . .

"Is anything a help?" Julius Penrose said. "Well, Marjorie's
coreligionists-to-be have a formula. They say: Offer it, or offer it
up. Possibly useful, one perceives. You set yourself to make believe that all misfortune, all pain, has point or purpose, can
earn you benefits. The worse the pain, the better—good, if, or as
long as, you can believe so! No go, with me, naturally. The un-
derlying idea of a source of merit—the fawning self-recommenda-
tion, the humble currying of favor—repelled me. No; vouchsafe
me no vouchsafements! If the supernatural is seen as entering,
to curse God and die would always, I can't but feel, better
become a man. So much for a religious attitude. Among the
opposed attitudes of irreligion, that one whose complaint is:
unfair, unfair, with its feeble indignation and tiresome self-pity,
manifestly doesn't become a man either. The becoming thing, in
any given situation, is for a man to try what he can do, not just
sprawl there whining. He should get up and walk."

Julius Penrose emptied his sherry glass. "But how are you to
walk when you can't even stand? Answer: What makes you think
you can't stand, or, at least, do something that will pass for that?
With a cheeriness all too unfailing, meant kindly to encourage
you yet hard to take, the specialists in these matters heartily cry:

Of course you can! They'll see me fitted with what they persist in calling comfortable braces. Then, I'll need crutches—here they are! Now, for it!"

He took another biscuit and chewed thoughtfully for a moment. "Yes; now for it. One try, and you see this is impossible, this can't be done. Tut, tut! they say; a child creeps before he walks! Was it the happiest image? Perhaps! Set your crutch ends a foot ahead of your feet. Now, can't you move your feet toward them? Don't try anything excessive—an inch will do. Fine! Now advance your crutches about an inch; now, move your feet another inch. Lo and behold, you're walking! I'm what? Well, you got from your bed to the wall and back, and it didn't take you ten minutes."

Julius Penrose smiled reminiscently. "Of course, even *they* didn't really consider that walking. Just a starter. The walking gaits, so called, are something else; and Rome wasn't built in a day. There's what's known as the four-point. When you're ready to try, you'll need someone behind you and someone in front of you; and you may keep needing them for quite a while. It's important not to fall and shatter your confidence, if nothing else. The technique is: first one foot, then one crutch; then the other foot, then the other crutch. Kindergarten stuff! After a certain number of weeks, or more likely months, the teachable lad may consider mastering the swing-through—what the crutch expert does most of the time when he's in the clear. Of course, you have to remember (no trouble, really) that you have ten pounds of steel on your legs which will affect balancing; so when you swing your pedal extremities forward, you must put your shoulders forward, too, and kept your body straight from the shoulders down —your shoulders swing you, your braces stop you. Amazing how you get over the ground, once you have the hang of it. You feel as though you were flying. And, of course, this—" he lifted a cane—"is ultimate art. You need muscle. Not many of us with both legs out ever graduate from crutches—"

Arthur Winner said: "What, exactly, do you propose?"

"Ah, my old friend," Julius Penrose said, "that's better! I propose that we let matters proceed as far as possible as they've been proceeding. I propose we concert our efforts and our wits on managing this—"

"Julius, the risks are terrible—"

"Agreed, agreed," Julius Penrose said. "But we are not children, nor unable, nor without resource. I think I am a man of judgment. I know you are. Let us put this judgment to use—"

"I don't think you realize just how great some of the risks are."

"If you mean there are some I don't happen to know about, you may be right. But I'm confident I'll be sufficiently sharp to see them as they appear; and I'm not unconfident that, as I see them, I'll see what to do about them."

"Perhaps I should tell you that Doctor Trowbridge is very much set on a move that would make an audit on behalf of Christ Church necessary."

"Indeed, you should! Like two heads, four eyes are better; you will be seeing things and I will be seeing things, and we can counsel together. If your rector is moving that way, you must, of course, yourself move to dissuade him—I assume he entertains ideas of transferring the corpus, otherwise investing the money. He must be advised that he can't, in law; that the donor's intent must be respected."

"I've already done that," Arthur Winner said. "For other reasons—" He broke off. "No, Julius!" he said. "I can't carry out such a plan—pretending to give honest advice. It's impossible."

Julius Penrose said: "Tut, tut! A child creeps before he walks! Think again. What's, here, material? Not, surely, delicacy-of-feeling's comforts or discomforts. Material, is: Can His Reverence be made to do as you say? He can; you can handle him. That risk, then, is already provided for, largely obviated. Yes; and I know there's talk of winding up the Union League, which would mean eventually auditing that account. But only eventually. The talk could take years, particularly if someone like me were helping to see that it did. Anyway, I think that there the deficit is manageable—I mean, Noah would probably be able to borrow enough from other accounts to meet it, if your church wasn't making a demand on him at the same time. What else?"

With bitterness, Arthur Winner said: "You consider that not

enough? Just think what you're saying, Julius. The course is desperate from start to finish. We evade; we misrepresent; we use secret influence—"

Julius Penrose said: "Clarissa remarked that the really terrible thing about Helen's business was that arrangements had been made for the charge against Ralph to be dropped—that was what you hadn't told Helen. I gather Garret Hughes let you know yesterday afternoon that the district attorney had been to Mechanicsville, and shortly after, prosecutrix decided not to proceed." He smiled faintly. "May I ask how you worked it, Arthur?"

"I didn't," Arthur Winner said. "I told Jerry, who came in to see me yesterday morning, that I believed the girl was lying, and if she were put on the stand, I had every hope of demonstrating that she was. Later, Garret, who had been to see her, must have told him Miss Kovacs wouldn't submit to a physical examination—"

"May I ask what J. Jerome came in to see you about? Am I to suppose nothing except Ralph's case was discussed?"

"No. He spoke of Ralph's case only in passing. What he came about was how I would stand on the bar association proposing his name to the governor for appointment to this fourth judgeship we're being given. You may not approve; but I told him I would not oppose him. Perhaps you feel he should be opposed."

Julius Penrose said gravely: "On the whole, no. It is true that as district attorney I find him rather offensive; but the thought occurs to me that the attaining of this ambition, this, as it's generally regarded, high honor, would have a salutary effect both on his manners and his—er—morals. I know Fred doesn't like the idea; but Willard and Mac McAllister won't mind. He's not lazy—they could unload a lot of work on him."

"And if you think I offered not to oppose him in an attempt to influence in any way his actions as public prosecutor, you do not know me very well."

"Gently, gently!" Julius Penrose said. "None of us, perhaps, knows any of us very well. Yet; yes, I'm satisfied I know you well enough; and I believe you. Imagine that, Arthur! Do you realize that I'm very likely the only person in the world who could or would believe what you've just told me?"

Arthur Winner said: "I cannot help what people believe or don't believe. I can only tell you that I have never—" (the voice of one dying said: *I've been among the luckiest of men* . . .) "I've never found myself in a position—yes; I can say it; I've never in my professional practice—"

"Nor, I can say, have I," Julius Penrose said. "No; do not look at me that way. Accessory after the fact, if you like, in this matter; but I, too, have never taken nor given a bribe; I, too, have never touched a penny that was not mine; I, too, have never borne false witness, never sworn a man away. Let us congratulate each other; but, also, let us for the moment attend to our grave problem. What else alarms you?"

"Julius, it's everything—" Where, indeed, to begin? Numberless, the general dangers, the uncertainties, the unchartable chances, of this—this wrongdoing, this frantic dice-throwing on which he must wildly stake his—yes, honor; his career; his reputation. (*Good name in man and woman, dear my lord, is the immediate jewel of their souls.* . . .) Ah, yes; how fond the the remembrance of yesterday's peace! Arthur Winner said: "Quite apart from whatever outright appropriating there may have been, the accounts, I know now, aren't even in ordinary order. Noah could be tripped up any time. Friday, he almost was. I've no doubt at all that if I hadn't just happened to ask this Mr. Woolf up to the lake for supper, got him—pure accident!—in good humor, when we resumed yesterday morning Woolf wouldn't have been half an hour forcing out what is the fact—that Noah, a couple of months ago, deposited twenty thousand dollars of McCarthy Estate money in his personal account. Helen had checked for me; and from what she said, I had to realize he does that sort of thing all the time, whenever it suits him. To let things just go on, as if we didn't know— there couldn't be a moment's peace of mind. No, Julius; if we do this thing at all, Noah's going to have to be told that we know, that we intend to do what we can to get the money paid back, and that we'll have to take charge of his accounts."

Julius Penrose said: "That, in the end, may be necessary; but I don't think we ought so to determine out of hand. Shun immediate evils is the wise, or at least the smart, man's maxim.

561

Never do today what doesn't have to be done until tomorrow. It is, I imagine, important to Noah to think nobody knows. Told, he'd not impossibly go all to pieces. That would be no service to us; and clearly no kindness to him. There is an unmanly streak in me. I was never able to be a sportsman. Games, when I had the use of all my limbs, yes; but sports, those blood sports of the man's man, no! To hook fishes, to shoot birds or animals, not because I needed them for food, but for fun— well, I could, and can, only ask: What fun? Even as touching food, I've often wondered. If I personally had to slaughter the beasts, would I learn to do without meat to eat? Or, if I had to do without meat to eat, would I learn to slaughter beasts? A nice question."

He looked seriously at Arthur Winner. "No," he said, "I think we should try for a while telling Noah nothing. Humanitarian considerations aren't, let me say candidly, my only ones. As you point out, the risks of what I'm suggesting are far from inconsiderable. We aim to buy time; we hope to see Noah live long enough to get the accounts squared. Intelligent recognition of the risks must include giving thought to what happens if time runs out, if our hope is not realized. If luck should fail us, if the law overtakes Noah, I would like him to be able to testify that we knew nothing of these shortages. The civil liability which must fall on you, and which I shall volunteer to, and will, share is quite sufficient. We do not need to make a criminal liability apparent, too. Since the crime is stealing, and we did no stealing, I can't feel that we cheat justice if we escape indictment in connection with it."

"Meanwhile, what we don't and can't escape is a whole life of lies," Arthur Winner said. "We can't trust Noah—" A seizure of impotent, not-controllable, anger overcame him. "How can a man do this, be this? That case of Sutphin's last week—no, no, not for us! Not perfectly honorable—dishonest intent; and all the time—yes, and Noah, if he only knew, can't trust us. We don't purpose to be open with him. How, when I know you knew this, and yet kept it from me, can I really—"

"No!" Julius Penrose said. "That's not you speaking, Arthur. That's unjust. I don't think you can fairly say I here deceived

562

you. I knew of something that it was my considered judgment you should not, need not, know. I don't think you can fairly believe my motive was any but a hope to spare you while Noah was allowed time to restore, if he could, what he had taken. We have known each other too long for either of us to honestly suppose untruths about the other. If you knew of something that you believed I didn't know, and that you thought it better I should not know, I'm persuaded you'd do as much for me—try every way to keep it from me." He paused. "Let me be more explicit. I'm persuaded, Arthur, that you *have* done as much for me. And, if unknown to you, I've always thanked you for it."

As though he, too, had an arm to offer and now offered it; as though Arthur Winner, too, might need an arm to rise, he said:

Arthur Winner had felt his surge of changed color—a crisis of consternation outside the control of consciousness; too quick for any summoning up of the mask for the face, the blankness for the eye, the calmness, if he should speak, for the voice. How, Arthur Winner must thunderstruck ask himself, could he have imagined otherwise? Friday night, pointing his cane, Julius said: *Few men of normal potency prove able to refrain their foot from that path!* The well-known habit of the finished phrases, in their level precision almost rehearsed-sounding, the familiar deliberately mincing tones that mocked themselves with their own affectation, that mocked, too, Arthur Winner (but without unkindness, without a wish or a will to hurt—let us consider together human passion and folly; let us smile together!)— could he seriously suppose those phrases had been selected, they had been intended, to tell him nothing, that, because the cane pointed at no one, no one was meant?

In Arthur Winner had succeeded, countersurging against the womanish blush, a coolness of clarity, of shame's sudden remission, a breathing-deep of the amazed, enlightened heart. Yes; thou art the man! Total, the exposure; he stood exposed; yet who condemned him, who scorned him, who triumphed over him? Unsmiling, compassionate still, still steady, Julius's gaze, the speaking clear dark eyes, rested on him, as though without use of words to say: Yes, I know that you have been afraid I would find out. But you had nothing to fear. Don't you see, I've known all along. Our pact is: As I am, you accept me; as you are, I accept you—yes; come, let us smile together!

Julius Penrose said: "We're agreed? I imagine there's no chance of Noah coming in here this afternoon. Lay me out the accounts, then; and I'll study them."

He waited while Arthur Winner stood up. "On my desk, if you will, Arthur. And if you will—"

Arthur Winner presented his arm. "Yes; thanks," Julius Penrose said. Erect, both canes in his left hand advanced skillfully to prop him, Julius smiled seriously. He put his powerful right hand into Arthur Winner's. "Yes; thanks," he said again. As though he, too, had an arm to offer and now offered it, as though Arthur Winner, too, might need an arm to rise, he said: "Be of good cheer, my friend. In this business, we're not licked, not by a long shot. We'll come through this. I have decided that we will. I now get to work. I now see where we stand."

Arthur Winner said: "But isn't Marjorie—"

"I informed her that I might have things to do, that her time for a while was her own. Poor dear, she is capable of amusing herself. Though I believe she was there this morning, in her present frame of mind, I suspect she has taken off for Our Lady of Mount Carmel, always, I understand, open. Amid the twenty-five-cent votive lights and the plaster images, prayer, I think, would be her purpose."

✦

O gentlemen, the time of life is short! To spend that shortness basely . . . Not in context—to recover the context Arthur Winner might have to think at length—the words, known only as a passage that some college course once required him to learn, repeated themselves, perhaps not reasonlessly. They witnessed, it might be, to an age of his innocence, continuing, succeeding, that of the child; more of the rapture of unknowing; more of the doubt-free ignorance; the folly of being wise still uncommitted by that useful football player, the important man in the college yard, the smartly golf-trousered and raccoon-skin-

564

coated part-time student of the plays of Shakespeare. He had been quite a happy fellow; mostly pleasant to people, he had not been such a bad fellow.

Arthur Winner's walk back up the hill had begun. That also I must watch out for, he thought. (Fred Dealey said: *I'd really like to be nicer to more people—the stupid bastards!*) I must not, because I find fault with myself, start finding fault with everyone. (Julius said: *Be happy, and you'll begin to be virtuous. . . .*) Virtuous, could you, like Julius, note no more than in passing, note unprovoked, that this age is cheap, this age is maudlin; that today's women must run to religion, that today's men must as well as work, weep—what good was deep feeling when you were quiet about it? How would anyone know you had it?

The stairs from the basement room, from the wrapped body on the stone slab, mounted, Arthur Winner had found there to meet him that tight uniform packed with Bernie Breck, that amiable face packed with flesh, and by consciously creditable feelings again illuminated. *We just got word, I wanted to tell you, Mr. Winner*—as if Arthur Winner had Ralph Detweiler on his mind, cared whether the brat was ever found! The philosophic cop, the tough cop, and so (without fail) the sentimental cop, the cop who slightly turned your stomach, said gruffly, said gently: "I don't think we need to send for him, Mr. Winner; he told them he'd come home. I mean, after giving himself up, I think he will. What it was; he told them he was having breakfast at this soda fountain, and he heard the radio. What I said! No, that boy's not bad; this shows that. Thing to do is, give him a chance to get things straight, give him a helping hand. . . ." Answering, Arthur Winner said: "I would rather talk about it some other time." He went down the police station steps. He began to walk up the street.

Elmer Abbott, only in part a man, said: *I will try to calm myself. . . .* Julius Penrose said: *I never thought the day would come when I would need to say it. . . .* Here were the yellow-brick, collected new buildings of Our Lady of Mount Carmel—church, rectory, sisters' convent, parochial school, impressive and expensive, in their architectural manner modern (modren?), but

565

at all events, advance indeed over the old church on Water Street, the humble edifice that the Pat-and-Mikes, the where-do-you-worka-Johns of another day had yielded their pennies to put up. Suppose, out of one of the church's arched triple doors on which the afternoon sun was falling, Marjorie, comforted by prayer, came suddenly? He strode faster, to get by them.

Federal Street, the shops all closed. On this side, on the whole stretch of sidewalk up to Court Street, to the bank at the corner, not a person was to be seen; though, quiet in the Sunday stillness, one or two cars had passed. Not improbably, those in the cars would know him, might see something strange, something odd—*wasn't that Mr. Winner?*—in his rapid walking all alone along the glass-faced line of closed shops; the straight tall solitary figure, his clothes of a kind which most of those who saw him would have seen in advertisements only, not in life. What phenomenon, what portent, they might ask, was this? Arthur Winner thought: If I'm to be at mother's at four, I haven't time to go out to Roylan and change.

In its wisdom, the law said: *No man shall be judge of his own cause.* Descending Federal Street, two troopers in a state police patrol car slowly drew near. The one not driving, who wore corporal's stripes, gave Arthur Winner a glance, plainly, from appearances in court, identified him; informally respectful, brought his hand to his hat brim, saluting as he passed. To return! *No man shall be judge*—yes, the law; the work of his life. The law, nothing but reason, took judicial notice of man's nature, of how far his conscience could guide him against his interest. For the sake of others, for his own sake, the law would not let him be led into temptation. In its wisdom, the law only aimed at certainty, could not, did not, really hope to get there. This science, as inexact as medicine, must do its justice with the imprecision of wisdom, the pragmatism of a long, a mighty experience. Those balances were to weigh, not what was just in general, but what might be just between these actual adversaries. (Judge Lowe said: *Caroline, you have done something very wrong and very serious. . . .*)

Walking, marching on, Arthur Winner came by the granite bulk of the shut-up First National Bank. Brocton, my Brocton! The courthouse in the trees; the façade of the Union League across the square. Walking, marching on, to his right, now, the building fronts; to his right went by the sober, proper name plate: TUTTLE WINNER & PENROSE ATTORNEYS AT LAW. Over beyond Christ Church's stone-mounded corner opened the vista of Greenwood Avenue, street of his yesterdays. Brocton, my Brocton— yes; and some thousands of other people's Brocton, its ordinary aspects, its well-known sights, owned by each of them—a Jerry Brophy's town, an old Joe Harbison's; the town, now, of the Reverend Whitmore Trowbridge, S.T.D., and, following her nuptials, the town-to-be of a little Miss Cummins; the town, now, of a Lower Makepeace Hughes, Garret, a respecter, looker-up-to of honorable men, who knew a good name is to be chosen before riches, and of Agatha, his wife, who must economize accordingly; the town of a Father Albright in his kingdom, his new yellow brick fortress-city of "Americanism" down there; the town of the tribe whose great name was Revere; the town of some uncertain newcomers called Moore, and Joan, their daughter.

To Helen Detweiler he had said: *Everything you do must be straight. No other way works, and there aren't any exceptions.* . . . Oh, indeed? To Helen, he said: *I can tell you something else; these things pass.* . . . Oh, they do, do they? *None of this will be easy.* . . . (Friend, you can say that again!) He would patch grief with proverbs? Walking, marching on, under the Greenwood Avenue trees, he walked indeed up yesterday. Here a child had passed a thousand times, whistling perhaps, perhaps taking ritual care not to step on the pavement cracks. Brocton, my Brocton! Away at school, somebody, a boy known as Hall II in fact, had said: *You mean Brockton, don't you? That's in Massachusetts. Brocton? There isn't any such place. Nobody ever heard of it.* Winner punched his nose. *Winner and Hall, take two hours' detention!* Yes; these things pass. In the bitter cold, the zero, New England nights, that boy, that Winner, waking in his snug enough dormitory bed had how many times with passion wished himself home; he would never,

never—the adverb, like "always," was inapplicable to this life, to living beings. Before spring came, Winner had forgotten that he once wished such a thing.

Freedom, Fred Dealey knew from reading, *is the knowledge of necessity.* All things pass. Yes; what of all the men who used to be? What of Time's manifold disasters and miseries, of Time's events, eventful or uneventful, that had been, and were no more? When you saw, any summer evening, the hollow of Roylan, how hard to throw off, to know as false, today's picture of seeming permanence—the houses long-standing, today—no expense spared; with all utilities, with all modern comforts—made so soundly new; the tended lawns and fields, the well-groomed roadsides along the smooth paving (once that Queen's, that King's, highway of ruts and mudholes) over which swept gleaming today's cars to take out and bring in those resident there. Yet, you had before your eyes the vine-grown walls of the old mill, the iron-railed plot with the little stone monument to speak to you of other todays—the once-present of the great water wheel going around, the millstones turning; and by the loading porch, the waiting wagons, the patient horses, the sacks of grain and sacks of flour, the knots of farmers gossiping; the once-present of the eighteenth-century night the Royal Anna Tavern was raided, the pound of hoofs, the hastily presented muskets making fire, the yells and roars of butchered and butcherers. The Roylan mill's great water wheel was fallen apart; loyalists and militiamen alike compounded were with clay, and who cared now?

Walking, marching on—here was the house; the boy was home. To Arthur Winner, his mother said: *It's absurd to suggest that you, or Julius Penrose either . . .* The station wagon from Roylan stood in the drive. Good; his mother would know, or would now be hearing. Up the walk! Quietly, Arthur Winner opened the screen door, quietly he entered the high hall. Able to see into the living room he saw that they were all upstairs; and, quietly, he went in—the Canton jar, the potpourri on the air; the *étagère,* the music box; still lying on that table by "her" chair, that faded green silk volume of Browning of his mother's —*For Miss Harriet Carstairs from her sincere friend . . .*

Alone, he stood motionless. To Clarissa, he said: *Whenever you don't tell all the truth you may expect to regret it. . . .* Sagacious words! Indeed, you may! You may look for hard moments, any number of them—very likely, hours together of them. "I'm tired," Arthur Winner said aloud. Speaking the words without intention, almost inadvertently, he felt their truth. He travailed, he was heavy laden. This weight was terrible; yet there was no way to put it off. And so, no knowing how far it would have to be carried, no knowing how long, burdened so, he must daily, hourly, affect to be unburdened. Yes; Julius wasn't wrong. This took courage, this took prudence, this took stoutheartedness. Do I have them? he thought. About that business with Majorie, I could say: *That* really wasn't I. But this is I. Of this, I am not going to be able to think: I must have been crazy.

Aloud again, he said: "I don't know." (*I don't know, I don't know,* Noah Tuttle mumbled.) In a minute, he thought, in a few minutes, they will face me; I am going to face them. *We are not children . . .* Julius said. Patient, Julius said: *In this life we cannot have everything for ourselves we might like to have. . . .* Yes; life which has so unfairly served so many others, at last unfairly serves me—really, at long last! Have I a complaint? Have I, or have I not, been shown a dozen times those forms of defeat which are the kinds of victory obtainable in life? Givings-up—my good opinion of myself; must I waive that? Compromises—the least little bit of crook? Assents to the second best, to the practical, the possible? Julius Penrose said: *Be of good cheer, my friend. . . .*

Agreed, agreed! Victory is not in reaching certainties or solving mysteries; victory is in making do with uncertainties, in supporting mysteries. Yes, Arthur Winner thought, I must be reasonable. I said how easily to Helen: *The question is: What's now the reasonable thing to do?* Is that hollow friend, myself, in spite of me to whine: *I would; but I can't, I dare not, I don't know how?* Never; not ever! (Never say never? Well, then; not for now!) This load, this lading, this burden—the need was only strength. Roused, rousing, he thought: I have the strength, the strength to, to—to endure more miseries and greater far, than my weakhearted enemies dare offer! With a start, he heard, down the stairs, a voice—his Aunt Maud's—calling in loud inquiry: "Arthur? Are you there?"

On the mantel, Arthur Winner saw the gilded, the ceaseless ticking clock. In its dead language: *Omnia vincit amor,* the metal ribband unchangeably declared. Timeless, the golden figures—on feeling's forever winning side, the smiling archer, the baby god; below, the peeping Tom, the naked girl—immobile held their pose; and now—the minutes how they run!—sudden, yet slow and melodious, the unseen mechanism was activated, struck a first silvery stroke, a second, a third, a fourth.

Raised to call back, to answer his Aunt Maud, Arthur Winner heard his own grave voice. He said: "I'm here."